Fire and Sword

Fire and Sword

SIMON SCARROW

headline
review

First published in 2009 by HEADLINE REVIEW
An imprint of HEADLINE PUBLISHING GROUP

2

Cataloguing in Publication Data is available from the British Library

ISBN 978 0 7553 2437 8 (Hardback)
ISBN 978 0 7553 3917 4 (Trade paperback)

Typeset in Bembo by Avon DataSet Ltd,
Bidford-on-Avon, Warwickshire

Printed and bound in the UK by CPI Mackays, Chatham, ME5 8TD

Headline's policy is to use papers that are natural, renewable and recyclable
products and made from wood grown in sustainable forests. The logging
and manufacturing processes are expected to conform to the environmental
regulations of the country of origin.

HEADLINE PUBLISHING GROUP
An Hachette Livre UK Company
338 Euston Road
London NW1 3BH

www.headline.co.uk
www.hachettelivre.co.uk

To Murray, Gareth and Mark,
in the hope that we can keep up with Glynne!

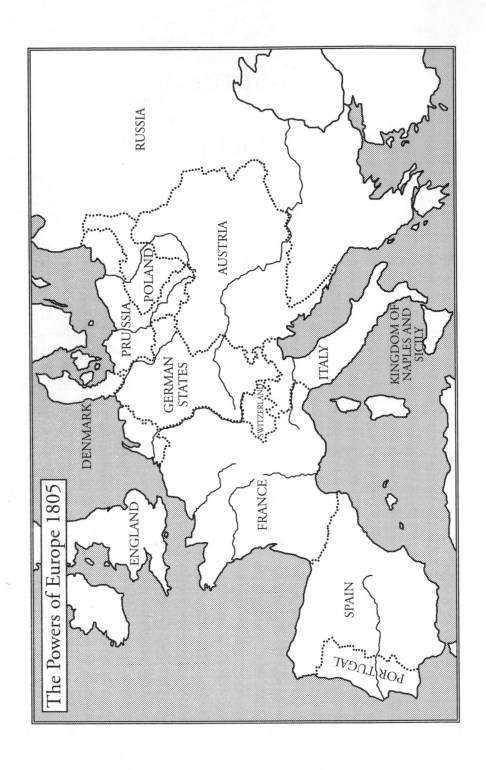

The Powers of Europe 1805

RUSSIA

AUSTRIA

POLAND

PRUSSIA

GERMAN STATES

DENMARK

SWITZERLAND

ENGLAND

FRANCE

ITALY

KINGDOM OF NAPLES AND SICILY

SPAIN

PORTUGAL

Chapter 1

Napoleon

Paris, December 1804

As Napoleon's carriage pulled up in front of Notre-Dame, the vast crowd that had been waiting in the chill air let out a cheer that echoed off the massive grey walls. The buildings that had once surrounded the great cathedral had been cleared to make space for the coronation procession, and the citizens of Paris had pressed tightly into the area cordoned off by the Emperor's grenadiers. The soldiers stood, two ranks deep, along the entire route, and their tall bearskins obscured much of the view, leaving those behind them to snatch glimpses of the ornately decorated carriages and their robed passengers as they trundled past. In between the carriages trotted squadrons of cuirassiers, their breastplates so carefully polished that they captured the surrounding scene in distorted reflections on their gleaming surfaces. The Emperor, his Empress, the imperial family and the marshals and ministers occupied over forty carriages that had been constructed specially for the coronation. Paris had never seen a sight like it, and at one stroke Napoleon had eclipsed the pomp and grandeur of his Bourbon predecessors.

He smiled with satisfaction at the thought. While the kings of France owed their crowns to an accident of birth, Napoleon had won his through ability, courage, and the love of the French people. It was the people who had given him the imperial crown, in a popular vote where only a few thousand souls in the whole of France had denied him their support. In return for the crown Napoleon had given them victory and glory, and already his mind was filled with plans to extend that glory even further.

There was a brief delay as a pair of elaborately dressed footmen scurried over to the carriage with a small flight of steps and then pulled the handle down and opened the door. Napoleon, sitting on the silk-covered seat in splendid isolation, took a deep breath and rose up,

1

emerging into view of the crowd. His grey eyes swept across the sea of adoring faces and his lips parted in a grin. Another great cheer rent the air and beyond the ranks of the grenadiers a sea of waving arms and plumed hats flickered in a confused storm of colours and motion.

Glancing round, Napoleon saw Talleyrand, his foreign minister, frown with disapproval as he stood with the other ministers on the approach to the cathedral. Napoleon could not help a slight chuckle at the sight of the aristocrat's discomfort over the Emperor's lack of decorum. Well, let him disapprove, Napoleon reflected. The old regime was gone, swept away by the revolution, and a new order had risen in its place. An order based upon the will of the people. Napoleon was grateful enough, and astute enough, to return their greeting as he turned to each side and waved back to the delighted crowd before he descended from the carriage. At once the footmen took up the train of his gold-embroidered red robes and followed him at a steady pace as he strode across the carpet towards the entrance of the cathedral.

Most of the guests, and his family, had already made their way inside and been ushered to their appointed seats. The ministers, as the senior servants of the state, would follow the Emperor and take up the most prestigious places close to the heart of the ceremony. Originally Napoleon had intended to lead his generals into the cathedral, but his brother, Joseph, and Talleyrand had urged him to present the coronation as a primarily civilian celebration. Even though the army had been the means by which Napoleon had assumed power over France, it was important that he present himself to the world as a political and not a military leader. Talleyrand still held out hope that a lasting peace might be achieved in Europe, as long as the other powers could be persuaded that the new Emperor was a statesman first, and a soldier second.

After so many years of war the short-lived Treaty of Amiens had given the people an appetite for peace and stability. Stability above all, and that meant the establishment of a new, permanent form of government. Napoleon had prepared the ground skilfully, proceeding from consul to First Consul, then First Consul for life, before he presented the people with the opportunity to approve his assumption of a new throne. Of course the senators had dressed it up as a necessary expedient to protect the Republic from its foreign and domestic enemies, but the Republic was no more. It had died in the birth throes of the empire. Already Napoleon had surrounded himself with the gaudy panoply of royalty and whittled down the powers of the senators, tribunes and representatives of the people. And there were plans to introduce a host of new aristocratic titles and awards to bolster the new

2

regime. In time, Napoleon hoped, the empire would be accepted by the other European powers and there would be an end to the attempts on his life by Frenchmen in the pay of foreign nations.

As he neared the entrance Napoleon paused and turned, then raised his hands and gestured towards the crowd, with a brilliant smile beneath the dark hair that framed his face. They let out a roar of joy and affection for their Emperor and surged forward so that the line of grenadiers bowed under the pressure and their boots scrabbled on the cobbles as they braced themselves against the surge and thrust back at the crowd with the lengths of their muskets.

Napoleon turned away and resumed his progress towards the high arched door. As he passed Talleyrand he inclined his head towards the foreign minister.

'It would appear that the people approve.'

'Yes, sire,' Talleyrand nodded.

'So, are you still concerned over my decision to accept this honour?'

Talleyrand shrugged faintly. 'No, sire. You have their trust, and I am sure that they will see that you honour it.'

Napoleon's smile froze as he nodded slowly. 'Today, I am France, and France is me. How can there be any dissent?'

'As you say, sire.' Talleyrand bowed his head and gestured faintly towards the entrance. 'Your crown awaits you.'

Napoleon straightened up, so that he rose to his full height, determined to look as regal as his slight frame permitted. It had been over four years since he had last been on campaign and the fine living he had enjoyed since then had added a slight paunch to his frame. Josephine had been tactless enough to point it out on more than one occasion, gently poking him in the side as they lay in each other's arms. He felt a lightness in his heart at the thought and glanced through the door, down the length of the cathedral to where he knew she would be sitting. It was nine years since they had met, when he had first emerged from obscurity. She could never have guessed that the slim, lank-haired young brigadier would one day become the ruler of France, nor that she would sit beside him as Empress. Napoleon felt his heart quicken with pride at his achievement. At first he had feared that she was too good for him, and would realise it all too quickly. But his rise to fame and fortune had killed that fear, and now, even as he loved Josephine as he had never loved another woman, he had begun to wonder if she was worthy of him.

With a last deep intake of the cold air, Napoleon paced forward, into Notre-Dame. The instant he crossed the threshold a choir began to sing from the far end of the cathedral and with a rustle of robes and gowns and scraping of chairs the audience rose to their feet. A length of dark green carpet stretched out before him towards the dais where the Pope stood waiting before the altar. The Emperor's smile withered at the sight of the Holy Father. Despite his efforts to reduce the role of the Catholic church in France, the common people were stubbornly attached to their religion, and Napoleon had needed the Pope's blessing to give his coronation the appearance of divine sanction.

Both dais and altar were new. Two old altars and an intricately carved choir screen had been demolished to create a more imposing space at the heart of Notre-Dame. On either side, statesmen, ambassadors, military officers and scions of Paris society bowed their heads as the Emperor passed by. His hand slipped to the pommel of the sword of Charlemagne that had been fetched from a monastery at Aix-la-Chapelle to swell Napoleon's regalia. Another part of the effort to lend the coronation the authority of royal traditions stretching back across the centuries. A new Charlemagne for a new age, Napoleon mused as he emerged from the avenue of silk and ermine picked out with the glittering jewellery of the ladies and the gold braid and gleaming decorations of the generals and marshals of France. At their head stood Murat, the flamboyant cavalry officer who had fought with Napoleon at Marengo, and later married his general's sister, Caroline. They exchanged a quick smile as the Emperor passed by.

Pope Pius VII sat on a throne in front of the altar. Beside and behind him were his retinue of cardinals and bishops, brightly illuminated by the shafts of light that angled down from the windows piercing the great stone walls high above. Napoleon stepped towards the three steps leading up to the dais. Glancing to his left he saw his brothers and sisters. Young Louis could not suppress a smile but Joseph nodded gravely as his brother passed. It was a shame that not all the family could be present, Napoleon reflected. Jérôme and Lucien were still in disgrace, having refused Napoleon's demand that they abandon their wives in favour of women he considered more suitable to be included in the imperial household. Napoleon's mother, Letizia, was also absent, protesting that she was too ill to leave Italy and attend the coronation. Napoleon had not been taken in by her excuses. She had made her dislike of Josephine quite clear from the outset and there was little doubt in her son's mind that Letizia would be damned rather than witness the crowning of Josephine alongside Napoleon. If only his father had lived long enough to see this day. Carlos Buona Parte would have talked some sense into his prickly wife.

A flicker of movement drew his eye to the other side of the cathedral and he saw the artist, Jean-Louis David, shuffle a fresh sheet of thick paper on to his draughting board as he prepared to start another sketch of the event. A monumental painting had been commissioned by Napoleon to record the coronation and David had told him that he would require as long as three years to complete the work. Truly, Napoleon thought, the spectacle of this day would shine down the years for centuries to come.

The Pope rose from his throne and extended a hand towards Napoleon as the Emperor went down on one knee, resting his white-stockinged leg on a heavily embroidered cushion that had been set in front of the pontiff. As the sound of the choir died away and stillness settled over the audience and participants the Pope began his blessing in a thin, high-pitched voice, the Latin words carrying down the length of the cathedral and echoing dully off the walls.

As the Holy Father continued with his incantations Napoleon stared fixedly at the carpet in front of him, seized by a sudden urge to laugh. In spite of all the pageantry, the gaudy costumes, the elaborate set-dressing, the months of preparations and weeks of rehearsals, it was this moment of religious ceremony that struck him as the most ridiculous aspect of it all. The notion that he, of all men, required divine sanction was not only laughable, but insulting. Almost all that he had achieved had been the result of his own efforts. The rest was down to blind chance. The idea that God was directing the trajectory of every bullet and cannonball on the battlefield was absurd. Religion was the affliction of the weak-minded, the credulous and the desperate, Napoleon decided. It was a shame that the vast majority of mankind held to such superstitions. But it was also to his advantage. As long as he paid lip-service to religious sensibilities he could use the church as yet another means of dominating the minds of those he ruled. The only difficulty lay in reconciling his needs with those of the papacy.

For the present Napoleon was content to be seen to have reached an accommodation with the church, and he knelt with bowed head while the words of an outdated language washed over his head. He shut out the noise as he once again concentrated on the part he had to play in the ceremony, once the Pope had finished his blessing. There would be no mass; Napoleon had been adamant about that. All that remained would issue from his personal authority. None but Napoleon was fit to crown Napoleon. And Josephine, for that matter. She too would receive her crown from his hand.

For a moment his mind turned to the other crowned heads of

Europe. He despised them for possessing such power merely on the basis of birth. Just like all those aristocrats who had made Napoleon's school years so miserable. But there was the paradox, he thought, gently chewing his lip. It was only through the hereditary principle that states enjoyed any kind of stability. The ferocious blood–letting of the French Revolution had proved the need for such stability and it was only when Napoleon had seized power and begun to rule with an iron grip that order had started to reappear in France. Without Napoleon there would be a return to chaos and that was why the people had been only too pleased to approve him as Emperor. In time there must be an heir. He shifted his head a fraction to stare briefly at Josephine. She caught his eye and winked.

Napoleon smiled, though he felt a heavy sadness in his heart. He had sired no children so far and the years were catching up on Josephine. Soon she would be too old to bear children. The sudden fear that he might be impotent struck him. If that turned out to be true then the dynasty that was being founded on this day would perish with him. It was a chilling thought and Napoleon hurriedly diverted his mind from it, fixing instead on the more immediate difficulties that threatened his position. Even though there was an uneasy peace on the continent France was still at war with her most implacable enemy.

Across the Channel the British still opposed him, protected from his wrath by the thin wooden screen of her warships, constantly patrolling the sea lanes and denying Napoleon the triumph that would complete his mastery over Europe. Already his mind had turned to the prospect of invasion and plans were being made for the construction of a vast number of barges in the ports and naval bases stretching along the French coast opposite Britain. When the time came, Napoleon would assemble a great battle fleet and sweep the British navy aside from the path of the invasion barges.

Once Britain was humbled, no other nation would dare to defy him, Napoleon reasoned. Until then, he would have to watch Austria and Russia closely, as his spies reported that they were arming for war even now.

He was suddenly aware that the Pope had stopped speaking and all was silent. Napoleon hurriedly mumbled an amen and crossed himself before he raised his head with a questioning look. The Pope was retiring gracefully to his ornate seat, right hand raised in a gesture of blessing. He caught the Emperor's expression and nodded faintly. Napoleon began to straighten up and nearly stumbled forward as part of his train was caught under his foot. Just in time he recovered his balance, and with a faint curse he rose to his feet and ascended the last step on to the dais. To one side of the Pope was a small golden stand on which rested the two cushions bearing the crowns fashioned for the Emperor and his Empress.

Napoleon approached the stand and hesitated for an instant to convey the due sense of awe demanded by the occasion. Then he reached forward with both hands and took the gold wreath of the imperial crown, designed to evoke those of the Caesars, and turned slowly as he held it aloft for all to see. He drew a deep breath, and even though he knew exactly what he was going to say he felt his heart pounding with nervous excitement.

'By the authority vested in me by the people I take this crown and assume the imperial throne of France. I pledge my honour to all present that I will defend the nation against all enemies, and that, by God's will, I shall govern in accordance with the wishes of the people, and in their interests. Let this moment signify to the world the greatness of France. Let this greatness act as a beacon to other nations so that they may join us in the glory of the age to come.'

He paused and then raised the crown directly above his head and slowly lowered it. The gold wreath was heavier than he anticipated and he was careful to ensure that it was firmly seated before he withdrew his hands. At once the choir struck up again from the balcony behind the altar and sang a piece composed to celebrate the moment. Napoleon tilted his head back a fraction and gazed out over the ranks of the guests stretching out before him. There were mixed expressions there. Some smiled. Some looked on with grave faces and others dabbed at the tears on their cheeks as the emotion of the great occasion overwhelmed them. He looked towards Joseph again and saw that his older brother's lips were quivering awkwardly as he struggled to restrain the pride and love he felt for Napoleon. The same pride and love that he had always felt, ever since they had shared the same nursery in the modest home in Ajaccio all those years ago when the proud Corsican family had struggled to find the money to ensure the boys had a decent education in a good French school.

Napoleon permitted himself to exchange a quick smile with his brother before his gaze passed on, over the ranks of his marshals and generals, many of whom had shared his perils and adventures from the earliest days of his military career. Brave soldiers like Junot, Marmont, Lannes and Victor. Men he would lead to yet more victories in the years to come, if the other powers of Europe dared to defy the new order in France.

As the choir came to the end of their piece and fell silent the Emperor turned to Josephine and she stepped forward, her train held by the two friends she had selected for the honour after Napoleon's sisters had refused the task. Like her husband she wore a heavy scarlet robe richly decorated with gold motifs, and even though her face remained composed her eyes glittered like priceless gems as she advanced gracefully towards the steps and took her place on the cushion, kneeling at Napoleon's feet. She inclined her head and was still.

There was a pause as Napoleon cleared his throat and addressed the audience. 'It is our great pleasure to confer the crown of the Empress of France on Josephine, whom we love as dearly as life itself.' He took the remaining crown and approached his wife. He held the gold circlet over her head and then slowly lowered it over the neatly coiled tresses of her brown hair. The moment he stepped back from her the choir began the piece that had been composed in her honour, their melodious voices carrying the length of the cathedral. Napoleon bent forward and took Josephine's hands, raising her up to her full height as she stepped on to the dais and turned to stand at his side to face their subjects.

The ceremony ended with a prayer from the Pope and then Napoleon led his Empress down the steps and back towards the entrance of Notre-Dame. As he passed his older brother he leaned towards him and muttered, 'Ah, Joseph, if only our father could see us now!'

Chapter 2

April 1805

Napoleon stood in front of the window, staring down into the neatly regimented gardens of the Tuileries palace. The first buds of spring had sprouted from the branches and the sky was bright and clear, following a brief outburst of rain and wind that had swept away the grimy shroud of smoke that habitually covered Paris. Such a fine morning would usually lift his soul, but today the Emperor regarded the scene with a blank expression. His mind was clouded with a succession of worrying thoughts over the report Talleyrand had just outlined to him. No man in Europe doubted that France was the greatest power on the continent. Her influence stretched from the shores of the Baltic sea to the Mediterranean. But there, at the water's edge, Napoleon's power failed. Out to sea, the warships of the British navy mocked his ambition and the defiance of Britain nourished the simmering hostility of Prussia, Austria and Russia.

With a weary sigh Napoleon turned away from the tall window and stared at his foreign minister. 'Our agents are certain of this?'

'Yes, sire.' Talleyrand nodded. 'The orders have been given to the Austrian generals to begin concentrating their forces outside Vienna from the end of June. The supply wagons are already gathering at depots along the Danube. Agents of Emperor Francis have been travelling the length and breadth of the continent buying up remounts for their cavalry. The fortresses that guard the passes from Italy have been strengthened and fresh outworks erected around their perimeters. Our ambassador has questioned the Austrian court about these issues and demanded an explanation.'

'And?' Napoleon cut in tersely.

'The Austrians are claiming it is no more than a long overdue adjustment of their defences. They deny that there is anything sinister about these developments.'

'They would.' Napoleon smiled grimly. 'Nevertheless, there is no mistaking it: these are preparations for war.'

'It appears so, sire.'

'What of the intelligence from our ambassador to Russia? Much as the Austrians might boast of their military prowess, I sincerely doubt that they would risk war with France without an alliance with at least one other European power. The question is, will Russia fight alongside Austria, or will Prussia?' Napoleon paused briefly. 'Or all three? All subsidised and cajoled into action by their British paymasters, of course.'

'Yes, sire.' Talleyrand nodded again. 'I imagine the British will be extending their usual lines of credit to our enemies, together with supplies of arms and equipment and a steady flow of gold and silver.'

'Of course.' Napoleon sniffed with derision. 'As ever, the British spend their riches, and save their lives, leaving the shedding of blood to their allies. So, what of Russia?'

Talleyrand briefly consulted a note on the sheet of paper he held in one hand, then glanced up at his Emperor. 'Ambassador Caulaincourt reports that the Tsar seems to be reluctant to enter into a war against us on his own. None the less there has been a degree of mobilisation of Russian forces that cannot simply be attributed to a defensive posture. If Austria does declare war on us, then I imagine that Russia might well be persuaded to join the cause.'

Napoleon folded his hands together and rested his chin on the ends of his fingers. As ever, his rivals seemed intent on the destruction of France. Almost for the sake of it. If only they would accept that France had changed. There would be no return to Bourbon tyranny. France offered a model of a better society, Napoleon reflected, and that was what they feared above all. If their own people began to realise that there was an alternative to the parasitical aristocracy of birth, then their governments would collapse like a line of dominoes. Given time, they would follow France down the road of revolution, and emerge at the far end more enlightened, more liberated, and inevitably drawn into a family of nations under the influence of France, and her Emperor. Napoleon frowned. That day was still a long way off. For the present his enemies were gathering, like wolves, and the first step to defeating them must be to find some means of dividing them. He looked up at Talleyrand. 'What do you make of the new Tsar?'

Talleyrand pursed his lips for a moment and composed his reply. 'Judging from Caulaincourt's reports and my conversations with the Russian ambassador here in Paris, it would seem that Tsar Alexander is an impressionable young man. And something of an idealist. He desires to improve the lot of his people, perhaps to the extent of abolishing serfdom. However, he is no fool. He knows well enough that his ambition is opposed by the landowners, and he knows how dangerous that can be.'

There was a flicker of a smile on Napoleon's face. 'Indeed, it is a rare thing for a tsar to die of natural causes.'

Talleyrand nodded. 'Quite, sire.'

Napoleon sat down at his desk and clasped his hands together. 'We are dealing with something of a radical, then. That is good. We might yet bend such a man to our point of view.'

'Especially as the Tsar has plans to extend the influence of Russia into the Mediterranean and the east.'

Napoleon glanced up. 'Where he will run foul of British ambitions.'

'Precisely, sire.'

'Good. Well then, see to it that Caulaincourt feeds the Tsar a steady diet of information about Britain's insatiable appetite for empire. As for Prussia,' he smiled briefly, 'let's dangle the prospect of a little reward in front of them. We'll offer the Prussians Hanover in exchange for neutrality. King Frederick William is no war hero. The man is weak and easily influenced. A bribe should be enough to buy his peace. The Tsar is our real problem. Especially as we are at war with Britain and are likely to be at war with Austria as well in the near future.'

'Yes, sire,' Talleyrand assented.

There was something in his manner that caught Napoleon's attention and he looked closely at his foreign minister for a moment before he spoke again.

'You have something to say.'

It was a statement of fact and not an enquiry, as the foreign minister recognised at once. He nodded.

'Then speak.'

'Yes, sire. It occurs to me that we might yet avoid a war with Austria, and perhaps even achieve a lasting peace with Britain.'

'Peace with Britain? That treacherous nest of vipers? I think you are deluded, Talleyrand. There is no taste for peace amongst the rulers of that island. You have read what their newspapers have said about me.' Napoleon stabbed a finger at his breast. 'Monster, tyrant and dictator. That's what they call me.'

Talleyrand waved a hand dismissively. 'A mere foible of their press, sire. British newspapers are renowned for their partiality. As are those of Paris,' he added with gentle emphasis. 'It does not make them the mouthpiece of their government. And there are men in high places who would be willing to entertain the prospect of peace with France.'

'Then why have they not announced their desire more vocally?'

Talleyrand shrugged. 'It is not always easy to speak up for peace in time of war. Yet the subjects of Britain must be as weary of war as the citizens of France. There must surely be scope for our nations to live in peace, sire. We must break the cycle of hostility, before it ruins us all. We must negotiate.'

'Why? What is the point?' Napoleon snapped impatiently. 'Britain has made it clear that she will be satisfied with nothing less than my destruction, the restoration of the Bourbons and the humbling of France. And then Britain will dominate the continent.'

'Sire, with respect, I disagree. Britain is at heart a nation of traders, a nation of businessmen. If we could show them that they may trade as freely with Europe as they wish, then we might convince them that this war is unprofitable, in every way. If we could only find some measure of compromise, there could be peace with Britain, and peace across Europe.' Talleyrand paused and looked keenly at his Emperor. 'Sire, if you would permit me to open negotiations with the British, then—'

'Then nothing!' Napoleon slapped his hand down on the table. 'Nothing would come of it. I will not compromise. I will not be dictated to by that nation of shopkeepers! There is room for only one power at the heart of Europe. Do you not see, Talleyrand? If you truly want peace, then Europe must be mastered. If we trust to compromise and talk to our neighbours as equals, there will always be differences, enmities and conflict.'

There was a brief silence as Talleyrand stared at Napoleon and then shook his head. 'That is the council of despair, sire. Surely it is better to negotiate to win others round than to rely on war?'

'Perhaps, but at least war has the virtue of granting the victor the right to dictate the terms of the peace. Then there is no need for compromise.'

'At what cost, sire? How much gold would be wasted? How many lives destroyed? War is simply the failure of diplomacy, sire.'

'You are wrong, Talleyrand. War is the continuation of diplomacy, in extremis. It is also the most powerful force for unity in a nation. It brooks no compromise and if it results in victory then a nation is rich in glory and self-regard and can remould the surrounding world in its own best interests. Negotiation is the first recourse of the weak. War is the preserve of the powerful. If France has an aptitude for war, then war becomes the most efficient means by which she can exercise her influence.' Napoleon leaned back in his chair and smiled. 'And have we not demonstrated a peculiar talent for war in recent years?'

'A talent for war?' Talleyrand's brow rose in surprise. 'War is a terrible thing, sire. One would think that such a talent, as you call it, would be an embarrassment rather than a virtue.'

'You do not know war as I do,' Napoleon countered. 'I have been a soldier for most of my life. I have been at war for the best part of twelve years. I have campaigned across the nations of Europe to the deserts of Arabia. I have fought in scores of battles and have stood my ground amidst storms of musket and cannon fire. I have been wounded and I have seen friends killed. I have seen the dead and the dying, Talleyrand. Vast fields of them. I have also seen men at their best. I have seen them master their fears and terrors and attack against overwhelming odds. I have seen them march, barefoot and hungry, for days at a time, and fight a battle at the end of it, and win. I have seen all this.' He smiled. 'You see, Talleyrand, I understand war well enough. But you? What do you know of it? An aristocrat by birth. A creature of the salons of Paris and the palaces of princes and kings. What do you know of danger? At the height of the revolution you were not even here in Paris. So before you presume to lecture me on the evils of war, please do me the courtesy of restricting your comments to the field of your own expertise. You deal with the diplomacy. You achieve what you can for France with your silver tongue and your intrigues. But remember this. You are a servant of France. A servant of the Emperor. You are a means to the end, and I, I alone, decide the nature of that end. Understand?'

'Yes, sire,' Talleyrand replied softly, through clenched teeth. 'I understand perfectly.'

Napoleon stared intently at his foreign minister for a moment and then suddenly smiled and waved his hands dismissively. 'Come now! That is that. Let us not talk of philosophies any longer, but of practicalities. At the present I no more desire war than you do. But one must guard against eventualities.'

'Of course, sire.'

'Then we must induce our friends, the Austrians, to believe that there is no advantage to be gained from waging war against us. We have driven them from Italy's domains. Now is the time to let them know that France is the new and permanent master of the kingdoms of Italy.'

'Sire?'

'I want you to make arrangements for another coronation.' Napoleon tilted his head back. 'No later than the end of spring, I shall be crowned King of Italy. And we shall extend all the benefits of our civil code and governance to the natives of that land. In short, we shall make Frenchmen of them as soon as possible, so that they will never again have to endure being ruled by Austria.'

'King of Italy?' Talleyrand mused. 'That is your will, sire?'

'It is. See to it that preparations are begun at once.'

'Yes, sire.'

'You may go now, Talleyrand. I have finished my business in Paris for a few days. If you need me, I shall be at Malmaison with the Empress and my family.'

'Yes, sire.' Talleyrand paused. 'And the other matter, sire?'

'Other matter?'

'The question of opening negotiations with Britain?'

'There will be no negotiations. Britain wants war, and war she shall have.'

Talleyrand nodded sadly and left the room, limping on his deformed leg. Once the door had closed behind the foreign minister, Napoleon's expression hardened. Much as he valued his diplomatic skills, he did not trust Talleyrand. The smooth charm and faintly mocking tone of his voice left Napoleon feeling bitter and angry, a sentiment the Emperor was obliged to conceal as much as possible in order to retain the foreign minister's services. All the same, he decided that he would have the man watched more closely by Fouché's spies. While Napoleon had little doubt that Talleyrand was a patriot, that sense of patriotism was tied to a very particular notion of France's best interests, one that did not conform to Napoleon's plans for the empire.

One thing was certain, however. Britain must be destroyed. Thanks to the improvident twenty miles of sea that separated France from the cliffs of Dover, there was only one way to crush the enemy: the British navy must be swept from the Channel so that Napoleon could lead the Grand Army in an invasion of Britain and dictate peace terms in London itself.

Chapter 3

'Well, why shouldn't I have ten new pairs of shoes?' Josephine frowned as she poured herself a fresh cup of coffee and then hesitated over a plate of pastries until her fingers alighted on a slender length of biscuit drizzled with honey. Holding it delicately between forefinger and thumb she raised it to her lips and took a bite, chewing for a moment before she continued. 'After all, I am the Empress, and it would not reflect well on you if I were seen in public in some threadbare sackcloth and a battered pair of clogs. Besides, you can afford it.'

They were alone in the private sitting room overlooking the gardens at the rear of the château. Outside, dusk was settling over the country-side and it was chilly enough to warrant the fire that glowed in the grate, occasionally emitting a sudden crack or hiss from the latest log to be tossed on to the embers. Napoleon was flicking through a tray of correspondence that was resting on his lap. He tapped another letter.

'And here's another. From a supplier of curtains in Lyons . . . Five bales of silk.' Napoleon's eyebrows shot up. 'Five bales of silk! Good God, do you know what he has charged you for that?'

Josephine shrugged.

Napoleon sighed as he nodded down at the letters piled on the tray. 'Most of these are from suppliers to the imperial household. Aside from the silk, they mention shoes, hats, dresses, horses, furniture, wine, cakes . . . In every case they respectfully state that the account has yet to be settled.'

'They had better be respectful, the little ingrates.' Josephine sniffed. 'After I have gone to the effort of appointing them to supply the imperial household with their wares. You'd think they would be sensible of the honour I do them.'

'They still have to be paid,' Napoleon admonished her. 'They are not charities. And you must not continue like this. I could equip an infantry brigade on what you spend on petty indulgences each month. It has got to stop, before this profligacy damages our reputation.'

'How can it? That little weevil Fouché controls all the news that gets into the papers. He's hardly going to permit the publication of any gossip that undermines his master.'

'Gossip is spread by tongues just as easily as it is through the news-papers,' Napoleon countered wearily. 'And I will not have people grumbling about you not paying your debts.'

'Well, it's your own fault,' Josephine said petulantly. 'If you would give me enough to make ends meet you would not have to deal with those petty misers and their petulant complaints.'

'A good wife knows how to live within her budget.'

'What's that?' Josephine sneered. 'Another pithy bit of Corsican wisdom from your mother?'

'I warned you before. You will respect my mother. Especially while she is under my roof.'

It had been over a month since Letizia Bonaparte had joined the imperial household, having recovered from her illness.

'That's another thing,' Josephine added. 'How long is she staying?'

'As long as she wishes.'

'Of course.' Josephine chuckled humourlessly. 'She makes herself at home here, and spends the days finding fault with almost everything I say or do. She despises me, and I know she drips poison about me into your ear at every opportunity.'

'Enough!' Napoleon snapped as he flung the correspondence at his wife. The tray struck the platter of pastries and the fine porcelain and its contents tumbled from the table to shatter on the floor. Josephine jumped back in her seat, eyes wide with fright. There were still crumbs on her lips as she swallowed nervously, staring at her husband. Napoleon rose up, stepped towards her and leaned in close, stabbing a finger to emphasise his words.

'You will not speak in that manner again, do you hear me?'

'Yes, husband.' Her voice trembled. 'As you wish.'

'That's right.' He nodded. 'As I wish. You will be polite and respectful to my mother, and the rest of my family, whatever they may say to you. In spite of everything, deep inside I am still a Corsican, and my family matters to me more than you can ever know. Understand?'

Josephine nodded, clutching both hands to her breast. The tears were already welling up in her eyes as she watched her husband fearfully. For a moment Napoleon glared back; then he let out a deep sigh and reached down and gently took her hands in his.

'I am sorry. My temper is not what it was. I have much on my mind. I have little patience for the small details that every husband must attend to. Forgive me.' He lowered his head and kissed her fingers.

Josephine nodded, and her chest heaved a little as she strove to control her tears. 'It's my fault. I know I should show her more respect, but . . . she hates me. As do all your family. They have always hated me. I can't bear it.'

'Hush.' Napoleon cupped her cheek in his hand. 'No one hates you. They're Corsicans with Corsican morals.' Napoleon's mind moment-arily flicked to his sister Pauline and the scandalous manner in which she conducted herself. Her numerous affairs were public knowledge. But she had always been promiscuous. Napoleon winced at the memory of catching her with a grenadier behind a screen in his map room during his first campaign in Italy, nine years ago. He shook his head. 'Most of them, at least. Anyway, you will not have to endure my family for much longer.'

'Oh?'

Napoleon smiled. 'We're leaving France for two, perhaps three, months.'

'Leaving France?' Josephine responded warily. 'Not another campaign?'

'Not unless Britain has decided to invade Italy.'

'Italy!' Josephine's expression lightened at once as she recalled the days of Napoleon's first army command, the almost regal court at the palace at Montebello where her days had been carefree and she had been surrounded by the brightest minds and most vivacious personalities of the Italian kingdoms. 'When do we leave?'

'Within the month.' Napoleon smiled. 'Just be sure not to order any new clothes for the journey that you can't afford.'

'Swine!' Josephine swatted him on the shoulder, then her expression became serious for a moment. She wrapped her arms round his neck and drew him down on to the chair and kissed him full on the mouth. Her pulse quickened and then his hands were on the straps that fastened her bodice.

'It will be like last time,' she breathed. 'No, better than last time we were together in Italy. I swear it.'

Napoleon softly grazed his lips down the arc of her neck towards the soft mound of her breast, and out of the corner of his eye he saw from the clock ticking above the fire that there would be time to make love before dressing for dinner with his family.

Usually Napoleon regarded eating as a necessary evil and ate swiftly before returning to his work. But not tonight. Around the table sat his wife, his brothers Joseph and Lucien, his sisters Caroline and Pauline, and at the far end of the table his mother, Letizia. When the main course was served and the servants had retreated from the room and quietly closed the doors behind them, Caroline cleared her throat.

17

'I hear you are to visit Italy.'

Josephine started a little at the statement and glanced hurriedly at Napoleon, who forced himself to keep his surprise in check as he asked, 'Where did you hear that?'

'From my husband. Joachim had it from his chief of staff.'

'Really?' Napoleon raised an eyebrow. Marshal Joachim Murat was the Emperor's most talented cavalry commander, but like most of his kind he was inclined to swagger about and be indiscreet. If he had heard the news of the pending tour of Italy, then there was every chance that it was the talk of half the salons in Paris.

He nodded at his sister. 'Very well then, since the secret is out, yes, it is true. I intend to make a tour of our territories in Italy.'

'Is it also true that you are to be crowned King of Italy?'

That could only have come from Talleyrand, Napoleon realised at once. But why would he spread knowledge of Napoleon's plans? Perhaps to forewarn any would-be assassins? The thought was no sooner in his head than Napoleon forced himself to dismiss it. Since the bloody attempt on his life four years earlier he had been inclined to see threats everywhere, but he realised he could not run his life effectively if he lived in a state of fear.

'It is true, Caroline.'

At the other end of the table his mother laughed humourlessly. 'Another coronation? Do you collect crowns, my son?'

Napoleon laughed, and the others followed suit for a moment, finally clearing the air of some of the tension that had hung over the dinner table since the meal had begun.

'I am prepared to collect crowns when it is expedient to do so, Mother. However, it would be unseemly to overindulge in such acquisitions.'

'Especially for one who was such an ardent Jacobin not so many years ago,' Lucien added quietly.

Napoleon turned to his younger brother with a weary expression. Lucien had always been the most radical of his siblings, dangerously so.

Lucien sipped his wine and continued. 'Do you remember, brother, when we overthrew the Directory and you became First Consul?'

'I do.'

'And do you recall that I drew my sword and swore an oath that if ever you betrayed France and became a tyrant I would plunge that blade into your heart myself?'

'I remember it.'

'Now you are Emperor, and about to take another crown.' He raised his glass in mock salute. 'That makes rather a mockery of my oath, wouldn't you say?'

'It would, if I had become a tyrant,' Napoleon replied evenly. 'But the people voted for me to become Emperor, and that makes me the embodiment of their will. In that case, I am no tyrant, and your honour is intact.'

'A lawyer would find no problem with that form of words,' Lucien conceded. 'But my oath is honoured in the letter rather than the spirit.'

'As you will, Lucien. But times have changed. The revolution was descending into chaos before we ended the Directory. Since then France has had order.'

'True, but we have traded order for freedom.'

'That may be, but do you really think it matters to the vast majority of the people? They need employment. They need bread, and more than anything they need a sense of stability. All of which it is my intention to provide. It all depends on what you mean by freedom, Lucien.' Napoleon paused as his mind enlarged on the idea. 'For you, and me, and those who frequent the salons, it is an ideal, and like all ideals it is a luxury. The only freedom that matters to the common people is the freedom from suffering.'

Lucien frowned, shook his head and stared down at the food on his gilt-edged plate. 'If men are not to aspire to ideals, Napoleon, then what distinguishes us from common beasts?'

'There is always a place for ideals, and for those men who will discuss them and advance their cause. But such men are scarce and must be nurtured and raised up to privileged positions.'

'In other words they must become aristocrats. It would seem that you are advocating a return to the evils of the Bourbons' regime.'

Napoleon shrugged. 'As long as a man has talent I won't hold his background against him, even if he is a stuck-up prick like Talleyrand.'

Joseph laughed, and after glancing round at the shocked expressions on the faces of the women, Napoleon joined in.

Even Lucien smiled at the remark. 'You have the measure of that man, brother.'

They raised their glasses to each other and took another draught of wine.

Letizia cleared her throat. 'Of course, it is very fine that you provide such rewards for talented men, but how can you ensure that they will remain loyal to the new order? Can you trust men who would be so easily dazzled by the baubles you offer them?'

19

'Of course, Mother. What greater spur to loyalty is there than the prospect of reward for good service?'

'Family,' she replied at once. 'There is no greater bond of loyalty than blood.'

Napoleon nodded. 'And that is why I must elevate my family and friends to high positions in France, and in time place them amongst the ruling houses of the European powers, and perhaps on thrones of their own.'

'You cannot be serious.' Joseph chuckled. 'You would make me a king?'

'One day perhaps, and sooner than you might think.'

'Preposterous!' Joseph shook his head. 'I was not born to be a king, any more than Lucien here, or Louis or Jérôme.'

'I disagree,' Napoleon replied. 'Any one of my brothers is worth ten tsars, or any ruler placed on a throne by right of birth. Why, one only needs to look to Britain to see the proof of that. King George is insane, and his heir is an irresponsible libertine. Are there not a hundred, a thousand, better men in Britain with the ability to rule? So, when the time comes, I will make kings of you all.'

'Whether we wish it or not?' asked Lucien.

'I need allies I can trust. As Mother says, what better bond is there than blood? Are you with me?'

Lucien thought for a moment, and shrugged. 'You are my brother. Of course I am with you. As long as you are no tyrant.'

'And you, Joseph?'

His older brother grinned and raised his glass. 'To the bitter end.'

'The only end I recognise is everlasting glory.'

'Everlasting?' Letizia pursed her lips and darted a glance at Josephine. 'That will only happen if you produce a successor. Without an heir the whole thing falls apart.'

'There will be an heir,' Napoleon said firmly. 'It's just a matter of time.'

'Time is very much the issue,' his mother said. 'You have been married for over ten years now. Josephine, remind me. How old are you?'

The Empress winced but did not reply as Letizia leaned towards her and tapped her finger on the table. 'Forty-two, I seem to recall. Am I right?'

Josephine nodded.

'Well, forgive me, my dear, but isn't that a little late for child-bearing?'

Napoleon rushed to his wife's defence. 'Older women have given birth to healthy children, Mother. There's still time.'

Josephine stared at him across the table and said flatly, 'Older women? Thank you.'

'You must have an heir,' Letizia insisted.

'And I will. Josephine has borne two healthy children—'

'That was a long time ago.'

'And she will produce more.'

'When?' Letizia asked sharply.

'When the time is right, Mother.'

'And if she doesn't?'

'She will,' Napoleon countered fiercely, although he knew in his heart that there was little chance of it.

'She has to, if she is to justify being the wife of the Emperor of France.'

'That is enough!' Josephine banged her hand down on the table, startling the others into silence. 'I will not be spoken of in this manner. Do you understand? I will not. Tell her, Napoleon.'

Napoleon stared back at her, then glanced towards his mother.

Josephine's lips quivered. 'I will not take this! What right does she have to speak to me in this manner?'

'What right?' Letizia drew her thin frame up in her chair. 'The right conferred on me by bringing thirteen children into this world, eight of whom have survived. Not just two.'

Josephine glared at her bitterly, then stood up abruptly. 'Damn you! Damn all you Corsicans!'

She turned and strode towards the door as tears choked her chest. She flung the door open and slammed it behind her. There was a shocked silence, broken by the sound of her footsteps retreating up the corridor.

Caroline glanced round the table and muttered, 'I always said she wasn't good enough for Napoleon.'

'Silence!' Napoleon snapped at her. 'You don't know what you are talking about, you little fool. Is your memory so short? When we arrived in France we were fugitives with no home, no money, no influence. Josephine was the wife of a count, the confidante of the most powerful politicians in the capital, and men lost their hearts to her. Yet she chose *me* for her husband. When I could barely afford the uniform on my back and I was living in a run-down slum. Do you have any idea what that means to me? I adored her. I still do,' he added quickly. 'With Josephine I can be myself. When I am surrounded by lesser men and lickspittles, only Josephine offers me honesty and understanding. I owe her my loyalty. And my love. So don't you dare try to come between us.'

Caroline shrugged. 'That's all very well, but in return she owes you an heir, Napoleon. Where is your child?'

Napoleon's expression darkened, but before he could respond his mother cut in.

'Does it matter? That woman is clearly too old for child-bearing. There is only one solution to the problem and the sooner you face up to that the better, my son.'

Napoleon shook his head. 'I will not do it. I will not.'

'Not now, perhaps. But regardless of your feelings for her, you have an obligation to your people. There must be an imperial successor.' Letizia wagged a finger at him. 'Sooner or later, you must provide France with an heir to the throne. Especially if you go off to war again and place yourself in danger.'

'Danger?' Napoleon laughed. 'Mother, have you not heard? I lead a charmed life.'

'Your luck will not last for ever.'

'Why not?'

Letizia shrugged. 'No man's luck ever does. I've lived long enough to know that. And so you must have an heir.'

'There will be time enough for that.' Napoleon emptied his glass and pushed his chair away from the table, signifying that the meal was at an end. 'But first there is the small matter of crushing Britain, once and for all.'

Chapter 4

Arthur

London, September 1805

For Sir Arthur Wellesley the sight of London was welcome and familiar after six months at sea on the voyage from India. It had been almost nine years since he had last set foot in the capital and he could not help rising from his seat and leaning out of the window as the coach clattered to the top of a gentle hill from where there was a fine view of London's sprawling houses, and glimpses of the gleaming Thames and a forest of masts from the shipping that brought raw materials and luxuries to Britain and carried her manufactured goods across the world.

Now, thanks to his efforts and those of his brother Richard, Britain's wealth and power was enhanced by the vast swathe of Indian territories they had won. While Richard had served as Governor General, Arthur had won his spurs in the army, rising from the rank of colonel to that of major-general at the head of an army that had won a string of great victories. Finally, his achievements had been rewarded with a knighthood and he returned to Britain a man of experience, wealth and influence.

At thirty-six, he felt that he was at the height of his powers, and could serve his country well in its titanic struggle with France. When he had left Britain the enemy had been a revolutionary republic. Now France was an empire, ruled by the tyrant Bonaparte. With much time on his hands over the last six months, Arthur had read every newspaper that the ship had picked up in ports along the way and had followed the progress of Bonaparte from strength to strength. It was a staggering tale of success, Arthur admitted grudgingly. The man was clearly a phenomenal force of nature to have achieved so much so swiftly. It was a pity that Bonaparte's qualities as general and statesman were not moderated by any desire for peace with his neighbouring kingdoms. At the end of the present war, Bonaparte would be master of the world, or France would be humbled. It was Britain's duty, as Arthur saw it, to bring about that defeat, however long it took, however many millions of pounds it cost, and however many lives it claimed.

The first chills of autumn were some weeks off yet and so the sky above the city was only covered with a faint haze of sickly yellow smoke. Once winter set in, Arthur recalled, there would be a perpetual smear across the sky on still days as the smoke from tens of thousands of fires wrapped itself over London. For a moment he fondly recalled the fresh breezes that had accompanied his recent sea journey. The ship had docked in Portsmouth only two days earlier and he had not yet lost his sea legs. Each time he stepped down from the coach the ground felt strangely unsteady beneath his feet, as if he still stood on a wooden deck that rose and fell with monotonous regularity for days on end. There had been a few weeks of wild weather as the Indiaman had fought its way round the Southern Cape in rough seas, but for most of the voyage he had been able to rest and recover from the strains of several years of hard soldiering in India.

The sight of the city lightened his sober mood, and he smiled at the prospect of being reunited with his family and looking up scores of former friends. More important still, Arthur was keen to discover how things stood between him and Kitty, the young love he had left behind in Ireland. The infrequent communications between them over the last ten years were a poor basis from which to judge the true nature of her feelings towards him. And what would he make of her? Ten years might well have wrought a significant change in Kitty's character, not to mention her looks. But it was not her looks that had first won his heart, Arthur reminded himself. It was that quirky vivaciousness of hers that set her apart from all the wide-eyed, demure and ultimately dull debutantes who decorated the social circle of Dublin Castle. If it remained undimmed, her personality would suit him admirably. The question was, how should Arthur proceed in the matter of winning her hand?

He had tried once before, some months prior to leaving for India, when he had asked her older brother, Tom, for permission to marry her. As a mere major, with little prospect of winning a fortune, and every prospect of a premature death, Arthur had had little to offer but love. To a practical man like Tom such an emotion was neither attractive nor desirable. And so he had refused Arthur's request, despite the fact that Kitty had already given her heart to the young officer. In a last attempt to hold her affections Arthur had written a letter stating that his feelings for her would not change, and if he returned with rank and riches and she was still unwed, his offer of marriage would stand.

The coach began to follow the road down a gentle slope and the view of London was lost behind a line of trees, so Arthur eased himself back on to his seat opposite the considerable bulk of the other passenger travelling to London. The man was wearing a dark coat with a white lace stock woven with an intricate design. They had exchanged a bare formal greeting at the start of the journey and few words since. Mr Thomas Jardine had announced that he was a banker and had clearly never heard of the young major-general when Arthur had offered his name in return. Mr Jardine had bought a newspaper at the last stop. Now he folded it up and set it down on the leather seat beside him.

Arthur gestured towards the newspaper. 'May I?'

'Of course, sir. Be my guest.'

'Thank you.'

Arthur picked up the newspaper and opened it out on his lap. One of the most prominent articles dealt with the preparations for battle by Britain's naval hero, Admiral Lord Nelson. Arthur was already familiar with the most notable of the man's exploits, namely his crushing victory over the French at Aboukir Bay, on the coast of Egypt. But Nelson was promising to eclipse even that with one of the largest fleets that the Royal Navy had ever amassed. Even now the warships were gathering at Portsmouth, loading shot, powder and supplies for a great test of arms against the combined navies of France and Spain.

Mr Jardine stirred. 'Quite the man, eh?'

Arthur looked up, lowering the newspaper on to his lap. 'Sir?'

'Nelson. Britain's best chance of humbling the frogs. Once he's given them a sound thrashing, that'll be the end of any talk of an invasion.'

'Yes, I suppose so.'

'Damned lucky thing we have the Royal Navy standing between us and Monsieur Bonaparte. If not for it, we'd all be forced to parler frog and eat the damned things before the year was out.'

'Yes, we are indeed fortunate to have Nelson and the Navy.' Arthur smiled. 'But one should not forget the part played by the army in defending Britain.'

'Of course.' Jardine nodded, his cheeks wobbling. 'Though I dare say that even you would admit that our, er, valiant redcoats have had little chance to distinguish themselves in this war.'

Arthur's smile faded. 'I can assure you, sir, that the army has played its part as much as the Navy.'

'Oh, come now, I meant no offence. I merely desired to point out that the burden of the war has largely fallen on the shoulders of our jack tars. You cannot deny it, sir.'

'Can't I?' Arthur thought back to his first campaign in the lowlands. Half of his men had died from want of food and the bitter cold of a terrible winter. Then there had been India, and the long marches through searing heat before taking on armies vastly superior in size and beating them. He fixed his eyes on the other man and cleared his throat. 'I am sure that if you were in full possession of the facts, you would not judge the contribution of the army so harshly.'

Jardine shook his head briefly. 'I am not being harsh. Forgive me if I appear to be. I merely point to the record of both services. On the seas our sailors have completely mastered the enemy, whereas our soldiers are no match for the French and have failed to secure the least foothold on the continent. Instead of taking the fight directly to the enemy they are merely nibbling away at his colonies, far from the heart of the struggle.'

'It is hardly the fault of the soldiers if the government chooses to deploy them in such a fashion,' Arthur protested.

'Precisely, sir. Take yourself.' Jardine gestured towards Arthur's tanned face. 'From your colour, I assume that you have been on service in the tropics, or some such?'

'I have just returned from India.'

'And what did you do there of any importance to this country?'

Arthur took a deep breath. The question was startling in terms of the breadth of the answer he could provide, but Jardine continued before he had a chance to begin.

'I warrant that you and your men spent most of the time chasing the natives off the property of the East India Company.'

'We achieved more than that, sir. It is thanks to the efforts of the army that Britain now rules over lands many times the size and population of the British Isles.'

'India is a mere detail of our struggle against France,' Jardine countered dismissively. 'Besides, you were fighting savages, not proper civilised armies. How could you possibly lose in such an unequal contest?'

Arthur leaned back with a weary expression. The man was clearly ignorant of the campaigns that had been fought across the heart of the subcontinent over the last decade. He knew nothing of the bloody assault on the Sultan of Mysore's fortress capital of Seringapatam. Nothing of the desperate march across the face of the vast Mahratta army at Assaye to attack their flank and defeat them. Nothing of the bold advance against the cannon and massed ranks of the enemy at

Argaum. Nothing of the long months of bitter skirmishes with the bandit columns led by the bloodthirsty Dhoondiah Waugh. Clearly, the exploits of Arthur and his men had been overlooked back home in Britain. Almost as if they were a forgotten army led by a forgotten general. He sighed.

'I can assure you that the troops I was honoured to command in India faced enemies every bit as dangerous as the French. When the time comes for our soldiers to face Bonaparte in pitched battle, they will be more than a match for him and his men.'

'Of course, sir. Of course.' Jardine nodded placatingly. 'I am sure that you know your business. But from the point of view of the well-informed layman, such as myself, it would appear that our best hope of defeating the French lies in the Royal Navy.'

'By God, you are wrong, sir. Quite wrong,' Arthur snapped. 'How can the Navy defeat Bonaparte? To be sure, Admiral Nelson can defeat his warships, but he can only pursue the French as far as their coast. And from there on, wherever there is solid ground, Bonaparte can defy his enemies. So it follows that the war between Britain and France can only be decided on land. When the time is right our soldiers will fight on the soil of Europe and there they will prove that they are more than a match for the very best of Napoleon's men. Mark my words, sir. You will see the day.'

'I hope so, sir. Sincerely I do. But that depends on our government's being prepared to land a force large enough to make a difference.'

Arthur nodded. 'And to keep it adequately supplied and reinforced when necessary. You are right, sir. The government has so far declined to commit to such an investment of its military power. But that will change. There are men with vision at Westminster. Men who can be persuaded to take the bold course.'

'Who will persuade them, sir? Most of our generals seem to be the very fount of caution and, dare I say it, indecision.'

'Then it will be down to men like myself to make the case for action.'

Jardine smiled. 'Pardon me, sir, but what makes you think that young officers will carry much weight in this affair?'

'Because I shall speak the truth. I shall present the facts clearly and logically so that there can be no doubt as to the correct path to take.'

'Ah, but you speak as a soldier. Those in Westminster are inclined to speak and listen as politicians. Facts and logic are as clay to their minds; soft and infinitely malleable. I fear you overestimate the influence of reason on such men.'

Arthur was quiet and still for a moment before he shrugged. 'We shall see.' He picked up the newspaper again. 'Now, if you don't mind, sir, I would like to finish this before the journey is over.'

Jardine nodded briefly and turned to look out of the window with a slight pout of piqued disapproval.

The coach soon emerged from the trees and entered the first of the villages that were slowly being swallowed up and overwhelmed by the sprawling capital. The cottages and small shops gradually gave way to dense housing that rose up on either side, crowding the cobbled streets. Occasionally the coach passed workhouses and the premises of small industries from whose chimneys smoke belched into the sky, adding to the brown pall hanging over London. At length they arrived at the yard of the coach station in Chelsea, and after a curt farewell to Mr Jardine Arthur tipped a porter to carry his travel case to one of the cabs waiting out in the street. The rest of his baggage was in the hold of the Indiaman and would be sent on to London as soon as it was unloaded.

'Cavendish Square, if you please,' Arthur called up to the cabby as he climbed aboard and pulled the small door to.

'Aye, sir!' The cabby nodded, and then flicked the reins, urging his horse forward. The cab rattled out into the traffic passing along the crowded thoroughfare. At once Arthur was struck by the stark difference between the streets of London and those he had become used to in India. As a boy, his family had mostly lived in the countryside of Ireland, and Arthur had been horrified by the squalor and the smoky, sweaty odours of Dublin and then London. But he had quickly become used to them, just as he had become used to the appalling poverty and stench of the primitive slums of Indian cities. Now he measured London by a new standard and marvelled at the obvious wealth of the capital and the fine facades it presented to the paved and cobbled streets.

As the cab turned into Cavendish Square, Arthur's mind turned to his family. The house that his mother rented was in a street off the square. It was modest by the standards of the aristocracy, but Anne Wellesley had been saddled with debts after her husband had died and what little was left of her private fortune was supplemented by loans from her sons. Arthur wondered what kind of greeting she would offer him after an absence of a decade. They had not parted on good terms, mostly because they had never been on good terms. She had regarded Arthur as the least able, and most indolent, of her sons, and had always been cold with him. Now that he was a major-general and the hero of

Assaye he wondered if his stock with her might have risen. Would she now embrace him and hold him in the same regard as Richard, William and Henry?

Arthur rapped the side of the cab and called to the driver. 'Stop here!'

The cab pulled up and Arthur stepped out on to the street in front of his mother's house, straightening his jacket as he waited for the driver to bring his travelling case down from the roof. Then, taking a deep breath, he climbed the steps and rapped the brass knocker sharply. There was a short delay before he heard footsteps inside and the door opened to reveal a footman.

'Yes, sir?'

'I am Arthur Wellesley. Is my mother at home?'

The footman scrutinised his face for a moment before he nodded and stood aside.

'Yes, Sir Arthur, my lady is at home. If you would care to wait in the front parlour I will see to your luggage and inform Lady Mornington of your arrival.'

Arthur nodded, paid off the cab driver, and made for the parlour as the footman brought his bags in. The floor of the parlour was carpeted and the furniture was neat and expensive. Clearly his mother had done well out of her sons' improved financial standing, Arthur mused. He took a seat and glanced round the walls. Above the fireplace were a series of small portraits of his brothers and sister, beneath a larger picture of his father, but no picture of Arthur.

Before his thoughts could become more melancholy, the door opened and his mother stepped into the room. Anne Wellesley was more gaunt than he recalled. Ten years had hardened the lines in her face and her bright eyes had sunk a little further into their sockets. She stood and examined him in turn.

'You don't look well,' she said abruptly. 'Your hair is cropped too close and your complexion is altogether too common and ruddy, as if you had been working the fields alongside common labourers.'

Arthur smiled faintly as he rose to his feet. 'It's good to see you again too, Mother.' He crossed the room and leaned forward to kiss the cheek she offered him. She forced a smile and took his hand.

'It has been a long time, Arthur. Too long, perhaps. You did not write to me very often.' Her tone was hurt, or affected to be hurt, Arthur thought.

'You hardly wrote to me either, Mother.'

'I was busy. A mother has to spend her time watching over her whole family. I did not have time to write in detail to every one of my children.'

It was a lame excuse and Arthur felt his heart harden a little. Ten years appeared to have changed very little between them. She gestured to the two seats opposite the fireplace. 'Sit down. I have asked for tea to be served to us. I expect you will want to stay here for some time, while you find your feet in London.'

'Yes, Mother. If that would not be too much of an imposition.'

'Of course not,' she shot back. 'And now that you are here I will send word to William and the others to let them know you have returned. They will want to see you again.'

'And I them.'

'Yes, I am sure you will have plenty of tales to relate of your adventures amongst the savages. You and Richard may have had a high time of it in India, but you have stirred up a veritable wasps' nest of criticism back here in London.'

'I gathered something of it from the newspapers I read on the voyage back.'

'It seems that not everyone is appreciative of your efforts on behalf of the nation. The East India Company is furious over the cost of Richard's wars in the subcontinent.'

'War is an expensive business.'

'Perhaps, but there are men in Parliament who say that Britain needs every penny just to continue the fight here in Europe.' She pursed her lips. 'It doesn't help Richard's case that he is reported to have been lavishing every luxury on himself out of the public purse.'

'If that's all they are saying I am not unduly concerned.' Arthur shrugged. 'Some people are envious, others are malicious and the rest are merely ill-informed. I shall make the case on Richard's behalf until he gets back.'

'Well, you had better make a better go of it than William has managed thus far. At times it has been as if Parliament was a pack of hounds baying for the blood of our family. Speaking of which, there was a message for you this morning, from the Colonial Office in Downing Street. You are required to attend Lord Castlereagh's office at your earliest convenience. It seems that news of your arrival preceded you.'

'By God, that was quick. Word must have been sent the moment I landed.'

'Then the powers that be are wasting no time in calling you to account.' Lady Mornington leaned forward. 'Be careful, Arthur. You are a soldier amongst politicians. You are out of your league. Do nothing to embarrass the fortunes of the family.'

Arthur stared at her for a moment, his heart filled with bitterness at her obvious disregard for his qualities. He swallowed and replied tersely, 'I will not discredit the name of Wellesley, Mother. I never have. And I never will, and I pray that we both live to see the day when you regard me with pride.'

Anne Wellesley smiled faintly. 'I hope so. Now, you'd better go. Don't make a hash of it.'

Chapter 5

In Downing Street, Arthur made directly for the office of Lord Castlereagh, Secretary of State for War and the Colonies. Arthur was surprised to find that his heart was beating fast and that he felt apprehensive over the coming interrogation, assuming that was the reason for his summons. It was strange, he thought, how he had faced shot and shell on the battlefield with less trepidation. Or was it that he had been so acutely focused on his duties as commander that there was no time for fear? Arthur had long since mastered the art of hiding his emotions, and he did so now when he approached the clerk seated at the large desk in the main hall of the Colonial Office.

'May I help you, sir?' asked the clerk, rising to his feet.

'Indeed. I have been asked to attend Lord Castlereagh.'

'Your name, sir?'

'Major-General Sir Arthur Wellesley.'

'Ah yes, you are expected, sir. Please follow me.' The clerk led the way up the stairs and along a narrow panelled corridor, passing several other hurrying officials and stopping outside an open door. 'If you would be so kind as to wait in here, sir, until his lordship is ready to see you.'

Arthur nodded and entered the anteroom. It was modestly sized, with a number of chairs and small tables arranged around the walls. A large window looked out on to Downing Street. There was only one other occupant, a slight naval officer, somewhat shorter than Arthur, who was sitting half turned away as he read an article in the newspaper spread across the table in front of him. From the heavy gold epaulettes and the ribbons and stars on his left breast Arthur knew he must be a senior officer. He did not look up as Arthur entered the room and took a seat a short distance away. Only when he had finished reading the article did he raise his eyes to examine the new arrival. His left eye was a brilliant blue and his features were sharp and sensitive, making him look much younger than his fine grey hair seemed to indicate. His right eye, by contrast, was dull and empty-looking and Arthur realised that there was no sight in it. Then he noticed that the naval officer's right sleeve was empty and pinned to his coat, and with a flash of surprise he realised who the man must be.

'Lord Nelson, it is a pleasure to meet you, sir.'

'I'm sure.' Nelson gave him a friendly smile. 'And might I know who you are, sir?'

'Arthur Wellesley, sir. Major-General Sir Arthur Wellesley.' Arthur could not help smiling back as he crossed the room and instinctively offered his hand in greeting. Then he drew up in embarrassment as Nelson glanced meaningfully at his empty sleeve and chuckled.

'I'm sorry, Sir Arthur, you'll have to pardon my rudeness, but I lack the wherewithal to shake your hand. Ah, but I see that I have discomfited you. I am sorry. Do take a seat so that we may talk.' He gestured to the chair opposite with his surviving hand and Arthur sat down gratefully.

'So what are you here for, Wellesley? Come to see Castlereagh?'

'Yes, my lord.'

Nelson gestured at his face. 'Seems you have spent some time in the sun. Jamaica?'

'India. I returned a few days ago.'

'India.' Nelson nodded. 'Bit out of my way. Can't say I know much about our affairs in that part of the world. But I'm sure you've acquitted yourself capably, Wellesley.' He frowned for a moment before nodding to himself. 'Ah, I have it now. Wellesley! Richard Wellesley is, or was, the Governor General. You must be related to him.'

'He is my brother.'

'So you were there helping him out in some capacity, no doubt. On his staff?'

'No, my lord. My brother Henry was his private secretary. I served with the army. In the field.'

'Quite a family affair, then. It must have been helpful for your brother to have two siblings to carry out his instructions.'

Arthur winced at the implied diminution of his achievements. 'The Governor General decided the policy. I was responsible for our forces on the ground.'

'Quite so.' Nelson nodded. 'And I'm sure you served him well, Sir Arthur.'

'I did,' Arthur replied tersely. 'And with a degree of success.'

'Good. That's good.' Nelson regarded him for a moment and then tapped the newspaper he had been reading.

'Exciting times, Wellesley. The French fleet is at Cadiz, our ships are massing for the big effort and all Britain wonders what my plan of action will be. You too, I'll be bound.'

Arthur was a little surprised at the direct display of the other man's sense of his own importance, but there was no denying that he was keen to know how Nelson intended to beat the French. He nodded.

Nelson's good eye glinted with pleasure as he leaned back and began. 'The trick of it, as I've always known, is to confound the expectations of the enemy. The thing is that the French have held fast to the old ways of fighting and assume that our line and theirs will sail up and down, parallel to each other, pounding away until the will of one side breaks. I have to confess that our admirals were equally culpable of a lack of initiative until the Battle of St Vincent, when I pulled out of our column and cut their line. Allowed our fleet to defeat them in detail. I did the same again at the Nile. That's the trick of it: break their line and destroy a division at a time. So we'll do the same again when we encounter Admiral Villeneuve, and as long as they come on in the same old way we'll defeat them sure enough.'

'Most interesting.' Arthur nodded. 'But surely, if you approach their line in column, they will be able to bring far more guns against you than you can reply with. At least until you reach their line.'

'A fair point,' Nelson conceded. 'But with French gunnery being what it is, and the stout-heartedness and good training of our men being equal to the occasion, we will prevail. I am certain of it. Certain enough to command my fleet from the first ship in our column. Where I lead, my men will always follow, Sir Arthur,' he added with a glint of pride in his good eye. 'They are devoted to me.'

Arthur shifted uncomfortably in his chair. 'Speaking for myself, I would prefer my men to be well trained and confident rather than devoted.'

'Perhaps you would, Sir Arthur. But when you have led men as long as I have, and won great victories, then the devotion of one's subordinates is as inevitable as it is useful. I am sure you will discover that for yourself in time, when you become more experienced.'

Arthur regarded the admiral coolly. 'I have already acquired a measure of experience, sir, and won my own victories, and I think I managed to understand my men well enough.'

'Ah, yes.' Nelson stared at the younger officer with a faint look of surprise. 'I am sure you are indeed a most competent officer. Do please excuse me for a moment.'

He rose abruptly and strode from the room, leaving Arthur tight-lipped and tense as he took up the newspaper and made himself read some of the small articles surrounding the hagiography that had fed the admiral's conceit. He could hear Nelson in conversation with someone out in the corridor, but their voices were low and the sounds of echoing footsteps from passing clerks made it impossible for Arthur to make out any words. A moment later the admiral returned and took his seat opposite Arthur. He was silent for a moment before he leaned forward.

'I now recall why your name seemed familiar to me a moment ago.'

Arthur looked up and raised his eyebrows enquiringly. 'Indeed?'

'Yes. You are the hero of Assaye and the victor of Argaum, are you not?'

'Hero?' Arthur smiled. 'I'm not so sure about that, my lord. But I had the privilege of commanding the men who won those victories.'

'And noble victories they were!' Nelson leaned forward with an eager expression. 'I read of them a while back. It was hard to fit such singular achievements to a man of your age. My word, it must have been a daunting affair to take on such odds as you faced at Assaye, Sir Arthur.' He nodded admiringly. 'Strikes me that we have something in common. The desire to take the fight directly to the enemy, without delay.'

'It seemed to be the most provident course, my lord. If one does not strike the enemy where one finds him, then the initiative is immediately lost.'

'Quite so! But that philosophy is shared by all too few of our military leaders, not to mention our politicians. They seem to hold to the notion that French power can be whittled away and worn down. They do not understand the nature of the foe. Emperor Napoleon is a new kind of leader. He has no comprehension of the balance of power that has maintained order across the continent in the past. He does not see himself as a member of the council of European rulers, as it were. Napoleon recognises no one as his equal. His sole ambition in this world is to win glory and gain control over all others. He will not rest until he can exercise his will without limit. So we must not rest until he is defeated absolutely. That is what our credo must be, Sir Arthur. A sentiment I feel that you might share.'

'I do, my lord.'

Arthur felt himself warming to the admiral, despite the overbearing self-regard that had spoiled his initial impression of the other man. It was clear that Nelson was well aware of the high stakes in the war against France and the need to see it through whatever sacrifices that entailed.

Arthur continued. 'The problem is that too few of our countrymen are aware of the danger. With Pitt back in power, that may change.'

Nelson's excited expression faded. 'Yes, thank God for Pitt. But have you seen the man lately? He looks old and drawn. I fear the burden of

35

steering our people through this conflict has broken him. I doubt he will survive to see the victory to which he has contributed so much.'

'You are certain we will win?'

'How can we not win, when there are men like you and me to command our forces on land and sea?' Nelson suddenly laughed. 'If you'll pardon the poor couplet.'

Arthur smiled and a moment later a clerk entered the room and bowed his head briefly. 'My lord?'

'Yes.' Nelson rapidly reined in his high spirits. 'What is it?'

'Lord Castlereagh will see you now.'

'Thank you.' Nelson rose from his seat, and Arthur stood up and paused an instant before offering his left hand. The admiral grasped it firmly and smiled. 'It was damned fine to meet you, Sir Arthur. I'm sure we shall meet again in less pressing times. I'll be certain to look you up when I return from beating Monsieur Villeneuve.'

'I will look forward to it, my lord.'

Nelson nodded, still holding Arthur's hand. 'God go with you, Wellesley. Britain needs men like you. Now more than ever.'

'Thank you, sir.'

Nelson gave his hand a final squeeze, then let go and turned to leave the room. When he was gone Arthur sat down again and stared out of the window. The glass had not been cleaned in a while and the smut from the city's fires had stained and pitted the outside surface so that it made the sky seem dirty and gloomy. Yet inside his heart felt warm with pride that a great man like Nelson should have recognised his ability. Particularly Nelson, who obviously had such a huge sense of his own self-importance that the fact he had recognised another man's achievements was high praise indeed. Arthur smiled wryly at the thought. At least Admiral Nelson was clear about his duty, and knew what needed to be done. Arthur picked up the newspaper again and turned the pages, scanning the stories. There was little of interest, save one small editorial piece, allegedly speaking up for the shareholders of the East India Company, demanding that Richard Wellesley be called to account for his actions in India.

He cast the newspaper aside in disgust and stared back towards the window while he waited to be summoned to his interview with Lord Castlereagh. At length, some half-hour after Nelson had preceded him, the clerk returned and led him up another flight of stairs to the offices of the senior ministers. Castlereagh was in a large room with two windows overlooking Downing Street. Opposite the windows was a large map of the known world. Notes were pinned to the map in places of interest to the policymakers in London. The Secretary of State for War and the Colonies stared at him briefly, and then gestured to the chair opposite his desk.

'Welcome back to England, Sir Arthur.'

'Thank you, my lord.'

'You are to be congratulated on your achievements in India. Even some of the most bitter of your family's political opponents grudgingly admit the brilliance of your victories over the native forces opposed to us.'

'That is good to hear. I am sure that those who have followed events in India understand that the credit for such achievements should be directed as much towards my brother as myself.'

'Alas, no.' Castlereagh folded his hands together. 'I am sure that you are aware that the directors of the East India Company are furious at his appropriation of their funds for the purpose of expanding our interests across the subcontinent.'

'I see,' Arthur replied evenly. 'Might I ask where you stand on the matter, my lord?'

Castlereagh indicated a large folder of reports on his desk. 'I have been reading through the material on your brother's term of office, and frankly, I can see why some might argue that his policies were not justified. Take the war against the Mahrattas as an example. The costs of that venture seem to vastly outweigh any perceivable benefits for the Company, and Britain. One might almost suspect that the real reason for fighting the Mahrattas was little more than personal glorification. It must be tempting for any Governor General to make his mark on so broad and unblemished a canvas as the lands of India. Who can blame him?' Castlereagh paused, and when he continued there was ice-cold steel in his tone. 'Nevertheless, the financial, and human, resources of the East India Company are not the playthings of the ambitious. Your brother will be called to account when he returns, and if he fails to explain himself to the satisfaction of Parliament he will be ruined . . . utterly. Now, I am not a vindictive man, Sir Arthur, and I see no reason why the disgrace of your brother should afflict you, or the rest of your family. Particularly if you should co-operate with the inquiry into your brother's actions.'

Arthur cleared his throat and stared directly at the Secretary of State for War. 'This is Britain's darkest hour, my lord. We are fighting for our survival, against a tyrant and his hordes. We are not simply another one of Bonaparte's enemies. We are the last hope of Europe. If we are defeated, then all other nations opposed to France will lose heart.' He leaned forward. 'That is why we must do everything we can to strengthen Britain's power around the world. If Richard had not taken the bull by the horns and strengthened our hold on India, then we would have been forced to contest every inch of the ground with the French and their allies. It is my belief . . . my utter conviction . . . that Richard was justified in his policies, and it is nothing less than a scandal that his political foes are seeking to ruin him. If Bonaparte ever defeats Britain, it will be due as much to the misdirected efforts of envious Englishmen as to his armies.'

He sat back in his chair with a defiant expression. Lord Castlereagh's lips were pressed into a thin line as he stared back. Neither man spoke for a moment, then Castlereagh rose from his chair.

'We have said all that needs to be said for now, Wellesley. I sincerely hope that you will not live to regret your decision to stand by your brother.'

Arthur smiled. 'The longer the war goes on, the less likely it is that I will live to regret any decision, my lord. A prospect that few politicians have to face, I'll warrant. I bid you good day.'

Chapter 6

Napoleon

Boulogne, August 1805

The encampment of the army tasked with invading Britain spread out for miles in all directions. From the top of the signal station Napoleon could make out row upon row of the shacks and shelters that his men had constructed across the countryside. Interspersed with the camps were the areas cleared for parade grounds, artillery parks, supply stockpiles and horse lines. Over a hundred thousand men were poised to board the invasion barges in ports along the coast.

Below the signal station the harbour was filled with clumsy flat-bottomed transports. According to the senior naval officer at the port, the vessels handled badly and were too exposed to the elements. His opinion was of little concern to Napoleon. As long as the barges were capable of crossing the channel to Britain that was all that was required of them. But before that crossing could be undertaken there was the small matter of clearing the path of the opposing fleet.

The wind suddenly howled round the signal station tower for a moment, threatening to dislodge Napoleon's hat, and his hand flew up to hold the brim firmly until the gust had passed. He waited a moment to be sure, then raised his telescope and rested it on the edge of the wall that ran round the top of the tower. He slowly tracked across the choppy white-capped waves out over the sea until he found what he was looking for.

A British frigate was cruising along the coast in a languid fashion, under topsails in the strong breeze. A handful of tiny figures could be seen climbing the rigging to make adjustments to the trim of the canvas that bloomed from the highest spars. Napoleon watched the warship for a moment, as it gracefully went about and put in a tack away from the coast. The same ship had been patrolling the approaches to the harbour for months, in an unceasing routine that varied only minutely according to weather conditions. Napoleon shifted the direction of the telescope towards the horizon and after a short search found the neatly spaced line of white topsails of the rest of the blockading squadron. At least ten ships of the line stood watch over the French port, great towering slabs of oak pierced by two or three lines of gun ports. Between them those ships carried twice as many cannon as the army surrounding Napoleon, and of greater weight too. As the situation stood, if the invasion fleet attempted to cross the Channel in the face of the British navy it would be blown to pieces long before it reached the English coast.

The situation was about to change, Napoleon reflected with satisfaction as he straightened up and closed his telescope with a snap. For months now the scattered squadrons of the French navy had been breaking out of their ports and heading across the Atlantic to a secret rendezvous off the coast of Martinique. If all went according to plan, Admiral Villeneuve would wait until he had forty ships of the line under his command. Then he would recross the ocean and fall upon the English Channel fleet with overwhelming force, and crush the enemy. Even if he failed to defeat them, Villeneuve would be able to clear the Channel for long enough to cover the invasion fleet.

Napoleon turned to his chief of staff. 'Still no word then, Berthier?'

'No, sire. Nothing in the morning despatches.'

'No signals from Paris? Nothing relayed from the watch station at Ushant?'

'I'm afraid not, sire.'

Admiral Villeneuve and his fleet were overdue. Napoleon turned to gaze out over the sprawl of shelters and tents of his army and slapped his thigh in frustration. A month earlier he had secretly quit Italy and travelled across France to be with the army by the time the French fleet appeared in the Channel. After his spectacular coronation in Milan he and his court had toured the great cities of northern Italy, moving from one civic reception to another, surrounded by cheering crowds who were delighted to be free of the iron fist of the Austrian empire. But all the time, Napoleon was thinking of his plans for the invasion of Britain. With luck, the enemy would think that he was still in Italy even as the army was boarding the transports, ready to cross the narrow channel under the protection of Admiral Villeneuve's fleet.

But luck, it seemed, was against him, Napoleon mused. That timid fool Villeneuve had failed to carry out his orders so far. The admiral had been present at the Battle of the Nile when Nelson's warships had annihilated the French fleet. Ever since then Villeneuve had been in awe of the British navy. On several occasions in the past year Napoleon had been driven to frustration and rage by the admiral's failure to put to sea, even when wind and numbers were on his side. It was only by directly threatening to dismiss Villeneuve that he had finally got his way. Napoleon pressed his lips together. Most of the navy's senior officers had been purged during the revolution, and the weak-minded Villeneuve was one of the few that remained. Otherwise he would have been removed from his post long ago.

'Well then,' Napoleon rounded on Berthier, 'I'm returning to headquarters for the rest of the morning. Are the preparations for this afternoon's review complete?'

'Admiral Bruix assures me that all will proceed as planned, weather permitting.'

'Weather permitting?' Napoleon glanced out to sea. 'Surely the admiral is not afraid of a few waves?'

Berthier shrugged. 'He says that there may be a gale brewing up, sire, in which case it would be dangerous for the transports and gunboats to put to sea.'

The anticipation and tension of waiting for Villeneuve to arrive had added to Napoleon's exhaustion after the journey from Milan, and he snapped back irritably to his chief of staff. 'The review will take place. I order it. I will not let a little breeze make a coward of the admiral. You tell him that!'

'A little breeze?' Berthier glanced out to sea where long grey rollers were sweeping in from the ocean. He bit his lip, and when he turned back and saw the dark expression on the Emperor's face he swallowed nervously. 'Yes, sire. I will tell him at once.'

The wind continued to grow in strength during the rest of the morning and by noon there was a gale blowing in over the coast, moaning as it whipped across the tiles of the inn that served as the imperial head-quarters. Napoleon sat at a large table strewn with maps marking the positions of the invasion army and the routes they would take once they landed in Britain. But his mind was not on the details before him. He was deep in thought over the latest news he had received from Paris.

Talleyrand's report told of the continuing preparations for war by Austria and Russia. The Tsar had apparently vowed to put an end to the 'monstrous regime of revolutionary France'. There was some good news, however. Talleyrand had managed to buy Prussian neutrality by offering them Hanover. King Frederick William was only too pleased at having won a new land without having had to fight a war. Napoleon smiled to himself. Clearly the man had no scruples, and, more importantly, no courage. Indeed, the main threat to French interests at the Prussian court was not the King but his wife, Louise, who hated France with all her passion.

'The only real man in the whole of Prussia,' Napoleon mused.

Berthier looked up from the end of the table where he was copying Napoleon's orders in a fair hand for distribution to the small staff of secretaries. 'Sire?'

'It was nothing.' Napoleon flicked his hand dismissively, glanced at the clock against the wall and then stood up abruptly. 'Is Admiral Bruix ready?'

Berthier shrugged. 'He has not sent word yet, sire.'

'Then find him and bring him to me at once. I want the review to commence within the hour. I will brook no further delay. Tell him.'

Berthier nodded, scribbled down the order and left the room in search of an orderly to carry the message to the admiral. Napoleon crossed to the window and looked out at the harbour. Down on the quay stood the men of the division waiting to be rowed out to their vessels. He had ordered Bruix to demonstrate the landing procedure with thirty barges. Once the men were aboard, the flotilla would pass along the shore while Napoleon and his staff watched their progress from a specially erected pavilion. After that the men would demonstrate a landing on the shore. It would be a useful experience for all concerned and Napoleon was looking forward to analysing the procedures to see if he could suggest any improvements. That would put Bruix and the other naval officers in their place, he reflected, and give his subordinates one more example of their Emperor's omniscience.

A sudden patter of rain against the glass drew Napoleon's attention back to the weather. Overhead a thick band of cloud had blotted out the last patch of blue sky and a fresh gust of wind hurled the rain against the window with a sharp rattle. A moment later the view of the harbour had dissolved in the blur of water running down the window panes.

There was a rap on the door and Napoleon turned away from the window. 'Yes?'

Berthier entered, followed by Admiral Bruix and two of his senior officers. The small party approached Napoleon and bowed their heads respectfully.

'I assume that everything is in hand for the review?' said Napoleon.

The admiral seemed to wince before he replied. 'Sire, it is not safe to proceed.'

'Not safe?'

Bruix gestured towards the rain-lashed window. 'There's a gale blowing. It would not be safe. I have given orders for the review to be cancelled.'

'You do not give the orders here, Admiral. I do. And I ordered you to prepare the review.'

'But, sire, in this weather it would be madness.' The instant the word was uttered Bruix realised his mistake and hurriedly tried to conceal the error in a rush of explanations. 'The boats ferrying the men out to the barges could be swamped. The vessels are already overloaded with supplies and equipment. The moment they try to tack out to sea they might be blown on to the shore.'

'Could be? Might be?' Napoleon snapped. 'Where is your courage, Admiral? Where is your determination to see your orders through? Have you no sense of duty?'

Admiral Bruix's face coloured at the attack on his integrity. 'I know my duty, sire. It is my duty to preserve the men and vessels under my command so that they are fit and ready to do battle with the enemy. As such, it is my decision to delay the review until the weather improves.'

'I see,' Napoleon replied icily. 'Then it is my decision to dismiss you from your post, with immediate effect.'

'What?' Admiral Bruix's eyes widened in astonishment. 'You can't do that.'

'It is done. Berthier?'

'Sire?'

'Inform the naval ministry at once. And then see that Monsieur Bruix is removed from our presence and sent home.'

'Yes, sire.'

Napoleon swept his gaze away from the hapless admiral and fixed it on the nearest of the other naval officers. 'You. What is your name?'

'Vice-Admiral Chaloncy, sire.'

'Well then, you will take command of the naval forces in the harbour, and give orders for the review to continue.'

'Sire, I . . .' The vice-admiral glanced helplessly towards Bruix and Napoleon slammed his hand down on the table, making the others jump.

'Damn you navy officers! Is there not one man amongst you ready to do his duty?'

The third naval officer stepped forward at once. 'I'll give the orders, sire.'

'You are?'

'Vice-Admiral Magon, sire.'

Napoleon stared at him and then nodded. 'Very well. You are now promoted to admiral. See to it that there is no further delay.' His glance flicked back to the other naval officers. 'As for you two, get out of my sight.'

By the time word arrived at headquarters to announce that the men had boarded their vessels and the review was ready to begin, the rain was lashing down across the coast and the sea was a heaving mass of lead-coloured waves, fringed with white caps and spume where the wind carried off the spray. The barges, under heavily reefed sails, and towing launches, battled to keep their stations as the flotilla prepared to sail past the imperial pavilion on the beach. Napoleon and his staff, wrapped in oilskins and clasping their hats on their heads with their hands, made their way down through the cobbled streets of the port and out along the strip of sand and shingle to the pavilion.

'Wild weather, sire,' said Berthier. 'I wouldn't fancy being out on the sea in this storm.'

'Storm?' Napoleon laughed. 'This is no storm, Berthier. Merely an unseasonable spell of bad weather. It'll soon pass, you'll see.'

'I hope so, sire. For the sake of our men.'

'A little seasickness never hurt anyone. Besides, they must be prepared to make the crossing in whatever weather there may be when our fleet arrives to clear the Channel.'

They reached the steps to the viewing platform and climbed on to the stage, which overlooked the beach and the sea beyond. In this slightly elevated position the wind was even stronger and the Emperor and his staff officers were forced to squint into the driving rain blowing in off the sea. Napoleon turned to the newly promoted naval commander. 'You may begin, Admiral Magon.'

'Yes, sire.' Magon nodded to the signals officer and a moment later the telegraph arms above the pavilion swung into place to pass on the order to the flotilla. There was a delay as the sailors on the leading barge scrambled aloft from the crowded deck and shook out a reef. Slowly the vessel got under way and cautiously crossed in front of the pavilion before approaching the shore, while the other barges struggled to follow in the heaving seas. One by one they lurched forward across the waves in a straggling line, and then hove to half a league from the pounding surf. At once they dropped anchor, hauled in their sails and swung head into the wind.

Napoleon gestured to Admiral Magon. 'Is this the usual practice, anchoring so far from shore?'

Magon nodded swiftly. 'Of course, sire. Under such conditions the barges' commanders dare not come any nearer to a lee shore.'

'So what happens now?'

'The unloading of the troops will begin.'

Berthier raised his telescope and watched as the longboats pitched up and down as they were hauled alongside the barges. He drew a sharp breath. 'Is it safe?'

Magon swallowed nervously and risked a quick glance at his Emperor before responding. 'I'm sure it's safe enough, sir. In any case, the Emperor has ordered it.'

'That's right,' Napoleon affirmed evenly. 'And we will proceed with the unloading. The men are more than able to cope in these weather conditions. Isn't that so, Admiral?'

'Yes, sire. My officers are in no doubt about what they must do.'

'Good. Then let's see how they handle it.'

Napoleon and his staff fixed their attention on the nearest vessel as the sailors hauled a launch alongside and held it in position with lines and boathooks as the first of the soldiers clambered down the side of the barge. The launch lurched up and caught three men just as they stepped into it, sending two tumbling into the bottom of the boat while the third fell over the side with a splash. He was seen to struggle for a moment, arms waving desperately, then a wave passed over him, sweeping him away, and he was lost from sight. As more soldiers boarded the launch, another two men were lost, and then, at last, the sailors pushed the boat away from the barge and unshipped their oars. But as the wind carried the launch away it turned side on to an oncoming wave and capsized. The staff officers around Napoleon gasped, but he continued to watch without expression as a handful of survivors clung to the bottom of the boat, which floated low in the water like the back of a whale.

'Sweet Jesus,' Berthier muttered. 'Those poor bastards.'

'Yes,' Napoleon said tonelessly. 'Let's see if we have any better luck with the next boat.'

Fortunately, the soldiers from the barge managed to board without incident and the sailors turned the launch smartly into the shore and rowed for their lives. The third boat was not so lucky, and a chaotic surge of foam along the side of the hull swamped her just as she was cast off, carrying away some of the men aboard before the rest panicked as the boat sank into the sea beneath them. Those who could swim struck out for the side of the barge a short distance away. The rest went down with the launch.

Berthier shook his head in horror. 'Sire, we must put a stop to this.'

'No. They handled it badly. The men in the other ships will learn from their example.'

Berthier rounded on his Emperor. 'It is not their fault. That sea is wild. Too wild for any man.'

'But not them, it seems.' Napoleon gestured to the tiny distant gleam of the sails of the British frigate keeping watch over the French exercise. 'If they can cope so far out to sea then surely our men can manage to cover the short distance to the shore?'

'But, sire . . .' Desperately, Berthier looked round the other officers for some support, but most avoided his gaze and those that did not hurriedly glanced away, not daring to defy the Emperor. Berthier turned helplessly towards Napoleon. 'We are doing murder, sire. Signal the ships to end the exercise. I beg you.'

'Berthier!' Napoleon snapped. 'You forget yourself. How dare you challenge my authority? You are to return to headquarters at once.'

'But sire—'

'At once!' Napoleon balled his hands into fists. 'At once, do you hear?'

Berthier stared back for a moment and then his gaze wavered. 'As you wish.'

He turned and strode away through the ranks of the silent officers standing behind Napoleon as the latter glanced back towards the sea. The surviving launch had made it as far as the surf and the sailors timed their oar strokes carefully before putting in a spurt as a large wave lifted the boat and carried it towards the beach. The launch grounded heavily and swerved slightly to one side as the terrified soldiers clambered out, splashed into the surf and ran from the sea. Napoleon noted sourly that some had even abandoned their muskets in their haste. A fresh wave caught the stern quarter of the launch and rolled it over on to the last of the men still aboard, crushing them underneath.

To one side, Napoleon heard a sharp intake of breath as Admiral Magon watched the unfolding disaster. Then the Emperor turned his gaze to the other barges stretching out behind the vessel he had been watching. Many more boats had capsized or floundered and hundreds of men were in the heaving waves, fighting for their lives as their heavy clothes and equipment dragged them down. Less than half the launches reached the shore, and as the dazed soldiers staggered out of the surf the officers and sergeants that remained tried to form them up in their companies on the rain-slick sand. Half an hour after the attempted landing had begun the remains of the division stood shivering, while behind them those men who had managed to swim ashore crawled out of the reach of the waves, exhausted.

Napoleon stared at the scene, thin-lipped and silent. Then he turned abruptly to the admiral and said in a low voice, 'Put an end to this charade, at once. Send the men back to their bivouacs and order the ships back into harbour.'

'Yes, sire.' Magon swallowed and forced himself to continue. 'As soon as they have finished picking up survivors from the sea.'

'What? Yes . . . yes, of course. Take over here, Admiral. But I want a full report on this mess, first thing in the morning. Find out which of your officers were responsible for the shambles and discipline them.'

'Yes, sire.'

Napoleon did not return the admiral's salute, but stalked away, head down and hands clasped behind his back. He could sense the fear of the officers and gave thanks for that small mercy at least. None would dare to confront him over the affair, and he would have Fouché see to it that the Paris newspapers made little of the event. Back in his private quarters Napoleon cast off his wet clothes and ordered his manservant to prepare a bath. Then, as he lay up to his chin in the steaming water, he closed his eyes, folded his hands over his chest and began to reflect on the day. There was no question of it. The navy was woefully unprepared to carry out the vital duty of conveying the invasion army across the Channel. The officers vacillated over every decision, and the men had little opportunity to train and carry out exercises, thanks to the vigilance of the British navy patrolling just off the coast.

Napoleon felt a surge of rage sweep through him. Barely thirty miles from where he lay were the shores of Britain. No more than a day's hard marching. And yet it might as well be three hundred miles, or three thousand, thanks to the wretched stretch of ocean that guarded the country like a moat. As things stood, there was only an outside chance that Britain would ever be invaded. Accepting the point, he suddenly gritted his teeth and thumped the side of the bath. Very well, then. Even if there was no invasion, he would keep an army here, and fill the ports and harbours along the coast with transport ships, just to keep the fear of invasion alive in the minds of the British. That at least would help to divert them from intervention elsewhere. Which was as well, since Napoleon's thoughts were already turning towards a more pressing situation to the east.

The gale blew itself out overnight and in the rosy glow of dawn the sea was calm and a gentle swell rolled in towards the beach. A few battered launches had survived, washed up amid a tide of fragments from the other boats and the bodies of soldiers and sailors who had been lost the previous day. Small parties of men dragged the bodies up from the surf and laid them out in rows where they could be counted and identified.

Berthier entered Napoleon's quarters as the Emperor was hurriedly eating his breakfast. Napoleon glanced up, chewing furiously on a slice of ham, and gestured to a chair on the other side of the table before he raised an eyebrow and stabbed his fork towards the sheaf of papers Berthier was carrying.

'The morning roll call of the division chosen to demonstrate the landing, sire,' Berthier explained. 'It appears that we lost over two thousand men yesterday. Of course, some might have been swept up the coast and may yet report back to their battalions. But they won't amount to many.'

Napoleon swallowed, and took a quick swig of water to clear his mouth. 'That doesn't matter now. I summoned you for another reason.'

'Sire?'

'I'm calling the invasion off. If Villeneuve ever arrives, he can still take on the British navy. Who knows, by some miracle he may even beat them. Be that as it may, the invasion army is to be reduced to one corps. As for the rest of the army, they must be prepared to march.'

'March, sire?' Berthier's eyes widened with surprise. 'Where to?'

'To the Danube, Berthier. It is time to confront Austria.'

Chapter 7

Paris, September 1805

'Not a very satisfactory state of affairs,' Napoleon muttered as he eased himself down into the bath. He sighed as Josephine leaned forward on her cushioned stool and stroked his hair. 'I leave Paris for two months, and that fool Mercurier turns a blind eye while his officials make off with a fortune from the National Treasury. As if that was not enough, Fouché tells me that thousands of those men called up to join the army have taken to their heels and are hiding in the countryside.' He frowned for a moment and then continued. 'Well, they'll soon learn the price of defying their Emperor.'

'Oh?' Josephine arched her eyebrows.

'I have ordered Fouché to track down those who stole from the treasury, and the deserters who betray their country. They'll be tried and shot, the lot of them.' Napoleon nodded vehemently. 'And good riddance. I do not need such distractions on the eve of a new war. I must leave Paris in a few days, a week at the most.'

'So soon?' Josephine pouted as she looked down at Napoleon.

He nodded. 'My dear, we should never have stayed in Paris this last month. It was never my intention.' He yawned. 'By now I had hoped we would have been with the headquarters at Strasbourg.'

'Strasbourg . . .' Josephine repeated vaguely. 'A nice enough city, I suppose, but it is not Paris. I sometimes wonder how those provincials cope with such lack of stimulation.'

Napoleon glanced at her with an amused smile. 'Sometimes you are such a snob, my dear. Not everyone enjoys your privileges. And it is not as if all this finery is something you were born into.' He gestured round the ornately decorated sleeping chamber with its heavy purple curtains, gold-leaf mouldings and thick carpets. 'Nor was I, for that matter.'

He stared at the room for a moment in thought. In truth he felt little for all these luxurious trappings. The Corsican streak in him tended to value the practical over the ostentatious, but the panoply of the imperial household was necessary to bolster the legitimacy of the new regime and set it on a level with the other ruling houses of Europe. It was a sad truth, he reflected, that men were so easily swayed by baubles. But a useful truth. Surround a man with the trappings of a king and he would be treated as one, even though he was of the same flesh and blood as those who bowed to him. That was why the moment he became Emperor Napoleon had insisted that all the old protocols of the deposed Bourbon household be consulted to ensure that the imperial court appeared authentic and traditional, and not spirited out of thin air. To be sure, the palaces, servants and procedures looked the part, but there was some nagging doubt in his mind and he looked at Josephine again.

'Do you think we are carrying it off?'

She raised a plucked brow at him. 'What do you mean, my darling?'

'All this.' He waved a hand at the room and then continued, 'And us. Emperor Napoleon and Empress Josephine.'

She shrugged. 'What does it matter? You are the Emperor. By law and by the will of the people. That's all that matters, surely?'

'I don't know.' Napoleon frowned. 'I feel that I have earned the right to call myself Emperor, as much as any man can.'

'And yet?' Josephine prompted.

'And yet I sometimes feel as if I am playing a role, and so are you, and all the others. All the chamberlains, stewards, equerries, masters of the hunt, and so on. We wear the costumes and speak the proper lines, but at the end of the day it appears to knowledgeable onlookers that we are just performers. Take our friend Talleyrand, for example. I can never shake off the feeling that he considers me his inferior.'

'He considers everybody his inferior.' Josephine chuckled bitterly. 'Why, I am sure that when the man dies the very first thing he will do when he reaches heaven is admonish the almighty for taking as many as six days to create the world.'

'If such a man as Talleyrand is admitted to heaven, then there is hope for us all.' Napoleon was silent for a moment before continuing. 'The man despises me. He thinks me a coarse upstart. And he's not the only one. I've seen the way some of the aristos look at me.'

'You are imagining it, my love.'

'No. They only serve me for as long as they can profit from it. They would as soon serve under a Bourbon as me. In fact, I imagine they would prefer a Bourbon ruler to a Bonaparte. I fear that's why we shall never know peace in Europe while I am Emperor.'

Josephine looked at him for a moment and then shook her head. 'I don't understand.'

'These endless coalitions of other nations are determined to defeat France, or rather to defeat me. Perhaps that is what all this is about. The revolution toppled the Bourbons and proved that the people could choose their own ruler, rather than have one imposed by divine right. That is what they cannot tolerate. As long as I stand as refutation of the birthright of aristocrats and monarchs they can never rest easy. I, and what I stand for, must be swept away in order that they can survive on their thrones.' He sighed wearily. 'There can be no peace. This is a war without precedent, Josephine. This is not about redrawing boundaries, nor redressing grievances, nor even about the shift in power between royal households. This is a war between two ideals. A war to determine whether we shall live in a world governed by birthright, or a world governed by raw ability.'

'Really?' Josephine looked at him and stifled a yawn. 'If you say so, my love. Now then.' She stroked a hand down his chest and slowly continued across his stomach, the tips of her fingers setting his nerves alight. 'If there is to be a war, we must make the most of our time together.'

Napoleon's eyelids fell as her fingers gently closed around his penis. As it stirred, he let out a faint moan. For a moment, at least, his thoughts on the destiny of Europe were put aside.

The following day, a signal reached Paris from the army headquarters at Strasbourg. The staff officer who had interrupted Napoleon as he approved the drafts of his orders and instructions in his office stood at attention breathing hard as the Emperor scanned the short note scribbled on the slip of paper. Napoleon rose from his desk and crossed the room to the map table that ran along one wall. Shuffling through the maps that were spread out on its top, he pulled out one that displayed the heart of Europe, from the eastern frontier of France across to the heart of the Austrian empire. Summoning the staff officer to join him, Napoleon tapped the uneven line that marked the passage of the river Inn.

'Murat's scouts report that an Austrian army under General Mack has crossed the Inn, and is heading for Munich.' He paused, and then nodded to himself. 'They mean to crush our Bavarian allies before turning on Strasbourg. Murat says that there is no sign of the Russians as yet. It seems that the Austrians are intent on grabbing the glory of defeating France before their allies can intervene. Very well, let them come.'

He turned to the staff officer, his mind made up. 'Send a signal to

Strasbourg immediately. Tell Berthier to give the order for the Grand Army to begin concentration. They are to be ready to cross the Rhine no later than the last week of September. Got that?'

'Yes, sir.'

'And have Berthier draft a general order to the troops. He is to tell them that all the riches of Vienna will be theirs for the taking, before the year is out.'

Chapter 8

Strasbourg, 24 September 1805

As two of the junior staff officers spread out the map and weighted the corners Napoleon looked round the table at the commanders of his army corps. There was an expectant and excited air about these men he had come to know so well over the years. They were the cream of those officers who had risen through the ranks during the wars that had followed the revolution. Unlike their Austrian and Russian counterparts most of Napoleon's marshals and generals were not aristocrats, and owed their present positions to their own efforts. They would need every last reserve of courage and quick wits in the weeks to come, Napoleon reflected as he watched them lean forward to examine the map spread out before them. Berthier had already marked out the dispositions of the Grand Army, and the possible locations and strength of enemy forces.

Clearing his throat, Napoleon motioned to them to take their seats on either side of the table.

'Gentlemen, before I begin let me say that you have all performed prodigious feats of organisation in preparing your men so swiftly for this campaign. I am in your debt.' He bowed his head. 'Now then, on to the plan. As you can see, it appears that our enemies have not yet realised that the main weight of our attack will be directed across the Rhine and on towards the Danube. Our spies report that there are nearly a hundred thousand Austrian troops concentrating to attack northern Italy. Meanwhile another twenty thousand are defending Tyrol, while a third force of seventy thousand, under General Mack and Archduke Ferdinand, is advancing towards the Rhine to try to cut us off from our Bavarian allies. It is likely that Mack has also been tasked with holding us back long enough to permit the Russian armies of Kutusov and Bennigsen to join forces with them.'

Napoleon paused to let his commanders take in the situation. 'The Austrians have already made their first mistake, in dividing their strength. They assume that this war will be like the last and fought out on two fronts, either side of the Alps. But this time we will undertake only one offensive, over the Danube. Our forces in Italy will merely contain the Austrians. The Grand Army has been given the best men and resources to carry out its task and there is no enemy in Europe that can match our men. The main danger facing us is the possibility of the Austrians' trading space for time in order to combine with the Russians. It is imperative that we seize the chance to strike at the Austrians, before the Russians arrive, and crush them individually.'

Napoleon leaned forward and tapped the area of the map that depicted the Black Forest. 'We begin by making a feint here. Murat's cavalry will move towards the upper Danube, as if screening our advance. While General Mack's attention is focused on the Black Forest the real offensive will begin.' Napoleon swept his hand in an arc across the map, from the Rhine through Bavaria and over the Danube. 'The Grand Army will strike east, as fast as it can march, until it is level with Munster, and then turn south, cross the Danube and cut General Mack's lines of supply. Then he will be forced to surrender, or be overwhelmed. Once Mack has been dealt with, we will attack the other Austrian armies in turn. If we move fast enough we will knock Austria out of the war before the Russians can intervene.'

Bernadotte seared his throat. 'Do we have any information about the location of Kutusov or Bennigsen, sire?'

Napoleon shook his head. 'Not yet. But Murat's scouts have orders to advance along both banks of the Danube as far as possible to give us the earliest news of the appearance of Russian troops.'

'And if they do appear before we have crushed General Mack?'

'Then it will be the job of your corps to hold them back, Bernadotte. As soon as you cross the Danube at Ingolstadt your men will turn east and guard our flank.'

Bernadotte quickly searched for the crossing point on the map and nodded. 'Very well, sire. But what if the Austrians attempt to bring up their forces from Tyrol, or Italy?'

'Davout's corps will block them,' Napoleon replied with a quick glance at the other officer. 'That leaves five corps to surround and destroy General Mack. Assuming he doesn't guess our plans before we can get across the Danube.'

'And if he does?'

'Then he will be forced to turn his army round and attempt to march out of the trap before it closes. However, as some of us have discovered in the past, our Austrian friends are not renowned for the speed of their marching.'

Those who had served with Napoleon on his Italian campaigns smiled in amusement at the comment as the Emperor continued.

'If Mack tries to retreat we should still have time to cut across his line of march, and destroy each of his columns in turn. Either way, we will compel him to fight on our terms, and most likely on ground of our choosing. With luck, the Russians will arrive just in time to witness the surrender of Austria.'

Soult raised his eyebrows and said mildly, 'That assumes that the Russians won't reach the Danube for at least another six weeks. Can we be sure of that, sire?'

'As sure as we can be of anything,' Napoleon responded dismissively. 'Time and surprise are on our side, gentlemen. Even the weather seems to favour our cause, for now. I sense that the Grand Army is about to take its place in history.'

At dawn the following day, Napoleon sat with his staff on a hill above the Rhine watching the dense columns of Lannes's infantry cross the river and climb up the slope on the eastern bank. The air was cool and overhead the sky was clear, promising fine conditions for the advance of the Grand Army. Away to the north, downriver, Napoleon knew that the other corps would also be on the move, tramping east behind a screen of Murat's cavalry, who were tasked with preventing the Austrians from discovering the vast army sweeping across Bavaria.

Over two hundred thousand men and fifty thousand horses were involved in the vast strategic manoeuvre, and with them went several hundred cannon, engineer columns, pontoon detachments and medical staff, together with the vast supply trains carrying ammunition and food. The latter would only be distributed when the French columns closed on their enemy and foraging became too dangerous. It was a vast enterprise, and not without its risks should the enemy discover the ruse, yet Napoleon felt confident that every detail that mattered had been accounted for. Even so, he turned to Berthier and quietly asked, 'Any news from Murat?'

'No, sire. I would imagine that he has little enemy contact to report at this stage.'

That was true enough, Napoleon reflected. Murat's light cavalry would only be sparring with the Austrian scouts for a few days yet. Not until the two armies approached each other would more substantial actions be fought and more definite intelligence gathered. Nevertheless, the whereabouts of the Russian armies marching to Austria's aid concerned Napoleon greatly. Everything depended on dealing a mortal blow to General Mack before he could be reinforced.

'Very well, but I want to know the moment we hear from Murat.'

'Yes, sire.' Berthier nodded and hurriedly scribbled a line in his notebook.

Napoleon watched his chief of staff approvingly. Now that the campaign had begun he would have the critical facts about his army at his fingertips, thanks to the detailed notebooks that Berthier kept at the field headquarters. Each day every regiment's strength returns and location would be updated so that the Emperor would be able to control his huge army and time its movements with precision.

Napoleon felt his heart swell with pride at his achievement. Truly there was no finer instrument of war than the Grand Army.

Marshal Lannes came riding up the slope towards him and saluted as he reined in. With a grin he swept off his hat and gestured towards the French host crawling across the landscape. 'Quite a sight! Never seen anything so fine in my life, sire.'

'Let's hope the Austrians feel the same.' Napoleon returned the grin. 'What is the mood of your men?'

'Never better, sire. For the most part.' Lannes smiled wryly. 'Of course there are the usual grumblers, but they'll never be happy. You know what the veterans are like. They'll moan about their boots, the rations and the weather, and blame it all on their officers. But the moment you march 'em on to the battlefield they can't wait to carve a path through the enemy.'

Napoleon looked him in the eye and lowered his voice as he spoke. 'And you, my old friend, how do you feel?'

'Sire?'

'Do you share the men's confidence? Do you think we can defeat our enemies this time?'

Lannes returned his look with a faint expression of hurt and surprise. 'Of course we can defeat them, sire. If you have planned this war, and you are there to lead us into battle, then how can we fail?'

Napoleon stared into his comrade's face, searching for any sign of insincerity. Lannes had been with him since the very first campaign in Italy. His face still bore the faint scar from the wound he had received as they had charged the bridge at Arcola. Napoleon recalled the other battles they had fought, as well as the hardships shared during the terrible marches across the deserts of Egypt. Lannes had stood by his side when Napoleon had snatched power from the corrupt politicians of the Directory, and he was there again in the second Italian campaign and the desperately close battle at Marengo. Napoleon nodded to himself. Lannes was as much a friend as a follower, and when so many had fallen along the way, a friend was to be valued indeed. Especially one so brave and blunt as Lannes.

Napoleon suddenly leaned towards Lannes and punched him lightly on the shoulder. 'My dear, dear Marshal! You are right. How can we fail? We have the best soldiers and by far the best leaders of men in Europe. Leaders like the great Marshal Lannes himself.'

The Gascon beamed with pleasure at his Emperor's praise and then nodded. 'Yes, sire. I shall never let you down.'

'I am counting on that, old friend. But please do me one favour.'

'Anything, sire.'

'Try not to get yourself wounded, or killed.'

Lannes laughed. 'That rather depends on the enemy.'

'Well don't give them any assistance, Lannes. You are a marshal of France. Your men will need you throughout the coming campaign. I will need you. You can let your subordinates lead the charges.'

'But sire!' Lannes protested. 'I was a grenadier long before I was a marshal.'

'No buts. I cannot afford to lose any of my best officers.'

Lannes frowned, and replaced his hat firmly before grumbling. 'Very well, sire. If that is your order.'

'It is. Make sure you obey it. Now you may return to your corps, Marshal.'

'Yes, sire.'

Lannes bowed his head and turned his horse away, then spurred it into a trot as he descended the slope and rejoined his staff. Berthier watched him go for a moment before muttering, 'A fine man, that.'

Napoleon watched the retreating figure of the marshal before he responded. 'One of the very finest.'

The Grand Army's columns tramped swiftly east. The soldiers rose before dawn, shivering as they shouldered their packs and shuffled into their companies, their breath pluming in the first grey glimmer of light. Around them came the snorts and whinnying of horses being saddled and harnessed for the day's march. Then, one by one, the regiments, brigades and divisions of each corps began to tramp forward. The infantry marched on either side of the route, with the wheeled traffic of wagons and artillery moving along the tracks and roads. As the sun rose the men cast an eye over the surrounding countryside, the youngest amongst them looking earnestly for any sign of the enemy, while the veterans turned their experienced gaze on the small villages and farms they passed through, minds focused on foraging, and, if the opportunity arose, a discreet looting expedition under cover of darkness.

Every two hours the order was given for a brief rest and the men lowered their packs and muskets and slumped down. Those that had pipes lit them while the air filled with animated conversations about the coming battles and the prospects for victory. Then an order would be barked out and the men hurriedly re-formed ranks and waited for each brigade's band to strike up a tune to get them on their way again. Sometimes it was a rousing patriotic piece, but more often a song that had become popular in the ranks, and the soldiers sang lustily as they marched on. Then, at noon, the army halted, and once the men had fallen out and made the best of whatever shelter was available, they were free to forage for the remainder of the day.

The fine weather lasted to the end of September before dark clouds closed in from the north-east and an icy wind swept across Bavaria, bringing with it rain that quickly turned to sleet and brief flurries of snow. Now the men of the Grand Army marched forward in sullen silence, collars pulled high and mufflers tied over their shakos as they trudged into the wind with bent heads. As October began, in the freezing cold and wet, Napoleon realised that the new conditions would hamper the march east and might give his enemies time to recognise the threat and turn to meet the Grand Army. So he gave the order for the army to swing south and march as quickly as possible for the Danube.

Five days later, French troops began to appear along the northern bank of the great river and they seized every bridge and ferry that could be found before pouring across. Napoleon, riding with the leading divisions of Lannes's corps, made for Augsburg, the town he had chosen for his field headquarters. He had spent much of the previous days in the saddle as he had moved from corps to corps to ensure that his marching orders were being rigorously applied. When night fell the Emperor and his staff were still some ten miles from Augsburg, so Napoleon decided to stop at the camp of one of Ney's divisions.

At the sound of the approaching horsemen the pickets emerged from the shadows on either side of muddy track and advanced their muskets warily.

'Halt!' a deep voice bellowed out. 'Who goes there?'

Napoleon was riding with a handful of staff and six cavalrymen from the guard, one of whom now bristled angrily at the challenge and stood erect in his stirrups to shout a reply.

'The Emperor!'

There was a brief silence before the voice called back. 'Bollocks! What's the password?'

The guardsman swore under his breath and then bellowed, 'Move aside, you fools, before we ride you down!'

'That's enough!' Napoleon snapped. 'They're only doing their duty.'

The guardsman stiffened. 'Sorry, sire. But they shouldn't address the imperial party like that.'

'Really?' Napoleon smiled wearily. 'Do you know what the password is?'

The guardsman breathed in sharply and hissed, 'No, sire.'

'Why not?'

The Emperor did not wait for a reply from his shamed escort, but spurred his horse on and trotted towards the line of dark figures barring his path, warily watching the dull gleam of their raised bayonets. His escort hurried after Napoleon as he reined in a short distance from the picket.

'And who are you?' asked Napoleon.

'Fuck me,' the voice muttered. 'It is him!' A moment later a burly sergeant stepped forward and saluted.

'Sorry, sir. But we had to chase off some Austrian dragoons earlier today. Can't be too careful.'

'At ease, Sergeant. You did well to challenge us. I'd have had you broken back to the ranks if you hadn't. Now then, what is this unit?'

'Sixty-third regiment of the line, sir. Dupont's division.'

'Dupont?' Napoleon recalled that the previous day General Dupont's four thousand men had attacked an enemy force four times their size in order to force a crossing of the Danube, and suffered heavy losses as a result. Now that he looked round the men of the picket, Napoleon could see that some of them were bandaged. Kicking his right foot from its stirrup, he swung his leg over the saddle and dismounted. He turned to face the sergeant, a huge man with several days' growth of beard darkening his chin.

'What's your name?'

'Sergeant Legros, sir.'

'Legros, eh? And why do you not address your Emperor correctly? It is sire, not sir.'

'If you please, sire, you were my general before you became my Emperor.'

'Your general?'

'I served with you in Italy, in ninety-five, sir . . . sire.'

'Ah!' Napoleon smiled and grasped the sergeant's arms. 'One of the first of my comrades. There are all too few of us left, Legros. And you may call me sir, if you wish.'

Legros smiled. 'Yes, sir.'

Napoleon glanced round at the other men. 'From the reports, your division had quite a fight.'

Legros nodded. 'We buried some good men yesterday. But the enemy buried more.'

Napoleon nodded with satisfaction and then nodded towards the small fire burning a short distance down the road. In its glow a man was hunched over a cauldron stirring the contents with a long wooden ladle. 'Would you share some soup with your general?'

'It would be an honour, sir,' Legros bowed his head and turned to lead Napoleon towards the fire. He called out to his corporal to take charge while he entertained the Emperor. With a quick gesture to one of his escort to take the reins of his horse, Napoleon strode quickly to catch him up. As they approached the man at the cauldron a number of other soldiers sat up. As soon as the first of them recognised the man at their sergeant's side there was an excited whispering and they jumped to their feet and stiffened to attention.

Napoleon raised a hand to them. 'Easy there! Just an old comrade come to warm himself at your fire, and share rations, if there is any soup to spare.'

As he stepped into the orange loom of the crackling blaze Legros took a battered bowl and spoon from his kit and proffered it to the Emperor. Even though rations were short, it was clear the sergeant felt honoured to share his supper with Napoleon.

'Thank you.' Napoleon took the bowl and turned to the man at the cauldron. 'May I?'

'Yes, sire!' The man instantly passed over the ladle. Leaning towards the steaming cauldron, Napoleon dipped the ladle in and gave the stew a quick stir before scooping up a portion and pouring it into his bowl. He returned the ladle and took up his spoon. Raising the bowl he gave it a cautious sniff, and found that the warm hearty smell was to his liking, particularly as he had eaten nothing since dawn. He took a spoonful and blew carefully across the surface before he sipped. It was hot, but not so hot as to burn his mouth, and he swallowed it eagerly before looking up at the expectant faces surrounding him. More and more shadows were emerging from the darkness as word spread through the camp that the emperor was present.

'Good soup!' Napoleon announced. 'A bit saltier than I used to have it when I was a junior lieutenant, but good all the same.'

He took another spoonful as he let the men marvel that their Emperor had once lived on the same fare as themselves. It was another chance for Napoleon to win their hearts and he smiled to himself as he observed the crowd gathering round him. After a few sips he handed the bowl back to Sergeant Legros and wiped his lips on the back of his hand. 'Thank you. I needed that.' He raised his voice. 'Soldiers! I know of your brave deeds yesterday. But tell me, who is the bravest man in this regiment?'

There was a pause before Legros's name was shouted, and at once there was a widespread roar of approval. Napoleon grinned as he turned back to the huge figure looking slightly embarrassed by the shouts of his comrades.

'It seems that you are the regiment's hero, Legros.'

'Just doing my duty, sir.'

'Of course. Well then,' Napoleon frowned slightly as if considering a problem and then suddenly laughed and clasped Legros's hand, 'I promote you to lieutenant. Your regiment is going to need good officers if it keeps fighting as fiercely as it did yesterday. Congratulations, Lieutenant Legros.'

The man looked astonished and tilted his head slightly from side to side. 'Don't know what to say, sir.'

'Thank you will do.'

The men around laughed, and then someone cheered for the newly promoted Legros and the others joined in. Napoleon let them indulge themselves for a moment before he turned to one of his staff officers to ensure that the promotion was noted and made official as soon as possible. As he was talking there was a pounding of hooves down the road and Napoleon glanced round to see a staff officer galloping towards the fire.

'Where's the Emperor?' the new arrival shouted as he saw Napoleon's escort. He jumped down from his hard-breathing mount as soon as he saw Napoleon and thrust his way through the soldiers. With some difficulty he composed himself enough to stand to attention and salute before he ripped a folded sheet of paper from inside his coat. 'Sire! Despatch from Marshal Ney.'

'What's happened?' Napoleon asked quietly as he took the message.

'We've got them, sir. The Austrians. Ney's vanguard captured an Austrian colonel. He told them that Mack's army is at Ulm. We've caught them on the wrong side of the Danube, sir. With their backs to the hills and the Black Forest, they're caught like rats in a trap.'

'As I always knew they would be,' Napoleon responded tersely, as he read the full details by the light of the fire. When he finished he crumpled the message and tossed it into the blaze, then turned to the crowd of soldiers who had gathered to see him.

'Tomorrow the Grand Army closes its fist round the throat of General Mack! First blood to the Grand Army!' Napoleon punched his hand into the air and the men roared their approval. He watched their excited faces for a moment and then turned to re-join his waiting staff officers and escort. Behind him the cheers echoed to the skies.

Chapter 9

Ulm, 16 October 1805

Hemmed in on all sides, the Austrians retreated to Ulm and prepared the hapless town for an assault. As nearly a hundred thousand men of the Grand Army closed around the defenders, the guns of the artillery reserve were brought forward and batteries were dug into the hills surrounding the town. At dawn, Napoleon was sitting on a campaign chair a short distance above the largest battery. Around him scores of staff officers talked in muted tones as they waited for the bombardment to begin. Napoleon ignored them. He was filled with an immense feeling of gratification that his plans had come to fruition so swiftly. The night before, he had received word from Marshal Bernadotte that the Russian army of General Kutusov had finally been located, two hundred miles from Ulm. Napoleon nodded faintly as he considered the situation. Kutusov was far enough away to give the Grand Army time to defeat the Austrians before turning to face the Russians. He pulled his coat more tightly about his shoulders and hunched down into the collar as he concentrated his gaze on the panorama stretching out before him.

Below his position lay the lines of the Grand Army, and a short distance beyond, the hastily erected redoubts and earthworks that ringed Ulm. A faint mist had risen from the Danube, on the far side of the city, and most of the buildings were grey and indistinct. Only the spires of churches and the roofs of taller buildings were high enough to be seen clearly. The air was filled with the shouts of artillery officers as they trained their guns on distant targets and gave the order for the weapons to be loaded with round shot. It was a cold morning, and a gleaming frost covered the frozen ground. Ideal conditions for artillery fire, as the cannonballs that did not immediately strike an object would take several bounces before coming to rest, thereby greatly increasing their range and capacity to do damage.

Out of the corner of his eye Napoleon saw a staff officer come trotting up to General Marmont. He saluted and spoke briefly before his superior strode across the slope towards the Emperor.

'Sire, I beg to report that the artillery is ready to commence the bombardment, on your order.'

Napoleon nodded, drew a draught of chilled air deep into his lungs and took one last look at the peaceful town of Ulm nestling beside the dull gleam of the Danube. Then he breathed out. 'Very well. You may open fire.'

'Yes, sire.' Marmont saluted and turned to bellow the order to the crew of the signal gun. 'Open fire!'

The gunner with the linstock lowered the smouldering end to the powder in a small paper cone poking into the vent. There was a brief flare, then a jet of flame and smoke billowed from the muzzle an instant before the booming report carried up the hill to Napoleon and his staff. A moment later the rest of the massed guns of the Grand Army opened fire with a deep rolling roar that filled the morning sky like thunder. Hundreds of plumes of flame and smoke spat from the muzzles of the French guns, and then roof tiles exploded off the buildings of Ulm to show where some of the shot had struck home. Those guns that had been ordered to direct their fire at the Austrian earthworks began to take their toll, gouts of soil bursting into the air as fascines and timber fortifications were battered down. The defenders soon returned fire and the French positions received their damage in turn. But such was the weight of the Grand Army's fire that General Mack's outlying batteries were gradually silenced as the morning wore on. The sun rose in the sky and the mist from the Danube cleared from the streets of Ulm, only to be replaced by a thick cloud of dust swirling up from the masonry being pounded to pieces by heavy iron shot. Thick banks of smoke hung over the artillery positions of both sides, making them fire blind as they trusted to the careful laying of the guns before the bombardment to stay on target.

The gun crews had been ordered to cease fire at noon, and within a few minutes of the hour the last of the guns had fallen silent. A short time later the Austrians gradually followed suit and the comparative silence and stillness that followed was initially unnerving to the men new to war. Those in the artillery batteries quickly took advantage of the break in the action to make quick repairs to their defences, and drag away damaged guns as well as the dead and injured.

Up on the hill, Napoleon was taking a light meal of cold chicken, bread and watered wine when his attention was drawn to an excited babble amongst his staff officers. Lowering the wicker basket that contained his makeshift lunch, he rose and turned to follow the direction of their gaze. A small party of horsemen had emerged from the

Austrian lines. Two men carried trumpets and were repeatedly blowing the same shrill call as they crossed the open ground between the two armies. Another man carried a large white standard, which he waved from side to side to ensure that it was clearly seen by the wary French skirmishers. The party was led by an officer with a broad red sash over his shoulder, and several decorations glittered brilliantly on his chest.

They were met at the French lines by a junior officer who directed them on to his regimental commander, who had them escorted to his brigade commander, and so on until they finally rode up the slope into the presence of the Emperor of France himself. Napoleon had resumed eating his meal and made a show of reluctance in putting it aside again as the Austrian officer dismounted and strode stiffly towards him. He was about to speak when Napoleon silenced him curtly with a raised hand. 'A moment, if you please!'

He slowly chewed the last mouthful, staring intently at the Austrian as he did so, until finally the other man's gaze wavered. Napoleon casually wiped his hands on a napkin and stood up to address the Austrian officer.

'There. You may speak.'

The Austrian's mouth sagged open in surprise at this curt treatment. Then he recovered, cleared his throat and began to deliver his message.

'I am Colonel Count Freudklein, on the staff of General Mack. He sends you his warmest compliments and an offer to open negotiations with you.'

'Negotiations?' Napoleon interrupted. 'To surrender?'

'Surrender? No, sir!' Colonel Freudklein frowned. 'General Mack wishes to discuss an armistice. That is all.'

'An armistice . . .' Napoleon considered this for a minute, and then folded his arms and stared intently at the officer again. 'How long does General Mack wish it to last?'

'Ten days, sir.'

'Ten days is a long time. Perhaps he has heard that Kutusov and his army are approaching?'

Freudklein kept his face expressionless and after a moment Napoleon grinned. 'My dear Colonel, I am kept fully informed as to the whereabouts of Kutusov. And I know full well that he is sufficiently distant to allow me to reduce Ulm and compel your surrender long before he arrives.'

'We shall see about that, sir. The Russians might be here sooner than you think.'

'Perhaps, but I doubt it. In any case, I am a compassionate man. My army might enjoy a brief rest from its exertions, as could yours. I grant your general his armistice.' Napoleon paused for effect. 'On one condition.'

'Yes?'

'That General Mack agrees to surrender his forces to me if the Russians have not relieved him within nine days of the signing of the armistice. That is my offer, and it is not negotiable. Now return to your general and let him know my terms.'

Colonel Freudklein saluted and returned to his horse and remounted. At a kick of his spurs his horse reared slightly and then galloped off down the slope, and his three companions quickly urged their mounts to follow him. Napoleon watched them go with a satisfied smile. His offer was generous, and acceptable to General Mack, who was desperate to buy time as he awaited his Russian allies. The Austrians no doubt assumed that Kutusov would reach them within ten days. But the latest report from placed at least two weeks' march from Ulm. So, Napoleon mused, let the Austrians have their armistice, as long as they agreed to his surrender date.

The next morning, representatives of both armies met on open ground and signed the truce. General Mack declined to be there in person so Napoleon sent Berthier to complete the agreement in his own place. If the Russians failed to relieve their allies by the expiry of the armistice then the Austrians agreed to surrender to the Grand Army. Once the document had been signed the men of both armies stood down and settled into their camps while their pickets continued to watch each other warily. As the enemy toiled to repair their defences the French soldiers, exhausted by the rapid advance of the previous month, rested and repaired their uniforms and equipment. Napoleon saw to it that they were kept supplied with wine and the best food that could be looted from the surrounding towns and villages. As the autumn evenings drew in the French lines were alive with the sounds of good-humoured banter, song and laughter. On the other side the Austrians sat and quietly waited for word of the approach of their Russian saviours.

In the days that followed, at the country estate chosen for the headquarters of the Grand Army Napoleon spent long hours with Berthier planning the next stage of the campaign. The daily reports from Bernadotte told of the plodding advance of General Kutusov's army, and as Napoleon scrutinised the maps spread over the floor of his quarters he knew there was no question of the Austrian army's being relieved before the armistice expired. Kneeling on the map and

measuring the distance with his dividers Napoleon nodded with satis-
faction. Then his eyes flicked to the area representing the lands of
Prussia and he stared fixedly at it for a moment before addressing
Berthier, who was sitting on a stool to one side taking notes.

'What's the latest news from Prussia?'

Berthier pursed his lips as he hurriedly recalled his examination of
the morning's despatches. 'According to our ambassador the war party
is still trying to goad Frederick William into joining the coalition, but
he's reluctant to take the risk.'

'Risk?' Napoleon sniffed with contempt. 'What risk could there
possibly be if he joined forces with the Tsar and the Emperor of Austria?
They would outnumber us three to one. The man is a coward and a
fool.'

'Just as well for us, sire.'

'Yes,' Napoleon replied quietly. 'So . . . It is imperative that we keep
our enemies divided. That means we must end this war swiftly, with the
kind of annihilating victory that will crush the very idea of further
opposition to France.' He shuffled round and tapped his dividers on the
Austrian capital. 'It will not be sufficient to occupy Vienna. We cannot
dictate terms until we have destroyed their army.'

Berthier nodded. 'Indeed. But the loss of Vienna would still be a
heavy blow to them, sire.'

Napoleon shook his head. 'It is only a city, Berthier. Bricks and
mortar. It can do us no harm. Still, in some ways it is a shame that old
niceties of war have perished. It would be far more convenient if our
enemies gave in once their capital cities had fallen. But this is a new age
for warfare. Only the swift and the ruthless will prevail. That is why we
win, Berthier.'

'Yes, sire.'

The sound of heavy boots echoed down the corridor outside the
room and both men turned towards the door as there was a sudden
sharp rap.

'Come!' Napoleon called out as he heaved himself up and stepped
carefully off the map. The door swung open and Marshal Lannes
entered, his face flushed with excitement.

'Sire, you'd better come and see this at once!'

'See what?'

'It's the Austrians, sire. They are breaking the armistice. There are two
columns advancing out of the Ulm defences.'

'Treachery,' Napoleon growled. 'This is what you get when you trust
the word of an Austrian aristocrat. Come on, Berthier!'

Snatching up his hat, Napoleon strode from the room. With Lannes and Berthier following, he hurried outside and gestured to one of the grooms to bring their horses. The small party galloped out of the stable yard and across the open countryside towards the observation point atop a low hill overlooking Ulm and its defences. All around them drums were beating and trumpets shrilled out, calling the men of the Grand Army to take up their arms and form in their regiments ready to face the enemy. On the hill, a handful of officers was watching the enemy positions fixedly and were only aware of the Emperor's arrival when he dismounted and snatched a telescope from a young lieutenant. He trained it in the direction of Ulm and took a breath to steady the view as he panned across the lines of defences. Sure enough, there were two vast columns advancing from the town. Away to the north a dense mass of cavalry, perhaps several thousand strong, was riding hard towards the French lines and already puffs of smoke were blossoming from the French batteries facing the Austrian lines. To the south-east of the town, a huge column of infantry was tramping out of the gates.

Lannes slapped his hands together. 'Damn fools are marching straight towards our guns. They'll be cut to pieces.'

'Maybe,' Napoleon replied softly, then fixed his attention on the head of the Austrian column. There was no glitter of bayonets there, and then he understood. The enemy were holding their muskets upside down. Quickly he scanned the banners at the front of the column and saw that most were furled. The rest were plain white. He lowered the telescope and smiled.

'They're surrendering.' He turned to Lannes and offered him the telescope. 'See for yourself.'

'What?' Lannes looked astonished and then hurriedly trained the telescope on the enemy. 'You're right, sire. Surrendering, by God. Five days before the end of the armistice. But why?'

'They must have heard news of the Russian army's location,' Napoleon mused. 'General Mack has realised that he could not be saved in time. That has to be it.'

'What about the other column, sire?' Lannes lowered the telescope and gestured to the distant cavalry charging through the French lines to the north.

'A break-out force. I imagine Mack is hoping that he can at least save his horsemen. Well, we'll see about that. Berthier, send word to Murat at once. Tell him what is happening and order him to pursue the enemy's cavalry. They are not to escape. We cannot afford to let them join the other Austrian armies, or Kutusov.'

'Yes, sire.' Berthier saluted and swung himself on to his horse to gallop back towards headquarters.

As they watched, the Austrian column began to deploy into line facing the hurriedly forming Grand Army. Then, regiment by regiment, the enemy lowered their weapons to the ground and stood to attention before the astonished eyes of the French soldiers. A large party of officers detached themselves from the Austrian lines and rode slowly towards the French pickets. They were quickly passed through and directed towards the headquarters of the Grand Army.

'Come on!' Napoleon ordered. Leading Marshal Lannes, he hurried back to his horse and climbed into the saddle and spurred his mount into a gallop. By the time they reached headquarters Berthier had issued orders for the formation of a guard of honour and the grenadiers of the Old Guard were hurriedly assembling either side of the gravel drive that led up to the country house. In their dress uniforms and towering bearskins the tough veterans looked as formidable as any men in Europe and Napoleon regarded them with pride as he joined the officers gathering in front of the entrance to receive the Austrians.

Just as the last men hurried into position there was a distant clatter of hooves and then Napoleon saw the first of the enemy's officers swing into the drive. They trotted forward between the still lines of the grenadiers. Then an order was barked out and the French soldiers presented arms in one fluid movement that momentarily startled the Austrians. They continued forward, reining in a short distance from Napoleon and his staff. Their leader, wearing a glittering uniform bedecked with ribbons and medals, dismounted and approached. He was a thin man with a gaunt expression, made worse still by exhaustion. He paused as he scanned the French officers, until his gaze rested on Napoleon. With a weary sigh he drew his sword with a metallic rasp and held the hilt out horizontally as he advanced the final few steps with bowed head.

'Emperor Napoleon, I have come to surrender my army to you.'

'And you are?' Napoleon asked casually, with an amused glint in his eyes.

The Austrian glanced up. 'Sire, I am the unhappy General Mack.'

Napoleon accepted the sword, and handed it to Berthier. 'I accept your surrender. Please permit me to entertain you and your officers here, while arrangements are made to take your army prisoner. How many men do you have, General?'

General Mack swallowed bitterly before he replied. 'Over twenty-seven thousand souls.'

There was an excited muttering amongst Napoleon's officers before he turned and shot them a withering glare and they fell silent at once.

'Marshal Lannes, see to our guests.'

Lannes grinned. 'It will be a pleasure, sire.'

Mack gave the order for his companions to dismount and as their horses were led away by French grooms the Austrian officers filed miserably through the entrance of the country house. Napoleon watched them for a moment, then turned to Berthier with a satisfied expression.

'The first half of the campaign is over. Now comes the time to turn our might against the remnants of the Austrians, and their Russian friends.'

Chapter 10

Arthur

London, November 1805

In the weeks that followed his return to Britain Arthur gradually renewed his former friendships and other contacts in the capital. Yet at the back of his mind there was always the thought of Kitty, still living in Dublin, as far as he knew. Much as he longed to see her again, he put off writing to her over and over, telling himself that he was too busy for such matters at present. Amid the whirl and glitter of the capital's social circles Arthur was flattered by the attention of women of quality, although he also spent many evenings in the clubs and drinking dens where he enjoyed the company of courtesans. Yet none of them excited his ardour as much as the mere thought of Kitty. Accordingly, he tried to occupy his mind with other matters.

It was vital that he fully understood the social and political terrain across which the Wellesleys would fight to secure their place at the centre of Britain's affairs. His older brother, William, was a member of the House of Commons and proved a useful guide to the complex relations between the various factions. In the eleven years since they had last seen each other William had aged poorly. He was growing stout, and his hair was streaked with grey. More disheartening still was the degree to which William had become so acclimatised to politics that he had come to see it as the means to all ends, and he vigorously encouraged his younger brother to align himself with the rising faction of Lord Buckingham.

One morning, the two brothers were sitting in the parlour of their mother's house as the first wet, windy days of winter closed in over London. Icy rain pattered against the windows and ran down the glass in dull streaks that blurred the details of the street outside. A servant had made up a fire, but even though the coals glowed brightly in the grate Arthur shivered and pulled his plain coat more tightly about his shoulders.

'There was a time I looked forward to returning to Britain,' he said quietly. 'I thought that anything was better than enduring another summer in India. But now? By God, I'd give rank, title and fortune to be back in Mysore. Now that was passing comfortable.'

William smiled faintly. 'Ah, yes. I'd heard that you and Richard were living like kings amongst the natives. What was the name of that palace you were using?' He frowned as he tried to recall. 'Dowley something?'

'The Dowlut Baugh,' Arthur replied. 'And it was a summer residence of Tipoo Sultan, not his palace. You really shouldn't believe everything you hear in London, brother.'

'I suppose not, but there were stories of the, ah, excesses of opulence that Richard bestowed on himself while he was Governor General. Rumour has it that you did not do so badly out of the situation either.'

'Stories, William. That's all. Just stories.'

William pursed his lips. 'I hope so, for all our sakes. As long as Richard can explain himself to the satisfaction of Parliament when he returns.'

'He will. And I shall back him to the hilt, as will you and the rest of the family.'

'Oh, of course.' William drew himself up in his chair. 'That goes without saying. And we must make sure that we have secured enough political support to help Richard when – if – there is an investigation.'

Arthur regarded his brother wearily. 'You are referring to Buckingham, I take it?'

'I am. The man is set to make his mark on the political scene. It would serve our family well if we allied ourselves to him.'

'Politicians come and go, William. What if your friend Buckingham fails to make his mark? What if we were dragged down with him? Then how could our family hope to wield enough influence to serve Britain effectively? It would be best if we did not align ourselves with any faction. Indeed it would be best if there were no factions for the duration of the war.' Arthur paused, and thought a moment before continuing. 'I think it would be risky to tie ourselves to Buckingham.'

'But what if he succeeds?' William's eyes gleamed. 'Then we might have the pick of the offices of state, and serve Britain to the fullest extent of our abilities. Think of it, Arthur. The Wellesley family would be at the heart of government, where real power resides. That is where we deserve to be.'

Arthur shook his head sadly. 'It seems to me that you care rather too much about power. As I said before, politicians come and go, Tory and Whig alike. They are an ephemeral detail, brother. I will not make political enemies when Britain's fate hangs by a thread. My ambition, my sole ambition at this moment, is to see Bonaparte and France defeated. I place nothing higher than that. Not party, nor faction, not even the political ambitions of my family. Do you understand? Nothing matters, save the defeat of France.'

William nodded slowly. 'Perhaps you are right. But one might argue that just as politicians come and go, so do our foreign enemies. And Bonaparte is, after all, just another politician. Might you not exaggerate the danger one man poses to Britain?'

'No,' Arthur replied firmly. 'I am certain that he is the greatest threat this island has ever faced. To be sure, Bonaparte is a politician, but he is also a soldier and a statesman and he holds the affections of the mass of his people in his hand. France is an extension of his will, and he means to crush Britain, once and for all. Surely that is obvious to you, William? And that being the case, no Englishman can allow himself to be diverted by petty politics.'

'Petty politics?' William's lip curled. 'Are you so naïve that you think there is any alternative to politics? Why, it is the lifeblood of government. You must embrace politics, Arthur, or let those who do sweep you aside.'

Arthur stared back at him, frowning. There had been a time when William had been principled, priggish even, but now Arthur saw that his brother had succumbed to the base values of those who had made Parliament their home. He felt tired, and unwilling to continue the discussion. If William wanted to play politics Arthur would not dissuade him. But he would not let himself surrender to the same temptation. Even so, however distasteful it might be, Arthur realised that he would have to bend a little in order to serve Britain's interests. He leaned towards the fire and shovelled some more coals on to the fire.

'Very well then, William. I will speak to Lord Buckingham.'

William smiled in warm satisfaction. 'I knew you would see sense. I will broach the matter with him as soon as possible.'

Arthur nodded, and then fixed his brother with a firm look. 'Mind you, I will not commit myself to his cause. You understand?'

'I understand. Trust me, you need only talk to the man.'

As the chilly winter days passed and Arthur made his rounds of the social events of the capital he felt as if he was surrounded by enemies, seen and unseen. So it was that when an invitation came from Lord Buckingham to meet him at his grand house at Stowe early in November, Arthur gratefully accepted the chance to escape London for a few days. It would be good to breathe fresh air. Buckingham was known for his love of the hunt and Arthur, who shared the passion, looked forward to the chance to ride again. William let Arthur use his carriage for the journey and, on the morning Arthur left, his brother gently took his arm as he settled into his seat.

'Remember, this man could be vital to our fortunes. Be careful what you say to him.'

Arthur smiled. 'Trust me.'

William did not reply immediately, and a moment later the driver flicked his reins. The carriage lurched into motion and William hurriedly withdrew his hand. Arthur settled back and pulled the travelling rug over his body in an effort to keep warm. As soon as the drab grey facades of the city gave way to open country he felt his spirits rise. Despite his fond memories of the kinder months of the Indian climate, Arthur felt a deep contentment in his heart as he gazed out at the English countryside. Even in winter there was a wholesome beauty to the gentle lines of the landscape, broken as they were by small woods of ancient trees whose bare limbs were stark against the sharp air of a clear sky. The route took the carriage past small villages of timbered and brick buildings from whose chimneys thin trails of smoke curled into the blue heavens. After so many years away from Britain, Arthur regarded it all with a keen interest, and a growing sense of passion that this land must never endure the tyranny of Bonaparte.

The latest news from the continent was grim. The first rumours had reached London that an Austrian army had been forced to surrender at Ulm. Despite this reverse, Arthur reflected that the combined weight of the remaining Austrians and the armies of the coalition powers would surely overwhelm France. He pushed the thought aside as he stared out across the gaunt countryside. There was a special history here, one that made its people unique. A tradition that was worthy of preservation and one that he would give the last drop of his blood to defend.

As dusk drew in, the carriage reached Stowe and turned through the entrance to a large sprawl of parkland. A long tree-lined avenue stretched away from the muddy turnpike towards the pitched roofs and towers of a stately home the other side of a small rise in the ground, enough to keep Lord Buckingham's country seat out of the sight of those travelling along the road that ran past his estate. As the carriage crested the rise, Arthur could see the full extent of the grand house with its lofty classical columns and tall windows. Light spilled out into the gloom and illuminated the neatly trimmed hedges that bordered the formal gardens lying to the side of the main house. The carriage drew up outside the main entrance and a footman trotted smartly down the steps to open the carriage door.

As he stepped down Arthur heard the unmistakable sounds of a large party: a loud hubbub pierced by the higher voices of women. He turned to the footman.

'Lord Buckingham is entertaining, it would seem.'

'Yes, sir.'

Arthur frowned. He had brought with him a minimum of formal wear in addition to his hunting attire. There had been no hint of a party in Buckingham's invitation. 'I am Sir Arthur Wellesley. I believe Lord Buckingham is expecting me.'

'Indeed, sir. Your rooms are prepared. May I take your bags and show you the way, sir?'

Arthur nodded, and a moment later followed the footman up the steps into the warm glow of a well-lit entrance hall. Lord Buckingham's wealth was conspicuously evident in every detail. Large paintings of family members adorned the walls, and gold leaf picked out the details of ornate mouldings in the ceiling high overhead. Opposite the entrance a marble staircase climbed up to a gallery that ran round the hall. On either side classical statuary filled niches painted a pale blue to enhance the lines of their contents. The footman led the way up the stairs and down a corridor into one of the wings, where he paused to open a door for Arthur before following him in with the bags. It was a comfortable chamber with a small dressing room and Arthur gestured to the chest at the end of the bed.

'Place the bags there, please. I'll need to change into something suitable before joining the party. How many guests is his lordship entertaining tonight?'

The footman paused to think before he replied. 'All told, more than a hundred, sir.'

'Any notables?'

'Indeed yes, sir. We have the Prime Minister himself here.'

'Pitt?' Arthur could not contain a look of surprise. 'Who else, besides the Prime Minister?'

'Lord Monterey, Lord Paget, Earl Portman, Sir Edward Walsey, to name just a few of them, sir. Quite a gathering.'

'Yes, it is,' Arthur said thoughtfully. 'Thank you. You may go.'

The footman bowed his head. 'I'll tell his lordship that you have arrived, then?'

'Yes, of course.'

As soon as the door had closed behind the man Arthur sat down on the bed with a sigh of frustration. He had assumed that he had been invited for a discreet meeting with Lord Buckingham, a mutual sounding out of opinions and positions. So it was with a heavy heart that he dressed in his best clothes: a plain dark coat, white breeches, silk stockings and buckled shoes. He knew full well that his attire would be rather drab in the whirl of fine lace and satin that would be adorning the great ballroom of his host. He left his room and made his way back downstairs, pausing to take a deep breath before he joined the party. Two footmen stood at the open doors and beyond them Arthur could see the guests, standing in clusters round the edge of the room talking and taking refreshment as a dozen members of a string orchestra took their places at the far end of the salon. Arthur knew Lord Buckingham by sight from his visits to Parliament and made his way across to his host, who was talking animatedly to a slight figure with grey hair standing with his back to Arthur.

'My Lord Buckingham.' Arthur bowed as he approached the two men.

Buckingham, a few years older than Arthur and rather more stout, turned his fleshy face towards the new arrival and raised an eyebrow.

'I'm sorry, sir, you have me at a disadvantage.'

Arthur mentally cringed with embarrassment as he realised that Buckingham had not recognised him. But before he could suffer the humiliation of announcing his name the other man turned round and Arthur saw the familiar features of William Pitt. This was the first time he had been so close to the Prime Minister, and the exhaustion and ill health that was etched into his face shocked Arthur. Fortunately Pitt smiled and grasped Arthur's hand.

'Why, it is Sir Arthur Wellesley, the conqueror of the Mahrattas.'

'You know me, sir?'

Pitt laughed. 'You have been pointed out to me, Sir Arthur. Besides, I have followed your career, alongside that of your illustrious oldest brother, with great interest over the years. Now I understand that you are seeking a seat.'

'Yes, sir,' Arthur admitted. 'Although I have not had much luck in that respect so far.'

'I'm sure you will not be kept waiting long. Britain has great need of men of your calibre, on and off the battlefield.'

'Thank you, sir.'

Pitt still held Arthur's hand and fixed him with a steady gaze as he continued. 'Of course, I would hope that you might support my premiership when you do secure a seat. I could use a man like you in government.'

Lord Buckingham suddenly laughed. 'You are ever the politician, William! Please spare my guest your wiles for the evening. Come, Sir Arthur, let me tear you away from this scoundrel and introduce you to some people of more honest disposition. You will know many here, but not all.'

Pitt released his grip, but raised his hand to stop Buckingham from making off with Arthur. 'In a moment. First I would like to hear the young general's opinion on the matter we were discussing.'

'Surely there is a better time for that,' Buckingham protested. 'Besides, the man is here to enjoy himself, not to be interrogated by scheming reprobates such as ourselves.'

Pitt glanced at his host shrewdly. 'Whatever his reason for being here, I am certain it is not wholly for pleasure. So let him speak his mind.'

'Oh, I doubt that Sir Arthur would be interested in our debate, William. He is a soldier, freshly returned from the battlefield. It would be unfair to expect him to have grasped the niceties of the governance of Britain and her foreign relations.'

'Perhaps, but then again Sir Arthur might be sufficiently unspoiled by political faction-fighting to offer a fresh perspective. Would you indulge us, Sir Arthur?'

Arthur nodded slightly. 'I would be pleased to offer what assistance I may, sir.'

'Very well,' Pitt responded decisively before Buckingham could make any further attempt to draw Arthur away. 'Now then, Sir Arthur, the heart of the debate rests on the course that Britain should chart in the near future. You may not yet be aware, but we have received a fresh peace overture from the French government.'

'I had not heard of this, sir.'

'Ah, but I am sure you soon will. Secrets have a way of leaching out no matter how closely my ministers and I attempt to keep them. In any case, it is not clear if the provenance of the French offer to talk peace is Bonaparte himself, or Talleyrand and his coterie.' Pitt arched an enquiring eyebrow at Arthur. 'The question is what to do about it.'

Arthur thought rapidly. He stood in front of two of the most powerful figures in Britain, men who could determine his destiny on a whim. Having decided that he would not play at partisan politics, he was now faced with a test of his ability to avoid taking sides. He cleared his throat.

'Well, sir, whoever may be behind this peace overture, I suspect that it is not Bonaparte.'

'Really?' Buckingham's brow creased faintly. 'On what basis?'

'It doesn't seem likely, my lord, when one considers what is readily known to those who read the papers in London. Even now Bonaparte has launched his army against the Austrians. That does not seem to be the action of a man who desires peace.'

'Quite so.' Pitt nodded. 'It seems we share a common view on the matter.'

'It is still possible that the Emperor does desire peace,' Buckingham insisted. 'He has disbanded the army poised on the French coast for the last year. Surely that is a sign of his good intentions with respect to Britain.'

'The army is not disbanded,' Arthur replied. 'It has merely been redirected against the Austrians.'

'Ah, well, then perhaps Austria's danger is to our advantage. Napoleon would not be wise to fight on two fronts.' Buckingham shifted his gaze to the Prime Minister. 'If the latest reports from the continent are to be believed, Russia is already marching to Austria's aid. Against the additional forces from Sweden and those we ourselves intend to send to Hanover, what chance has the Emperor? Faced with the threat of defeat, Napoleon will make any peace deal he can get.'

Pitt shook his head wearily. 'You misunderstand our enemy, my lord. Even if Bonaparte did make peace with us, do you imagine he would actually honour the terms of any treaty he put his name to?'

Buckingham looked surprised. 'He is Emperor of France. His name would be signed on behalf of every man, woman and child of that country. To break the terms of such a treaty would bring down infamy on France.'

'Infamy?' Pitt snorted. 'If Britain falls under the heel of this Corsican tyrant, the charge of infamy will be of poor comfort to those who live here.'

Buckingham was silent for a moment before he continued, in a low voice, 'It seems that you have not lost your appetite for war, Mr Pitt. For over ten years now you have been instrumental in keeping our nation in a state of conflict. How much longer must our people be forced to endure this obsession of yours? How many millions of pounds have been expended? How many good men have died because of it?'

Arthur glanced towards the Prime Minister to gauge his reaction to Buckingham's harsh accusations. There was no anger in Pitt's expression, nor even a trace of moral indignation, just the weary resolve of a man who had long since committed his life to one end.

'Sir,' Arthur intervened. 'It is the lot of a soldier to face danger on behalf of his country.'

'Of course it is,' Buckingham replied soothingly. 'But there is no virtue in fighting an unnecessary war, particularly when an offer of peace is on the table.'

'There can be no peace with France,' said Pitt. 'Not while she is ruled by Bonaparte, and those responsible for the revolution. That is the melancholy truth of the situation, my lord. So there can be no rest for men like Sir Arthur until Bonaparte is defeated once and for all. Now, you may disagree with me on this. That is your privilege. But I assure you, if Britain falls, then we will be ruled by a man who does not tolerate disagreement. Would you have us live under such a tyrant, my lord?'

'You should not believe everything you read in the London papers,' Buckingham replied bitterly. 'The Emperor is open to reason.'

'I wish you were right. Truly.' Pitt sighed sadly. 'But in my heart I know, with certainty, that you are wrong. Since we disagree, I see no purpose in prolonging this discussion. Now, if you will pardon me?' Pitt bowed his head, stepped back a pace, and turned away to walk slowly across to a group of women clustered around the handsome young Lord Paget. As he approached, the crowd parted and flowed around him while the women glowed with pride at the attention being paid to them by the Prime Minister. Arthur watched him for a moment, noticing that Pitt was clearly exhausted and did little to hide his frailty as his slender shoulders slumped.

'Come, Sir Arthur!' Buckingham suddenly grasped his arm and drew Arthur in the opposite direction. 'A friend of mine wishes to speak to you. I told her you would be here tonight, and you and she have a close friend in common, it would seem.'

Lord Buckingham did not elaborate, and a short while later Arthur found himself being presented to a couple somewhat older than himself. The man was tall and thin and had the reserved air of one who held himself in high regard. Beside him his wife was short and plump, with an ample bosom and bright sparkling eyes that gleamed with an easy-going hint of mischief.

Buckingham bowed to the lady as he made the introductions. 'Sir Arthur Wellesley, it is my pleasure to present General Charles Sparrow and his charming wife, Olivia.' Buckingham exchanged a quick smile with the woman and then continued. 'Now, if you'll excuse me I have to attend to some other guests. I am sure that you will have plenty to say to each other, Olivia, my dear.'

Once their host had moved on General Sparrow gave Arthur a cursory examination. 'Wellesley? Any relation of the recent Governor General of India?'

'My brother.'

Mr Sparrow's wife swatted him playfully. 'Oh, Charles! You know that perfectly well. Don't play the fool with the young man.'

'Oh, very well.' General Sparrow's face creased into an amused smile. 'I've heard a great deal about your recent exploits, as it happens.'

'Really?'

'Unfortunately, most of it is second hand, gleaned from the letters my wife receives.'

'Letters?' Arthur frowned. 'I'm sorry, I don't quite understand.'

'Sir Arthur.' Olivia took his arm and beamed, revealing two rows of small, sharp-looking teeth. 'I am a firm friend of someone you know, or knew, exceedingly well. Miss Kitty Pakenham, to be precise.'

Arthur stared at her for an instant, a sudden surge of passion coursing through his heart. He swallowed and tried hard to contain his feelings as he tilted his head slightly to one side. 'Miss Pakenham . . . Kitty. And might I enquire after her health?'

'I should hope so!' Olivia Sparrow burst into laughter. 'Especially since she has written simply volumes to me concerning her feelings regarding you, Sir Arthur.'

'She has?' Arthur could not hide his surprise. In the years he had been in India, he and Kitty had exchanged a handful of letters, mostly about the affairs of friends and family and more general news. Arthur adopted a neutral expression. 'I am sure that you exaggerate, Mrs Sparrow.'

'Me? Exaggerate?' She clasped a hand to her breast with a pained look and then quickly broke into another smile. 'Well, perhaps just a little. But I know the girl's mind, Sir Arthur, and her heart. She has missed you greatly. You should write to her.'

'That's enough, my dear,' her husband broke in. 'As ever, you go too far with other people's confidences.'

Olivia stared meekly at her husband before leaning closer to Arthur and squeezing his hand. 'Write to her.'

'Er, yes, of course,' Arthur replied awkwardly.

General Sparrow cleared his throat. 'Sir Arthur, as a soldier, tell me, what chance has Bonaparte got of beating the Austrians in the present conflict?'

It was a clumsy attempt to divert the conversation away from his wife's gossip, but Arthur was grateful not to have to talk about Kitty in front of them. His mind was filled with a jumble of images and emotions, and he needed time to consider his intentions towards her. For now he forced himself to focus on General Sparrow's question.

'The Austrians have a large enough army to counter Bonaparte,' he began. 'If the Russians join forces with them in time, they will outnumber the French overwhelmingly. I am no expert on the relative merits of the soldiery, but I have heard that the Austrians are well disciplined and brave, and their cavalry is without equal. However, the Frenchman has proved time and again to be a most valiant and hardy individual. He can outmarch any enemy, and fight like a demon at the end of the day. He is also well led by young commanders who can inspire their men to great acts of courage. And then, of course, there is Bonaparte himself. That man is perhaps the most brilliant general of our age. His very presence on the battlefield is worth ten thousand men.'

'You speak as if you admire him, Sir Arthur.'

'Admire him?' Arthur thought for a moment and then shook his head. 'I might have admired him once, when he was just a soldier. But now? No. He is a tyrant, and all his achievements are mere symptoms of that evil.'

His attention was abruptly drawn to a man who had just entered the salon, and stood at the threshold scanning the guests. His boots, breeches and cape were spattered with mud and his chest heaved with the exertion of his ride and final sprint into the house. Then, spying the Prime Minister, the man hurried across to him and spoke hurriedly in a low voice. The conversation in the room died quickly as the guests became aware of the man, and the warm air grew tense with excitement.

Pitt and the messenger conversed a moment longer, and then Pitt patted the man's shoulder and turned to face the silent crowd. It was clear to Arthur that the Prime Minister was torn by mixed emotions. For a moment Pitt said nothing and stood ashen-faced, a shaking hand stroking his chin. Then he took a deep breath and addressed his audience.

'I have just heard news of a great victory. From first reports it seems that Admiral Nelson has met and engaged the combined fleets of France and Spain off Cape Trafalgar. The enemy was annihilated.'

'Good God,' Arthur muttered as the impact of the news struck him. The immediate danger of invasion was over. Bonaparte had been humbled.

Some of the younger men began to talk excitedly and a voice bellowed out, 'Hurrah for Nelson! Three cheers for Admiral Nelson!' The orchestra hurriedly made ready to play a patriotic jingle, scrabbling through their sheet music.

'Hah!' General Sparrow clapped Arthur on the back. 'They'll make him a duke for this!'

But Arthur was still watching Pitt. There was no joy in the Prime Minister's expression, only grief and despair as he raised his hands to attract the audience's attention once more.

'Please! Quiet, please, I beg you. There is more.'

Gradually the crowd hushed and stared expectantly, hardly daring to believe there was even better news to follow.

'It is with the very greatest regret that I have to announce that Admiral Nelson fell in the battle, at the hour of his greatest service to the nation.'

'Dead?' Olivia Sparrow whispered and clutched her hand to her mouth. 'Nelson is dead?'

The silence was total in the salon as the party guests stood, stunned into stillness. Pitt tried to say something further, but the words died on his lips. He shook his head and turned to leave the room, the first tears gleaming in his eyes.

Chapter 11

The following morning Lord Buckingham's guests returned to London. They were desperate to discover the full details of the victory at Trafalgar. The politicians were also aware that it would be useful to be seen in Parliament paying tribute to the fallen hero. A few choice words of sorrowful rhetoric would be sure to be quoted somewhere in one of the country's newspapers.

As Arthur rose from his breakfast at one of the tables that had been set in the salon, he felt a hand on his shoulder and turned to see the Prime Minister.

'Sir Arthur, I take it you are returning to London today.'

'Yes, sir.'

'Are you leaving soon?'

'As soon as my bags are packed and my carriage is ready.'

'Ah, that is good. I wonder if you would do me the honour of sharing my carriage on the road to London?'

Arthur was taken aback. It would indeed be an honour, but for Arthur rather than William Pitt. Instinctively he wondered if the offer was being made in order to derive some kind of political benefit for the Prime Minister. Perhaps he was trying to drive a wedge between Arthur and his host, Lord Buckingham. Arthur glanced across the room and saw Buckingham engrossed in conversation with a fat, pasty-faced man whom Arthur recognised as one of the Whig members of Parliament who had made a reputation for himself in constantly advocating peace with France. Pitt saw the direction of his gaze and smiled thinly.

'Put your fears at rest, Sir Arthur; I will make sure that your presence in my carriage is not detected. I suggest you take your own carriage as far as the nearest village and send it on from there while you wait for me.'

It seemed a strangely covert arrangement and Arthur was tempted to turn the offer down politely, for fear that he would be seen as something of a conspirator if the ruse was discovered.

Pitt lowered his voice and leaned closer. 'Sir Arthur, I do not make this suggestion lightly. I was impressed by your directness last night. In government one finds oneself surrounded by placemen, and those who would be placemen. They cut the cloth of their advice to suit their audience, and I would be glad to hear a more honest opinion on two pressing matters. Now then, will you drive with me?'

Arthur stared at the Prime Minister for a moment and came to a decision. He nodded.

'Very good, then I shall see you later.' Pitt leaned back and raised his voice. 'A pleasure to meet you in person, Sir Arthur. I wish you a safe trip back to London.'

They exchanged a brisk shake of hands before Pitt moved off, heading for his host to take his leave. Arthur waited a moment before he followed. Buckingham clasped Arthur's hand and composed his features into an expression of regret.

'It is a shame that we did not have time to talk properly, but events have overtaken us. We will speak again soon, you have my word.'

'Thank you, my lord. I will look forward to the occasion.'

'As will I.' Buckingham looked meaningfully at his guest. 'In the testing times that lie ahead of us a man should be careful that he picks the winning side. Eh?'

Arthur smiled. 'It is always my intention to win the struggle against the French, sir.'

Buckingham frowned. 'I was referring to conflicts somewhat nearer to home.'

'Of course, my lord. I misunderstood,' Arthur replied smoothly, and then bowed his head. 'I thank you for the invitation to your house.'

Lord Buckingham smiled graciously and acknowledged the bow before turning to the next of his departing guests. Arthur made his way out of the salon and into the entrance hall. A small crowd of guests stood in clusters with their baggage while they waited for their carriages. Footmen hurried in and out of the door, laden down with bags, chests of toiletries and hat boxes. To one side, Arthur spotted the Sparrows, but before he could avoid their gaze and move off Olivia caught sight of him and raised her laced glove to wave excitedly.

'Sir Arthur! Good morning to you!' Pulling on her husband's arm, she hurried across the hall towards Arthur, who stood torn between a desire to hurry off for his meeting with Pitt and the obligation to be well mannered. Stifling a weary sense of resignation, he smiled a greeting.

'Good morning to you, madam. Good morning, sir.'

'Joining the stampede back to London, Wellesley?' asked General Sparrow. 'It's going to be busy on the turnpike this morning, eh?'

'Indeed.' Arthur, still musing over their mention of Kitty the previous evening, was tempted to ask for more news of her. Before he could speak Olivia took his hand and gave it a squeeze.

'Sir Arthur, do please look us up in London. And there's one other thing: the moment you get back to London, make sure you write to our mutual friend. A letter from you would warm her heart.'

'I, er, will give it some thought, madam.'

'Make sure you do. A lady can only be kept waiting for so long.'

'Do get in.' Pitt smiled as he held the carriage door open, and Arthur bent his head to climb inside. Although the interior was large by the standards of most carriages, it was upholstered in plain leather, which was heavily worn. Pitt noticed Arthur's searching glance and could not help laughing.

'A bit spartan, is it not? Not quite what you expected the Prime Minister to be travelling in. Well, this is not France and I am not the Emperor, so there is no need for an ornate toy with which to impress the common herd.' Pitt laid his hand down on the cracked leather and stroked it with a fond expression. 'I have been using this carriage for over ten years, on and off, and it has served me well enough. Though I think I shall not be able to use it for much longer.'

Arthur looked across into Pitt's face and noted the ashen pallor of his flesh, and a strained expression he had tried to keep in check while at Lord Buckingham's country house. Arthur cleared his throat. 'You are to retire soon then, sir?'

Pitt smiled thinly. 'No. It is my duty to remain in my post for as long as I am able to work towards the defeat of our enemy. But I fear I shall not live to see the victory.'

'How can you know that, sir?'

Pitt raised a hand to silence Arthur. 'Before you say another word, and spoil my growing regard for you, spare me any of the polite platitudes men lavish on those they know will die. I am a sick man, Sir Arthur. My doctor's opinion, for what it's worth, is that I will endure for a few months, a year at the most, before my life gives out. Therefore I must not waste a moment of what time is left to me. If Britain is to win this war of wars I must do all that is in my power to ensure that I leave my country in the hands of the best men, and give them the means to defeat Bonaparte. That is why I wish to speak to you now. There are two matters I want to discuss. Firstly there is the question of what happens to your brother, Richard, when he returns to Britain.' The Prime Minister stared at Arthur for a moment before continuing. 'I know that the Wellesleys are a close-knit family. I know that you served your brother loyally, and with great credit, while you were in India. However, I am generally a good judge of character, Sir Arthur, and I believe you will be straight with me.'

'I will do my best to be as honest as I may, sir,' Arthur replied carefully.

'I could expect no more,' Pitt conceded. 'So, then, I have read the reports sent to me by the board of directors of the East India Company, as well as your own representations and those of your brother William. The Company's main allegation is that your brother misappropriated vast sums of Company funds and equipment. Is that true?'

'Establishing peace and order across India did not come without cost, sir. It is true that Richard authorised the use of several million pounds of funds and equipment belonging to the company. But there was no dishonesty. He did not misappropriate anything. You have my word on it.'

'Your word?' Pitt was silent for a moment as he gazed shrewdly at Arthur. Then he nodded slowly. 'Very well. I think I am satisfied that the, er, Wellesley system of government in India was sound. I will do my best to see that your brother, and you, are protected from political persecution. But I offer no guarantees, do you understand?'

'I would ask for none, sir. Only a fair hearing and a just outcome.'

Pitt smiled wryly. 'If you think you'll get that in Parliament then you are a madman, Sir Arthur.'

'Then maybe I had better stay as far from Parliament as I can.'

'Yes, that would be wise. I sense that you do not yet have the venal temperament that a career in politics requires. Such a gross deficiency dictates service to your country in some other sphere.'

'A sacrifice I am willing to make, for Britain,' Arthur replied, and they both laughed, Pitt so much so that he suddenly began to cough violently, and he clutched a hand to his mouth as his lined features clenched into a grimace. Arthur, fearful for the man's health, leaned closer and reached out hesitantly.

'Sir? Are you all right?'

Pitt waved a hand dismissively, and closed his eyes as he fought off the coughing fit. When at last it was over he took a deep breath and puffed out his cheeks.

'God, I needed that. It has been a while since I laughed so heartily, Sir Arthur.'

'It is perhaps as well, given the effect on your constitution, sir.'

'I am fine, really I am. Laughter is the best medicine, so they say, though there has been precious little to laugh about in the last few years. And now this business at Trafalgar . . .' Pitt's expression hardened. 'It is a bad blow for Britain that Nelson has been taken from us. The people need heroes. They need men who can win victories and prove that Bonaparte can be defeated.'

Arthur nodded.

'The difficulty for us,' Pitt continued thoughtfully, 'is that our military power rests on the shoulders of the Navy. The army will never be strong enough to take on the hosts that Bonaparte can summon. To be sure, we can pour money into the coffers of our allies on the continent, but it is no secret that such subsidies demean them as much as they impoverish us. So what are we to do, Sir Arthur? That is the question. How can we defeat France?'

Arthur considered the question for a moment, bringing into focus the ideas and plans he had been pondering ever since his return from India. He cleared his throat and Pitt looked at him expectantly.

'You are right, sir. We cannot defeat Bonaparte if we continue our current strategies. France's colonies are a mere detail to him, and even if we capture them or disrupt their trade, he will still be master of the continent. If he is to be laid low, then we must defeat him on land, and ultimately on French soil. This is a war we shall have to carry to the very heart of Paris. At some point Britain must assemble an army powerful enough to confront Bonaparte himself. That will not be possible for some years. The men who defeat France will have to be trained well, and fully equipped and provisioned. They must gain plenty of campaign experience and be convinced that they are more than a match for any man in the French army.' Arthur paused a moment. 'And they will need to be led by the best officers that can be found. They will need a commander who stands beside them whatever the danger, one who is flexible in his methods, and resolutely fixed on his goal.'

'And would you be such a man?' Pitt asked with an amused expression.

'I would. But there are others who would serve as well.'

'And many who would not.'

Arthur did not respond to the comment, and continued with his train of thought. 'Then there is the question of where such an army might gain the experience it requires to defeat Bonaparte. Too often Britain has hurled her forces piecemeal on to the continent to support our allies, with little tangible benefit to our war aims. Sir, we need to concentrate our forces in an area on the periphery of Europe where the men can be forged into a fine weapon.'

'Where do you have in mind, Sir Arthur?'

'The Iberian Peninsula.'

'Spain?'

'Portugal, to begin with. That would serve as a fine base of operations for taking the war to Spain, and ultimately France.'

'A most indirect route to Paris, I should say.'

'That is the beauty of it, sir. It would stretch Bonaparte's resources to the limit. Given France's position on the continent, he enjoys interior lines of communications for all his forays into northern Italy, Austria and the German states. But Spain and Portugal are out on a limb. Any troops he sends to support Spain will be drawn from the armies opposed to Russia, Austria and Prussia. Even Bonaparte cannot endure if he is fully committed to fighting on two fronts. He will have to divide his attention, and his men, between the two. And there is a third front to consider, sir. The home front, as it were. While Bonaparte races from one end of his empire to the other there will be ample scope to encourage discontent amongst his own people.'

Arthur paused to give the Prime Minister time to take in the details and then continued in a more deliberate tone. 'Of course, there will be risks. If our army is defeated on the Peninsula I have little doubt that public support for the war will fail. That means that whoever is commanding the army must look to its safety as his first priority. Furthermore, the government will need to accept that this is no mere incursion to discomfort our enemies. They will need to commit men and resources to the Peninsular army on a scale that has never been seen before. They will also need to be prepared to maintain it in the field for some years. I do not see this as a question of striking one mortal blow at the enemy, rather a methodical and incremental destruction of his will to continue the fight. Our army will be com-pelled to fight on the defensive at first, but as it gains experience and confidence it can be deployed to attack, the moment circumstances are propitious. I have seen our men fight in India and I have little doubt that our infantry, in line, can cut down the French columns as they advance to attack.'

'Then why the need for time to harden our army, if the men are ready?'

Arthur smiled slightly. 'I said the infantry, sir. Our cavalry, alas, is fairly lamentable in terms of quality and discipline. They need toughening up. There should be more of them and they must understand their role both on campaign and on the battlefield. We have the raw ingredients of a fine army, sir. We just need the time to mould the different elements together.'

'I see.' Pitt mused for a moment and then leaned back into his seat, his body jolting lightly as the carriage trundled along the turnpike. Then he nodded. 'Your arguments make fine sense, Sir Arthur. I will have the matter looked into thoroughly. Spain, then, will be where Bonaparte's empire begins to unravel . . .'

Chapter 12

The mood in the capital was mixed. The news of the great victory won at Trafalgar had brought great excitement and joy to the people of all classes. But the sense of triumph was muted by the public grief over the death of Nelson, and as Arthur passed through the streets and saw the black-ribboned portraits of the admiral in the windows of shops, offices and homes, he could not help wondering at it. Here was a man known to the vast majority of Britain only by virtue of his reputation and yet the people grieved for him as if he was one of their family. In spite of the irrationality of such a seemingly universal response, Arthur felt moved that one man could have such a hold on the emotions of all those in Britain. He wondered if, when his time came, there would be a similar outpouring of grieving, and then shook his head with a bitter smile. The achievements of the Wellesley brothers in India were of minor signifi-cance to the British public. If a soldier was to achieve any kind of reputa-tion in this world, it had to be won on the battlefields of the continent.

Arthur had not forgotten Lord Buckingham's mention of an exped-itionary force to be sent in support of the coalition armies marching against Bonaparte, and he was determined that he should be part of it. He made his request for a posting immediately on his return to London and anxiously awaited a response.

Meanwhile, his thoughts turned to Kitty, and Olivia Sparrow's insist-ence that she had not cooled towards him. It hardly seemed credible after so long a time apart. And yet he felt a warm ache in his heart at the thought of her as she was, and as she might be now. He murmured her name idly to himself as he entered a coffee house. The atmosphere inside was thick with the aromas of tobacco smoke and coffee, and a fire glowed in the centre of the shop. There were no spare tables and Arthur asked if he might share one that sat in the bay window overlooking the street. The other customer at the table, a bewigged man who looked to be younger than Arthur, barely glanced over the top of his newspaper as he nodded his assent, and then carried on reading.

Arthur ordered tea, and sat and stared out through the recently cleaned glass. Outside the passers-by, wrapped up and hunched into their collars, strolled quickly along, oblivious of his gaze. Life continued as normal, then. Despite the war on the continent, the triumph at Trafalgar and the death of Nelson. What would Kitty think of it all, he wondered. Would the constant procession of officers in gaudy uniforms in Dublin's streets impress her, or would the whittling down of her old acquaintances have depressed her spirits? And would she be old enough now to have outgrown the careless pursuits of youth? Would she have changed that much?

His tea was served, and Arthur raised the cup and gently inhaled the steam curling up from the clear brown liquid that brought back faint memories of India. For a moment he stared down into the cup, frowning faintly. Then he set it down with a sharp rap and sat back. Fumbling for some coins to pay for the drink, he rose and left the shop. Outside he turned deliberately in the direction of the address that Olivia Sparrow had sent to him on her return to London.

'Sir Arthur! What a delightful surprise!' Mrs Sparrow smiled widely as she flowed into the parlour and held out her hand. Arthur took it and kissed it lightly before waiting for her to be seated, and then following suit.

'Well, it's not such a great surprise really,' Mrs Sparrow continued with a mischievous sparkle in her eye. 'I assume there is more to this than a passing visit.'

'Indeed. There is something that is perhaps dear to my heart and I would know more.'

'Something? Surely you mean someone?'

'Yes. Kitty.' Now it was out, he would not indulge in coyness. 'You said that she had written to you about me. I should be grateful to know what she has said.'

Mrs Sparrow smiled. 'Of course. But first, Arthur, there are a few things I should tell you about what has occurred since you left for India.'

'Oh?' Arthur felt a sick feeling stir in the pit of his stomach. 'Go on, please.'

'You do know that she loved you before you left?'

'She intimated as much,' Arthur replied carefully. 'And I returned the sentiment. But that was not sufficient for her older brother. He was kind enough to point out that no man with any integrity would let his sister wed a lowly army officer with few prospects.'

'And now you have wealth and title.' Mrs Sparrow nodded. 'And every prospect of further fame and fortune. So there can be no further objection on that front. You must admit that her brother acted correctly in defending her best interest.'

'Perhaps.'

'You were not the first, nor the last, to be rebuffed on those grounds.'

'Not the last?' Arthur felt his heart quicken with anxiety. 'What do you mean?'

Mrs Sparrow folded her hands in her lap. 'Arthur, you must understand that ten years is a long time.'

'I think I know that,' Arthur responded with bitter feeling.

'Of course. But while you were busily occupied with your duties in India, Kitty was sitting at home. Losing you broke her heart, I think. She did not go to the soirées at Dublin Castle. In fact she rarely ventured out to any social event for some years. At length, however, she felt that you might not return from India, and even if you did you were sure to have transferred your feelings to someone else. So she re-joined the world.' Mrs Sparrow noticed his pained expression and leaned forward to pat his hand reassuringly. 'Please, Arthur, don't think that she had forgotten you. After all, the odd letter did pass between you from time to time. Kitty just felt that she had to continue with her life. That's when she met young Galbraith Lowry Cole.'

She paused to let the implication of her words sink in. Arthur swallowed and nodded. 'Please continue.'

'Galbraith was a handsome young man. And very earnest, much like you in many respects. He fell for Kitty and courted her as only a young man desperately in love can, bombarding her with notes and letters and gifts until he wore Kitty down and she began to form an attachment to him. I could see that he was not suitable for her, but she just said that you would never be coming back for her and she must make do. By and by I think her affections did begin to turn towards him, once she had convinced herself that she could not have you.'

Arthur closed his eyes for a moment and breathed in steadily. Even though he had known that there was every chance that Kitty would meet another lover, somewhere deep in his heart he had hoped, fervently, that she would believe theirs to be as real and enduring a love as two people could ever know. Now he cursed himself for a fool. He should have written to her more often. He should have told her of the depth of his feelings for her, of his dreams for their future together. The sense of loss cut him to the soul and waves of bitter self-reproach coursed through his heart. With great difficulty, he repressed his despair. Opening his eyes, he stared bleakly at Mrs Sparrow.

'What happened?'

'Galbraith proposed to her.'

'Proposed?' Arthur repeated softly through clenched teeth. 'When was this?'

'Nearly three years ago. It came as no surprise to anyone observing the two of them. Just as the consequence came as no surprise.'

'Why? What do you mean?'

'Her brother refused to give his permission. One thing you can say for Tom Pakenham, he is consistent. Galbraith, like you, was a junior officer with no fortune of his own. Once again, Kitty's heart was broken. Honestly, Arthur, you should have seen the poor, dear thing. She has been wasting away ever since. Thin as a stick.' Mrs Sparrow shook her head sadly before continuing. 'But all is not lost, as far as you two are concerned.'

'Oh?'

'I said that Tom Pakenham was consistent, did I not?' Mrs Sparrow smiled faintly. 'I seem to recall Kitty once telling me of a letter you wrote. Not long before you left for India. In it you said that if you came back, having won your spurs and some wealth, your offer of marriage to her would still stand. Is that true?'

'It is.'

'Well, now it seems that you are Major-General Sir Arthur Wellesley, returned from India with a handsome fortune. In which case, what reason could Tom Pakenham possibly have for refusing you a second time? If your offer still stands, that is.'

Arthur stared at her, for the first time feeling his pulse quicken with hope, and excitement. 'Do you really think I would be accepted?'

'I am sure of it. I know Kitty's mind well enough. I know that you have but to write to her and tell her of your enduring feeling for her and she is yours.'

Arthur was silent for a moment before he rose to his feet. 'I must go. I am meeting my brother William at the House.'

'Of course.' Mrs Sparrow nodded sadly. 'You must be a very busy man. But do not let that delay you in contacting Kitty. She has waited long enough.'

'I will find the time to write to her soon.' Arthur paused. 'If she will have me, then I am hers. I always was.'

In the week that followed the party at Stowe, Arthur received an invitation to attend the Lord Mayor's Guildhall banquet. He was still waiting to hear if he had been appointed to the army destined for service in Hanover, and hoped that he might have the chance to further his ambitions at the dinner.

Crowds drew William Pitt's carriage through the streets to the Guildhall, where they cheered him to the heavens as he descended. He acknowledged their acclaim with a bow and a smile. Then he entered the building, between ranks of applauding merchants, politicians and noblemen who fully realised the part he had played in making the victory at Trafalgar possible.

The banquet was held in a grand chamber, filled with long tables heavily laden with fine silverware, crystal and ornate dinner services. The worthy gentlemen of the capital and their guests were decked in their finery and Arthur, in his dress uniform, found himself seated opposite Lord Castlereagh. The Prime Minister, according to tradition, was seated at the head table next to the Lord Mayor, and Arthur was shocked to see that Pitt appeared to be in even poorer health than a few days earlier. Unnaturally pale, with sunken eyes, he hardly touched his food and spoke few words to those either side of him.

'You seem preoccupied, Wellesley.'

Arthur glanced away from the Prime Minister and saw that Castlereagh was looking at him as he dabbed a spot of sauce away from the corner of his mouth. Arthur pursed his lips. 'I was just considering the latest news of the war, my lord.'

'Ah, yes. Grim tidings indeed.'

The details of Bonaparte's victory at Ulm had reached London a day earlier. It seemed that nearly half of Austria's army had been destroyed or taken prisoner. French forces were striking towards the very capital of the Austrian empire and there was little chance that Vienna could be saved before Russia and the other coalition powers could intervene.

Castlereagh cleared his throat and continued. 'It would appear that the best chance of defeating Bonaparte now seems to hinge on the massing of the coalition forces for one decisive battle.'

'I agree, my lord. That is why it is vital that a British army is landed on the continent as soon as possible.'

'Of course.' Castlereagh nodded. 'The government understands that well enough, and the task is in hand. Despite the setback at Ulm, the Prime Minister is confident that we have the beating of France. It won't be long before our soldiers are chasing the Corsican tyrant all the way back to his bolt-hole in Paris.'

'I hope so, my lord.'

Castlereagh took a sip of wine and looked shrewdly at Arthur. 'I imagine you are wondering if you will be assigned to the expeditionary force.'

Arthur kept his face expressionless as he stared back, and composed his reply. 'Naturally. It is every officer's desire to serve his country at any opportunity.'

'Opportunity?' Castlereagh chuckled drily. 'I sometimes wonder at you fellows in uniform and your desire to go to war. It's almost as if you derive some strange pleasure from proximity to death.'

'No, my lord. I have already seen enough of war to know that it is an evil. A necessary evil on occasions, but an evil for all that. I shall be glad when Bonaparte is finally defeated. Until then I will not rest, nor avoid any chance to bring about his downfall.' He paused. 'I believe that I have served my country well enough to merit a position in the army being sent to the continent.'

Castlereagh was silent for a moment and then smiled. 'You Wellesleys seem to have a very high opinion of yourselves. Fortunately, it seems that Pitt shares that opinion. He has recommended you for a command in the army.'

'Has he, by God?'

'Indeed, he insisted on it. You have won yourself a powerful patron there, Sir Arthur. My advice to you is to ensure that you avail yourself of as much advantage of Pitt's high regard as you can.' Castlereagh nodded in the direction of the Prime Minister. 'I fear that Britain will not be enjoying his leadership for very much longer.' He lowered his voice. 'He is a very sick man. And the news about Ulm weighs heavily upon his heart. I doubt that he will be able to bear the burden of high office for much longer. And once he is gone, your family will lose a powerful ally. Perhaps it is time you considered your political position, Wellesley. Find a new patron, while there is still time. I could always use an able subordinate myself.'

'That is generous of you, my lord,' Arthur replied in an even tone. 'However, I feel that I could best serve my country in uniform.'

'As you will.' Castlereagh shrugged. 'I suppose that at least warfare has the virtue of allowing a man to identify his enemies. In that respect there is much to be said for a life in uniform. See the noble features lining every table here? Not one of 'em dressed like a frog yet many of them pose an equal danger to our country. Blasted appeasers will be the ruin of us all yet!'

A sudden sharp series of knocks rang out in the chamber and Arthur turned to see the master of ceremonies striking his staff on the floor to demand silence. Quickly, the hubbub of conversation died away, cutlery was laid aside and the guests sat back in their seats, their attention drawn to the head table where the Lord Mayor had risen to begin his speech.

He began in a subdued manner, praising the sacrifice of Admiral Lord Nelson and emphasising the great sorrow of the nation, then continued in praise of the heroic efforts of the king's soldiers and sailors to defeat France.

Arthur quickly lost interest. These were sentiments he had heard over and over again in recent days and he simply followed the cue from other guests as he nodded and applauded at the appropriate moment. His mind was consumed with the implications of his exchange with Castlereagh.

There was no doubt that Pitt was ill. But ill enough to have to surrender office? That would be a sore blow to the nation. As great, perhaps, as the death of Nelson. Few men of good sense doubted that Britain's survival thus far in the struggle against France was down to the determination of William Pitt to see that his country maintained the struggle, whatever the cost. Lesser men would have compromised on the expense of Britain's army and navy; Nelson's triumph at Trafalgar was built on the sound governance of Pitt and his followers.

After William Pitt, what? Arthur pondered. There were statesmen of considerable talent in Westminster, men like Castlereagh, Canning, Grenville and Jenkinson. But each was mired in his own ambitions and there was every danger that their followers would indulge in the petty obstructionism that plagued Parliament. That could only be of benefit to Bonaparte, who was sure to rejoice if his most inveterate enemy was to quit the office of Prime Minister. The loss of Pitt would be a serious blow to the Wellesleys, who had few enough friends in Parliament. Arthur looked again at Castlereagh and wondered if the Colonial Secretary fully shared the vision of the man he had served faithfully over the years. Certainly Castlereagh wanted to prosecute the war with the same zeal, but there was a prickly pride in his nature that could easily turn him against people. A man to cultivate, Arthur concluded, but only with the utmost care and tact.

The Lord Mayor had finished his oration and the guests clapped and cheered for a moment before he raised his glass and held his hand up to silence his audience.

'My lords, gentlemen! I give you the Prime Minister – William Pitt, the saviour of Europe!'

The chamber echoed as the guests stood, raised their glasses and loudly repeated the toast. Then the Lord Mayor took his seat and the guests followed suit, falling quiet as the Prime Minister slowly rose to make his speech of thanks to his host. For a moment he stood and silently gazed round the room, and when he spoke the tone was clear and measured. 'I return you many thanks for the honour you have done me; but Europe is not to be saved by any single man. Britain has saved herself by her exertions, and will, as I trust, save Europe by her example.'

He stood a moment longer, as if there was more that might be said, but then he bowed his head to his audience and resumed his seat.

There was a silence, before Arthur heard a voice near him whisper, 'Is that it?' Another voice grumbled in reply, 'Well, really . . .'

Arthur shook his head. 'One of the best and neatest speeches I have ever heard in my life,' he said firmly. Across the table Castlereagh nodded solemnly. Arthur stood up and pounded his hand on the table. 'Bravo! Bravo!'

With a smile, Castlereagh followed suit, then more men rose and soon the chamber was filled with a deafening roar. Soon only Pitt remained seated, basking in the deserved acclaim of his countrymen.

When the banquet ended, Pitt left the building first. The crowd that had cheered him into the Guildhall was still waiting outside, in the flickering glow of street lamps and the torches that some had brought with them. Another roar filled the night as he paused on the steps to give them a final wave before climbing unsteadily into his carriage and being driven away.

Arthur and Castlereagh watched him depart before the latter spoke. 'That was well done, Sir Arthur. At the end of his little speech back there.'

'My appreciation was sincere enough. Pitt said what needed saying without wasting one word more than was necessary. What better way to stir men's hearts?'

Castlereagh nodded. 'Anyway, Wellesley, I bid you good night. I trust you will serve your country well in Germany. I shall be watching your career with interest.'

A few days later the letter came from Lord Castlereagh's office appointing Arthur to the command of an infantry brigade billeted at Deal. At once he was thrown into the business of preparing himself for the post. Uniforms and a wardrobe fit for a winter campaign had to be bought and packed, bookshops scoured for reference works and maps on the regions through which the British army might be expected to march. His mother watched proceedings with a critical eye and made occasional sharp comments about children who left her almost as soon as they had bothered to return home.

Amongst his other preparations Arthur hurriedly composed letters to friends and acquaintances informing them of the forthcoming campaign. He wrote a brief note to Kitty telling her of his return and imminent departure. He carefully expressed his wish to see her again as soon as he was home again. To Richard he wrote of the political situation, and the encouraging views he had heard from Pitt and even Castlereagh with respect to Richard's treatment once he arrived back in

Britain. Before leaving London he paid a final visit to the Sparrows' house, hoping to hear more of Kitty.

Mrs Sparrow received his news with a sad expression. 'Well, I suppose a soldier must do his duty.'

'Yes.' Arthur nodded. 'There is always duty, and will be until the war is ended for good.'

'And then?'

'Then I can enjoy the fruits of peace with a full heart, lay down my duties and resume my life.' Arthur cleared his throat. 'I wondered if you had heard anything from Kitty?'

Mrs Sparrow nodded. 'She told me she had a letter from you. She said it was a bit stiff and stilted, but all the same it has raised her spirits, although it has given her no little cause for concern.'

'Concern?' Arthur frowned. 'Why?'

'Because she is unsure how to respond to it. Suffice to say that you have reawoken her old affection for you. The difficulty is that she is nervous that the Kitty you express feelings towards is no more than a memory, a person gone from your life these ten years.'

'Ten years,' Arthur mused, 'in which she has always been in my heart.'

'And you in hers.'

'Not always, it would seem,' Arthur replied sharply, still feeling a cold jealous rage at Galbraith Lowry Cole for all the time he had shared with Kitty while Arthur was in India. Then, with a deep sigh, he fought the unworthy impulse.

'What did you expect, Arthur? Besides, it could be worse. What if she had found someone whom Tom Pakenham would have allowed her to marry? What then?'

'Then . . . I think I would rather have died,' Arthur replied with quiet sincerity. 'But at least she is uncommitted for the present.'

Mrs Sparrow shook her head. 'She is committed rightly enough, but only to you, Arthur. The poor girl is in an agony of indecision. She wants to see you, but fears it too much at the same time.'

'Then I must put an end to her indecision,' Arthur resolved. 'Once and for all.'

'How?'

'I will write to her again. This time I shall make her an offer. I shall honour the letter I left her with ten years ago. If you speak accurately of her feelings, then surely she will accept?' Arthur looked at Mrs Sparrow almost pleadingly, and she smiled.

'Surely!'

★

For the rest of November Arthur and his men waited to board their ships, but the winter gales were against them and the British army could only stand helpless as their allies marched against Napoleon on the continent. Rumours and fragments of news seeped across the Channel, some claiming another French victory, others that the Russians had joined their Austrian allies and were closing the trap on Bonaparte.

At the end of November the wind changed at last and the British soldiers embarked on their transport for the rough crossing of the North Sea. The convoys of troopships and their Royal Navy escorts beat their way over the slate-grey water towards the coastline of northern Europe, where they entered the River Weser. There they anchored and prepared to land, making ready to advance towards the Danube.

As light faded on the afternoon of their arrival, Arthur stood on the deck of a frigate, wrapped in his coat as he surveyed the bleak winter landscape on either bank. A light shower of snow had fallen earlier and coated the roofs of the nearest hamlet in a pale sheen. The sky was dark and grey and threatened yet more snow.

Behind Arthur the lieutenant of the watch was pacing up and down as his sailors completed the furling of the sails and descended below decks for their evening meal. Arthur took one last glance at the sky and was about to head back to his cabin when there was a shout from aloft.

'Deck there! Boat approaching!'

Arthur paused, and then turned to scan the river behind him in the gathering gloom.

Sure enough, a ship's gig had rounded the nearest bend and was making straight for the frigate, which was anchored at the head of the line of transports. An army officer was seated in the stern and as the boat drew up to the side of the frigate he jumped up, and nearly tumbled over the side in his lubberly eagerness to clamber up on to the deck. A moment later, with the helping hands of the sailors in the gig, the officer, a young major on the headquarters staff, scrambled on to the deck and addressed the nearest midshipman.

'You! Where can I find Major-General Wellesley?'

Arthur strode towards him. 'Here!'

The officer, panting, hurried up to Arthur and fumbled inside the breast of his coat for a despatch. 'From the flagship, sir. We got the news just over an hour ago.'

'What news?'

'There's been a great battle, sir.' The man's eyes were wide with excitement. 'Not far from Vienna. At a place called Austerlitz.'

Napoleon's Campaign Against Austria and Russia in 1805

Chapter 13

Napoleon

As soon as the arrangements had been made for the paroling of some of the prisoners captured at Ulm and sending the rest into holding camps in Bavaria and France, the Grand Army wheeled about and marched against the Russian army led by Kutusov. For the remainder of October, and into the early days of November the soldiers trudged towards Vienna, driving the enemy before them. The weather continued to worsen as autumn began to give way to winter.

On some days, there were bright spells when brilliant white puffy clouds billowed serenely across a clear sky. Then there were times when thick banks of rain and mist blotted out the sun and icy squalls lashed down, soaking the men through to the skin and turning the routes along which they marched into glutinous slippery bogs. At night the temperature dropped swiftly and the men huddled around their campfires, trying to dry their clothes and get some warmth into their shivering frames as they supped on whatever food they had managed to forage during the afternoon. The lucky ones, mostly veterans who had long since learned the knack of finding good shelter, slept under cover, while the rest made themselves as comfortable as they could in the open. There were frequent frosts in the morning when the men woke to find their belongings covered in a gleaming patina of tiny ice crystals that gleamed pale blue in the hour before dawn. After a quick meal the men formed up, stamping their feet to keep warm, and then, when the order was given, they advanced towards the enemy again.

As his carriage lurched forward with the long train of headquarters wagons and mounted staff, Napoleon glanced through the streaked glass of the window and muttered to Berthier, 'This mud may yet undo us.'

Berthier had been dozing, but he blinked his eyes open and looked round. 'Sorry, sire, what did you say?'

'This mud is slowing our advance down too much.'

'It hampers the enemy as much as us, sire.'

'True,' Napoleon conceded. 'But time is more against us than the enemy. We have to finish the war, swiftly and decisively. They only have to hold out long enough to demonstrate to the rest of Europe that France, that I, can be held at bay.'

Berthier nodded. 'That is the danger, sire. But you have acted as quickly as you can.' He paused for a moment to consider the disposition of his master's forces. 'As long as Murat keeps pressing the Russians back they will have no chance to concentrate their forces with the Austrians.'

Napoleon smiled faintly. 'I can't say I feel terribly comforted by the thought of depending on a hothead like Murat.'

Berthier kept his silence. Not only was Murat senior to him, but he was also married to the sister of Napoleon, and any criticism of the impetuous cavalry commander was likely to be taken as a criticism of the Emperor's family. Berthier knew that he was useful to Napoleon, but his position was not so secure that he dared to offer criticism of Marshal Murat. So he remained quiet and waited for Napoleon to continue.

'We have to keep driving the enemy back towards Vienna,' Napoleon said firmly. 'If we can threaten their capital, then they will feel compelled to turn and fight us.'

'What if they don't, sire?'

Napoleon considered this for a moment. If the Austrians followed tradition they would see the fall of their capital as marking the end of the war. Therefore they would fight, must fight, to defend Vienna. And for that they would have to stop retreating and turn to face the Grand Army. The only doubt in Napoleon's mind concerned the actions of the Russians. Kutusov could decide to stand alongside the Austrians, or continue to fall back and await the arrival of reinforcements before facing Napoleon. As long as Murat kept driving Kutusov away from Vienna and the Danube, then Napoleon would be free to destroy the divided allies one at a time. He turned his attention back to Berthier.

'The Austrians will fight. They are too proud to surrender their capital, and too foolish to do anything else.'

Berthier's eyebrows flicked up for an instant. 'I trust you are right, sire.'

There was a rap on the door of the Emperor's carriage and Berthier lowered the window. Riding alongside was a hussar, his saturated coat glistening in the rain. He leaned towards the window and offered a sealed despatch to Berthier.

'Signal from Paris, sir. Marked urgent.'

Berthier took the despatch with a nod and slid the window up as the hussar wheeled his horse round in the mud with some difficulty and rode off. Berthier broke the seal and held the paper out to Napoleon, who shook his head wearily.

'You read it.'

'Yes, sire.' Berthier unfolded the message and scanned it hurriedly, then read it again more slowly as he took in the details with a growing sense of shock and anxiety over the Emperor's reaction to the news.

'Well?' Napoleon asked softly as he leaned his head back on the cushioned seat and closed his eyes. 'What do those fools back in Paris want with me now?'

Berthier cleared his throat nervously. 'There has been a naval battle, sire. Admiral Villeneuve and his fleet encountered the British navy off the coast of Spain.'

Napoleon's eyes snapped open and he sat up straight. 'Ah! At last he's got off his arse and done something! What happened?'

'Sire, it appears that he was defeated.'

'Defeated?' Napoleon sneered. 'I can imagine. He ordered his men to turn tail the moment the first ship lost a mast. The man is as cowardly as he is incompetent.'

'No, sire. Not on this occasion, it appears. He stood his ground and fought the British.'

'And?'

'He was beaten, sire.'

'Beaten? How badly?'

Berthier glanced at the message from Paris, then replied, 'It seems we have lost upwards of twenty sail of the line, sunk or taken. The rest were dispersed as they broke off the engagement.'

Napoleon took a deep breath and glared at his boots resting on the seat opposite. When he spoke it was with a bitter intensity that Berthier had never heard before. 'God damn that coward Villeneuve to the most fiery pits of hell. We will never beat the British at sea now.' He paused, and then continued in a low voice, 'My plans for the invasion are finished. We must find another way to beat Britain. If we can't defeat them on the battlefield, we must strangle their economy.' His eyes glittered cruelly. 'We must ruin them, and when their money has drained away and their people are starving they will beg us for peace, rather than face a revolution of their own.'

There was a brief silence as the carriage rumbled and slid along the muddy track, and then Berthier asked, 'What do we do now, sire?'

'Now?' Napoleon nodded in the direction the carriage was heading. 'Now we fix every thought on crushing our Austrian and Russian friends as ruthlessly and completely as possible.'

★

That night, as word of Villeneuve's defeat spread through the army, there was a subdued atmosphere in the camp. Napoleon could not help being aware of it as he strode through the tent lines and attempted to raise the men's morale by stopping to talk to them as they crowded round their fires. The temperature had dropped still further and every so often a light flurry of snowflakes swirled out of the dark heavens. The usual greetings were more muted, and Napoleon was conscious of conversation stopping as soon as men were aware of his approach. His dark mood over the defeat was made worse by the latest report from Murat.

His cavalry commander had barely been able to contain his excitement as he wrote to tell Napoleon that the road to Vienna was open. Murat had given orders for his corps to advance on the Austrian capital. As a result Kutusov was no longer being pursued, and according to further reports the Russians had crossed the Danube and were making good their escape along the northern bank. Now they would have time to gather their strength, and manoeuvre closer to their Austrian allies to combine their forces and face Napoleon on more equal terms.

There was nothing left but to retrieve whatever political advantage there might be in taking the enemy capital. That at least would humiliate Austria in the eyes of the other nations of Europe, and make them think hard about defying Napoleon. The Emperor frowned as he reflected on the coming confrontation with Murat, who had been summoned to headquarters to report to him in person. Like any good cavalry commander, Murat was fearless in attack and resolute in defence, but his kind tended to suffer from far too much pride, arrogance and impetuosity. In Murat these qualities, both good and bad, had been refined to an unusual degree. It was time to rein Murat in, Napoleon mused humourlessly.

When he returned to the large farm commandeered by the headquarters staff, Napoleon heard a loud roar of laughter coming from within. He nodded at the sentry, who saluted, and then opened the door of the farmhouse. He paused on the threshold as he heard Murat's voice carrying across the merriment of his staff officers and members of the imperial headquarters. Napoleon removed his hat and quietly made his way inside, to stand at the side of the hall in the shadows as he watched Murat holding court. The glow of the fire and the candles flickering around the room picked out the elaborate gold braid and bejewelled decorations that covered the cavalry commander's tunic.

'You should have seen it!' Murat continued. 'The bastards were on the far side of the bridge, with guns covering it and a brigade of infantry formed in line across the end on the far bank. The Austrians had mined it as well, just to make sure. Any attempt to cross would have ended in a bloodbath. So, there's Marshal Lannes and myself looking across the Danube and Lannes calls up the grenadiers and tells 'em to keep out of sight on our side of the river and wait for his signal. Then Lannes and I start walking across the bridge to the Austrian side. Just him and me. Alone.' Murat paused, milking the suspense and relishing every moment of it, before he continued. 'Well, soon as they see us the Austrians raise their muskets, and the gunners bring up their linstocks, and wait for the order to open fire. Then Lannes and I raise our arms and wave 'em, and start shouting "Armistice! Armistice!" for all we're worth.' Murat accompanied his words with great sweeps of his arm to dramatise the point. 'You should have seen their faces! The colonel in command of the defences just stood there as we walked up.' Murat assumed an aristocratic falsetto. ' "Armistice?" he says. "What armistice? No one's told me." '

This provoked another roar of laughter from his audience, and he held his hands up to quieten them down. 'So I stroll right in and give the uppity bastard a bollocking for not having his superiors there to negotiate. Meanwhile Lannes has marched up to the fuses on the mine and ripped them out and thrown them in the river. And while I'm bawling at the colonel, Lannes tips his hat to the grenadiers and they come on at the double. Soon as the Austrian gunners see 'em they make ready to fire. "Not so bloody fast!" I shout at 'em. "What the hell do you think you're doing? This is an armistice!" And I shove them away from the guns. By the time they'd recovered their wits the grenadiers were already across and disarming them.' Murat puffed out his chest and concluded, 'And that, my friends, is how just two men of the Grand Army took a bridge across the Danube from a whole brigade of Austrians.'

At once the officers burst into wild applause and Murat made a few stage bows to them in return. Napoleon stepped out of the shadows into the room and pushed his way through the rearmost officers. As soon as the crowd realised that the Emperor was present, a path opened for him as if by magic and he strode forward towards the beaming Marshal Murat.

'Sire! I bring you great news. We have Vienna!' Murat was taken aback by the frigid expression on the Emperor's face, and continued in a blustering tone. 'Vienna, I tell you. The enemy's capital is ours. The Austrians declared it an open city and bolted away to join their Russian allies. Left the place undefended. As I was telling our friends here, we even captured a bridge over the Danube.'

'So I heard,' Napoleon replied flatly. 'I would speak to you, Marshal Murat. In my office.'

'Of course, sire. But first join us, and toast the capture of Vienna.'

Several officers cheered the suggestion, but others had become aware of Napoleon's mood and stayed silent, watching warily. Napoleon shook his head. 'Now, Murat, if you please.'

Murat stared at him, half smiling, and then glanced round the room looking for moral support, but all the other officers had fallen silent and lowered their glasses. Napoleon turned away and strode through the crowd to the back of the farmhouse where the kitchen now served as his office, its long table covered with maps and notebooks. As he entered the room Napoleon saw a clerk busy updating one of the notebooks filled with the strength returns of the Grand Army's units.

'Out.'

'Yes, sire.'

The clerk lowered his pen at once and hurried from the room, squeezing to one side of the doorframe as Murat followed the Emperor inside.

'Close the door.'

Once Murat had obeyed, Napoleon gestured to a simply constructed bench on one side of the table, and then seated himself on the room's single chair at the head of the table.

'You've come to make your report, I understand.'

'Yes, sire.'

'So, do tell me what you have achieved.'

Murat looked surprised and then puffed out his cheeks. 'We have taken the enemy capital. So far my men have discovered over five hundred guns and perhaps as many as a hundred thousand muskets in the Austrian arsenals, besides huge stockpiles of supplies and equipment. Sire, we could replenish the entire Grand Army for some months from what we have seized. Enough to carry us through the rest of the campaign.'

'No doubt,' Napoleon responded. 'But if you had followed your orders there would be no reason why the campaign need continue for a matter of months.'

'Sire?'

Napoleon slapped his hand down on the table. 'You let the Russians get away! Now they will be licking their wounds, waiting for the Austrian forces to join them from Italy. All the good work of this campaign may be undone by your foolhardy drive towards Vienna. The entire point of my strategy was to divide our enemies. Now you have given them the chance to concentrate their strength and we must fight a much harder battle than I had hoped. Thanks to you.'

'Sire, I – I had no thought of compromising you when I gave the order.'

'You had no thought at all, as far as I can see.'

Napoleon glared at his subordinate. Murat wilted and looked down, crestfallen. 'I had hoped to please you, sire.'

'You had hoped to win the glory for yourself, you mean,' Napoleon snapped. Then he drew a deep breath, and closed his eyes to control his rising temper. Murat had made a mistake. One that would cost Napoleon the lives of many of his soldiers and might indeed prolong the campaign by a matter of months, unless the situation was speedily resolved. Very well, then. Let Murat make amends by reverting to his original orders. His eyes flicked open.

'I want you to return to your command at once.'

'Sire, my staff and I have only just arrived at headquarters. We've been in the saddle for the best part of two days.'

'At once.' Napoleon ignored his protest. 'You are to pursue the Russians immediately. When you make contact, stay on them. Give Kutusov no chance to stop and rest. Drive them back, away to the east and north, as far from any Austrian forces as you can. Then pray that you have acted in time. Do you understand?'

'Yes, sire.'

'Then go.' Napoleon leaned his head forward on to his knuckles. 'Now.'

Murat nodded, rose from his bench, and paused a moment, trying to think of some words of self-justification to say. Then he gave up and strode back towards the door, yanked it open and bellowed at his staff to get outside and mount up at once. There was a chorus of scraping chairs and the pounding of heavy boots as the cavalry officers hurriedly gathered their capes and hats and left the building, calling out to the grooms to fetch their horses from the stables.

Chapter 14

After a brief rest to gorge themselves on the supplies stockpiled in Vienna the men of the Grand Army crossed the Danube into Moravia as the winter began to settle across the landscape in earnest. Even during the day the temperature rarely rose more than a few degrees above freezing and the frequent rain chilled the men to the bone. It was nearly two months since the campaign had begun and the weariness of the troops was readily apparent to their commanders as they tramped miserably across the rolling countryside in pursuit of the Russians. All the time reports were reaching Napoleon that Prussia was preparing for war and mobilising its army in readiness to strike. From the south came yet more disturbing news: Marmont was expecting ninety thousand Austrian troops to march from Italy any day.

Towards the end of November, Napoleon halted the army near Brunn, to rest and consider the increasingly dangerous situation. Murat's scouts had reported that Kutusov's army had been swelled by reinforcements so that he could field nearly a hundred thousand Russians and Austrians against the Grand Army.

'What is our strength?' Napoleon asked Berthier that night.

'We have fifty thousand here, sire. If Bernadotte and Davout are ordered to concentrate with us, then that will give seventy thousand men.'

'Which will still leave us outnumbered,' Napoleon mused. Numbers were not everything, he reminded himself. Man for man, the Grand Army's soldiers and officers were the best in Europe. And it was also a matter of leadership. Kutusov was a capable enough commander, but old and schooled in ways of war that Napoleon considered outdated. In addition, the Russian general was leading a polyglot force, and would have to contend with interference from Austrian generals. To make matters worse for Kutusov, the Tsar had loudly proclaimed that he would lead his men in person to victory over France and had set off from Moscow to assume command. So the disparity in numbers was bearable, Napoleon reflected – provided a battle was fought soon. But time was on Kutusov's side. With the Prussians mobilising, and a large Austrian army about to emerge from the Alps, Napoleon would be caught between his enemies and overwhelmed. He was also troubled by the lack of supplies for his men. They had been on the march for over two months and were at the end of a very long and vulnerable supply chain. Foraging was difficult given that the Russians had stripped the land ahead of the Grand Army and left little in their wake.

He nodded to himself and then looked up at Berthier. 'We are in a dangerous position. It would seem that our best course is to retreat to Ulm and wait for reinforcements before continuing the campaign.'

'If you think that is wise, sire,' Berthier said carefully.

Napoleon smiled. 'Well, you obviously don't.'

Berthier folded his hands together and chewed his lip for a moment before continuing. 'It will appear to the wider world that we have been forced to retreat, sire. That we have been worsted. Once our enemies trumpet that view of events, they may find ready allies to join them in a war against France.'

'My thoughts exactly. So we dare not retreat, and we dare not advance, and we dare not sit here and wait.'

Berthier shrugged. 'A dangerous position indeed, sire. What are you going to do?'

'The only thing I can.' Napoleon stretched out his arms and yawned before he continued. 'We must persuade Kutusov and his Austrian allies to attack us.'

'Persuade them?' Berthier's eyebrows rose in surprise. 'How?'

'We give Kutusov an opportunity he will not be able to resist.' Napoleon reached forward over his campaign table and pulled a map towards him. He scanned it for a moment and then tapped his finger on a feature indicating high ground. Leaning forward he read the inscription.

'We will bait the trap here, on the Pratzen Heights, close to this town.' His finger moved fractionally across the map. Berthier bent his head forward to read the name.

'Austerlitz. Very well, sire.'

'Austerlitz,' Napoleon repeated softly as he began to consider the details of the plan that was forming in his mind. It would entail a degree of risk and fine timing, as well as a good deal of subterfuge. 'We must crush them at Austerlitz, or be crushed in turn.'

The following day Napoleon gave orders that the corps of Soult, Murat and Lannes were to advance and occupy the Pratzen Heights, where their fifty thousand men would be in full view of the Austrian scouts.

The very next day an Austrian officer arrived in the French camp with an offer to open negotiations for an armistice. He was led through to the first line of the Grand Army to await the Emperor. The Austrian officers' sharp eyes took in every detail of the worn-out soldiers and their threadbare uniforms. Some looked back with sullen expressions of vague curiosity, but most simply sat around their campfires in dejected silence.

Napoleon and Berthier came riding forward shortly afterwards. The Emperor's coat was stained with mud and his uniform jacket unbuttoned. He had not shaved and he wore a weary expression. He lowered himself from the saddle with a grunt and turned to meet the enemy envoy.

'I bid you welcome, sir. Might I know your name?'

'Count Diebnitz, at your service.' The Austrian was immaculately turned out and had to restrain a sneer at the unkempt appearance of the French Emperor. He bowed his head briefly, then began to state his terms without any preamble. 'The Emperors of Austria and Russia graciously offer you an armistice, of ten days' duration.'

'An armistice?' Napoleon raised an eyebrow and pursed his lips as if deep in thought. So, the allies were trying to buy time for Archduke Charles to join them with the army from Italy, he thought. He forced himself to keep hidden any sense of amusement at the transparency of the armistice offer. Instead, he nodded and smiled. 'Yes, yes, an armistice would serve both sides well. It would be the humane thing to do.' Napoleon gestured at his men. 'I imagine your army is as tired of running as we are of pursuing you.'

Count Diebnitz's lips pressed together briefly before he replied through clenched teeth. 'The Austrian army does not run, sir. I cannot speak for the Russians, but the Austrian army does not run.'

'No, of course not,' Napoleon said in a placating tone. 'I did not mean to offend you.'

'You did *not* offend me,' Diebnitz replied fiercely. 'Now, sir, will you accept the terms or not? I must have your answer at once.'

'At once?' Napoleon looked anxious. 'How can I reply at once? I need to know the precise terms of the offer. You can't expect me to accept at such short notice.'

'That was the demand of my emperor.'

Napoleon glanced helplessly at Berthier before he turned back to the officer. 'I offer my compliments to the Emperor. Tell him that I am more than willing to negotiate, but I must have the terms in writing before I can agree to anything.'

'I doubt that he will brook any such delay.'

'Nevertheless, return to the Emperor and ask him.'

Count Diebnitz frowned for a moment, then replied, 'As you wish, sir. I doubt the Emperor will be in the mood to talk. But I will carry your words to him all the same.'

'Thank you,' Napoleon replied with an expression of relief. He maintained the expression as the Austrian remounted, wheeled his horse and rode back through the lines towards the enemy outposts around the small town of Austerlitz. Once Diebnitz was a safe distance away Napoleon relaxed and muttered to Berthier, 'Well, what do you think?'

'I think that the theatre lost a great actor when you decided to become a military man, sire.' Berthier could not help chuckling. 'I just hope that every Austrian over there is as easy to fool.'

'We shall see soon enough.' Napoleon straightened his jacket and refastened the buttons. He nodded to the nearest men of the regiment that Diebnitz had ridden through. 'Find some wine and spirits for those men. They deserve it after such a fine performance.'

The soldiers overheard and one instantly rose to his feet and raised his cap to cheer the Emperor, but froze as Napoleon glared at him.

'Sit down, you fool! If the enemy see everyone jump up and shout their heads off they'll see through the ruse in an instant!'

The soldier slumped down and was immediately nudged by the men around him as they teased him about his over-reaction. Napoleon turned away, nimbly remounted his horse and trotted back towards headquarters, cheerfully acknowledging the greetings from soldiers as he passed by. Back in his tent Napoleon and Berthier examined the map of the surrounding area.

'Assuming they take the bait,' Napoleon said quietly, 'they will think we are far weaker than they are. I doubt they will be able to resist the chance to defeat the Grand Army, and humble Emperor Napoleon.' He smiled grimly as he tapped the map. 'The moment they make their move we fall back, behind the Goldbach stream, and send for Davout and Bernadotte. We'll keep the main bulk of the army hidden behind the Zurlan hill there, and then leave Soult to hold the centre. If he spreads his men thinly and keeps them in open view, then even Kutusov won't be able to resist the opportunity to throw his columns against us, weak as we shall appear.'

'It's a fine plan, sire. A clever trap,' Berthier said approvingly. 'I just hope the enemy fall for it.'

Napoleon drummed his fingers on the map as he examined the ground he had chosen for his battle. 'We shall know soon enough.'

General Kutusov waited two days before he gave the order to advance. As the Austrian columns advanced on the Pratzen Heights Napoleon gave the order to retreat. The men had been ordered to give the impression of being in a panic and they hurried from the enemy in a disordered mass. Several damaged guns and supply wagons were left behind to enhance the impression of a hasty retreat and the leading elements of the Russian and Austrian army jeered after the French as they took the abandoned positions on the Heights.

As the first day of December wore on, fine and bright, the French formed a line behind the Goldbach stream, facing the slopes now dominated by enemy troops. Napoleon was satisfied that he had played his hand as well as he could. From the vantage point of the Prazen Heights the French position would look weak and poorly defended. The looming mass of the Zurlan hill on the French left would easily conceal the corps of Lannes and Bernadotte, together with the Imperial Guard. From the enemy's position it would seem that the enfeebled Grand Army was ripe for destruction.

All through the day Napoleon kept watch on the Heights, until at last, as the late afternoon sun began to sink towards the horizon, he started to pick out the dense columns of infantry moving opposite the centre and right of the French line.

'There!' He pointed the enemy out to Berthier. 'I told you it would work. Send word for Davout and Bernadotte to join us at once. And issue a general order to the army. Let them know that there will be a battle tomorrow. Tell them that we shall win a great victory.'

'Yes, sire.'

As night fell over the winter landscape Napoleon entertained his senior officers with a simple dinner at the inn in Bellowitz, a small village at the foot of the Zurlan hill. The main course, a steaming bowl of fried potatoes and onions, was consumed with relish and accompanied by some of the wine looted in Vienna. As they ate, reports continued to come in of the loom of campfires on the Heights, directly opposite the French centre, so there could be no doubt over the enemy's intentions for the next day. Then, at midnight, Napoleon and his officers heard the beating of drums and wild cheering close at hand.

'What's that?' Napoleon asked. 'Berthier, find out what is going on.'

Berthier smiled. 'Sire, have you forgotten?'

'Forgotten?'

'The date.' Berthier pulled out his pocket watch. 'It is past midnight, sire.'

'So?'

'It is the second of December. The first anniversary of your coronation. The men are celebrating.'

'Of course,' Napoleon replied quickly, angry with himself for letting such an important detail slip his mind. 'Then I must let the men see their Emperor.'

He left the table and went outside, followed by the others. It was a cold night and his breath plumed in the light cast by the brilliant stars scattered across the heavens. All around the village, and up on the Zurlan, bright campfires flickered in the night, and the cheers of the soldiers carried clearly to the Emperor. As he emerged from the inn, there was a burst of applause and greetings from the men of the Imperial Guard who stood in the street. Some carried torches made from twisted straw and Napoleon could see the warm grins and smiles of his veterans, men who had served with him in previous campaigns. One of the grenadiers took off his bearskin hat and placed it over the muzzle of his musket before hoisting it high into the air as he cheered. Others followed suit and as Napoleon descended the small flight of steps into the street an avenue of cheering soldiers opened before him. He walked slowly down the street, smiling back at his men with genuine warmth.

'Long live the Emperor! Long live Napoleon!' The cries echoed down the street and were quickly taken up by the troops outside the village until the night resounded with the chant. Napoleon felt his heart swell with affection and gratitude to these men who had followed him through the years, and now trusted him with their lives. He turned to Berthier and muttered, 'Did you put them up to this?'

'No, sire. They do it because they love you.'

'Love me?' Napoleon smiled, and for a moment he was tempted to think Berthier must be flattering him. But there was no guile in the faces around him and he in turn realised that Berthier spoke the truth. He patted Berthier on the arm. 'I think this has been the finest evening of my life. And with the dawn will come my finest day.'

Chapter 15

Austerlitz, 2 December 1805

At four in the morning the officers and sergeants of the Grand Army began to rouse their men. Most of the campfires had died down but there was still enough light from the glowing embers for the soldiers to pull on their boots, adjust their uniforms and prepare their weapons for the coming battle. It had been a bitterly cold night and a thick mist had risen from the Goldbach stream which now blanketed the land on either side, so that the French troops were all but invisible to their enemy up on the Pratzen Heights. The celebratory mood over the Emperor's first anniversary had given way to a quiet contemplation of what was to come. The veterans, for the most part, went about their preparations with a fatalistic calm. The younger and more inexperienced soldiers either were anxious and filled with dread of being wounded or were full of bravado and spoke with a cheery loudness that fooled no one except themselves.

To the south of the Zurlan hill lay the vast sprawl of Murat's cavalry lines where the troopers were carefully saddling their mounts, checking every strap and buckle to ensure they would be well seated if they needed to charge. The cuirassiers helped each other into their polished chest and back plates before pulling on their helmets with their flowing horsehair crests. In other regiments the dragoons, hussars and lancers made ready and then led their horses into line to await the start of the battle.

On the great mound of the Zurlan the artillery crews carried the first charges from the caissons up to the massed batteries, where some guns were trained on the Heights opposite while others were aimed to the south to pour an enfilading fire on the enemy's attacks across the Goldbach stream. Even though it was still dark there was no doubt about where the strongest concentration of the enemy forces lay. A faint loom across the skyline in the direction of the village of Pratzen revealed their position and the French gunners marvelled at the strength of the forces ranged against them.

Napoleon led his staff up the hill to the command post that had been prepared for him the afternoon before. He had slept in a barn at the foot of the hill on a bed of straw, and had managed to snatch three hours of deep sleep. Like most of his veterans Napoleon had long since developed the knack of quickly falling into a deep sleep when the chance arose. He felt the familiar light ache of excitement mingled with anxiety in the pit of his stomach. Even now, his mind raced over the details of his plan and the disposition of his troops, and there were still doubts in his mind.

If, for any reason, Davout's corps failed to arrive on the right flank in time to stiffen its defence, then the enemy might turn the flank and roll up the French line. Davout had visited headquarters the previous evening to report and give his word that his men would reach the battlefield in time to play their part. The marshal had looked weary, and no wonder, Napoleon reflected. He and his men had marched over eighty miles from Vienna in two days after receiving Berthier's summons. The corps would be exhausted, and yet the fate of the Grand Army might well rest on their shoulders.

Then there was the question of the timing of the main attack on the Pratzen Heights. Too soon and the enemy would spot the danger and be able to respond in time to block the thrust. Too late and the French right might be broken and both armies would merely have wheeled round, locked on each other like a pair of battling stags. Napoleon knew that the attack would have to be perfectly timed to achieve its purpose, and the decision when to give the order would depend on how long the weakened centre and right of the French line along the Goldbach could hold its ground. He stared to the right and cursed the heavy mist. It might well be useful to conceal the French positions from the enemy, but it also concealed the men from the eyes of their commander and it was essential that Napoleon knew exactly what was happening along the length of his battle line throughout the coming day.

He turned to Berthier. 'I want regular reports from the commanders, down to brigade level. On the half-hour, understand? Make sure that there are adequate messengers to carry it out.'

'Yes, sire.' Berthier added a note in his log and then turned to one of his junior staff officers to pass on the Emperor's order. As they talked behind him, Napoleon closed his eyes for a moment, and mentally projected a map of the surrounding area in his head. Marshal Lannes was on the left flank, with orders to hold any Austrian attacks. Murat's cavalry would form up in support of Lannes, and be launched in pursuit of the enemy if things went well. If they didn't it would be Murat's responsibility to cover the retreat of whatever was left of the Grand Army. Then there was Bernadotte's corps, entrusted with the defence of the Zurlan, but ready to exploit any weakness in the enemy line should the opportunity arise. Behind the Zurlan was the Imperial Guard acting as a reserve, and the two divisions of Soult's corps chosen to lead what should be the decisive attack – if the battle went as planned, Napoleon reminded himself. He allowed himself a wry smile as he recalled something he had heard years before: once a battle began the very first casualty of the day was always the plan. Just one division, commanded by General Legrand, was entrusted with holding back the main weight of the enemy attack along the bank of the Goldbach. Legrand must hold on until Davout's hard-marching corps arrived on the right flank and could support him.

'Dawn, sire.' Berthier drew his Emperor's attention to the east, where the dull pink orb of the sun was rising over the crest of the Pratzen Heights, picking out the Russian and Austrian troops massing to attack.

'Very well. Give the order for Soult's assault columns to cross the stream and form up. Tell Soult to make good use of this mist, and keep his men hidden for as long as possible.'

'Yes, sire.'

A dull boom echoed across the valley from the direction of Pratzen and the assembled officers turned towards the sound of the signal gun. A moment later there was a sudden detonation of cannonfire away to the right, followed by the faint rattle and pop of muskets.

Napoleon glanced down as he fished his watch out of its fob pocket. 'Just short of seven o'clock.'

Berthier strained his ears and eyes as he stared towards the right flank of the French line. But the mist and the smoke from the campfires still obscured the view and only the crest of the Heights and the Zurlan itself stood proud of the miasma. Several columns of enemy troops were marching swiftly down the opposite slope into the mist, and more troops could be seen moving from the Russian and Austrian centre to reinforce the attack. Berthier concentrated on the flank again. 'Looks like they are attacking the village at Tellnitz.'

Napoleon listened for a moment and nodded. 'Tellnitz. Send someone to find out what's happening.'

As Napoleon stood waiting, the firing intensified all along the line, and when the first reports came in it was clear that the enemy was indeed mounting a powerful attack on the French right. Within an hour word came that Tellnitz had fallen and the village of Zokolnitz soon followed.

Napoleon nodded grimly as Berthier told him the news.

'We must retake those villages. The Goldbach has to be held for a while longer. Long enough to draw in more men from the enemy centre.' He paused. 'How close is Davout now?'

'His light cavalry is already supporting the men defending Tellnitz.'

'What about his infantry?'

Berthier flicked through the messages he had received until he found the most recent one from Davout. 'His lead brigade, under General Heudelet, should be close to Tellnitz by now.'

'Then send Heudelet forward to retake the village, and hold it at all costs.'

'Yes, sire.'

Almost the moment Tellnitz was retaken a fresh assault was launched against the French, and though Heudelet reported that his men had fought heroically they were completely outnumbered and forced to give ground, so for the third time the village changed hands. But Napoleon's attention was fixed on the Heights. The mist and fog were slowly beginning to lift, revealing more of the slope, but thankfully still concealing Soult's two divisions, whose general had come up to the command point in person to receive his orders. Above them the enemy continued to reinforce their attacks on the right of the French line. Napoleon watched carefully, his mind rapidly estimating the speed with which the enemy columns were crossing the battlefield to join the assault. Then he turned to Soult and gestured to him to come forward, indicating the Heights opposite.

'I want your assault force to attack in the direction of Pratzen, understand?'

'Yes, sire.'

'How long do you think it will take them to reach the crest?'

Soult looked over the rising ground in front of his two divisions and thought quickly. 'Twenty minutes, sire, maybe less.'

Napoleon looked up the slope and estimated the timing for himself. It was too soon. The enemy must be given as much chance to commit himself to the right of the French line as possible. Raising his telescope, Napoleon trained it on two large columns of Austrian troops marching south along the Heights. He watched them for another quarter of an hour before he snapped the telescope shut and turned to Soult. 'Go now. Move as swiftly as you can and strike the enemy hard.'

'Yes, sire.' Soult saluted. 'You can depend on me.'

'I know.' Napoleon punched the marshal lightly on the shoulder. 'Go.'

Soult hurried to his horse, mounted and rode down into the mist. All was still to Napoleon's immediate front. Over to the right the firing had intensified once again as yet another enemy attack was thrust home. Napoleon nodded with grim satisfaction. There were sure to be heavy casualties in Legrand's division, but it was necessary if the enemy were to be lured into the trap he had set for them. A trumpet blared out from the mist at the bottom of the slope and a moment later the deep rattle and boom of drums announced the advance of Vandamme's and St-Hilaire's divisions. There was something quite otherworldly about the shouted orders, beating of drums and throaty roars of 'Long live the Emperor!' when there was still nothing to see. Then the first spectral shapes began to emerge from the mist, the dispersed screen of skirmishers advancing ahead of the main columns. Perhaps a hundred paces behind them came the colours of the leading units, followed by the dense mass of infantry striding up the slope. Sunlight glinted off the gilded eagles atop their standards, and the bristling mass of bayonets, and the men cried out again, 'Long live the Emperor! Long live Napoleon!'

'They're cheerful enough,' Napoleon mused.

'So they should be, sire,' Berthier replied. 'Soult saw to it that they had three issues of spirits before they formed up.'

'Three issues?' Napoleon shook his head slightly. 'God, I pity the Russians and Austrians once those men get in amongst them.'

The two divisions cleared the mist and climbed the slope up to the Heights at a brisk pace. Too brisk, Napoleon thought. No point in reaching the crest out of breath and unable to fight. As the two divisions approached the Heights the skirmishers exchanged fire with the first line of enemy soldiers. Tiny puffs pricked out along the edge of the Heights before the Austrians disappeared behind a bank of smoke as they fired a massed volley. A moment later the sound, a sharp rattle, carried across to Napoleon's command post. Calling one of the orderlies over to him, Napoleon rested the end of his telescope on the man's shoulder and watched as the skirmishers fell back around the advancing divisions. The right hand division, commanded by General St-Hilaire, angled towards the village of Pratzen. As the leading troops entered the village Napoleon glimpsed, through the smoke, a small force of Austrians hurriedly trotting back along the Heights towards the village and he allowed himself a smile. Even though General Kutusov was aware of the threat to his centre he would not have time to do much about it.

Napoleon glanced round at Berthier. 'Now is the time for our left flank to go forward. Give the order.'

'Yes, sire.'

As soon as the order was received, the corps of Lannes, Bernadotte and Murat marched forward from the Zurlan. Faced with this new threat, the enemy commander dared not weaken his right to reinforce his beleaguered centre. Napoleon nodded with satisfaction before turning his attention back to the Heights.

St-Hilaire's division had cleared the village and was advancing on the remaining enemy forces on the Heights, while General Vandamme's attack had stalled around some earthworks protecting a small clutch of peasant houses. Thick smoke and the darting flames of artillery pieces told of the fierce resistance being put up by the defenders. Napoleon cursed softly as he saw that Vandamme was being delayed long enough for a gap to develop between the two divisions. The right hand column had penetrated some distance on to the Heights when it was brought to a halt by fire from its front, as well as the enemy units on either side. The attack was already in danger of being beaten back, Napoleon realised. If it failed then there could be no clear victory, merely a bloody battle of attrition right along the line.

'Damn,' he muttered. 'We need to support St-Hilaire.'

'Yes, sire,' Berthier replied, but then thrust his arm out and pointed to the slope opposite. 'That's Soult, isn't it? What the hell is he doing?'

Napoleon lowered his telescope and followed the direction Berthier was indicating. Six artillery pieces were being hurriedly hauled up to the Heights by their crews and soldiers detailed to help them. At the head of the horse teams drawing the guns was a figure on a powerful mount, who had raised his white-plumed hat and was urging the artillery teams on towards their comrades.

'It's Soult,' Napoleon confirmed tersely. 'And he's doing what is necessary.'

Soult led his guns through Pratzen and forward to the head of St-Hilaire's division where they unlimbered and opened fire, immediately tearing great holes in the Austrian line as they discharged case shot at close range. Heavy iron balls blasted out from each gun in a tight cone that tore the stolid Austrian infantry to pieces. Their discipline wavered and they began to give way, falling back towards the town of Austerlitz on the far side of the Pratzen Heights. As soon as Vandamme had taken the earthworks from their zealous defenders he came up in support of the other division, and an hour and a half after the attack had begun French standards dominated the Heights.

Napoleon snapped his telescope shut and called for his horse before turning to Berthier. 'We're moving the headquarters forward to Pratzen.'

'Pratzen? But sire, what if you lose touch with our right flank?'

'The men on the flank are holding their own. Once Davout arrives with the rest of his men they can retake Tellnitz and Zokolnitz. I need to be close to the heart of the battle. Come, Berthier, we must ride there at once!'

As the church clock chimed noon Napoleon and his staff approached Pratzen. The slope before the village was spotted with the blue uniforms of the French skirmishers who had been cut down as they approached the enemy-held houses. Once they entered the village Napoleon and the other officers had to slow their mounts to a walk as they picked their way over the French and Austrian bodies strewn across the narrow street. When they reached the church Napoleon reined in and turned to Berthier.

'Set up in the church. Then give orders for reinforcements to be sent to Davout. I want Bernadotte's corps up here as soon as possible, and order the Guard up to the Heights.'

Leaving his staff behind, Napoleon rode on with ten men of the Imperial Guard chasseurs to a small rise beyond the village from where he could get a better view of the battle's progress. To the left, Lannes was steadily pushing back the Russians, away from the Pratzen Heights, allowing Murat and his cavalry to charge into the enemy line, threatening to cut them in two. To the right, Napoleon saw that the enemy was still fully engaged with Davout's corps. Even though he was out-numbered by at least three to one, Davout was holding his ground. Beyond the right flank stretched a series of frozen ponds and small lakes surrounded by marshes that hemmed in the men fighting at that end of the battlefield. Napoleon immediately saw his opportunity. Once the enemy centre was broken, then the French could wheel round and trap nearly half of the allied army against the ponds and lakes.

Turning his attention to the east, Napoleon saw that Kutusov had only one body of men left that could still challenge the French mastery of the Heights. Moving up from the direction of the town of Austerlitz came the elite soldiers of the Russian Guard. As many as three thousand of them, Napoleon estimated. Their fine banners billowed in the cold air and sunlight glinted off their bayonets as they advanced in neat lines. Napoleon could not help admiring their brave appearance as they held their formation and marched steadily up the slope towards the lines of Vandamme's infantry silently waiting for them. Spurring his horse on, he led his escort over to General Vandamme, who was shouting encouragement to his men as they watched the enemy approach. The general turned at the sound of approaching hoofbeats.

'Sire.' He bowed his head briefly. 'You've joined us at an interesting moment.'

'So I can see. I am sure your men will stand their ground.'

'They will,' Vandamme replied firmly.

At that moment, while the nearest Russians were still over three hundred paces from the French, they suddenly let out a great roar and surged up the slope.

Vandamme raised his eyebrows. 'They must be mad. They'll be blown by the time they reach us.'

'That may be so.' Napoleon nodded. 'But what they lack in brains they seem to make up for with courage.'

They stared fixedly as the Russians came on, hurling themselves up the slope, mouths agape as they shouted their war cries. The standards jostled above the thick shivering sea of bayonets, broken here and there by a sword as the officers urged their men on. Any pretence of form-ation was soon lost and it seemed to Napoleon as if the French were about to be engulfed by a raging mob.

'Ready muskets!' Vandamme bellowed out and the order was repeated along the front line as the men brought their weapons up and levelled them at the face of the oncoming enemy. When the foremost Russians were little more than fifty paces from the tips of the French bayonets, Vandamme bellowed, 'Fire!'

A ragged volley crashed out along the front line and the enemy was instantly obscured by a billowing veil of powder smoke. A light wind was blowing over the Heights and the smoke quickly dispersed enough to reveal that scores of the Russians had been struck down, but already their comrades were leaping over them, bayonets levelled as they raced towards the French. Vandamme's men hurriedly grounded their muskets and drew fresh cartridges from their pouches, biting the ends off and pouring the powder into their muzzles, before spitting the balls in and ramming the charges home. There was just enough time to fire a second desperate volley before the charge reached them. Once again smoke filled the air, but before it could disperse the Russians charged through and ran full pelt in amongst the French. Within seconds the front line had turned into a chaotic tangle of blue and green uniforms as the Russians fought like ferocious beasts. There was no attempt at bayonet drill, just violent thrusts of the blade and bone-crunching thuds as the butts of their weapons were used like clubs.

The first line of Vandamme's division reeled under the impact and for a moment it held, before the first of the Russians burst through and the line quickly dissolved into a general melee.

'Your men are going to break,' Napoleon said quietly.

Vandamme was silent for a moment before he conceded, 'I fear so, sire.'

'Then you must hold them with the second line. Understand?'

'Yes, sire.'

Napoleon turned to one of his escort. 'Get back to headquarters. Tell Berthier I want the Guard cavalry sent to support Vandamme at once.'

The trooper saluted and wheeled his horse away, spurring it in the direction of Pratzen. Napoleon turned to see the first men of the front line turn and flee. The fear was contagious and at once scores more men followed suit, some throwing down their weapons as they ran for their lives. The braver hearts amongst them fought on, and died as the Russians cut them down and bludgeoned them to death where they lay. As the fleeing soldiers ran towards the second line their comrades there whistled and jeered and roughly cuffed and kicked those who attempted to run through their formation. A handful broke through and continued to run even though they were safe, and Vandamme rode up to them with a fierce scowl.

'Get back into line, you cowards!' He thrust his arm towards Napoleon. 'Would you disgrace yourself in front of the Emperor himself, you curs?'

One of the soldiers scurried past, hands raised protectively above his head. As he saw Napoleon he called out, 'Long live the Emperor!' and dashed on by, sprinting towards Pratzen. One of Napoleon's escort angrily snatched a pistol from his saddle holster and twisted round in his stirrups to take aim.

'Leave him!' Napoleon ordered. 'Save your bullet for the Russians!'

Hot on the heels of the survivors of the front line came the Russian Guard, chests heaving from their uphill charge and the frantic fight with the first French line. Some, still fired by their earlier success, came rushing on, faces fixed in snarls or shouting incoherently. The volley from the second line crashed out at less than forty paces and as the smoke cleared Napoleon saw Russian bodies littering the ground in front of the French. Behind the killed and wounded the others had stopped in their tracks. Some just stared wildly at their enemies, others looked aghast at their fallen comrades. Those with harder hearts lowered their muskets and fired into the blue ranks ahead of them. Several of Vandamme's men spun round and collapsed under the impact of the Russian bullets, while their comrades swiftly reloaded and brought their muskets up for another volley. Another cloud of smoke, pierced by bright orange flashes, billowed out and a hail of lead tore through the head of the Russian mob. When the smoke cleared this time Napoleon smiled grimly as he saw the enemy recoiling with fearful and panic-stricken faces.

Before them, their comrades lay in bloodied heaps. A third, ragged volley sent them fleeing from the French line, back to where a line of officers stood with drawn swords, and behind them a line of impassive grenadiers with lowered bayonets. A short distance beyond the grenadiers stood a body of Russian cavalry, still unbloodied and ready to charge. As the first of the Russian soldiers slowed to a halt the officers raised their swords and bellowed orders for their troops to rally to their colours and re-form, beating the slower men into place with the flats of their blades. Force and discipline soon reasserted control and, as Napoleon watched, the Russian Guard formed into a dense column, ready to renew the attack.

Then he sensed the ground rumbling beneath his mount, and turning his head he saw Bessières and the first of the Imperial Guard cavalry squadrons, with a battery of horse guns, gallop over the crest of the Heights and make for the right flank of Vandamme's remaining line. Bessières came charging towards Napoleon and slewed his horse to a halt.

'Sire? Your orders?'

Napoleon thrust his arm out towards the Russian column. 'Charge them immediately. They must be broken at any cost. Any cost. Is that clear?'

'Yes, sire.'

'Then go!'

Bessières saluted, and spurred his horse forward, pounding along behind the rear of Vandamme's division as he re-joined his men. Riding to the front of the cavalry column, whose mounts breathed through flared nostrils and stamped and pawed the frozen ground, Bessières stood in his stirrups and raised his sword towards the heavens. He paused a moment and then swept the point down until it aimed directly at the Russian Guard. A bugle call shrilled out, and the squadrons rippled forward in a trot, hooves rumbling over the hard ground. The distance to the enemy was short and the slope lent the cavalry extra momentum as the pace increased into a gallop, and then, fifty yards from the Russians, they charged. Drawn swords glittered above the flickering horsehair crests on their gleaming helmets and then, as Napoleon and the men of Vandamme's division watched in breathless awe, Bessières's cavalry plunged into the dense mass of the first battalion of Russian infantry. Swords plunged down, flickered up, spattering gleaming crimson droplets, and the air was filled with the cries of men, the sharp whinnies of wounded horses and the crackle of musket and pistol fire.

Behind the first battalion men were hurriedly forming into two squares as the Russian cavalry formed line to counter-charge. As the helpless men of the first battalion scattered and ran for their lives, Bessières and his horsemen broke through the rush of fugitives and bore down on the nearest square. Meanwhile, the horse guns jingled across the slope in front of Vandamme's men and began to deploy, their teams loading them with case shot and waiting for a clear target. The Russian infantry, closed up, presented a dense front of gleaming bayonets and no amount of urging could persuade any of the French mounts to throw themselves into the enemy square. Volleys flashed out from each side, unseating the passing cavalry and bringing down several horses, who pitched forward and rolled as their iron-shod hooves lashed out. Bessières quickly realised that his men were being cut down uselessly as they surged about the squares, and ordered the recall. Strident notes carried above the noise and the French cavalry drew off, trotting back up the slope to form on their standards.

There was a brief lull as the last of Bessières's men hurried clear of the enemy squares, and the French gunners and the Russians stared at each other over ground strewn with dead and wounded men and horses. Then the captain in charge of the battery bellowed the order to fire and the six guns bucked in recoil as they spat lethal cones of lead balls into the closely packed enemy. The case shot ripped bloody holes through the Russian lines, which were quickly filled as the sergeants dressed their ranks. But no men, no matter how brave, could withstand such carnage for long and after several rounds from each of the guns, when hundreds of Russians lay heaped about the squares, those left began to waver, instinctively backing away from the French. This time there was nothing that the officers could do to rally their men and the formations broke as the Russians fled down the slope, straight towards their own cavalry.

As soon as he saw his chance to catch the enemy cavalry in disorder, Bessières ordered his men to charge again. They pounded down the slope once more, narrowly avoiding the last blast of case shot sent after the Russians. Then they were in among the tide of running infantry-men, hacking wildly as they ran the broken enemy down. Ahead, the Russian cavalry was in disarray as their routing comrades forced their way through the horse lines, thrusting bayonets or musket butts at any horseflesh that threatened to bar their escape from the French cavalry. Then Bessières and his men thundered in amongst them, shattering any last vestige of order in the ranks of the Russian cavalry. The impetus of the charge and the chaos caused by the fleeing infantry was more than the Russian horsemen could bear, and quickly they turned their mounts and fled down the slope, riding down their own comrades as they raced for safety.

Napoleon regarded the scene with grim satisfaction. His forces controlled the Heights and the enemy centre had disintegrated. The battle was as good as won. Only the scale of his victory was yet to be determined. He turned to Vandamme.

'Your men have fought well, General, but there is one last effort I must ask of you.'

'Yes, sire?'

Napoleon gestured to the southern edge of the Heights, where Davout and the French right were still engaged in a desperately uneven fight against the Austrians. 'Wheel your division and advance on the enemy flank. If you are in time, then the trap will be closed, and the most glorious victory is ours for the taking.'

Vandamme smiled. 'Yes, sire. It will be done.'

Napoleon nodded and turned away, galloping back up towards the crest of the Heights. As he reached it and reined in, he saw Bernadotte's corps advancing to cover the French centre. Beyond them came the men of the Imperial Guard, streaming south across the Heights to close round the Austrians before they became aware of the danger now that their allies had been cut off from them. Soult's other divisions followed Vandamme south at a quick step, driven on by their officers. Napoleon rode ahead to the southern edge of the Pratzen Heights and gazed down on the densely packed formations of the Austrian army as they waited their turn to be launched against the right flank of the Grand Army. The survivors of Legrand's division and Davout's corps were not content with holding back the Austrians, but had already driven them back across the Goldbach and were attempting to retake the villages of Zokolnitz and Tellnitz in the face of withering fire from the massed batteries of the enemy.

As soon as Soult's corps reached the edge of the Heights they deployed and began to advance on the Austrians as the first gun teams to unlimber poured fire down on to the enemy formations below. It was hard to miss their targets and soon the French batteries were sweeping away files of Austrian soldiers and smashing the guns that were hurriedly brought to bear on Soult's forces. The French infantry descended from the Heights, driving the enemy back before them at bayonet point. As the first Austrian battalions reeled back from the attack on their flank, they broke and poured away from the French, who were taking no prisoners. The fugitives ran straight into other units that were still holding their ground, and as the fear leaped from man to man like a contagion the Austrian army crumbled, battalion after battalion, and fled away from the French forces closing round them. There was only one line of escape, across the frozen lakes and marshes to the south, and soon the landscape seethed with men and horses desperately seeking a path over the ice.

Marshal Soult came riding up to Napoleon with a gleeful expression on his face as he pointed out the spectacle.

'We have beaten them, sire! You have won a famous victory.'

'Not quite yet,' Napoleon replied in a grim tone, his eyes on the fleeing army. 'We must make their defeat more crushing still, if we are to convince them to come to terms and end the war.' He was silent for a moment before he turned to Soult. 'Order your guns to open fire on those men.'

Soult stared at his Emperor for a moment and then responded quietly, 'Sire, they are beaten. They can do us no harm.'

'Not today. Not tomorrow, perhaps. But they will re-form soon enough, ready to face us again. We must remove that threat, Soult. Now carry out your orders, at once.'

Soult's lips tightened into a thin line as he saluted and spurred his horse away from the Emperor towards the nearest of his batteries, which had ceased fire as the French infantry closed with any Austrian units that still offered resistance. As soon as the order was given Napoleon watched Soult move on to the next battery. Round shot howled over the heads of the Austrians streaming away from the battlefield. Thousands were slithering across the frozen lakes as the heavy iron balls fell around them, shattering the ice and pitching men, horses, gun carriages and cannon into the freezing water beneath. Many were carried under by the weight of their uniform and equipment, but the strongest flailed for purchase on the unstable chunks of ice, struggling for a while before the cold sapped their energy and they slid beneath the dark surface of the water to join their comrades. Napoleon watched in silence as his enemies drowned in their hundreds. It was a sickening sight, and he was tempted to order the guns to cease fire, but he reminded himself of the brutal necessity of breaking the enemy's will to continue the fight. The more Austrians who perished in this battle the greater the chance of peace.

As the late afternoon sun angled down across the battlefield the guns and musket fire finally died away, and the quiet and stillness were strangely unsettling after the din of long hours of fighting. In the cool blue haze of a winter dusk Napoleon surveyed a landscape of bodies and wrecked guns and wagons. Smoke still swirled into the sky from buildings that had been set on fire during the fighting along the Goldbach stream. Most of the soldiers of the Grand Army sat on the ground, or leaned on their muskets as they looked on the devastation around them. Already the more opportunistic were walking amongst the heaps of enemy corpses looting the bodies of the dead, and finishing off any of the wounded who tried to resist their predations. Elsewhere thousands of Austrian prisoners were herded together under the watchful eyes of a screen of guards.

Napoleon bowed his head in a brief greeting as Soult rode up to him. 'Congratulations, sire. A famous victory.'

'It will be,' Napoleon agreed. 'Once Fouché applies a little pressure to the newspapers back in France.'

Soult chuckled at what he thought to be his Emperor's self-deprecation. 'A great victory by any measure, sire.'

'We'll know the measure soon enough.' Napoleon gestured to the bloodied ground of the battlefield. 'Have your men do a body count, then you send in your report to headquarters. I'm returning there now.'

'Yes, sire.'

Napoleon could see that his sober tone had deflated Soult's moment of triumph and he paused a moment before riding away. 'You and your men were as gallant as any in the field today. Let them know that. And when I next have to call on them, I'll be sure to grant them another triple issue of spirits.'

Soult laughed. 'Thank you, sire. I will let them know.'

Napoleon spurred his horse into a gallop and crossed the Heights back to the village of Pratzen as darkness began to close in over the battlefield, hiding its horrors until the morning. The gloom was pricked with the fires being lit by the men of the Grand Army before they settled to sleep, exhausted by the day's fighting and the fear and tension that had knotted their stomachs. There were a handful of the veterans of the Old Guard on duty around the army's headquarters and they offered a cheer as the Emperor dismounted and entered the church. Inside, Napoleon found Berthier sitting at a trestle table making notes from the reports that had started to come in from all quarters of the battlefield. The chief of staff rose quickly to his feet and bowed.

'Congratulations, sire.'

Napoleon waved aside any further words and cut in curtly, 'What news from the left wing?'

'Lannes and Murat have forced the Russians back. They are retreating towards Olmutz.'

'Is Murat pursuing them?'

Berthier shook his head. 'Marshal Murat reports that his cavalry are too weary to mount a pursuit, sire. Nearly all his force was committed today. His horses are blown.'

Napoleon was still for a moment as he thought. Crushing as his victory had been, the Russians might not have lost heavily enough to persuade them to consider peace. If they could only have been pursued and forced to abandon their artillery, if they had left behind a long tail of stragglers for Murat to deal with, then their spirit would have been utterly broken. Napoleon shrugged. 'A pity. But then we are all tired.'

Thought of his men's weariness served to remind the Emperor of his own exhaustion, and he could not help shivering for a moment. Berthier saw the tremor and his eyes widened in concern.

'Sire, are you all right?'

'I'm fine. I need some rest. Is there a bed in here?'

Berthier gestured to a small arched door opening on to a small cell. 'In there, sire. A bunk belonging to the local priest.'

'Good. I'll sleep now. Wake me before the third hour. Have the reports ready to present to me then.'

'Yes, sire.'

Napoleon wearily made his way into the priest's humble sleeping quarters, where a single candle guttered in a bracket on the crudely plastered wall. There was a small table and stool, a cupboard, and the bed: a simple straw mattress covered in worn blankets. Napoleon undid the buttons of his greatcoat and spread it out on top, then sat down and pulled off his boots before easing himself under the blankets and laying his head on the rough hessian of the bolster. He was asleep almost as soon as he shut his eyes and Berthier smiled to himself as his master began to snore. Then he turned back to his reports and began calculating the cost of victory.

'The enemy losses are over fifteen thousand killed; another twelve thousand are prisoners. In addition we have captured nearly two hundred cannon and fifty standards,' Berthier read from the summary he had prepared.

Napoleon stretched his shoulders until he felt the muscles crack, then straightened his spine and clasped his hands firmly behind his back as he braced himself for the other side of the balance sheet. 'And our losses?'

'One thousand three hundred dead, six and a half thousand wounded and a few hundred taken prisoner.'

Napoleon breathed a sigh of relief and nodded. 'Better than I had feared.'

'Yes, sire.'

'Very well, make provision for the wounded to be taken to Vienna. The prisoners can follow. They can be held there until the campaign is over. Now, I want you to issue orders for the army to re-form and be ready to march by noon.'

Berthier nodded and made a note. Outside, the first rays of dawn pierced the church windows with hazy orange shafts of light. Napoleon was grateful for the clear skies and cold air, which would aid his pursuit of the Russians. He was determined to drive them far to the east before the surviving Austrian forces could concentrate and re-join their allies.

The sound of hooves on cobbled stones came from outside the church and there was an excited challenge from one of the imperial guardsmen protecting headquarters. Napoleon glanced at one of Berthier's clerks. 'See what that is.'

While the man hurried off to do the Emperor's bidding Napoleon sat down on one of the pews that lined the walls of the church and buried his face in his hands to rest his eyes for a moment. There was a brief exchange of voices in the street before the clerk returned, with another man.

'Sire?'

Napoleon took a deep breath and puffed his cheeks as he sat up and regarded the clerk. Behind him stood Count Diebnitz. The Austrian was no longer scrupulously neat. His cheek was covered with bristles and his uniform was spattered with mud and there was a tear in one sleeve. He eyed Napoleon with a sullen, bitter expression.

'Well, Count Diebnitz, I am glad that you survived yesterday's encounter. Many of your countrymen did not, alas.'

Diebnitz's nostrils flared angrily but he kept his mouth shut and reached inside his jacket and pulled out a folded and sealed document.

Napoleon cocked an eyebrow at it. 'What is that?'

'A message, sir. From the Emperor of Austria.'

'Tell me what it says,' Napoleon continued wearily. 'I am a busy man, Count. Spare me the need to read it.'

Diebnitz swallowed his pride and lowered the document on to the pew beside Napoleon before he spoke. 'His imperial majesty wishes to discuss an armistice.'

'An armistice?' Napoleon smiled thinly. 'And why should I agree to one now, when I hold every advantage? Unless, of course, this is merely a preparatory step . . .'

He waited for the Austrian nobleman to get over his discomfort and come to the point.

Diebnitz spoke in a monotone. 'His imperial majesty requests an armistice, in order to negotiate a peace agreement.'

'Ah! I thought so.' Napoleon smiled triumphantly. 'Then you may tell the Emperor that I would be happy to discuss peace, on my terms.'

'Yes, sir.' Diebnitz bowed his head stiffly. 'I will inform him at once.'

'Wait.' Napoleon narrowed his eyes as he stared at the Austrian. 'Before you leave, you must know that there can be no peace while Russia is still your ally.'

'Ally?' Diebnitz sneered. 'Our ally is in full retreat, towards Russia, sir. The Tsar has abandoned Austria to run and hide and lick his wounds. We have no ally, sir. Not any more. It would appear that your victory is complete.'

Napoleon nodded. 'Yes, it would. You may go, Count Diebnitz.'

The Austrian bowed his head and turned to march out of the church. Napoleon waited until he was out of earshot before springing up and rushing over to clasp Berthier's hand in delight.

'It's over then. The war is over. The coalition is humbled.'

'Yes.' Berthier grinned back. 'A triumph for you, sire.'

'Indeed, my friend. We have crushed our enemies,' Napoleon said with relish. 'I'd give a small fortune to see Prime Minister Pitt's face when news of Austerlitz reaches him.'

Chapter 16

Arthur

London, February 1806

'It was Austerlitz that killed him,' said William as he leaned back in his chair and lowered his soup spoon. 'It broke Pitt's heart. He never recovered after hearing the news. Austerlitz changes everything.'

Arthur shook his head. 'Austerlitz changes nothing. We are still at war with France and the future peace of Europe can only be achieved if we defeat Bonaparte. Pitt knew that well enough and devoted his life to the prosecution of the war.'

'Well, now Pitt is dead, and so is his grand alliance against France,' William continued gravely. 'Austria has been humbled, Prussia is too afraid to fight and the armies of Sweden and Russia have retreated back inside their national boundaries. Our new Prime Minister and his government are of a very different line to Pitt and his followers. More's the pity. There are many men in Parliament who argue that now is the time to make peace with France.'

'Then they are fools.' Arthur reached for the decanter and topped up both their glasses. They were dining at William's London house. Richard had been invited but had sent word that he was too ill to attend, so they had started eating without him. Arthur had only recently returned from the abortive attempt to land an army in Germany to march and join with the Russians and Austrians against the French Emperor. News of the crushing defeat at Austerlitz had reached the expeditionary force before it had even landed, and the transports and warships had been recalled to Britain. A frustrated Major-General Wellesley had returned to London to seek a new opportunity to serve his country on the battlefield. But the national mood was far from bellicose and he had been offered, and reluctantly accepted, command of a brigade based at Hastings.

It was over a month since William Pitt had died, his declining health given its death blow by the news of Austerlitz. The nation had marked his passing with solemn respect. Arthur knew the worth of the man who had given the best years of his life in the service of his nation. Not only had Pitt's single-mindedness and administrative genius made it possible for Britain to counter the threat of France, but also he had made it possible for the powers of Europe to join the fight against the Republic, and the Corsican tyrant who usurped it. Vast sums of money, and convoys of supplies and equipment, had flowed to Britain's allies thanks to Pitt's vision. Now that he was dead, and Napoleon had crushed the alliance forged by Britain, the will to continue the fight was ebbing away swiftly, Arthur reflected sadly. The newspapers were filled with items bemoaning the continuation of a war that had yielded little in the nation's interest and only served to deepen the national debt. The talk in the coffee houses was dominated by those who proclaimed the invincibility of Bonaparte.

There had been no obvious successor to Pitt. There were men with the ability to take on the responsibility of the office, Arthur mused, but none had sufficient support in Parliament to form a stable government. The mercurial Canning was not trusted by the political class, and Castlereagh was unpopular with the people. In the end it was Pitt's cousin, Lord Grenville, who had emerged as a compromise candidate and persuaded the King to confer the position on him. But at a price. Gone were all the old friends and supporters of William Pitt and in their place was a mixed bag of politicians of all political persuasions. When Arthur attended a handful of debates in Parliament, the Whigs, who had opposed the war for many years, made smug speeches about the unnecessary cost in lives and bullion and demanded an end to the war. The so-called government of 'all the talents' even included the populist liberal Charles Fox. Arthur frowned.

'What's the matter?' asked William, noting his brother's expression. 'Something wrong with the soup?'

'No, it's not the soup. I was just thinking about that scoundrel Fox. If Pitt could see it now he would groan in his grave. I can't believe that Grenville would make such a man Foreign Secretary. Good God,' Arthur shook his head, 'Fox betrayed us to the rebels of the American colonies, and I've even heard people mutter that he is in the pay of Talleyrand.'

'You should not believe everything you hear, Arthur, but I agree with you that Fox holds some questionable views.'

'Questionable!' Arthur's eyes widened. 'You've heard the man often enough in Parliament. Time and again he has spoken out against the war. And now he would even have us open peace negotiations with

France! He would dishonour all that we have sacrificed over the years.'

William shrugged. 'Charles Fox is a political animal, Arthur. As such he is a pragmatist, and a weathervane in the cross-currents of popular opinion. He knows that the people are weary of war and desire peace, so much that they would even treat with the Corsican tyrant himself. So Fox will use every ounce of his charm to persuade Grenville to open negotiations with Talleyrand.'

'God help us,' Arthur responded bitterly. 'Is the man so foolish that he thinks he can persuade Bonaparte to agree to terms that are remotely in the interests of Britain?'

'His position is a little more subtle than you think.' William spoke evenly as he raised his glass and sipped it contemplatively. 'Consider for a moment the question of Napoleon's primary virtue.'

'Virtue?' Arthur smiled thinly. 'There! You have me already, brother, for I cannot think of a single virtue pertaining to Bonaparte.'

William sighed irritably. 'Indulge me, then. Let us suppose that Napoleon's ability finds its truest expression in the art of war. Would you agree with me on that at least?'

Arthur considered this for a moment and then nodded. 'For the sake of argument.'

'I do not see how you can deny it, Arthur. He has defeated his enemies comprehensively, and, indeed, seems to relish the substance and trappings of a martial existence. All of Europe, and many of our own countrymen, regard the French Emperor as the greatest commander of the age. Now, whether you agree with that or not is immaterial. The point is that Fox believes it. So, being the shrewd thinker that he is,' William laced his words with irony, 'the Foreign Secretary has concluded that the best way to frustrate our enemy is to deny him that which he craves above all things, namely war. To which end Fox has persuaded Grenville to allow him to approach Talleyrand with some preliminary proposals for a lasting peace.'

Arthur had lowered his glass as his brother spoke and now stared at him across the table. 'Good God . . . Do you have any detail on these proposals?'

'Oh, yes.' William smiled. 'Fox was good enough to discuss his ideas when I met him in the House earlier this week.'

'You met him? Why?'

'I wanted to discuss the prospect of finding you a seat in Parliament.'

'Parliament?' Arthur's eyebrows rose. 'Why would I want such a thing? I am a blunt soldier. I lack the necessary tact and guile to be a politician.'

'Come now, Arthur, false modesty is a vice, not a virtue. You are as capable of being a politician as any man, and besides, I dare say that a bit of blunt speaking would be a welcome change in the House. I must talk to some people and see what I can do.'

Arthur stared at his brother for a moment before shaking his head. 'I'd rather not, all the same. I had my fill of politics back in the Irish Parliament.'

'Ah, but you were nothing then,' said William, and then waved a hand in apology as he saw his brother's expression darken. 'I mean no offence. But then you were young and inexperienced, with little achievement to your credit. Now, you are Sir Arthur Wellesley, hero of Assaye. Your voice would count and you would be able to influence events. Besides,' William's tone became more serious, 'our brother Richard needs all the friends he can get in the House. His political future is at stake, and that of our family. Without influence, Arthur, what hope have you of being given any worthwhile military appointment? Do you know how many major-generals there are on the army list? One hundred and forty-eight, and the majority of them are senior to you. That is why you have been assigned to that tedious backwater down in Hastings.'

Arthur laughed lightly. 'You have done your homework, William. At least the Hastings command keeps me on the active list.'

'Really? I wonder just how active a soldier can be in such a place. I imagine the gravest danger one must face is being pelted with guano by the seagulls.' William sat back with a brief sigh and folded his hands over his stomach. 'You will need political friends if you are to rise to import- ant military commands. Now then, I have arranged a quiet meeting with Grenville and Fox. Primarily as an opportunity for Richard to see them and put his case in private before he is exposed to the full rigour of parliamentary examination. If you come with me as well, as a prospective member of the House, it will add strength to our cause. Besides, I think you will have something to say on the matter of Fox's peace proposals that it might do him good to hear.'

Arthur listened wearily. In truth, he accepted that William was right. The plain fact of it was that no man ever rose to prominence purely by his own efforts and abilities. It seemed that to become a successful general one must also become something of a successful politician as well. He nodded. 'Very well, I'll come.'

William had arranged for the meeting to take place in a private dining room in one of the gentlemen's clubs off Park Lane. Crauford's was a club favoured by clients with an interest in card games, and when Arthur entered on the stroke of nine in the evening and gave his name to a footman he was ushered through a room containing half a dozen tables at which men were playing whist. Their concentration was absolute. Not one looked up as Arthur passed by, and he realised why his brother had chosen this club for the encounter between the three Wellesley brothers and the two most powerful men in the government. Beyond the card room was a short corridor with two rooms leading off each side. The footman opened the second door on the right and bowed his head as Arthur stepped inside, then closed the door behind him. The others were already seated at the end of a long dining table, which was bare save for a large decanter of port and the glasses set out for the guests. The other four men were already seated.

'Arthur, delighted you could join us.' William smiled. 'Do take a seat.'

Arthur glanced at his brothers as he strode round the table. William appeared to be his usual robust self, but Richard was as wan and pale as when he had returned from India and looked to be in poor health as he rested his chin on the knuckles of one hand and steadily regarded the two men on the other side of the table. Arthur knew both Grenville and Fox by sight, having seen them both in parliamentary debates and at social events. Grenville was tall and slender but Fox was by far the more arresting of the two. Tall, broad-shouldered and rotund, he had a jowly, good-humoured face and his eyes sparkled with energy. He returned Arthur's gaze with an intense searching look and then rose and offered his hand as Arthur approached.

'Ah! One of the younger brothers of the Wellesley family!'

'Yes, sir.' Arthur shook his hand, returning the powerful grip with a tightening of his own fist, until he sensed the other man slacken his hold and release his hand. Arthur turned to Grenville, who had risen to his feet a moment after Fox. 'Prime Minister.' Arthur bowed his head respectfully. 'My condolences on the loss of your cousin. Mr Pitt was a fine man.'

'My loss is the nation's loss, Sir Arthur. Make no mistake about that.' Grenville nodded sadly. 'But we must move on, and take full advantage of the stable condition in which my brother left our nation.'

'Stable condition?' Fox chuckled. 'I hardly think such a vast mountain of public debt and a state of war with the most powerful nation in Europe constitutes stability.'

Grenville turned to his companion with an irritated air. 'Pitt's legacy is that he saved us from revolution and defeat. I think that is more than enough justification for describing Britain as stable.'

'If you say so.' Fox chuckled. 'Although some of my friends in the House might disagree.'

'And we must always consider the views of your friends,' Grenville responded in an acid tone.

The two men stared at each other for a brief moment, and Arthur wondered how such a political partnership could work. In Britain's present rudderless state perhaps such compromises were inevitable.

Fox cleared his throat. 'This is a free country, and a man should be free to speak his mind. After all, those are the values that we are fighting for, or so it appears to me.'

Richard's sickly white face seemed to drain of the very lost drop of blood. When he spoke, it was in a cold, hostile tone. 'I do not need any lectures on freedom from a man who has been in open communication with the very nation that is determined to end the liberties enjoyed by every man in Britain.'

There was a faint smile on Fox's lips, but he replied with a hard edge to his voice. 'That is hearsay and rumour, and you would be well advised not to repeat such scurrilous untruths.'

Arthur tapped his finger on the table and interrupted. 'And yet you would have us negotiate peace with France, if I understand correctly?' He glanced at Grenville, who nodded.

'Times change,' Fox continued. 'What might once have been considered a lack of blind patriotism might now be seen as the best hope for Britain, under the present circumstances.'

'Circumstances change,' Arthur responded. 'Bonaparte's enemies will not long tolerate his power over Europe. Equally, I doubt whether he would tolerate a prolonged peace. Bonaparte will always want more territory, more power and more glory. He needs these things as other men need food and water. Unless Britain is prepared to continue submitting to his demands, however humiliating, there will be further wars. You cannot appease such a despot for ever, Mr Fox.'

'You may have a point, young man. But try telling that to the merchants of this country who increasingly find themselves closed off from continental markets. Try telling it to the hungry mobs of unemployed in our great industrial cities whose jobs have gone as trade has withered. Try telling it to those countless families up and down this land whose sons and fathers have been killed in the wars against France, or have come home crippled by wounds and incapable of earning a crust. Do you really think they will rejoice at the prospect of war unending?'

'No one is asking them to rejoice. And the war will end, the moment France is free of Bonaparte.'

Fox suddenly sat back in his chair and took a swift draught of port from his glass. Then he looked closely at Arthur. 'It's peculiar that you should say that.'

'Really? Why, sir?'

'I was approached by a French dissident earlier this week, who had come to London in secret in order to present me with a plan to assassinate his Emperor.'

'Good God!' Grenville stared at his Foreign Secretary. 'And you didn't think to tell me?'

'You are a busy man, Prime Minister. The fellow's plan seemed madcap when he broached it, and he needs a large sum, in gold, to pay the assassin. So I declined the offer. Moreover, I decided to inform my opposite number in Paris of his countryman's plan.'

'You would reveal this to Talleyrand?' Richard could not hide his amazement. 'By God, why would you do such a thing? This Frenchman and his agent would be caught and killed. Would you have that on your conscience?'

'No more than I would the killing of an emperor. Considerably less, in fact. Besides, you are missing the point. By exposing this conspiracy we could demonstrate our good faith to Talleyrand, and, through him, to Napoleon. It would surely help our attempt to open peace negotiations. In any case, the argument is academic. I have already sent a message to Talleyrand to warn him of the plot.'

There was silence in the room as the others took this in and showed their surprise, and some disgust. Grenville was the first to recover and he turned fully towards Fox and glared. 'You go too far, sir. The dissident's approach to you should have been reported to me directly. The decision as to whether to back the man, or turn him down, was not yours to make.'

'It was a foreign policy issue, sir, and therefore well within the responsibilities of my office.'

'That is enough! You should have discussed this with the Cabinet, or me at the very least. In future, I demand that you report any further such activity to me directly. Understand?'

'Yes, Prime Minister. I understand.' Fox smiled faintly, then suddenly reached down and examined his pocket watch in the candlelight. 'Ah, I'm afraid I must beg your pardon and leave you, gentlemen. I have a prior engagement. I am taking my wife to a late recital.'

'A recital?' Grenville gently stroked his frown-streaked brow. 'Don't you think this meeting is more important than a recital?'

'In truth? No. A man who neglects his wife is no man at all, sir. So I must go. Gentlemen.' Fox stood up and bowed his head to each of the brothers on the opposite side of the table. 'I will leave you to your politics, then. Good night.'

He clasped his hands together, stretched his back and strode towards the door. 'I'm sure I will be seeing you all again soon. Especially the Wellesleys, who will have to face some tough questions in the House if I am any judge of my own supporters. Once again, good night, gentlemen.'

Taking his cape and hat from the stand, Fox opened the door and left the room. The others stared after him as the door clicked shut. Richard let out a low dry laugh and was the first to speak.

'Well, Grenville, it appears that you have your work cut out for you with that man. I should not like to work alongside him.'

'You can't begin to imagine . . .' muttered the Prime Minister. 'But on one thing he is right. There is no avoiding the need to have him in government. At least it keeps his supporters relatively quiet. It is both a pity and a paradox that Fox is less of a danger inside the Cabinet than without.'

'I wonder,' Richard mused. 'If only there was a dissident Englishman in Paris with the desire to assassinate a member of our government. If the frogs wouldn't back him I'd certainly invest in an attempt on Fox's life.'

Grenville stared at him for a moment. 'I fear that you have imbibed too many uncivilised values during your time in India, Mornington.'

Richard shrugged. 'It was just a thought. Besides, I know full well that Fox and his friends are behind the corruption allegations levelled at me.'

The Prime Minister casually clasped his hands together as he composed his reply. 'I will, naturally, do my best to protect you, and the interests of your family. After all, my late cousin held you in high esteem and greatly valued your service to our nation. However, you must understand that I can only shield you so far. This government hangs by a thread and has to be sensitive to every shift in opinion, within Parliament, at Windsor and in the streets.'

'I thank you most humbly for your reassurance,' Richard sneered.

'Mornington, you must understand. I act as I have to for the good of the country. If it is in the country's interest that you are forced to endure the attacks of Fox and his associates, then you must accept it.'

'I am tired, and I am sick, Grenville. I know in my heart that I have done right by my country, and that truth will be accepted in the end.'

'I hope so. But in the meantime, I think it would be wise to cultivate as much support as you can within Parliament. You have William here to speak for you, and it would make good sense for Arthur to enter the House as well. He has won an enviable reputation on the battlefield, as well as social and military rank. His voice would carry considerable weight in support of you, Richard. I would willingly assist in finding him a seat. After all, people would hardly be surprised to find Arthur speaking up in defence of his brother.'

Arthur smiled. He could see through the Prime Minister's motives at once. It would be politically inconvenient for him to have his supporters openly defend Richard. This way, he would oblige Arthur to repay his patronage and at the same time avoid the risk of taking sides over the dispute concerning Richard.

Grenville continued. 'What is your position at the moment, Sir Arthur? Still on the active list?'

'I have been given command of a brigade at Hastings.'

'Hastings?' Grenville thought for a moment. 'Excellent. There is a seat at Rye that is available. Not so far from Hastings. I am sure the War Office can be persuaded to grant you leave to stand.'

Arthur bowed his head respectfully. 'Thank you.'

Grenville reached for his glass and raised it. 'Gentlemen, a toast. I give you the next member of Parliament for the constituency of Rye!'

Chapter 17

Hastings, February 1806

As the long winter months dragged on Arthur was determined to make the most of his small command, billeted in the quiet coastal town of Hastings. The men of the brigade had become used to the relative inactivity of winter quarters and were surprised and not a little unenthusiastic when their new major-general gave orders that they should be roused for drilling and exercise every morning. Come rain, snow or hail, the men of each battalion assembled at dawn and were put through their paces under Arthur's keen eye as he rode over the fields that had been chosen for exercise grounds. His experience in India had proved to him the need to keep his men fit and healthy through regular exercise. They might well curse him for it, but when the time came for them to endure long marches and hard battles while on campaign they would cope more easily, even if they never thanked him for it.

He was aware that some of the men grumbled that there was little point in training since the government seemed adept at sending British soldiers to join campaigns just in time for them to be sent home again. Arthur sympathised with their frustration, but that was no reason to relent on regular drill and the maintenance of uniforms and equipment to the highest standards. He recalled an expression he had once heard that an army's drills should be bloodless battles, and its battles bloody drills.

Arthur smiled at the thought one morning in late February, when he rode out to find one of his battalions formed up on frozen ground. A thick frost coated the surrounding trees and hedges with gleaming white against a backdrop of a pale grey sky. This morning the men had been joined by a commissariat wagon loaded with boxes of cartridges and Arthur gave orders for each man to be issued with twenty rounds. He was well aware that the penny-pinching officials of the War Office frowned upon live fire practices since the cost of the powder and balls discharged was considerable. But Arthur well knew that men who were familiar with the din of firing and the rolling clouds of stinking smoke on the training ground were far less likely to be perturbed by musket fire when it happened on the battlefield.

The prospect of live fire practice lifted the mood as the battalion went on to form column a half-mile from a long low hedge that bordered a little-used turnpike. When the men were ready the order was given to advance on the hedge and the column rippled forward. As the front rank closed to within a hundred paces of the hedge Arthur abruptly reined in his horse and bellowed, 'Form line!'

The orders were repeated and the redcoat companies tramped out at an angle across the frost-gilded meadow until the senior sergeants reached their positions and lowered their pikes to indicate the line along which the following ranks were to form. As the last men stepped into place on the gently rolling pastureland Arthur snapped his watch shut and trotted over to where the lieutenant-colonel of the battalion stood a short distance ahead of the colours.

'Chambers, that took your men a shade under three minutes. If you can't do it in two, a Frenchie column will be upon you before your men can fire a single volley.'

'Yes, sir.' Colonel Chambers took the rebuke stolidly, and stared to the front. 'I will attend to my men's timing, sir.'

'See that you do. Now then.' Arthur looked up and indicated the brow of a hill half a mile away. 'Let's assume your men have just fought off a French column. You have just sighted a regiment of cuirassiers over there. What do you do?'

'Sir?' Chambers glanced at the hill. 'I don't understand.'

Arthur spoke evenly. 'Use your imagination, man. That hill is covered in cuirassiers. Except by now they have gained at least a hundred yards on you. So what do you do?' Arthur pulled out his watch again and thumbed open the cover. 'Well?'

Chambers immediately took a deep breath and roared, 'Battalion will form square and prepare to receive cavalry!'

Once again, Arthur kept an eye on his watch as the companies steadily folded back from the wings and formed a square three men deep, the front rank kneeling with their muskets braced against their boots so that the bayonets pointed up and out, creating a deadly obstacle that few horses would dare to hurl themselves at.

Arthur nodded to Chambers. 'Much better that time. Very well. Your men can do you credit when they want to, Chambers.'

'Yes, sir. Thank you, sir.'

'Now it's time for some live firing. Have some men posted on the turnpike to hold off any travellers. Now then, the hedge is a line of French soldiers, Chambers. What now?'

This time Chambers did not delay and instantly gave the order to form line at the double. His men trotted into place, their haversacks and water bottles slapping up and down as they hurried across the trampled grass to their positions.

'Battalion will make ready to fire by companies!' Chambers called out. 'Fire when ready! Five rounds!'

The sergeants called time as the men grounded their muskets and began the loading procedure. Then they raised their weapons and waited for the order.

'Fire!' bellowed the sergeant of the first company to be ready, and a sharp crashing thud reverberated off the hard ground as a cloud of smoke swelled into life in front of the battalion's Light Company. A moment later one of the other companies fired and then the rest came in with a ragged discharge along the line. Over by the turnpike, bits of twig and small branches leaped into the air as the musket balls raked through. The companies continued to fire their volleys, and such was the efficiency of the Light Company that they had managed to loose their final round before the slowest company had finished loading their fourth.

Gradually the fire slackened. As the last echo died away and the dense clouds of choking powder smoke began to dissipate, Arthur waited a moment for the men's ears to clear and then called out, 'Gentlemen! Bonaparte has eight soldiers for every man in King's uniform. Man for man they are not your equal, but we are not fighting man for man. We are outnumbered, and the only thing that will save us is killing them faster than they can kill us. That means we must be able to fire more volleys than our enemy on the battlefield. Today, the Light Company took nearly eighty seconds to fire the first three rounds. That will not do!' Arthur paused and turned towards the battalion's commander. 'Colonel Chambers!'

Chambers stiffened his back as he replied. 'Sir?'

'I want your men to be able to fire the first three rounds within a minute by the end of the month. You may continue with the live firing, and then drill the men in the movements for the rest of the morning.'

'Yes, sir.'

'Very well, carry on.'

The two officers exchanged a salute, then Arthur wheeled his mount round and galloped back towards his billet on the hill east of Hastings. He could trust Chambers to drill the men to the standard he required of them so that they would perform well whenever the time came to send them off to war. Arthur smiled grimly to himself. With Bonaparte's present run of successes it was unlikely that his brigade faced the prospect of any action in the immediate future. Especially if Fox held to his purpose of attempting to negotiate a peace with France. The more Arthur thought about it the more frustrated he became with his political masters. Even if the French Emperor was prepared to negotiate, there was every chance that the talks would follow the pattern of the earlier Peace of Amiens, where France added further demands each time the treaty was about to be signed. After the peace took effect, Bonaparte blithely snapped up further territory and made preparations for forcefully expanding French interests as far afield as India and the West Indies. The Corsican tyrant was truly insatiable, Arthur reflected, and he did not care how many bodies were buried on the path to realising his ambitions.

As he entered the town, Arthur slowed his horse to a walk. Fox's plans for peace, however well intentioned, were doomed to fail. The war would continue. Britain must choose the ground to wage land war against Bonaparte very carefully. Somewhere on the periphery of Europe where the small but highly trained and highly disciplined British army could pick its battles carefully and gradually wear down Bonaparte's marshals and their armies, and prove to the rest of Europe that the men who marched under the tricolour could be defeated again and again. Once more Arthur's mind turned to the Iberian Peninsula, where such a scheme would most readily bear fruit. If only a British army, under a competent commander, could be landed in the Iberian Peninsula there was no telling how much it could achieve, and perhaps shift the balance of victory in favour of those nations allied against France.

When he arrived back at the riding school that served as brigade headquarters Arthur dismounted and handed the reins to a groom. Then, stepping into the entrance hall, with its smell of leather and polish, he hung his coat on one of the pegs outside his office and entered. Corporal Blake, his personal clerk, rose from the ledgers on his desk and stood to attention.

'Good morning, Blake.'

'Morning, sir.'

'Better put in a request for ten thousand more rounds of ammunition.'

'More live firing exercises, sir?' There was a hint of disapproval in

143

the corporal's tone and Arthur paused at his desk to stare levelly at the man.

'Yes. If they have been issued with muskets, then it's as well that they have the opportunity to learn how to use the bloody things. Wouldn't you say?'

'Yes, sir. But then I'm not in supplies. And you know what they're like, sir.'

'I do. Can't bear to deal with 'em. That's why you have the job, Blake.'

'Thank you, sir. Much obliged.'

Arthur smiled and strode on, through the door into the small adjoining room where he had his personal office. One wall had shelves floor to ceiling on which Arthur kept his paperwork in an orderly manner. His desk, unlike rather too many desks of commanding officers, was bare. It had long been his practice to deal at once with every letter, report, request chit, leave application, disciplinary form or any other piece of paper that landed on the in-tray. That, in addition to the regular training and exercise, is why the men under his command were always amongst the best soldiers in the service of the King.

He sat heavily in his chair and stared out of the window for a moment. The riding school sat atop a hill overlooking Hastings and the sea beyond. Down on the shingled shore the fishing boats were being hauled up from the surf towards the large cluster of net-drying sheds that rose above the tiled and thatched roofs of the town. Beyond the sheds the beach became a mad jumble of large rocks beneath the looming cliffs, and Arthur looked forward to the afternoon walk he regularly took there for exercise. He always found it a fine opportunity to think, uninterrupted by the duties and minutiae of commanding the brigade.

Foremost amongst his concerns at present was the upcoming election for the seat at Rye. He had submitted his name, and been approved by the local landowners who largely dictated the manner in which their tenants would vote. All that remained was to take a short period of leave from the brigade to wine and dine the voters, as was the custom, make a few fine speeches and, after the brief formality of winning the vote, accept the honour of representing his constituents. After that Arthur would be able to support his brother in Parliament, while at the same time promoting his views on the most effective way of defeating France.

There was a knock on the doorframe and Arthur turned away from the window to see Corporal Blake standing beyond the threshold, holding a leather pouch.

'Excuse me, sir. Just had the mail off the post coach from London.'

'Thank you, Blake. On the desk there.'

Blake laid down the pouch and returned to his accounts in the other room. With a sigh Arthur unfastened the pouch ties and flicked back the flap. Inside were several letters. He took them out and examined the first, a brief note from the War Office acknowledging his request for permission to conduct live firing exercises, and regretfully urging him to take the matter no further due to the stringent financial constraints the Treasury was placing on army and naval expenditure. Arthur tossed it to one side and opened the second letter, from his mother, Anne Wellesley. It was curt and precise and Arthur thought it read like a mere series of diary entries as it related the most recent social events she had attended in London. There were a few references to the family, including a caustic comment about Richard's being too arrogant to defend the family's good name in Parliament. It concluded with a brief expression of good will to Arthur, who she trusted was looking after his health. Arthur set the letter aside with the familiar sense of resignation over his mother's evident lack of maternal affection for him. Then his eye fell on the next letter and he froze for an instant as he read the name of the sender.

Lord Longford, Rutland Square, Dublin. Arthur held the letter up and stared at it as he felt his pulse quicken. Then he broke the seal, unfolded the paper and began to scan it quickly. He read it once again, more slowly, to be sure that he had understood it fully. Kitty's brother acknowledged his letter requesting permission to propose to her. In view of the rank that Arthur now held in the army, as well as the knighthood bestowed on him, and the private fortune he had accrued after his service in India, Thomas Pakenham deemed Arthur worthy of his sister's hand in marriage. Therefore he would raise no objection if Sir Arthur Wellesley were to send a formal proposal of marriage to Kitty.

'Good God,' he said as he laid it on the desk. 'What a pompous idiot.'

'Sir?' Blake leaned out from his desk so that he could see his commanding officer.

'It's nothing. Pray continue with your work.'

Arthur was cross with himself for uttering such an uncharitable thought about his prospective brother-in-law. After all, Thomas had given him permission to marry Kitty, having rebuffed him eleven years previously on the grounds that Arthur was unworthy. Well, now the wait was over, and Kitty would be his wife, if she accepted his offer. Arthur realised, with some surprise, that the feeling uppermost in his mind was not unbridled joy at the prospect, but a sense of relief that all the uncertainty of his feelings for Kitty was almost over.

He did not dwell on the sentiment but immediately drew a sheet of paper from his stationery drawer, flipped the lid back on his inkwell and took up his pen to write to her at once. When he had finished, he glanced over his words critically. It was no love letter, to be sure. It stated his intentions clearly and tersely and requested that he might know her mind on this as soon as possible, since they had waited long enough already and he would wish to make arrangements for the marriage at once, if she would do him the honour of accepting his hand. Satisfied that the letter was adequate to the occasion Arthur signed it, blotted the ink and folded the paper, sealed it and wrote Kitty's address on the front.

'Blake!'

'Sir?' the corporal called. His chair scraped back and he hurriedly stepped into the room to stand stiffly before Arthur's desk.

Arthur carefully placed the letter in the despatch pouch and held it out to Blake. 'See that this gets on the coach back to London at once.'

'Sir?' Blake looked uncertain.

'What is it, man?'

'The coach stops down in the town just long enough to change the horses and pick up the passengers and post. Then it goes straight back to London, sir. It's most likely too late for the letter to go today, sir.'

'Well, there's only one way to find out, Corporal. Get it down there yourself. Right now.'

'Yes, sir.' Blake saluted, then turned away, and Arthur could almost sense his irritation at being ordered away from his warm office. But, he reasoned with an amused smile, the corporal was rather too corporeal and would benefit from the exercise. Then, as the man's footsteps receded, Arthur sat back in his chair and closed his eyes, recalling as best he could Kitty's face and the sound of her voice and the touch of her hand, and slowly a host of other memories from many years before played out in his mind and filled his heart with warm delight.

A month later Arthur went to London to see William in order to plan their defence of Richard. William ensured that he was introduced to many of the leading figures of the day and briefed him on those who could be counted on to speak up for Richard, and those who could be numbered amongst his enemies. Richard did himself no favours by remaining contemptuously aloof and refusing to counter the charges laid against him. Arthur had sent Kitty a brief note informing her that he would be staying at William's London home temporarily and that any letter should be sent there in the first instance.

While he waited for her reply Arthur made the most of the chance to see old friends, visit the theatre and attend social events. It was at a raucous party at Swann's, a Chelsea club favoured by the cavalry, that he ran into Richard Fitzroy, an old friend with whom Arthur had served since his earliest days in the army. The main salon was filled with army officers, mostly youngsters, and as ever it was the hussars who were making the loudest noise. Arthur had been invited to join an acquaintance from his days in India, but the man had not turned up and so Arthur sat at a table in one corner and watched the antics of the younger men with an amused detachment as they competed to see who could throw a goose feather the furthest. Their frequent roars of encouragement echoed round the room and drew the occasional disapproving glance from more senior, or serious-minded, officers sitting at the other end of the salon. As Arthur watched, a cheery-faced individual in a red jacket pushed through the throng towards him. Arthur grinned as he recognised an old friend.

'Hello, Arthur!' Fitzroy beamed as he reached Arthur's table and clasped his friend's hand warmly. 'Haven't seen you in a while. What brings you here?'

'The search for decent companionship,' Arthur replied with mock weariness.

'Ah, yes. I had heard that you were thinking of entering Parliament. My commiserations. But why do it at all?'

Arthur shrugged. 'The family requires it. And so it is. Anyway, how about you? I see you are a colonel now.'

'Ah, yes.' Fitzroy glanced awkwardly towards the epaulette on one shoulder. 'My father finally stumped up the money for a colonel's commission, and he's never going to let me forget his generosity. Best make the most of it, I suppose. Before a lucky shot, some bloody campaign fever or the wedding bells do for me.'

'No plans to get married yet, I assume?'

'Hardly. I've been back in Dublin for a while. The place is growing a little more tame than it was in our day, but there's still enough going on to warrant remaining a bachelor for a while yet. Ran into a few old faces. One in particular asked to be remembered to you.'

Arthur suddenly knew exactly what Fitzroy was going to say and felt his stomach knot itself with anticipation.

'Really? Who might that be?'

'That Pakenham girl you used to be so attached to. What was her name?' Fitzroy frowned for a moment and then snapped his fingers. 'Kitty! That's it. Ran into her at a castle ball. She saw me first and made a charge straight at me. Else I'd have bolted for cover!'

'What are you talking about?'

Fitzroy chuckled. 'Well, she has changed a good deal since we last saw her. I barely recognised the girl. Well, girl is hardly the word to describe her. And has not been for a while, I'd hazard.'

'I expect we have all changed,' Arthur replied coolly. 'We've matured, Fitzroy. That's all.'

'Matured?' Fitzroy's eyes twinkled. 'I dare say. But in some cases I think the better word would be weathered. And the once fair Kitty, and she was very fair as I recall, has turned into something of a thin old stick. Shame, really. Ah well . . . Anyway, she asked me about you, and about our campaigns in India. I gave her the abridged version, since there were some fine girls about and the hour was already late. Before I got away she said to send you her warmest regards if you and I should meet. And here we are!'

'Yes, here we are.' Arthur forced himself to smile. Inside, he had felt his heart sink at Fitzroy's words, and then his conscience pricked with guilt and he felt the beginnings of anger. 'Despite her mature looks, I am sure she is the same Kitty that we once knew.'

'Perhaps. But I'd say that she has lost a lot of that spark that she used to have. Quite the lively filly, she was. I think you'd be surprised by the change in her, Arthur. Damn good thing you didn't marry her back then, I'd say.'

Arthur's expression froze and Fitzroy's brows knitted together in bewilderment. 'Are you all right, Arthur?'

'Quite fine, thank you.'

'Ah, good! Thought you were having a turn there.'

'No, nothing like that.' Arthur took a deep breath and shrugged. 'It's just that I have sent Kitty a formal letter of proposal and I'm waiting for her reply.'

Fitzroy stared at him a moment, mouth slightly agape. Then he roared with laughter and slapped Arthur on the shoulder. 'Oh, that's a good one! For a moment there I thought you must be serious.'

'But I am.'

Fitzroy started to smile again, then his lips froze as he took in the mirthless expression of his friend. He swallowed nervously. 'I see. Well, I, er, I don't quite know what to say, Arthur. Are you quite sure she's the woman you want to marry?'

'Quite sure.'

'I had no idea. I mean, Kitty said nothing about having seen you since we got back from India.'

'That's because I haven't seen her. We have been in touch by letter.'

'Good God!' Fitzroy looked astonished. 'You've proposed to Kitty without so much as seeing her? That's madness. But tell me truly, Arthur. You really haven't see her since we left Ireland?'

'Yes.' Arthur's irritation with his old friend was growing more acute with each utterance from Fitzroy. It was bad enough that he had such a low regard for Kitty, but it was worse that he so obviously thought Arthur a fool. Trying to thrust aside the description of Kitty as she was now, Arthur felt compelled to defend her character, and his pride. Besides, he had made a promise to her to renew his offer, before he had left for India. He had given his solemn word, and Arthur was bound to honour that. His breeding, his family name, his feelings for Kitty and his conscience ruled out any other course of action. He drew a long deep breath as Fitzroy shuffled with embarrassment.

'The thing is, Fitzroy, that I am a man with sound judgement and integrity. I know that my affection for her is not based on the superficial attraction of beauty, but on the substance of her character. I love her for her mind, Fitzroy. I don't imagine for a minute that you could comprehend such a thing.'

'Steady on, Arthur. I meant no offence. You are one of my oldest friends. But I have to say that it seems a little unwise to me for a fellow to commit himself to a wedding with a woman he has not seen these eleven years.'

'She has not accepted me yet.'

'There is some chance, then?'

'I think you misunderstand me. I live in earnest hope and anticipation of her acceptance.'

'Oh . . .'

They stared at each other in silence for a moment before Fitzroy could not bear the embarrassment any longer. He smiled weakly and clasped Arthur's hand. 'Well then, I hope . . . sincerely hope that it all works out for the best, my dear Arthur. Really I do. Now I'd love to talk some more, but I'm here with some friends from the Guards, and we really only just came by for a quick drink. Look here, I'll make sure I look you up in a day or so.'

'I'll look forward to it. Now, don't let me stop you re-joining your friends. Goodbye, Fitzroy.'

'Goodbye.' Fitzroy nodded solemnly and turned away to walk unsteadily back towards the crowd of officers on the far side of the salon. Arthur stared after him for a moment, then made his way to the entrance, where he retrieved his hat and cape and stepped out of the lively atmosphere of the club into the cold dark street. He paused to breathe deeply of the chill night air and then marched quickly back to William's house.

For the first time he was assailed with doubts about his offer to Kitty. It had been so easy to assume that she would still have that same essence of being that had won his heart years before. After all, Arthur reasoned, did he not feel himself to be substantially the same character as ever, beneath the layers of experience? But what if she had changed as much as Fitzroy claimed? Granted, her looks were bound to have faded. No, not faded, he corrected himself, but what, then? Surely someone who had been as beautiful as Kitty would have acquired grace rather than lost her looks. Yes, that was it. No wonder Fitzroy had perceived her as lacking beauty. The man was facile enough to not make the distinction. By the time he returned to William's house Arthur was in a cold fury over his friend's dismissal of Kitty.

The footman who let Arthur into the house took his cape and hat and motioned towards a silver salver on a table close to the door. A letter rested on the tray.

'That came while you were out, sir.'

Arthur crossed the hall and picked up the letter. By the dim light of the handful of candles that William permitted as illumination he raised the letter and read the name of the sender. Katherine Pakenham. Dismissing the footman, he took up a candle and hurried into the parlour next to the front door, making for William's writing table. He set the candle-holder down, sat at the table and hurriedly opened the letter. The very sight of her handwriting, spidery and cramped, evoked an excitement that filled him with a warmth and affection he was sure was love.

Kitty wrote that she had received his proposal, and that while she was minded to accept it she felt it only fair not to hold him to his promise until he had met her face to face so that he could be certain that he truly wanted to marry her. If his heart was unchanged then Kitty would be overjoyed, and proud to be his wife and companion for life.

The encounter with Fitzroy still smouldered in his heart, and as Arthur read through the letter several more times he warmed to Kitty's honesty and integrity. He set the letter down, drew out a sheet of writing paper, a pen and a small pot of ink from the desk drawer and began to write a hurried response. He told her that if she would marry him he would be the happiest of men. There was no need to see her first. His heart was true and his mind was set on becoming her husband. That being the case, all that remained was to set a date for the wedding. He urged her to accept a date in April, so that no more time be lost before their loving union was blessed. He would settle his immediate duties in Hastings and set off for Dublin at the earliest possible date. If Kitty was agreeable, the ceremony would be conducted by Arthur's brother, the Reverend Gerald Wellesley, who he was sure would be honoured to be asked. Having signed off the letter with a few hurriedly chosen endearments, Arthur blotted the paper, folded it, sealed it and addressed it before returning to the hall and setting it down with the others in the rack by the door that were waiting to be sent off.

Then, with a weary mind and heart, Arthur climbed the stairs towards the small suite of rooms that William had set aside for him. In a matter of weeks he would be marrying Kitty. The sudden reality of it was quite shocking, and though he felt his spirits rise a little at the prospect of having her for a wife at long last, he could not quite shake off the doubts that Fitzroy had instilled.

Chapter 18

Dublin, April 1806

The ship from Bristol fought its way across the Irish Sea to Dublin in the teeth of a spring gale and Arthur was gripped by seasickness as the vessel lurched from end to end, accompanied by a pitching and rolling motion that made his stomach churn violently. Unlike most of the other passengers who remained huddled down in their tiny fetid cabins below deck, Arthur preferred to be in the fresh air where he could see the horizon and use it as a fixed point to give him some sense of control over his nausea. Not that it worked all the time, as every so often the ship would soar or swoop without any warning and the sickness would return with a vengeance.

'Good day to you, Sir Arthur!' a voice called out cheerily, and Arthur turned to see Captain Acock striding up the deck towards him. His years at sea had accustomed him to the motions of the ship, to which he adjusted his pace with confidence. 'Bit of a breeze today, I think.'

'Bit of a breeze?' Arthur shook his head ruefully. 'I shall never understand what you sailors enjoy about your profession.'

'Oh, it's not so bad, sir.' The captain laughed. 'There's nothing like cutting your ties with the land and setting out into the wild.'

Arthur nodded. Perhaps there was something to be said for such a life, though it had its own dangers. 'I think, on the whole, that I'd rather avoid sailing through such tempests as this.'

'Tempest, you say?' The captain smiled and shook his head, blinking as a shower of spray drenched them both. 'Hardly. This weather is typical for the time of year, sir. You get used to it. I dare say that you've not had much experience of sea travel, then?'

'Oh, I've had my share, and my fill. I've been out to India and back.'

The captain turned to glance at him with raised eyebrows. 'India. Now that's real sailing. I've only ever crossed the Atlantic, on the Jamaica run. Some hard times in those days, I can tell you. But I've only ever heard sailors' stories about the passage to India. Not many men do that in their lifetime, sir.'

'Nor should they,' Arthur replied with feeling as he recalled the cramped accommodation, the week-long storms, the lack of fresh food and above all the raw agony of the days, and sometimes weeks, before one found one's sea legs and grew accustomed to the motion of the ship. The very thought had him gripping the side rail tightly as he struggled with another wave of giddy nausea.

'So, what's your business in Dublin then, sir?' the captain continued in a light tone.

Arthur swallowed and replied through gritted teeth. 'I'm going to be married. My intended is waiting for me in Dublin.'

'Is she now?' The captain grinned. 'Ah well, a fine city to be married in, sir.'

'Not in this weather.'

The captain raised his eyes to the grey clouds rolling over the white-capped sea. 'It'll blow itself out soon. Like as not the moment we dock.'

'With my fortune, I'd imagine so.'

'Are you planning on living in Ireland, sir?'

'Certainly not. I can think of few climates I'd rather avoid. No, the moment we are wed, and have had a honeymoon, I will be bringing my wife back to London with me.'

'Ah well,' Captain Acock mused; then a swinging motion aloft caught his eye and he turned away from the rail. 'Beg your pardon, sir, I must attend to my ship. Hope you have a fine wedding then, sir.'

He made his way across the deck to the foredeck gangway and bellowed an order to one of his sailors to go aloft and secure a loose block. Arthur had no desire to watch a man clamber up the rigging in such rough seas, and kept his gaze resolutely on the horizon as he fixed his thoughts on Kitty once again. Kitty would be the same Kitty he had delighted in and loved all those years before. She would be as opinion-ated and mischievous as ever, and there would be the same bright twinkle in her eye and the same becoming bloom in the rounded cheeks he had so loved to kiss on the few occasions it had been permitted. And he would love her just as before. They would be married, and live happily, he resolved.

The gale had moderated by the time the ship approached the dockside on the Liffey, but even as the wind dropped the rain continued to fall in an icy downpour that exploded off the surface of the river like newly minted coins. The passengers had all come up on deck to view the approach to the city and huddled in their coats and hats as they stared out at the slick walls and roofs of Dublin under a leaden sky. Using staysails and reefed topsails the captain eased his ship in towards the wharf, and then gave the order to loose sheets before letting the forward motion of the vessel carry it the remaining distance. Ropes were cast ashore to the dockers who looped them round the mooring posts and drew the ship in until it rested gently against the tarred hessian fenders.

Shortly afterwards the passengers wearily descended the gangplank, desperately grateful to be back on firm land. Arthur hired a porter to carry his travelling chest and set off for Gerald's house. Dublin did not seem to have changed much since Arthur had last seen it. He recognised many of the same shops, taverns and clubs that he had frequented in the days when he had served as an aide to the Viceroy at Dublin Castle. There were some new names on the shopfronts and there was the same mix of poverty and affluence amongst those he passed by, but there was something lacking in the ambience. The streets were less crowded than he remembered, and somehow less spirited.

By the time he reached the house, Arthur was soaked through. He stood dripping in the hall as he paid off the porter and handed his coat to a servant. The sound of footsteps on the stairs caused him to turn and he saw his younger brother, Gerald, descending to greet him with a broad smile.

'My goodness, did you swim all the way here?'

'Very funny,' Arthur grumbled. 'I imagine your sermons must be the very model of wit.'

'Now, now, don't take on so. I'm delighted to see you again.' Gerald grasped his hand and shook it warmly. 'Especially to celebrate such a happy event. It's about time you took a wife, Arthur.'

'Is it?' Arthur mopped the rain from his brow. 'That's what everyone seems to say to a man of my age. Still, maybe they have a point. A man must have heirs and someone to care for him. And someone to care for.'

'Of course.' Gerald stepped back and looked his brother up and down. Arthur's skin still had a faint brown hue from so many years exposed to the burning Indian sun, and his hair was cut closely enough to subdue any hint of the wavy curls that he had worn before he went overseas. He was thin, but in a sinewy, fit way that few men of his years managed to retain as they surrendered to the temptations of good living and complacency. Gerald smiled to himself and gestured towards the door leading to the front room. A coal fire glowed in the grate and Arthur stood in front of it and held his hands out towards the flickering flames, relishing the warmth.

'I'll have some dry clothes found for you. Would you like something to eat and drink?'

Arthur nodded. 'I'd be very grateful, thank you.'

Gerald turned towards the door and was on his way out of the room when Arthur said quickly, 'Gerald, I forgot to say, it is good to see you again too. And I am so very grateful that you are going to perform the service.'

What are brothers for?' Gerald laughed lightly and left Arthur alone by the fire.

Half an hour later, as the two sat on either side of the hearth, Arthur finished the platter of cold meats, cheese and bread that had been brought to him. He drained the last of the Madeira from his glass and sat back in his dry clothes, contented. The shutters had been closed and muffled the sound of the rain pattering against the window panes.

'I imagine you are delighted to return to civilisation after so many years amongst the natives of India,' said Gerald.

'It is said that travel broadens the mind.'

'But does it though, Arthur? Can you truly say that you are a better man because you have seen the world?'

'Not better, perhaps. But wiser. I feel that I know the minds of other men more fully than I did, and I know my own mind more clearly. So I suppose I am glad I have experienced something of the world.'

'And yet here you are, back in Britain, and now about to take a wife from amid the self-same stock that you were raised amongst. That seems to be a refutation of the wider world if ever I heard it.'

'That is unfair, brother. How can a man truly value what he has until he has seen the depths and the heights of human activity? Gerald, how can you know for certain that the immediate world around you is all that is good? Surely you could only know that if you had the chance to compare it to something else?'

'If you love your country, and you have faith, then what need is there to strive to make such a comparison?'

'Sometimes I wish I could see things as you do, Gerald. I wish that I could have faith in the goodness of men. I wish that I could understand God's will in all the suffering that I have witnessed.' Arthur paused a moment. 'What I crave is some certainty in my life. The certainty of feeling. The security of a home and the chance to raise a family. Once that is gained then a man has something he can believe in. Something that is truly worth fighting for.'

'And you think Kitty will provide you with that, when you marry her tomorrow?'

'I hope so,' Arthur replied thoughtfully. 'If not her, then who?'

★

The following morning Arthur hurriedly bought himself a fine set of clothes and arranged to hire a carriage for the week-long honeymoon he had decided on. They would be driven round the places he had known as a child, where he and Kitty had been together before Arthur left for India. It would help to rekindle memories of the times that had meant so much to them both, or so Arthur reasoned.

At noon, Arthur and Gerald set out from the house for the short walk to the rather more imposing Pakenham residence on Russell Square. Arthur felt more tense than ever, but said nothing of it as he responded to his brother's light-hearted small talk. For the first time in days the skies had cleared and a bright sun bathed the world in its warm glow. Arthur wondered if this might be a good omen. The people they passed on the streets were in good spirits and exchanged greetings with complete strangers in a cheerful manner. On arriving at the square the brothers paused to quickly examine each other's appearance. Gerald was wearing a simple black frock coat and his clerical collar was just visible. He carried his Bible, prayer book and other religious accoutrements in a large leather bag.

'Well?' said Arthur. 'How do I look?'

Gerald cocked an eyebrow. 'To be sure, I am not certain whether I will be officiating at a wedding or a funeral. You might try smiling a little.'

Arthur took a calming breath and tried to compose his expression into that of a happy and contented man. 'Any better?'

'It will serve,' said Gerald. 'Come.'

They crossed the square and approached the Pakenhams' house. The front door had been decorated with white ribbon that looped across the fanlight and it was evident that their approach had been watched, since the door swung open even as they were climbing the steps from the street. A footman bowed his head and gestured for them to enter.

'Sir Arthur, Mr Wellesley, the service is being held in the drawing room. If you would follow me?'

They stepped inside and the footman led them down the hall. More ribbon adorned the chandeliers and freshly cut flowers filled urns that lined the length of the hall. At the end, double doors opened on to a large room with high ceilings and long windows overlooking the neat garden behind the house. A score of chairs had been arranged in rows in front of a makeshift altar. A handful of Kitty's closest friends and relatives were already seated, and turned to glance curiously as the groom and his brother entered. Arthur nodded a curt greeting and then went and sat on one of the two chairs that had been set for bride and groom to one side of the altar. Gerald sat beside him and they waited in silence, until Arthur found it too awkward not to speak.

'She must know we have arrived,' he said quietly. 'Why is she keeping us waiting?'

'Because she can,' Gerald replied with an amused expression. 'The woman's prerogative, Arthur. I've seen this sort of thing at countless weddings. Don't worry yourself, she will join us when she is good and ready.'

'Woman's prerogative be damned. I'll not have my time wasted in this fashion.'

'Arthur, calm down. It's quite natural to be nervous before the ceremony.'

'It's not nerves, damn it. I just don't see any need for a delay.'

'Arthur, this is a marriage ceremony, not an army drill. It's probably not a good idea to confuse the two if you want a lifetime of married bliss.'

Arthur clamped his lips together and folded his arms, staring rigidly ahead as the clock on the mantelpiece behind the altar ticked away. The other guests did their best to ignore his mood and talked in muted tones. An hour after the Wellesley brothers had arrived, and twenty minutes after the service had been due to begin, Tom Pakenham appeared at the door to the drawing room and cleared his voice. 'Ladies, gentlemen, my sister is ready to join us.'

'Not before time,' Arthur whispered.

'Shh!' Gerald nudged him, then rose to take his place before the tiny congregation who had come to witness the wedding of Arthur and Kitty. Tom waited at the door and a moment later was joined by his sister. Arthur turned his head and looked directly at her. His first reaction was to deny that this woman could possibly be Kitty. She was as thin as a stick, with sunken cheeks and eyes, and her hair, though still brown, was wispy and had lost the unruly curls of her youth. Only her lips, and something of her eyes, even reminded him of the Kitty he had known, and at that moment Arthur realised he had made a mistake. The most awful mistake of his life. What made it worse was the dawning realisation that there would be no undoing of this mistake. He could not withdraw from his commitment to marry her any more than he could stop drawing breath.

'My God,' he muttered under his breath. 'She has grown ugly.'

Gerald glanced sharply at him, then turned to the bride and her brother, who was to give her away, with a welcoming smile. Kitty smiled back nervously and then squinted slightly as she stared at Arthur. Her

157

smile flickered a moment, and for all his misgivings Arthur could not help but smile back rather than hurt the poor creature as he rose to his feet along with the other guests.

Tom Pakenham offered his arm to his sister, and led her towards the altar. When they drew up abreast of Arthur, Tom released her and stepped aside as Gerald raised his hands and began.

'Dearly beloved, we are gathered together here to join together this man and this woman . . .'

As his brother continued with the ritual Arthur stared straight ahead, as if he was on a parade ground. Inside he felt his heart sink like a lead weight in mud. The years had settled on Kitty like a tattered shroud and the passion that he had once felt for her so strongly taunted him as a mirage taunts a thirsty man in the desert. On the periphery of his vision he sensed her sidelong glances at him, and he wondered if she felt the same way about him. Perhaps the years had been kind to neither of them. In that thought he managed to find some small scrap of hope. Even if their looks had faded, then surely their personalities would have escaped the ravages of time? Arthur clung to that belief as the ceremony wore on, and spoke his lines in a wooden manner that would have disgraced the very poorest of actors.

At length the service came to an end and Gerald pronounced them man and wife. The words fell heavily on Arthur's ears and as he turned to face Kitty he forced himself to smile. He took her hands in his, and sensed her tremble.

'There, my dear. As I promised all those years ago, I have married you the moment I was deemed suitable.'

Kitty smiled shyly. 'I always dreamed you would.'

'Thank you, my dear. You have no idea how much that means to me.'

Kitty blushed, and Arthur gently dipped his head towards her. Kitty closed her eyes as her lips pressed forward, but Arthur kissed her quickly on the cheek and withdrew. Kitty's eyes flickered open and she looked at him with a faintly hurt expression.

Tom Pakenham cleared his throat again and announced that refreshments were available in the dining room.

'Excellent!' said Arthur. 'I'm quite famished. Come on, my dear Kitty!'

He slipped his arm through hers and led the guests out of the drawing room and down the hall towards the dining room, before she could think of kissing him again.

The wedding's informality meant that speeches were kept to a minimum, and once a light meal had been eaten, the couple toasted and the cake cut, the newly-weds were escorted out to the carriage that Arthur had hired for their honeymoon. They climbed aboard amid the congratulations of the guests, and some of the passers-by, and once the door was closed the driver flicked his whip and the horses lurched forward. Inside Kitty and Arthur were jolted against each other and shared a quick laugh of embarrassment before they stared at each other, uncertain of what to say.

'That was a beautiful wedding,' Arthur blurted out finally, and then hurriedly groped for the most appropriate sentiment to express. 'And this is the best day of my life. You have made me a very proud and happy man, my dearest Kitty.'

She looked at him, her expression flitting between doubt and hope, and then she took his hand and squeezed it. 'Arthur, this feels so strange. I feel I know you and yet I don't.' She paused and swallowed nervously. 'And I fear that I disappoint you.'

Arthur kissed her, on the lips this time, and made himself linger there a moment before drawing back. 'My darling, I have waited for this moment for all these years. How could you possibly disappoint me?'

Kitty smiled briefly and turned to look out of the window. 'I will do my best to be a good wife to you, dear Arthur. I will try to be worthy of the faith you place in me, and the honour you do me by holding to the promise you made so many years ago.'

'Kitty, it is you who honour me.'

'Shh! I know the truth of the situation. Just promise me that you will be fair and honest with me. I could not bear to be hurt by you, Arthur.'

'I promise, my darling,' Arthur replied as earnestly as he could, and then he turned to stare out of the other window as the carriage rumbled through the cobbled streets of Dublin, closed in on both sides by tall drab buildings that mocked the unblemished blue heavens above.

They stopped for the first night at an inn on the road to Dangan and ate a cheap but hearty stew in the small back room reserved for the better sort of guest. The landlord built up a small fire and then left them alone with their meal and a jug of his best ale. The conversation was stilted at first, and then, as they shifted the topic of conversation on to the times they had shared many years ago, a genuine warmth entered their exchanges. For Arthur it went some way towards rekindling affection for Kitty, but every time he looked closely at her there was only a shadow of the young woman he had known, and it was hard to stem the growing sense of lost opportunities as the evening wore on.

At length, they finished the meal and there was an awkward silence before Kitty cleared her throat.

'I think I will go and prepare for bed, my dear. I won't be long. Give me a quarter of an hour before you join me.'

'Yes. As you wish.'

They exchanged a brief, embarrassed smile, then Kitty turned and hurried from the room, leaving Arthur alone in the warm glow of the dying fire. He stared at the embers, wondering at the perverse combination of honour and indolence had led him into this predicament. There had been chances to avoid it. He could have ignored Olivia Sparrow's entreaties to renew the correspondence. He could have taken up Kitty's offer to meet her before committing himself to marriage. He could even have walked out of the ceremony. But the more he considered these things the more clearly he saw that he was a man driven by a sense of duty. Duty in all things. He could no more have abandoned his obligations to Kitty than he could abandon his obligations to King and country. Once set on a path he would travel it all the way to the end and apply himself to overcoming every obstacle set before him.

With a sigh he drew out his pocket watch and marked that nearly half an hour had elapsed since Kitty had gone to bed. He put the watch away, drained the last dregs of his ale and rose from the table. Outside, he passed the landlord as the latter wiped down his counter.

'Good night, sir.' The landlord smiled knowingly. 'I hope you and your bride will be comfortable.'

Arthur felt something give way inside and felt the urge to snap at the landlord and tell him to mind his own damned business. But just as quickly as the urge arose, he mastered it and suppressed his anger.

'Thank you,' he said coolly. 'I am sure we will. Good night.'

There was a narrow flight of stairs to the few rooms the inn provided as guest accommodation and Arthur paused as he stood outside the door of the room he had rented. He looked at the brass handle gleaming dully in the light of the candle flickering in a wall bracket. Then, stiffening his resolve, he entered the room. It was a modest size with clean plaster walls. A large bed rested against the far wall, and a candle burned in a holder on the small table to one side. Under the thick bedcovers he could make out the slender shape of Kitty, lying quite still. Her nightcap covered her hair and only a small expanse of her face was visible above the covers.

'Won't be a moment, my dear,' said Arthur as he crossed to his travelling chest. He undressed unhurriedly, slipped on his nightshirt and turned towards the bed. Kitty did not seemed to have moved, and she made no sound. The only noise in the room was the faint rustle of the branches of a chestnut tree just outside the window. Arthur slipped under the covers and lay facing his wife. She had her back to him and for a moment Arthur wondered if she might be asleep, and he did not move. Then the covers stirred and her hand reached back towards him, groping across the sheet for his hand. Finding his fingers, she interlaced her own and gave a gentle squeeze.

'Are you ready, my love?' he whispered.

'Yes,' came the reply, soft as a light breeze.

Arthur edged closer and drew Kitty over so that she lay on her back. Her eyes were wide as she stared up at him, terrified by this new intimacy. Arthur leaned over her and kissed her on the lips, feeling hers tremble. He kissed her again, and let his fingers caress her neck, down to the breast of her nightshirt. As the tips brushed her nipple Kitty gave a small cry and Arthur felt a sudden hot stirring in his loins. His hand continued to move over her stomach, and then he began to draw the material of her nightdress up until he could feel the smooth bare flesh. His hand paused a moment before tracing its way down to the soft tuft of hair. Kitty gasped.

'Are you all right, my love?' he asked.

'Yes, yes.' Her eyes were tightly shut. 'Arthur, my dear, please . . . please don't hurt me. Please be gentle with me.'

'I will.'

He was now fully aroused and he gently eased her legs apart and climbed over her. Kitty's sex was dry and unyielding as he pressed the tip of his penis against her. There was resistance for a moment, and then he entered her. She cried out in surprise and a little pain and her hands grasped his shoulders tightly. Arthur thrust home, again and again, working his way up to a quick, joyless climax, and as soon as it was over he rolled to one side and lay gazing at the ceiling as his heart pounded passionlessly. Kitty lay still for a moment, and then began to cry silently, though he could feel the little judders through the mattress.

For a moment he thought about trying to comfort her, but no words came, and he turned away and blew out the candle on his side of the bed and lay in the dark, not sleeping and filled with a deadening sense of despair.

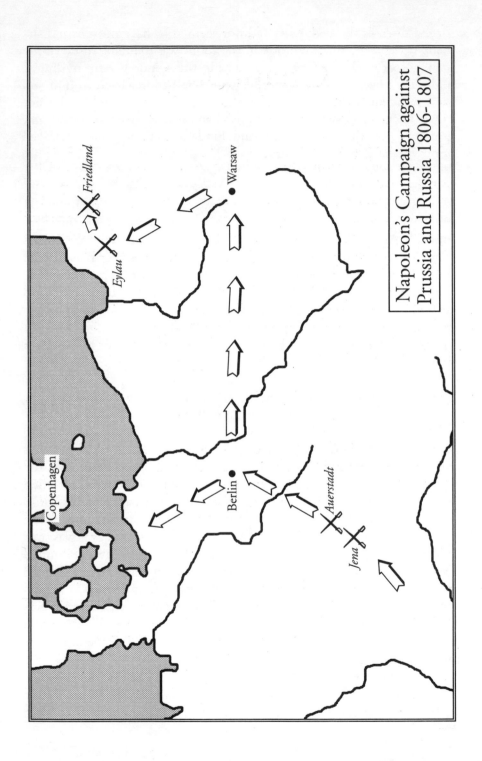

Napoleon's Campaign against
Prussia and Russia 1806–1807

Friedland

Eylau

Warsaw

Copenhagen

Berlin

Auerstadt

Jena

Chapter 19

The honeymoon was over in less than a week and when the newly married couple returned to Dublin Arthur was riding on top of the carriage with the driver, while Kitty sat alone in the cab. Gerald immediately offered to accommodate his brother and his bride. The following morning Arthur booked passage on a ship leaving for Bristol the same afternoon, and then made arragements for Gerald to escort his wife from Dublin once she had settled her affairs in Ireland. With his travelling chest packed Arthur sent for a cab and made ready to leave. Gerald and Kitty were sitting in the front parlour when Arthur joined them, his coat and gloves already on.

'My goodness,' said Gerald. 'You don't waste any time!'

'Alas, I have none to waste,' Arthur replied briskly. 'Duty calls me back to London. I have to support Richard in Parliament, and there is a brigade to command. Not only that,' he turned to Kitty and forced a smile, 'I have to find a home worthy of my bride.'

Kitty smiled back and it pained him to see how easily she could be pleased. As easily as she could be hurt, he realised. Arthur felt shamed by his duplicity. In truth he was burdened by the dreadful knowledge that he had made the mistake of his life in marrying Kitty. That had become clear enough in the long days of the honeymoon as they travelled in frequent silence, the gulf between them merely becoming even more starkly apparent when they did start to talk. While Arthur had voyaged to India, fought battles, commanded armies and become the ruler of the kingdom of Mysore in all but title, it was as if Kitty had sat on the shelf gathering dust. Conversation was awkward. There was much he wanted to tell her, to discuss. Yet Kitty's world had been utterly different from his own these eleven years and they struggled to find common ground on many issues. Their talk was stumbling and broken and the silences filled with self-consciousness. The only comfort was that their lovemaking at least had improved as Kitty's initial apprehension about the act dissolved. Even so, after five days Arthur found her company stifling and was desperate to return to London, where he could busy himself and not dwell on the mistake he had made.

'When are you going?' she asked.

'As soon as the footman finds a cab.'

Kitty's expression crumpled momentarily, then she swallowed and recovered her composure. 'I will come to the dock with you.'

'There's really no need. It's cold out and, in any case, the cab won't afford you much space.'

'Nevertheless, I wish to come with you and say goodbye.'

Arthur was silent for a moment, and then nodded. 'Oh, very well, then.'

By the time Kitty had got her coat, bonnet and gloves the cab had arrived. The driver loaded Arthur's chest on to the rack on the roof and then held the door open. Arthur shook hands with Gerald and hurried down the steps. He turned and saw Kitty standing in the hall adjusting her bonnet, and his foot tapped impatiently as he waited. Having satisfied herself about her appearance, Kitty emerged and exchanged a chaste kiss with Gerald before stepping lightly down the steps and into the street. Arthur handed Kitty up into the cab and quickly climbed in after her, squeezing on to the seat beside his wife. An instant later the cab lurched into motion and turned out of the street and down towards the forest of masts and furled sails of the ships thronging the Liffey.

They did not speak for a while, and then Kitty asked, 'Will you look for a house immediately, Arthur?'

'Yes, of course.'

'Good. I could not bear to be apart from you a day longer than necessary.'

'I know, my dear. It is the same for me. But we must be patient so that I can find something suitable.'

'I understand. But really, Arthur, there's no need for me to wait here in Dublin while you hunt for a house. I am sure that I could live with Olivia Sparrow in the meantime. And if I was there in London, I could help you look for a house.' She glanced at him and smiled weakly. 'Would that be entertaining?'

Arthur nodded. 'I imagine so.'

'Then I will make arrangements with Olivia to join you there as soon as possible.' Kitty took his hand tentatively and gave it a squeeze. 'I will be a good wife to you, I swear it.'

'Of course,' said Arthur. 'And I will be a good husband, as far as my duties permit.'

The cab rattled out of a side street and on to the broader thorough-fare that ran alongside the wharves. Moored ships clustered as far as the eye could see and the driver flipped down a small hatch and called through. 'Which vessel, sir?'

'The *Ardent*, about two hundred yards further on.'

The hatch clacked shut as the driver slowed his horse and began to look for the names of each vessel as they passed. A short distance further on he drew up and stopped. Opening the door, he indicated a sturdy-looking merchant vessel moored a few paces away.

'Here you are, sir.'

Arthur climbed out and offered his hand to Kitty as she stepped down on to the cobbles. Her nose wrinkled at the smell: salt, fish and tarred cordage.

'Wait here,' Arthur told the driver. 'The lady will be taken back to my brother's house shortly.'

'As you like, sir.'

Arthur summoned a porter to carry his chest aboard and then walked with Kitty to the end of the gangway. 'Well, here we are, my dear. Now we must say our farewells. Just for the present,' he added quickly.

Kitty stared at him with wide eyes and her lips trembled as she responded. 'Can I not stay and see the ship off?'

'There's really no point. She won't be leaving Dublin for some hours yet. Best if you didn't, Kitty. You'll only get cold and might catch a chill. Come, be brave. Give me a kiss and hold me.'

He opened his arms and Kitty stepped into his embrace, pressing her face against his chest so that he would not see her tears, but he could feel her thin frame shudder all the same. At length she drew back slightly, dabbing at her eyes with a lace handkerchief, which she hurriedly stuffed down her sleeve. Arthur cupped her cheek in his hand and tilted her face towards him and kissed her on the lips. It was not a passionate kiss, merely perfunctory, and he drew his head back quickly and smiled.

'There! Now you must get back into the cab and go, Kitty.'

'I don't want to go just yet. Please don't make me.'

Arthur looked at her in silence. Inside he was struggling to contain a growing sense of irritation. At the same time he did not want to hurt her and the tension between the two impulses only made the situation even more intolerable. He took her hand and guided her gently but firmly back towards the cab, where she climbed in and took her seat with a show of reluctance. Arthur closed the door on her and stepped back.

'Goodbye, Kitty. I will see you in London, my love.'

'Goodbye, dear Arthur.' She raised a hand and waved it weakly.

Before she could speak again Arthur nodded to the driver. 'Take her straight back to my brother's house.'

'Yes, sir.'

At a crack of his whip the horse broke into a trot and the cab began to move away. Kitty's face appeared at the window and she waved her hand as the cab drew off. Once she was no longer visible Arthur drew a deep breath and puffed his cheeks in relief, but he had the good grace to wait until the cab turned up a street and disappeared, with one last frantic wave from the occupant, before he turned to climb the gangway on to the deck of the *Ardent*. A fresh breeze was blowing up the river Liffey and Arthur paused to fill his lungs and relish the sense of freedom.

Five days later he was back in London. Arthur quickly hired some rooms for himself and arranged to meet his brothers to discuss their strategy for dealing with the accusations being made against Richard, and by extension the rest of the family. Richard was still claiming to be ill, but his scandalous disregard for the opinion of his social peers meant that he openly consorted with courtesans, with little regard for the effect this had on his wife, Hyacinthe, and their children: a state of affairs that was prejudicing more and more of the non-committed amongst the members of Parliament, not to mention provoking the wrath of those who owned the newspapers that seemed to fill every coffee shop and club in the city. But try as he might Arthur could not shift his brother from his course and matters came to a head one Sunday towards the end of April when Arthur paid a visit to Richard's home in Chelsea.

The servant showed him into the drawing room, and Arthur picked his way over the toys and dolls that lay scattered about the floor. He took a seat by the window that overlooked the street and waited. After quarter of an hour had passed the door clicked open and Richard entered. He had not shaved for some days and his thin jaw was dark with stubble. His hair was roughly tied back with a ribbon and he wore a silk gown of the type favoured by Indian nabobs. He greeted his guest with a tired smile and stepped over the obstacles to join him at the window.

'You look terrible,' Arthur began.

'I thank you. So kind of you to say so. How is married life, brother? Not that you can have enjoyed much of it as yet. I heard from William that you left Kitty in Dublin when you returned.'

'She will be joining me soon enough.'

Richard looked at him with a sharp expression. 'Too soon, from your tone.'

'I'm here to discuss *your* problems.'

'Rather than your own?' Richard sat back in his chair and winced. 'Ahhh. Sorry, too much drink last night. I can't cope with the consequences as well as I used to. Anyway, you mentioned problems.'

'Richard, I have the seat for Rye, as you know, and will be taking my place in Parliament tomorrow. Naturally I will speak up for you.' Arthur paused to ensure his next point was given its full impact. 'The thing is, Richard, that your behaviour is not helping our cause.'

'My behaviour?'

'This flagrant cavorting around the capital with your latest mistress on your arm. Have you no sense of decorum?'

'Decorum is for asses and hypocrites,' Richard sneered. 'I love the woman, and I don't care who knows it. We are exceedingly happy together. How many men of our class can say that?'

'That's all very well, but you cannot ignore the impression it is creating on other people. They regard it as a scandal, Richard. And as long as they do, there is no hope of your achieving the high office you deserve, and no hope of Britain's benefiting from your talents.'

Richard chuckled. 'Quite the patriot, aren't you, brother? Perhaps I am not quite so public-spirited as you think.'

'I know you, Richard. I know that you gave several years of your life to promoting the fortunes of our country in India. And I know that you feel aggrieved over the scant recognition of your achievements that has been accorded to you by the people here in Britain. It is most unjust, I grant you that. But squatting here in your self-pity and indulging yourself in outraging public morals is a self-defeating form of revenge, I'd say. Richard, you cannot continue like this, for all our sakes.'

Arthur fell silent and stared at his brother earnestly for any sign that his words had had their intended effect. Richard sighed and stared out of the window. At length he shrugged, then coughed to clear his throat and winced at a sudden pain in his head.

'Look here, Arthur, I appreciate your concern. But there is little I can do about it now.'

'Rubbish!' Arthur snapped back. 'There is everything. Sober up. Smarten up. Go back into Parliament and defend yourself and your policies. If you can't stop whoring around then at least attempt to keep your private life private, and for God's sake start cultivating a following amongst the newspaper editors here in London.'

'Newspaper editors?' Richard frowned. 'Why should I want to associate with such vermin?'

'Because they influence public opinion.' Arthur spoke patiently. 'And public opinion influences those in government. You might try to be seen in public with Hyacinthe more often and give the impression of being a dutiful husband.'

'What is the point?' Richard asked wearily. 'My enemies mean to destroy me. I hear that votes of censure are being planned in the Lords and the Commons. Of course I will try to defend myself, but you know how slowly these things progress, Arthur. It will be years before my name can be cleared, if it ever is. I will have to employ lawyers to defend me, and they are sure to bleed me dry in the process. So you can see why I feel little desire to play along with public opinion, or deny myself what few pleasures life affords me. I am not the only man in London who indulges his physical needs outside marriage.'

'True,' Arthur conceded, 'but you are one of the few who elevates it to the level of popular spectacle. It has to stop, Richard. For your own good.'

'For the good of the family,' Richard countered mockingly.

'Yes, that is true. Britain has need of us as never before. We have proved what we can do in India. Think what we could do for Britain with you in government and I on the battlefield. Our country needs us, and if we serve her to the fullest extent of our abilities, then people a hundred years from now will honour the name of Wellesley.'

Richard looked at his brother sadly. 'You seem to have quite an appetite for posterity. But I want my rewards now, in this life. Alas, those bastards on the board of the East India Company, and their friends, are hell-bent on ruining my career.'

Arthur was growing tired of his brother's obstructive state of mind, and he hissed through his teeth for an instant before continuing in a low, flat tone. 'I can see there is no point in prolonging this discussion, Richard. I'll leave you to enjoy your misery, then. Meanwhile, you may rest assured that at least William and I will be defending the honour of our family name. Perhaps, when you come to your senses, you might join us. I bid you good day.'

So saying, he rose from his chair, and strode across the room, leaving Richard to stare after him with a surprised and pained expression.

★

168

Once Arthur became the new member for Rye he wasted no time in securing permission to take leave from his command in order to attend Parliament. After he had delivered his maiden speech on the need to be wary of making peace with France, he spoke up on any matters relating to India and the army. Despite the efforts of the Foreign Secretary to promote the notion of peace with France, Arthur and many other members of Parliament watched events on the continent with growing concern.

Early in April news arrived in London that Joseph Bonaparte had been made King of Naples. Then, in June, more worrying news reached Britain: Louis Bonaparte was on the throne of Holland. Meanwhile the French Emperor had been hard at work on the Rhine, consolidating the hundreds of tiny German states into a more manageable number, under the protection of France. Against this background the ambitions of Charles Fox found less and less support in Parliament.

Some weeks after Arthur had returned to London, he was joined by Kitty. At first she stayed with the Sparrows, until Arthur found a house to rent in Harley Street. Once all the furnishings, dinner services, bedding and plethora of other household necessaries had been purchased, Arthur and Kitty moved in. The first days were as awkward as the honeymoon had been and Arthur did his best to play the part of a loving and dutiful husband at home, and in public. For her part Kitty seemed keen to please him, and to be considered a worthy companion, and wife.

As they grew more used to the intimate touch and feel of each other, it became easier to make love. Even so, Arthur felt an aching despair at the loss of the years he might have had if only Kitty had been allowed to marry him before he had gone to India. Then he would have had the Kitty he had loved, and carried in his heart through the years they had been apart. As it was, he felt she was almost a different person, and one he would never have picked as a wife had he encountered her more recently. But he had kept his word and married Kitty, Arthur reflected fatalistically, and he had satisfied his personal sense of honour in doing so. Therefore, he must commit himself to the marriage as best as he could.

Then one day, early in September, as he returned home from a day of wearisome debate in Parliament, Kitty came hurrying downstairs and held her arms out to embrace him.

'Good God, Kitty!' Arthur laughed. 'What was that for?'

She looked up at him and smiled nervously. 'Are you happy with me?'

'Of course I am!' Arthur leaned his head down and kissed her lightly on the lips. 'How could I fail to be?'

Kitty stared at him searchingly. 'I know you think I am weak-willed, Arthur, but I had to hear you say that. Just to know.'

'Well, now you have heard it, so tell me, my love, what vexes your mind so obviously?'

Kitty swallowed, and licked her lips before she replied. 'Arthur, dear, I am expecting.'

Arthur froze for a moment before the full import of the news hit him. He kissed Kitty again, with warm excitement this time. 'Expecting, by God! That's wonderful news, my love. Quite wonderful.'

'Do you mean it?'

'Of course I do!' Arthur stepped back and took her hands in his and stared into her wide eyes. 'It is the best news I have had in a very long time. We must celebrate.'

'The doctor said I am to rest and avoid excitement.'

'Stuff and nonsense!' Arthur replied cheerily. 'This is something worthy of celebration. Oh, I forgot! When is the child due?'

'Late January or early February next year.'

'Wonderful,' Arthur muttered as his mind began to race. 'We must tell our families and friends.'

'I'd really rather we didn't, in case . . .' Kitty's gaze fell away from his face as she stared at the ground. 'In case we lose it for any reason. I could not bear facing people if I lost our child before it was born.'

'Hush, my dear. That is not going to happen. I will ensure that you are well looked after, by the best doctors that can be found in London. I swear it.'

'Thank you,' she replied softly.

Arthur smiled at her, and then leaned forward to kiss her lightly on the forehead. 'Dearest Kitty, it is I who should be thanking you.'

The prospect of becoming a father relieved Arthur of some of his gloom over the news from Europe that France had abolished the Holy Roman Empire and made itself ruler of a confederation of states in the Rhine area. The mood lasted until one morning, a week later, when there was a sharp rap on the front door. A footman showed his brother William into Arthur's study. Looking up, Arthur was surprised to see his brother's strained expression.

'William? What is it?'

'It's Charles Fox,' William said baldly. 'He died late last night.'

'Fox is dead?' Arthur stroked his chin. 'Dead, do you say? Then there will be no treaty with France. Not now. No other Englishman would dare to treat with Bonaparte.'

'Well yes, quite,' William responded quietly. 'And you know what that means?'

Arthur nodded soberly. 'No peace. Just war to the bitter end. And only one of our nations will survive.'

Chapter 20

Napoleon

Paris, August 1806

The air was heavy and still and already the first distant rumbles of thunder could be heard amid the dark clouds edging across the city skyline. Napoleon dabbed at the perspiration along his hairline as he stared out of the open window. Even though he was naked he was hot and his skin was clammy. There was a sudden brief puff of breeze and the lace curtains ballooned around him before settling and sliding over his skin, making him shudder at the light sensation. Behind him, on the bed, Josephine stirred.

'Sounds as if a storm's coming.'

'Yes,' he replied softly, without turning round. Beyond the end of the Tuileries gardens the buildings were fading into the gloom and a dull band of shadow was creeping across the lawns towards Napoleon. There was another breath of wind, colder this time, and the first chilly pinpricks of rain on his face and chest. Still he did not move, and just watched as the leafy boughs on the trees lining the avenues began to shimmer and sway. Then there was a brilliant flash of sheet lightning that bathed the gardens in a ghostly white glare and almost at once the crack of thunder rolled across the city. The concussion rattled the windows of the imperial bedchamber. It reminded him of the sensation of the battlefield as the artillery of the Grand Army reverberated through the air and the earth itself.

'Napoleon!' Josephine sat up in alarm, staring across the room to where her husband stood gazing up at the sky as the lace curtains billowed round him like a shroud. His hands were clutching the window frame and he did not move, or respond to her. Throwing back the bedsheet, Josephine snatched up her silk gown and slipped into it as she hurried across the room and took his arm.

'Napoleon? My love.'

The rain was sweeping in through the window now and he blinked as if recovering from a trance, and looked at his wife. 'What? What is it?'

'Close the window. Close it and come back to bed. Before you catch a chill.'

Josephine gently drew him away from the window and closed it behind them, securing the latch firmly. Outside the rain pattered off the glass, streaking the view of the gardens as they were brilliantly illumin- ated by lightning again, before the thunder crashed out over Paris. Napoleon walked slowly back towards the bed and climbed in under the sheet, while Josephine lay down on the other side and then edged across so that she could cradle his head against her breast.

'What's worrying you so?' she asked softly.

Napoleon was silent for a moment, his eyes wide open and staring at the gilded mouldings on the ceiling. His brow furrowed slightly. 'There is going to be another war. It cannot be avoided.'

'We are already at war. Unless the British have changed their minds.'

He smiled her light-hearted tone. 'We are always at war with Britain. I'm talking about Prussia. I thought we'd humbled them for some years yet. Seems that I hadn't counted on that vixen wife of Frederick William's. He is a weak fool and Talleyrand can play him like a fiddle. But that Queen of his, Louise, is made of tougher material. She has been agitating against us from the moment the peace treaty was signed.'

Josephine smiled, and wound one of his dark curls around her little finger. 'You should never underestimate women, my love.'

Napoleon's gaze flickered away from the ceiling and he tilted his head round so that he could look into her eyes. 'I know. I made that mistake once before.'

Josephine felt an old anxiety well up in the pit of her stomach as she recalled the affairs she had conducted while Napoleon had been away campaigning in Italy and then Egypt in the early years of their marriage. She had nearly lost him when Napoleon discovered her infidelity. There was a quick flicker of anger as she recalled that he had been unfaithful himself. Then the thought was banished and she turned her mind back to Prussia as Napoleon continued.

'I had thought the Prussians lacked the nerve for war. There we were, on the eve of Austerlitz, and the Russians and Austrians thought I was as good as beaten. It was only then that the Prussians decided to throw in their lot with my enemies and demand that I let them broker a peace. And after Austerlitz?' He sniffed with contempt. 'Frederick William sends me his congratulations on a magnificent victory. The man has the heart of a mouse. He could not sign a treaty with us fast enough. At one stroke of the pen I had humiliated Prussia and left Britain to continue the fight alone . . . And now my spies tell me that Prussia is planning to make war on France. Why? Why do they want war?'

Josephine tugged his hair gently. 'Perhaps because you humiliated them too much. You might have heeded Talleyrand's advice and treated them more leniently. I'm no diplomat, but I would have thought that another nation is more likely to remain an ally if it is treated well, rather than having its pride ground underfoot.'

Napoleon rolled over and propped himself up on an elbow so that he could look down at his wife. 'I treated them as leniently as they deserved under the circumstances.'

Josephine raised her eyebrows. 'You might think so, but from their point of view the treaty might not look lenient. I think that's your trouble, my love. You cannot see the world through other people's eyes. You live only for your ambitions, and are inclined to treat others as a means to that end. Talleyrand is always telling me that there can never be a lasting peace while nations are unwilling or unable to see things from each other's perspective.'

'Talleyrand. What does he know?'

'More than enough to make a fine statesman. Otherwise you would not depend upon him so much.'

'I do not depend on him at all. I do not depend on anyone,' Napoleon added coldly, and then his mouth flickered into a smile. 'Except you, my darling. And as you pointed out, you are no diplomat. You could not understand such affairs. Prussia, and the other powers of Europe, resent the dominance of France. They resent me. They will not be won round by reason. They must be controlled with an iron fist, and once they know the limits of my tolerance and abide by them, then we shall have peace.'

'Perhaps this peace of yours will, in their eyes, look like subjugation.'

'It is possible. But that is not important. As long as they do as I wish they can have their peace.'

Josephine smiled. 'That is precisely the kind of imposition that they resent so much. Why, take that business with Hanover. That's typical of the way you treat other nations and why we are surrounded by wary enemies rather than allies. First of all you offer Hanover to the Prussians to bribe them to stay out of the war with Russia and Austria. Then, when the British approach you about holding peace negotiations, you go behind Frederick William's back and offer Hanover to them as a bargaining counter.'

'It was a rational enough move,' Napoleon protested.

'Really? And did you not consider the possibility that the British would inform Frederick William of your duplicity? How indignant, how angry do you think such a ploy might make the Prussians? Or did you think they might see it as a rational enough move as well?' Josephine shook her head. 'Sometimes you shock me, Napoleon. You make your grand plans with so little regard for the opinion of others. And now, as a consequence, you face dragging France into another war.'

'I do not drag France. She goes willingly wherever I lead her.'

'I think you will find that many of the people are considerably less willing than they were.'

'That is not true.'

'Because you say so? On what evidence?'

'I have the evidence of my own eyes, Josephine. Wherever I go crowds cheer me.'

'Of course they do. They could hardly do otherwise with Fouché's men scouring the streets looking for any signs of disloyalty as an excuse for arresting your political enemies.'

'Perhaps there is some truth in that. But my soldiers love me as a father.'

'An army is apt to idolise any general who is in the habit of leading them to victory. But the soldiers are only a small portion of any nation.'

Napoleon laughed. 'They are the most important portion of a nation, my dear Josephine. Without the army I am nothing.'

'Then you had better look after your soldiers more carefully. You cannot continue to call young men to arms indefinitely to replace those you lose in war. I read the newspapers too, and I know that there are thousands who go into hiding to avoid military service. Hardly proof of their devotion to the army of France and her Emperor, I'd say. The people do not want any more war, my love. They want genuine peace and a chance to prosper, that's all.' She paused and considered a new thought, before continuing, 'Why must there be war? Why not give Talleyrand a chance to negotiate a peace with Prussia? Let them keep Hanover and let us have peace. If you showed willing, I am sure there could be peace with Prussia, and all the other European powers, even perhaps a lasting peace with Britain.'

'A lasting peace with Britain?' Napoleon shook his head at the fanciful suggestion. 'If that was possible, we would have had it years ago.'

'Well at least there could be peace in Europe. The other nations might be prepared to live in harmony with us, as long as you don't continue to treat Europe as if it was your personal property.'

'What do you mean?'

Josephine was surprised. 'Why, my love, you have been distributing kingdoms to your family and your marshals as if they were sweets.'

'They have earned their rewards,' Napoleon answered firmly. 'Unlike those who merely inherit their titles.'

Josephine stared at him for a moment. 'Is that what it is all about? A crusade on behalf of the worthy?'

'Don't be so foolish.'

'I don't think that I am being foolish,' Josephine reflected. 'It seems to me that you have resented aristocratic and royal blood as long as I have known you. And you seem to go out of your way to raise men up from the lowest stations in life to the highest posts of state. Napoleon,' she reached for his hand and squeezed it affectionately, 'you are the man I love. You have achieved more in your life than any ten kings or emperors. Every man in Europe considers you its finest living general. Most of the people love you. All that remains is to establish your place in history. Now is the time to think carefully about the future. Will you be remembered as the man who loved war and glory above all else? Or as the man who led France to greatness and lasting peace? You can choose that, and history will remember you as one of the finest rulers that ever lived.'

There was a pleading tone in her voice, but Napoleon brushed her concerns aside. 'A man is only a ruler if he is free to exert his will over others. I would have peace, Josephine, I really would. But only on my terms.'

She shook her head sadly. 'Then there will be war. Always war, until you conquer all, or you are destroyed, and France falls with you.'

'If that is what God wills.'

'God? Since when did you acknowledge His authority?'

'Since it became good politics to.'

'And if God wants peace?'

'Then He will bless my cause and abandon all those who oppose me.'

Another sheet of lightning illuminated the Paris skies and burst into the bedchamber, painting their exposed flesh deathly white for an instant. There was a pause of a few seconds before the thunder cracked the heavens and then rumbled away. Napoleon spoke again. 'I think the storm is passing.'

Josephine shook her head. 'The worst is yet to come.'

★

That night, the air in the capital was hot and humid and those who met in the Emperor's private office wore only shirts, save Talleyrand, who refused to make any concession to climate and still wore his coat and cravat. Napoleon sat at the head of the table, with Berthier and Fouché to his left, and Talleyrand to his right. The meeting was lit by the glow of candelabras suspended from the ceiling and the heat of the little flames only added to the stifling atmosphere. Napoleon finished reading the report that his foreign minister had prepared for him, and slapped it down on the table.

'It seems that you do not think it wise for France to risk another war at the moment?'

Talleyrand nodded. 'Indeed, sire. We would risk being isolated and fighting another war against a coalition of enemies.'

Berthier patted a handkerchief against his temple. 'I thought it was only Prussia that constituted a threat.'

'No,' Talleyrand replied flatly. 'My sources in Moscow tell me that even though the Tsar was overawed by our victory at Austerlitz he is still an implacable enemy of the Emperor. If Prussia goes to war, then the Tsar will pledge his support to Frederick William. Worse still, since we defeated Austria and imposed harsh terms on them, there has been no shortage of resentment in Vienna and the danger is that the war party may yet sway the opinion of Emperor Francis towards intervention.' Talleyrand paused a moment and then continued, addressing Napoleon directly. 'I am sure that your army could defeat Prussia on its own, sire. But could it prevail against the armies of three nations? Four, if we count Britain.'

Napoleon pursed his lips. It was true that a victory against such odds was unlikely. Worse still, the last campaign had cost him the lives of many fine men who would be difficult to replace. The fresh drafts of conscripts that had filled out the ranks of the Grand Army were younger than ever and lacked experience of war. And yet his enemies, who had suffered so many defeats, still seemed able and willing to raise fresh armies to oppose him. In the end they must be defeated once and for all, before they bled France dry. He looked up at his foreign minister.

'What would you advise me to do, Talleyrand?'

'Sire, war with Prussia would not serve the interests of France. Our true enemy is Russia. She looms across Europe from the icy wastes of the north to the Black Sea in the south. Her lands are vast, and her people countless. The Tsar's inner circle have ambitions to spread the influence of Russia into Poland towards Prussia, and into the Balkans, the Ottoman empire and even across the mountains that border India. All the while the powers of central Europe are fighting each other Russia is biding her time, and waiting for the opportunity to snap up the lands that border her frontiers. You cannot guarantee the predominance of France while Russia remains undefeated, sire.'

'And how would you propose to defeat Russia?' asked Berthier. 'To reach Moscow would take a march three times as long as between Paris and Berlin, across trackless lands that are baking in summer and as cold as hell in winter. No hostile army could conquer such a vast country. It is unthinkable.'

'Nothing is unthinkable, Berthier,' Napoleon cut in. 'But I agree. At present, we are not ready to march on Moscow.'

'I doubt that we will ever be ready to undertake such a campaign, sire.'

'We shall see.'

'In any case, sire,' Talleyrand continued, 'there is no need to wage war on Russia, provided we can secure alliances with the other European powers against the Tsar. Given our current difficulties with Prussia the obvious move would seem to be repairing our relations with Austria.'

'Austria?' Berthier raised his eyebrows. 'But we were at war with them only eight months ago.'

'Precisely. A large dose of magnanimity on our part, at present, would go a long way towards securing their gratitude. And once we have that, we can cultivate Austria on our side of the balance of power.'

Napoleon suddenly laughed. 'You are a schemer to the very core of your soul, Talleyrand. You talk of a balance of power. We do not need to concern ourselves with such things. One either has power or one does not. That is all.'

'Surely, sire, power consists in getting others to do what one wishes them to do. If that is achieved bloodlessly, then it has to be the optimum result.'

Napoleon wagged a finger at his foreign minister. 'No! It is not enough to trick them into doing what you want. They have to be aware that they do it because it is your will. That is the true meaning of power, my friend.'

Talleyrand stared expressionlessly at the Emperor for a moment, and then bowed his head a fraction as he responded, 'If you say so, sire.'

'I do. Now then, gentlemen, enough philosophy. We must concentrate our thoughts on Prussia. Let us assume for the present that they intend to wage war on us. If that is the case then what chance of victory do we have?' Napoleon turned to Berthier. 'You have assessed the intelligence reports?'

'Of course, sire.' Berthier reached for his notebook and flipped to the right page. He cleared his throat and began to read. 'King Frederick William has over a hundred and seventy-five thousand men available to him at present. If he mobilises, then another seventy-five thousand could be under arms within ten weeks. That said, we know that the Prussian army has inherent weaknesses. It marches slowly and there is hardly a general under sixty years of age. The only officer with any outstanding ability is Prince Louis. As for the rest, they still conceive of war as it was thirty years ago.'

Napoleon smiled. 'That is why I shall defeat them. What of our own forces?'

Berthier ran his finger across on to the facing page. 'A hundred and sixty thousand infantry are available in southern Germany for the campaign, plus another thirty thousand cavalry.' Berthier glanced up. 'The cavalry are in particularly fine form, sire. Murat helped himself to the best of the Austrian horses after Austerlitz. We have the finest cavalry in Europe now. Like the rest of the army, their officers report that the men's morale is high. I'd say that the Grand Army is as ready for war as it has ever been.'

'Good!' Napoleon clasped his hands together. 'Then it only remains to isolate Prussia as far as possible before the war begins. Talleyrand, you must make it quite clear to the Austrians that if I detect the slightest hint that they are mobilising, or that they are even considering an alliance with Prussia, then they will feel our wrath and next time I will not spare Vienna.'

'As you wish, sire.'

'And it would be as well to try to keep Russia out of this as long as possible. Send word to the Tsar that we earnestly wish to discuss peace with him. Tell him we propose a treaty to end hostilities and, as proof of our good intentions, we are willing to give him a free hand in Poland. That should tempt him long enough to fit our purpose.'

'Yes, sire,' Talleyrand replied flatly.

Napoleon fixed him with a penetrating stare. 'You wish to add something?'

'Only that you are taking France to war yet again, sire. Barely half a year on from the end of the last.'

'So?'

'So, the people are growing weary of war, sire. I hear it all the time in the Paris salons.'

Fouché stirred. He had been sitting still and silent until now. 'If that is true, then give me the names of these defeatists. They will need watching.'

Talleyrand turned to regard the police minister disdainfully. 'I am terribly sorry, Fouché, but I cannot recall their names.'

Fouché smiled coldly. 'Really? I have men on my staff who might be able to help cure your memory.'

'Is that a threat?'

'No . . . at least not yet. Besides, I only said they needed watching. That's all.'

'That's all, *for now*,' Talleyrand replied quietly. 'Until they are arrested and sent into exile, or simply disappear.'

Fouché shrugged. 'As the saying goes, you can't make an omelette without breaking some eggs.'

'But I am not talking about eggs, my dear Fouché. I am talking about people.'

Napoleon slapped his hand down on the table. 'Eggs, people, no matter. Fouché, if the war happens I want any opposition to it put down at once. Once the mobilisation is authorised I suspect there will be the usual malcontents who'd rather abscond than serve in the army. When they are caught you may hang some of them to serve as an example. And Berthier, you will give the order for the corps of the Grand Army to begin concentrating about Bamberg. Understand?'

Fouché and Berthier nodded. Talleyrand regarded them coolly and then rose from the table. 'Sire, it would appear that you are determined to go to war against Prussia, in which case my work is done, and you have no further need of me.'

'On the contrary.' Napoleon paused and stared at his minister, until Talleyrand resumed his seat. 'You have one more service to perform for your country, for your Emperor, before any war begins.'

'Really, sire? And what service would that be?'

'When war comes, then I will not be seen as being responsible for causing it. So we need a *casus belli*.'

'Evidently, sire,' Talleyrand replied drily. 'What did you have in mind?'

'The Prussians have made little secret of their desire to annex Saxony. I would like you to let them know that we would not take exception to such an eventuality. Naturally, I want this to be an informal understanding. There is to be nothing on paper, do you understand?'

Berthier frowned. 'Saxony? But, sire, that is part of the Confederation of the Rhine. It is under your protection. I don't understand.'

Napoleon sighed wearily. 'Berthier, please confine your contributions to areas where you have expertise. Leave diplomacy to others.'

Berthier's lips pressed together, and he bowed his head and looked down at his notebook. Napoleon returned his attention to Talleyrand. 'Let Frederick William know that Saxony is his, provided Prussia keeps its peace with France. I doubt that he will turn up the chance to add Saxony to his inventory. And when he does, we will have our reason to go to war.'

Chapter 21

Bamberg, 7 October 1806

'And, unless his imperial majesty replies to this ultimatum by the eighth day of October, and pledges to order his forces back from the frontier, a state of war will exist between Prussia and France . . .'

There was silence in the imperial headquarters as Talleyrand finished reading aloud from the document that had been sent from Berlin. He stepped towards Napoleon's desk and laid the despatch down. Josephine stood behind the Emperor and rested her hands on the back of his chair as she glanced down at the despatch and saw the seal of Frederick William on the document. There was no doubt that the threat was genuine and that Prussia was set on war.

'When did this arrive?' Napoleon asked coldly.

'It was delivered in Paris only five days ago, sire, and immediately forwarded here.'

Napoleon nodded slowly. 'This is a calculated insult. Not by that weakling Frederick William. He would not have the nerve. This is the work of that witch, Queen Louise, and her war party of cronies. Very well then. If they wish to insult us, then we will deliver our reply in kind.'

Talleyrand cleared his throat lightly. 'I beg your pardon, sire. But the deadline is tomorrow. There is no question of a reply's reaching Berlin in time.'

'Nevertheless, they will have their reply in the clearest possible manner. The invasion of Prussia will commence tomorrow. I imagine that will communicate our intentions unmistakably. Wouldn't you agree?'

Talleyrand arched an eyebrow. 'Invasion is eloquence itself, sire.'

Napoleon smiled at the comment and then continued, 'At least our enemies had the kindness to fall into our trap.'

As Napoleon had hoped, the Prussians had annexed Saxony the moment they had been told that Napoleon would not oppose the move. As soon as the Prussian troops had marched in, a formal protest was sent to Berlin and the men of the Grand Army had begun to concentrate close to the border with Prussia. The Imperial Guard had been sent to the front in a fleet of hired carts and wagons, and finally at the end of September the Emperor himself had set off from Paris, accompanied by Josephine and Talleyrand. They arrived at Bamberg to find that Berthier had co-ordinated the preparations for the coming campaign with his usual efficiency. A hundred and sixty thousand Frenchmen, and ten thousand Bavarian allies, were poised to cross the border into Prussia in three vast columns led by Soult, Bernadotte and Lannes. Ahead of them, as ever, would ride Murat's cavalry, screening the Grand Army from the prying eyes of Prussian scouts.

Before the Grand Army lay the Thuringer forest, a dense mass of ancient trees sprawling across rolling hills, through which many roads and tracks had been cut. It would take the Grand Army two days to pass through the woods and emerge deep inside Prussian territory. Since there had been little firm intelligence on the location of the Prussian armies Napoleon had arranged his columns in such a way that should any one of them run into enemy forces, it would pin them in place while the rest of the army converged on the location, a manoeuvre that would take little more than a day. Even with the earliest of reports to go on Napoleon estimated that his army would encounter the Prussians shortly after passing through the Thuringer forest. The most logical position for the Prussian army would be across the route towards Berlin.

And that was where Napoleon intended the Grand Army to find and defeat them.

He turned to Berthier. 'Very well, then. Give the orders for the army to advance. At dawn tomorrow the Prussians will have their reply.'

'Yes, sire.' Berthier bowed his head to the Emperor. 'At once.'

As the chief of staff strode off to implement his master's will, Josephine leaned forward and spoke quietly into Napoleon's ear. 'It seems that you have contrived yet another war for yourself.'

Napoleon twisted round in his chair and looked up at her with an angry expression. 'I did not ask for this.'

'You have done all but that.' Josephine smiled faintly. 'You manipulated the Prussians into this war.'

'They made their choice,' Napoleon replied bluntly. 'They could have chosen peace, but they chose to wage war on France, to wage war on me. And they will learn the price of such folly soon enough.'

'And once they are humbled, what next? One day you will run out of enemies, my love, and then what will there be left for you to do?'

Napoleon stared at her for a moment and then shrugged. 'Enjoy the peace.'

She was silent for a moment and then shook her head sadly. 'War and peace. I don't think you even know the difference between the two any more.'

'Difference?' Napoleon thought for a moment. 'I wonder if there is a difference in the end. One cannot have one without the other. War is an extension of diplomacy by other means, and peace is merely the continuation of war by other means. There will always be war and peace, Josephine, just as surely as the rising of the sun. All that one can do is try to keep winning, however one can. Else there is only surrender or defeat. To me, war is not an aberration, but the essence of human nature.'

Josephine straightened up and regarded him with a look of despair. 'God save us,' she muttered in a low tone that only the two of them could hear. 'You are a monster.'

'No.' He shook his head. 'I am Napoleon.'

As the first hint of dawn lightened the horizon, the men of the Grand Army formed into their battalions and tramped across the border. The night had been cold and the chilly dawn air about the marching columns was marked with the swirling puffs of exhaled breath as the soldiers hunched in their coats, waiting for the warmth of their exertions to spread through their bodies. The din of nailed boots crunching over the hard ground was accompanied by the jingle of harness and rumble of heavy wheels as the limbered guns and wagons of the Grand Army rolled forward between the columns of marching infantry.

Napoleon had taken his leave of Josephine in a soured atmosphere. She had kissed him dutifully, but there was no warmth in her embrace, no affection in her eyes, and he felt an ache in his heart at her cold expression. He hoped that it did not portend an ill outcome for the coming campaign. Fortune had blessed him in the past, and where many men had been killed or crippled on the field of battle Napoleon had come through unscathed. The odds against his survival must surely be growing with each new campaign, he mused, as he took her hands and squeezed them.

'I will return, my love.'

'Yes,' she responded softly. 'I know. Until the next war.'

Napoleon looked sadly into her eyes, then released her hands and turned away to mount the horse that was held ready for him by one of his staff officers. Once he had heaved himself into the saddle, Napoleon adjusted his stirrups and took up the reins, and at a click of his tongue and a nudge from his heels the horse walked forward.

'Napoleon!' Josephine suddenly called out. 'Be careful, my love. Come back to me.'

Napoleon turned to her with a smile and waved his hand, then spurred his horse into a trot and rode away to lead the Grand Army to war.

Berthier and his staff proved their worth once more as the three columns of the French army followed their carefully planned marching orders. They passed swiftly through the Thuringer forest in an orderly manner and emerged into open countryside towards the end of the second day of the campaign. The reports from Murat's scouts still provided no conclusive intelligence as to the location the Prussians had chosen to concentrate their forces.

Then, on the morning of the third day, a hurried despatch from Lannes informed the Emperor that he had encountered a Prussian corps blocking his advance through the town of Saalfeld. After a brief struggle the Prussians had been routed, leaving their commander, Prince Louis, dead on the battlefield. Napoleon read the report with a degree of satisfaction. Prince Louis had been one of Prussia's finest generals and they could ill afford to lose him in such an insignificant battle.

Berthier had chosen an inn in a village ten miles from Saalfeld for the imperial headquarters. The rest of the houses and barns of the village had been occupied by the officers and orderlies attached to the staff. After a day visiting some of his marshals Napoleon returned to the inn and saw Berthier bent over a large table in the main room. Around him several other officers sat at smaller tables hunched over their paperwork. One of them looked up, and called out, 'The Emperor is present!'

At once the room was filled with the sound of scraping chairs as the officers rose and stood at attention.

'At ease!' Napoleon waved them back to their desks as he crossed the room towards Berthier. He quickly related the details of Lannes's victory at Saalfeld and then asked, 'What are the latest reports on the main enemy force?'

Berthier reached to one side of the table and pulled a map over. He unrolled it and weighted the corners before leaning forward and tapping his pencil where the town of Plauen was marked. 'I've had word from Soult that he has beaten an enemy column here. They are now retreating towards Gera.'

'Gera?' Napoleon leaned over the map and traced a line from Plauen, through Gera and on towards Leipzig. 'It's as I thought. They are in this direction.' He paused and frowned and thought aloud. 'Then why send that column of Prince Louis's so far to the west where it would be cut off and powerless to act on its own? It doesn't make sense. What reports have we had from Murat?'

'I'm still waiting for today's reports, sire.'

'Very well.' Napoleon took a last look at the map before he straightened up. 'I am going to rest. As soon as you hear anything about the enemy's location wake me.'

'Yes, sire.'

Napoleon took a seat by the inn's fire and helping himself to a staff officer's rolled-up coat to act as a pillow he eased himself down and closed his eyes. It seemed like only a moment before he was gently shaken by the shoulder.

'Sire?'

Napoleon's eyes snapped open and he saw Berthier looking down at him.

'Sire, we have a report from Marshal Lannes, and news from Murat.'

Napoleon sat up, wincing at a stiffness in his neck. 'What time is it?'

'Five o'clock, sire.'

Little more than an hour and a half had passed, then. Napoleon stood up. 'Well?'

'Lannes's prisoners say that the main Prussian army is situated towards Erfurt. That's confirmed by Murat's scouts.'

'Let's see.' Napoleon yawned as he led the way back to Berthier's table and examined the map. 'Erfurt, eh? Seems that I was mistaken, Berthier.'

His chief of staff remained silent and Napoleon could not resist a small smile. 'It happens, Berthier. So, our enemy is to the west of us. Well, once he receives word that Lannes is at Saalfeld, he will know that we have got between Berlin and the Prussian army. They will try to march round us to get back on to their lines of communication. So we must march faster than them and cut them off.' Napoleon made a sweeping gesture across the map. 'The Grand Army will turn west. Davout and Bernadotte can outflank the enemy to the right, at Auerstadt. The rest of the Grand Army will concentrate here.' He thrust his finger on the map. 'At Jena. That's where we will humble Frederick William. That's where we will crush Prussia and end the campaign.'

186

Chapter 22

Jena, 13 October 1806

'I would say that there are perhaps forty, maybe fifty thousand Prussians to the west of us,' said Marshal Lannes as he slowly scanned the enemy positions through his telescope.

Beside him Napoleon considered the estimate for a moment and nodded. 'In which case, that should be the main body of the enemy. There will be other formations nearby, guarding their flanks, but that *must* be the main body. Very well then, we must concentrate the Grand Army at once. I want every available man here within twenty-four hours. Meanwhile, you and the Imperial Guard must hold this position.' Napoleon gestured to the surrounding heights that rose up between the town of Jena to the east and the plateau to the west where the Prussian army was making camp for the night. 'What do the locals call this place, Berthier?'

'The Landgrafenberg, sire.'

Napoleon shook his head. 'These Germans come up with some incomprehensible place names. When the campaign is over, I will make it a priority to cut them down to size.'

His staff officers laughed, and Napoleon was grateful for their good humour. There were risks involved in choosing this ground for what he hoped would be the decisive action of the campaign. Given a full day he could summon nearly a hundred and fifty thousand men to the area around Jena. Until then, Lannes and the veterans of the Guard must hold the heights. If the Prussians decided to attack in the remaining hours of daylight, or even early the next morning, the French troops who had crossed the river Saale to occupy the Landgrafenberg would be hopelessly outnumbered. If they were forced down the heights into Jena there would be a bottleneck at the bridge and the Prussians would inflict heavy losses. Everything depended on holding the hill, Napoleon decided, looking up to the highest point half a mile away.

He turned to Berthier and indicated to the ridge. 'We have to fortify that position. I want as many guns up there as possible. Twelve-pounders would be best, so that we can command the approaches to the slopes.'

Berthier stared at the steep rise that led up to the ridge, then sucked in a sharp breath. 'Twelve-pounders? That won't be easy to do, sire.'

'I didn't say that it would be easy,' Napoleon replied quietly. 'I said that it will be done.'

'Yes, sire. I will give the orders at once.'

Napoleon nodded, then folded his arms as he turned to regard the Prussian army again. The autumn evening was drawing in and already the fine spirals of the first campfires were marking the clear, still sky. Apart from a handful of cavalry pickets patrolling across the plateau there was no sign of any activity that presaged any attack. Napoleon called for his horse.

'I'm going back to the headquarters in Jena. Lannes, you can stand your men down. But be ready to form up at the first sign of any movement the Prussians make.'

Lannes bowed his head. 'Yes, sire.'

'Good. If the enemy are content to sit on their arses through the night and into the morning, then they're in for the surprise of their lives.'

As night fell the staff officers of the imperial headquarters worked at a frantic pace to issue the orders to concentrate the separate columns of the Grand Army. The Emperor had decided on a battle the following day and marching schedules had to be drafted and issued to every division. Ammunition trains had to be brought forward ready to replenish the cannon and muskets of the army. Since foraging was not possible so close to the enemy the rations carried with the army had to be distributed along the approaches to Jena.

Napoleon and Berthier had taken over a large room and at once spread out maps of the surrounding lands across the floor. Napoleon took note of the scale of the main map and adjusted his dividers accordingly to measure half a day's march. He knelt down on the map and leaned forward to inspect the details of each unit Berthier had marked in pencil. Every so often Napoleon walked the dividers across the map towards the area around Jena and then made appropriate allowances for night marches, and the reported conditions of the roads and tracks his men would have to march along. Any questions he asked about the strengths of the units sent Berthier scurrying to the small chest of notebooks, which were updated every day from the returns sent directly to headquarters from each brigade.

At length Napoleon was satisfied that he would be able to amass sufficient strength before noon the following day to mount a successful attack on the Prussians. The critical phase of the coming battle would occur well before midday. In order to provide room for the advancing French columns to cross the Saale and make their way through Jena, the bridgehead would have to be pushed forward. That meant that Lannes and his men were going to have to advance against the Prussians on their own at first light, and hold the enemy back long enough for the rest of the Grand Army to deploy. Napoleon stared at the map again. Not the whole of the Grand Army, he decided. There was an opportunity here for an outflanking movement by Davout and Bernadotte's columns. If they could cross further along the Saale and move against the enemy's left, then the Prussian army would be caught in the jaws of a vice and crushed.

Napoleon dictated the final details to Berthier, then stood up and announced his intention to return to the Landgrafenberg and spend the night there with the Imperial Guard. He took up his hat and buttoned his greatcoat and strode outside. After the warm fug of the crowded headquarters the air outside was cold and crisp and the clear heavens were scattered with the brilliant pinpoints of stars. Napoleon paused a moment, head tilted back, and admired the view. He had read that astronomers claimed that each star was like the sun and that vast distances separated them so that the earth, and all who dwelt there, were as insignificant as dust on the great scale of the universe. For the briefest instant Napoleon felt a tremor of despair in his heart, then quickly dismissed it with a snorted inhalation of the cold air, and strode towards his horse and let one of his escort help him up into the saddle.

Above the roofs of Jena loomed the dark mass of the Landgrafenberg, lit here and there by the dancing flickers of torches and campfires. There was a concentration of torches on the lower slope and by the dim loom of their light Napoleon could just make out the forms of some wagons and gun carriages. He frowned, dug his heels in and galloped down the street towards the road that led up to the heights. A short distance outside the town he came across the tail of the artillery train that had been ordered to the summit of the Landgrafenberg. On either side of the track, the battalions of the Imperial Guard were waiting to move up to the heights and some of the men stirred at the sound of approaching hoofbeats. Even in the dark the keener-sighted of the men recognised the distinctive shape of Napoleon's hat and a voice cried out excitedly, 'It's the Emperor! On your feet for the Emperor!'

As word spread along the line of vehicles dark figures rose up and waved and cheered as Napoleon and his escort trotted past without acknowledging them. The road began to climb the slope and as the gradient steepened the road ended and a crude track began, snaking up the hill. Here Napoleon found the head of the artillery train, where a small crowd of gunners and their officers stood in the light of several torches and lanterns. Scores of men were labouring on traces to haul a twelve-pounder up the narrow track, and every pace gained came with painful slowness.

'What is going on here?' Napoleon called out sharply as he reined in. 'Why the delay? These guns should be halfway up to the ridge by now.'

The brigadier in charge of the artillery train stepped forward with an apprehensive expression and gestured towards the track. 'Sire, you can see for yourself. It's the track. Little more than a bridle path. It's poor going for anything larger than a dog cart.'

Napoleon swung himself down from the saddle, took a lantern from one of the artillerymen and began to examine the ground just in front of the leading gun. The path was narrow, uneven and littered with small boulders, some wedged into the soil and loose gravel. More than enough of a challenge to the artillery train, he conceded. Nevertheless, the guns had to be in position on the ridge and ready to fire at first light. Napoleon strode back down the hill towards the brigadier.

'Order the artillery train to halt.'

'Yes, sire.'

'Then give the order for every pick and shovel in the artillery train, and from the engineers back in Jena, to be brought here.' Napoleon turned to one of his escort. 'I want each battalion of the Imperial Guard to work for an hour on improving the track before they move up to the ridge. Pass the word.'

While the two officers hurried off to carry out his orders Napoleon walked a short distance up the narrow path, inspecting the ground closely. In places the track was little more than a pace wide and that width would need to be tripled before the twelve-pounders and artillery caissons could pass along it. In addition, the boulders would have to be dug out to make the route as level as possible for the heavy wheels of the wagons and gun carriages. It would be back-breaking work and the men would curse him for it, but there was no other way to get the guns to the top of the Landgrafenberg by dawn.

As the first of the Imperial Guard battalions reached the head of the artillery train the gunners handed the small supply of ready tools to the men and the sergeants directed them to begin cutting into the embankment beside the track. As more tools came forward other companies moved further up the route to work by the light of lanterns set up on posts by the engineers who had hurried forward from Jena. The air was filled with the thud of picks, the soft scrape of shovels and the grunts of the men labouring in the chilly night air. Napoleon walked slowly up and down the track for the next half-hour, offering encouragement, cajoling, and swapping greetings with his veterans. Then, satisfied that the work was well in hand, he passed the lantern to an artilleryman, climbed back on to his horse and made his way up the track towards the ridge.

He found Marshal Lannes and a handful of his officers on the knoll on the crest of the heights. They were staring out across the plateau to where the campfires of the Prussian army sprawled across the darkened landscape.

'Any signs of movement?' Napoleon asked as he slid down from his saddle.

'No, sire.'

'Any reinforcements?'

'None that we have detected.'

'That's strange,' Napoleon mused. 'They know we're here. They will want to concentrate their forces to make or meet any attack. Are you certain there's been no sign of activity, no fresh columns arriving in the enemy camp?'

'As certain as we can be, sire.'

Napoleon was still for a moment, and then shrugged. 'Very well, then. That has to be the main Prussian force. And we have the enemy where we want him. The first thrust of the Grand Army will fix the Prussians on the plateau, while Davout and Bernadotte cross the Saale and march on to their flank and rear. If all goes well, they will crumble under assault from two directions and the day is ours.'

Lannes was silent for a moment before he responded. 'Assuming that is the entire Prussian army out there. What if the enemy has split his force, sire? What if there is another column we have not accounted for?'

'Another column?' Napoleon snorted dismissively. 'Why would there be another column? Why would the enemy divide his strength on the eve of battle? Not even the Prussians are that foolish, my dear Lannes.'

He turned away from the enemy and indicated an even stretch of ground a short distance from the crest of the ridge. 'I'll spend the rest of the night there. Have a fire made up, and then I want the first units of the Imperial Guard to take up position around the crest.' Napoleon turned to the nearest of his staff officers. 'See to it.'

'At once, sire.'

As the night passed the first of the guns arrived at the top of the Landgrafenberg and was eased into position on the forward slope. A steady stream of cannon and caissons rumbled past Napoleon's makeshift command post, while the columns of infantry from Lannes's corps and the Imperial Guard took a direct route to the summit and filed past in the darkness as they were directed into line for the dawn advance on to the plateau. By the light of his campfire Napoleon issued the last of his orders, and read through the most recent reports from his corps commanders. There was only one that concerned him slightly. Davout claimed to have detected a large enemy force ahead of him and suggested that it might be the main Prussian army. Napoleon considered the possibility for an instant and then dismissed it as he glanced towards the enemy campfires once more. There was no doubt about it, he decided, that had to be the main Prussian army. So, wrapping his coat about his shoulders, he settled on a camp chair and warmed himself at the fire as he waited for dawn and the coming battle.

The cold night brought up a dense fog from the plateau as the first glimmer of day thickened along the horizon. The ground in front of the Landgrafenberg was wreathed in a pallid gloom that hid much of the detail of the landscape. During the night, the corps of Soult and Augereau had arrived and taken up positions alongside Lannes's. Over forty thousand French troops were ready to advance and open the way for the bulk of the Grand Army crossing the river Saale behind them. The men were standing still and silent as ghosts as they waited for the attack to begin and Napoleon was pleased with their good discipline, since they were well within cannon range of the enemy position. If the Prussians were to detect any sign of the coming onslaught they would be ready in time to inflict fearful casualties amongst the leading French units.

As he stood behind the batteries on the heights Napoleon flipped his pocket watch open and glanced down now and again as the hands slowly crawled towards six o'clock. Then there was a distant shout as the order was given, and the signal gun boomed, announcing the start of the attack. An instant later the batteries on the Landgrafenberg thundered out and Napoleon's gaze was caught by the thin dark smear of a ball as it arced towards the Prussian lines, until it dropped into the fog. Then the drums rolled as they beat the advance and Lannes's divisions began to tramp down the slope until they too were lost in the fog.

Moments later Napoleon saw a bloom of orange in the murk and then heard the dull thud as a Prussian battery fired in the direction of the approaching French divisions. More enemy guns opened up and the rattle of musket fire accompanied the din as the skirmishers of both sides came into contact. On the Landgrafenberg the French gunners shifted their aim to target the dim flashes that revealed the positions of the enemy cannon. The firing from both sides grew more intense, but the fog prevented Napoleon from seeing how the attack was progressing. Then the first of the casualties came limping up the slope, nursing their injured limbs as they found what cover they could to wait out the battle and then find medical help.

'I have to know what is going on,' Napoleon snapped to one of the hussars of his personal guard. 'Ride down there. Find Marshal Lannes and tell him to report his progress back to me at once.'

'Yes, sire.'

The firing continued with growing intensity, as if a storm were raging below the smooth surface of the fog, and even though the rising sun began to burn off the mist thick banks of powder smoke still obscured much of the detail as the first hours of the battle raged. The first reports arrived from the leading divisions and Napoleon scanned the hurriedly written notes to learn that the nearest villages on the plateau had been taken, with heavy losses inflicted by enemy cannon firing at close range on the densely packed French assault columns. But the enemy had been driven back and Lannes had won sufficient space for the other corps of the Grand Army to join the attack.

By ten o'clock Soult's men had reached their position on the right flank and launched an immediate attack on the Prussians, pushing them back. To the left, Augereau's columns were striding out to take up their positions, and in the centre Ney's fresh troops were marching up the road from Jena to reinforce Lannes. Only the last wreaths of fog lay in dips in the ground and now Napoleon had a clear view of the battle-field. The bodies of men from the assault columns littered the plateau, piled in small heaps where Prussian grapeshot had blasted into the French line. Beyond the villages of Closwitz and Lutzeroda the men of Lannes's corps had paused to re-form in the face of fresh troops the Prussians had brought forward to meet the attack. There was a gap of nearly a mile between the reduced ranks of the men of Lannes's corps and that of Augereau, and, as Napoleon watched, Ney's column made for the gap and then continued forward alone towards the waiting Prussian artillery that had already done so much damage to Lannes's men.

'What is Ney doing?' Napoleon fumed. 'What is that fool up to? He has no orders to advance yet. He can't attack by himself.'

Behind the Emperor the staff officers and messengers stood silently and watched helplessly as Ney's men closed on the enemy and began to deploy as the first of the Prussian guns ahead of them opened fire, orange flames stabbing through puffs of smoke that looked like tiny flowers at a distance. Through Napoleon's telescope the effect on the delicate-looking lines of French soldiers was all too real, however, as round shot swept away whole files of men at a time. With painstaking steadiness Ney's men completed the manoeuvre and advanced towards the enemy line. The bright colours of each battalion's standard led the way and the waving swords of the officers glittered like far-off stars as they caught the morning sun. The enemy cannon continued to cut scores of men down as the French advanced and then, as they closed up on the Prussian line, they halted and made ready to fire.

There was a pause, then a final volley flashed out from the Prussian guns. An instant later, Ney's men replied. Scores of men fell on each side, and then Ney's infantry charged through the musket smoke and made for the enemy artillery positions. There was no time for the Prussians to reload and they fled from their guns, abandoning them to the French.

Berthier clapped his hands. 'They've done it! They have the guns!'

'Yes.' Napoleon nodded. 'And at what cost? The fool has advanced too far, and has no support. Look there, now Ney will really have his battle.'

Napoleon pointed out the dense mass of enemy cavalry already edging forward from the rear of the Prussian lines. They had been moving forward to counter Lannes's attack, but the Prussian general had seen his chance to crush Ney's isolated formation and the long lines of mounted men closed in on the French infantry. Ney did the only thing that he could under the circumstances, and Napoleon watched the distant infantry hurriedly form squares and prepare to receive the charge of the enemy cavalry. The Emperor had little doubt that Ney and his men would hold off the Prussian horsemen, but they were not the real danger. While Ney's corps held off the cavalry the Prussians would bring forward more guns and infantry to blast the static French formations to pieces. They could not possibly endure such punishment for long, and the squares would break down. At that point they would be entirely at the mercy of the Prussians.

Napoleon frowned bitterly. 'Ney has forced my hand. We have to save that Gascon fool and his men.' Napoleon turned away from the scene, his mind swiftly conceiving the necessary orders. 'We need cavalry. Where is Murat?'

'Still on the road to Jena, sire,' Berthier replied. 'His advance elements have just begun to cross the Saale. We only have two cavalry regiments in the reserve.'

'Then we must use them. Send them forward to support Ney.'

Berthier's eyes widened. 'Two regiments against that host, sire? They won't stand a chance.'

'Neither will Ney if we don't act at once. I will not lose Ney's corps,' Napoleon stated firmly. 'Send those two regiments forward immediately. And order Lannes and Augereau to advance and take position on either flank of Ney's corps.'

'Yes, sire.'

Napoleon turned back towards Ney's embattled corps and saw that the enemy cavalry had now engulfed the squares. Each pocket of blue was surrounded by thick smoke amid which the dashing shadows of Prussian cavalry galloped past, their riders firing pistols at point blank range, and threatening to charge any weak points in the French lines. Napoleon's heart was heavy with a mixture of dread for the fate of his men, cut off from the rest of the army and threatened with annihilation, and rage at Ney for his hot-headedness. Bravery was one thing, and Ney was as brave as they came, Napoleon conceded, but rashness was irresponsible at best and a positive peril at worst. If Ney survived the battle, there would be words spoken about his cavalier approach to orders.

Napoleon dismissed his anger towards his subordinate and concentrated his attention on the battlefield once again. For the moment, the initiative had passed to the Prussians and they had the opportunity to crush Ney, and force the entire French line back to the foot of the Landgrafenberg, if they acted quickly. Already Napoleon could see a dense mass of enemy infantry moving towards Lannes and as the two sides came together in a fury of musket flashes and plumes of smoke the overwhelming numbers of the enemy began to tell. Lannes's men were forced back on to a small hamlet halfway across the plateau. Napoleon could see at once that there was no chance that the Prussians could be halted there, and he cursed the speed at which his other corps were marching towards the battle. If only there was one more corps here to throw into the fight, to stabilise the line long enough for more men to arrive and swing the balance in favour of the French. He cursed Ney once more, and then Murat for failing to have his cavalry on hand, and then the enemy general for having the temerity to be a good enough soldier to seize the advantage.

'Who would have thought that a Prussian general would take the initiative?' he muttered to himself.

It was Berthier who noticed it first. He stared over the battlefield for a moment, and then frowned as he spoke. 'Sire, the enemy have halted.'

'What?'

Napoleon strained his eyes to make out the details of the battlefield to Lannes's front. There was still a good deal of smoke obscuring both sides. But then he could see that Berthier was right. The enemy line had indeed halted, and even as Napoleon raised his telescope to look more closely he could make out the sergeants dressing the Prussian formations as if they were on a parade ground. As French fire plucked men out of the line, so they dressed ranks again and stood to attention, waiting.

'What on earth are they playing at?' asked Berthier. 'Why don't they continue to advance?'

'God knows,' Napoleon replied, and then swung his telescope across the battlefield. Ney was barely holding his own against the enemy cavalry but the Prussian artillery and infantry that had been advancing to trap his corps had also halted and were standing still, almost within musket range of the nearest French square. At first Napoleon could not understand it. Why would the Prussians throw away such a splendid opportunity to send the French line reeling back? Why delay? What were they waiting for?

Napoleon swept his telescope across the landscape, and then steadied it on a fresh mass of Prussian soldiers approaching the battlefield from the west. He estimated their strength to be at least ten thousand, and smiled as he realised what was happening. The enemy general was waiting for reinforcements before he launched what he hoped would be the decisive attack on the battered French line. So, the Prussians were performing true to form, Napoleon mused. Still the same cautious, plodding foe. Well, they would pay for their foolishness. Indeed, they already were. Lannes's men sheltering in the buildings of the hamlet were pouring a withering fire on the smartly dressed Prussian lines. As soon as Lannes became aware that the enemy had halted he had given the order for his artillery to unlimber in range of the Prussians and open fire. Now, blast after blast of case shot smashed into the enemy lines, leaving ten or more men dead and wounded with each discharge. Napoleon watched with a grudging sense of admiration as the enemy stood their ground in the face of such fire. All the time they were being steadily cut down by French fire, each battalion contracting amid the carnage dealt by the cones of heavy iron balls blasted at them from the muzzles of the French guns.

The Prussians continued to take the punishment for the next two hours. Once Lannes's skirmishers realised that the enemy were not going to move, they crept forward and added their fire from the houses of the village, and from behind the low walls that surrounded the villagers' vegetable gardens. In return the Prussians fired volleys by company, reloading and firing again with little hope of causing any harm to the sheltered Frenchmen. The worst casualties suffered by Napoleon's men came from a handful of lucky shots from Prussian howitzers that landed amongst the artillery caissons of the French batteries and blew up one of the powder wagons, scattering fragments of the vehicle, its horses and their handlers across the surrounding ground.

While the duel on the right flank continued, more French troops were arriving on the battlefield and taking position as they waited for the order to attack. As the last of Murat's cavalry formed up behind the centre of the French line Napoleon glanced down at his watch and saw that it was half an hour after noon. He glanced round at Berthier.

'Send an order to all divisions. The army is to execute a general attack at one o'clock.'

'Yes, sire. All divisions,' Berthier repeated, and then gestured to the neat ranks of the Imperial Guard standing ready behind the Emperor's command post. The men in the front rank had eager and excited expressions and there was no mistaking their desire to take part in the attack. 'Does that include the Guard, sire?'

'No.' Napoleon shook his head emphatically. He had nearly suffered a defeat at Marengo for want of adequate reserves. In any case, he reasoned with himself, this battle was as good as won and there was no need to commit the veterans of the Guard to the fight. He glanced over at the heavily moustached faces of the nearest men of his elite corps and could see their disappointment at his decision. 'The campaign is not yet over,' he added loudly enough for them to hear. 'The grumblers will have the chance to win their share of glory another day.'

On the hour the entire French line began to advance and once more the plateau was engulfed in acrid powder smoke, and the air resounded with the ear-splitting roar of artillery and the crackle of musket fire. For a while the Prussian line held and the men of the Imperial Guard began to mutter bitterly about their inactivity. Napoleon kept his back to the men and resolutely refused to acknowledge their discontent, until a voice cried out, 'The Guard must advance! For pity's sake, sire, do not shame us!'

Napoleon turned abruptly and stabbed a finger towards the nearest men. 'Who said that?'

There was a sullen silence, and then one of the younger soldiers stepped a pace forward and presented his musket. 'Sire!'

Napoleon strode over towards the man and stood in front of him, crossing his arms as he glared at the soldier. 'Your name?'

'Guardsman Bercourt, sire!'

'So then, Bercourt, you want to charge at your enemy?'

'Yes, sire. As does every man in the Guard.'

'Is that so?'

'Yes, sire. We are the best men in the army. In any army. It is our right to prove our worth in battle.'

'Your right?' Napoleon frowned. 'You are a soldier, you have no rights. Just orders, and you will obey them. Look here, Bercourt.' Napoleon gestured to the stripes on the man's sleeve. 'You have served the minimum number of campaigns to qualify for the Guard. Yet you presume to know how to command the army better than your Emperor?'

The guardsman's gaze flickered guiltily towards Napoleon's face before snapping back to his front and staring over his Emperor's shoulder. 'No, sire.'

'No, sire,' Napoleon mimicked. 'Of course not. Let me tell you, Bercourt, only when you have commanded in as many battles as I have should you even dare to offer me advice on how to run the army. Understand?'

Bercourt swallowed nervously. 'Yes, sire.'

'Very well, return to the ranks.'

'Yes, sire,' Bercourt replied in a humbled tone.

Once the man had resumed his position Napoleon glared at the massed ranks of his finest soldiers and called out, 'Is there any other man amongst you who would presume to command his Emperor?'

The words were met by silence and Napoleon nodded as he addressed them again. 'Thank you, gentlemen. Now, if you don't mind, I have a battle to fight.'

He turned away and strode back to join Berthier and the other staff officers. They had been watching the confrontation, but now turned to follow the progress of the French line as it gradually pushed the Prussians back. Napoleon shook his head as he approached Berthier.

'Damned glory-hunters! There are a sight too many of them in the army for my taste. It's young men like that who end up like Marshal Ney.'

Berthier shrugged. 'Is that such a bad thing? It is only a measure of the men's élan, sire.'

'Élan?' Napoleon frowned. 'I command an army, Berthier, not a duelling society. What use is élan if it leads to recklessness? The Grand Army is an instrument of my will, and the men must understand that first and foremost. Otherwise they threaten us all with disaster.'

'Yes, sire.' Berthier conceded. 'I will have that soldier and the rest of them reprimanded.'

'No. That's not necessary.' Napoleon thought for a moment before he continued. 'Promote him to sergeant. I need men who are keen to fight. But tell him that if I ever hear him, or any man in his company, challenge my orders like that again, I'll have the lot of them sent to rot in the navy.'

'Yes, sire.' Berthier grinned. 'That'll put the fear of God in them, sure enough.'

'They can fear God if they like, just as long as they obey their Emperor.'

Napoleon concentrated his mind on the battle spread out before him across the plateau. Except for a few isolated positions where the Prussians were putting up a spirited resistance, the enemy was falling back. Behind the front line the Prussians were forming up into columns and preparing to march away from the battlefield. Napoleon felt the tension in his body. If there was to be a decisive result it was vital that the enemy did not have the chance to retire in good order and fight another day. He clasped his hands together behind his back and began to pace up and down in front of his staff as he continued to watch the battle. It was swiftly apparent that he need not have worried that his subordinates were up to the task. They had fought enough battles at his side to be fully aware of the need to press the enemy to breaking point.

As the Prussians fell back and attempted to disengage from the struggle, Lannes sent his artillery forward to continue blasting grapeshot into the enemy ranks. Already demoralised by having to retreat, and still under withering fire from the advancing French, the Prussian regiments quickly became disorganised as they fell back and disorder spread through their ranks. There was no need for Napoleon to issue any order to Murat, as the cavalry commander instantly grasped that the time had come to begin his charge. The shrill call of trumpets sounded across the plateau, and as Napoleon and his staff looked on the French cavalry, eight thousand strong, edged forward, building up to a trot as they passed beyond their comrades in the infantry and then finally surging forward into a gallop as they approached the Prussians.

Napoleon could well imagine the terror of the enemy, already shaken by defeat, as they faced a glittering wave of horsemen, swords and lances readied to strike as the pounding hooves of their charging mounts shook the earth beneath them. Then they were in amongst the Prussian formations, shattering all but the most brave and professional of the Prussian regiments who had been able to form squares. A tide of fugitives fled from the battlefield, and even the column of reinforcements that Napoleon had sighted earlier fell prey to the panic that now gripped the Prussian army as it broke and streamed back across the landscape in the direction of Weimar.

Berthier consulted his watch and made a note in his logbook before he addressed his Emperor. 'My congratulations, sire. Your victory is complete, and there are still at least three hours of daylight left for Murat to continue his pursuit. The enemy has lost the campaign.'

'Let's hope so,' Napoleon replied. 'But the day is not over, and I have yet to hear from Davout and Bernadotte. They should have reached Apolda by now, and cut off the retreat of some of the men we have defeated here.' He glanced to the north, where faint smudges of powder smoke were visible towards the horizon. 'I trust that they have dealt with the Prussian detachment at Auerstadt. Any reports from them yet?'

'Only that Davout had encountered a large enemy force.'

'Nothing more?'

'Not so far, sire.'

Napoleon pursed his lips for a moment and then started towards his horse. 'I am sure that Davout will have defeated them as readily as we defeated the main army. I'm surprised we won as easily as we did. Anyway, I'm riding down on to the plateau to speak to the men. If there is any news from Davout or Bernadotte, send word to me at once. I shall be returning to the headquarters at Jena for the evening.'

'Yes, sire.'

The gently rolling landscape was covered with the dead and wounded from the battle. Napoleon rode from regiment to regiment to offer his congratulations and rewards to those who had distinguished themselves. His men knew that they had won an important victory and cheered him as he approached, clustering round his horse as he acknowledged their greetings with a broad smile, and a wave of his hat. As he passed amongst them Napoleon gave orders for the wounded to be carried down to Jena where they could be sheltered from the cold of the coming night. He also instructed that any captured enemy colours were to be taken to headquarters at once, together with the count of casualties suffered by both sides.

Dusk was gathering over the town as Napoleon entered Jena with his escort and clattered through the cobbled streets. On either side wearied men, many wearing bloodied dressings, rose up and cheered as the Emperor passed by. When he reached headquarters an excited staff officer showed him the stack of enemy colours that had been brought in from the battlefield.

'Over twenty so far, sire! Quite a haul.'

'Yes.' Napoleon smiled, and then yawned. He rubbed his jaw as he looked at the trophies. 'Make sure that the men who captured these are awarded promotions.'

'Yes, sire.'

Napoleon had turned away, and was about to go to his quarters and order a meal, when the staff officer addressed him again.

'Sire! There's a messenger waiting to see you. He has come straight from Marshal Davout at Auerstadt.'

'Auerstadt?' Napoleon turned back quickly. 'Where is he?'

'Waiting outside your quarters, sire.'

Napoleon strode away through the main hall of the hotel that had been commandeered for the temporary headquarters of the Grand Army. The place buzzed with the excitement of victory as the officers toasted each other with wine taken from the hotel's cellar. Napoleon ignored them all as he climbed the stairs to the hotel's best suite of rooms, which was serving as his personal quarters. An officer rose from a bench outside the door leading into the private dining room as Napoleon approached. He was spattered with mud and a bandage had been crudely tied about his head. Nevertheless, there was no hiding the triumphant gleam in his eye as he greeted his Emperor.

'Sire, I have come from Marshal Davout.'

'I know that.' Napoleon waved a hand dismissively. 'Make your report. Wait, who are you?'

'Captain Tobriant, of Marshal Davout's staff, sire.'

'Very well, Tobriant. What news from Davout? Did he manage to contain the enemy's flank guard?'

'Flank guard?' Captain Tobriant looked surprised. 'Sire, I don't think you understand. Marshal Davout begs to inform you that he met with the main body of the Prussian army on the Auerstadt road and defeated it today.'

Chapter 23

Napoleon stared at him for a moment and then shook his head. 'What nonsense is this? The main Prussian army fought us here at Jena.'

Captain Tobriant's exultant expression faded. 'Sire, Marshal Davout estimates that his corps faced more than sixty thousand Prussians today.'

'Sixty thousand?' Napoleon laughed. 'Impossible! How could Davout have defeated so many? Why, that would mean he was out-numbered by more than two to one.'

'Yes, sire. That's right.' Tobriant nodded, then reached into his jacket and pulled out a slim despatch. 'His report, sire.'

Napoleon took the document and hurriedly broke the seal, unfolded it and read through the briefly recounted details. Then he lowered the report and glanced up at Tobriant. 'This can't be true. Your commander is seeing double. He could not possibly have overcome such odds. The real battle was here. The victory is mine. Mine. Davout's fight was merely a flank action. Does he think he can usurp my glory?'

Captain Tobriant opened his mouth to protest, then thought better of it as he made his reply. 'Sire, you have Marshal Davout's report. I can only say that I witnessed the battle from his headquarters, close enough to the fighting to be wounded by a spent musket ball. I know what I saw, sire, and Marshal Davout speaks the truth.'

'Then he must be a fool,' Napoleon snapped. 'You return to him at once and tell him to present himself here first thing in the morning when he can make a more sober, and accurate, account of his . . . skirmish.'

'Skirmish?' Tobriant looked astonished for a moment before he recovered his composure. 'I will go and report to him, sire.'

Napoleon dismissed Tobriant and entered the dining room, where he sat down at the long table. He called for his secretaries and ordered food to be brought to him. While he ate he dictated a despatch to be sent to Paris immediately to let France know of the great victory that had been won over the Prussians at Jena. Then there were orders to be written so that the army might take advantage of the situation and make a rapid advance on Berlin to end the war. As he dictated, the first of the detailed reports from Davout's headquarters arrived. Reading the tally of enemy and French losses, as well as the description of the battle at Auerstadt, Napoleon began to wonder if he had judged Davout too hastily.

It had been some days since Napoleon had last slept well and towards midnight exhaustion finally got the better of him: he fell asleep, head cradled in his arms as he slumped over the table. Berthier waited a moment to see if he would stir, and then quietly rose up and fetched a thick coat from one of the pegs by the door and gently placed it over his shoulders as he began to snore. Then he ushered the secretaries from the room and, with a last glance at his master, followed them out and shut the door behind him.

Napoleon woke with a start as the first rays of the dawn filtered into the room. Tossing the coat aside he stood up and rolled his neck cautiously until the stiffness had worn out of his spine. Then he strode to the door and pulled it open.

'Berthier!' he called out into the corridor. Receiving no reply, he pointed at a passing staff officer. 'You there! Where is Berthier?'

'Sire, he has just retired to his room to rest.'

'Then wake him up and send him to me at once.'

'Yes, sire.'

'And then have the latest reports from Davout and Bernadotte brought to me.'

The staff officer saluted and hurried away to do the Emperor's bidding. By the time Berthier reached the room, bleary-eyed and dishevelled, Napoleon had read through most of the reports that had reached headquarters during the night. He lowered the steaming cup of coffee he had been drinking and tapped the sheaf of documents.

'Have you seen these?'

Berthier twisted his head as he approached the table so that he might see the reports, and then nodded. 'The despatches from Marshal Davout. Yes, sire, I have read them.'

'And what do you make of his claim to have defeated the main body of the enemy's forces?'

Berthier was quiet for a moment as he tried to gauge the Emperor's mood, and then spoke carefully. 'I have to say that I was sceptical at first, sire. But as I read more, it was clear that his assessment was backed by the reports sent in by his divisional commanders. It would appear that he is speaking the truth, sire.'

'I see . . . So you believe that while nearly a hundred thousand men of the Grand Army were tied down here, taking on the enemy's flank guard, Marshal Davout and his single corps attacked and defeated the main body of the Prussian army?'

'That is what seems to have happened, sire. Based on those reports.'

'Preposterous!' Napoleon shoved the documents across the table in frustration. 'It is not possible. Why, he even claims that he received no assistance from Bernadotte and his corps.'

'Yes,' Berthier said evenly. 'If what he says is true, then Bernadotte disobeyed a direct order to march to Davout's aid. That will require an investigation, sire.'

'If it is true, then Bernadotte deserves to be court-martialled and shot,' Napoleon decided. 'Be that as it may, I cannot bring myself to believe the full extent of Davout's claims. Why, if it were true, then he would have won a victory far greater than the one I achieved here yesterday. Is that not so?'

Berthier did not respond at once but raised his eyebrows and tilted his head slightly to one side as if he was considering a very complicated proposition.

Napoleon shook his head. 'No, the real victory was won here, at Jena. That is what people will say.'

'Yes, sire. I imagine so.'

Napoleon eyed him coldly. 'You imagine so?'

Berthier shifted uncomfortably but did not reply and Napoleon sighed with exasperation. He did not want to believe that one of his corps commanders had taken on the main Prussian army and won a victory that so clearly eclipsed his own. Yet all the evidence of the reports was that Davout had achieved precisely what he claimed to have done. There was no denying that the victory at Auerstadt was an astonishing achievement, and one that Napoleon could not help feeling a surge of jealousy over. Once word of Davout's success spread through the army, and then across Europe, any attempt made by Napoleon to claim that the real glory was won on the field at Jena would be seen through at once as a petty attempt to outshine his subordinate. People would laugh at him, Napoleon reflected bitterly. There was no avoiding the painful humiliation that the true glory of the previous day belonged to Davout. Very well then, Napoleon resolved. He would be magnanimous and accord Marshal Davout the praise and recognition that was due. Besides, a show of respect for the man would be sure to play well with the rankers, and in the newspapers. By such gestures he would be seen to remain a man of the people, and not the petty despot and tyrant his enemies tried to depict him as.

Napoleon took a deep calming breath and eased himself back in his chair as he looked at Berthier. 'Send Davout to me the moment he arrives.'

'Yes, sire.'

'In the meantime, have the army newspapers prepare an article on the magnificent victory a handful of French soldiers achieved over an enemy army many times their strength. The writers are not to stint in their praise of Davout. You are to let them know that the Emperor himself pays his profound respect and gratitude to the marshal and adds his voice to the honour that the rest of the Grand Army bestows on Davout and his heroic men. Is that quite clear?'

Berthier nodded.

'Then leave me. I must be shaved and properly dressed to receive France's hero of the hour.'

Once Berthier had gone, Napoleon clenched his fists and gritted his teeth as he indulged in a seething rage over the mistake he had made in assuming that he had attacked and defeated the main Prussian army at Jena. The reasons behind the ready success of the previous day were now apparent and the words of triumph he had penned for the newspapers in Paris the night before now mocked him. Napoleon hurriedly searched through the morning paperwork left on the table for his signature until he found the despatch announcing the victory at Jena. He glanced over the neatly transcribed paragraphs and then folded the letter and tore it in half, and then again and again until there was only a scattering of paper fragments on the table.

Marshal Davout arrived at headquarters as Napoleon was finishing his breakfast and the Emperor instantly rose to his feet and thrust his napkin aside as he smiled at his subordinate.

'Marshal Davout, it is a pleasure to greet the victor of Auerstadt! Please, sit down and join me. Coffee? Something to eat?'

'Thank you, sire. Coffee would be most welcome.'

Once Napoleon had ordered a clerk to bring refreshments for the marshal, he glanced over at his guest. Davout had ridden through the night, and had not slept for three days. A thick stubble encrusted his cheeks and his eyes were red-rimmed and bloodshot. He eased himself stiffly into the chair opposite the Emperor and smiled wearily. 'May I offer my congratulations to you, sire, on your victory here at Jena?'

Napoleon laughed. 'Two triumphs in one day. Providence was surely shining on French arms yesterday.'

'Yes, sire.'

'So tell me, Davout. What happened? According to Murat's scouts you should have been facing a small corps protecting the enemy flank.'

'Even Marshal Murat makes mistakes from time to time, sire,' Davout replied wryly and they both smiled before he collected his thoughts and continued. 'I crossed the Saale ten miles along the river from here, in accordance with your orders, sire. I deemed it best to march on Apolda as quickly as possible in order to block any Prussian retreat from Jena. So I advanced with Gudin's division and ordered the others to follow as swiftly as possible. We were over the Saale by dawn, and there was a dense fog covering the landscape. You must have had the same here.'

Napoleon nodded.

'So we continued to advance and our cavalry patrols ran into enemy scouts. The prisoners told us that they belonged to Brunswick's army. I doubted their word, as you can imagine, and continued advancing as far as the village of Hassenhausen, when the fog began to lift and we saw for the first time the Prussian army spread out before us. I sent word to you at once, sire, and also to Marshal Bernadotte to march his corps to support mine. There was very little time to do anything else before the Prussians attacked. Gudin's men formed squares and held them off and they fell back. There was a delay while they prepared to attack again, but by now Friant's division had reached the field and I could see that Brunswick would attempt to get round our right flank, so I sent Friant to the right and shifted Gudin's centre in the same direction.'

'What of your other flank?' Napoleon asked sharply. 'You can't have left that unguarded, surely?'

'No, sire. It was covered by one regiment.'

'One regiment?'

'It was all that could be spared, sire. Until the last of my divisions arrived,' Davout explained. 'The Prussians threw in a massive attack against our right, which we beat back with heavy losses on their part. But then they immediately advanced on our left, and broke the regiment I had left there. As soon as the right flank looked safe I rode across to the left, taking two of Gudin's regiments, and rallied the broken regiment. We charged the enemy and drove them back and retook the village.'

'You led the charge in person?'

Davout looked at him steadily. 'Yes, sire. As I said, we needed every man who could hold a musket. There were no exceptions. I even had the men in the supply wagons armed and brought forward as a final reserve.'

Napoleon nodded approvingly, as he realised how desperate Davout's situation had been. 'What then?'

'The Prussians mounted four more assaults on the village, but we drove them off.'

'Must have been a hard fight.'

'Yes, sire. I have never seen my men so resolute. So brave.'

Napoleon smiled. 'I am equally certain that they have never seen a marshal fight at their side before. Your men are a credit to you, as you are to them.'

Davout shrugged modestly. 'We were fortunate, sire. The Prussians played their part as well. They were slow to attack, and when they did it was always piecemeal and poorly co-ordinated, so I was able to move men along my line to meet any dangers. But we were losing men all the time, sire, and Morand arrived only just in time to hold the left flank. But there was no sign of Bernadotte, and I heard nothing from him until noon, when a message arrived saying that he would not move without instructions from you, sire.'

'Really?' Napoleon folded his hands together. Bernadotte's orders had been clear enough. He was to work in concert with Davout, with the latter acting as his immediate superior. His refusal to march to Davout's aid could have led to the latter's defeat and the victory at Jena would have amounted to nothing. Napoleon resolved to have Bernadotte called to account for his dangerous inactivity. 'Continue.'

'Yes, sire. Once I had all three of my divisions in line, I could see that the Prussians were still disorganised, and I decided that our best chance of survival lay in attack, so I ordered the corps to advance in the direction of Auerstadt. As we marched forward the enemy cavalry counter-attacked. But they could not break our squares, and for some reason they did not bring any guns or infantry forward to support their cavalry. By contrast, I kept our guns as far forward as I could and each time we encountered any attempt by the Prussians to make a stand, our guns cut them down and scattered their formations.' Davout paused and rubbed his brow. 'So it continued through the afternoon, as I was determined to push them back as far to the south as I could while my men were still capable of advancing. But by four o'clock it was all over. The Prussians were in full retreat. I could not mount a pursuit, sire. The only fresh units I had by then were three regiments of cavalry.' He broke off and took a deep breath. 'If Bernadotte had joined us, then it might have been different.'

'Yes. I can see that,' Napoleon said quietly. 'But still, you tell an extraordinary story, Davout. It's as fine a victory as any French general has achieved since the revolution.'

Davout bowed his head. 'Thank you, sire. On behalf of all my officers and men.'

'There is only the question of the butcher's bill now. I can imagine your losses were severe.'

'Yes, sire. Gudin's division suffered worst. Nearly half his men have been lost. In all my corps has lost perhaps as many as seven and a half thousand men.'

'And the enemy's losses?'

'When I set off from my headquarters we had accounted for a least ten thousand killed and three thousand prisoners. And we have captured over a hundred cannon.'

'A fine result, Davout. I am proud of you and your men. I am sure that France will be equally proud when news of the victories at Jena and Auerstadt reaches Paris. Now I imagine you need some rest.'

'Once I have attended to my wounded, fed my men and gathered weapons from the battlefield, sire.'

'Of course, but at least enjoy your coffee and a quick meal with the other officers downstairs before you go. I am sure they will be as enthralled by your tale as I was.'

'Yes, sire.'

Once Marshal Davout had left the room, Napoleon's expression hardened and he stared at the opposite wall until there was a knock and Berthier entered. 'Sire? Do you wish me to summon the staff for the morning conference?'

'In a moment. First, send a message to Bernadotte. Tell him the Emperor demands an explanation of his conduct yesterday. Marshal Bernadotte is required to justify the fact that his corps did not fire a single shot in anger yesterday when the rest of the Grand Army was inflicting a great defeat on the Prussians.'

The Grand Army set off in pursuit of the enemy later the same morning. Murat's cavalry led the way, followed by the columns of Ney and Soult. The shattered men of Davout's and Lannes's corps were permitted a day's recuperation before they had to march swiftly to catch up with an advance column that had set off round the flank of the retreating Prussians in order to cut them off from Berlin. The only men fresh enough to lead the flanking force were those of Bernadotte's corps and Napoleon reluctantly handed him the responsibility for the task. So it was over a week later before Napoleon finally caught up with the advance column and rode into Bernadotte's headquarters. He swiftly dispensed with any formal greetings and offers of hospitality and demanded an interview with Bernadotte alone. As soon as the other officers had cleared out of the marshal's office and closed the doors behind them, Napoleon took off his mud-stained cloak and tossed it one of the ornate couches that Bernadotte took with him on campaign, eased himself into the marshal's chair and for a moment stared hard at his subordinate.

Bernadotte stood stiffly, hands clasped behind his back, head slightly aloof and gleaming boots shoulder width apart. He was clean shaven and his uniform was spotless. It was dark outside and the room was lit by the candles burning in several gilded candelabras. Despite the heat of the fire in the grate and the comforting hue of the candlelight there was no warmth between the two men. Bernadotte returned the Emperor's hostile gaze unflinchingly.

'I assume this is about your request for an explanation of my actions at the recent battle, sire.'

'No,' Napoleon replied flatly. 'I seek an explanation of your *inaction*. And I don't request it, Marshal Bernadotte. I demand it. Why did you disobey Davout's instruction to come to his aid?'

Bernadotte smiled faintly. 'I am of the same rank as Davout. I am not obliged to obey his instructions.'

'Yet I specifically directed you to take orders from him.'

'A direction is not an order, sire. In any case, I was already obeying your orders in advancing towards Dornburg.'

'That was written the previous day,' Napoleon snapped back. 'And it was superseded by the order to obey Davout.'

'The order did not reach me until after I had set out for Dornburg.'

'You dissemble, Marshal. Only your advance elements had begun to march. The rest of your corps had not even left their encampment.'

Bernadotte frowned irritably. 'I judged that it would be best to continue with my existing orders rather than cause any delay in my corps's movement by rerouting the line of advance towards Davout. It was a professional judgement, sire. If you wish to hold me accountable for anything, then let it be for making an unfortunate decision for the right reasons.'

Napoleon stabbed a finger towards him. 'There was nothing professional about your judgement. You disobeyed an order. You endangered Davout and his entire corps and the snail's pace of your advance towards Dornburg makes even the Prussians look quick-witted by comparison.'

Bernadotte shrugged dismissively. 'There were certain difficulties along the route.'

'That is a lie. I have had an officer retrace the route and he can find no explanation for the tardiness of your advance.'

'The officer was not there on the day, sire. What could he know of the difficulties faced by my men? The roads were narrow and we were obliged to halt frequently to drive off enemy scouts.'

'Good God, man! If the army stopped to fight every scout it encountered we would never advance far beyond the borders of France.' Napoleon slapped a hand down on the table. 'Your excuses are feeble, Marshal Bernadotte. You are guilty of a gross dereliction of duty and I can tell you that there is a widespread feeling in the army that you must be called to account, and punished severely.' Napoleon reached into his breast pocket and pulled out a document and placed it in front of him. 'Do you know what this is? An order for your court-martial. I have already signed it.'

Bernadotte stared at the document and for the first time his arrogant composure slipped and Napoleon saw a flash of anxiety in his expression.

'You mean to court-martial me?'

'The army is expecting it,' Napoleon replied coldly. 'You deserve no less. I dare say that any trial before your peers would find you guilty. The other marshals would support such a verdict, and order that you be shot.'

Bernadotte bit his lip. 'You would countenance that?'

'If that was the verdict of the court, what else could I do? I will not side with you against the will of the Grand Army.'

Bernadotte took a half-step towards the table and gestured in the direction of the signed order. 'Sire, this is absurd. I am no traitor. I would never betray the interests of France. I am your loyal servant, and I am married to the sister of your brother Joseph's wife.'

It was a desperate gambit, and Napoleon could not help feeling contempt at such a naked appeal to place family concerns before national interest. He stared back at the miserable Bernadotte and let him suffer through a prolonged silence before he spoke again.

'I have made my decision, Bernadotte. You have brought disgrace upon yourself, and upon your men, who little merit it. There is no question that you deserve to stand trial.'

Bernadotte clasped his hands together. 'Sire, I know I made an error of judgement, but I do not deserve this. I swear to you, on my life, that I will never let you down again. I swear it by all that I hold dear!'

Napoleon's lips curled in contempt for a moment, then he reached for the order and held it in his hands. He stared at the document for a moment before he spoke again. 'I know full well that if I issue this it is the same as giving the order for you to be shot.'

Napoleon stood up and walked slowly towards the fire. He ripped the order in two and tossed the pieces into the blaze. He watched as flames flared along the edges of the paper and a moment later there was nothing left of the document but charred flakes and ash. Then he turned back to Bernadotte and noted the amazed expression on the other man's face.

'You have made your great mistake in life, Bernadotte. Every man is entitled to one such error. There will be no more chances. You must atone for your failings with every breath of life that remains to you. If there is any sense of honour in you, then you will own up to your disgrace and see that neither I, nor any of your comrades, ever have cause to regret my leniency.'

Napoleon picked up his coat and strode towards the door. Bernadotte finally managed to recover from his shock and surprise, and muttered, 'Sire, I thank you with all my heart, and I swear you shall never regret this. I swear that I will devote my life to your service.'

Napoleon paused at the door and looked back at the man, feeling sickened by his grovelling display of gratitude. 'Very well. That is a promise I will hold you to as long as you live.'

Bernadotte nodded gravely. 'And it is one that I shall honour above all else, for ever.'

Chapter 24

Warsaw, January 1807

Napoleon pulled the thick fur robe more closely about his shoulders as he stared into the fireplace. A servant had built the fire up before retiring and leaving him alone in the study. That had been over an hour ago, and the split logs had long since burned through. The charred timber was gilded with bright orange specks that pulsed slowly amid the slender fingers of flame flickering up from the heart of the fire. Outside, the wind moaned round the castle as the blizzard that had begun at dawn continued into the dusk, blanketing the city in a thick mantle of white snow. Winter gripped the land and across Poland the men of the Grand Army huddled in their billets and only ventured abroad to search for food and firewood, or when required for patrol and sentry duties.

As the previous year had come to an end the Emperor had finally sent his army into winter quarters, before exhaustion and a sharp decline in morale caused it to fall apart. Despite the victories at Jena and Auerstadt and the subsequent pursuit of the remnants of the Prussian army until its almost complete destruction, the Prussians had not surrendered. Even as Marshal Davout had led his corps in triumph through the streets of Berlin the Prussian King, Frederick William, had fled east to join his Russian allies and continue the war against France. All that was left of his army was one rag-tag column scraped together from the survivors, barely a match for a single corps of the Grand Army. Yet, Napoleon knew, the Russians were massing formidable numbers of men to confront the French army once the worst of the winter had passed. Or so he had thought until the first reports of Russian movements had reached imperial headquarters. It seemed that the Russian soldiers were injured to the effects of winter and were already advancing towards the French outposts.

Napoleon idly stroked his chin as he considered the situation. Berthier had updated his notebooks the previous night, and examining them the following morning Napoleon had been shocked to learn how his army had been ravaged by the onset of winter. Almost half of the men were absent from their units as they ranged across the frozen countryside stealing food and looting whatever valuables they discovered in the villages and estates surrounding Warsaw. Discipline was breaking down and already there had been reports of men killing officers and sergeants who had attempted to hold them back from committing the worst excesses.

Napoleon had been shocked by the backwardness of Poland compared to the rest of Europe. There were few good roads, and those that existed became impassable the moment the autumn rains turned their surfaces into a glutinous mire that sucked down the wheels of wagons and cannon and made an effort of every step taken by men and horses. Such conditions meant it was impossible to bring supplies forward and Napoleon had been forced to call a halt to operations. It had been his intention to wait until spring came to continue his advance against the Russians, but it looked as if his hand would be forced if the Russians decided to attack while Poland was still in the grip of winter.

Life was not hard for all the men of the Grand Army. Those at imperial headquarters, and the men of the Imperial Guard quartered in Warsaw, were comfortable enough, and had plenty of diversions to entertain them through the winter. For many years the Poles had suffered at the hands of their Russian, Austrian and Prussian neighbours and they had greeted the French as liberators. Napoleon had been pleased to play such a role and had made every effort to befriend them and offer promises of independence once the Russians had been driven out of Polish territory. Thousands of Poles had already volunteered to serve with the French and Napoleon needed the reinforcements. But if his men continued to plunder the countryside the Grand Army would not be welcome for much longer. While the soldiers could march swiftly when they lived off the land it did mean that they tended to operate like a plague of locusts, leaving discontent and hunger in their wake. Napoleon frowned as he considered the matter. If he attempted to supply his men on the march, it could only be achieved by advancing more slowly, and operating with smaller armies with which it would be impossible to overwhelm the nations that opposed him.

In any case, however an army was supplied, it could not hope to march far and fight in the depths of such a winter. Napoleon leaned forward in his chair, closer to the fire, and stretched his hands out to warm them. For a moment he cursed his enforced stay in Warsaw. But only for a moment as his thoughts turned to the young countess,

Marie Walewska, who had arrived in Warsaw a few days earlier. Her breathtaking beauty had instantly captured the attention of the French officers at headquarters, and Napoleon had felt his heart quicken when she was introduced to him at a ball given in his honour. They had talked briefly, then he had invited her to join him for a late supper after the ball, and before midnight had struck they were in each other's arms beneath several blankets in the Emperor's bed. She was as good a lover as he had ever known and he felt his lust return as he recalled the smoothness of her skin, the gentle curves of her limbs and the smooth fullness of her breasts. He resolved to send for her again that very night.

There was a knock on the door and with a hiss of frustration he thrust Marie from his mind and turned away from the fire.

'Yes? What is it?'

The door clicked open as a young staff officer stepped into the room and bowed neatly. 'Sire, a deputation from the senate in Paris has arrived.'

'A deputation? What on earth are they doing here?'

'They requested an audience with you, sire.'

'Now?' Napoleon frowned. 'No. Let them rest for the night. They must have had an arduous journey. Let them rest.'

The officer hesitated a moment before he continued, 'Sire, they were insistent on seeing you tonight. They are led by your brother Lucien.'

At the mention of his brother Napoleon was tempted to change his mind. Lucien would not have made such a trip without good cause, but Napoleon was too weary to contemplate any business of state that evening. Besides, the prospect of another evening making love to Marie Walewska was more than enough reason to defer meeting Lucien and his senatorial companions until morning. Napoleon cleared his throat.

'Welcome them to headquarters in my name. Feed them and find them the finest quarters available. Find out why they are here and report on that to me by tomorrow morning. Is that clear?'

'Yes, sire.'

'Good. Then tell my cook to prepare a light supper, with champagne, and send an invitation to Countess Walewska to join me at ten o'clock. Before then I shall want a hot bath. Now go.'

'Yes, sire.' The officer bowed his head and left the room, closing the door softly behind him. The room was quiet again, and the only sounds were the muffled moan of the wind, the occasional hiss and crackle from the fire and the distant sounds of voices of the younger staff officers at a drunken party somewhere in the castle. Napoleon eased himself back into the chair with a faint smile as he contemplated the evening that lay ahead.

It was not until ten the following morning that Lucien and the other senators were admitted into the Emperor's presence. Napoleon had chosen to wear the uniform of a Colonel of Chasseurs of the Guard, set off by a jewelled star on his breast and a sash across one of his gold epaulettes. He sat at a desk on a dais in the castle's best reception room with two grenadiers of the guard standing to attention a short distance away on either side, like statues. It was draughty, but Napoleon considered that he must let his guests know that though they were far from the splendours of Paris they were still in the presence of the Emperor of France. The deputation had been entertained graciously according to his order, but had remained tight-lipped about the purpose of their mission across the heart of Europe in the middle of winter. That in itself was an indication of the seriousness and secrecy of their business. Nevertheless, Napoleon did not look up from the fair copy of a letter he was reading as they entered the chamber and advanced towards the dais. The footsteps stopped in front of him, then after a brief delay there was a light cough and Lucien spoke.

'Sire, we—'

'Wait!' Napoleon held up a hand to silence his brother, and continued reading a moment longer. Then he picked up his pen, dipped it into the inkwell and signed his name with a flourish before setting the pen down and looking up with a stern expression. 'Now then, gentlemen, what can I do for you?'

Lucien stared back at his brother coldly. 'We requested an immediate audience with you last night . . . sire.'

'I know. I had other business that needed attending to first.'

'Really? More important than attending to a deputation of members of the government of France?'

'You are senators, Lucien,' Napoleon responded quietly. 'It is I who am the government of France, whether I am in Paris, or here in Warsaw. You would do well to remember that when you address me.'

Lucien bit his lip, then took a sharp breath and nodded. 'Yes, sire. Of course.'

Napoleon inclined his head slowly. 'Very well. I will permit you to make your presentation.'

Lucien shifted uncomfortably and glanced at the guardsmen before he continued. 'Sire, might we speak with you in a more private setting?'

'Forgive me, but I was given to believe that your business with me was of some importance.'

'Well, yes.'

'Then let us accord it the setting it deserves. Now, I have plenty of other business to attend to today and I'd be obliged if you got to the point.'

'Yes, sire.' Lucien drew himself up. 'We have been sent from Paris to represent the views of the senators, as well as the members of the other houses of the legislature. In the first instance we are required to congratulate your majesty on the defeats you have inflicted on the enemy, and to wish your majesty well in your ongoing campaign against Frederick William and his Russian allies. It is hoped that you will crush the enemy swiftly and bring the war to a conclusion.'

Lucien paused and Napoleon bowed his head in acknowledgement. 'I thank the senate for its kind wishes. But I don't think that you have come all this way just to congratulate me.'

'There is more,' Lucien admitted. 'It is the view of the senate that the time has come for France to make peace and enjoy all that your majesty, and our courageous soldiers, have laboured so long to win. Austria has been humbled. Prussia is occupied and the Tsar's armies dare not venture far from their homeland. Your triumph is complete, sire, and now you can enjoy the fruits of peace.'

'My triumph will be complete when Russia joins my alliance against Britain and I finally dictate the terms of peace in London. Then, and only then, can there truly be peace.'

'But since the defeat of our fleet at Trafalgar there is no prospect of defeating Britain, sire.'

'Which is why I issued the Berlin decrees,' Napoleon explained with forced patience. 'If we cannot beat them at sea, and they do not dare to face us on land, then we must strike at their Achilles heel. Trade. Trade is the lifeblood of Britain. That is why I have forbidden trade with Britain from any port in Europe over which we hold influence. As their trade with the continent withers so the British merchants will lose markets for their goods. Their factories and mills will begin to close. There will be popular unrest, and when the people of Britain are hungry and desperate enough they will rise up and Britain will have a revolution, just as we did, gentlemen. And when that happens King George and his aristocrat followers will share the fate of King Louis and his aristos. And then there will be peace.'

He paused to let his words sink in and Lucien licked his lips nervously. 'That is a fine strategy, sire. In principle.'

'And it will work in practice,' Napoleon insisted. 'Given enough time.'

'That is to be hoped. But at present the decrees are being flouted openly. Our brother, King Louis of Holland, turns a blind eye to trade with Britain, and word has reached Paris that Marshal Masséna is selling licences to Italian merchants to trade with Britain.'

Napoleon felt a surge of anger at the last comment. That fool Masséna would spoil everything with his greed. He might be a fine general, Napoleon conceded, but there was none as corrupt and avaricious as Masséna. If it was true that he was selling licences he must be dealt with the moment the present campaign was concluded. He looked steadily at Lucien and gestured dismissively. 'Teething problems, brother. That is all. Once I have the time to ensure that the Berlin decrees are enforced effectively it will only be a matter of time before Britain falls and our triumph is complete. Then you and your companions can have your precious peace.'

'But first you must defeat Russia,' Lucien said deliberately. 'Might we ask how you propose to undertake such a task? There are not enough men in the whole of Europe to conquer and occupy such vast tracts of land as there are in Russia. So great an achievement is beyond even your undoubted abilities, sire.'

'Enough!' Napoleon stabbed a finger towards his brother. 'Nothing is beyond my abilities in this world. If I decide to conquer Russia then it will be so.'

Lucien shook his head. 'It cannot be done. Ask your officers, sire. We already have, and those with any experience agree that the subjugation of Russia is impossible. If that is the case then there is no alternative to making peace with the Tsar. And Britain.'

'There will be no peace with Britain,' Napoleon replied firmly. 'Not until they are beaten.'

'Then let there be peace with Russia at least. For the sake of the people of France. Sire, they grow so weary of war. The cost of your armies constantly threatens to bankrupt the nation. Your battles rob families of their fathers and sons, and tens of thousands of those men who have avoided service now wander the land in bands of brigands. War has exhausted France, and you would be wise to heed the popular mood, sire. When the news of Jena and Auerstadt reached Paris there were few celebrations. You won yet another battle, sire, but still the war goes on. The people are tired of war.'

'I know my people, Lucien. I know that they are loyal to me. They proved that when they voted to approve the senate's proposal that I become their Emperor. By millions of votes to mere thousands. So don't presume to tell me what the people think. I know what they think. The people love me.' Napoleon smiled coldly. 'Even if your precious senators don't.'

His brother froze at his words. Behind him the other senators glanced fearfully at each other before Lucien spoke again.

'Sire, do you not recall the day when you became First Consul? We stood side by side in order to save France from the tyranny of corruption and incompetence. It would be dangerous if the people began to wonder whether they have not simply exchanged one form of tyranny for another.'

'Do you call me a tyrant?'

'Not I, sire. But others do.'

'Then pass their names on to Fouché and they will be dealt with.'

'That is precisely why I do not pass their names on to Fouché, sire.'

The two brothers stared at each other for a moment, and then Napoleon looked past Lucien at the other senators and pointed to the door. 'Leave us.'

They looked to Lucien for a lead. He nodded slightly and they retreated from the room. No word was spoken until the door was closed and then Napoleon pointed towards the chairs set against the walls of the chamber. 'Bring one of those here and sit with me, brother.'

After an instant's hesitation Lucien did as he was told and settled stiffly on his chair under the penetrating gaze of his brother. At length Napoleon leaned forward and rested his elbows on the desk. 'Is it true what you say about the public mood?'

'Yes.'

'I see.' Napoleon nodded as he considered the situation. He could count on the loyalty of the army without question. Some of his marshals on the other hand were clearly ambitious men in their own right. Men like Bernadotte, Augereau and Masséna. Then there were men of influence in Paris who could not be trusted either. Talleyrand, and even Fouché, who would submit to any master who served his own ends. There were dangers to his position, then. Yet Napoleon could not believe that the French people would abandon him. Not while he gave them victory. He decided to change the mood and smiled at his brother.

'That's enough of politics for now. I will think on what you have said. I promise. But for now, let us be brothers. What news of the family?'

Lucien's posture relaxed a little as he composed his reply. 'They are all well enough. Our sisters continue to argue bitterly and Mother gathers up every titbit of gossip that she can that confirms her opinion of Josephine. Our brothers are well enough. Joseph rules Naples effectively and is winning over the people with his reforms. The same goes for Louis in Holland. Jérôme is as much a liability as ever and trades heavily on the family name for advancement and influence. He wants all the privileges of being a Bonaparte without any of the obligations.'

They shared a chuckle over their younger brother's hubris.

'Have you seen Josephine recently?' Napoleon asked.

'Yes, she was at Mainz when we stopped there. She's been there for some time, it seems. Waiting for permission to come and join you.'

'I know. She writes to me regularly.'

'So why not let her come?'

Napoleon shrugged. 'The roads are difficult. The climate is uncomfortable and there are only my officers here for company. Hardly the cosmopolitan life she enjoys so much in Paris.'

'It's not so bad,' Lucien countered. 'From what I've seen so far Warsaw seems to offer enough diversions. I'm sure Josephine would be happy enough here.'

'I'm sure she would.' Napoleon's thoughts turned to Marie Walewska and the uncomfortable prospect of having to juggle a wife and a mistress in the same small social circle. At present the physical charms of the young countess appealed more to him than the familiar comforts of the Empress. 'However, as you helpfully pointed out, we are still at war and I am occupied by my duties. I would not have much time to spare for Josephine and it would be unfair to summon her to Warsaw only to neglect her.'

'Yes, it would.' Lucien looked at him closely. 'I heard something of your, er, duties from the officers in the mess last night. The countess is a true beauty, apparently.'

'She is. And I consider it a sacred obligation to create good relations with our hosts.'

'Well, I've never heard it called that before!' Lucien laughed. 'But seriously, Napoleon. You cannot put Josephine off for long. She will get to hear of this and be hurt.'

'So? She has hurt me in her time. Besides, there are other issues that divide us.'

'Oh?'

'She has yet to provide me with an heir, and the years are drawing on. I fear that she may no longer be capable of giving what is most needed. A son to succeed me and provide France with the stability she needs. Without an heir there is little chance that you will have your peace, Lucien. If Josephine fails me in this respect then I will need to find another wife to bear me children.'

'That is a little cold-blooded,' Lucien responded quietly. 'I thought you loved her.'

'I do. In my way. But the needs of France outweigh the needs of any one man, even the Emperor.'

Lucien raised his eyebrows briefly. 'Perhaps. But she will be hurt.'

'As will I. Sometimes pain cannot be avoided. When you and your companions return to Paris please tell her to travel with you from Mainz. There is no point in her waiting any longer. She might as well be where she is most comfortable.'

'And when shall I say that you will return to her?'

'When the war is over. When Prussia surrenders and I have beaten Russia.'

'Do you seriously intend to invade Russia?'

'If I need to. With luck, the Tsar will send his armies to face me. If not, then some day the Grand Army will need to find and defeat his armies. Even if that means chasing them to the very gates of Moscow.'

Lucien contemplated this for a moment and then asked, 'Can you truly do that?'

'I think so.' Napoleon smiled. 'We shall see. Let's just hope that the Tsar obliges me by marching on Warsaw when spring comes.'

The door to the chamber suddenly burst open and they both turned to see Berthier hurrying across the tiled floor towards them, a piece of paper clutched in his hand. Napoleon saw the anxiety in his chief of staff's face.

'What is it, Berthier?'

'A message from Bernadotte, sire. He says that a Russian army has appeared in front of him and he is falling back towards Ney.'

Napoleon shut his eyes and pictured the disposition of his forces in his mind. It made sense that the enemy should march on Bernadotte. His corps was the most advanced and if the Russians moved quickly they might envelop it and destroy Bernadotte before the rest of the Grand Army could intervene. However, Napoleon calculated, if the Grand Army manoeuvred swiftly, the tables might be turned and the Russians could be trapped in turn. His eyes flicked open.

'Send word to all corps commanders to concentrate their forces immediately. We will advance towards Bernadotte. Once we have joined with him, Ney is to close in from the north and Davout from the south.' Napoleon paused as he mentally projected the coverging lines of march. 'We will pursue the Russians in the direction of Eylau.'

'Eylau?'

'A town a hundred and fifty miles north of Warsaw. If we can close the trap there, we will destroy the enemy.' He turned to his brother. 'If that happens, let us pray that the Tsar gives you the peace that you and your companions want.'

Lucien nodded. 'I will pray for your victory, Napoleon. And that peace will follow. After you face the enemy at Eylau.'

Chapter 25

Eylau, 8 February 1807

From the church bell tower Napoleon had a good view over the snow-covered roofs towards the distant lines of Russian soldiers waiting a mile and a half away to the east. According to the reports from the scouts the enemy had spent the entire night standing to, in case the French attacked under cover of darkness. Indeed, Murat and Soult had pressed the Emperor to launch an attack as night fell, but Napoleon had had no desire to take the risk. Instead the Grand Army would wait until Ney and Davout approached before initiating any attack. Staring at the stolid Russian lines Napoleon could only guess at the discomfort of the enemy soldiers who had stood in their lines through the freezing cold of the night and were still ready for battle. They must be as hardy and disciplined as they came to endure such conditions, Napoleon reflected. His own men had emerged from their winter quarters in a bitter, surly mood and only the promise of a generous pay bonus and a free issue of new clothing and equipment had persuaded them to follow their colours against the Russian army.

'A hard fight last night, sire.' Berthier nodded down into the streets where the blackened remains of several wagons of the imperial baggage train littered Eylau's main square. Scores of bodies were still sprawled around them, half hidden by the flurries of snow that had swept across the white landscape since dawn. Napoleon frowned. The officer commanding the baggage train had blundered into the town, ahead of the main army, late the previous afternoon and had run into the rearguard of the Russian army. Both sides had thrown more men into the skirmish until a bitter battle raged through the streets as night fell over Eylau. Thousands of men had died on both sides before the Russians finally gave up the town and the last shots died away. A pointless waste of men on the eve of the main battle, Napoleon reflected.

He nodded at Berthier's words. 'Yes. But it will be as nothing compared to today's fight. I am sure it will snow again at any moment.'

The sky was overcast and an even darker band of clouds was already edging over the town as the first tiny flakes began to drift through the still air. The thick snow on the ground already muffled most sounds and Napoleon was struck by the quiet as the men, horses and guns of the Grand Army took up their positions east of the town, opposite the enemy spread out along a low ridge. The most recent reports from Davout and Ney indicated that they would reach the battlefield later in the morning. Until then Napoleon would be outnumbered, and he had taken the precaution of having the Imperial Guard brought forward to strengthen the French line.

The snowflakes began to fall more heavily and within minutes the last of the bodies lying in the street had disappeared under a white mantle to become little more than vague lumps beneath the snow. Occasional breezes swirled the thick white flakes and obscured the view of the Russian lines as the sun continued to rise unseen and unwarming in the gloom.

As the bells in the church chimed eight there was a muffled thud from the direction of the enemy line. Looking up, Napoleon saw a brief flickering glow in the blizzard and then heard a dull rumble as the Russian guns opened fire. With thick snow on the ground there would be no ricochet as the balls struck home and the men would be spared the worst of the preliminary bombardment. Even so, the tower shuddered momentarily as a lucky shot hit it halfway down. A moment later bright stabs flared out along the French line as the Grand Army's guns returned fire, trusting to the accuracy with which they had been laid before the blizzard closed in over the battlefield.

Napoleon's plan depended on Davout's corps arriving on the enemy's left flank once the battle was under way. With good timing he should be able to roll the enemy line up and fall on their rear. Then the Russians must surely break and be crushed under the hooves of Murat's cavalry as they were chased down. Meanwhile the artillery duel continued as both sides fired blindly into the swirling snow. As Napoleon gave up trying to penetrate the gloom and lowered his telescope with a curse there was a faint whistling noise.

'Mortar shell!' Berthier yelled. 'Down!'

Before Napoleon could duck there was a bright orange flash to one side as the shell burst in the air. Fragments of iron rattled off the masonry of the tower and the slates of the church's roof as the concussion from the blast struck the Emperor and his staff. For a moment Napoleon was deaf, and he shook his head to try to clear his ears. His hearing began to return as voices and the continuing cannonade cut through the ringing sensation in his head. He glanced round.

'Anyone injured? Berthier?'

His chief of staff shook his head and the other officers in the tower seemed dazed but otherwise unharmed.

'Lucky shot,' someone said loudly as he rubbed his ears.

'Lucky for who?' replied Napoleon, wincing from a stabbing pain in his own ears. 'Still, ten paces closer and it would have killed us all. Given a choice, I'll take being deafened every time.'

Some of the officers laughed and smiled, then all of them flinched as another mortar shell detonated down in the streets. As the morning continued some of the shells landed in the wooden buildings in the town and set fire to them. Smoke billowed into the leaden skies, adding a grim pall to the clouds that hid the sun.

'Time to draw the enemy's attention to their right,' Napoleon said to Berthier as he glanced at his watch. 'Order Soult and Augereau to advance. They must draw the enemy into a fight while Davout approaches from the south. Go.'

Once Berthier had sent the orders off Napoleon and his staff strained their eyes to follow the progress of the attacks. The snow deadened the sound of the drums as they beat the advance and the cheers of the men were muted as they set off through the snow towards the Russians waiting silently along the ridge. For a moment the enemy's guns ceased their bombardment of Eylau as their crews brought forward and loaded case shot to meet the approaching French infantry. There was a palpable tension on the church tower as Napoleon and his staff waited for the Russian guns to open fire again. Then there was a rippling glow from the direction of the ridge and a dull rumble like distant thunder as grapeshot blasted into the advancing French columns, before a fresh blizzard obscured the view.

'What is the latest news from Davout?' asked Napoleon. 'How long before he reaches the battlefield?'

Berthier consulted his log book. 'Marshal Davout estimates that he will be able to commence his attack at eleven o'clock, sire.'

'That's not soon enough. Send a message. Tell him to attack as soon as he can.' Napoleon chewed his lip as the cannonfire from the Russian lines intensified. He could well imagine the destruction being visited on his infantry as they tested the Russian centre. 'Tell him to attack even if it means he cannot deploy his entire corps at first.'

'Yes, sire.'

A short while after the order was given the snowstorm began to thin out and then stopped, to reveal the battlefield stretching east of the town.

'Good God almighty,' Berthier muttered as he and the other staff officers stared towards the Russian lines. 'What the hell's happened?'

In front of the main Russian battery stood the remnants of Augereau's corps. Thousands of men lay sprawled and heaped in snow where they had been cut down as they marched blindly through the blizzard straight into the teeth of the enemy's cannon. Napoleon felt an icy fist clench round his heart at the sight. It was clear what had happened. Augereau and his men had lost their sense of direction and blundered to the left, straight into the path of the enemy's guns. Worse still, they had come under fire from their own guns, still engaging the enemy artillery. Mercifully, the French gunners had ceased fire the moment the blizzard cleared to reveal the carnage spread across the frozen ground between the two armies.

'Sweet Jesus,' one of Napoleon's officers said. 'What a bloodbath.'

'It's not over yet,' another officer added and pointed to a movement behind the Russian guns. 'Look there!'

A dense mass of cavalry was forming up to charge the disorganised survivors of Augereau's corps. The Frenchmen had already seen the danger and had begun to fall back, pacing away at first, then breaking into a fast walk across the bloodied ground, then running straight for the handful of regiments in the reserve line. As the fugitives fled past the reserves the enemy cavalry charged, sweeping past their guns and surging down the slope towards the shattered corps, cutting down those wounded who could not keep up with their comrades. Augereau's reserves hurriedly formed square, the foremost regiment edging up on to a small hillock directly in the path of the oncoming enemy cavalry. Their brave move served to halt the charge long enough for the survivors of the first line to reach the safety of Eylau's cemetery, where their officers attempted to rally their terrified men and force them to man the walls of the cemetery to defend it against their pursuers.

The men on the hillock were engulfed by the cavalry charge, but as Napoleon watched in pained admiration of their heroism the small square held its own and was still there when the cavalry pulled back and re-formed. At once the Russian gunners had clear sight of the square and began to fire round shot into the ranks of French infantry, cutting bloody paths through the blue lines. The sergeants quickly dressed the ranks to close the gaps and the square steadily shrank as the bombardment continued, leaving the ground around them littered with the bodies of their comrades. It continued for quarter of an hour until the enemy guns fell silent and with a throaty roar the Russian cavalry surged back up the hill, curved blades gleaming, and cut the survivors to pieces.

As the horsemen turned away and re-formed Napoleon could see that not a man was left standing on the hillock. A moment later the blizzard began anew and thick snowflakes blotted out the battlefield.

'Damn that fool, Augereau!' Napoleon growled through gritted teeth. 'His corps is finished. He has caused a gap in our line by shifting to the left. Now there's nothing left for it but to bring the Guard forward, before all is lost.'

Berthier was familiar with his master's reluctance to commit his veterans to battle. 'The Guard, sire? There are only two battalions close to the town. The rest are already committed to the line. Are you sure?'

'Of course I am, damn it! They are all that I have left. Give the order at once. They are to advance through Eylau and take up position along the eastern side of the town. At the double. Hurry, or we may lose this battle, Berthier!'

Napoleon turned back to observe the battlefield, but the new flurry of snow blotted out all sight of any detail beyond a hundred paces. Once again the sounds of cannon and musket were muffled and it was impossible to judge the distance, or even the direction. Napoleon gripped the parapet of the church tower as he stared anxiously into the swirling white specks and strained his ears. Down below in the streets of Eylau he could see the occasional dark shapes of men fleeing from the Russians. Survivors of Augereau's corps, Napoleon surmised. Thanks to their commander, there was now nothing between Napoleon's command position and the enemy.

A burning sensation in his fingers made Napoleon gaze down and he realised that his hands were losing feeling in the biting cold. He cupped them against his mouth and blew hard for a moment before rubbing them vigorously until the circulation returned, painfully. He pulled his gloves out of his coat pocket and put them on. The conditions under which the battle was being fought were truly appalling, he thought. He had hoped to pin the Russians while Ney and Davout crashed into their flanks to inflict a stunning defeat on the Tsar's army. Instead, there was no sign of Ney and Davout's men were arriving piecemeal, and the rest of the French line was in danger of collapsing. With a sudden frightening clarity, Napoleon saw that this day might well mark the loss of the Grand Army and with it all his dreams for dominion over Europe.

It was Berthier who saw the danger first as he leaned forward over the parapet and stared into the blizzard. 'Sire, I think the enemy are sending infantry forward.'

'What?'

'There, look!' Berthier thrust his arm out and pointed over the roofs of Eylau to the edge of the town. Sure enough a dark smudge was just discernible as it emerged from the gloom. A fluke in the wind provided an instant when the sky was clear and Napoleon could see the approaching Russian column plainly. No more than two hundred paces away, marching swiftly through the snow as the officers and sergeants urged their men on, scenting the chance of victory if only they could shatter the French centre before it could be stabilised.

Napoleon turned and ran across to the far side of the church tower and stared towards the French reserves, but the lines of the Imperial Guard had still not moved forward; Berthier's order could not have reached them yet. The Russians would be upon the men of the imperial headquarters before help could arrive. Napoleon whipped round towards his staff officers.

'We're going to have to fight, gentlemen.' Napoleon stabbed his finger at the snow-covered floor of the tower. 'This is the centre of the French line. If we lose the church then all is lost. Berthier, get downstairs. I want every available man to defend the church, and the doors barricaded as best you can. We have five minutes at the most. Go!'

Once Berthier had rushed down the stairs Napoleon turned to the others. 'Dupuy, get ten of our men up here with muskets. We need to slow the enemy down.'

'Yes, sire!' Dupuy hurried off as Napoleon turned to the remaining officers. 'It seems we are all in the infantry now. Find a weapon and prepare to fight for your lives.'

His officers nodded gravely and then clattered down the tower steps. For a moment Napoleon was alone and he made his way back to the parapet and stared at the approaching Russians. Already the first of the enemy had entered the streets of Eylau. The rest of the column led back into the snowy wasteland and was swallowed up as the blizzard intensified again. Napoleon straightened up and folded his arms as he surveyed the enemy.

'Is this how it all ends?' he muttered. A brief skirmish around the church before the Russians broke in and slaughtered the defenders? He smiled bitterly as he imagined the joy of his enemies when they received news of his ignominious death. Then he balled his hands into fists and shook his head. He would not give them that satisfaction. Never, as long as he drew breath.

The sound of nailed boots clattering on the steps caused Napoleon to turn round and he saw Dupuy emerge from the staircase, musket in hand, at the head of a section of the Emperor's personal escort.

'Over there!' Dupuy pointed to the parapet facing the enemy and Napoleon stepped aside as the burly soldiers took up position and held their muskets ready. The blizzard had begun to slacken again and fine flakes drifted down across the town. Overhead the sky was noticeably lighter and Napoleon sourly cursed the bad timing of the weather. If the skies had cleared earlier then Augereau would not have led his corps to its destruction. It was pointless to indulge in such regrets, he admonished himself. Then all thought stilled as his ears caught the sound of voices speaking an unfamiliar tongue and he realised that the enemy were close at hand. Sure enough, the first Russian skirmishers appeared at the end of the broad street leading to the church, cautiously picking their way forward from the shelter of one doorway to the next.

Napoleon touched Dupuy's shoulder. 'As soon as they are within a hundred paces, open fire.'

'The lads won't stand much chance of hitting anything at that range, sire.'

'They don't have to. Just as long as they slow them down.'

'Yes, sire.'

The men in the tower lowered their muskets and aimed down into the street, tracking the nearest enemies. Napoleon could hear shouts from below and the crashing of glass as the defenders prepared to shoot from the church's windows. At the sound the Russian skirmishers paused for an instant, and then crept forward again. Then the head of the enemy column appeared at the end of the street and came on in a silent shuffle through the snow.

Napoleon spoke softly. 'Aim for the column. It's a better target.'

Dupuy nodded and said, 'Make ready to fire.'

The guardsmen thumbed back their hammers and took aim and stood still, waiting for the order.

Napoleon watched the column start down the street, and heard the loud, jovial cheers and laughter of men whose spirits had most likely been raised by a generous issue of vodka before they had advanced. Once the column was well down the street he turned to Dupuy and nodded. 'Now.'

'Open fire!'

At Dupuy's shout the guardsmen pulled their triggers and the air around Napoleon filled with resounding cracks that were startling after the muffled sounds of the battle so far. At once the French soldiers grounded their muskets and began reloading. As soon as the smoke cleared from the top of the church tower Napoleon could see that two of the men at the front of the column had pitched forward and lay crumpled in the snow. A third had dropped his musket and was clutching at his shoulder. The head of the column had halted and there was instant confusion as the succeeding ranks pushed forward.

'Well done, boys!' Napoleon smiled. 'Keep firing as fast as you can.'

The Russian column was on the move again, stepping over the bodies in the snow. The skirmishers, much closer to the church, had taken a moment to determine the direction of the enemy fire and now aimed up at the tower, the muzzles of their muskets foreshortening before disappearing behind a flash of flame and puff of smoke. Musket balls clattered off the stonework and one of the guardsmen cried out as a chip of masonry gashed his cheek. With a shamed glance at his Emperor the man quickly turned his attention back to his weapon as he rammed home the wad.

Napoleon nodded. 'Carry on, Dupuy.'

The officer nodded as he finished reloading his weapon and Napoleon hurried to the staircase and ran down the ancient stone steps as fast as he dared. Down in the nave of the church there was turmoil as staff officers and the men of the Emperor's bodyguard hurriedly piled most of the heavy wooden pews against the church doors. The remaining pews had been arranged along the walls to act as firing steps. The officers of the headquarters staff stood alongside the soldiers, armed with a mixture of muskets and pistols and even swords for those who did not possess a firearm. A loud detonation echoed round the nave as the first of the guardsmen fired through his window and a moment later there were more shots as the head of the enemy column entered the square that lay before the church. The remains of the stained glass windows splintered as Russian musket balls crashed through, showering the defenders momentarily before they continued firing and reloading.

Napoleon made his way towards the main door of the church where Berthier stood behind the piled pews, sword in hand. A mixed squad of grenadiers and staff officers stood by, ready to defend any attempt to break through the makeshift barricade. Berthier nodded towards the pile of pews and a stone font. 'Best we could do, sire.'

'It will do.' Napoleon nodded. 'Until the Imperial Guard arrives.'

Before Berthier could reply there was a thud on the timbers of the church door, then another, and then more, before the latch was lifted and the door pressed against the barricade.

'With me!' Berthier called out as he sheathed his sword and pressed against the nearest pew. His hastily assembled squad followed his lead and heaved against the barricade as the doors slowly began to shift under the pressure of the Russian soldiers massing outside. Already there was a crack of light between the heavy timber frames and Napoleon could see a bearded face contorted with effort as the man shoved against the door. As the gap widened the muzzle of a musket poked through the gap and there was a flash and a roar as it fired. The ball passed over the heads of Berthier and his men and slapped into a tapestry at the back of the church. Napoleon shouted at the nearest guardsman.

'Shoot back!'

The man nodded and moved to one side so that he had a clear view through the slowly growing gap. He raised his musket, thumbed the cock back and shot into the tight mass of bodies on the far side. There was a sharp cry of pain, and then a roar of rage from the other Russians and renewed pressure as the gap continued to widen and the pews scraped back despite the efforts of Berthier and his men. The guardsman reloaded and fired again, and the moment he grounded his musket there was another shot through the door and this time it found its target as he was flung back and fell spreadeagled on the stone slabs of the floor. Napoleon glanced down and saw that a ball had struck him in the forehead, shattering his skull into a bloody ruin of bone and brains.

Now there was enough space for a man to pass through the gap between the doors and the first of the Russians thrust his way inside the church and raised his musket overhead to stab at one of the staff officers straining to hold the barricade in place. The tip of the bayonet caught the Frenchman in the neck and he fell away with a cry of agony. He clamped a hand to the wound, spurting gouts of blood across his uniform and spattering across Berthier's cheek as he stood next to him.

'Shoot him!' Napoleon called out and one of the officers at the nearest window swung round at the shout, raised his pistol, took aim and fired. The ball slammed into the Russian's chest, and he gasped at the impact, then looked down and roared with laughter when he saw that it had struck a buckle and not injured him. With another shove the door grated open even further and more enemy soldiers pushed their way into the church and stabbed their bayonets at Berthier's men.

'Leave the barricade!' Napoleon ordered. 'Defend yourselves!'

As Berthier and the others stepped back and raised their weapons Napoleon snatched up the musket from the dead guardsman and stepped forward to join the squad defending the doors. The barricade scraped backwards as more Russians pressed into the church, and those with loaded weapons attempted to aim as they fired them at the defenders. Berthier and his men fired back, killing and wounding a handful who fell beneath the boots of their comrades and were trampled as the Russians surged on. Then both sides were locked in a vicious melee over the jumbled pile of church pews, striking out with bayonet and musket butts as weapons fired around them.

Napoleon advanced his weapon, his heart pounding with the excitement and terror of battle. He saw the sash of an officer in front of him and thrust his weapon forward, over the barricade. The officer saw the danger at the last moment and ducked, leaving the point to thrust into the air beside his head. Then he snatched out a pistol and aimed it at Napoleon, his lips parting in a triumphant grin as he took aim. Napoleon could not help flinching, but he was caught between two burly guardsmen and there were more men behind him so that he could not move. The Russian cocked his weapon and slipped his finger inside the trigger guard. Before he could fire, a French bayonet stabbed through the sleeve, thrusting the extended arm to one side so that the pistol fired harmlessly into the wall as the officer cried out in pain.

'Sire!' Berthier cried out in alarm. 'You must get back!'

Napoleon shook his head and turned on another enemy, gritting his teeth as he made to thrust with the bayonet. Then hands grabbed his arm and hauled him roughly back from the barricade. Napoleon turned round with a fierce expression and looked up to see one of his grenadiers looking at him with wide eyes.

'What are you doing?' the Emperor demanded.

'Saving your fucking life, sire,' the guardsman replied through clenched teeth. 'You trying to get yourself killed? Then where would we be?'

Napoleon opened his mouth to protest, but the soldier firmly steered him away from the fight.

'Leave the fighting to us as gets paid for it, sire,' he said firmly, and turned away to re-join his companions as they faced a steadily growing number of enemy pressing into the church, forcing the barricade and its defenders back. Napoleon could see that it was only a question of time before the Russians' superior numbers forced Berthier and his men to give way and then the defenders would be quickly overwhelmed and cut down. He tightened his grip on the musket and prepared to step back into the fight.

There was a crash from outside the church as a volley was fired. Both sides started momentarily and stared out into the street. Then there was a cry from one of the men at the windows.

'It's the Guard! The Imperial Guard is here!'

The men of the bodyguard and the staff officers cheered and flung themselves back against the Russians who had made it into the church. Already panic had seized the enemy and they backed away, cramming themselves through the entrance and into the street. Another volley ripped through their ranks and then, with a roar, the men of the Imperial Guard charged down the street, scattering the Russians who stood before the church. There was a brief skirmish as the guardsmen killed those who resisted and then chased after the stream of enemy soldiers running back down the street.

Inside the church the defenders cheered and clapped each other on the shoulder. Napoleon drew a deep breath as he handed his musket to one of the guardsmen. Berthier came up to him, grinning like a boy, bloodied sword in hand.

'Haven't seen action like that in years, sire.'

'Let's hope we never have to again,' Napoleon replied. 'Now then, we must act quickly. Those two battalions aren't going to restore the centre of the line by themselves. As soon as the enemy re-form they will counter-attack and sweep them aside.' He thought for a moment and then nodded grimly to himself. 'There's only one thing I can do to save the army. Murat must charge the Russian centre.'

'But he will be needed for the pursuit, sire. Once the battle is won.'

'It won't be won. Not now. Not without Murat. He must charge. Murat must buy us the time to re-form our line and for Ney and Davout to move into position. He must charge at once. See to it.'

The snow had almost stopped as Murat's cavalry, eighty squadrons of superbly mounted men, trotted forward to the right of the town in a vast column of brilliant uniforms and gleaming horseflesh. The officers in the church tower gazed on the spectacle with awe, and desperate hope. Only Murat could save the Grand Army now. The chasseurs led the charge, carving a path through the re-forming infantry column that the two battalions of the Imperial Guard had driven out of Eylau. Across the front of the French centre the enemy recoiled and then fled, running for the main Russian line stretching across the ridge one and a half miles away. Murat's cavalry chased them down without mercy, sabres flashing as his men struck again and again at enemy fugitives, leaving bodies scattered across the battlefield to add to the corpses of Augereau's men.

As Napoleon watched the charge through his telescope he could just pick out the flamboyant uniform of Murat at the head of the second wave of cavalry, brandishing his riding crop as he urged his men on. The vast column of horsemen charged, through the remnants of the first Russian line and up the slope towards the ridge. The crews of the cannon that had cut Augereau's men to ribbons fired a few last shots at the oncoming French cavalry and then turned and ran for the safety of the squares that were forming along the Russian centre. The cavalry raced on, engulfing the squares and passing on through the heart of the enemy army. A handful of men paused by the abandoned guns to drive iron spikes into the vents with small mallets to make the cannon unusable for the rest of the battle.

Even Napoleon was taken aback by the grandeur and shock effect of the cavalry charge. Europe had seen nothing like it, and mounted as they were on the pick of the Prussian horses captured after Jena the French riders were invincible. The enemy's cavalry attempted a counter-attack but their mounts were lighter and easily brushed aside. The last wave of French horsemen disappeared over the ridge and for a moment a brief lull hung over the battlefield as the battered French soldiers took full advantage of the respite Murat had bought them and began to re-form their line. A message arrived from Davout informing the Emperor that the marshal's corps was in position and ready to begin its flanking attack.

'But where is Ney?' Napoleon fumed. 'Does he not know that he is needed if we are to deliver a fatal blow to the enemy? Where the devil is Ney?'

As noon passed and the skies began to clear, there was a sudden flurry of activity along the ridge and a moment later the French cavalry reappeared over the crest, scattering some of the enemy soldiers before they rode back down the slope, cutting down any Russians that remained in their path, and returned to the flat area south of Eylau where they had been positioned at the start of the battle.

The sound of cannon fire from the right flank announced that Davout was beginning to launch his attack on the Russian left and all eyes in the church tower turned in that direction. As the afternoon wore on and the sounds of fighting intensified the first reports from Davout claimed that the enemy to his front was steadily being forced back. Still there was no sign of Ney and Napoleon's frustration and anger at his subordinate's tardiness tore at his self-control so that he stamped a foot angrily.

'Why does Ney not march to the sound of the guns? Has he not learned the first principle of command?'

Berthier finally brought news of Ney late in the afternoon, just as word arrived from Davout that the Russians had heavily reinforced their left flank and were pressing Davout's men back in the gathering dusk.

'Sire, report from Marshal Soult's headquarters,' Bethier panted after his hurried climb up the stairs. 'Ney's corps is arriving on the left flank. He intends to attack at once.'

'How good of him,' Napoleon replied acidly. 'He may be just in time to save us from defeat rather than complete the victory that should have been mine.'

The rolling thunder of artillery sounded from the north, and as the Emperor and his staff waited for further news the winter night drew in and darkness crept across the battlefield, punctuated by squibs of bright light as cannon and musket volleys from both sides were fired into the gloom. As Napoleon hoped, Ney's attack forced the Russians to ease the pressure on Davout. Slowly, as the night dragged on, the firing on both sides petered out. By midnight the battlefield was silent, save for the pitiful cries of the wounded still lying on the frozen, snow-covered ground.

Napoleon had descended from the tower and stood in the nave warming himself at a fire that had been made from the pews. He had summoned his marshals to consider the next day's action. His officers gathered round the fire, faces lit in the wavering glow of the flames. The exhaustion of the day's fighting was etched into their faces as they attended their Emperor. Napoleon turned first to Ney.

'Would you care to explain why it took you so long to join us today, Marshal?'

Ney frowned and there was no hiding the anger in his reply. 'I did not receive your order to close up on the main army until after two in the afternoon, sire.'

'Did you not hear the guns? You must have done.'

'The wind and the snow prevented the sound from carrying to us, sire.'

Even though it was true, it still sounded like an excuse and Ney shifted uneasily under the gaze of the other officers. Napoleon stared at him for a moment before taking a deep breath and turning to the rest.

'We have been hit hard, gentlemen, according to the first strength returns to reach headquarters. Only a quarter of Augereau's corps are still fit to fight and there have been heavy casualties to all formations, except Ney's. We can only hope that the enemy have also suffered badly.'

Soult sniffed. 'They have, sire. Our bullets were not made of cotton.'

'Thank you, Soult,' Napoleon said testily. 'The question is, will the Russians still have any fight left in them come the morning? If so, will our men be able to withstand an attack? Should we even consider a withdrawal? Your thoughts, gentlemen?'

'We should attack,' Ney said firmly. 'Now. While the enemy are still shaken. Seize the initiative, sire.'

Napoleon shook his head. 'The army is in no condition to attack. The men are exhausted and I dare say their only thought at the moment is finding somewhere warm enough to spend the night so that they don't freeze to death.'

Augereau cleared his throat. 'Sire, we cannot attack. Equally we cannot retreat. The men's morale is low enough as it is. If we turn from the enemy now we risk a general breakdown in discipline. If the enemy pursue us, we're finished. We must hold our position, for a day at least. While the men recover.'

Several of the other senior officers nodded and Napoleon considered the matter as he rubbed the bristles on his chin. There seemed to be little choice. 'Very well, then. The army stands to for the night, in case the enemy mount an attack. When dawn comes, Ney's corps will open an assault on the enemy's flank. The entire Imperial Guard will move up to the centre of the line and attempt to break through the Russian position. That's the best we can hope for, gentlemen. Return to your commands to await orders. You are dismissed.'

Before the sun rose over the battlefield, a pale orange disc against a grey sky, Napoleon's fears for the losses incurred by the Grand Army were borne out as the last of the strength returns reached headquarters. There had been over twenty thousand casualties, nearly a third of the army. By the gathering light of the dawn the battlefield looked like an open-air slaughterhouse. A vast expanse of corpses, individual and heaped, men and horses, marked the passage of Augereau's ill-fated advance, the Russian counter-attack, and Murat's charge. The bodies had frozen in the night and the cold had claimed the lives of many of those who had lain wounded on the field.

At first light the French outposts had reported no sign of the Russians and now cavalry patrols reported that the enemy army had pulled back during the night and was retreating to the east. As Napoleon inspected the battlefield in the company of his marshals he could see that his men had reached the end of their endurance. As he approached, they rose sullenly to their feet, and when their officers called on them to cheer their Emperor there were few cries of 'Long live the Emperor!' and many more calls of 'Long live peace!' instead.

Napoleon's expression was fixed in a cold fury as he passed on and his staff eyed him anxiously as they approached the small hillock where the square of French infantrymen had perished the day before. As they stood on its crest, surrounded by thousands of stiffening bodies, Ney shook his head. 'What a massacre. And without result.'

Napoleon rounded on him. 'Enough! We have won a victory here. The enemy are in full retreat and left us in possession of the battlefield.'

'Battlefield?' Ney spoke wearily. 'This is no battlefield, sire. It is the graveyard of the Grand Army.'

'Silence, Ney! It is a victory, I tell you. Berthier, you will draft a despatch to send to Paris. You will tell them that I won a great victory at Eylau, after a gallant fight by our men. You will say that we suffered seven thousand casualties, and inflicted at least twice that on the enemy. The despatch is to be copied and distributed across Europe.'

'And published in the army newspapers, sire?' asked Berthier.

Napoleon was silent for a moment and then shook his head. 'Not for the present. The men are too tired to read even good news.'

He stared round at his officers, challenging anyone to defy him. No one dared speak. Napoleon clasped his hands behind his back and abruptly turned and began to pick his way through the bodies as he made his way back towards Eylau. After a moment's hesitation his officers filed after him, in silence.

Despite what he had said Napoleon was under no illusion about the damage done to his men. The Grand Army could not continue the campaign. Cold, weary, hungry and badly shaken, they were in no condition to fight. There was nothing for it but to pull back, return to winter quarters and wait for spring to arrive.

Then the Russians must be beaten decisively and forced to make peace. Before the rest of Europe saw through the pretence that Eylau was any kind of victory and closed on Napoleon like wolves circling wounded prey.

Chapter 26

Arthur

London, February 1807

The cries from upstairs reached a new pitch and Arthur dropped the cards on the table and rose up from his chair to make for the door.

'Easy there, Arthur,' Richard said calmly from the other side of the table as he looked through his hand and made a quick calculation of the odds. 'I'll have another card, if you please.'

Arthur stared at him. 'Damn you and your cards! My wife is in pain. She needs me.'

'She is in labour, Arthur,' Richard replied with the casual indifference of a man. 'It is a natural part of the process of giving birth. The pain will pass and you will have a child. Kitty is in good hands. There is nothing you can do to help, so come and sit, and continue the game.'

A fresh cry of agony came from the room above and Arthur hesitated for an instant before he made himself resume his seat and pick up the deck of cards. However, his eyes fixed on the ceiling and his brother had to cough lightly to get his attention.

'Another card, if you please.'

'What? Oh, yes.' Arthur glanced down and flipped the top card over on to the table in front of Richard. A nine of diamonds.

'Damn.' Richard frowned.

Arthur absent-mindedly gathered in the cards and added his brother's stake to the small pile of coins in front of him. As he dealt the next hand he spoke with forced calm.

'Is it always like this?'

'What?'

'All this pain? The suffering of the wife and the anxiety of the husband?'

'Oh, yes.' Richard smiled. 'It was the same every time with

Hyacinthe. A lot of noise, shouting, insults and so on. I soon learned that it was best to keep out of it and let the womenfolk tend to her.'

'I think it would be best if I went and comforted her. Kitty needs me.'

'No she doesn't,' Richard replied firmly. 'Trust me. Now deal me another card.'

Arthur obliged and his brother examined his hand and laid it down. 'I think I'll stick with that.'

Arthur flipped his over. An ace and a king. Richard frowned as his stake was swept away once more.

'I came here to offer you comfort and support and you insist on fleecing me. I've had enough of cards. Besides, your mind is not on the game.'

'How could it be?' Arthur replied with a nod to the ceiling as Kitty cried out again. 'My mind is on my wife and her suffering.'

'Then we must find other means of diverting your attention.' Richard poured himself another glass of port from the decanter and topped up Arthur's glass. 'Drink. It will help. Now then, I've been meaning to ask you, how long do you think the present government will last? It seems that the so called ministry of all the talents is missing the most vital talent of all in the field of politics, namely that of self-preservation.'

Arthur could not help smiling as he nodded his agreement. 'They do seem intent on failure.'

'As well as undermining me as much as they can.'

'That is just the Whigs, Richard. Most of the Tories are ambivalent about the charges against you, if not actually supportive of your position.'

'That is small comfort. And I do question why my own brother lends his support to such a coalition of my enemies.'

Arthur sighed wearily. 'Our country is at war, Richard. We cannot afford any unnecessary dissention in Parliament. So I must support the government, even if some of its members are hell-bent on ruining your reputation.'

'War?' Richard mused. 'A strange kind of war it seems to me. After Trafalgar and Austerlitz Britain rules the seas while France rules the land, and we are condemned to regard each other warily, but unable to fight.'

'That will change one day. And Britain has the advantage of being able to take the war to the enemy. Bonaparte does not have that choice. As for your situation, I wish it were otherwise. However, I doubt the present government will last much longer. And if Grenville and his coalition government fall, I pray to God that the next ministry is more determined to continue the fight against France.'

'I pray so.' Richard paused at a fresh cry from upstairs. When it had passed he continued, 'Grenville is doomed if he persists in attempting to mollify the Irish and the Catholics.'

Arthur nodded. As ever, the opponents of British rule in Ireland had drawn great comfort from Napoleon's triumphs and once news of Jena reached the ears of the Irish revolutionaries there had been uprising in the countryside. Several land agents had been murdered and some estates burned to the ground. As usual, the officials in Dublin had called out the army and the militia and suppressed the rebels mercilessly, hanging any ringleaders they captured and scattering the bands of rebels with a volley or two of musket fire. The spirit of rebellion still festered in Irish hearts and in an attempt to assuage such passions the government had proposed to ease some of the restrictions placed on Catholics.

'What else can the government do?' Arthur shrugged. 'Any prospect of peace with France died with Charles Fox. Britain is renewing the struggle and needs order. If that means satisfying the demands of the Catholics, so be it.'

'Whatever the feelings of people here in England? Surely you remember what happened when that man Gordon stirred up the rabble the last time there was an attempt at Catholic relief?'

'How could I forget?' Arthur vividly recalled the days of rioting, the burning down of public buildings and the bloody manner in which the army had restored order to the streets of London. 'But we were not at war then. People are more mindful of the need to do what is necessary to beat Bonaparte.'

'You think so?' Richard looked surprised. 'Arthur, you are a fine soldier, but a poor politician. Forgive me for saying so, but the national interest is not at the top of most politicians' list of priorities. If political capital can be made out of resisting Catholic relief, then it will be so. As surely as night follows day. Why, I have even heard that the King himself intends to intervene to prevent the passage of any such bill through Parliament.'

'That would be an act of madness. He would not presume. Surely?'

'Would he not?' Richard smiled. 'And as for madness, let us say that his majesty has hardly availed himself of a full measure of sanity since he came to the throne.'

Like many Englishmen Arthur did not wish to be reminded of King George's mental infirmity in an age when the very principle of monarchy was under widespread attack. He cleared his throat nervously. 'I am certain that the King would not challenge the authority of Parliament over such an issue. Especially when Britain is at war and a man's service to his country is more important than the question of his faith.'

Richard was about to reply when Arthur raised his hand to still his brother's tongue. He felt a sudden icy grip of terror fix on the back of his neck.

'Whatever's the matter?' Richard asked.

'It's gone quiet.' Arthur glanced at the ceiling and muttered, 'By God, if anything's happened to Kitty . . .'

The two brothers sat in silence for a moment, and Arthur felt his chest tighten anxiously at the sound of footsteps on the stairs. A moment later the door to the drawing room opened and Dr Hoxter entered. His shirtsleeves were rolled up as he wiped his hands clean on a bloodied piece of cloth. Arthur instantly feared the worst and swallowed nervously.

'Kitty . . . is she all right, doctor?'

'She is fine, sir.' Dr Hoxter nodded and then smiled warmly. 'And so is your son.'

'My son?' Arthur felt the tension drain from his body, to be replaced by the warmth of love and unbridled joy. 'I have a son.'

'Indeed, sir. A fine-looking young fellow if ever I saw one.'

Richard stood up, reached across the table and grasped Arthur's hand. 'Then I'll be the very first to offer my congratulations!'

Arthur turned to his brother, still dazed by the realisation that he was a father. 'Thank you. Thank you, Richard.'

Dr Hoxter tucked the cloth into his waistcoat pocket and strode across the drawing room to shake Arthur's hand in turn. 'And here's my congratulations to you too, sir.'

Arthur was no longer able to contain his delight and smiled broadly at the doctor and his brother. 'Bless my soul. I'm a father!'

Richard laughed. 'Welcome to the club. Once the first flush of pride and novelty has worn off you'll soon discover what a mixed blessing paternity can be. Take it from one who knows.'

'Amen to that,' said the doctor.

'May I see the boy? And my wife, of course.'

'I rather think Lady Wellesley would be rather aggrieved if you didn't.' Dr Hoxter grinned. 'Come along, sir.'

As the doctor turned towards the door Arthur looked to his brother with an awkward expression. 'Do you mind?'

'No.' Richard grinned. 'I have had more than my share of such events. You go ahead. I'll leave now.'

Arthur nodded his thanks. 'I'm sure we will speak soon.'

'You can count on it. New fathers are inclined to be boorishly persistent in telling all and sundry about their status. I was no exception to that rule.'

Arthur said a quick farewell and followed the doctor upstairs to the master bedroom. As they entered he saw Kitty in their bed, propped up against several cushions as she rested from her exertions. Her hair was plastered to her scalp by perspiration and her skin was pallid and waxy in appearance. She smiled weakly at her husband.

'Arthur. Dear Arthur. Come to me.' She raised a hand and he saw it tremble with the effort as he strode across the room and sat down beside her, taking her fingers and giving them a gentle squeeze.

'I hear that we have a son.'

Kitty smiled. 'Yes.'

'Where is he?'

'The midwife is just cleaning him up,' Dr Hoxter explained.

Arthur nodded and turned back to Kitty. 'And you, my dear, how do you feel?'

'Tired.' She smiled bleakly. 'Very tired.'

Arthur leaned forward and kissed her on the cheek. 'Kitty, you have made me so proud. I have never felt so happy.'

'I am glad, Arthur dear.' She stared into his eyes and he felt her fingers tighten around his. 'I so want to make you happy, my love.'

'And you have.' Arthur smiled back and felt a stab of guilt in his heart as he recalled the bitter disappointment of their wedding and the days, weeks and months that followed it. He took a deep breath and continued, 'I could not have asked for a better wife. And mother to my child.'

The door to the adjoining bathroom clicked open and Dr Hoxter clapped his hands together. 'Ah! Here's the little fellow. Come to say hello to his father.'

Arthur turned and saw the midwife approaching the bed with a bundle in her arms. She laid the swaddled infant gently down beside Kitty and Arthur leaned forward for a better look at his son. The face was tiny, wrinkled and pink and the lips moved slightly. The eyes were shut and the hands were raised on either side of the head, each one half clenched and no bigger than a penny.

Arthur felt his heart swell with such emotion as he had never felt before. He had a strange impulse to cry and only just stifled it as he swallowed and spoke with a tremor. 'May I hold him?'

The midwife looked across the bed. 'Why, of course you can, Sir Arthur. The moment he has fed.'

'Fed? But he's only just been born. By God, is the boy determined to eat me out of house and home the instant he is brought into the world?'

The midwife leaned towards Kitty. 'If you'd pick the child up, my lady, and offer him your breast.'

'Breast?' Kitty looked round, startled. 'Offer him my breast?'

'Why yes, my lady. Of course. How else is the young 'un to feed?'

'Oh, yes. I see.' Kitty looked up at Arthur and the doctor apprehensively. 'Would you mind leaving the room? I would feel more comfortable.'

'Yes,' Arthur replied awkwardly. 'Certainly, my dear.' He turned to the doctor. 'I imagine you could use refreshment, sir.'

'Indeed I could!' Dr Hoxter paced towards the door, then stopped abruptly and turned towards Arthur and Kitty. 'Have you decided on names for the lad yet?'

Arthur nodded. 'He is to be called Arthur Richard.'

'Capital!' Dr Hoxter rubbed his hands together. 'Then let us go and toast the health and long life of Master Arthur Richard Wellesley.'

The child thrived well enough, in spite of Kitty's misgivings that she would not be able to feed him adequately. The pregnancy had not been comfortable on her thin frame and the birth itself had taken the best part of a day before the baby was delivered. She remained in bed for several days to recover from the ordeal. Arthur would have spent more time with his wife and son but for the increasingly serious situation in Parliament. The government was besieged by opposition to some of its more progressive measures. In addition to the Catholic relief bill there was the vexed question of the abolition of the slave trade. The debates raged on through the remainder of February and into March. It was on the seventeenth day of that month, emerging from the chamber as dusk fell across London, that Arthur caught the first scent of a new crisis. Members and clerks were clustered about the hall talking in excited tones. Arthur crossed to the nearest group and nudged the elbow of a Tory member he recognised.

'Hello, Sidcup. What's the news?'

Sidcup glanced round. 'Have you not heard? The King demanded a meeting with the Prime Minister this morning.'

'What for?'

'To discuss the Catholic relief bill, what else? You know as well as any how bitterly he opposes it.' Sidcup raised his eyebrows. 'Now it seems that his majesty has told Lord Grenville that he will not give his assent to the bill, if it is passed. Not only that, but he has demanded that the Cabinet swear an oath never to bring such a bill before Parliament again.'

'By God,' Arthur said in shock. 'The King can't be serious.'

'He is. Deadly serious by all accounts and he won't take no for an answer. And you have to admire his complete lack of tact in making his demand today.'

'Eh?' Arthur frowned a moment before he got the point. 'Ah, I see. St Patrick's day.'

'Quite. Ever the sensitive monarch, our George.'

'But this is madness,' Arthur said quietly, glancing round to make sure that he was not overheard. 'The country is already divided enough over the issue. Now the King threatens to make it a constitutional matter.'

'So it seems,' Sidcup agreed, and smiled ruefully. 'We live in interesting times, Sir Arthur. Pray that his majesty comes to his senses before it is too late.'

Arthur returned to his home on Harley Street filled with a sense of growing despair over King George's intransigence. It was a divisive enough prospect for England, but in Ireland it would play straight into the hands of those who wanted an end to British rule. Arthur could think of nothing so calculated to foment a general uprising. His dark mood was evident to Kitty the moment he joined her in the parlour. She sat in a chair by the fire. Beside her the infant lay in his crib, fists twitching furiously as he wriggled on his back and made a strained gurgling noise.

'Arthur, what is the matter?'

He forced himself to soften his expression and smiled as he leaned over Kitty and kissed the top of her head. 'It does not matter now, my dear. How are you today?'

'Well, thank you. My strength is returning.'

'Good. And our son?' Arthur knelt down and tickled the infant's stomach gently.

Kitty smiled fondly as she glanced down into the crib. 'He has been feeding like the five thousand. I don't know where he fits it all. He's like a bottomless well.'

Arthur wrinkled his nose as a familiar odour rose up from the crib. 'I fear that the boy's bottom has welled up somewhat.'

Kitty laughed and swatted her husband gently. 'I will have him changed. Then he can be put to bed before we eat.' She looked at her husband closely for a moment and then touched his arm. 'Is there a problem? What happened today?'

'It's not important. Not yet, at least.'

'Can you tell me about it?'

Arthur shook his head faintly. 'I'd rather not even think about it.' He stood up. 'I'll be in the study while you attend to the boy. Send for me when dinner is served.'

'Yes, my dear.' Kitty looked at him reproachfully. 'You can talk to me about whatever it is that concerns you.'

Arthur smiled and patted her on the shoulder. 'I know. But not tonight, my dear. In any case, there is nothing we can do about it.'

He took a last look at his son and then turned to leave the parlour. Kitty watched him go, with a sad expression at his subdued mood, and then rose from her chair to call the nursemaid and have the nappy changed.

Eight days later the bill to abolish the slave trade was put to the vote before Parliament. When the count had finished and the members were allowed back in the chamber the house waited in silence as the spokesman for the tellers turned to address the speaker.

'The ayes, two hundred and eighty-three. The nays, sixteen. The ayes have it.'

The house erupted with a mixture of cheers from the abolitionists, drowning out the cries of protest from the supporters of the trade. As tears of triumph glistened in his eyes, William Wilberforce was surrounded by supporters eager to offer their congratulations on the success of his lifetime's work. Despite his ambivalence Arthur was moved by the sight and could only hope that the man's moral victory did nothing to undermine his nation at the hour of its greatest peril. The shouting and excited hubbub gradually died down as the speaker rapped his rod on the floor and called for silence. Eventually the chamber was quiet again and the speaker waited a moment before he indicated Lord Grenville.

'The Prime Minister wishes to address the House.'

The attention of the members was fixed on Lord Grenville as he rose from his seat and paused a moment to draw a breath before he spoke. When he did, there was no mistaking the weary frustration in his tone. Arthur was surprised, since Grenville was a firm supporter of Wilberforce's long campaign, and he leaned forward to hear the Prime Minister's words as clearly as possible.

'I can think of no better piece of legislation to honour the service this government has given to our people. The abolition of such an abhorrent trade in humanity will send a message to the world concerning the finest values that Britain holds dear even in this darkest hour, when we are beset by an enemy intent on tearing the very concept of liberty to shreds.'

A murmur of approval rippled through the chamber, and Grenville raised a hand to signal silence before he continued. 'As all gathered here will know, the abolition of the slave trade is just one measure of the freedoms the government intended to deliver to the people. It had been my wish, my dream, to offer freedom from religious prejudice. I had ordered the drafting of a bill to permit the entry of Catholics into the armed forces of our country. It was my hope that this would be the first of many measures to end the unjust oppression of so-called dissenters in these islands of ours. However, his majesty saw fit to demand that my ministers and I disown the bill, and swear never to bring similar legislation before this House again. After due consideration I have to tell the House that we are not prepared to swear such an oath.'

Grenville paused and looked round at the members watching him intently. Arthur could already sense the importance of the Prime Minister's next words and felt his stomach tighten with anxiety as Grenville cleared his throat and concluded his announcement.

'It is, therefore, with the greatest of regret that I announce my resignation, and that of all my Cabinet ministers, with immediate effect.'

Arthur felt his heart sink. At a time when it was vital for the nation to be united, it was folly for the King to undermine his government. If a coalition of the political factions could not succeed, then what hope was there for the future of Britain?

Chapter 27

'The Duke of Portland? You can't be serious.' Arthur shook his head. 'The man is almost permanently dosed up to the eyeballs with opium. One can hardly ever get a coherent word out of him. In any case, he's too old for the post.'

'Nevertheless, he has a powerful faction behind him and the King has asked him to form a government,' Richard replied as he helped himself to another lamb chop and then sent his servant away from the breakfast table. 'At least it means the Tories will be in power again, and we'll have no more Whiggish liberality for a while. For that at least I am grateful.'

Arthur could understand his brother's feeling well enough. It had been the Whigs who had been behind the calls to prosecute Richard for exceeding his authority during his term as Governor General of the colonies in India. With the Tories back in power there was a good chance that any prosecution could be delayed for years, or better still quietly abandoned in the fullness of time. No wonder Richard was in a fine mood this morning, when he had invited Arthur to join him for breakfast.

'Of course,' Richard continued, as he cut the fat from his chop, 'I will have some influence in the new government, even if Portland does not immediately offer me a Cabinet post. That's understandable under the circumstances. Once the cloud of impropriety has lifted from my shoulders I will be back in office. Meanwhile, it would be most useful if something could be found for you, Arthur.'

'Me?' Arthur had been about to bite into a slice of buttered bread, and now lowered it as he stared at his brother. 'But I am a backbencher. And I supported the last government. I hardly think Portland will be in such a forgiving mood as you imagine.'

'You supported Grenville out of a sense of patriotism. The need for order and all that. You were not the only Tory to take his shilling. In any case, Portland's position is not so secure that he would turn down the opportunity of recruiting another member of Parliament to his side, particularly as you are my brother and my opinion counts for something.'

Arthur pursed his lips and made no comment on Richard's hubris. Besides, there was truth in what he said. The present situation offered opportunities for those ready to grasp them, and at present Arthur's military career had stalled in the absence of any major operations against France. That meant abandoning his disdain for political factions, and joining the ranks of the Tories. In truth, Arthur felt that his values were largely the same as those espoused by the Tories, but he was wary of allowing himself to become embroiled in a web of political obligations that might tie his hands at a future date when it might be best to exercise independent judgement. It would be an even more bitter pill indeed if he were forced to act against his conscience.

Arthur glanced across the table at his brother. 'Is there any word on who Portland intends to include in his Cabinet?'

Richard nodded and finished chewing a mouthful of lamb before he replied. 'It's no secret that he wants Castlereagh to return to the War Office, and George Canning is likely to be offered the post of Foreign Secretary.'

'That will make for some interesting Cabinet meetings,' Arthur mused. 'Those two are hardly on speaking terms as it is.'

'I know.' Richard smiled. 'What wouldn't I give to be there when the altercations begin? Of course, the tricky bit will be finding someone willing to take on the role of Lord Lieutenant of Ireland. With all the trouble there has been there recently, it's something of a poisoned chalice. Unless the war is prosecuted more actively and with greater success, we shall have a perpetual state of resentment and rebellion in Ireland.'

'Well at least with Canning and Castlereagh behind the war effort we can be sure that it will be prosecuted with vigour. It will need to be, for I can see no early end to the conflict.'

Richard glanced up, knife and fork poised over the remains of his lamb chop. 'Indeed? Why is that? Do please tell me, Arthur.'

'Very well.' Arthur collected his thoughts. 'Foremost because of Bonaparte's continued run of victories. Even if Eylau was no triumph, the Russians were still forced to retreat and will continue to be cautious while they have but a few Prussians left to aid them in continuing the war with France. If Bonaparte strips men from his garrisons across Europe he will be able to renew his advance in the spring, and no doubt force a decisive enough victory to persuade the Tsar to negotiate. The only hope for us is that the Tsar continues to defy Bonaparte and retreats into the heart of Russia, drawing the French army after him. But I doubt that Bonaparte would be rash enough to take the risk.'

'Risk? What risk?'

Arthur looked at his brother in surprise. 'Why, Richard, have you any idea of the distances involved? Even the best supplied and disciplined of armies would be broken by such a campaign. Believe me, such an undertaking would dwarf the marches our forces had to make in India. Nor would Bonaparte be able to conduct his operations for long. Any invasion of Russian soil would have to be complete by the time autumn came for fear of being caught in the Russian winter.' Arthur shook his head. 'I can't think for a moment that Napoleon would be so rash as to lead his army against the Tsar. It would be sheer madness to attempt it.' He paused and sipped his coffee before continuing. 'Let us assume that he makes peace with Russia. Then Britain alone remains at war with France. The Royal Navy makes French invasion unlikely, and our lack of manpower makes British invasion of the continent an impossibility. So we have a stalemate. For the present. Fortunately Bonaparte has committed a grievous error in banning trade between the continent and Britain. He has caused great resentment amongst his allies and subject territories. In time that will play into our hands. Meanwhile, we must offer the European powers some hope.'

'It would make a fine change from offering them money,' Richard interrupted sourly. 'Pitt nearly bankrupted the country with the vast sums we handed over to our allies. And much good it did us.'

'I'm afraid that Britain will still have to finance any allies we may find in the future. But there are other means to inspire them. Since you mentioned Pitt, let me tell you of a viable scheme I suggested to him not long before he died. A way to keep the war open on land. One that would vex Bonaparte, and prove that he was not quite so invincible as his propaganda machine makes out. That is to wage war in the Iberian Peninsula.'

'Spain and Portugal? How would that profit Britain?'

'While Spain is an ally of France she is a legitimate target for hostility. Spain is also weak militarily and even a modestly sized British army could create havoc. Perhaps enough to force Napoleon to send forces to assist his Spanish allies. And thereby provide the means for us to demonstrate that French soldiers and French generals can be defeated. News of such defeats would be music to the ears of other continental powers.'

'That may be,' Richard agreed. 'But what if Napoleon himself took to the field in Spain? What if he inflicted a crushing defeat on your modestly sized British army? Then such an intervention would only serve to enhance his reputation, diminish ours and discourage any potential allies.'

'There is that risk,' Arthur admitted. 'The commander of our forces would have to be very circumspect indeed. He would have to avoid any battle where there was any risk of defeat. The key to our strategy would have to lie in tying down enemy forces and defeating them in detail as and when the opportunity arose. We would also enjoy certain advantages denied to the French. Since we have won the war at sea we could freely supply our men along the coast, and even land detachments to cause trouble at our whim. Our enemies, however, would have long land-based chains of supply and communication stretching back to France. Better still, the French army's custom of living off the land would win them few friends in Spain. To the extent that it might well cause Spain to switch her allegiance to our side.'

'That is a far-fetched supposition, some might argue.'

'It is only a possibility,' Arthur conceded. 'But I can see no other profitable deployment of our land forces on the continent. Certainly not one that offers as much chance of undermining Bonaparte.' He drained his cup and set it down in its saucer. 'It is certainly what I would do if I were deciding Britain's military policy.'

Richard thought for a moment and then nodded. 'It makes sense. I might mention it to Castlereagh when I next speak to him. It would be interesting to see what he makes of it.'

Arthur nodded, though he did not put much store in the prospect of politicians understanding such a strategic vision. Few of them had any military experience to speak of, and those who did could be readily discounted for having abandoned a military career in favour of a political one.

'In any case,' Richard continued, 'it would be useful to put your name in front of Castlereagh, should he be considering any military appointments in the near future.'

It was little more than a week after his breakfast with Richard that Arthur was invited to an interview with the Duke of Richmond. In the intervening time the Prime Minister had confirmed the appointments of Castlereagh and Canning and most of the other cabinet positions. The Duke had been tipped for high office but as yet there had been no public announcement and Arthur was curious to discover his reasons for requesting an interview.

They met in a small office in Whitehall. The Duke of Richmond, a rounded, grey-haired man with a good-humoured twinkle in his eyes, clasped Arthur's hand and greeted him with a warm smile before ushering him to a worn leather chair and then pulling another up so that they sat close together beside a grimy window overlooking the street.

'Your brother, Richard, tells me you have a fine mind, and a great deal of integrity.'

Arthur smiled slightly. 'It seems he forgot to mention my modesty while he was at it, your grace.'

The Duke laughed. 'Well, perhaps he knew that you would mention it. Anyway, let's not waste time on pleasantries, Sir Arthur. I imagine you are burning with curiosity concerning the purpose of this interview. Let me quench those flames forthwith. I take it that you have heard that Portland has had the devil of a job finding someone to take on the Lord Lieutenancy of Ireland. Beaufort and Rutland turned it down before the Prime Minister approached me.' The Duke puffed his cheeks out with a stage sigh. 'And so I have accepted the position.'

'May I offer my congratulations, your grace?'

'Commiserations would be more appropriate under the circumstances, eh?'

Arthur did not reply and merely smiled back as the Duke continued. 'Be that as it may, I accepted on condition that I had a free hand in appointing my subordinates. Can't be doing with having a pack of well-connected but ignorant young men to carry out my orders. Not with the current sensitivity of the situation in Ireland. I need men with ability, discipline and organisation. In short, men like you, Sir Arthur.'

'It's kind of you to say so, your grace,' Arthur responded. 'Do you intend to offer me a position in your administration, then?'

'Yes, of course. I am sure you did not think you were here on the basis of some casual social appointment?'

'Well, no, your grace.'

The Duke leaned forward and prodded Arthur on the chest. 'I am offering you the post of Chief Secretary. What do you say?'

Arthur struggled to hide his astonishment. The Chief Secretary was the most powerful office in Ireland beneath that of the Lord Lieutenant. A responsible position indeed, and one that might well make his political career. The only difficulty that occurred to Arthur concerned the obligation that such a favour might carry in the future. Was this the first step in selling his soul to the venomous world of political factions? In truth he would far rather be fighting the French, but at least this offer was a chance to serve his country usefully while he waited for a military command.

Arthur looked directly into the Duke's eyes as he responded. 'It is a very generous offer. Might I ask why you have made it to me?'

'It's simple enough. Your brother recommended you, and I know that you have served as an aide at Dublin Castle. You were a member of the Irish Parliament before it was abolished with the Act of Union, and you had some experience in the Treasury before you were sent away to serve in India. From what Richard tells me, you as good as ruled the kingdom of Mysore for some years, and made a damned fine fist of it. Just the sort of man to help me bring order to Ireland, I'd say. That's why. Now, young man, will you accept?'

'Yes, your grace,' Arthur replied at once. 'It would be an honour to serve you.'

'Chief Secretary?' Kitty's eyebrows rose as she held the baby to her shoulder and rubbed his back gently. Little Arthur had wind and duly obliged with a faint burp. 'That's quite a step up, isn't it?'

'To be sure.' Arthur held his arms out. 'May I hold him?'

Kitty smiled as she handed the infant over and returned to her seat by the fire as her husband held his son in the crook of his arm and began to sway in what he assumed was a comforting motion. As he smiled down at the tiny face Arthur continued, 'It's a fine preparation for high office here in London, and it carries a salary of six and a half thousand pounds.'

'Goodness!'

'I thought that would please you, my dear. Now even that brother of yours might cease to look down his nose at me.'

'Oh, I'm sure that it won't be too long before the positions are reversed.'

Arthur recalled the years before India, when Kitty's brother had been adamant that she could not marry a man with as few prospects as Arthur. The memory was like an open sore and he said quietly, 'I wish I could say that the thought does not appeal to me.'

Kitty ignored the comment. 'We are to move to Dublin, then?'

'Yes, my dear.'

'When?'

'As soon as I am confirmed in office. By the end of April at the latest.'

Kitty sighed. 'It does not seem so long ago that we moved in here. I imagine it would be nice to feel settled into a home.'

'That day will come, Kitty. For now we are off to Dublin. I will keep this house on as I will need accommodation in London when I am here on parliamentary business.'

'Oh.' She looked at him reproachfully. 'Are you to be away from me, from us, often?'

'Quite often,' Arthur replied lightly, 'but not for long. Be thankful I have been given a civil post, and not some military command in some godforsaken corner of the Caribbean. Then you would not see me from one year to the next.'

'I should hate that.'

'Well, it is not going to happen, my dear. Not now, at least.' Arthur laid his son down in the crib. The infant was fast asleep and lay still and silent. Arthur stared at him fondly for a moment and then took his wife's hand. 'Kitty, I am certain that this is a fine opportunity for me. Provided I perform sterling service for the Duke of Richmond, then I can surely make a name for myself. Something I can be proud of.'

'I am already proud of you, Arthur.'

He leaned forward and kissed her gently on the lips. 'Thank you.'

Arthur drew his head back and stared at her for a moment. Though she still seemed thin and wan he caught an echo of the young Kitty he had known in Ireland many years before and his heart quickened at the thought.

Kitty frowned at his intense expression, then asked tremulously, 'Arthur, what is it, dear?'

He smiled. 'Tell the nursemaid to take the boy to his room. I think we should have an early night.'

There was a flash of anxiety in Kitty's eyes and she bit her lip before replying. 'Very well, my dearest. But please, be gentle with me. I am still not fully recovered from childbirth.'

'Of course, my dear. I will be as gentle as I can.'

Chapter 28

Dublin, April 1807

The new Chief Secretary and his small family moved into his official residence in Phoenix Park and while Kitty arranged to take on staff, and set up accounts with suppliers of wines and fine foods in the city, Arthur set to work at once. The parliamentary elections were being held, with the usual excitement, and not a little violence. In Wexford the Tory candidate had challenged his Whig opponent to a duel and shot him dead. It was not appropriate that so disputatious a politician should be allowed to sit in the Commons, and he was duly persuaded by Arthur to step aside for another candidate less disposed to settling political differences with firearms.

On his first day in his new appointment Arthur was introduced to his staff by the senior clerk, an elderly Dubliner named Thomas Stoper. Once Arthur had been escorted down the line of officials, failing to take in more than a handful of names and faces, Stoper showed the new Chief Secretary to his office, a large, panelled room with windows overlooking the courtyard. Arthur's attention was drawn to a pile of letters lying in a wooden tray on one side of the desk.

'What's all that?'

Stoper's gaze flicked briefly to the letters. 'They were delivered this mórning, sir.'

'Good God, all of them?'

'Yes, sir. It is not unusual for the first morning of a new appointment.'

'Not unusual?' Arthur frowned. 'Then be so good as to tell me what reason could possibly prompt so many letters.'

'That's easy enough, sir. I'll warrant that they are nearly all from people requesting appointments for themselves, or for friends and family.'

'Well, they can damn well wait then,' Arthur growled as he took his seat behind the desk and gestured to the chair opposite. 'Please sit down, Stoper.'

The senior clerk arched an eyebrow in brief surprise and then did as he was bid, settling stiffly as he met Arthur's gaze, his grey eyes steely in his thin face with its pinched cheeks.

'Now then, Stoper,' Arthur began briskly. 'My first duty is to see to the appointments that are in my purview. It is the will of the Lord Lieutenant that the best men are found for the job. That is to be given priority over patronage for its own sake.'

'Indeed, Sir Arthur?' Stoper smiled faintly. 'That would make a most welcome change. If it could be put into effect.'

'And why should it not be put into effect?'

Stoper eyed his superior closely for a moment before he replied. 'Forgive me, sir, but it is not the first time that I have heard of such an intention, and, laudable as it is, such an ideal does not long outlive its utterance. Forgive me for being blunt, sir.'

'You disapprove?'

'It is not my place to approve or disapprove of such affairs, sir. I merely wish to point out to you that his grace's intention of appointing on the basis of ability may not translate so easily into reality. I follow the affairs of the London Parliament closely, sir, and I know how finely things are balanced between the various political factions. Every favour counts, and the political capital conferred on a post such as Lord Lieutenant is not to be squandered recklessly. Any more than is the case with your position, sir. It follows that whatever his grace may intend, the reality is that patronage will be exercised according to political expediency rather than the requirements for the offices concerned.'

Arthur stared at the senior clerk in silence. The man had spoken out of turn and had offered opinions on affairs well outside the realms of his particular duties. Yet there was an earnestness about him and Arthur resolved to hear him out.

'It seems to me that you do not approve of political patronage.'

'I have no quarrel with it in principle, sir. I know only too well that it is the grease that makes the political axle turn. My concern is with practice, and it is my belief that the situation in Ireland must be handled with extreme circumspection at present.'

'Really?' Arthur could readily guess the man's concerns, but wished to hear them all the same, if only to better gauge Stoper's capability and breadth of mind. 'Why do you say that?'

Stoper folded his hands together as he began to explain. 'Sir, before I continue you should know that I am in my thirtieth year of service at Dublin Castle. I have seen viceroys come and go and most have been good men and well intentioned to those they govern. Some, alas, have not and have tended to think ill of most Irishmen, and all Catholics. You were born here, sir. You know as well as any man the harsh conditions the poorest of this island have to endure. So you might understand the forces that compelled them to rebel back in ninety-eight.'

'I understand them well enough,' Arthur replied evenly. 'But I do not condone rebellion. Nor treachery. The rebels got what they deserved.'

'I suppose so, sir. I understand that you were not here at the time. In which case you might not know the full details of the revolt, and its aftermath.'

'I was told that the rebels were treated harshly enough.'

'Harshly?' Stoper replied bitterly. 'A fine euphemism, if I may say so, sir. The truth of it is that the British army, the militia and the loyalist mobs committed all manner of atrocities. Thousands of prisoners were massacred, hundreds of wounded burned alive in their beds. Then there was the rape and murder of women as well as the cold-blooded cutting down of hundreds of women and children after the battle at Vinegar Hill.'

'I've heard all this,' Arthur cut in. 'I have also heard of the atrocities carried out by the rebels.'

'That's right, sir. There were some reprisals.' Stoper nodded and continued carefully. 'It would be surprising if there were not. However, the numbers of casualties suffered by each side speak for themselves. The suppression of the rebels was out of all proportion to the harm they did. And even those of us here in the castle who were loyal servants of the crown were moved by the suffering of the rebels. There are some who still question the treatment of the common people and wonder if it is fair to discriminate against the majority of those living in Ireland solely on the basis of their religion. It is no wonder that the rebellion took over a year to quell. Still less that there was another uprising here on the very streets of Dublin four years ago, after the Act of Union. The reasons for abolishing the Irish Parliament were clear for all to see. A crude attempt to remove any prospect of independence. The members of Parliament were promised Catholic relief measures in exchange for supporting the abolition. Now that his majesty has quashed any prospect of such measures the people feel that they were cheated, sir.'

Arthur stared at the senior clerk for a moment before replying in a low tone. 'I'd be careful what you say, Stoper. It strikes me that your words could be construed as lacking in loyalty to the Crown.'

'I know that, sir. But it is my intention to retire within the year, and such a prospect tends to loosen the shackles that bind a man's tongue.'

'That may be so, but I would urge you to be careful of speaking too freely on such matters again. You sound like a Catholic.'

'I am no Catholic, sir. I am an Anglican. Yet I am also an Irishman, and I have compassion for the people of my country, no matter what their religion may be.'

'Religion be damned. There is no such thing as an Irishman any more, Stoper. We are all subjects of the United Kingdom of Great Britain and Ireland now.' Even as he spoke Arthur could not help wincing at the clumsiness of the official title.

Stoper shrugged. 'Very well, sir. I just thought it would be best if you were aware of the situation you, and his grace, are inheriting.'

'Well, I thank you for your briefing. I can assure you that it is my intention to carry out my duties for the good of all Ireland's people. But I will not brook any disloyalty, especially not from those who work directly for the government. Do I make myself clear?'

'Admirably, sir.'

'Very well then, we'll speak no more of this, Stoper.' Arthur eased himself back in his chair with a deep sigh. 'And now, I'm afraid we must deal with the first item of business. Namely answering all this correspondence.'

He reached for his letter opener. Slitting the first missive open he unfolded it and quickly read through the contents. Lady Ellesmere humbly requested that her sister's daughter's husband be found a minor office at the castle in order that he might earn an income to befit his newly married status. Young Henry was a gracious young man and not without some ability and charm. Arthur put the letter to one side and opened the next as Stoper sat and waited patiently. This time it was from a former army officer whose leg had been crushed under a supply wagon, who as a consequence had been discharged from his regiment. Knowing that the new Chief Secretary was a soldier, this former comrade in arms wondered if Arthur might be prevailed upon to find a position for a brother officer down on his luck.

Arthur looked at the pile of letters. 'All these arrived today?'

'Yes, sir.'

'And am I likely to receive more in the days to come?'

'I'm afraid these are only the first of many, sir.'

Arthur glared at the pile with undisguised malevolence. 'Is there any procedure for dealing with such correspondence?'

Stoper coughed. 'If you refer it to me I can prioritise these for you, sir.'

'On what basis?' Arthur asked as he reached for the next letter.

'Political expediency, sir. The letters will be arranged according to the rank of the sender. Those from titled persons I will place on your desk and those from commoners I will answer on your behalf, declining their services in suitably apologetic tones.'

Arthur looked at his chief clerk for a moment. 'Can't say I care for such a system'

'It worked well enough for your predecessors, sir.'

'Oh, very well then.' Arthur opened the next letter and felt his heart sink as he recognised the handwriting. It was from his mother, Lady Mornington, in London. She began by congratulating him on his new position before moving swiftly on to make the first of her recommendations on behalf of those who were deserving of Arthur's patronage. Arthur read to the bottom of the page, and then leafed through the other sheets.

'By God, there's over four pages of requests here!'

Stoper leaned forward. 'That is highly unusual, sir. Might I ask who the letter is from?'

'My mother.'

'Ah, a matter of some delicacy then.'

'You can't imagine.' Arthur tapped the letter and smiled ruefully. 'And where does a letter from one's mother fit into your scheme of political expediency?'

'Mothers are a special case. I would advise you to attend to it at once, sir.'

Arthur took a deep breath and prepared to read the whole letter in detail. He gestured to the piled correspondence. 'I'd be obliged if you took those with you and dealt with them. I shall be busy enough with this one letter as it is.'

Despite the Duke of Richmond's aspiration to find the best men for the jobs, it soon became clear that this was no more than a pious hope. It seemed that any person with whom Arthur had ever been remotely connected had written to him with a favour to ask. There was even a letter from Richard asking if some post might be found for a boatman who had served him when he was Governor General of India. Accordingly Stoper was left to apply his system for dealing with such requests while Arthur turned his attention to other tasks.

The first of these was the delicate matter of dealing with a request from the city councillors who wished to hold a parade through the streets of Dublin to celebrate the battle of Vinegar Hill. The mayor and a small deputation of corporate worthies came to Arthur's office to seek his permission and co-operation for the parade. As soon as formal greetings had been exchanged the mayor, a tall, broad man with red cheeks, spread out a street map of the capital across Arthur's desk.

He gestured to Arthur's inkwell. 'Sir, if you would kindly deploy that on the corner to hold it down. Thank you. Ah! That's it.' The mayor grinned happily and pinned the other side of the map to the desk with the letter opener. 'Now then, sir, I have taken the liberty of illustrating the intended route of the procession in pencil. As you can see, we shall pass through the middle of the Catholic districts and end here, in front of the castle gate, where I hope his grace will be kind enough to take the salute. And if his grace is unavailable then I would consider it an honour if you would take his place.'

'Doubtless,' Arthur responded awkwardly. 'I have to confess that I am somewhat confused, gentlemen. It was my understanding that the purpose of this meeting was to request permission for the procession to take place.'

'Well, of course, sir.' The mayor continued to smile. 'But that is, of course, a formality. Such an event as the decisive victory over those papist rebel scoundrels must surely be celebrated.'

'Why?'

'Why?' The mayor frowned. 'Why what, sir? I don't follow you.'

'Why must this battle be celebrated?' Arthur asked evenly. 'Surely a conflict between our people should be mourned, not celebrated?'

'But sir! Vinegar Hill was a victory of patriots over traitors.' The mayor drew himself up and clasped his hand over his heart. Arthur felt a cold shudder of contempt at the man's theatricality as the mayor declaimed, 'I consider myself to be a true patriot, as do my colleagues. It is our duty to celebrate our triumph over the papists.'

Arthur nodded. 'Our triumph, eh? I take it you were on the battlefield in person and fought the traitors hand to hand?'

'Me, sir?' The mayor frowned. 'Not in person, sir. But there in spirit, by God!'

'Trust me, then. It is a very different thing to be there in person. And had you been then perhaps you would not be so impressed with yourself. Nor so eager to celebrate the event.' Arthur let his words sink in and continued. 'This battle took place nearly a decade ago. Since then it has been the policy of the government to bring peace to Ireland. With mixed success, I admit. But the question that I would ask you fine gentlemen to consider is whether this procession of yours is more likely to encourage peace, or enmity. Well?'

The mayor drew a deep breath and puffed out his cheeks. 'The enmity was on the part of the rebels, sir. It is vital that the loyal men of Ireland are reminded of the sacrifices made to ensure that they do not have to live through bloody revolution. Why, if it were not for the victory at Vinegar Hill there would be a tricolour flying above Dublin Castle and not the Union flag! Think on that, sir, before you presume to upbraid me!'

Arthur shook his head. 'I do not mean to upbraid you. I do not mean to discount the sacrifices of the men at Vinegar Hill. I mean to ensure that the people of Ireland can enjoy the fruits of the subsequent peace. Accordingly we must not revive the divisions of the past. The conflict between our people should be forgotten if there is to be any chance of contentment in this troubled island. Do you not agree, sir?' Arthur continued before the mayor could reply, 'Therefore I do not give permission for your procession to take place.'

The mayor's eyes bulged and there were some angry murmurs from those in his deputation. The mayor swallowed and hastily gathered his map in and rolled it up. 'Then, sir, I shall take this matter to a higher authority, to someone who knows the true value of patriotism, and subscribes to the belief in no surrender to papist plotters.'

'You are welcome to try,' Arthur said with cool politeness. 'Now, I bid you good day, gentlemen.'

As the mayor and the deputation strode out of his office, Arthur caught the eye of Stoper and beckoned him over. Once he was sure that he would not be heard by his departing visitors Arthur spoke.

'Better send a quick note to his grace. Inform him of what has happened and my decision on this matter. Send it at once, before those men have a chance to drive a wedge between the Lord Lieutenant and his Chief Secretary.'

'Yes, sir.' Stoper pencilled a hurried line in his notebook. 'Will that be all, sir?'

'Quite enough, thank you.'

'Very well, sir.' Stoper bowed his head and made his way to the door. There he paused and looked back.

'Well?' Arthur raised an eyebrow. 'What is it?'

'If I may say so, sir, you did the right thing.'

'Of course I did,' Arthur replied coolly. 'Any bloody fool can see that.'

'Yes, sir.' Stoper smiled and left the room, closing the door behind him.

Chapter 29

In an effort to better understand the public mood across Ireland, Arthur took his carriage and, together with Stoper, toured the counties with an escort of dragoons. What he found did not encourage him. In village after village he saw the same ramshackle cabins of the poor who barely eked out a living on the scraps of land they could afford to rent. The landowners were, for the most part, living in England – far from the troubles they had helped to provoke by keeping rents high and leaving their estates in the hands of agents who were intent on earning a comfortable commission by squeezing every last penny out of the hard-pressed tenants.

Each town and large village was garrisoned with redcoat soldiers who patrolled the streets and country lanes with the swagger of those who knew they had complete power over the local inhabitants, who dared not even meet their eye for fear of earning a hard beating. Conversely, it was a brave soldier who ventured out from his barracks alone. Though cowed, those with rebellion still in their hearts were still capable of isolated acts of violence, and Arthur received reports of soldiers and loyalists who had simply disappeared. Once in a while a body might turn up in a bog, or weighted down in a river, too badly decomposed to be identified.

After two weeks spent mostly in his carriage, closely confined with Stoper, Arthur finally gave the order to return to Dublin. As they rumbled along a rutted lane, Arthur stared out of the window at the passing fields, seeing the bent backs of Irish peasants as they laboured at their crops, or made improvements to their lands or rude cottages and shacks.

'The danger to our interests here does not come from France,' Arthur mused.

Stoper looked up sharply, having been trying his best to sleep as the carriage bumped along the crude track.

'Sorry, sir. What did you say?'

'I was just thinking. Following Trafalgar I doubt whether Bonaparte would consider another attempt at landing a force here in Ireland. He could never amass enough transports to carry the number of men necessary to guarantee the conquest of Ireland.'

'No, sir. I suppose not.'

'In which case the danger comes not from without but within.' Arthur nodded towards the peasants in the field they were passing. A family of perhaps a dozen were busy seeding the tilled soil: a father, mother and children, some barely old enough to walk, let alone work. An infant was tucked in a sling round the mother's chest. 'As long as they endure such conditions, they will hold England responsible. Every time a child dies for want of a decent meal, they will blame England.'

Stoper nodded. 'And it would be hard to blame them for doing so, sir. Not while they feel themselves to be oppressed.'

'That may be true,' Arthur replied quietly. 'Yet, whatever the rights and wrongs of the situation, one thing is certain. Britain cannot dismiss the threat posed by the prospect of an independent Ireland. The French would be interfering here in a trice, landing guns, equipment and men and encircling Britain in an iron fist so that Bonaparte need only clench it to crush us. That cannot be allowed to happen.

'The trick of it is to instil an innate sense of superiority in those appointed to control Ireland, right down to the last soldier in every garrison. At the same time the people must be made to accept the superiority of Britain. They must believe it so that they shrink from taking action against our rule.'

'Our rule?' Stoper repeated the phrase thoughtfully. 'You already speak as if we were two different peoples and not one.'

'Yes,' Arthur replied sadly. 'That is so. It strikes at my heart to say it, Stoper, but we need to be cruel and heartless long before we can afford to make any kind of move towards relieving the burdens of the people of Ireland. We can only make concessions from a position of strength, or else open the doors to a flood of cries for reform. That would be a flood we could not control. So, for now, there is nothing I can do, save encourage the security of the state by whatever means are necessary.'

Stoper stared at his superior for a while before he pursed his lips. 'If you say so, sir.'

It was long after dark when the carriage returned to the lodge at Phoenix Park. The driver wearily unloaded Arthur's baggage as the Chief Secretary stepped down from the carriage and dismissed the dragoon escort before turning to his senior clerk.

'You have the notes, Stoper. I want a report on our findings before the end of the week so that I can present them to his grace.'

'Yes, sir.'

'Now then, you may take my carriage to convey you home. I expect to see you in my office before eight in the morning. Clear?'

'Yes, sir.'

As the carriage rattled off, Arthur climbed the steps to the house and rapped on the door. For a moment there was silence, then he heard the rapid patter of approaching feet and an instant later the door was opened. A footman peered cautiously round the jamb, holding a lantern up to inspect the late-night caller. He relaxed when he recognised Arthur.

'Thank God it's you, sir.'

'Why, who else were you expecting? Now see to my baggage.'

'Yes, sir.'

The footman's face resumed its fretful expression and he glanced past Arthur into the drive until Arthur snapped at him. 'Well? What are you waiting for?'

'My apologies, sir, but we are expecting the physician at any moment.'

'What?' Arthur felt a stab of fear and anxiety. 'What has happened, man? Tell me.'

'It's young Arthur, sir. He's fallen ill.'

'Ill?' Arthur felt his stomach clench. 'Out of my way.'

He ran up the steps and into the house. Taking the stairs two at a time, he raced to the first floor and along the corridor towards the bedrooms, the sound of his boots echoing off the walls. A door opened at the end of the corridor and Kitty emerged from the baby's room. By the dim light of the candle burning in a bracket outside the door Arthur could see that she had been crying and even in the warm glow of the flame she looked ashen. Arthur's footsteps faltered as he approached and a sick certainty that their son was dying struck him like a blow to the whole body.

'By God, Kitty, what has happened?'

'Our son is stricken,' she replied softly, her lips trembling.

Arthur took her hands and squeezed them, before leading her back into the room. A nurse was leaning over the crib and dabbing at the child's face with a damp cloth. The baby stirred and moaned pitifully for a moment before crying. Arthur looked down and saw that the boy's face and arms were marked by red spots and he trembled feverishly.

'What is it? What ails him?'

'It's measles, sir,' the nurse replied.

'He's dying,' Kitty whispered. 'I know it.'

The nurse shook her head. 'I've seen measles come and go, my lady. Most get over it soon enough. He's a bonny lad. He'll live, so he will.'

'Measles,' Arthur repeated. From what he knew of the sickness it was common enough and most who caught it recovered fully. He felt his anxiety begin to ease as he took Kitty's hand and gave it a gentle squeeze. 'The boy has measles, Kitty. I am sure he will recover. As the nurse says.'

'We must wait for the doctor,' Kitty replied. 'In case she is wrong.'

Arthur glanced at the nurse and they exchanged a brief look of understanding before he addressed his wife again. 'I am sure the doctor will confirm what she says. Now you must take control of yourself, my dear. It does you no good to react so. And it certainly sets a bad example for the other members of the household.'

Kitty looked up at him with a confused expression. 'But our son is gravely ill. How do you expect me to react?'

'He is not gravely ill,' Arthur replied tersely. 'He will recover. There is no point in over-reacting. You cannot affect the outcome by indulging yourself in emotion. Come, let us go to the drawing room and I will give you something to drink. Something to fortify your mind.'

She shook her head, stunned by his apparent cold-heartedness. He took her gently by the arm and steered her towards the door, where he paused to look back towards the nurse. 'Let me know when the doctor has been, and tell me what he says. We shall be in the drawing room.'

'Yes, sir.'

Once he had settled Kitty on a sofa Arthur poured them both a glass of brandy and sat down opposite her on the other side of the fireplace, in the light of a single lantern placed on a small table. Kitty winced as she sipped the fierce spirit, while Arthur tipped his down his throat in one go, relishing the warm glow that spread through his body. He set the glass down with a sharp tap, then watched as Kitty sipped from her glass.

He smiled. 'That's better. You are more yourself, my dear. I think it would be best to refrain from such outbursts of emotion in future. The boy is in the hands of a good doctor. He will recover soon enough. Trust me.'

Kitty nodded. 'I know, my dear. I know.' She was silent for a moment and took another sip of brandy before speaking again, looking at her husband furtively from beneath her brow. 'I know that I am a disappointment to you, Arthur. I am not the woman you wished to marry.'

'Nonsense, my dear. I will not hear it.'

'Arthur, you are a good man. An honourable man. You have proved it in holding to your promise to marry me, when a lesser man would have recanted. By that token alone, I adore you. I know that I am not learned as you are. I have little experience of the world and have achieved naught of value in my life. Any propensity to beauty that I once had has faded. All that I have to offer you is my love and admiration. And yet, I am painfully aware that I disappoint you. That you consider me an unworthy partner.'

Her words fell on his heart like rocks, because he recognised the truth of them, and when he replied the falseness of his assurances left a foul taste in his mouth. 'Kitty, my dear. I married you for love, and I honour you as my wife, as the mother of my son, and as the woman I will be proud to have by my side until the end of my days.'

She stared at him for a moment and then gave a resigned shrug. 'If you say so, Arthur. If you say so.'

'Is this all because of the boy's measles?'

'Not entirely. There have been other burdens to bear while you have been away, and I am not sure that I can run the household by myself. There seems so much to it.'

'Other burdens?'

She bit her lip and looked at him uncertainly. 'There is something else I need to tell you.'

Arthur felt yet more weight descend upon his shoulders and depress his spirits, even as he responded in an understanding manner. 'What is that, my love?'

'I believe . . . I think that I am expecting another child.'

'That is good,' Arthur replied softly, then beamed. 'What am I saying? That is better than good. That is excellent news!' He raised Kitty's hands to his lips and kissed them. 'Thank you, my dear.'

A smile flickered across Kitty's face as she saw the genuine happiness in her husband's eyes. 'At least I can do something that pleases you.'

Chapter 30

My Dear Brother,

I write briefly to let it be known to you that his majesty's government has determined to land a significant body of British soldiers on the continent before the year is out. The object of such an expedition is to offer encouragement to our allies who readily complain that Britain is only prepared to pay in gold what they pay in blood in opposing Bonaparte. As yet I have not been able to discover the destination of the expeditionary force, and will communicate any further information to you on this matter as soon as it is available to me. Arthur, I know that you believe that you best serve your country in a military rather than a civil capacity and I would commend this opportunity to you. However, there are sure to be plenty of officers of equal or superior rank, albeit inferior in ability, who will be competing furiously to be included in such an operation. Therefore, I would urge you to repair to London as soon as possible in order to make your representations in person to the War Office.

Richard.

Arthur folded the letter and set it down on the table beside his plate, with the others that he had opened and read since the meal had begun. He picked up his knife and began to cut into his steak.

There was a light cough from the other side of the table as Kitty gestured towards the letter. 'No bad news there, I trust?'

'No. None.'

'It's just that I recognised Richard's hand and wondered what he had written that caused you to frown so.'

Arthur thought quickly before replying. There was no sense in upsetting Kitty over something that might never happen. 'I was not frowning, my dear, just concentrating. Richard merely wishes to know if we are well, and if our son is thriving.'

'I see. That is all?'

'Yes,' Arthur replied, and hurriedly impaled a piece of meat and popped it into his mouth. His mind raced as it dealt with the message that Richard had sent him.

It was true that he saw himself as a soldier first, a politician a poor second. The chance of joining an expedition to the continent to fight the Corsican tyrant was tempting in the extreme. Yet, as Richard had said, it was vital that he present his case for inclusion in person. He must leave Dublin as soon as possible.

'I find it strange that Richard should write with such trivial concerns,' Kitty continued. 'It is unlike him.'

'He must have time on his hands,' Arthur replied. 'There is no hope of returning to high office for a while yet.'

'No. I suppose not.' Kitty raised another small piece of meat to her mouth and chewed a moment before continuing. 'Which makes it all the more odd that he did not take the time to write to you at more length.'

Arthur lowered his knife and fork and stared across the table at his wife. 'Kitty, I do not know the man's mind. Whether he chooses to write at length or not is a matter for Richard.'

'I'm sorry, Arthur dear. I did not mean to upset you.'

'You have not upset me,' Arthur said coldly.

Arthur did not like to deceive his wife and he knew well enough that the idea of his going off to war would alarm her. Besides, it was one thing to be excited by the possibility of a military command on active service, and quite another to be fortunate enough to be granted such an appointment in practice. He smiled to himself as it occurred to him that it was perverse to think of the prospect of danger as an opportunity to be grasped. Yet without the war with France, he would never have had the chance to improve his lot in life, doomed for ever to be a younger son of a minor aristocratic family casting about for a well-heeled wife to save him from penury.

'What are you thinking of, my dear?'

Arthur glanced up guiltily, and at once composed his expression into a mask of indifference. 'Just something someone said to me today.'

'Oh? And what was that?'

'It does not matter. It is of no consequence,' Arthur replied abruptly and instantly regretted his tone as he saw the hurt look flit across his wife's face. She had been attempting to make small talk, to play the part of the dutifully attentive wife, only to be curtly rebuffed. He decided to attempt to divert her attention from the pain he had caused and clapped his hands together. 'So tell me, how is our son today?'

Kitty started at the sudden noise and then smiled nervously. 'Arthur is much better. I think he has almost recovered from the measles now.'

'As I always knew he would. Good, good,' Arthur continued quickly. 'He is a robust little boy, sure enough. Make a fine soldier one day, eh?'

'Soldier?' Kitty nodded faintly. 'Yes, that would be nice. A hero, like his father. That would make me so proud, my dear.'

Arthur cleared his throat. 'My dear, it seems that I may have to travel to London soon.'

'London? Why?'

'Official business. I am minded to brief the Prime Minister on the situation in Ireland. With all this trouble we have been having with rebellious spirits, he will be keen to be kept abreast of events.'

'But I thought the situation was calming down? You told me so yourself.'

'It is, my dear. Which means that my presence here is not quite so vital at the present. Now would be a good time to absent myself.'

'How long will you be away?'

'Hard to say. Some weeks.' Arthur picked up his cutlery and began to cut at his steak again as he continued, 'Months, possibly. I cannot say.'

Kitty looked at him with large sorrowful eyes. 'So long? I don't think I could bear it.'

'Of course you can, my dear,' Arthur said smoothly. 'You will need to take charge of the household in my absence. It will be good practice for you.'

'Practice for what?'

'Ah.' Arthur paused and cursed his tongue. 'It is possible that I may be required to serve in the army again at some time. In which case, we may be separated for a while. Naturally, I could not fight well for my country if I was concerned that you were not coping with running the family's affairs and seeing to the upkeep of the household. So it would be wise to treat this trip to London as a chance for you to get some experience of managing without me. I'm certain that you will make a fine job of it, Kitty, my dear.'

'I will try to,' she replied softly. 'But do come back to me, to your son, as soon as you can.'

'I will endeavour to do so with all my might,' Arthur replied, forcing a smile.

It felt good to be back in London again, even though it had only been a matter of months since he had departed for Dublin. The streets, the coffee houses and the halls of Parliament itself were buzzing with news from Europe. With the coming of spring the French Emperor had renewed his campaign in the east and was marching towards the Russian armies in pursuit of a decisive battle. Few people in London seemed to doubt that he would achieve it. For his part Arthur was not so convinced. It all depended on how far Bonaparte was prepared to advance from his supply depots. If the Russians laid waste to the countryside behind them, then the French army must starve the further east it advanced. In time the Russians could pick their ground and turn on the tired, hungry and demoralised remains of the Grand Army. At least, that is the strategy that should be employed, Arthur reflected. Whether Tsar Alexander would see things the same way was another matter.

As soon as he had returned to the house in Harley Street, Arthur sent a message to Castlereagh at the War Office to request a meeting. He had already written to the minister at the start of June explaining his wish to be included in any army sent to fight the French, even if that meant giving up his current post and all the political prestige that went with it. Castlereagh's response had been swift and he had promised to discuss the matter in person if Arthur came to London.

So it was that on a fine bright day in the middle of June Arthur was strolling briskly along Whitehall to the War Office. Turning through the gates at Horseguards he passed between the sentries at the main entrance and presented himself at the desk at the end of the hall.

'Major-General Sir Arthur Wellesley. I have an appointment with the minister.'

The clerk glanced down the list of names and then nodded to one of the orderlies seated behind him. 'Take the general upstairs. Minister's office.'

'Yes, sir.' The orderly bowed his head. 'If you'd follow me, sir?'

As they climbed the staircase and passed along corridors Arthur was aware of a good deal more activity than had been the case on his previous visit. Clerks and officers were busy at their desks in each room they walked by. Others hurried along the corridors with sheafs of paper clutched tightly to their sides.

'It would appear that the War Office is engaged in planning something rather grand.'

'Yes, indeed, sir.' The orderly glanced back and nodded, before lowering his voice. 'Word is that there are plans to invade France itself, sir.'

'Really?' Arthur doubted it. There was no sense in such a direct approach to the enemy. Not when there was no earthly chance of success against the numbers the French could bring to bear against a British army setting foot on their soil. 'Any news from the continent?'

The orderly nodded. 'I heard from a clerk upstairs that the latest despatch says that Boney has forced the Russians to make peace. The beggar's unbeatable.'

Arthur glanced at him sharply. 'No general is unbeatable, it is just a question of time. Bonaparte will be beaten one day.'

'Really, sir?'

'You have my word on it.'

'That's a comfort,' the orderly replied and Arthur felt a brief spark of anger at the man's tone, before his mind fixed on the news. So Bonaparte had defeated the Russians. Arthur shook his head at the Tsar's rashness. He was doing Bonaparte's work for him. This was the price an army paid when it was led in person by a monarch, rather than a professional soldier. Arthur smiled wryly. France was indeed fortunate that her ruler and the very best of her generals were one and the same man. Fortunate for France, but a curse to her enemies.

'Here we are, sir.' The orderly stood aside at a doorway and bowed as Arthur passed inside. He rang a bell further down the corridor and then left Arthur alone. The anteroom was the same small room where he had met Nelson nearly two years before. As he recalled the moment and vividly pictured the admiral sitting there that day, Arthur felt a sudden sense of what the man's loss meant to those who had met him, however briefly, and to the nation as a whole. King George and all his subjects had slept more easily since Trafalgar. While that great battle had not won the war, it had made Britain's defeat unlikely. As the thought came to him, Arthur wondered on whose shoulders it would fall to complete the great project that Nelson had given his life for.

'Sir? If you would come in.'

Arthur looked up and saw a thin-faced young man in a neat dark coat standing in the doorway to Castlereagh's office.

'I'm twenty minutes early.'

'The minister wishes to see you at once, sir.'

'Very well, then.' Arthur strode across the room and followed the man inside. Castlereagh rose and stretched out a hand as soon as he saw Arthur. The young man settled himself at the side of the table and picked up a pencil and notebook.

'Good to see you again, Wellesley!'

'Thank you, sir,' Arthur replied as he took the man's hand and gave it a firm shake.

'Sit you down, man!' Castlereagh smiled. 'How are things in Ireland?'

'I am sure you have seen my reports, sir. I believe I have been thorough enough in those documents.'

'I'm sure you have. They are models of clarity and conciseness. And like any such things, they lack the personal perception that the reader so often craves. So I ask you again.'

Arthur smiled back, pleased by the minister's candour. Yet he knew that whatever admirable qualities Castlereagh possessed, he was still a politician and needed to be spoken to in a circumspect manner. For a moment he wondered if he should speak frankly in front of the third man, whom he assumed to be the minister's personal secretary. But if Castlereagh asked such frank questions in front of the younger man, then Arthur should answer them in a similar fashion. He cleared his throat.

'Sir, we hold Ireland, as a strong man holds a weaker one – by the throat. We can keep Ireland under control as long as we don't grow weary of the strength it takes to subdue the natives. Unless we can make Englishmen of them there will never be peace there, except under the muzzles of British guns.'

Castlereagh was still for a moment as he stared directly at Arthur. Then he nodded. 'I see. No peace, then.'

'No peace, but order. And that can be maintained as long as we have the will to do it, however forcefully it needs to be carried through.'

'Spoken like a soldier.' Castlereagh smiled. 'Alas.'

'Alas?'

'If you should cleave to a political career you will find such candour a considerable burden. Then again, you did not come here to pursue a political career. Carstairs, the letter if you please.' Castlereagh held out his hand and his secretary quickly flipped open a file in front of him and flicked through a couple of pages before he found what he was looking for and proffered it to the minister. Castlereagh held it up for Arthur to see. 'Your letter of the first of June.'

'Yes, sir.'

Castlereagh examined it briefly. 'You say that you cannot tolerate being in Ireland when an operation on the continent is being planned.'

'Yes, sir.'

'You still hold to that view?'

'That is why I am here, sir,' Arthur replied evenly.

'Yes,' Castlereagh lowered the letter and tapped his finger on the final paragraph. 'You say you would be willing to give up your post as Chief Secretary in order to have a military command. May I ask why?'

'For the reasons you have stated, sir. I am more a soldier than a politician. At a time of war I believe it is every man's duty to serve his country in whichever capacity best utilises his proven abilities.'

'A sound enough principle,' Castlereagh conceded. 'Yet the Duke of Richmond assures me that he could have picked no finer man for your current post than yourself. Do you doubt his word?'

270

'It is kind of him to say that,' Arthur replied cautiously. 'And I could quite easily continue serving his grace from here in London, until such time as my appointment in the expeditionary force is confirmed or denied. If I am denied then I could return to my duties in Dublin.'

Castlereagh considered the suggestion for a moment and then frowned. 'That is a highly irregular suggestion, Wellesley. I am not convinced that it would work.'

'I disagree, sir. I believe that I could conduct the business of government from a distance. Besides, I believe the true path of service to my country lies in being a soldier.'

'It is true that the late William Pitt regarded you highly in that capacity, and there are plenty of other men of influence who would agree that you are an officer of unusual ability and promise.' Castlereagh paused to collect his thoughts, and then nodded. 'Very well, I shall do my best to see that you are included amongst the general officers picked for the expeditionary force.'

Arthur felt a rush of relief sweep through his chest and tried to control the smile that was keen to play on his lips. 'Thank you, sir. You won't regret it, I swear.'

'See that I don't. Now then, is there anything else?'

'Yes, sir.' Arthur nodded. 'I am given to understand that Bonaparte has forced the Russians to come to terms.'

The minister exchanged a quick glance with Carstairs before he responded. 'Good God, that news has only just reached London this morning! Are there no secrets in this damned country? Where did you hear that?'

Arthur had no desire to have the orderly and his friend held responsible for slackness higher up the chain of command. So he shrugged. 'A chance comment overheard as I made my way to this meeting, sir.'

Castlereagh stared closely at him. 'I see. Fair enough. It seems certain that it will be only a matter of days before we hear that the latest coalition against France has collapsed. I sometimes wonder if that bloody frog is invincible.'

'Bonaparte can and will be defeated, sir,' Arthur replied firmly. 'Given the chance I shall prove it.'

Castlereagh smiled. 'I believe you would. You see, Carstairs, the fighting spirit of our commanders burns as bright as ever.'

Carstairs nodded. 'As you say, sir.'

'Well then.' Castlereagh rose to his feet suddenly, indicating that the meeting was over. 'Wait to hear from me, Wellesley. I will do all that I can to give you the chance to bloody the nose of our enemy.'

'Thank you, sir,' Arthur replied as he stood, and shook the minister's hand.

'In the meantime, you will need to settle your affairs in Ireland, and break the news to the Duke of Richmond, who, I dare say, will not be too pleased at losing the services of so able a subordinate.'

As he left the War Office Arthur felt a lightness in his heart at the thought of returning to active service. He had proved himself in India, but the real test was about to come. Here, in Europe, where the stakes were so much higher. He had little doubt that the Duke of Richmond would understand his sense of duty, but informing Kitty was a different proposition, and he frowned as he strode through the streets back towards his house.

Chapter 31

Napoleon

The River Niemen, near Tilsit,
25 June 1807

The early morning mist had burned off quickly as the sun rose into a clear blue sky. As he sat on the cushioned thwart at the rear of the barge Napoleon stared across the glassy flow of the Niemen towards the far bank. The dense ranks of the Russian Guard stood in columns a short distance from the water. There was not a breath of wind and their standards hung limply from their gilded staffs. The Tsar's barge was still tethered to a small jetty and as Napoleon watched there was a sudden burst of activity as the boatmen piled into the vessel and hurriedly took up their oars. Napoleon smiled to himself. Once again he had stolen the initiative by setting out from his side of the river first. He would reach the large raft that had been moored in the middle of the current before Tsar Alexander and so would be in a position to welcome the enemy sovereign aboard. That would give him a small but definite advantage over the Tsar before they even began to speak.

As his gaze moved to the raft Napoleon was pleased with the work carried out by the Grand Army's engineers. It was less than two days since Prince Lobanoff had ridden into the French camp to offer an armistice on behalf of his master, Tsar Alexander. Since then, the raft, twenty paces on each side, had been constructed on the banks of the river. A generous apartment had been built on the middle and comfortably furnished with a table and chairs, and extensively decorated with tapestries bearing the eagles of France and Russia. There were two doors so that the Emperor and the Tsar could enter the apartment from their side of the river. Once completed, the raft had been carefully floated out into the middle of the Niemen and anchored securely in place from a stout post at each corner.

As the French barge angled across the current towards it, Napoleon could see the fine craftsmanship that had gone into the hurried construction and made a mental note to have Berthier reward the engineers who had made such a fine thing so quickly. If the meeting with the Tsar went well, then perhaps there would be peace and the men who had been campaigning for the last ten months could at last rest after all their exertions.

Despite the battles of Jena and Auerstadt and the occupation of Berlin, the Prussians had not surrendered, and it was only after the bloodbath at Eylau and their subsequent defeat at Friedland that the enemy's will to continue the fight had finally broken. The men of the Grand Army sensed it at once and had been in high spirits ever since at the prospect of peace, on French terms. All the bitterness and demoralisation that had plagued Napoleon's soldiers through the long, freezing winter months had gone and even the slaughter at Eylau had faded from the thoughts of most. Though his men once again cheered him heartily as he passed through their ranks, Napoleon knew that their morale, what he called their 'sacred fire', was a fickle thing, and if Russia refused to come to terms and the war continued, then they would soon slip into the familiar morose despair of men who had been marching and fighting for too long.

The truth was that Napoleon needed peace as much as his enemies did. He had been away from Paris for too long, and from Fouché's reports it was clear that his opponents in the French capital were growing ever more bold and outspoken. It was vital that he returned at the earliest opportunity to re-exert his control over the politicians and people of Paris. In addition, he had not seen Josephine for several months, and her most recent letters were filled with a bitter petulance about his prolonged absence. Napoleon had no doubt that word of his affair with Countess Walewska had reached the Empress's ears and that she had been hurt by his infidelity.

The barge approached the mooring post on the edge of the raft and as the oarsmen, men from the engineers attached to the Imperial Guard, raised their oars, the boat glided gently in at an angle. The man in the prow grunted as he grasped the wooden side of the raft and strained his powerful arms as he braced himself and brought the craft to a standstill. With a quick flick of a rope he fastened the bows to the mooring post and then leaped nimbly on to the raft, where he took the rope thrown to him from the stern and pulled the barge alongside. Napoleon rose unsteadily from his seat and one of the men carefully supported his arm as he stepped on to the deck of the raft. He straightened up and smoothed down his coat and breeches. He was wearing the uniform of a Colonel of the Imperial Guard, and had deliberately left his decorations and sash back at his quarters. The impression he wished to make on the Tsar was that of a commander of men, not some pampered peacock at a royal court.

'Stay here,' he ordered quietly, and then crossed to the door facing the French bank of the Niemen. He pushed the handle down and entered the apartment, closing the door behind him. There he paused a moment, admiring the fine construction and decoration that his men had crafted. Napoleon nodded. The Tsar could not help but be impressed by the raft, not to mention the feat of putting it together so quickly, and positioning it so precisely in the middle of the river. Which was good, Napoleon mused. If the preliminary talks went well, he had resolved to put the Grand Army on display to impress the Tsar with its efficiency and élan. Napoleon crossed to the other door, opened it and emerged on to the far side of the raft.

The Tsar's barge had put out from the other bank and the men at the oars were rowing lustily to speed their passenger to the encounter with Napoleon. They were making a meal of it as they splashed furiously through the smooth ripples of the river. Napoleon focused his attention on the figure sitting at the rear of the barge. Alexander was wearing a green jacket adorned with heavy gold epaulettes, and diamond-encrusted stars were pinned to his breast. A broad red sash hung from his shoulder and a white plume rose high from his cocked hat. He sat stiff and erect as the boat neared the raft and seemed to look straight past Napoleon as the latter waited, alone.

The Russian barge bumped into the side of the raft, causing those aboard to lurch forward, and the Tsar hurriedly snatched a hand to his hat to keep it on his head. Once the boat was alongside, the Tsar stood and held out his arms and two of his men lifted him bodily from the boat on to the raft, where he paused and looked his adversary over without expression. Alexander was a tall, slender man with a rounded face and soft feminine features, and as he removed his hat and bowed he revealed a high forehead and receding hair.

Napoleon strode the few paces between them and grasped the Tsar's hand, smiling warmly. 'Your majesty, it is a pleasure to finally meet you in person. I had begun to fear that the tragic war that existed between our nations would deprive me of the pleasure of your company for ever. But here we are!' Napoleon gestured to the finely appointed raft.

The Tsar glanced round and nodded approvingly. Speaking in accentless French, he said, 'A fine piece of work, your majesty.'

Napoleon noticed the slight hesitancy before the Tsar addressed him by title, and fought back his anger over the man's reluctance to accord him the honour he was due. For an instant he was reminded of the ridicule he had endured at school in Brienne, when he had been mocked by the sons of aristocrats for his provincial background. However, he took a sharp breath and calmed himself before he replied, the welcoming smile still fixed on his face.

'It is the work of my engineers. They are capable of turning their hand to almost any task.'

'So I can see.'

'Please come this way.' Napoleon gestured towards the door, then led the Tsar inside the apartment and indicated the seats on either side of the table.

Alexander laid his hat on the table and then eased himself cautiously on to the chair, as if expecting some kind of French treachery. Napoleon could not help smiling at his suspicion. It would only help to keep the Tsar preoccupied while he conversed, and again hand the initiative to Napoleon. Flicking back his coat-tails, Napoleon sat down, and the two rulers looked at each other unflinchingly for a moment in silence. Napoleon waited for the other man to begin, and in due course the Tsar cleared his throat.

'I have come here to discuss peace.'

'It is what we both desire,' Napoleon responded. 'I can assure you that whatever my enemies say, I am a man of peace. War profits no man and is the regrettable outcome of poor communications. Why, here we sit, as easily as two old friends. Peace is a natural state of affairs between such powers as ours, would you not agree?'

'Yes, that is so.' Alexander nodded. 'Though there are other nations in Europe who would seem to hold on to warfare as a drowning man might a lifeline.'

'Ah, you speak of Britain.'

'I do.'

'As pernicious a race of shopkeepers as ever existed,' Napoleon continued. 'They fight to make the rest of the world customers for their goods and they will not rest until their industries dominate all of us, no matter how many men must be killed in order for them to succeed.'

'That is so.' The Tsar nodded. 'I have only to consider the efforts that they have taken to curtail Russian interests in the Mediterranean and in India. I can assure you that I hate the British as much as you do yourself.'

Napoleon leaned a little closer as he replied, 'If that is the case, then peace is already made between France and Russia.'

The Tsar could not hide the look of relief that flitted across his face. 'Peace. Thank God!' Then his expression hardened and he continued in a more even tone, 'On what conditions?'

'No more than you can afford and no more than you would wish. I propose an alliance between France and Russia. After all, we are not by nature enemies. Our borders do not encroach on each other and we have more to gain as allies than as enemies. Why, the natural enemy of us both can only be one nation.'

'Britain?'

'Of course. Britain is determined to frustrate the rightful ambitions of both our peoples. Either one of us would be sorely tested to defeat Britain on our own, but if we were united then neither Britain, nor any other nation of the world, could stand in our way, my dear Alexander. We have but to will it to make it happen.'

'Yes,' the Tsar responded softly, stroking his jaw. Then he glanced towards Napoleon. 'We are forgetting one thing.'

'That is?'

'Prussia. What is to be her part in these peace negotiations? Will Prussia be admitted to the alliance you propose?'

'No,' Napoleon replied firmly. 'Our two nations would not have been at war were it not for the calculated mischief of the Prussian court. It was they, and particularly Queen Louise, who brought about the conflict in the first place. Prussia must pay the price for the French and Russian lives lost in this unnecessary war.'

Alexander frowned. 'But Prussia is my ally.'

'An underserving ally if ever there was one. Where is the Prussian King at this moment?'

Alexander gestured over his shoulder. 'The King and his Queen are located in a mill a short distance north of here. Together with what remains of his army. I had hoped that he might be able to join us here.'

'He is a spent force.' Napoleon waved his hand dismissively. 'All that remains is to decide on the magnitude of his punishment for making war against France. Rest assured, my dear Alexander, that Russia will gain as much from Prussia's misfortune as France. Now then, I think we have a common understanding. I am sure that our diplomats can be left to discuss the details. So let us leave Prussia aside for a moment and talk of other things. There is much we can learn from each other.'

★

As soon as he returned to imperial headquarters Napoleon summoned Berthier and began to dictate a rapid series of orders.

'First,' he began as he strode up and down the map room outside his office, 'send for Talleyrand. I want him here as soon as possible to negotiate a peace agreement with the Tsar. The basis of the peace will be an alliance with Russia, and a declaration of war between Russia and Britain. Second, the town of Tilsit is to be made a neutral area. All hostilities between French and Russian forces, together with their Prussian allies, are expressly forbidden within the town limits of Tilsit. I wish to make the town freely available to the Tsar and his court, together with their senior officers. All French soldiers must accord the Russians full honours and respect. Any man who fails to obey this order will be severely disciplined. Got that?'

Berthier glanced up from his notebook. 'Yes, sire.'

'Then, once you have issued the orders, I want you back here. Summon the other marshals and have them join us.' Napoleon's eyes sparkled. 'We are going to offer the Tsar such displays of military power that he will never consider going to war against France again!'

The following day was hot, and as midday drew close the last of the preparations to receive the Tsar was hurriedly completed. Napoleon, his marshals and the staff officers stood waiting on the bank of the Niemen. A special landing stage had been constructed and decorated with the eagle emblems of Russia. From the end of the landing stage the route into Tilsit was bordered by two lines of guardsmen. They had been hard at work since before dawn cleaning and polishing their kit and now stood to attention in full dress uniform. Every button gleamed, and pipe clay had been applied to the cross straps until they attained a dazzling whiteness. Each line stood three men deep and stretched down the side of the road, thence along the sides of the streets leading up to the fine townhouse acting as imperial headquarters, and from there to the mansion Napoleon had chosen for Alexander's accommodation. The mansion was the most gracious house in Tilsit and Napoleon would have claimed it for himself in normal circumstances. But now everything depended on impressing the Tsar with the good intentions of France and her Emperor. On either side of the guardsmen, batteries of the Imperial Guard artillery stretched out along the banks, their crews standing silently by.

Napoleon paced up and down at the end of the jetty, hands clasped behind his back, as he waited for Alexander and his entourage to arrive.

Ney puffed his cheeks out and crossed his arms. 'Hope those bastards don't keep us waiting much longer. It's too hot out here. I could do with a drink.'

Napoleon rounded on him and stabbed out a finger. 'That's enough of that! I need the Tsar for an ally and I will not risk any man here offending him, or his entourage, or even that milksop the King of Prussia. No one is to cause our guests the slightest offence. Is that clear, Marshal Ney?'

'Yes, sire.' Ney stiffened his spine. 'Clear as day.'

'Good. Don't forget what I have said.' Napoleon swept his arm round at the rest of his officers. 'That goes for everyone.'

Berthier nodded towards the far bank. 'Sire, they're coming.'

Turning round, Napoleon could see that several barges had emerged round a bend in the river and were making for the landing stage. The leading barge was gilded about the prow, and the standard of imperial Russia rippled languidly from the bows as the craft struck out across the Niemen towards the French bank.

'Telescope.' Napoleon held out his hand and a staff officer hurried forward and handed his master a spyglass. Napoleon snapped it out and raised it to his eye, tracking across the gleaming surface of the river until he found the barges. He saw Alexander in the stern of the leading boat, sitting beside another man in uniform, equally glittering and encrusted with decorations. That had to be the King of Prussia, Napoleon realised with a faint smile. No wonder he looked so dour. He would be more depressed still once he discovered the terms Napoleon was going to demand from the peace agreement with his country. If he was abandoned by Russia the Prussian King would have little choice but to accept the demands that Napoleon intended to set before him. As the boat approached the west bank of the Niemen Napoleon lowered the telescope and handed it back to the officer.

'Right, everyone in position. Stand to attention and make this look as formal a welcoming ceremony as possible.'

The band of the Imperial Guard struck up with the Russian national anthem as the Tsar's barge drew up alongside the jetty. The oarsmen had learned their lesson from the previous day and were far more cautious in their approach, and Napoleon could almost sense their relief as the boat gently eased itself into position and was held in place by one man at the bows and another in the stern. The two rulers rose up from their cushioned bench and were helped ashore. The King of Prussia landed first and there was no movement from the French ranks until the Tsar stood upon the jetty.

Then Napoleon nodded to Berthier, who waved a hand towards the nearest gun crew.

'The artillery will commence the salute!' a sergeant roared out. The cannon had been loaded with blank charges and as the first linstock was applied there was a brief fizz and then the gun belched flame and smoke as it boomed across the river. At regular intervals the other guns followed, one by one, a hundred of them, giving a formal salute to the Tsar of Russia.

Napoleon stepped forward to greet Alexander. Clasping his arms, he planted a kiss on each cheek.

'I bid you welcome, your majesty.'

Alexander smiled. 'I offer you my thanks, imperial majesty. And may I introduce Frederick William, King of Prussia?'

The Prussian ruler smiled awkwardly as he stepped forward. Napoleon took his hand and shook it briskly. 'And I welcome you too, Frederick William. I trust that you will enter into peace negotiations with France as readily as your ally.'

'Yes. Yes, I will,' Frederick William stammered. 'Prussia wants peace as much as anyone.'

'I am gladdened to hear it,' Napoleon replied without a smile. 'Now, if you would both do me the honour of accompanying me I will show you to your accommodation in Tilsit.'

The three rulers led the procession up the designated route. The tall figures of the men from the Imperial Guard stood like statues as they stared straight ahead, their gaze hardly flickering as Napoleon and the others passed by. A respectful distance behind them came the marshals and staff officers of the Grand Army, interspersed with Russian and Prussian officers as they disembarked from the boats queuing up to unload their passengers on to the jetty. All the while the guns of the Grand Battery continued their salute, the crash of their shots echoing across the river.

Alexander looked closely from side to side, noting the decorations on the chests of the veterans lining the route. 'A most impressive body of men.'

'Indeed.' Napoleon smiled. 'I can assure you that they can fight as well as put on a smart display.'

'So I have been told,' Alexander replied wryly, and flashed a smile back at the Emperor. 'Those of my officers who faced them at Eylau say they will never forget how hard they fought to dislodge us from the town.'

'And today they are assembled to greet you, Alexander. To welcome you as a new ally of France.'

The Tsar nodded his head in grateful acknowledgement and at his side the King of Prussia shot his erstwhile friend a quick look of anxiety.

'I hope you don't mind,' Napoleon continued in a conversational tone, 'but I have given instructions that your accommodation is to be furnished from my personal stores. I have taken the liberty of sending you my best campaign bed.'

'Thank you,' Alexander replied. 'Most kind of you.'

'It was my pleasure,' said Napoleon. He turned to the King of Prussia, who was wearing a wretched expression. 'Sadly, my stores are somewhat limited by virtue of being on campaign, and I have been able to send you only what is left after having provided for the Tsar. I am sure you understand.'

'Of course.' Frederick William nodded. 'I appreciate it.'

The procession wound through the streets until it reached the headquarters of the Grand Army. There a banquet had been laid out for the guests, and once Napoleon had formally greeted the Tsar and the King of Prussia before the assembled officers and courtiers, toasts were drunk and the officers fell to talking. As Napoleon had ordered, his marshals and generals approached their opposite numbers and engaged with them in an animated manner regarding the features of the recent campaign. The reception continued through the hot afternoon, and Napoleon turned every measure of his charm on the Tsar, flattering him in every credible way while at the same time making clear their similarities and those of their respective nations and national interests. Meanwhile the King of Prussia stood by, occasionally included in the conversation and looking more and more bereft and humiliated as the hours wore on.

Late in the afternoon the Tsar took leave of his host, and the Russian retinue, and the handful of officers accompanying Frederick William, drifted off towards the accommodation prepared for them. As the last of them left imperial headquarters, passing once again between the ranks of the guardsmen, Napoleon watched them go with a weary sigh.

'Well, that's done.'

'Thank Christ for that,' Ney muttered sourly. 'Never had to entertain such a bunch of dunderheaded dandies in all my life.'

'This is only the start of it.' Napoleon yawned. 'I want to put the Grand Army on display while we conduct our negotiations. I want Alexander to be in no doubt about the quality of the men he must face if he ever decides to wage war on France again. Pass the word to Berthier. He is to give orders for a review of each corps. We'll start with the Guard in two days' time.'

'Yes, sire.'

Now that the strain of the day's preparations and performance were over, weariness descended on Napoleon like a dead weight. He rolled his head to ease the stiffness in his neck. 'I am retiring to my quarters to rest. I am not to be disturbed.'

'Yes, sire.'

Napoleon turned away, and then paused. 'Don't forget to have the Imperial Guard dismissed. Poor fellows have been out there for the best part of six hours.'

Ney grinned. 'Do 'em good, sire. Keep them on their toes ready for action at the drop of a hat. That's what I say.'

Napoleon stared at him and shook his head. 'The Grand Army has had its fill of war for the present, Michel. We need peace. Time to rest the men and rebuild our strength.' He turned away, adding under his breath, 'Ready for the next time it is needed.'

Chapter 32

While the preliminary articles of the peace negotiations were drawn up by the staff officers of the Emperor and the Tsar, Napoleon entertained his guests with a series of military pageants and reviews. A makeshift parade ground had been prepared by the engineers outside Tilsit complete with a grandstand where Napoleon, Alexander and the wretched Frederick William could sit in comfort as formation after formation of infantry, cavalry and artillery performed drills for their audience.

Napoleon intended these displays to serve two purposes. First to awe the Russians with the quality and quantity of troops at his disposal, and second to buy time until the diplomats gathered at Tilsit to begin the process of agreeing the precise terms of the treaty and drafting the final document for ratification and signatures.

A room had been set aside at the imperial headquarters to serve as the negotiating chamber, and the moment Talleyrand arrived from Berlin the talks began in earnest. The foreign minister arrived at night and was immediately ushered into Napoleon's private quarters, where he was met by the Emperor in a loose dressing gown. The air was humid and heavy, as if a storm was about to be unleashed over the Prussian countryside.

'Sire.' Talleyrand bowed his head. 'May I congratulate you on your victory over the Russians. I imagine that the news has reached Paris by now and all France is celebrating.'

'I'm sure of it,' Napoleon replied curtly. 'Sit down. I have sent for refreshments. I trust you had a comfortable journey.'

'It might have been comfortable had these barbarous Prussians ever bothered to maintain proper roads. As it was my internal organs feel as if they have spent the last few days in a butter churn.'

Napoleon chuckled. 'You were never one for the hard life, Talleyrand.'

'Indeed, sire. Some are bred for the harsh conditions of waging war, and some are naturally inclined to the comforts of the salon. Sadly, I fall into the latter category and would be of little use to my country on the battlefield.'

'True, you are weak and soft,' Napoleon mused, and then decided it would be of benefit to humour his foreign minister. 'But your skills at the negotiating table are every bit as valuable to me as the martial talents of my generals.'

'Thank you, sire.' Talleyrand nodded, and then leaned back in his chair and pulled out a silk cloth to dab his heavy jowls. 'Once I have had some rest I will be ready to talk to our new friends.'

'You can sleep later,' Napoleon responded. 'Once we have conferred.'

'Can we not wait until morning?' Talleyrand glanced down at his fob watch and saw that it was already past midnight. 'Dawn is no more than five hours away.'

'We will talk now.'

There was a light tap at the door and a moment later it was opened and two servants entered carrying a platter of meat, cheese and bread, and a bottle of wine and two glasses. They set them down and retired in silence, closing the door behind them. Napoleon gestured to the food. 'Eat, if you are hungry.' Then he poured them each a glass of wine and eased himself back in his chair. He held the glass in both hands and fixed his stare on the foreign minister. Talleyrand hurriedly picked at some of the food before he took a sip from his glass and cleared his throat.

'Well then, sire, what advantage do you intend to wrest from this situation?'

Napoleon drank from his own glass before he replied. 'The real threat to us is Russia. So, we must make Russia the partner of our labours. At the moment I have the Tsar eating out of my hand. He believes us to have everything in common, and I have indulged him in that thought. I have let him believe that it is my intention to divide Europe into two spheres of influence. While France is to be given power over the western half of the continent, Russia will have a free hand in the east. I have also said that I will not oppose any action the Tsar decides to take against the Turkish possessions in the Balkans.'

Talleyrand sighed. 'Sire, I have only recently concluded an agreement with the Sultan to improve relations between France and Turkey.'

'That does not matter now,' Napoleon cut in dismissively. 'I only ever intended to befriend the Turks in order to open a second front against Russia. Now that Russia is about to become an ally, we can offer them Turkish lands to sweeten an agreement with the Tsar.'

Talleyrand drew a breath and continued patiently. 'Diplomacy is a long game, sire. It takes time to build trust, to persuade others that we share common interests and ambitions. It is not an ad hoc process. It has taken years to win the Sultan round. If we abandon him now, I doubt we will be able to repair the damage to our relations for a generation at least. As for Russia, a month ago they were our mortal enemy. Now you would have them as our dearest friend. It is my experience that any friendship of value takes time to build. A friendship forged on the expediency of the moment is of little value, and can be broken just as swiftly as it was cobbled together. I urge caution, sire. We are not dealing simply with playing pieces that we can arrange on a board as the whim takes us. We are dealing with people, their instincts, their prejudices and their traditions. It is a sophisticated process, sire.'

'I thank you for the lesson,' Napoleon replied tersely. 'But like all teachers, you are prone to see complications where a more direct approach works just as well, if not better. It is my judgement that Russia will serve as a powerful and useful ally. Therefore it is my command, and your duty, to see that Russia is befriended.'

Talleyrand stared at the Emperor for a moment, as if considering further protest. Then he took a sip of wine and laced his fingers together. 'Very well, sire. What else do you intend to ask of our new friends?'

Napoleon set his glass down on the table and folded his arms. 'First, in exchange for giving the Russians a free hand against the Turks we will be permitted to occupy some of the islands and coasts around the Adriatic. That will help consolidate our hold on Italy. Second, Russia is to join our embargo on trade with Britain, and put pressure on the other Baltic nations to follow suit. Third, the kingdoms of Portugal and Spain are trading openly with Britain. That must cease forthwith, and if it doesn't it is my intention to remove their royal dynasties and replace them with monarchs selected from amongst my brothers. In these matters we will clearly need the consent of the Tsar.'

'Clearly,' Talleyrand agreed and pursed his lips doubtfully. 'In your estimation, do you think Alexander can be persuaded to support such sweeping demands?'

'Yes. I am sure of it. And with your silver tongue, my friend, our demands will be irresistible.'

'Let us hope so.' Talleyrand helped himself to another slice of cold sausage. 'And what of Prussia? What terms do we offer King Frederick William?'

Napoleon laughed coldly. 'For our dear cousin, the King of Prussia, I have little but contempt. Only when all seemed to go against me before Austerlitz was that coward prepared to throw in his lot with our enemies. The present war was caused by his folly and his ambition to humble France.' Napoleon paused. 'There can only be one fate for

Frederick William and his nation: abject humiliation. We will strip Prussia of her present borders and offer to share the spoils with Russia. We will demand reparations, the scale of which will cripple her for years to come, during which time French troops will be garrisoned on Prussian soil. Furthermore, Prussia will be obliged to uphold the trade embargo against Britain, and declare war on Britain if I deem it necessary. Finally, I will require Frederick William to recognise the existing and any future kingdoms that I confer upon members of my family and other monarchs nominated by me.'

Napoleon smiled with satisfaction as he concluded his list of demands. Talleyrand was quiet for a moment before he responded. 'Are you quite serious, sire? You propose nothing less than the dismantling of Prussia as it now stands.'

'That's right. Let it serve as a warning to any nation who even considers dealing dishonestly with France, and her Emperor.'

'Is it wise to go that far, sire?'

'Wise?' Napoleon frowned.

Talleyrand shifted uneasily. 'It appears to me that you are pinning your hopes on winning the Tsar over as a permanent ally, sire.'

'Yes. So?'

'Is that prudent? I think not. To my mind Russia poses the greatest of dangers to European nations. Her influence spreads from the Baltic in the north to Turkey and India to the south. Given time, I dare say the Tsar would consider swallowing up Poland, the Baltic states, and possibly Scandinavia. Unless those nations that lie in her path have the wherewithal to defend themselves, what is to prevent the Tsar from expanding his borders right up to the lands we claim for ourselves? Rather than allying ourselves with Russia we would be better off building an alliance with Austria, and providing Prussia with generous enough terms to swing their loyalty over to us, sire. Magnanimous terms for Frederick William could change Prussian opinion. Besides that, we would need to make sure that the Prussians retained sufficient military potential to discourage any further Russian expansion into Europe.'

'I will not permit Prussia to retain any such potential while that scheming witch Queen Louise is able to influence her husband and the Prussian court against me. I have not defeated an enemy only to present them with the chance to do me further harm at a future date. No. Prussia will be made to suffer so that she learns the cost of defying me. As for the Tsar, you will do what is necessary to secure the best terms for France while offering Alexander anything that might cement the peace between our nations. Within reason, of course.'

'Of course.' Talleyrand nodded. 'Though I would still ask your majesty to consider what I have said. Russia is not our natural ally, and it would serve France better to end the war with Britain than take Russia as an ally against her.'

'Thank you, Talleyrand. I have noted your opinion. You have your instructions, and I require you to carry them out. Is that clear?'

'Yes, your majesty.' Talleyrand bowed his head.

'Then you may go.'

The foreign minister eased himself up and walked stiffly to the door, where he bowed again before leaving the room. Napoleon stared at the door for a moment, his lips compressing into a thin line. He felt a cold rage in his heart at Talleyrand's questioning of his judgement. The foreign minister seemed to think that diplomacy must be conducted at the speed of a glacier. The truth was that people had short memories. Yesterday's villain was interchangeable with today's hero. Napoleon sniffed with derision. He knew that the very same mob in Paris that had cried out for the blood of the Tsar would be cheering him the moment peace was announced. Talleyrand was wrong. Diplomacy was like war. It was largely a question of arranging the pieces correctly, with a certain amount of bluff and luck. Rising from his chair, Napoleon yawned. As he made his way back to his sleeping quarters he decided that he must write to Fouché and order him to have his agents watch Talleyrand closely. It would be an easy step from disagreeing with the Emperor to plotting against him.

July had arrived and the days were long and hot. Even though the tall windows of the chamber were left open, the atmosphere inside was uncomfortable and heavy. There were no concessions to the summer temperature, however, and all those in attendance wore their finest uniforms and coats. Sweat pricked out on every man's brow and the hours dragged on as the terms of the treaty were put forward and debated. Some sessions were attended by representatives of all three nations, but most concerned only the Russians and the French, and the hapless Prussians were excluded.

As Talleyrand set out the harsh terms demanded by his Emperor as the price of peace with Prussia, Frederick William's envoys were shocked by the scale of the humiliation being heaped upon their nation. Their protests were met with cold disdain by the French diplomats, and on the sixth day of July the Prussians decided to try a more personal appeal for mercy.

Napoleon was seated at his desk, reading through the latest

correspondence to reach imperial headquarters, when a clerk entered and proffered a sealed letter.

'What's this?' Napoleon looked up irritably. 'Why has it not been opened?'

Then he saw the royal seal of Prussia neatly applied to the folded paper. He took it and waved the clerk away. It had been addressed to 'his imperial majesty, Napoleon, for his personal attention', in a neat, fine hand. He broke the seal and opened the letter.

Your imperial majesty, it is a tragedy that our two nations should have been locked in so bitter a struggle for so many months. Now that peace is at hand Prussia looks forward to a new era of friendship with France. In token of this, I wonder if I might meet with you in person to convince you of the lasting benefits of an equitable peace between our nations. I look forward to your response.

Your faithful friend, Louise, Queen of Prussia.

'Well, well,' Napoleon smiled. 'So it has come to this.'

He stood and strode across the room to the open door and clicked his fingers at his chief clerk. 'Méneval, send for the Master of the Imperial Household.'

'Yes, sire.'

'Tell him we are entertaining tonight. The best dinner service and the finest wines and food will be required.'

There was no polite preamble to the dinner. Queen Louise was shown into a private dining room at imperial headquarters. A small table occupied the centre of the carpeted room, covered with a lace cloth and set with fine china, glasses and cutlery from the imperial household. The room was lit by a single chandelier hanging above the table, which bathed the room in a soft orange glow. The Queen was shown to her seat by a footman and then left alone to await the Emperor, who, she was told, was completing his orders for yet another military review to be held the following morning. He would not be long, she was assured.

And so she sat, quite still and expressionless, as the clock ticked on the mantelpiece. The windows of the dining room were open and the faintest of breezes wafted in, just enough to cause the candles to flicker fractionally from time to time. At length Louise rose from her seat and went to the window. Below lay a small courtyard and the scent of herbs drifted up to her. Beyond the wall of the courtyard lay open fields, now covered with tents and the crude bivouacs erected by the French soldiers. Their campfires spread across the landscape like a vast constellation of twinkling red stars.

'An impressive sight, is it not?'

She gasped with surprise and whirled round, hand clutched to her throat. Napoleon had entered and trodden quietly across to the table, where he now stood behind her chair, hands resting on the seat back. He stared back at her, frankly appraising her looks. The Queen of Prussia was a slender woman with black hair and strong, almost masculine features. For all that there was a cold, ethereal beauty about her, Napoleon conceded. He smiled. 'I am sorry. I did not mean to startle you.'

'Really?' She arched an eyebrow. 'I rather think that was precisely what you meant to do.'

'Oh? And why would I do that?'

'You employ the same strategy off the battlefield as you do on it. You move quickly, achieve surprise and disconcert your enemy.'

'But you are not my enemy. I do not make war on women, your majesty.' Napoleon laughed. 'But I admit that you have a good grasp of my method of waging war.'

'It has been a hard lesson,' she replied coldly. 'One which has cost the lives of many of our subjects.'

'Well, the war is over, and our meal is about to begin. Please?' Napoleon nodded to the chair she had been sitting on. After a slight pause, the Prussian Queen glided back across the room and sat down, allowing Napoleon to edge her chair a little closer to the table. Then he took his place opposite, flicked his napkin loose and laid it across his thighs. 'I took the liberty of sending my chef to your quarters to discover what food appeals to your palate. How is your accommodation, by the way?'

'It is as good as most we have had to endure for several months.'

Napoleon shrugged. 'If your husband had come to terms after Jena you would still have the comforts of your palace in Berlin. But then, I imagine that you would not let your husband come to terms. My ambassador to Berlin told me how much Frederick William depends upon your advice. Other men have even said that you are the true ruler of Prussia.'

'Other men are fools,' she replied flatly. 'My husband is a good man and a sound ruler. But he is inclined to caution in dealing with a crisis. I merely acted as a spur to that course of action he knew he must take.'

'You are too modest, madam.' Napoleon stared at her. 'I sense that you are a far more formidable woman than you choose to appear.'

'Perhaps.' She smiled, showing a fine set of strong white teeth. 'For my part I sense that you are a far more sensitive man than your reputation as an all-conquering general would imply. Sensual even.'

'Sensual?' Napoleon tipped his head slightly to one side. 'It's not a word I have often heard used to describe me.'

'You surround yourself with soldiers, so that is hardly surprising.'

They were interrupted by the arrival of the first course, a thin soup of duck and herbs, and sat in silence while the steward carefully poured a ladleful into each of their bowls and then retired. Napoleon watched as his guest delicately filled her spoon and raised it to her lips, sipping the hot liquid with caution. 'Do you like it?'

Louise looked at him. 'A touch too much garlic, perhaps, but palatable.'

'I am so pleased.' Napoleon took a mouthful, and winced at the scalding sensation in his mouth. He glanced up to see her smiling at him, and mumbled an apology. 'I am sorry, it was hot. Painful.' He took a sip of wine to cool his tongue.

'Yes. The trick is not to let anyone know that it hurts.'

Napoleon lowered his spoon for a while, to let the soup cool. 'Tell me, your majesty. Why are you here? Why did you request to see me in this intimate manner? Did your husband send you to try to charm me?'

'He does not approve of the meeting,' she replied. 'I insisted. I hope to discuss the question of the terms you demand for peace with Prussia.'

'The terms are already being discussed, by our diplomats.'

'Diplomats . . .' She uttered the word with contempt. 'They talk and talk and resolve little in the longest possible time.'

'You have Talleyrand precisely.' Napoleon laughed.

Louise's expression remained serious. 'I wished to negotiate more directly with you.'

'Negotiate? What is there to negotiate? You already know my terms. I will not change them. Not even for you, your majesty.'

'But you must realise that your demands go too far. You seek to reduce Prussia to the status of a minor power. You would shame us before the rest of the world.'

'No more than you have shamed yourselves already.'

She was silent for a moment, and then continued in a calm tone, 'I accept that my husband vacillated before Austerlitz. If I had been king then Prussia would have fought alongside your enemies from the outset.'

'And very likely you would have defeated me. I must make certain that Prussia is incapable of challenging France for many years to come.

That is why I do not wish to have your husband removed from the throne. His presence there is as good a guarantee of peace as I could wish for. If he was weak before you decided to wage war against France, then he will be even more afraid now. I doubt that you, even with your undeniable charms and force of personality, will be able to persuade him to make war again.'

'I see.' Louise nodded, and sipped again from her spoon. 'You must know that the terms you have demanded of Prussia are sure to win you nothing but the hatred of our people.'

'What do I care?' Napoleon shrugged. '*Vae victis.*'

They ate in silence for a few minutes before Louise looked up again. 'Has it occurred to you that you might well need the friendship of Prussia one day?'

'Yes. There may be a time when I need all the friends I can get. But as long as you sit by the side of your husband and drip your poison into his ear, then I suspect that I need not look to Prussia for any hope of salvation. So what have I to lose by making the terms as harsh as possible?'

Queen Louise lowered her spoon, got up from her chair and walked slowly round the table until she was at his side. Napoleon instinctively lowered his spoon, as he felt his body tense at her closeness. She kneeled beside his chair and took his hand. She spoke softly. 'Your imperial majesty. If I need to I will beg you not to destroy Prussia. On my hands and knees if you say so.'

She grazed her lips over the back of his hand and Napoleon felt a bolt of fire streak up his arm. For an instant he closed his eyes, relishing the feeling, and the Prussian Queen continued to play her lips over the back of his hand before she turned it over slowly and kissed his palm with infinite tenderness.

'There is nothing I would not do for my country,' she whispered. 'Just ask me, your majesty, and I will do anything for you.'

'Anything?'

'Yes. Anything.' She moved her head so that her lips closed softly round the end of his middle finger and he felt her teeth press gently into his skin. He felt his sex stirring and shifted in his chair as he indulged the sensation. Then cold reason reasserted itself and he firmly pulled his hand away from her and opened his eyes. She was looking up at him with fierce intensity blazing in her brown eyes. Napoleon chuckled.

'Good God, but you are beautiful. Now I understand why Frederick William is your slave. However, I will not sacrifice the needs of France for the sake of a good fuck, your majesty.'

She stood up and backed away, her eyes narrowing. 'You bastard,' she muttered. 'You cold, cruel, contemptible bastard.'

Napoleon smiled faintly and raised an eyebrow. 'As you say.'

'Truly, you are a tyrant. I pray that I live to see the day when you are brought down and destroyed.'

'Of course you do. You are my enemy. I am your conqueror. It is only natural for you to hate me. Just as long as you and your people fear me, I shall be content. Now then, may we continue our meal?'

The Queen glanced at her soup and her lip curled. 'I would rather eat the scraps refused by swine.'

'Then I suggest you return to your husband and share his repast, before you share his bed. I have no need for you. No desire. Now you may leave me.'

She glared at him, and then with a swirl of her skirts she turned and strode for the door. Wrenching it open, she rushed through and slammed it behind her. Napoleon stared after her for a moment, then picked up his spoon and finished his soup.

The following day, Napoleon and Alexander signed the peace treaty in the negotiation chamber before an audience of dignitaries. Then Talleyrand read out the public version of the treaty, which expressed the great pleasure of both leaders that their countries were no longer at war. Both the Emperor and the Tsar looked forward to sharing the bounties of peace and prosperity. Napoleon seemed to listen indulgently and nodded his head at the applause that filled the chamber, but his mind was dwelling on the details of the secret articles that had been agreed and signed. Now, at last, he could turn all his attention towards crushing Britain. With Russia as his ally and all Europe under his sway, he could deny Britain access to her markets, and slowly but surely she would be starved into defeat.

Two more days passed before Napoleon deigned to sign the peace agreement with Prussia, shortly before he departed for France. This time the Prussian witnesses to the signature stood in mute despair as their King picked up his pen, dipped it in the ink pot and then held it poised above the treaty as he chewed his lip. Talleyrand leaned forward and indicated the blank space at the foot of the document.

'If your majesty would be kind enough to sign there?'

Frederick William nodded, then lowered the pen to the paper and wrote his name slowly, as if each letter was agony to write. At the end he lowered the pen and sat back abruptly, staring straight ahead, refusing to look at the French Emperor sitting at his side. Talleyrand slid the treaty across the table towards Napoleon. Behind a mask of regal calm Napoleon felt consumed by the pleasure of his triumph. He took up his pen, dipped it in the ink and signed the treaty, ending with a flamboyant flourish. The French officers and diplomats at once burst into applause, with Ney stamping his foot as he roared out 'Bravo! Bravo!' at the top of his voice.

There was a dull scrape as the Prussian King slid his chair back and abruptly rose from his seat and strode towards the door. As soon as he had left the room, his staff and courtiers filed out behind him, their ears deafened by the thunderous celebration of the French.

Talleyrand leaned close to his ear and said, 'Congratulations, sire.'

'Thank you.'

'I pray that you have won us a lasting peace.'

Napoleon turned to look up at his foreign minister. 'What is there to pray for? Prussia is humiliated, and I have the Tsar wrapped round my little finger. Trust me, my dear Talleyrand. Russia has been tamed, completely.'

Chapter 33

The streets of Paris echoed with the sound of the salute being fired from the heights of Montmartre. Tens of thousands of people lined the route of the procession and waved coloured ribbons and tricolour flags the instant they caught sight of the head of the imperial convoy. A cuirassier regiment led the way, breastplates sparkling in the bright sunshine as their glossy mounts clattered over the cobbles. Behind them came a battery of the Guard artillery, caissons and gun carriages freshly painted and every brass fitting polished to perfection. The crews sat erect in their best uniforms as the wheels rumbled beneath them. Then came a battalion of the Old Guard, their bearskins making every man look like a formidable giant. Two companies of light infantry followed, bearing captured enemy standards. A short distance behind came the imperial carriage bearing the Emperor and Empress, and immediately behind them rode the marshals who had fought in the long campaign to subdue Prussia and Russia.

At the sight of Napoleon the cheering of the crowd increased in a deafening crescendo that drowned out even the sound of the salute being fired by the guns on Montmartre. Napoleon was sitting on a large cushion to elevate him above his wife and every now and again he waved to each side of the route, smiling as he acknowledged his people. At his side, Josephine sat still, as she knew that it was not her place to respond to acclaim that she had not won. As the procession turned down the rue St-Honoré and made for the Tuileries, she touched her husband's leg.

'Seems that you are the saviour of the nation, my love.'

Napoleon leaned over and kissed her on the cheek, prompting a fresh roar of approval from the crowds. They both laughed and Napoleon lifted his hat and raised it high.

'I promised them victory and now they have it.'

'Yes.' Josephine nodded. 'But the taste of victory will fade soon enough. The people tire of war.'

'Nonsense!' Napoleon flashed a frown at her. 'As long as war provides them with glory and spoils then I can lead the people anywhere. To the ends of the earth, if I should wish it.'

Josephine noted his tone and thought better of continuing that line of conversation. Instead she turned to the side and bowed her head serenely towards a group of veterans sitting on a wagon on the corner of a street leading off the procession route. Some had patches over their eyes. Others had lost limbs or were horribly disfigured, and yet they cheered as lustily as the people around them.

The procession passed across the Carrousel and through the wrought-iron gates that surrounded the entrance to the Tuileries palace. The Emperor's carriage drew up in front of the steps that led up to the palace doors and footmen rushed to put in place a set of steps before opening the carriage door and bowing low. The emperor stepped out, and turned to offer his hand to his wife as she descended to join him. Then they steadily made their way up the steps, between the grenadiers forming a guard of honour on either side, and paused at the doors for one last wave to the crowds packing the Carrousel square before disappearing inside.

The following morning, with Paris unusually quiet as its people slept off the celebrations that had lasted long into the night, Napoleon held a meeting in his private office in the Tuileries. He sat at the head of a small table and tapped his fingers impatiently. Talleyrand sat to his left and Fouché to his right, and the chair opposite Napoleon was empty.

'How dare Lucien be late,' he muttered.

Talleyrand smiled. 'Your brother is a man of the people, sire. I imagine he celebrated your achievements with the same spirit as the rest of Paris.'

'Be that as it may, he should know better than to keep his Emperor waiting.'

'Indeed, sire,' said Fouché with a faint smile. 'It is disrespectful.'

The door to the office opened and a footman bowed his head as Lucien entered, looking flushed but happy. 'My apologies, brother! My coachman is nowhere to be found and I had to come on foot.'

'Never mind,' Napoleon responded tersely. 'Sit down.'

Once Lucien was settled, Napoleon leaned back in his gilded chair and folded his hands together under his chin. 'Gentlemen, you are my closest advisers. The reason I have summoned you here is to discuss what happens next. Despite our successes, we have work to do.'

'Work?' Lucien raised his eyebrows. 'You have only just returned to the capital. The war is as good as over. Now that you have Russia as an ally, and Britain is denied access to any port on the continent, she cannot endure much longer. She must come to terms soon. Why, I have read reports of riots in the towns in the north of the country. The blockade is a success. Work is drying up in the mills and the people grow hungry and rebellious. Soon their King will be begging us for peace. Let us enjoy this moment. Surely you of all people need a rest after your exertions?'

'I will rest when I decide to rest,' Napoleon responded coolly. 'And I will thank you not to interrupt me again.'

Lucien lowered his gaze. 'I apologise, brother.'

Napoleon stared at him for a moment before he spoke. 'The correct mode of address to your Emperor is your majesty, or in informal situations such as this you may call me sire.'

'Yes . . . sire.'

'Then let us proceed.' Napoleon collected his thoughts and began. 'The treaties signed at Tilsit have extended the influence of France from the Channel coast to the eastern frontier of Prussia, and from the Baltic to the toe of Italy. The Grand Army has proved that it has no equal on the continent and every enemy of France has been humbled, or is now an ally, save Britain alone. As Lucien has kindly pointed out, the Continental System is starting to undermine our last enemy. If we can ensure that the system is observed in all those ports directly under our control, it only remains to cut off the last remaining markets for British goods and then they will be compelled to sue for peace.'

Napoleon paused a moment. 'While I have been away from the capital I have kept abreast of events in Europe, and it is clear that our attention must now focus on the Iberian Peninsula. Thus far Portugal has refused all our entreaties to cease trading with Britain. I will not tolerate this situation any longer.' Napoleon looked at Talleyrand. 'It would appear that the usual diplomatic channels have proved worthless.'

Tallyrand opened his hands. 'As I have pointed out before, sire, diplomacy is a gradual process. In time I hope that I might be able to persuade the Portuguese to accept our position.'

'In time you *hope* that you *might* . . .' Napoleon shook his head impatiently. 'You prevaricate and vacillate far too much, Talleyrand. I have no more time for such diplomacy. I must have a result. You will inform the Portuguese that unless they close their ports to British trade by the first day of September, I will be obliged to occupy their country and remove their royal family from the throne.'

There was a stunned silence from Talleyrand before he swallowed and replied, 'But sire, that is tantamount to a declaration of war.'

'Yes, it is.'

'But we have only just achieved peace on the continent.'

'I want peace across the whole of Europe, on my terms. Nothing less will guarantee France's pre-eminence above all nations.'

'Or your pre-eminence above all sovereigns,' Lucien added.

'Quite.' Napoleon nodded.

'This is impossible,' Talleyrand said bitterly. 'The people will not be happy about another war, sire. I can assure you of that.'

Napoleon turned to Fouché. 'What do you think?'

Fouché leaned forward and stroked the back of his hand with a finger as he replied. 'Sire, there is already some discontent over the existing conscription laws. If we introduce further measures it will only exacerbate the situation.'

'That is obvious enough,' Napoleon agreed. 'The question is, can your police and your agents contain the malcontents?'

'Of course, sire. It merely depends on a judicious use of force and rewards, and ensuring that the newspapers print what we want people to read. If you grant me the powers I require, I can guarantee that any such rebels will be dealt with.'

'Rebels?' Talleyrand shook his head. 'Sire, they are not rebels. They are not traitors. They are simply tired of war. Now that you have given them peace they will be as loyal to you as any man.'

'He's right,' Lucien added. 'For pity's sake, sire, let France enjoy the peace.'

'In good time,' Napoleon replied. 'After we have dealt with Portugal.'

Talleyrand leaned forward with an earnest expression. 'But sire, how can you wage war against Portugal? Our fleet was destroyed by the British navy. The warships we have left would not be adequate to protect any convoy carrying an army to the coast of Portugal.'

'I know. That is why we must invade Portugal by land.'

'By land?' Talleyrand's eyes widened. 'By marching across Spain?'

Napoleon smiled. 'I am not aware of any other route. In which case, I require you to secure agreement with Spain that our army be given free passage from the Pyrenees across Spain to the border of Portugal.'

'And if they refuse our request?'

'Although the King of Spain is our ally, you must make it quite clear to him that I ask for his agreement out of courtesy. If he refuses, my army will march across his territory regardless of his wishes.'

'If the Spanish oppose our forces it will mean war.'

'Which is why they will not refuse.'

Talleyrand stared at the Emperor. 'This is madness, sire. There is no other word for it.'

'Be careful, Talleyrand. You go too far.'

'Even if you do not provoke a war with Spain, you will earn their bitter resentment. They are a proud people, sire, and they will be shamed by a French army marching across the breadth of their country. Besides, our men are accustomed to living off the land. If our soldiers do that in Spain they will make us enemies wherever they pass. Sire, you cannot do this. I implore you. I will not have any part in such a scheme.'

'Then I will have to entrust the task to another man.'

The Emperor and his foreign minister stared at each other for a moment in silence, each waiting for the other to respond. At length Talleyrand shook his head in despair.

'So be it.' He pushed his chair back and stood up. For a second there was silence around the table as the others regarded the foreign secretary with surprise. He drew a deep breath and composed himself before he spoke again. 'Sire, I regret that I can no longer serve you as foreign minister. You ignored my warnings over a treaty with Russia and now this . . . I am compelled to tender my resignation.'

Napoleon forced a smile. 'My dear Talleyrand! There is no need for such drastic action. If you have no wish to oversee this aspect of our foreign relations, then let another handle the matter for you. I can see you are tired, and no wonder after all the hard service you performed on behalf of your country at Tilsit.'

'Enough!' Talleyrand raised his hand to silence the Emperor. 'Sire, you ignored my advice at Tilsit. I tell you again, no good will come of our treaty with Russia. Now you are intent on dragging France into another conflict. Sire, your wars are bleeding the nation dry. The Grand Army is like a great beast devouring gold and men and leaving nothing but a wasteland where it passes. War is the greatest evil to afflict men, yet it appears to me that you worship at its altar. Where will it end, sire?' He shook his head and sighed. 'I am no longer prepared to share the responsibility for your policies. I will not serve you as your foreign secretary. You will have my letter of resignation before the day is out.'

Before Napoleon could respond, Talleyrand turned and stumped across the room, leaving the others staring after him in shocked silence. As the door closed behind him, Napoleon collected himself and sneered. 'It seems that Talleyrand lacks the stomach for a fight.'

Lucien leaned across the table and fixed his older brother with an intense stare. 'You cannot let him leave your service.'

'It is his choice whether he leaves or not.'

'But Talleyrand has connections in every country in Europe. He is well known in every court. Brother – sire, we need him.'

Napoleon shook his head. 'No. If he is fool enough to quit his position, then he is of no use to me, or to France. I can do without him. Besides, I doubt the man's loyalty.' He turned to Fouché. 'Have him watched. Closely. If there is the least sign of disloyalty I want to know about it at once.'

Fouché smiled and bowed his head in assent. 'Of course, sire. I will see to it.'

There were more processions and military reviews in the weeks that followed as the capital continued to celebrate France's triumph over her enemies and give thanks for the prospect of a profitable and secure peace. Napoleon, and the imperial court, played host to elaborate musical and theatrical entertainments where the highest-ranking officers of the Grand Army wore their best uniforms and glittering decorations, and mixed with the elite of French society. For his part Napoleon was keen to demonstrate to the rest of Europe that the court of the Emperor would rival, and surpass, that of any other sovereign on the continent. All eyes would turn to Paris and marvel at the gorgeous spectacle that he would put on display. Over it all would loom the presence of Napoleon, the master of Europe. He had made it possible and he wanted to ensure that all France was reminded of the fact.

At the same time he quietly gave orders for the formation of a new army, based in Gironde. The first corps of the new force was formed early in August and soldiers began to march to the south of France to join the army as Napoleon instructed the Portuguese ambassador to tell his government that henceforth France would refuse to permit Portuguese shipping to enter any French port.

Meanwhile, as France basked in long days of sunshine, the imperial court left the humid confines of Paris to seek its pleasures in the countryside. Berthier, who had proved his competence in supervising every last detail of the Grand Army's campaign, was now given the task of organising a series of shooting parties for the imperial court. Late in August, having enjoyed blasting pheasant and quail out of the skies, the Emperor gave orders for another shoot, this time aimed at land-based targets. Accordingly Berthier hurriedly made preparations for a rabbit shooting party.

On the appointed day a large convoy of carriages conveying Napoleon and his guests set off from Fontainebleau into the surrounding countryside. Earlier, at first light, a somewhat larger convoy of carts had set off carrying tents, tables, chairs, crockery, cutlery, silverware and glasses. More wagons groaned under the burden of the finest foods and wines the imperial court could provide for the luncheon. Still other vehicles carried the musicians who were to provide the entertainment while the members of the imperial court dined. At the tail of the convoy came the wagons carrying the hundreds of rabbits destined to be targets. Beside them walked the beaters and those assigned to load guns for the Emperor's guests. Long before the first of the imperial retinue arrived at the chosen site, everything had been prepared for them.

Napoleon was riding in his carriage with General Junot and Berthier, and had spent most of the short journey swapping memories of the campaigns they had shared. At length there was a lull in the conversation, and then Napoleon suddenly leaned forward and tapped Junot's knee.

'You have not asked me why you are travelling in my carriage.'

Junot shrugged. 'It is not my place to question your decisions, sire.'

'Of course not.' Napoleon grinned. 'But you are curious, eh?'

'Yes, sire.'

Napoleon leaned back and crossed his arms, enjoying his friend's suspense for a moment. 'General Junot, I have the pleasure of offering you the command of the newly formed Army of the Gironde. Do you accept?'

Junot smiled broadly. 'It would be an honour, sire. I thank you with all my heart. What are my orders?'

'You will have them in good time. Suffice to say, you will in all probability be enjoying the sights of Lisbon before the year is out.'

'Lisbon?' Junot's eyes widened. 'You mean to attack Portugal, sire?'

Napoleon frowned. 'Lower your voice! There are foreign diplomats ahead of and behind us, including, I might add, the Portuguese ambassador.'

'I apologise, sire.'

Napoleon dismissed it with a quick wave of his hand. 'We will talk more on this later, Junot. I just wished to let you know about your appointment. No doubt you are wondering why I picked you.'

'It had crossed my mind, sire.'

'You have proved to be a good soldier, Junot, and a loyal one. We have known each other since you were my sergeant at Toulon, and I was a mere captain of artillery.' Napoleon glanced out of the carriage window. 'It seems so long ago now.'

The Emperor fell silent and Junot glanced towards Berthier with a questioning look. The chief of staff shrugged faintly.

Napoleon's gaze fixed on his hands. It was over twelve years since he and Junot had won their spurs in the siege of Toulon. Much had happened between then and now, and suddenly Napoleon felt older than his years. The strength of will and swiftness of mind that had singled him out from his peers as a young man were starting to fade. His once thin face and slender body had been replaced by rounded, over-indulged features and a creeping portliness. He was suddenly overwhelmed by a sense of disgust at the changes in his body. Very well, then. If he could stay young in body, he would stay agile in thought. His eyes flashed up towards Berthier.

'Is everything in hand for the shoot?'

'Yes, sire. It has all been taken care of. Even the weather.' Berthier nodded towards the cerulean sky and laughed.

But Napoleon just nodded, absent-mindedly, and muttered, 'Good. That's good.'

Once the guests had arrived, and been served with wine and snacks by the imperial footmen, they began to congregate in groups, filling the air with good-humoured conversation, punctuated by laughter. Napoleon, with a small entourage, moved amongst them, greeting his guests, sharing jokes with old comrades and making flirtatious exchanges with the most beautiful of the women. Then he paused as he saw the Portuguese ambassador in earnest conversation with a small group of foreign dignitaries on the periphery of the party.

'Excuse me,' Napoleon said tersely to his followers. 'Wait here.'

He strode across the trampled grass and the Portuguese ambassador fell silent as the Austrian diplomat, Prince Metternich, nudged his arm.

'A word with you,' Napoleon called out as he strode up to them and the other men at once stepped back to make space for the French Emperor. Napoleon rounded on the Portuguese ambassador. 'I am still waiting for your King to respond to my demands. Well? Heard anything?'

The ambassador bowed his head and replied in a subdued tone, 'Alas, no, your majesty.'

'I see.' Napoleon frowned. 'This discourtesy has gone on long enough. I will not endure it, do you hear? If your King does not do what I want, then he and the house of Braganza will no longer rule Portugal a few months from now. You tell him that. And tell him that with Russia as my ally there is nothing that can stand in the way of France now. Nothing!' Napoleon glared round at the other diplomats and continued in a menacing tone, 'And if there is any other nation in Europe that chooses to defy me by receiving any British envoys, I will declare war on them too. I will not be defied, gentlemen.' He stood there a moment, to make sure they could see that he was serious, then wagged a finger at them and turned to stride back towards his entourage.

All the guests had fallen silent at the sound of his raised voice, and now there was a pause before conversation resumed, a low, nervous muttering which only gradually built up to the former light-hearted hubbub.

After lunch, the male guests strolled down to the shooting line on a raised bank and took up their weapons. Before them lay a vast cropped meadow, and beyond that a small forest. The cages containing the rabbits had been set up a short distance in front of the shooters with the beaters standing ready to drive them forward, in front of the guns of the imperial party. When all the guests had loaded guns held ready and stood in tense expectation, Bethier gave the signal to the senior huntsman, who cupped his hands to his mouth and bellowed, 'Loose the rabbits!'

The pegs were pulled free and the doors swung open as the beaters whacked the rear of the cages with their sticks. At once scores of rabbits bounded free, their tails bobbing up and down like balls of cotton. They hopped a short distance and then began to stop and turn, glancing round curiously.

Napoleon hissed impatiently, waiting for the rabbits to move beyond the beaters so that he could get a clear shot. But the rabbits, as if of one will, had turned round and were already hopping back, darting between the cages and the legs of the beaters as they made for the bank where the shooters stood watching in growing astonishment.

'What the hell?' Napoleon growled. He glanced towards Berthier. 'What is going on? Why don't they run away?'

Berthier shook his head in bewilderment as the rabbits surged up the bank. He called out to the senior huntsman. 'What is the meaning of this?'

The huntsman ran over and bowed his head. 'Sir?'

'What are the rabbits doing?' asked Berthier anxiously as he watched Napoleon lower his gun and kick out at a small crowd of rabbits clustered at his feet.

The huntsman bit his lip. 'These rabbits, sir. Can I ask if you bought 'em wild, or tame?'

'They're from a breeder. Why?'

'So they're tame.' The huntsman nodded. 'That's it then. They must think the shooters have come to feed them.'

The blood drained from Berthier's face. 'Oh, no . . .'

He looked round and saw the line of shooters besieged by the wave of hungry rabbits. Already some of the Emperor's guests were in a retreat, some angered and some amused as the little beasts followed them. Then, as a fluke waft of breeze brought the scent of the banquet down the slope, the rabbits rose on their haunches, tiny noses quivering, and then surged up the slope. Berthier's heart sank at the sight.

'Berthier!' Napoleon called out furiously. 'You fool! You dunderhead!'

Throwing down his weapon in disgust, the Emperor stalked back up the hill towards his carriage. The first of the rabbits had reached the tables and the more hysterical of the female guests were rushing for the shelter of the carriages, some screaming. Berthier looked round, mouth agape, as picnic tables were upset and men and rabbits ran hither and thither in the chaos.

Reaching his carriage, Napoleon climbed the steps and threw himself down on the seat, slamming the door behind him. And then froze. Sitting on the opposite seat was a small rabbit, watching him warily.

'Bastard,' Napoleon muttered, launching himself across the gap and grasping a handful of writhing fur and kicking feet. Holding it at arm's length, he thrust the rabbit towards the carriage window and dropped it on the ground. 'Driver!'

'Sir?'

'Take me back.'

'To Fontainebleau, sir?'

'Where else, you idiot?'

The driver cracked his whip and the carriage lurched forward. Ignoring the scene outside, Napoleon slumped down, arms crossed, the darkest of expressions on his face.

He did not move until the carriage stopped in front of the entrance to his country house, and then he climbed down from the coach as swiftly as possible and strode up the stairs to the door being held open for him by a footman. Inside, the hall seemed dark and cold after the dazzling light and warmth of the summer day, and Napoleon paused to let his eyes adjust. Halfway down the hall a figure abruptly rose from one of the padded benches outside the Emperor's suite of offices.

'Who's that?' Napoleon called out as the figure marched towards him.

'Courier from Paris, sire.' The figure halted and dimly Napoleon made out the features of a young dragoon officer. The officer saluted crisply and held out a despatch. 'From the War Office.'

Napoleon tore open the seal and opened the document out. He moved back into the light beaming from the entrance and read the contents through quickly, then the main points once more, before he folded it up again and thrust it towards the courier.

'Take this. Do you know the estate at Cerbière?'

'Y-yes, sire. I think so.'

'Well, do you or don't you?'

'I do, sir.'

'Then ride there as fast as you can. Ask for the shooting party, and then find Marshal Berthier. Tell him I want him back here immediately. Tell him the British have landed an army in Denmark. Got that?'

'Yes, sire.' The officer nodded. 'Denmark.'

Denmark, Napoleon mused. Why Denmark? The Danes were not allied to France; they were neutral. So why invade them? He frowned, and muttered, 'What are they thinking? What are the British devils up to now?'

Chapter 34

Arthur

Sheerness, 31 July 1807

There was no putting it off any longer, Arthur realised. It would be the very last task he carried out before he boarded HMS *Prometheus*. The warship lay at anchor, a quarter of a mile from the wharf, and he could see her clearly through the window of the room he had taken in a Harwich inn. In the dying light he stared at the dark hull with the two broad stripes of yellow indicating her gun decks. Above towered the masts and spars, seemingly caught like insects in the intricate web of her rigging. The brigade that Arthur commanded had already boarded the *Prometheus* and the large merchant ships anchored astern of the warship. The men were packed along the decks, crowded in with the sailors and marines. More men, together with equipment and supplies, were loaded in the holds of the merchant ships.

The loading was complete and it only remained for Lord Cathcart, the commander of the expeditionary force, to give the order for the fleet to put to sea. As yet the destination of the force was known only to a handful of men in the government and Lord Cathcart, who had been told in the last few days before departure. He had told his senior officers where they were headed – Denmark – but nothing about the purpose of sending the army there. It was puzzling, since Britain was not at war with the Danes. Not yet. Arthur shook his head wearily. Portland's government seemed hell-bent on provoking neutral powers. The recent policy allowing the Royal Navy to seize vessels, of any nation, suspected of trading with France had outraged them all.

With a sigh, he pulled a sheet of paper across the desk and reached for his pen. He dipped the nib into the inkwell, tapped off the excess and held the pen over the blank sheet. This was not going to be an easy letter to write. As far as Arthur knew, Kitty had no idea that he was about to sail off to war. He knew that he should have told her long before, but Kitty being the nervous, uncertain creature that she was he had told himself that it would be best to present her with a *fait accompli*, rather than letting her fret for weeks while he prepared his men for war. It did occur to Arthur that this delay in informing her might be construed as ignoble, and have the odour of cowardice, but those who knew Kitty as he did would be well aware that the delay was for the best. He drew a deep breath and began.

> *My Darling Kitty, I write to tell you that I am to embark on a ship this night to join a small army being sent to fight the French. I have been given command of a brigade and you will be delighted to know that your younger brother Edward is to serve under me. Hopefully it will be the making of him. As for me, I must apologise for being reticent in informing you of my inclusion in this expedition. Given that you are expecting our second child, I did not want to burden your excitable nature with the news that I am returning to active service. Please forgive me, my dearest Kitty, I did not mean to be deceitful.*

He paused and frowned as he re-read his last words. She would see through that in an instant, he mused. Of course he was being deceitful; there was no other word for it. But it could not be helped. If Arthur had felt confident that Kitty would receive the news with stoic calm he would have had no hesitation in telling her. As it was, his wife was a very long way from being stoic in disposition and so a measure of deceit was necessary, he told himself, for her own good. He dipped the pen into the inkwell again and continued.

> *I entrust the running of our household to you and have instructed the family's agent in Dublin to assist you in your duties, and advance you whatever sums you require, within reason. Try to be brave, my dearest Kitty, and God bless you.*

Arthur laid down his pen and read over the brief note. It was very brief, he decided. Perhaps too brief, given that it might well be the last word she ever had from him, apart from being the first intimation she would receive of his involvement in the coming campaign. There was no helping that. He had said what needed to be said and that was that. Folding the paper briskly, Arthur sealed it and thrust it on to the pile of letters he had already written to family, friends and sundry creditors promising to clear accounts the moment he returned. He rang the handbell on the corner of his small desk and a moment later the door opened and the corporal who served as his chief clerk entered.

'Sir?'

Arthur indicated the letters. 'Add these to the post bag, and once that is done get yourself aboard the *Prometheus*, Jenkins.'

'Yes, sir.'

When the corporal had closed the door behind him Arthur stretched back in his chair and folded his arms behind his head. His work was finally done. All preparations and obligations had been tended to and now he was about to set off on campaign. There would be dangers to be sure, a voyage by sea not the least of them, but there was great contentment to be gained from the prospect of leaving behind all the petty duties and annoyances of his post as Chief Secretary in Dublin.

No more patronage to dispense. No more wearisome attempts to balance the interests of the various religious communities in Ireland. No more poring over the reports from secret agents paid to sniff out the faintest whiff of disloyalty and rebellion amongst those who aspired to independence for Ireland. There was a brief lull in his thoughts before he was prepared to admit that the prospect of escaping Kitty and her cloying affection and anxiety over his feelings towards her pleased him as well. It was a sad state of affairs when a husband felt that way, he chided himself. But then not every husband had to deal with someone like Kitty. Still, he would be free of it all for some months, and be able to dedicate himself to the unambiguous duty of fighting the French.

Leaning back, Arthur crossed his hands behind his head and gazed out of the window again towards the shipping resting peacefully at anchor in the sunset. That dog, Bonaparte, had the very good fortune of being the absolute authority in every situation, martial or civil, he mused with a touch of envy. And while the Emperor might have to suppress plots against him, at least he did not find himself enmeshed in the sensitivities of others, as Arthur was. He stared out of the window a moment longer, before wearily rising up and quitting the room.

The small fleet of ships from Sheerness put out to sea at first light and joined the larger convoy that had sailed from Deal. As the ships braced up and began to heel to windward Arthur stood on the quarterdeck and watched as the officers and sailors of the *Prometheus* completed the final adjustments to their sails and the warship settled steadily on her course. Only then were the soldiers permitted on deck, and those who were suffering from the unfamiliar motion rushed to the side and hung their heads over. The rest examined the vessel with curiosity, or simply sat and watched the restless patterns of the waves. The coast of England was little more than an irregular strip of grey between the sea and the sky, and Arthur was slightly surprised that he felt no sense of regret at leaving his country behind. Instead he clasped the ship's rail and closed his eyes as he relished the salty wind sweeping across his face and ruffling his cropped hair.

An hour later, the coast was no longer in sight, and Arthur drew one last deep breath of the fresh air before he turned away and made for the gangway leading towards the officers' cabins that lined each side of the wardroom. He had been allotted the cabin of the first lieutenant of the warship, who had simply moved into the next cabin and obliged the ship's most junior lieutenant to bed down in the midshipmen's berth. Despite being the quarters of the second in command of the ship, the cabin was barely large enough to contain a cot, a desk and a chair. One of Arthur's chests was tucked under the cot; the others were in the hold with the rest of the brigade's baggage. His writing case lay on the desk, and sitting down he flipped back the flap and drew out the orders that had come to him from the War Office a few days before. A short note on the cover of the sealed package instructed him not to open them until out of sight of land, and now he drew a small letter knife from one of the pockets of the writing case and slit the seal. He felt his heart quicken a little as he opened the papers out on the desk. Now he would finally discover the reason for despatching Lord Cathcart's expeditionary force to Denmark.

His eyes skipped over the preliminary formalities and focused on the main section. He read that the current mission was of the utmost importance to the safety of Britain. The Foreign Secretary, George Canning, had discovered through agents the secret clauses of the recent treaty signed between France and Russia, one of which had detailed France's intention to seize the fleets of Denmark and Portugal, the last neutral powers in Europe. There was already an army of thirty thousand Frenchmen gathered at Hamburg, poised to invade Denmark the moment the Emperor gave the word. Accordingly, Canning had instructed Denmark to sail her ships to British ports where they would be safe from the Emperor's clutches for the duration of the war. Denmark had refused to comply and so Lord Cathcart and a fleet of warships had been sent to take the vessels by force.

'Good God,' Arthur muttered, and paused a moment to reflect on the situation. Canning was certainly taking the bull by the horns. Arthur could understand and agree with the strategic necessity of such a move, but he was astonished by the gall of the Foreign Minister. Canning would surely be vilified by the Whigs, and some of his own party, and by almost every nation in Europe for such an act. He picked up the orders and read on.

Once the Danish fleet was removed from Copenhagen, the government would be turning its sights on the Portuguese navy. A diplomatic solution was sought, but if that failed it was possible that Lord Cathcart's force would be required to perform a subsequent operation in Lisbon. The orders ended with a reminder that should either fleet fall into French hands the Emperor would have adequate naval power to force a crossing of the Channel and an invasion of Britain.

Arthur lowered the sheet of paper. He carefully folded it and returned it to his writing case before he leaned back and stared at the stout timber of the bulkhead above the desk, deep in thought.

There would be a fight. There was no doubt of that. Even though Denmark had little sympathy with France, she would be sure to resist any attempt by Britain to remove her fleet. Equally, it was possible that Bonaparte had already given orders for the invasion of Denmark and the seizure of the fleet at Copenhagen. If that was the case then Lord Cathcart might well be caught between the Danes and the French and his position would be precarious indeed. Everything would depend on the speed of the operation. Copenhagen must be taken, and the Danish fleet captured, before the French could react.

The fleet sailed due north, out of sight of land, to avoid being sighted. A screen of frigates sailed in an arc ahead of the convoy to ward off any merchant ships, privateers or the few enemy navy vessels that dared to venture on to the high sea. On the second day the convoy turned east and the ships' crews busily wore their vessels round and began the final approach towards the coast of Denmark. Arthur had informed his officers of the final destination, but not the men, and they now crowded the ship's side to see the low coastline, punctuated by tiny islands and rocky outcrops.

The sails were reefed in as the ships closed on the coast, and as the daylight faded the flagship gave the order to heave to and drop anchor. Several small craft sailed closer to the shore to reconnoitre the approaches to the Danish capital, while on board the *Prometheus* Arthur passed the word for the men under his command to be ready to begin landing at short notice. The night passed slowly and the dark hulks of the British fleet gently pitched and rolled at their anchors, while the men aboard huddled expectantly against the sides. As he walked down their lines, dimly illuminated by bulkhead lanterns, Arthur could sense that they were in high spirits. The younger men were full of nervous excitement, while the veterans sat and waited with stoic expressions, or simply took advantage of the opportunity to sleep, not knowing when the next chance would come.

Then, as the first glimmer of dawn lit the horizon, the flagship gave the signal to make sail. Across the calm surface of the sea came the steady clanking as the crews strained at their windlasses to haul in the thick anchor cables with the great weight of the iron sea anchors at the ends of them. One by one, the ships edged forward, taking up their stations as best they could in the light breeze and making towards the coast at an angle until at noon the signal came to drop anchor a mile from the shore opposite a long sandy beach fringed with grassy dunes.

When Arthur took out his spyglass and examined the horizon he could just make out some spires and perhaps the faint mass of buildings away to the east.

'I think that's Copenhagen,' he muttered as he handed the glass to General Stewart, his second in command. 'Over there.'

Stewart was an experienced officer with a steady, though unspectacular, history of promotion. Even though he respected the man, Arthur suspected that someone at Horseguards had appointed him to Arthur's brigade to nursemaid its young commander.

Stewart squinted through the eyepiece as he steadied the instrument and adjusted for the slight roll of the *Prometheus*. 'I believe you are right, sir. And there's the reception committee.'

He lowered the glass and pointed towards the beach. A group of horsemen had emerged from the dunes and ridden to the water's edge to examine the shipping spread out across the sea. There was a brief flash as a telescope was trained on the fleet, and then the horsemen turned and rode off at a gallop, disappearing back into the dunes.

'There goes the element of surprise,' said Arthur. 'The Danes will be ready enough for us soon.'

'Aye.' Stewart nodded. 'There'll be plenty of blood shed before this is all over. One way or another.'

'Deck there!' a voice called from aloft and Arthur turned and tilted his head back to see one of the sailors high up on the mainmast thrusting his arm out. 'Boat approaching!'

A launch was advancing from the direction of the flagship and Arthur could see the red coat of an army officer sitting at the stern beside the midshipman in command of the boat. The oars rose and fell rhythmically as the small vessel approached the towering sides of the

Prometheus, and as it hooked on to the chains the army officer scrambled awkwardly up the side and on to the deck. Glancing round, he spied Arthur and came striding towards him.

He saluted and held out a folded slip of paper. 'Orders from Lord Cathcart, sir.'

Arthur nodded. He unfolded the paper and skimmed over the contents before he looked up. 'Very well. Tell his lordship that I will begin at once.'

'Yes, sir.'

Arthur turned to Stewart, who was watching him expectantly. 'Lord Cathcart intends to land the army today. Our brigade is to go in first and establish a beachhead, before advancing towards Copenhagen.'

Stewart grinned wolfishly and rubbed his hands together. 'That's the ticket! At bloody last. I've had enough of this tub and need to get my boots on dry land.'

Arthur nodded. 'Pass the word to all officers. They are to have their men ready to go ashore at once. We'll have the first three companies on deck ready to load. The rest can wait below.'

'Aye, sir.' Stewart saluted and turned to march away across the quarterdeck. He cupped a hand to his mouth and bellowed, 'All officers on me! Sergeants, form your men up. First three companies of the battalion only on deck! We're ordered to lead the attack, lads!'

One of the soldiers punched his fist into the air, and cheered at the top of his voice. Instantly the cry was taken up by the other men as they hurried to their stations. Arthur could not help smiling at their high spirits. Then he turned towards the shore and his smile faded. Within a matter of hours the gleaming sands of the beach and the dunes beyond might well be covered in blood and bodies. The prospect of action did not scare him in the least, he reflected calmly. Only the consequences of it.

He turned away and made for the gangway to collect his sword and pistols from his cabin before he led the first wave of British troops to land on Danish soil.

Chapter 35

'Easy oars!' the midshipman cried out and the sailors ceased rowing, allowing the *Prometheus*'s launch to continue forward under its own way through the gentle waves breaking on the flat stretch of sand. Overhead the sky was a deep blue and the sun blazed down from its zenith. Fortunately a comfortable breeze cooled the faces of the men in the boat and the air was punctuated with the shrill cries of curious seagulls as they whirled above the boats. There was a sudden lurch under the keel and the launch slid to a halt, rested a moment, then was carried forward another few feet by the next wave. Two seamen in the prow hopped over the side and held the launch steady. Arthur was sitting close to the bows and when the boat was solidly grounded he was the first of his men to rise up. He clambered over the side into the knee-deep surf with a splash, and waded ashore.

'Over yer go, lads!' a sergeant bellowed. 'Don't want the general to fight 'em all on 'is own now! Move yerselves!'

The redcoats climbed out of the launch, muskets held clear of the water, and made their way ashore, emerging from the sea with drenched boots and trousers from the thigh down. On either side, the other boats from the warship ground softly on to the sand and more men piled over the side and surged ashore, until the first company was complete and the sergeant ordered them to form up ten paces beyond the surf. The moment the last of the soldiers was out of the launches the crews pushed their boats back into the sea until they had cleared enough distance to turn round and return to the ship to collect the next company of redcoats.

Stewart made his way over to Arthur and nodded to the dunes rising up ahead of them. 'Shall I post some pickets up there, sir?'

'Yes, of course. See to it, please.'

Stewart took the nearest ten men of the Light Company and trotted away across the sand. Arthur watched him with a thoughtful look. He had been about to order the pickets forward himself and now Stewart would no doubt assume he had scored a point over his superior. At some point the man was going to have to be firmly reminded who was in charge. But there was no time for that now. Arthur turned towards the gap in the dunes, a quarter of a mile further along the beach, where the Danish horsemen had appeared earlier. He called the captain of the Light Company over.

'Sir?'

'See that gap?'

The captain followed the direction that Arthur pointed out. 'Yes, sir.'

'Take the rest of your company over there and form them in line across it. They are not to fire on any Danish soldiers they may encounter. If we can avoid a confrontation we must.'

'And if they fire on us, sir?'

'Make every attempt to parley, first. If they are still not amenable to persuasion you may fire on them. Now off you go.'

As the captain led his men down the beach at the double Arthur glanced back towards the ships. The first boats were still rowing back and it would be at least half an hour before they returned. More boats were putting out from the other ships to help convey the rest of the brigade ashore, but Arthur estimated it would be some hours yet before his command was safely landed. He turned and strode up the beach to join Stewart and the pickets, spread out along the dunes.

From the top of the highest dune close to the beach there was a clear view over the surrounding landscape. The dunes continued inland for a few hundred paces before giving way to pastureland, where the tiny figures of cows and sheep dotted the fields. A vague haze and the spires Arthur had seen earlier indicated the direction of Copenhagen.

'Any signs of activity?'

'No, sir,' Stewart replied. 'But we can be sure the men we saw will have made their report by now. I'd guess we will have some company before too long.'

Arthur nodded. 'It would seem likely. Tell the pickets to keep their eyes open. I'm going to join the Light Company. Send a runner the moment you sight anything.'

'Yes, sir.'

They exchanged a brief salute before Arthur turned away and strode off through the dunes towards the men blocking the opening to the beach. The air was still and hot and insects buzzed drowsily amid the tufts of grass that clung to the sandy soil. He removed his cocked hat and mopped his brow, puffing his cheeks out as the heat became decidedly uncomfortable. Even so, he infinitely preferred to fight in such fine weather rather than the bitter freezing cold he had experienced the last time he had fought on the continent. That had

313

been in the Low Countries early in the war, when a terrible winter and incompetence had cost the British army dear and convinced Arthur that he would always look to the welfare of his men first, wherever and whenever he was called upon to fight.

Once Arthur's brigade had secured the beach, the rest of Lord Cathcart's army began to land, and as night fell the dunes were illuminated by hundreds of campfires built from the stunted trees that grew on the fringes of the sand. Scores of cattle and sheep had been taken from the nearest farms and slaughtered, and now were roasting over the fires. Arthur was angry over such looting, knowing full well how it would be bitterly resented by the locals and make the task of securing the Danish fleet that much more difficult. But Lord Cathcart was unmoved by his protests.

'Come now, Sir Arthur, we are here to steal a fleet!' The commander of the British army smiled as he carved a large chunk of meat from his steak. He was entertaining his senior officers in his command tent, erected in the shelter of the dunes. It had proved a poor spot to choose as the air was thick with midges. 'I think the odd bit of beef and mutton along the way will hardly matter.'

'Precisely, sir,' Arthur's immediate senior, David Baird, added. 'Spoils of war and all that.' The conqueror of Seringapatam turned to Arthur and wagged a finger. 'Ah, but I was forgetting. Seems you still harbour the same scruples concerning the local people as you did back in India.'

Arthur ignored the goading and kept his attention focused on Lord Cathcart. 'It makes little sense to antagonise the local people if we can avoid it, sir. We are a small enough force as it is, and it would be better if we maintained good relations with the people whose lands we are obliged to pass through. It is my conviction that it always pays dividends in the long run.'

'And it costs a small fortune to pay for local produce in the short term,' Cathcart countered. 'Besides, it is not as if the practice of living off the land is not without precedent. Why, Napoleon's soldiers have all but turned it into a way of life.'

'To their detriment, sir. Now farmers and landowners conceal their stock and grain stores at the first sign of the advance of a French army. With the result that the French troops are obliged to use force to discover the location of concealed supplies, which in turn promotes a bitter hatred and thirst for revenge amongst those whose lands they pass through. In the end they will be obliged to deploy as many men to protect their communications as they have available to fight the main force of their enemy.' Arthur shook his head. 'I would rather not burden the British army, small as it is, with such concerns if I could avoid it.'

Lord Cathcart thought about it for a moment, as he chewed on another large piece of steak, and then nodded. 'It's a fair point, Wellesley. But what would you have me do? Hang those who purloin the odd specimen of livestock?'

'Yes, sir,' Arthur replied seriously. 'I would. The lesson would be learned soon enough.'

'Good God, man,' Baird protested. 'You would value an enemy pig or a sheep above the life of a British soldier?'

'No. I would value the safety of a man's comrades over the life of one looter. I would value the reputation of a British army over the needs of an individual soldier. That is all.'

Baird shook his head. 'Mad. Quite mad,' he muttered.

As they neared the city Arthur could see that the inhabitants had made some efforts to defend themselves. A ring of simple earthworks surrounded the approaches to Copenhagen and the muzzles of cannon could be seen protruding from the embrasures of some formidable-looking redoubts. In the distance, towering above the buildings of the city, were the masts of the Danish fleet, the prize the army had been sent to seize.

There was no question of the brigade's leading an immediate attack and Arthur ordered his men to form an extended line around the earthworks to keep watch on the enemy until Lord Cathcart and the main body of the British army arrived, with the siege train that had been landed to batter the Danes' defences.

As Cathcart and his staff came trotting up the turnpike Arthur turned his horse and saluted.

'What's this, Wellesley?' Cathcart frowned. 'Why have we halted?'

Arthur indicated the earthworks. Flags were fluttering above each one, and the heads and shoulders of their defenders were clearly visible as they watched Arthur's brigade deploy. 'The Danes have been preparing for us, sir. It seems that we won't be permitted to simply walk in and seize their fleet. I had hoped that they would see reason.'

'Well, no one really imagined they would simply roll over for us.' Cathcart surveyed the defences briefly. 'Very well, gentlemen, it seems we are in for a short siege.' He turned to his aide and dictated a brief order. 'The army will disperse around the city and form a cordon. The engineers are to begin constructing siege batteries and approach trenches at once. Then we'll see how long it takes them to come to their senses and offer their terms for surrender.'

As the last days of August came to an end the small British army laboured under the hot sun digging a series of trenches that zigzagged across the fields towards the enemy redoubts. By night, another relay of men went forward to work on the batteries that were to blast the city's defences to pieces before bombarding Copenhagen itself in an effort to compel surrender. If the Danes continued to resist there would be no alternative to an assault, which would be bloody and would spare neither the Danish militia nor the civilians of the city. There was no possibility of Danish reinforcements arriving by sea, or of escape by the same means, since the warships of the Royal Navy lay anchored off the approaches to the capital, beyond the range of the guns in the forts that guarded the harbour.

Arthur watched the preparations for the siege with a growing sense of unease. The work was proceeding too slowly, to his mind, yet Lord Cathcart seemed content with the present pace and spent much of his time entertaining his officers in his command tent, which was dominated by a long dining table that had been brought ashore in his personal baggage train, together with an ample supply of wines, brandy and fine foods.

Every evening the senior officers dined with their commander, waited on by half a dozen footmen who had accompanied Lord Cathcart from Britain. And outside the sounds of picks and shovels came faintly from the direction of the siege works, together with the occasional shouted order or dull thud of a musket being discharged as the nervous sentries of both sides fired at shadows.

One night, just over a week after the British army had arrived before the city, Arthur was the last to arrive at the usual evening gathering.

'Wellesley!' Cathcart shouted a greeting from the head of the table. 'Sit yourself down, man! What kept you?'

'My apologies, sir, but I had to discipline one of my corporals for looting.'

'Looting?' Cathcart chuckled. 'Hope you didn't have the man shot! Eh?'

'No, sir. He is to be broken back to the ranks and given the lash at dawn.'

'Ah, well, I'm sure it will teach him a lesson,' Cathcart concluded dismissively. 'Anyway, eat up. My steward has managed to prepare a fine saddle of mutton, though I fancy it will have gone cold by now.'

Arthur helped himself to a few cuts of meat from the platter offered to him by one of the footmen. Major Simms, commander of the small contingent of engineers attached to the expeditionary force, was sitting opposite and Arthur leaned towards him. 'What news, Simms? How long before the batteries are completed?'

'Two more days, sir. Three at the most.'

Arthur nodded and was about to ask another question when General Baird, two places further along from Simms, interrupted. 'What's the matter, Wellesley? The Danes aren't going anywhere. We have 'em bottled up like pickled onions. We can take as much time as necessary.'

'I'd like to think so,' Arthur replied evenly, 'but by now the whole of Denmark will know that we are here, not to mention the French. We need to finish the business before they can react.'

'Pah!' Baird shook his head. 'You fuss so, Wellesley. But then you always did.'

Before Arthur could reply a young lieutenant entered the tent, breathless. He strode up to Lord Cathcart and leaned down to talk softly to the commander.

'There's trouble,' Simms said quietly.

Lord Cathcart nodded to the lieutenant and waved him aside before tapping his wine glass with the edge of his knife.

'Quiet, gentlemen! I pray you, be quiet.'

Once all had fallen silent and were looking in his direction Cathcart lowered his knife and cleared his throat. 'One of our cavalry patrols has spotted a column of Danish soldiers marching on Copenhagen, no more than twenty miles away.'

'What is their strength?' asked Baird.

'At least a division.'

Not enough to have any hope of defeating Cathcart's force, Arthur decided, but if they managed to break through to Copenhagen it would make any assault on the city a much greater risk.

'They must be halted,' said Cathcart. 'Halted, or, better still, driven off. But we must move swiftly.'

Before any of the other officers could speak, Arthur rose to his feet. 'My men march as fast as any men in the army, my lord. Let me deal with the Danes.'

Cathcart considered the offer. 'I admit your men are fine soldiers, Wellesley, but setting a brigade against a division? Those are not good odds.'

317

'I beg to disagree, sir. A brigade of good British soldiers is worth a division in any foreign army.'

Cathcart grinned. 'Well said, sir! Well said. Then you may put your confidence to the test. Take your brigade and drive those rascals before you.'

'Thank you, sir. If you'll excuse me, I must rouse my men. We'll march within the hour.'

Chapter 36

'What town is that?' Arthur asked, nodding across the fields towards the modest-looking settlement two miles away. Even at this distance he could see the figures of a line of men well in advance of the buildings. Skirmishers most likely, he decided. Beyond them scores of men were busy barricading the streets that led into the town. The Danes must have been alerted to the approaching column of redcoats at first light and had used the intervening hours to prepare to make their stand.

His question was greeted with silence by his staff officers and Arthur looked round with an irritated expression. 'Well?'

General Stewart came to their rescue. 'It's called Køge, sir.'

'Køge.' Arthur nodded. 'Well, it seems that the Danes have reached the place before us and dug themselves in. That could be a promising sign.'

'Promising?' Stewart cocked an eyebrow. 'How is that, sir?'

'If the Danes have stopped and are setting up defences, that means they are not confident of advancing any further, not without reinforcements. So we have a moral advantage over them already, and I intend to exploit that to the full.'

'You will attack then, sir?'

'Of course.' Arthur fished for his fob watch and glanced down. 'Just after eleven. Plenty of time to clear them out.'

'Good! I'll give orders for the brigade to deploy. Two battalions in the front line and the third in reserve,' Stewart announced. 'Better send our guns forward to soften them up first. Then a rapid advance while they're still reeling should do the trick.'

Arthur listened to his subordinate's plan with a growing sense of irritation. Before Stewart could elaborate Arthur raised a hand to still his tongue and smiled genially. 'Come, come, General Stewart, it is my turn to command.'

'What?' Stewart looked puzzled for an instant before he realised he had overstepped the mark and was being put back in his place. He stiffened his back and nodded. 'Yes, sir. Of course. What are your orders?'

'That's better. Now then, I'll have the brigade formed up, as you suggest. No closer than a mile to the town. No sense in exposing the men to any cannon fire unnecessarily.' Arthur smiled at Stewart. 'Be so good as to see to it.'

'Yes, sir.' Stewart saluted and turned his mount away to ride back down the column and pass the orders on to the battalion. Arthur concentrated his attention on Køge once again. If there really was a division there, and they had entrenched themselves effectively, it would present a sizeable challenge for his brigade to overcome. They would be outnumbered at least two to one, and would have the further disadvantage of being forced to attack regular troops in prepared defences. Normally, it would be rash to even contemplate such an action, Arthur mused. But he had meant what he had said to Cathcart. His men were more than a match for the Danes. Provided they were manoeuvred and fought well, they should win the day.

As the British battalions marched up the road and then turned off it to deploy into line, Arthur and his staff rode ahead until they reined in just outside the range of the Danish skirmishers. It occurred to Arthur that he had not once referred to them as the enemy. The only enemy that mattered was the French, the common enemy of all the nations of Europe, if they but realised it. This conflict with the Danes was a matter of tragic necessity. Britain could not afford to let the Danish fleet fall into Bonaparte's hands, just as the Danes could not let their national pride be shamed by submitting to British demands. Even so, Arthur decided, there might still be a chance to avoid bloodshed. He turned to his staff.

'Wait here. I will return shortly.'

Spurring his horse forward, he trotted along the road towards Køge, making directly towards a small party of Danish soldiers spread across the turnpike. They advanced their muskets and eyed him warily as Arthur approached. He slowed his mount and halted no more than ten paces away from them, and saluted.

'Good day. Is there any man amongst you who speaks English?'

There was a pause before a sergeant nodded. 'A little.'

'I am Major-General Wellesley and I have a message for your commander. Would you be kind enough to ask him to speak to me? I will wait here for his reply. Do you understand all that?'

'Yes, sir.' The sergeant saluted and summoned one of his men, to whom he passed on the message. The soldier handed his musket to a comrade and ran back along the road to Køge. While he waited, Arthur took the chance to examine the Danish defences as discreetly as he could. They appeared to have sited all their cannon to cover the road leading into the town. The same was true for all the infantry that Arthur could see. To his right the country was open and sparsely dotted with trees and farms, offering little cover or concealment from that direction. In the other direction, however, a dyke angled across the flat fields to the edge of the town before bending round the houses there and continuing across the landscape in the direction of the sea. Looking back over his shoulder, Arthur saw that his brigade had completed its deployment and the thin lines of scarlet with white cross–straps looked neat and bright in the sunshine, like toy soldiers.

A quarter of an hour after he had ridden up to the Danish skirmishers a small party of horsemen appeared from the town and galloped up the road towards him. Their leader wore heavy gold epaulettes and a broad scarlet sash across his chest. The sergeant snapped an order and the skirmishers fell in and stood to attention as their general and his staff slowed to a walk, and then stopped just in front of Arthur.

'General Wellesley at your service, sir,' Arthur said firmly, and bowed his head.

'General Schmeiler at yours,' the Danish commander responded in slightly accented English. 'You asked to speak to me.'

'Yes, sir.' Arthur indicated his men. 'We have orders to prevent your column from approaching Copenhagen. I would ask you to withdraw your men from Køge and retreat. You can do nothing to prevent the surrender of Copenhagen. If you remain here, or attempt to continue your advance, then there can only be unnecessary loss of life.'

Schmeiler smiled. 'I thank you for your concern, General Wellesley. But you must know that it would be unthinkable for me to retreat, particularly in view of the minimal threat that your force offers.' He squinted at the redcoats standing in the distance. 'You must have no more than what . . . two thousand men? I have over five thousand. It is I who should be requesting that you fall back.'

Even though he had known that the chances of persuading the Danes to retreat were slight, Arthur felt a heavy sense of sadness in his breast. 'General Schmeiler, I understand your sense of duty, and I commend it. But I implore you, sir, to be rational. My brigade is only a small contingent of the army that is besieging Copenhagen. You cannot hope to penetrate through to the city. If you are not defeated on this ground, then you will surely be crushed further along the road. And to what end? Copenhagen will still surrender.'

Schmeiler's expression hardened. 'We shall see about that. Nothing is certain in war, General Wellesley, but I think that you are perhaps too young and inexperienced to have learned that. I only pray that you survive today and learn a valuable lesson. Now, unless there is anything else, I would ask you to return to your men. Good day, sir.'

Arthur touched the brim of his hat in a parting salute, turned his horse away and galloped back to his staff. He gestured for them to follow him and they returned to the brigade, where Stewart was waiting beside the colour party.

'They mean to fight us,' Arthur announced. 'Their general thinks that we can be swept aside easily enough.'

'Does he now?' Stewart growled. 'Then we must teach him a lesson!'

'Quite,' Arthur responded. He had made his plan of attack on the ride back from his interview with Schmeiler and gave the orders immediately. 'Stewart, you are to take the Light Companies of all three battalions, the Thirty-Second Foot and the Twentieth, and advance directly on the enemy line until you are within musket range. Then you are to halt and engage the enemy. But you are not to advance any further until I give the order. Is that quite clear?'

'Yes, sir. But in the event that I discern an opportunity to—'

Arthur cut him short. 'You will not move until you receive orders.'

'Yes, sir.' Stewart nodded. 'And what of the last battalion?'

'I shall be leading the Thirtieth in person,' Arthur replied, 'together with the Grenadier Companies of the other battalions. I mean to attempt an outflanking manoeuvre, there beyond that dyke, as soon as the gunpowder smoke obscures the enemy's vision.'

There it was, he realised with a slight shock. The Danes had become the enemy. He had tried to prevent it from happening, but now there was nothing for it but to fight and to kill. To win victory, or suffer defeat. Perhaps even to perish here in some obscure skirmish in an unregarded corner of Europe. Arthur shook off the morbid thoughts and glanced round at his officers. 'Gentlemen, we are outnumbered, but we are superior in training, discipline and morale. Set the right example and make sure that your men fight hard, and die hard if necessary, and the day is ours. Now, if you please, to your positions.'

As soon as he saw that his officers and men were ready Arthur nodded to the drum major standing beside the colour party and the brigade's drummers struck up the advance, a harsh rhythmic rattle that set the redcoats on their way. The Light Companies trotted ahead, opening up a gap between themselves and the rest of the brigade as they closed on the enemy and began to fire at will at their opposite numbers. On the flanks, the two nine-pounders attached to the brigade opened fire with a deep roar, firing solid shot against the defended buildings on the edge of the town.

As the leading battalions caught up with the skirmishers, Stewart took command of the whole formation. They continued forward to within two hundred yards of the town, then halted and began to exchange fire with the Danish infantry formed up in front of them. After the first half-dozen volleys a thick pall of gunpowder smoke hung in the still air, obliterating each side's view of the other.

This was the moment Arthur had been waiting for. He filled his lungs and turned in his saddle to bellow an order. 'The Thirtieth will form column to the left!'

The line of redcoats turned swiftly and doubled their ranks so that they formed a column, four abreast, facing the dyke a few hundred yards away.

'Advance!'

With Arthur riding at their head, the battalion, led by the Grenadier Companies, quick-marched over the pastureland, scattering the sheep before them as they trampled down the grass. Glancing to his left, Arthur saw that the smoke was building up nicely. Even the roofs of the buildings were barely visible in the thickening haze hanging over the acrid yellow smog that consumed Stewart's men, and the front line of the enemy.

As he reached the dyke Arthur spurred his mount up the grassy slope. As he had thought, there was a broad expanse of polder on the far side, and the hot weather had dried out a thin strip of land alongside the mound of the dyke. The battalion swarmed up and over and set off parallel to the far side, following Arthur as they headed at an angle towards the town. The sounds of battle to their right were now muffled by the dyke and as they tramped on Arthur could not help noticing the brightly coloured butterflies and drowsy insects flitting through the long grass and wild flowers growing along the bank, quite oblivious of the bloody affairs of men.

Turning round, Arthur urged his column on. General Stewart and the rest of the brigade would be able to keep the Danes occupied for some time before the enemy was able to concentrate superior fire and force the redcoats back. The flank attack had to be made before that happened. When he estimated they had gone nearly a mile, Arthur halted his men and dismounted. Leaving the reins in the hands of one of the battalion's drummer boys, he made his way carefully up the dyke. As he approached the top he removed his cockaded hat and peered over the crest.

The outskirts of the town were no more than two hundred yards away, guarded by two companies of Danish regulars and a small artillery piece that had been laid to cover any attempt by Stewart to filter men round the side of Køge. Away to the right came the continuous crackling of musket fire. Arthur re-joined his men and summoned the battalion's officers.

'It is as I'd hoped. The enemy have left us an opportunity to attack from this flank. Have your men fix bayonets. When I give the word we cross the dyke and approach the town at the trot. We will halt at fifty paces and fire a volley, and then charge. After that, stop for nothing. You strike hard and you strike fast. Give them no time to recover, and make as much noise as you can. Stewart will hear and make his charge, and taken from two directions I doubt that the Danes will stand. Questions?'

There was no reply and Arthur shook his head. 'Very well. Carry on.'

The officers trotted back to their companies and Arthur drew his sword and rested the flat of the blade on his shoulder. There was a low scraping and rattling as the men drew their socket bayonets and fixed them over the muzzles of their muskets. With the weapons advanced, the men charged their flash pans with powder and firmly closed the frizzens. Then all was still and Arthur glanced round to see that the officers were watching him expectantly. He stepped forward, and climbed halfway up the bank where he could be clearly seen.

'Thirtieth will advance at the run!' He raised his sword, and the blade glittered in the bright sunshine for an instant before he swept it towards the town. 'Advance!'

The redcoats swarmed up the bank, grunting and scrabbling as a handful slipped in the long grass. Then they poured over the crest and started towards the town, their boots rumbling softly over the dry ground. The Danes saw them coming at once. Snatching up their muskets they turned towards the threat, and glanced uncertainly at their officers for a moment until the latter recovered from their surprise and began to shout out orders. At once the Danish regulars hurried into formation and stood at ease, muskets grounded, facing the British battalion rapidly approaching them. Meanwhile the crew of the solitary artillery piece had rushed to their weapon and grabbed the trail, struggling to turn the gun round to face the oncoming enemy.

Arthur led the way, setting the pace, urging his men on. At a hundred yards he saw the gun crew drop the trail and make ready to blast the redcoats. The portfire flared above the firing tube for an instant and then a bright yellow jet of flame leaped from the muzzle as a plume of smoke billowed out. The weapon had been loaded with case shot and the deadly cone of iron balls swept through the company on the right flank of the British line, knocking several men to the ground. The battalion did not even pause, but continued rushing forward as one of the gunners sprinted round to the front of the gun and began to sponge it out.

Gauging the distance between his men and the two companies of Danes, Arthur waited a moment and then drew up, thrusting his sword into the air. 'Thirtieth! Halt! Make ready to fire!'

The battalion drew up, swiftly dressed their ranks and then advanced their muskets, the men panting for breath.

'Aim!'

The muskets came up, the bayonets pointing directly at the enemy. The Danish officers were busy bellowing their own orders and their men raised their weapons in response.

'Cock your muskets!'

'Fire!'

The two sides fired within an instant of each other and the volleys thundered out. Arthur felt the wind of a ball pass close by his head and heard the thudding impact and gasps of his men as they were struck down. From the right came the sound of another blast from the cannon.

'Charge!' Arthur bellowed, the cry torn from his throat. Thrusting his sword forward, he raced through the thin cloud of gunpowder smoke and saw through the opposing veil that the Danes had already grounded their muskets and begun to reload. On either side the men of the Thirtieth burst through the smoke and raced across the open ground directly at the enemy. As they closed the gap Arthur could see that the Danes would not have time for another volley and already some of them were stepping back in the face of the line of bayonets sweeping towards them. Only a handful managed to discharge their weapons before the redcoats were among them. Arthur made for a tough-looking veteran, who had managed to fix his bayonet and now advanced the point towards Arthur's stomach. With a vicious slash, Arthur parried the thrust and slammed the hilt of his sword into the man's face, crushing his nose and knocking him senseless. On either side the men of the Thirtieth tore through the enemy line, stabbing with their bayonets and using the butts of their muskets like clubs as they smashed into skulls with savage roars. The Danes, outnumbered and stunned by the ferocity of the charge, died where they stood, or broke and ran, fleeing towards the shelter of the town.

'Keep after them!' Arthur roared. 'Charge! Charge!'

The officers and sergeants took up the cry and the redcoats rushed over the last stretch of open ground before plunging into the town. Arthur drew up, and grabbed the arm of one of the young ensigns.

'Circle round the town. Find Stewart and tell him to charge. Got that?'

'Yes, sir.' The ensign nodded, wide-eyed and breathing fast.

'Then go!' Arthur thrust him in the right direction and turned to re-join the tide of screaming British soldiers charging into the town.

Their blood was up and they cut down any Danish soldier they came across, whether they attempted to surrender or not. Arthur joined a loose column of men surging up one of the wider streets leading into the heart of Køge. Ahead of them, at an intersection with another broad thoroughfare, stood another company of soldiers, formed up and facing the redcoats. They raised their muskets and thumbed back the cocks.

'Get down!' Arthur cried over the heads of his men. Most instinctively obeyed, falling to their stomachs or crouching on hands and knees. A few slower souls reacted too slowly and were cut down as the Danish volley crashed down the length of the street.

'Up and at 'em!' Arthur shouted and the charge surged forward again. This time the Danes put up more of a fight and there was a heaving scrummage as the soldiers were thrust against each other and then pressed on from behind. The war cries subsided into agonised groans and the grunts of men straining to push their foes aside. The weight of numbers was on the British side and the Danes were steadily forced back, the men striking at each other with their fists as well as their weapons as the resistance eased. Again the enemy broke and fled and Arthur and the others pursued them down the street towards the heart of the town.

One of the redcoats stopped outside a door and kicked it in, splintering the wood around the latch. There was a female scream from within, then Arthur grabbed his arm.

'Move on!'

The man stared at him, wide-eyed and wild, his teeth bared in a snarl.

'That's an order!' Arthur shouted into his face and thrust him away from the door. 'Move yourself!'

The soldier's snarl faded as some sense returned, then he turned and ran after his comrades, and Arthur had a glimpse of a terrified young woman clutching a child before he ran on after his men. A short distance ahead the street opened out on to a large square, filled with a milling confusion of Danish soldiers. Those who had fled from Arthur's columns had run headlong into the formed units of their comrades and caused confusion and chaos, a situation made far worse the moment the grenadiers and the men of the Thirtieth burst into the square and threw themselves on their enemies. Arthur stopped, heart pounding, gasping for breath. Seeing a supply wagon parked close by he thrust his way through his men and climbed up on to the driver's seat for an overview of the struggle.

Now that he could see right across the square Arthur realised that his men were hopelessly outnumbered. With surprise and shock on their side they would hold their own for a short time yet. But beyond the nearest mob of Danish soldiers stood over a thousand more men, formed up and ready to fight. In their midst Arthur could make out Schmeiler and his staff officers. He watched for a few more minutes as his men pressed the enemy back, and then the impetus of their wild charge died and the melee formed a static line across the edge of the square. Then, almost imperceptibly at first, the British soldiers began to give way, forced back by weight of numbers, and they began to be cut down by the vengeful Danes. Arthur looked in the direction from which Stewart would come and prayed that the ensign he had sent had managed to get through. If the other two battalions did not appear now, the Thirtieth's attack would fail and they would be hunted down and killed in the streets.

Seeing that his men were now winning the fight, General Schmeiler rode through the ranks and drew his sword, bellowing encouragement to his soldiers. He looked over the heads of the combatants and for a brief instant he met Arthur's gaze and his lips curled into a smile of triumph.

Just then a volley crashed out to Arthur's right, then another, as musket balls swept into the square from the side streets. The range was close and scores of Danes went down. A moment later the first of Stewart's men surged into the square, charging home with wild abandon.

'We're saved, boys!' a grenadier sergeant close by Arthur cried out, then his head snapped back in a welter of blood and brains as an enemy officer fired a pistol into his face at close range. But it was too late for the Danes. Those who had been facing Arthur's men stopped moving forward and glanced over their shoulders in panic at the sound of a new threat.

'Thirtieth!' Arthur cried. 'One more effort and the day is yours!'

Someone cheered, the cry was taken up and the tide reversed as the men of Arthur's column pressed forward again, thrusting the Danes back across the square. Assailed from two directions the enemy's discipline broke and the weaker-willed were already fleeing from the redcoats, racing off down the streets that were still clear. As the panic spread more and more men turned and ran, many casting aside their weapons in a bid to escape. Jumping down from the wagon Arthur thrust his way through the ranks of his men towards General Schmeiler, who was caught in a tight press of bodies. His horse's nostrils flared in terror at the shouts and screams that filled its ears. It lashed out with its hooves, breaking the bones of those immediately behind the general, and the Danish soldiers tried to make space for it. Ahead of Arthur a burly sergeant of grenadiers clubbed aside two Danes before grasping Schmeiler's sleeve and hauling him bodily from the saddle. The general crashed on to the cobblestones, emitting an explosive gasp as the air was driven from his lungs. The grenadier laughed, grasped his musket tightly in both hands and raised the bayonet ready to strike.

'No!' Arthur yelled, pushing his way to the side of the sergeant and grasping the barrel of the musket with his spare hand. 'This one lives!'

The sergeant growled a curse and lowered his musket, then strode forward a few paces and slammed the butt into the side of an enemy officer's head. Already the Danes were little more than a mob, each man running for his life, and the square was beginning to empty, leaving the redcoats to claim their prize and their victory. Arthur stood over General Schmeiler, who was still badly winded and dazed by his fall. Schmeiler shook his head to try to clear it, and then his hand groped for the hilt of his sword. Arthur lowered his blade and let the point rest on the Danish general's breast.

'Sir, I must ask you for your surrender.'

Schmeiler did not reply and his lips pressed into a thin line as his hand closed round his sword hilt. Arthur applied a little pressure with the point of his blade.

'General Schmeiler, I insist that you surrender.' Arthur paused. 'Or die.'

Schmeiler stared back with a bitter expression, and then nodded, letting his hand slip to his side. Arthur breathed a quick sigh of relief and then leaned down, grasped his opponent's arm and hauled the Dane to his feet. General Schmeiler bowed his head for a moment and then drew his sword and offered the hilt to Arthur. 'I surrender. My sword is yours.'

Arthur accepted the ornately decorated weapon with a nod and tucked it under his arm.

'General Wellesley! Sir!'

Arthur turned towards the voice and saw Stewart striding towards him. He had lost his hat and blood streaked his face from a cut in his scalp, but he was grinning like a madman. 'We did it, sir!' Stewart laughed self-consciously. 'My apologies, General. You did it, sir. The town is yours.'

'I thank you.'

'What are your orders, sir?'

'Orders?' Arthur forced himself to calm his thoughts. 'Right. Pass the word to all officers to continue the pursuit only as far as the limits of the town. Have the grenadiers take charge of any prisoners, and weapons collection. Find somewhere for the treatment of the wounded, and let the men know that there is to be no looting. No rape and no drunkenness. Clear?'

'Yes, sir.'

'Oh, and one other thing.'

'Sir?'

'Send a messenger to Lord Cathcart. Tell him I have the honour to report that the brigade has taken Køge, and that the Danish relief column has been routed. Nothing can save Copenhagen now.'

Chapter 37

The preparations for the siege were completed shortly after Arthur's brigade returned to the British lines outside Copenhagen. Several batteries had been constructed within range of the city, and the engineers had ensured that the guns would be well protected by great ramparts of earth, fortified with fascines and stout wooden props. Behind the defences the siege guns were hauled into place and stores of powder and shot brought forward by long lines of redcoats sweating under the late summer sun as they toiled along the trenches that zigzagged towards the Danish positions. All of which activity was scrutinised by the defenders of Copenhagen as they helplessly watched their enemies crafting their doom.

There had been one attempt to disrupt the work when a Danish battalion had crept out from the city on a moonless night. Stealing across the open ground they had soon run into British outposts and after a brief skirmish, illuminated by orange flashes of musket fire, the Danes had been forced back having done little more than smash a score of fascines, and inflict a handful of casualties.

When the last of the siege guns was eased forward, and aimed at the outer works of the city, Lord Cathcart nodded with satisfaction as he inspected the biggest of the batteries in the company of his senior officers. In addition to the siege guns there were several peculiar iron contraptions that looked like cooking tripods except that one leg was longer than the others and was angled inside like a length of guttering. After a moment's reflection Arthur realised that these must be the launch beds for the modest supply of Congreve rockets the army had brought with them from Britain. Sure enough, a small column of men approached carrying the experimental weapons, which looked to Arthur's eye like large fireworks.

'Damn fine work.' Cathcart nodded happily as he leaned forward and squinted down the length of one of the rockets, which was lined up with a church tower the best part of a mile away. In the far distance lay the delicate-looking masts of the fleet that would be the prize of a successful siege. Outside the entrance to the harbour lay the fleet of Admiral Gambier, bottling the Danish vessels up and ready to bombard the city from the sea if necessary.

Cathcart clapped his hands together. 'Those bloody Danes will have to come to terms now. If not, then we'll pound their city to dust, and good riddance.'

Arthur cleared his throat and Cathcart turned towards the sound with a frown. 'D'you have something to say, Wellesley? Speak up.'

Arthur glanced towards the distant roofs of Copenhagen gleaming dully in the sunshine. A faint haze hung over the landscape, adding to the peaceful appearance of the setting. He turned his attention away from the city and looked steadily at his commanding officer. 'We have been sent here to secure the Danish fleet, my lord.'

'I know that well enough, thank you. What is your point?'

'Well, it seems to me that the most prudent course of action would be to do all in our power to take those warships with the least loss of life and damage to property.'

'Damn it, man.' Cathcart thrust his hand out towards the Danish warships. 'There is the fleet, Wellesley. In case you had not noticed, the city lies between us and those ships. We must overwhelm the one to win through to the other.'

'I agree, my lord. We must have those ships. But we do not want this affair to damage Britain's reputation unnecessarily. Surely it would be better to try to persuade the Danes to surrender before any more blood is shed? If we can demonstrate that violence is our last recourse then we may yet emerge from this with more credit than we brought into it.'

Lord Cathcart shook his head. 'Do not if and but me, Wellesley. That is no way for a soldier to think. We have our orders and we will obey them to the best of our ability. Now then.' Cathcart forced a smile. 'Since you insist on using those terms, then *if* the enemy can be persuaded to surrender as soon as possible, then so much the better, eh? *But* if he is resolved to fight, then we must make sure that we crush him without mercy. Then all Europe will know the dreadful price that comes with defying the interests of Britain.'

Arthur thought about this for a moment before responding. 'You are probably right, my lord. It might well be better to be feared than be-friended.' He paused and tried to restrain a small smile as he continued. 'However, I would rather not have our country compared to France in terms of the lessons we teach other nations. We make war as a last resort and even then we should not make enemies if we can avoid it.'

'Stuff and nonsense!' General Baird snorted. 'War is war. It's a bloody business. Besides, the Danes have brought this on themselves. They should have given way when they had the choice, Wellesley.'

'That is so,' Arthur conceded. 'But their pride was affronted. Now that they have suffered a number of reverses, and are looking upon the muzzles of our siege guns, they might be more willing to negotiate.'

Cathcart shut his eyes for a moment and breathed heavily, as if struggling to control his temper. 'Look here, Wellesley, if you think you can talk them round then you are welcome to try. I don't give a damned fig for their city, but I will do what I can to spare our boys.'

Arthur felt his heart lift at Cathcart's words. He saluted. 'I'll see to it at once, my lord.'

'You do that,' Cathcart replied flatly and turned away as he raised his telescope and examined the Danish defences.

Arthur galloped back to his brigade headquarters and hurriedly briefed Stewart.

'If anything happens, you will take command of the brigade.'

'Yes, sir. Be careful.'

Arthur stared at him a moment as he sensed the man's sincerity, and then bowed his head. 'Thank you, Stewart. Now you have your instructions. I will need an officer to carry a flag of truce. Also I want General Schmeiler brought forward.'

'Schmeiler?'

Arthur nodded. 'I have a feeling he may prove useful.'

Stewart saluted and strode off to carry out his instructions leaving Arthur staring out of his tent flaps towards Copenhagen, shimmering in the heat. He reached down and unbuckled his sword, and laid it down on his campaign desk. Now that he was about to approach the Danish lines unarmed and with just one of his men, Arthur felt the first cold tingle of fear trace its way up his spine. At once he was furious with himself for the unworthy sentiment, and forced it from his mind. A general simply could not afford to succumb to such moments of weakness. He drew a cloth from his pocket and mopped the sweat from his brow before pressing his cocked hat firmly down over his crown. Taking a deep breath, he strode out into the sunshine and called for his horse.

Shortly before noon, the three men rode out from the British lines, down the turnpike leading towards Copenhagen. Arthur rode a short distance ahead. To his left a young ensign bore a white flag aloft, gently waving it from side to side in the breathless air to ensure that the Danes would see that it was a flag of truce that he carried. To Arthur's left, General Schmeiler sat erect, a strained expression on his face. He had cracked some ribs when he had crashed to the ground back in Køge and was in some pain as his horse walked slowly forward.

They passed between the last of the British outposts and emerged into the open ground between the two armies. The air was still and a slight haze wavered off the dried track in the distance. The hooves of the horses scraped and clopped as the saddlery creaked under the three riders. Now and then one of the horses snorted or ground its teeth on its bit. As they approached the Danish outposts several of the militiamen emerged from shelter, holding their muskets at the ready.

'General Wellesley,' Schmeiler said softly. 'What is to prevent me from joining my countrymen when we reach their lines?'

'Just your word of honour. You have given your parole and I will not release you from it until this conflict is over.'

Schmeiler eased his mount forward until he was alongside Arthur. 'And then you will release me?'

'Of course. What would be the point of holding you prisoner any longer than was necessary? As I explained, we are here for your fleet and nothing more. Once France is defeated the warships will be returned to Denmark.'

'So you say.'

'So I mean.' Arthur looked at the Danish general. 'You have my word on it.'

They continued forward until they were no more than fifty paces from the nearest of the militia. Then one of them, a junior officer, raised his hand and shouted to the three riders.

'He says we are to halt,' muttered Schmeiler.

Arthur reined in. 'Would you be kind enough to explain that I wish to speak to the senior officer of the gallant defenders of Copenhagen.'

Schmeiler translated the request and after a further brief exchange the officer saluted and trotted off towards the nearest redoubt. A moment later Arthur saw him emerge on horseback from behind the earthworks and gallop off towards the town a quarter of a mile beyond. They waited patiently in their saddles as their mounts ambled towards the grass growing along the side of the turnpike and lowered their heads to feed. Arthur turned to Schmeiler.

'It is a shame that Denmark does not join us in the fight against Bonaparte. Surely you must see the danger he poses to us all?'

'Of course. But what can we do about it? Denmark is a small nation. Our army is no match for soldiers of France, or Britain for that matter, as I have discovered. If we defied the Emperor he would swallow us up in a matter of days. So we bide our time, and attempt to keep out of the wars of greater nations. Now you have brought war to us and we find ourselves caught between Britain and France without even the consolation of making a friend out of an enemy's enemy.'

'What's that?' Arthur looked at the Dane sharply.

'Copenhagen is besieged by Britain and Denmark is besieged by France. Before I encountered your brigade, I had just been informed that a French army was massing on our border. I think their intention is clear enough. They mean to let you weaken our defences before marching on your rear, and taking Copenhagen the moment they have dealt with you. They could arrive within a week. Ten days at the most.'

Arthur nodded towards the militiamen watching them closely from a short distance away. 'Did you say anything about the column to that officer?'

'No. I will save it for his commander.'

Arthur felt his pulse quicken. This was bad news indeed and made it essential that the Danes surrender as soon as possible. He cleared his throat and continued calmly. 'It would seem that Denmark faces a choice of giving way to us, or to France. I need not tell you that the consequences of the latter option are far more dire than permitting Lord Cathcart to remove your warships. Once we have those there is no purpose to our remaining on Danish soil. I doubt the French would leave your country quite so readily.'

Schmeiler thought on this a moment and then nodded slowly. 'I think you are right.'

'Then can I count on your assistance in helping to persuade the commander of the Copenhagen garrison to lay down his arms?'

'I will not go that far,' Schmeiler replied. 'But I will present your case fairly.'

'Thank you.'

A quarter of an hour later a small party of horsemen reined in a short distance from Arthur and his two companions. Some were dressed in civilian clothes and one, their leader, wore a gaudy uniform. He saluted Arthur as he approached, and then frowned as he saw General Schmeiler. He addressed the latter sharply and there was a brief exchange before he turned his attention back to Arthur.

'Sir, I am General Peymann, commander of the garrison. Whom do I have the honour of addressing?'

'Major-General Sir Arthur Wellesley at your service, sir.' Arthur touched the brim of his hat.

Peymann eyed him appraisingly. 'Is it true that your brigade defeated a division of regular troops?'

'Why, yes, sir.' Arthur sensed Schmeiler flinch at his side and decided it would be best to spare the man as much embarrassment as he could. 'But only after a stiff fight, sir. Your compatriots did all that they could before yielding to my men.'

'I am gratified to hear that,' Peymann responded flatly. 'Though it would have been better if our men had fought with more zeal. I can assure you that the defenders of Copenhagen will fight with rather more heart than General Schmeiler and his men.'

'I have no doubt of that,' Arthur replied politely. 'I am sure that they are all good patriots. Like any man who volunteers for the militia. Be that as it may, they are up against regular soldiers, the best trained infantry in Europe. Our fleet anchored off the approaches to your harbour is manned by the victors of Trafalgar. Sir, there can only be one result if you should make the tragic mistake of opposing our demands. Admiral Gambier's fleet will bombard Copenhagen. Thousands will die and many fine buildings will be crushed to rubble. Then the army of General Cathcart will storm the city. You know the rules of war, sir. If you fail to come to terms with us before the assault begins then our men will be fully within their rights to sack Copenhagen and take what, and whom, they like.'

General Peymann eyed him coldly. 'You would let them do that?'

'I regret to say that I, or any British general, could do little to stop them,' Arthur replied. The redcoats were fine soldiers on the battlefield but could be perfect devils when given their head and Arthur dreaded to consider the consequences should a drunken host of British soldiers descend on the helpless population of the Danish capital. He decided to make one final effort to persuade General Peymann to see reason. 'Sir, much as I admire your determination to defend your country's honour, I would beg you to spare your people the horrors of war. What glory is there in such an end? I implore you. Surrender your fleet to Admiral Gambier while there is still time.'

'You know that we cannot do that. Do you think for a moment that the French Emperor would tolerate such meek behaviour? No, he would punish Denmark severely.' General Peymann smiled bitterly. 'So it seems that my people are damned either way.'

It was true, Arthur reflected sadly. There was no easy choice for the Danes.

General Peymann stiffened his back and continued. 'Besides, what gives your government the right to demand possession of our warships?'

'Only the right of self-preservation. Britain cannot let those ships fall into French hands. You would do the same in our position.'

'Perhaps,' Peymann conceded. 'And what about you, General

Wellesley? If our positions were reversed, would you surrender your capital city and your warships?'

Arthur thought for a moment and shrugged. 'I doubt it. But we must deal with the present realities, sir. Will you surrender?'

'No.'

'Then there is nothing more to say.'

Peymann shrugged. 'I bid you farewell.'

The Danish commander tugged on his reins and turned his mount away. Arthur glanced at Schmeiler and thought quickly. There was still a chance that General Peymann might yet be persuaded to see sense. He reached over and touched Schmeiler's arm.

'I release you from your parole.'

Schmeiler looked at him in surprise. 'You release me? Why?'

'There is no point in keeping you prisoner any longer. It serves no purpose. You are free. I hope that you live through what is to come.' Arthur offered the Dane his hand and Schmeiler shook it warmly before Arthur turned his mount away and spurred it back towards the British lines, hurriedly followed by the ensign still carrying the flag of truce.

That night the British fleet sailed within range of the city and began to bombard Copenhagen. Arthur watched from one of the British outposts close to the coast. Scores of flashes illuminated the sides of the warships as their solid shot arced across the harbour and pounded the buildings of the Danish capital. Fire was returned from the citadel that guarded the harbour until the guns there were silenced, and for the rest of the night the ships of the Royal Navy continued to pour a devastating barrage of shot on the Danes.

From the landward side the siege guns added their weight, pounding the defences before them, while the rockets shrieked out from their launchers, inscribing a flaring parabola across the night sky before they fell inside the city and exploded with bright flashes that brought cheers from the ranks of the excited British soldiers who had gathered to watch the spectacle. Some fires began to start where the rockets had landed and wavering orange flames steadily spread across expanses of the city as the night drew on. Only as the first glimmer of dawn appeared did the fire begin to slacken as the British warships made sail and withdrew out of range of the remaining Danish guns. As the light strengthened and Arthur trained his spyglass on the city his heart sank at the sight of the shattered roofs and the clouds of smoke billowing up from the fires that still raged.

The bombardment continued for the following two nights, increasing in intensity. Once the initial exuberance of the first night had worn off the redcoats watched the terrible pounding in awed silence, their faces dimly lit by the distant glow of flames and the sudden flare of explosions as they witnessed the death of a great city. Then, on the morning after the terrible destruction of the third night, General Peymann sent a message to Lord Cathcart offering to surrender both Copenhagen and the fleet. A treaty was signed two days later and the garrison laid down its arms and opened the city to the victors.

When Arthur inspected the town he was horrified to see the damage that had been inflicted. Wide stretches of ground were little more than charred ruins and most buildings had been damaged by round shot that had carried away chimneys, smashed through roofs and walls and left the streets littered with debris. Then there were the bodies. In places they had been laid out neatly and covered with blankets. There had been little time to bury them as the citizens had struggled to fight the fires and find shelter for themselves and their families. But there were still hundreds sprawled in the street or buried in the ruins and the air was thick with the sickly sweet smell of corpses rotting in the heat of the late summer.

By the terms of the treaty the Danes gave up their fleet, together with those naval stores and supplies that had survived the bombardment. In return Britain agreed to quit Copenhagen as soon as the troops could be embarked. Over the following days the heavy guns were carefully loaded back on board their transports and then the infantry battalions followed suit. Arthur's brigade was the last to go aboard the final squadron of warships that lay at anchor in the harbour. He had received reports that a French corps was on the march towards Copenhagen and the leading elements were already little more than a day's march from the city. While the other battalions waited on the quay to be rowed out to the warships Arthur took command of the rearguard and positioned them in a cordon around the dock area.

The streets were eerily silent as the Danish inhabitants hid away, bolting their doors and shuttering their windows before retreating further inside to pray for their deliverance. Arthur stood in the tower of the customs house resting his telescope on the back of a chair as he fixed his attention on a French cavalry patrol that had appeared on a low rise inland that overlooked the capital. Well, let them look, he mused to himself. They were already too late. The Danish fleet had weighed anchor and was already on its way across the North Sea to Britain. Eighteen ships of the line together with twelve frigates. Those ships undergoing repairs in the dry docks had been fired a few days earlier and only the skeletal remains of their great timbers remained.

He turned at the sound of footsteps and saw General Stewart climbing into the tower behind him.

'How is the loading proceeding?'

'Almost done with the first battalion, sir.' Stewart saluted. 'The second should be aboard within an hour or so. Then it's just the rearguard.'

'Very well. I shall be glad when we have quit this place.'

Stewart nodded. 'I am sure that some in Britain will say that this was not our finest hour.'

'That is true. However, we must let them say what they like as long as they leave the soldiering to us.'

'Yes, sir.'

'Right then, time to be off.' Arthur took a last look at the enemy cavalry scouts, and was about to collapse his spyglass when a new movement caught his eye. Just to one side of the enemy horsemen the head of a column of infantry had appeared and was already pouring down the far slope and marching towards Copenhagen as swiftly as they could. Arthur waited a moment longer so that he could ascertain their strength. When the first three battalions had crossed over the rise he snapped his glass shut and stood up stiffly. 'We have company.'

Stewart scanned the horizon, saw what Arthur had seen and nodded. 'They'll reach the city within the hour.'

'Yes,' Arthur responded dully. 'Best prepare for them. Have the rearguard occupy the buildings along the waterfront.'

'Yes, sir.' Stewart saluted and disappeared back down the stairs. Arthur stared at the French for a few minutes longer, gauging the pace of their advance. They were making good time and he felt a sick feeling in the pit of his stomach as he realised they would reach the quay well before the last men of the brigade could quit the city.

'This is going to take some careful timing,' he muttered to himself. 'Very careful timing.'

Down on the quayside, the last companies of the other battalions were being herded aboard the launches as Arthur emerged from the customs house. He marched along the quay making sure that his men were well placed to guard the approaches to the embarkation area. Time seemed to crawl as the boats rowed steadily to and fro between the ships and the waiting soldiers, and Arthur tried not to let himself fret at the time it took his men to climb aboard and take their seats on the thwarts before each small vessel was fended away and the oars dipped into the calm sea to power the boat to the waiting warships.

Then at last he heard the drums of the approaching French soldiers and almost at once the crackle of musketry as they ran into the first of the British outposts. The sound quickly increased in intensity as General Stewart came striding up to join him.

'Now we're in for it, sir.'

'Yes, quite,' Arthur replied absently as he tried to gauge the direction of the main thrust of the enemy. 'Seems to be heaviest towards the left flank. As soon as the next boat reaches the quay pull back one company at a time from our right and have them embark as swiftly as possible. Have the Grenadier Company form up on the quay.'

'Yes, sir.'

As the firing continued to the left, the battalion's line began to shorten from the right as one company at a time withdrew and trotted along the quay and down the stone steps to the waiting boats. Arthur was glad to see that one of the warship captains had taken the initiative of placing two launches armed with carronades in the bows to cover the evacuation of the last troops. When there were only two companies left ashore, Arthur had one form up around the steps and then sent a runner to the flank company still holding the houses that covered the approaches to the quayside to order them to fall back. A short time later a handful of redcoats came trotting into sight, then some more, and finally the stragglers and wounded, with several men fighting a rearguard action as they fired and then retreated to new cover.

Arthur filled his lungs and called out calmly, 'Grenadier Company! Stand to!'

The men in front of the steps dressed their line and stood waiting with muskets grounded as their comrades from the Light Company hurried towards them. The captain, breathing heavily, drew up in front of Arthur and saluted.

'Enemy's going to be on us any moment, sir. I also saw some parties making off down side streets to try to outflank us.' He turned and gestured towards the buildings crowding the edge of the quayside. Just then Arthur caught sight of a figure in one of the narrow alleys leading into the dock quarter. An instant later there was a flash, a puff and a crack and a musket ball whirred overhead.

'Very well, Captain. Get your men aboard the launches.'

The officer saluted and stood by the top of the stairs as he urged his men on. As the wounded were helped into the first boat and the rearguard turned and trotted to catch up with the rest of the company, the head of the French column swarmed out on to the quay, a tricolour swirling through the air above their shakos and glinting bayonets. At the same time, more enemy soldiers were emerging from the alleys, cheering as they caught sight of the small band of redcoats remaining to face them.

'Time for you to go, Stewart,' Arthur said quietly.

'Aye.' Stewart nodded. 'Mind you follow on as soon as you can, sir.'

'I will.' Arthur patted him on the back and then turned to face the approaching enemy. 'Grenadier Company, make ready to fire!'

Primed and cocked, the muskets came up and were levelled towards the leading Frenchmen, who drew up at sight of the line of muzzles facing them.

'Fire!'

There was a deafening crash as the volley went off, sending a blast of deadly lead shot through the leading ranks of the French. As the gentle breeze swiftly cleared the smoke Arthur saw that a dozen or more of the enemy were down and it took a moment before those behind pressed on, over the bodies of the dead and wounded. A man close to Arthur suddenly doubled up with a deep grunt and collapsed on to the ground, kicked once and died. Looking round, Arthur saw that those enemy soldiers who had managed to find other routes to the quay were firing into the Grenadier Company from the shelter of the nearest alleyways.

'Fire at will!' he ordered, then glanced round and saw that two launches were approaching the stone steps below the quay. He strode over to the company sergeant and grasped his arm. 'Get the wounded into those boats as soon as they are alongside.'

'Yes, sir.'

The French had halted a short distance away and both sides were firing freely at each other, and Arthur had to steel himself not to react to the whirr of balls flying past, and the thuds as they struck his men. The wounded were carried down to the first boat and then the sergeant began to pluck men out of the line and send them down until the first boat was full and it pulled off, heading back to the nearest warship. As the second boat came up to the steps Arthur bellowed the order to cease fire.

'Quick as you can, lads! Into the boat!'

Together with the last men of the grenadier company, Arthur clambered down the steps and stepped into the launch, half falling on to one of the thwarts. The company sergeant came last and the seamen thrust the launch away and began to row. With a triumphant shout the French surged forward and Arthur realised that he and the others in the boat would be easy targets from the top of the quay.

'Row for your lives!' the midshipman, little more than a boy, in the stern of the launch cried out in a high-pitched voice.

The enemy began to appear along the quay and a shout went up at the sight of the launch. As the first muskets were raised in his direction Arthur felt utterly vulnerable and afraid, yet forced himself to sit quite still and not flinch. There was nothing he could do. Only providence could save him now.

There was a sudden roar from one side, and then the other, and a hail of grapeshot swept the top of the quay clear of enemy soldiers. Startled, Arthur turned and saw that the launches on the flanks had fired their carronades, and were already reloading as the men on the oars began to stroke the vessels away from the quay. One of the seamen in Arthur's boat let out a cheer.

'Shut your bloody mouth!' the midshipman shouted. 'Keep rowing!'

For a moment there was no further sign of the French soldiers, and then the more stout-hearted of them showed themselves along the quay again and took aim on the retreating boats. Shots slapped into the water close by, sending up narrow spouts of silver into the salty air. But the range was already long and within a minute the lusty strokes of the men at the oars had carried the launch to safety. Arthur felt the tension and fear begin to drain from his body as he turned to stare back towards Copenhagen and the tricolour flag waving over the heads of the French soldiers as they hurled insults after their enemy.

Even though the operation had been a success and the Danish fleet was on its way to Britain, he could not help feeling a sense of failure. Once again a British army had secured a small foothold on the continent, only to have to give it up. As long as that remained the pattern of the conflict, Britain would never defeat Bonaparte. As he stared at the enemy flag, swaying defiantly from side to side, Arthur made a resolution. The instant he returned to London he would do whatever he could to persuade the government to commit itself to a full-blooded campaign on the continent. It was only through such action that Britain could begin to topple the edifice of Bonaparte's vast empire.

Chapter 38

Napoleon

Paris, December 1807

The Emperor sat at his desk, hands folded together and supporting his chin as he stared into the middle distance. It was the day after Christmas, yet he felt not the slightest inclination to share the festive mood of the rest of his household and the people of Paris. Before him, on the desk, lay the report from General Junot, detailing his operation in Portugal. Despite marching across Spain and through Portugal with commendable speed, Junot's corps had captured Lisbon only to discover that the royal family, the government and the warships of the Portuguese navy had fled to their colonies in Brazil just two days before. They had quit the capital so swiftly that they had abandoned on the quayside scores of wagons carrying chests of gold and silver, works of art, linen, dinner services and fine furnishings from the palace. None of which compensated for the loss of the fine ships of the Portuguese navy, Napoleon reflected ruefully.

Now that he had lost the chance of seizing both the Danish and the Portuguese fleets there was no chance of redressing the imbalance in naval power that had existed between France and Britain since the disaster at Cape Trafalgar. The only hope of defeating Britain now lay in the full implementation of the closure of European ports to British trade and British vessels.

Napoleon let out an explosive, exasperated sigh. He rose abruptly to his feet and crossed over to the long windows overlooking the courtyard of the Tuileries and the open square beyond. A thin veil of snow had descended on Paris the night before and much of it had been trampled into the cobblestones during the morning so that the streets looked peculiarly grimy compared to the gleaming white mantles that covered the roofs of the capital. Overhead the sky was filled with thick grey clouds that wholly obscured the sun and threatened further snow.

342

Down in the square a large crowd of street urchins were engaged in a snowball fight and their shouts and shrill cries of laughter carried faintly through the glass as Napoleon gazed down. He felt a brief twinge of envy as he watched them.

A memory flashed into his mind and he recalled a time when he had led a team of students in a snowball fight at the school he had attended in Brienne. A smile flickered across his lips. That had been a fine day. One of the few pleasurable days he recalled from a childhood spent far from his family; a lone Corsican amongst a crowd of haughty and wealthy boys from the finest families in France. At times they had made his life a torment. And now he was their Emperor. Fate played peculiar games, Napoleon mused. Yet despite all his power and all that he had achieved, he fervently wished that he could be an anonymous young boy once more and run across the square and join those engaged in the snowball fight, heedless of the duties and burdens of his office. The thought filled his heart with an aching sense of loss as he looked at the children and he felt his throat tighten.

'No,' he muttered, angry with himself. He turned away from the window and returned to his desk, forcing his mind to fix on the high affairs of state. The Portuguese ruler and his government may have escaped Junot and taken their fleet with them, but their country was now in French hands and their ports would soon be closed to British ships. It was a different situation in Spain, however, where the corruption and incompetence of the government meant that British merchants openly flouted the embargo. The King, Charles IV, and his heir, Ferdinand, were both fools who loathed each other, and were in turn loathed by their people. Both the King and his Queen were under the spell of Manuel Godoy, a nobleman who had once been a mere soldier in the royal guard until he had become the lover of the Queen and been showered with honours and riches.

Napoleon smiled to himself. Godoy's corruption knew no bounds, and for some years he had secretly been in the pay of the French. It was through Godoy's influence that French troops had been permitted to march across Spain to reach Portugal, and to leave garrisons in their wake to protect the communications with France. Even now, three small army corps had crossed the border into Spain and were well placed to intervene in Spanish affairs the moment Napoleon gave them their orders. He turned his chair round and stared up at the large map of Europe that hung on the wall behind his desk. His eyes fixed on Spain and he pressed his lips together. Very well then, he decided. The time had come to act.

That evening Napoleon returned to his country estate of Malmaison, not far from Paris. A fresh fall of snow had made the road difficult going for the horses; in places the snow had drifted and the men of the mounted escort had been forced to dismount and clear a path with the butts of their carbines before the carriage could proceed. It was past midnight before they finally pulled up outside the main entrance and a mufflered footman jumped down to place the steps beside the carriage and open the door for the Emperor. Napoleon cast aside the thick sheepskin covering that he had been using to try to keep warm and climbed stiffly down. The door to the house had been opened and a welcoming shaft of warm yellow light fell across the steps and out on to the snow-covered drive. He hurried inside and allowed a footman to take off his coat before he warmed himself at a small fire burning in a hearth to one side of the lobby.

'Is the Empress still awake?'

'I do not know, sire. Her majesty retired to her quarters over an hour ago.'

'Ah.' Napoleon frowned. He had sent word earlier in the day that he would arrive in time for the evening meal. That was before the snow had started again.

'Do you wish me to have some food brought to you, sire?'

'Yes. Some soup and wine. I'll be in my study. Is the fire made up?'

'Yes, sire.'

'Good.' Napoleon nodded and strode off down the corridor to the rear of the house, the stamp of his boots echoing off the tiled floor. The air in the study was warm and the glow from the fire was comforting as Napoleon eased himself into the chair at the desk that looked out over the gardens. At night the windows were shuttered and heavy curtains drawn across them to cut off any chilly draughts. He lit a lantern and by its light drew a piece of blank paper from the top drawer and then reached for a pen. He thought for a moment, and then dipped the nib in the inkwell and began to make notes in his usual swift, scarcely legible hand.

There was a soft tap on the door and a servant quietly entered and set down a tray on the corner of the desk. The Emperor did not look up from his work. At length he set the pen down, pulled the tray closer and began to drink his soup as he read over his thoughts on the situation in Spain. As he was finishing the soup he became aware of another presence in the study and glanced up to see Josephine standing just inside the door.

'Can't sleep?' he asked.

She smiled thinly. 'Not easy when you have been waiting anxiously all evening for your husband to arrive in a blizzard.'

'Hardly a blizzard.'

She shrugged. 'In any case, I was worried.'

'Well I am here, safe and sound. Come, sit.' Napoleon thrust his chair back and patted his lap. Josephine crossed the room and eased herself down, wrapping an arm round his neck and dangling her hand from his shoulder. She bent her head down and kissed him on the lips.

'We haven't done this for some time.'

'No?' Napoleon frowned, and then chuckled and kissed her again. 'You are right. It is a pity. I have been neglecting you.'

'You have.'

There was a serious edge to her tone, but before Napoleon could comment she had turned to read his notes, her eyes flicking over the uneven lines and figures. 'What is so compelling about Spain at the moment?'

For a second Napoleon considered brushing the matter aside. He was tired and wanted to rest his head against her naked chest and fall asleep there. But his mind was still working, still turning over various possible actions and consequences. He drew a breath and sighed. 'It is time the regime in Madrid was changed.'

'Why? Spain is our ally.'

'Some ally.' Napoleon sniffed. 'That wretched little mercenary, Godoy, has been taking our money for years and France is not seeing as much benefit from her investment as I would like. Many of Spain's ports openly trade with our enemy. Godoy schemes with other powers and now it seems that he is trying to block the marriage between Ferdinand and Lucien's daughter.'

'Louise? I thought that matter had been settled.'

'So did I. The marriage would have gone a long way to cementing the alliance. But now it seems that Ferdinand is not keen to hold to the agreement, and Godoy refuses to use his influence with King Charles and the Queen to force the issue.'

Josephine thought for a moment before looking directly at Napoleon. 'So what do you intend to do about it? Not another war, surely?'

Napoleon shook his head. 'There's no need. Madrid is riven by dissent. The members of the royal household spend their lives plotting against each other while the people look on in despair. So it will be simple enough to engineer a crisis. The King will ask me to intervene.

I imagine Ferdinand will make a similar request as well. Then my soldiers who are already in Spain can seize control of the towns along the frontier and I will adjudicate the grievances between Charles and his heir.'

'While disposing of Godoy, naturally.'

'Yes.'

'What then?' Josephine asked as she moved her hand and began to softly stroke the back of his neck.

'If Godoy goes, then so must Charles. I will make Ferdinand King, and ensure that he knows who his master is.'

'And if Ferdinand does not like being your puppet?'

'Then he must go as well.'

'Then who will rule Spain?'

Napoleon smiled. 'That is a matter for contemplation at a later date, my dear.' He took her other hand and raised it to his lips and kissed her fingers softly, one by one. They kissed again, and Napoleon's hand glided down her neck and across her cleavage before slipping inside her nightdress and caressing her breast. He felt her shudder as her nipple swiftly hardened. Napoleon withdrew his hand.

'We will be more comfortable by the fire.'

Josephine glanced round at the rug lying on the floorboards before the hearth. 'Can't we go up to bed, my love?'

'Why? It is warm enough in here, and the fire will give us light.'

Josephine sighed. 'I am tired. I want to be in a nice comfortable bed. Besides, I am getting too old to make love on a hard floor. Come, husband. To bed.'

She rose from his lap and took his hand, pulling him gently after her, but Napoleon did not move and after a moment she released her grip and looked anxiously at him. 'What is it?'

'I want to make love to you. In here. Now.'

'Wouldn't the bed be more comfortable? It's a cold night.'

'It's warm enough in here,' he responded flatly.

'I know. But I would still prefer to go to bed, my love.'

They stared at each other for a moment, and as they did so Napoleon felt the passion for her die in him. The feeling had passed, and he felt a wave of weariness wash through him. 'You go on first. I'll join you. There's something I need to finish first.'

'You don't love me any more . . .' she whispered.

'What?'

'I said that you don't love me.'

'Don't be a fool.'

'I'm no fool, Napoleon. I have known you for twelve years. Well enough to know what you are thinking.' Her voice caught and she had to bite her lip to stop it trembling. 'You don't love me. Why? Is it because of that young Polish whore?'

'What are you talking about?'

'Marie Walewska. Did you think I wouldn't find out?'

Napoleon took a deep breath to calm his racing heart. 'I had hoped you would not find out, but since you have I won't deny it. Why should I? After all the lovers that you have entertained in the years of our marriage? I am entitled to whatever solace I can find when I am away on campaign.'

'As long as it does not harm your feelings for me.'

'I still love you,' Napoleon said firmly.

'But you are not in love with me. Not in the same way. Not any more. Isn't that what you mean?' Josephine smiled sadly and the tone of her voice cut into his heart like a knife. He could not reply, and she moved a step away from him, towards the door.

'I knew this would happen, my love,' she continued. 'One day. When I had grown old enough for my looks to fade. I suppose she is far younger, fresher. The kind of girl who would make love in front of a fire on a cold winter's night. Am I right, husband?'

His silence was answer enough and she laughed mirthlessly. 'I knew it.'

Napoleon swallowed nervously. 'I am a man, Josephine, with a man's appetites. If you cannot satisfy them, then I must look elsewhere. Besides—'

He shut his mouth abruptly and looked away.

'Besides?' She narrowed her eyes and continued sharply. 'Besides what?'

When he did not reply, she raised her voice, fists clenched by her sides. 'Besides what? Speak up.'

'Very well, then.' Napoleon raised his chin. 'Since you insist. You are right. Marie excites me more than you do. Besides which, you have never given me any children. At least Marie could. She was carrying my child before it was lost. That proves my seed is fertile. And it is clear to me that your womb is barren. If we cannot have a child together, then what is the point of lying with you? But that does not mean that I don't still love you, in a way.'

'In a way,' she mimicked mercilessly. 'What way? Like a young man's affection for an aged aunt, or an old pet? Is that it?'

Napoleon looked away wearily. 'Leave me. Go to bed. I will not have this discussion with you. Not now.'

'Well, what if I want to discuss it now?'

'Go, Josephine. I will not argue with you. Not tonight. Now go.'

'Bastard,' she muttered through clenched teeth. 'You faithless bastard.'

Napoleon jumped to his feet and thrust his arm towards the door. 'Get out! Go! Now!'

Josephine was startled by the instant transformation and backed away nervously. She started to speak but he took two paces towards her, eyes blazing, and she feared that he might strike her. Turning, she hurried out of his study and quickly closed the door behind her.

For a minute or so, Napoleon stared at the door, then slumped down in a chair by the fire and stared into the glowing embers. At first he was inclined to angrily refute everything she had said, everything that she had accused him of. As his temper began to calm, and his heartbeat slowed to a more regular rhythm, he realised that she was right, and had only put into words those thoughts and feelings that he had refused to acknowledge within himself. Now that he had been forced to confront them the sense of failure was deadening. Worse, he knew more certainly than ever that the order he had brought to France could not endure while there was no heir to the imperial crown. The time must come when Napoleon would be forced to find a woman who could provide him with a son. There must be a divorce, he accepted. But not until he had found himself a princess, of Austrian or Russian stock, in order to cement his ties with another powerful dynasty. Once he had chosen, only then would he break the news to Josephine.

Two days later Napoleon was back at his office in the Tuileries. No more snow had fallen and that which still lay across the roofs was stained by soot and ash so that Paris had taken on the appearance of a grimy, mottled wasteland. The cheerful mood that had filled the city had soon faded as its citizens huddled round their fires, or hurried through the cold, damp streets, hunched down in their coats. Napoleon turned away from the window towards the two men sitting at the table waiting for him. Berthier sat ready with a notebook opened in front of him, pen in hand and poised close to a small pot of ink. Beside him, Fouché glanced at the chief of staff with a faintly amused expression of contempt. Napoleon found himself earnestly wishing that Talleyrand still served as foreign minister. His advice and wisdom was sorely needed at present and his replacement, Champagny, had proved to be of little worth. The Emperor sighed with frustration as he took his seat.

'Gentlemen, I have decided that the time is ripe for us to bring Spain within our sphere of control. Since our enemies have removed the fleets of Portugal and Denmark from our grasp, the last navy of any significant size that we might gain possession of lies in Spanish ports. I mean to have those ships. We can no longer count on Spain as a loyal ally. Godoy is a man whose only loyalty is to himself and he will sell his influence to whoever pays him enough gold. Charles is an indolent fool, a trait he seems to have passed on to his heir. I cannot afford to permit the Bourbons to remain on the throne in Madrid any longer.'

Berthier looked up from his notebook. 'Do you propose an invasion of Spain, sire? If so, we will need to shift the balance of the Grand Army to the Pyrenees as swiftly as possible. That's no small task.'

Napoleon shook his head. 'That won't be necessary. There will be no need for an invasion, as such.' He smiled. 'What I had in mind was an armed intervention to assist our Spanish allies in restoring order. To which end we must set them at each other's throats. That is where you come in, Fouché.'

'Sire?'

'I want our newspapers to play up the business about Ferdinand's proposed marriage to my niece. I want the papers to express outrage over the bad faith the Spanish court has shown us. I want them to fix the blame on Godoy. At the same time I want your agents to feed Godoy information that Ferdinand is planning to oust his father.'

'Very well, sire.' Fouché bowed his head. 'I will see to it. And might I suggest a refinement?'

'Well?'

'You might instruct our ambassador in Madrid to let Godoy believe that the Prince has asked for our support in his attempt on the crown, and having failed to tempt us has gone to the British to request their backing. With luck that should set the cat amongst the pigeons, sire.'

'Indeed.' Napoleon nodded approvingly. 'It is a good thing you are my creature, Fouché. I would hate to have you as an enemy.'

'There is no question of my ever being an enemy of your majesty.'

'Of course not,' Napoleon responded. 'Besides, if you ever did contemplate any disloyalty to me I would ensure that you suffered as a consequence.'

Fouché smiled nervously, and Napoleon turned back to Berthier. 'Once we have undermined the Bourbons in Madrid, our forces already in Spain must be prepared to take control of the largest towns and cities the instant the order is given. I want the main routes across the frontier in our hands as swiftly as possible. My generals are to achieve that with the minimum loss of blood. It is imperative that we are seen as liberators and not invaders. To that end our men must not be permitted to loot any property or supplies. Discipline must be maintained at all costs. Make sure that every soldier who crosses the border into Spain has money in his pockets.'

'Yes, sire. Of course.'

'Give immediate orders that our men already in Spain are to start gathering intelligence on every road and town in the north of the country. I want to know where every Spanish soldier is positioned. I want to know their state of readiness, their morale, and most important how loyal they are to either Charles or Ferdinand. When the time comes to act, we must have a column ready to march on Madrid and take control of the city as soon as possible.' Napoleon paused and thought for a moment before he came to a decision and nodded. 'Murat is to command the column. He can be trusted to drive his men on and do what is necessary to achieve our ends. Yes, Murat is the man for the job.'

Berthier nodded, and added to his notes. 'Anything else, sire?'

'Just the timing. Our preparations must be complete by early February. I plan to begin our operations in the middle of the month and have Spain in our hands by the summer. No later.'

Chapter 39

Pamplona, February 1808

It was a freezing morning and the Spanish sentries guarding the entrance to the citadel struggled to keep out the cold while they waited for their watch to come to an end. The thought of retreating to their barracks and settling round a fire was a source of comfort. Meanwhile they stamped their feet and cupped their hands and breathed warm air on to their cold palms. They had stood guard since first light over the approaches to the drawbridge which spanned the wide defensive ditch that surrounded the citadel. As the first rays of the sun peeped over the snow-covered hills and began to cast warmth across the land, the Spanish soldiers started to feel their spirits rise.

Before them, the city was starting to come alive. A handful of market traders began to set up their stalls on the edge of the plaza in front of the citadel. Over to one side a large bakery had opened its doors and the aroma of fresh bread wafted across to the sentries and made them feel hungry. Shortly after eight in the morning the sentries' attention was drawn to the sound of boots echoing down one of the streets that led on to the plaza and a short time later a crowd of French soldiers emerged, talking and laughing cheerfully as they crossed the open ground towards the bakery.

They were not armed, and were wearing their forage caps in place of shakos. They shouted good-humoured greetings at the Spanish soldiers as they passed by the drawbridge, and there was no reason to suspect that anything was amiss. After all, the French were allies and they had lived alongside the local people comfortably enough for the past few weeks. Their commander, General Mouton, had explained to the governor of Pamplona that his men were waiting for the worst of the winter to pass before they marched west to reinforce General Junot in Portugal. The French soldiers had not been unwelcome in Pamplona. They treated the locals in a sufficiently courteous manner and paid their way with gold and silver. Indeed, the inhabitants of Pamplona had come to embrace the custom they provided for the local sellers of food and wine.

While the officer in charge of the party entered the bakery to negotiate the sale of a bulk order of bread his men waited in the plaza. It had not snowed for a few days and the snow on the ground had become icy and hard to compress into a decent snowball. Nevertheless the Spanish sentries guarding the entrance to the citadel watched with amused curiosity as a handful of French soldiers spontaneously bent down and began to scrape up snow to throw at each other. Within moments others had joined in and soon the snowball fight was general. Little by little some of the soldiers came closer to the drawbridge and then one of the snowballs struck a Spanish soldier, bursting off his shoulder in a spray of white. For an instant the man glared at the foreigners, searching for his assailant. Then, slinging his musket across his back, he swooped down, scooped up a handful of snow, packed it tight and hurled it into the crowd of French soldiers. There was a shout of protest and then several missiles were thrown back at the sentries as the nearest Frenchmen turned on them and began to exchange a flurry of missiles with the Spaniards. Soon the men of the bread party were on the drawbridge itself, mingling with the outnumbered sentries as they hurled snow and ice at each other.

As the sounds of the shouting from the drawbridge increased in volume the officer emerged from the bakery and stared towards the entrance to the citadel, examining the scene carefully. Then he drew a whistle from his pocket, raised it to his lips and blew three sharp blasts.

At once, his men on the drawbridge threw down their snowballs and seized the startled sentries, snatching away their muskets and knocking them to the ground. At the same time more French soldiers, fully armed, burst out of a side street and crossed the plaza at a dead run, surging across the drawbridge and into the citadel. The officer watched for a moment, hearing muffled sounds of shouted protests and harsh commands. Within a matter of minutes it was all over, and as the first of the bewildered Spanish prisoners emerged on to the drawbridge to be marched to a holding area in the plaza, the flag of the Bourbons fluttered down from the flagstaff on the central tower of the citadel. A moment later a new flag was hoist, and as it reached the top of the flagstaff a faint breeze caused it to ripple out. The blue, white and red colours of the French flag gleamed in the bright rays of the morning sun.

In the days that followed, many more towns and fortresses fell into French hands through similar ruses and more French troops poured across the frontier until, by the end of February, over a hundred thousand French soldiers were on Spanish soil. In Madrid many members of the junta and supporters of Prince Ferdinand were outraged by the French and openly cursed Godoy and the King for their complacency over such an affront to Spanish national pride. Napoleon read the reports of these events with glowing satisfaction. Everything was going according to plan. There remained only one last piece to fall into place: the final humiliation of King Charles, his Queen and their scheming Prime Minister, Manuel Godoy. A message from Napoleon was sent to the latter, via Fouché's agent in the Spanish court, suggesting that the court would be well advised to quit Madrid before the mob gave vent to their anger. At the same time, the agent hinted to Ferdinand that his father was planning to quit Spain altogether and flee to Spanish possessions in the Americas.

One night early in April Napoleon was woken in the early hours by a servant. He blinked his eyes open and winced as he stared into the bright flame of the candle the man was holding over him.

'Get that away from me,' he grumbled, and the servant hurriedly retreated a couple of paces as his master stirred irritably. 'What time is it?'

'Past two in the morning, sire.'

Napoleon turned his back to the man and instinctively reached his arm across to the other side of the bed. But there was no one there. Josephine had refused to sleep with him since that night in Malmaison, and a frosty cordiality often divided them when they were together now. Napoleon thrust her from his mind.

'What is the reason for waking me at this ungodly hour?'

'Sire, there is a messenger from Marshal Murat waiting in your study. He bears urgent news from Madrid.'

Napoleon was fully awake in an instant, and throwing back his bedclothes he rose to his feet and clicked his fingers. 'Bring me a warm gown.'

'Yes, sire.'

Slipping his feet into soft slippers, Napoleon allowed the servant to slip the woollen gown over his shoulders. He pulled the folds tightly around his body and quickly tied the sash before pacing from the sleeping chamber and down the dimly lit corridor to the suite of offices at the far end. The courier stiffened to attention as he entered the study. Flames flickered in a candelabra set on the desk and by their light Napoleon saw that the messenger was a young colonel of hussars, splattered with mud and trying not to collapse with exhaustion.

'You can eat and rest when we are done.' Napoleon forced himself to smile. 'I understand you have a report for me. From Murat.'

'Yes, sire.' The courier opened the flap of the bag at his side and took out a waterproofed and sealed leather tube, which he handed to his Emperor.

'I will read this later,' said Napoleon. 'First, are you able to give me a detailed verbal report?'

'Yes, sire. That was why the marshal chose me.'

'Very well.' Napoleon smiled. 'Proceed.'

The colonel rapidly collected his thoughts, cleared his throat and began. 'In accordance with his orders, Marshal Murat was advancing towards Madrid. As far as the Spaniards knew we were marching south, to lay siege to Gibraltar. The story seemed to hold up well enough, sire. We met no resistance of any kind and were still four days' march from Madrid when we heard that the King and his court had made an attempt to escape to Cadiz. They had got as far as Aranjuez, some twenty leagues south of the capital, when a mob of Ferdinand's supporters caught up with them and surrounded Godoy's palace, where they had stopped for the night. The mob stormed the palace and beat Godoy close to death before Ferdinand intervened and saved his life.'

'A pity.'

'Yes, sire. After that the King and Queen were placed under house arrest, before the King was forced to abdicate in favour of his son. Ferdinand immediately proclaimed himself Ferdinand VII of Spain and returned to the capital to secure the junta's confirmation of his title. But the junta is split, sire. Some back Charles, although most support Ferdinand. There was violence in the streets when word of the coup got out. The marshal took an advance force of cavalry and entered Madrid the following day. The people actually came out and cheered us, sire. They are heartily sick of the civil strife that has plagued Madrid for months now. They assumed that the French army had been sent to restore order.'

'Good.' Napoleon nodded. 'Carry on.'

'Well, sir, Marshal Murat was not certain how to proceed. Events had rather superseded his orders. He was not sure whether to back Charles or Ferdinand. The marshal says that Charles is far too unpopular amongst his people to survive for long on the throne. On the other hand, Ferdinand makes no secret of his hatred for the French, and cannot be trusted.'

'And what has Murat done to resolve the situation?' Napoleon asked anxiously.

'Nothing, sire. He has placed Charles under protective custody and he has refused to recognise Ferdinand as King. He awaits instructions from your majesty.'

'Murat has done the right thing.' Napoleon was relieved. For once his cavalry commander had managed to act with discretion. The situation was very promising, he mused. Very promising indeed. There was much that could be gained if he acted quickly. He focused his attention on the colonel again. 'You must return to Madrid in the morning.'

'Yes, sire.' If the young officer was dreading the prospect of several more days in the saddle, he had the sense not to show it.

'I will have instructions drafted for Marshal Murat. But in case there is any misunderstanding of the written word you are to make it clear to Murat that he is not to intervene on either side at any cost. Nor is he to permit our soldiers to be quartered in Madrid. They must remain in the suburbs and be kept in check. The very last thing we can afford is any of the usual high-handedness with the local people. Murat is to make it clear to the Spanish that he is there to keep the peace and to help Spain improve its institutions in the interests of the common people. Lastly, I want him to instruct Ferdinand to meet me at Bayonne later this month. He is to tell Ferdinand that I wish to discuss the best way to reconcile the differences of opinion that currently divide Spain. Once Ferdinand is on his way to Bayonne, Murat is to wait two days and then send Charles to join him at Bayonne, on the same pretext.' Napoleon looked closely at the weary officer. 'Is that all clear, Colonel?'

'Yes, sir. Quite clear.'

'Good. Now I suggest you have something to eat, and sleep for the remainder of the night. Your orders will be given to you at first light. You have a long journey ahead of you, so get some rest. Dismissed.'

'Yes, sire!' The colonel stiffened to attention, saluted and turned to march out of the room, his heavy boots echoing off the floor. Once he was alone, Napoleon sat a moment in silence, his mind swiftly processing what he had been told. Then he broke the seal on the leather tube and pulled out several sheets of paper that made up Murat's report. By the time he had finished reading through the document Napoleon had decided on his course of action. One that would for ever bind Spain and France together and deal a crippling blow to British interests.

The decision to hold a conference at Bayonne had been made some months before the crisis in Madrid occurred. For a long time Napoleon had intended to assemble his family to explain what he required of them. The purpose of awarding them the lands and titles he had bestowed on them was to provide a close-knit dynasty that would bind Europe together. As it was, some of his brothers were taking their status as rulers a little too much to heart and acting with a degree of independence that ran counter to Napoleon's interests. He was determined to make them understand what he wanted and that they should do his bidding as efficiently as possible.

The finest houses in Bayonne and the best of the nearest estates had been commandeered for the conference and every luxury prepared for the arrival of the Emperor and his brothers: Joseph, King of Naples and Louis, King of Holland. A spate of last-minute preparations were hurried through in order to welcome Ferdinand and Charles and their immediate retinues. The townspeople had never seen so much royalty gathered together before and the excitement in the town was tangible. Napoleon waved at the crowds lining the streets to greet him, but his mind was elsewhere. The coming days were vital to his ambitions for France, and he would have to play a very careful game in order to secure the desired end.

Then there was still the question of his relationship with Josephine. She had remained in Paris and scarcely a word had passed between them since that night in Malmaison. Napoleon felt his heart soften as he thought of her. She had been the love of his life, until he had discovered her infidelities when he was away campaigning in Egypt. Since then their love had been qualified and based on an affection whose strength drew more on the habit of years than any remaining physical desire and romantic ardour. They had sought pleasure in other arms for years now and had only come together for familiar and comfortable undemanding lovemaking. Nevertheless, Napoleon would not hurt her any more than he had to when the time came to find a more fertile wife to provide France with an heir to the imperial throne.

Napoleon met Louis and Joseph before Ferdinand was due to arrive. Once the pomp and ceremonies of a meeting of three kings had been observed and the parades and the banquets concluded, they met as three brothers in the privacy of the estate that had been taken over by the imperial household. Even though it was spring a cold rain had fallen all day. They met in a small salon with paintings of hunting scenes adorning every wall. A freshly lit fire crackled in the grate of an enormous fireplace that seemed far too large for the room. The three brothers pulled up chairs in an arc around the fire and a servant left them with a decanter of wine and some glasses on a small table at Napoleon's side. He poured his brothers a glass and then one for himself, raising it for an informal toast.

'To the family, and a dynasty that will be the master of Europe.'

They drank and then Napoleon set his glass down and turned to the business of the evening.

'We stand on the verge of a great victory, my brothers. Britain has but one ally left in the world. Thanks to her decision to seize any neutral vessel on the high seas that has entered any port on the continent she has played into my hands. Now even America is contemplating declaring war on Britain. As an inducement I have promised their ambassador that they can take possession of the Spanish Floridas if they join the fight on our side.'

'Isn't that a bit precipitate?' asked Louis. 'Given that those lands are not yours to give.'

'Not yet.' Napoleon smiled. 'But I am getting a little ahead of myself, my dear brothers. First, we must discuss our wider strategy.'

'Ah.' Louis nodded. 'You mean your wider strategy. Your interests.'

'We are one blood,' Napoleon replied in an irritated tone. 'Our interests are the same. We must not forget that. Which is why I must confess to a little disappointment in your affairs. Both of you, that is.'

'Disappointment?' Louis leaned forward. 'In what respect?'

'Your failure to ensure that your subjects adhere to the trade embargo with Britain, my dear Louis. Surely you must know that many of your harbour masters turn a blind eye to cargo landed from Britain. If my agents are aware of it, then I am sure your officials must be. This is not the first time I have mentioned it to you. But I hope it will be the last.'

Louis was silent for a moment before he responded. 'Napoleon, this Continental System of yours is unworkable. I cannot police every fishing village and strip of coast in Holland. Besides, I risk incurring the anger of my people should I try to enforce your laws too rigorously. They ask me whether I am their king, or your puppet.'

'If you were truly their king, they would not dare to ask.'

'Perhaps that is your way. It is not mine. There are other ways to rule a country than by just cowing the people or offering them bread and circuses.'

'Louis is right.' Joseph spoke up. 'You cannot sever trade between the continent and Britain. Your policy is ruining businesses the length and breadth of Europe. Besides, it is impossible to police.'

'It is not impossible,' Napoleon said evenly. 'Provided the will is there to see it through. I appreciate that my measures hinder trade. But they are only required for as long as it takes to ruin our oldest enemy and drive her to the negotiating table. Once Britain is defeated then trade can flow as freely as ever, with my full blessing. Until then, I depend upon my allies, and I particularly depend upon you, my brothers, to secure the victory and the peace we all want to bring to each of our realms. This cannot be if you permit your subjects to defy me. And, as you are my family, if they defy me they defy you, and neither one of you will be able to rest easy in his bed if rebels and traitors are allowed to go unpunished. If you will not rule your people, Louis, perhaps it is time that someone else did.'

There was a brief pause as Louis stared coldly at his brother. 'Are you threatening me?'

'I made you the King, and I can unmake you just as easily, should I wish it.' Napoleon let the words sink in and then smiled suddenly. 'Come now! There is no need for any unpleasantness between us. Indeed, my brother, one of the reasons I have asked you here is to offer you an even greater proof of my trust and faith in you.'

Louis's eyes narrowed. 'What are you talking about?'

'Holland is a fine enough kingdom, I grant you. I have heard that you rule it well and the people respect you. But Holland is a small nation, and one that is barely fit for a Bonaparte to rule.'

'I like it well enough,' Louis replied uneasily.

'Yes, yes. Of course, and I admire your sense of duty. However, I may need your skills as a ruler to be applied with respect to another kingdom. One that has long suffered under the vicious and baleful influence of the Church and its inquisition. A land where every aspect of public life reeks of corruption.'

Joseph cleared his throat. 'You refer to Spain.'

'Yes. Spain. Her people are crying out for a new ruler. A man who will lead them out of the Middle Ages and into the modern world. I believe Louis is the man who can do that. Would you accept such a challenge, brother?'

'Aren't you forgetting something?' Louis replied. 'Spain already has a king.'

'Really?' Napoleon could not help smiling. 'At present it seems that there are two claimants to that title, neither of whom is worthy of that honour, or any other. We shall have to see if either of them has a viable claim to the throne in the days to come. For the sake of argument, let us assume that the Spanish throne falls empty. In that case, would you accept the crown if it was offered to you?'

Louis stared at him and Napoleon continued, 'You would not just be master of Spain. Think of it, Louis. There is a vast empire in the Americas with untold wealth in gold and silver waiting to be discovered in its hinterlands. With your rather idealistic concern for the welfare of the common man you could transform Spain into a country that would be proud to take its place amongst the most advanced nations in Europe, rather than languishing as a decadent backwater. Greatness beckons to you, Louis. You have but to answer the call.'

Louis eased himself back into his chair with a faint smile. 'I am not a fool, Napoleon. I have heard about conditions in Spain. It is a patchwork of a country, riven by superstitions and suspicions. Its people are proud, and while they may be at each other's throats at the moment, they would surely unite against any foreign power that presumed to dictate their affairs. That is what my advisers have told me.'

Napoleon could see that his brother would not be persuaded so easily to do his bidding, and raised a hand in a placating gesture. 'There is no hurry, Louis. The matter is not yet settled. All that I ask is that you consider the prospect.' He paused. 'And if you should decide that you would rather rule in Holland, it is possible that Joseph might be prepared to lead where you will not.'

'Me?' Joseph stiffened in his seat. 'You would ask me to become King of Spain?'

'If Louis does not want to, I can think of no better alternative. You at least I know would never let me down. You never have, my dear Joseph. So you too can think on my offer.'

Napoleon poured himself another glass of wine and continued in a low, menacing tone, 'In the meantime, I must deal with young Ferdinand, and his father.'

Chapter 40

'His majesty insists on being referred to as King Ferdinand VII of Spain,' the chamberlain informed Napoleon anxiously.

'Does he now?' Napoleon muttered as he smiled politely at the uninspiring figure seated opposite him. The claimant to the Spanish throne was a corpulent young man in his mid-twenties. His eyes were large and dark and his hair was thick and wiry. He wore a fine silk coat, encrusted with bejewelled stars and ribbons of several noble orders. His lips were thick and coarse-looking. He was the very image of his mother, Napoleon had been told, and he repressed a shudder at the thought of ever encountering her.

Ferdinand and Napoleon were meeting in the largest hall in the Emperor's château, as befitted their status. In accordance with the instructions of the Spanish protocol official, a dais had been set up for Ferdinand, large enough to accommodate a gold-leafed chair for the man who would be king. Napoleon's courtiers had arranged for another dais to be positioned opposite with an even more ornate chair, and steps slightly higher than those of the Spanish dais so that Napoleon might look down on his guest. Behind each of them stood the ornately dressed courtiers of their respective retinues.

Napoleon waved the chamberlain aside and bowed his head. 'Ferdinand, Prince of the Asturias, I bid you welcome to Bayonne.'

Ferdinand's lips compressed into a tight grimace for a moment before he relaxed and spoke in accented French. 'I am Prince no longer, but King, proclaimed by my people, following the abdication of my father, and the consent of the Madrid junta.'

'Of course, your highness,' Napoleon conceded. 'Under normal circumstances that would be sufficient authority for the title you lay claim to. But the circumstances are far from normal, which is why we are meeting here today. I am sure that the details will be resolved satisfactorily in the days to come. Meanwhile, it will be more agreeable to all if you restrict yourself to the rank of prince.'

Ferdinand did not reply immediately and glared stupidly at his host, as if waiting for him to retract the comment. At length he cleared his throat and shrugged. 'As you please, your majesty. For now I will revert to my previous title. But I am King, and I will be until almighty God deigns otherwise. Only out of respect for you do I make this temporary concession.'

'I thank you.' Napoleon nodded graciously. 'Now then, we are told that there is some dispute between you and your father over who is the legitimate King of Spain.'

'There is no dispute,' Ferdinand interrupted. 'My father abdicated in my favour. In front of these witnesses.' He waved a hand at the Spanish noblemen behind him on the dais. 'Every one of them will attest to that. Therefore, I am King, regardless of how you, or anyone else, might choose to address me.'

'Alas, there are those in Spain, and elsewhere, who deny that you have any right to the title. Your father claims that he was forced to abdicate under duress. If that is proved then the abdication is not legal.'

'He lies,' Ferdinand replied bitterly. 'As I said, there were witnesses.'

'Who are hardly impartial,' Napoleon countered. 'We shall investigate the matter thoroughly, my dear Prince. I am deeply concerned to resolve the divisions that beset our Spanish neighbours.'

'No doubt that is why so many French soldiers have descended on Spanish soil. To help us.' Ferdinand could not help sneering a little as he continued. 'I trust they will be removed the moment the crisis is over and I am duly crowned King of Spain.'

'I give you my word that my soldiers will be withdrawn at the earliest opportunity.'

'And when will that be?'

'When my military operations in Portugal, and against Gibraltar, are concluded.'

'And what if I ordered you to withdraw your men at once?'

There was a sharp intake of breath from some of the officials behind the Emperor. Napoleon paused and then spoke very deliberately. 'I would find that difficult to accomplish, your highness. If it were not for Marshal Murat there would be chaos in Madrid and the streets would run with blood. Our soldiers are there out of concern for the well-being of your people. I could not begin to contemplate the horrors that would ensue if I gave the order for my men to withdraw from Spain during the present crisis. So there they must stay, for the present.'

'Some might call them an army of occupation,' Ferdinand countered. 'That is what the British newspapers are saying.'

Napoleon felt his stomach clench in anger and he had to take a deep breath to steady his temper before he continued. 'The British lie in this, as in all things. You should pay no heed to their twisted words. They are as much your enemies as my own. My soldiers entered Spain with the full permission of your father. You have nothing to fear from their presence. After all, have not the French and Spanish shed their blood side by side in fighting Britain for many years now?'

'That is true, but only because that vile worm Godoy was bought with French gold and used his silver tongue to mislead my mother and father into obeying his every whim. I have always doubted the wisdom of the alliances Godoy made with France. They have invariably been one-sided, and very costly to Spanish interests. I shudder to think how many warships have been lost, how many men have been lost, thanks to the treaties Godoy made with France. But now Godoy is gone, your majesty. He can no longer betray his country and serve your interests. Those days are over. I will lead Spain into a glorious new age, *without* your assistance.'

'I see.' Napoleon nodded slowly. 'It seems we understand one another's positions well enough. I will need to confer with my ministers before we speak on these matters again. Meanwhile, your highness, you and your companions are free to enjoy the pleasures that Bayonne has to offer. We will meet again, soon, and discuss your claim to the throne in more detail.'

Napoleon rose from his chair and bowed briefly before he descended from the dais and left the room, his staff bowing their heads until he was out of sight, and then filing out as well, leaving the chamber to the Spaniards. Ferdinand turned round to face his retinue with a broad smile. 'There! I told you the Emperor would not dare to defy me!'

The members of his retinue nodded their agreement with little conviction and darted nervous glances after the French.

Outside, Napoleon gestured to Fouché to follow him and marched to his private study, head down and hands clasped behind his back to hide his thunderous mood from those he passed by. Once the door was closed behind them Napoleon gave vent to his temper.

'Just who does that fat bastard think he is?'

Fouché coolly raised his eyebrows. 'I rather assumed he thinks himself to be the King of Spain, sire.'

'That arrogant fool? You heard him, Fouché. He means to throw his lot in with the British the moment the last of our soldiers quits Spain.'

'He did not say that precisely, sire.'

'It was clear enough to me. We cannot afford to let him stay on the throne. There is no question of it. Ferdinand must be persuaded, or forced, to renounce the crown.'

'Even if he is, sire, I do not see how Charles can remain in power without our protection, and then we will share the hatred of his people in full measure.'

'No. Neither of them is fit to be King,' Napoleon reflected. 'And I dare say neither of them will be willing to abandon their claim to the crown. This is going to require some deft handling.'

Charles and Marie-Louise arrived two days later. Their carriage and retinue had been escorted from the border by a regiment of Napoleon's finest cavalry. Entire villages and towns turned out to watch the cavalcade pass and wave to Charles and his wife as though they were still the King and Queen of Spain. Their arrival at Bayonne was greeted with a deep boom at regular intervals as the artillery of the Imperial Guard welcomed them with a sixty-gun salute. The carriage rumbled down streets lined with guardsmen standing at attention, before finally turning into the courtyard where Napoleon and his two regal brothers were waiting.

The carriage ground to a halt and steps were hastily set in place as a footman opened the door. Charles heaved himself awkwardly out on to the steps, with the support of the footman. He was a large man, and Napoleon could instantly see where the son had got his appetite from. Charles smiled at his host with a kindly expression and then turned as his wife descended from the carriage. She was every bit as ugly as Napoleon had feared and combined severely masculine features with a furrowed brow that betrayed a fiery temper.

Napoleon descended all but the last step of the château and bowed. 'I trust the journey was comfortable.'

'Oh?' Charles raised his eyebrows and then thought a moment before nodding. 'Comfortable, well, yes. I suppose it was.'

His wife snorted with derision. 'It was a long journey on rough roads and I'm heartily glad it's over! Still, it is better than living under house arrest.' She fixed her beady eyes on Napoleon. 'We were living in a virtual prison. Can you imagine that? It seems we have raised a treacherous viper in the bosom of our family. Once this is over, we'll banish him for life, at the very least,' she added in an ominous tone. 'And then we will see to all his supporters.'

Napoleon bowed graciously before her. 'You must be the radiant Marie-Louise. Your beauty does not do justice to the reports I have had of you, madam.'

Marie-Louise stared at him with narrowed eyes as she wondered if she was being mocked, but Napoleon kept his expression neutral, even as Charles looked at him in surprise. Napoleon bent low, took her hand

and kissed it. On cue, there was a ripple of applause from his officers and Marie-Louise beamed delightedly.

'It seems we are amongst friends, Charles, my dear.'

'Friends? Oh, good.' He smiled and beamed happily. 'I have so missed having friends.'

'If you would come with me.' Napoleon gestured up the steps. 'I have arranged a modest reception for you.'

Inside the château's ballroom a table laden with delicacies and decanters of the finest wines stood at one end. A large crowd of dignitaries and officers in their finest uniforms parted to permit the Emperor and his guests to enter the centre of the room. The small retinue of the former King and Queen of Spain followed and assumed a haughty air in front of the curious gaze of their hosts. Napoleon clapped his hands together to attract attention. When every eye was on him, he quietly cleared his throat and addressed the crowd.

'All France welcomes Charles and Marie-Louise of the house of Bourbon. It is our fervent wish that we may be able to help Spain overcome the division and dissent that has plagued her in recent months. But for now, we will celebrate your arrival and help you to forget the rigours of the journey that brought you to Bayonne.'

From a gallery, hidden by a great tapestry, a small orchestra struck up the Spanish national anthem and Napoleon began to introduce his senior officers and officials to Charles and his wife.

Later, when night had fallen outside and all the guests had long since departed from the ballroom, Napoleon met Charles and Fouché in a small private sitting room with doors and windows that overlooked the geometrically perfect flowerbeds of the château's garden. His sister Caroline, together with the wives of some of the generals, had led Marie-Louise off to a picturesque orangery in the grounds to be entertained by an opera singer from Paris, while Napoleon dealt with Charles alone.

'I must say, it is most good of you to step in to sort this ghastly business out,' Charles began affably. 'You're not quite the tyrant that some of your enemies make you out to be.'

'Really? That is good to know.' Napoleon smiled warmly. 'It is a shame that there are those who mistake my motives. But who can blame them, with all the lies that are spread by British agents?'

Charles frowned. 'I have to confess that my own son was easily misled by such devils. Truly, the British will stop at nothing to undermine every royal house in Europe.'

'Sadly, you are right,' Napoleon said solemnly. 'And the Spanish Bourbons are no exception. Why, when I spoke to your son, he was little more than a mouthpiece for Britain, and damned your alliance with France as the work of a fool and a madman.'

Charles's eyes narrowed. 'He said that? Of me?'

Napoleon nodded with a pained expression. 'I wish it was not true, but . . .' He gestured helplessly, and watched as his words worked their way on the weak-minded Spanish ruler.

Charles's lips trembled with rage as his jaws worked furiously. 'That damned boy! Always was ambitious, and treacherous as a snake. To turn on his own father. And his King!' Charles fixed his watery eyes on Napoleon. 'He must not be allowed to be King. I will not permit it.'

'Ah, you see, there's the problem,' Napoleon responded with feigned embarrassment.

Charles frowned. 'Problem? What do you mean?'

'Well, I don't mean to sound defeatist. As far as France is concerned you are the King of Spain. Those others who forced you to abdicate are clearly traitors. The problem is that they have managed to persuade most of your people to believe their lies. I fear it may already be too late to undo such villainy.'

'Too late?' Charles looked pained. 'But I must have my crown back. For the good of my people.'

'Naturally. But the reality of the moment is that it would not be good for your people if you were to return to the throne. Later, perhaps, when Spain has had the opportunity to forget these troubled times.'

Charles leaned forward anxiously. 'But who will rule Spain? We cannot let Ferdinand remain on the throne.'

'Indeed not,' Napoleon agreed firmly. 'He must be deposed at once. After that, I suggest that Marshal Murat is permitted to oversee the government for a limited period before we prepare the way for your majesty to return. That would seem like the best way to proceed.'

'Yes . . . yes, I suppose so,' Charles muttered as he gently rubbed his forehead, and nudged his wig slightly off centre so that his head looked unbalanced. 'You are right.'

'I am glad that you think so, your majesty. In which case I have taken the liberty of having two despatches drawn up for you to consider.' Napoleon nodded at Fouché and the latter lifted a folder from his lap and passed it to the Emperor. Flipping it open, Napoleon took out two sheets of neatly written prose and glanced through the first.

'This is a statement condemning the actions of Ferdinand, and stating quite clearly that he and his followers threatened you with violence in order to force you to abdicate. It says that you condemn him utterly for this course of action and wish to expose before the whole of Europe that Ferdinand is a usurper. Here you are, your majesty. You can read it for yourself.'

Napoleon handed the statement to Charles and sat back as the old man held it at arm's length. Squinting, Charles read through the document carefully. At length he set it down. 'It is a fair account of what took place. But what is the purpose of this document?'

'Merely to let the other royal courts of Europe know the truth of what happened so that they are not fooled into recognising your son's claim to the throne. It will have a limited circulation, your majesty. No point in risking the shame of your family in public.'

'Quite so!' Charles nodded emphatically. 'And I must thank you for being so sensitive.'

'Not at all. It is the very least I could do.' Napoleon smiled warmly and then tapped the bottom of the document. 'All it needs is your signature, your majesty. Fouché, a pen, if you please.'

'Yes, sire.' Fouché lifted a small case from beneath his chair and opened it out to reveal a writing pad with an inkwell and several pens in holders. He quickly laid the set down on a small table at Charles's side and dipped a pen in the inkwell before offering it to the Spaniard. Charles hesitated, and for an instant Napoleon was not sure that he would sign. Then, with a bold flourish, Charles leaned over the letter and printed his signature. As soon as it was done, Fouché whisked the letter away.

'There,' Napoleon said encouragingly. 'It's done. Now, if we can move on to the second document. It is little more than a minor formality.'

He set it down on the table next to the writing set and sat patiently as Charles examined it painstakingly, at length looking up with a hurt and confused expression. 'This confirms that I have abdicated.'

'Yes, your majesty. As we agreed, in the interests of Spain it would be best to delay your return to the throne for a while, at least until the situation is resolved.'

'Really?' Charles frowned.

Fouché dipped the pen into the ink again and held it out to Charles. 'Sire?'

'I'm not sure that I should abdicate. I don't think it is the right thing to do.'

'It is the only thing you can do for the moment,' Napoleon said soothingly. 'And it's only a temporary arrangement. Please sign. Just here.' He tapped the blank space awaiting a signature. 'At least you will have given the crown up without duress. It will help to smooth Murat's way to re-establishing order.'

Once again Charles took the pen. He signed quickly and eased himself away from the table.

'It is done.'

'Thank you, sire.' Napoleon nodded. 'You won't live to regret this, I assure you.' He handed the signed documents to Fouché, who placed them back in his case and began to fasten the straps. 'Now, I think it is time that we re-joined the womenfolk and stopped speaking of politics.' He rose from his chair and took Charles's arm, helping him up and guiding him towards the door. 'I will join you shortly.'

'Good, good,' Charles mumbled. 'About time we sat down and talked, over a glass of brandy.'

'Yes, of course, sire.' Napoleon eased the old man out of the room and closed the door behind him. At once he turned to Fouché. 'Keep that document safe.'

'Yes, sire. I will.'

'Now then,' Napoleon smiled. 'We need to get to work on Ferdinand.'

The clock on the mantelpiece chimed a quarter past two. All was quiet within the house and the only noise from outside was the occasional crunch of gravel as a sentry passed by. Napoleon sat alone in the room with Ferdinand. There was a small table between them with an inkwell and a pen. The Spanish Prince had been summoned at midnight and Napoleon had waited impatiently for him to arrive, and then handed him the document Charles had signed attacking his actions. When Ferdinand had finished reading he lowered the statement with a quick raise of his eyebrows.

'The old man does not hold any of his anger back.'

'No,' Napoleon responded coldly. 'Nor would I if I had received such treatment from you. This document is going to be copied to every capital in Europe. Soon all will know how you came to steal his crown.'

'It would have been mine in the long run,' Ferdinand countered. 'Besides, if I had waited much longer the people would have risen up and taken the crown from him, and then we would have had a full-blown revolution on our hands. And we know where that leads. I would spare my people such terror, and tyranny.'

Napoleon ignored the gibe. 'It is true that you might have acted for the good of the people. It is equally true that you might have acted out of naked ambition and a hunger for power. That is for people to decide for themselves. Either way, you cannot command the respect of other nations while your assumption of the crown is shrouded in confusion and suspicion over its legality.'

Ferdinand shrugged helplessly. 'So what am I to do?'

'You must return the crown to your father and apologise, in writing, for what you have done.'

'No. That is not possible.'

Napoleon smiled. 'You have little choice, your highness. If you are permitted to seize power in the manner that you have, you will have set a precedent. What if every royal prince thought to emulate you? No ruler would be able to sleep. Nations would be paralysed by fear, Spain most of all. I tell you, Ferdinand, you would forever be jumping at shadows, until the day when the conspirators came for you. And on that day there will be no Marshal Murat and his soldiers to save you from the wrath of the mob.'

Ferdinand pondered for a moment and then opened his hands. 'So what am I to do?'

'You must return the crown to the King and then wait your proper time to inherit the throne. It will come soon enough. Charles is old and weak. When he is no more, then you will have your crown, legally and without recrimination from any royal court in Europe.'

'I suppose so.'

'There is one other thing,' Napoleon said evenly. 'You must apologise for your treatment of the King.'

'Apologise?' Ferdinand's eyes widened. 'Never.'

'You must. Your recent actions will not be forgotten. Would you want people to still regard you with suspicion and misgiving when the time comes for you to assume the crown? There must be some act of contrition first. You must issue a public apology and return the crown.'

'What if I refuse to do either?'

Napoleon stared at him a moment before continuing in a low, menacing voice. 'You cannot refuse. I will not permit it. I could easily place you under arrest and keep you here until you renounce the throne. I might even try you for treason, on your father's behalf, and have you shot.'

Ferdinand's jaw dropped in astonishment for a moment before he recovered and shook his head. 'You cannot threaten me.'

'No? Why not? You threatened your father into signing a document. Why should I not do the same to you?'

'But you would not cause harm to me. You would not dare.'

'What makes you so certain?' Napoleon asked curiously. 'I have sent far better men than you to their deaths and slept well for it.'

There was a long pause. At last, Napoleon produced a statement Fouché had copied earlier in a fair hand. 'Sign this.'

'What is it?' Ferdinand asked suspiciously.

'Your announcement that you are returning the crown to your father with immediate effect, and your apology for having wrongfully usurped the throne.'

Ferdinand laughed. 'You are not serious! I cannot sign that. I will not.'

'You must.'

'No.'

'Sign it!' Napoleon snapped. 'Sign it now, or suffer the consequences.'

He flipped the lid of the inkwell open, dipped the pen in and thrust it towards Ferdinand. 'Sign it! Or I swear you will suffer.'

Ferdinand sat quite still for a moment, his face fixed in an agonised expression as he stared at the pen, and then at Napoleon as if beseeching him to change his mind. But Napoleon held firm and said nothing, and returned his look with cold, hard eyes. At length Ferdinand hesitantly reached out and took the pen. Leaning forward, over the statement, he began to sign in a slow, trembling hand. As soon as he had raised the pen from the paper, Napoleon took the document away and laid it on the floor next to his chair to allow the ink to dry.

'It is done. Now you may go.'

Ferdinand bit his lip. 'You guarantee that there will be no revenge taken by my father?'

'I can guarantee it.'

'I have your word on that?'

'You have my word. Your father will not cause you, or any of your supporters, any harm.'

Ferdinand nodded, and rose from his seat. 'Very well, then. I bid your majesty good night.'

He turned away and paced wearily across the room, and closed the door quietly behind him. Napoleon's lips slowly curled into a smile, then he reached down and picked up the signed statement. Turning towards a partion doorway, he called out, 'Fouché!'

The door opened at once and Fouché entered the room.

'You heard?'

'Every word, sire.'

'He crumbled more quickly than I had anticipated. A disappointing young man, in almost every respect. Still, we have all we need now. Take

369

this confession and have it published along with Charles's attack on his son, and his abdication, in every newspaper in Paris and Madrid.'

'Yes, sire.' Fouché took the proffered document. 'Will that be all?'

'Yes. It is done. So falls the Spanish house of Bourbon,' Napoleon said with quiet satisfaction.

Chapter 41

Even before the reports had been published in Europe's newspapers Napoleon had settled the affairs of Charles and Ferdinand. The latter was sent into exile at Talleyrand's estate at Valençay, to spend his remaining days under close watch. He would live comfortably enough, but in isolation from the rest of society and his countrymen. Charles, meanwhile, had hardened his position and negotiated a much better deal than his son received. A number of estates in France and an annual pension of some seven and a half million francs was the price he demanded for surrendering any claim to his former kingdom.

Napoleon announced to Europe that Murat would remain in charge of the government in Spain until a new ruler was chosen. Again Napoleon approached Louis, who once more refused to abandon his palace in Holland, and so the Emperor turned to his older brother, Joseph.

One day, soon after the conference at Bayonne had ended, Napoleon and his staff, together with his brothers, went out to shoot in the surrounding countryside. Berthier had learned from his experience with the rabbits and made sure that this time there would be no question of the event's turning into a farce. It was early in May and the first growths of spring were bursting from every tree, while new flowers sprinkled bright colours across the rolling, verdant countryside. Birds sang lustily in the trees, little knowing that the band of laughing men passing beneath them in open carriages would shortly be turning their guns on any feathered prey that came into their field of vision.

The hunting party arrived at the site chosen for the shoot: a small hillock overlooking an expanse of flat, marshy ground. A light buffet had been prepared, and Napoleon chewed on a savoury game pie as he spoke to his brother, who was sitting beside him on a grassy bank.

'Joseph, you will recall the conversation we had about what might happen should the throne of Spain fall vacant.'

'I recall it very well,' Joseph replied flatly.

'Well, what do you say to my offer now?'

'It is very generous of you, but I am not sure that I am the right man to rule Spain. Besides, I am in the midst of reforming the government of Naples. It is a task I must complete if we are to win the people over.'

'That work can be easily continued by another,' Napoleon said dismissively. 'And you would have the chance to improve a much more significant country. In time your reforms could make Spain a great power once again. You would be loved by the people and envied for their affection by many of the other rulers in Europe. What say you?'

Joseph was silent for a moment as he considered his reply. 'I say that it is a generous offer. A tempting offer, but for the present the throne of Spain needs to be occupied by a better man than I. Someone like Murat, perhaps? He has been in Madrid long enough to make useful connections amongst the local people and officials. He has even intimated in letters to me that he would be pleased to take the crown if it was offered to him.'

'He has said that to you, has he?' Napoleon mused, instantly realising that Murat meant to use Joseph to support his claim to the throne, because he dared not broach the matter with the Emperor himself. With good reason, Napoleon decided. Murat was a fine soldier and an inspirational commander. He was also headstrong and easily corrupted, and could be breathtakingly tactless. Hardly the right choice of ruler for a country like Spain where the sensitivities of the people had to be handled with great care and a degree of compassion. That required the attributes that Joseph possessed and Murat did not. A lesser crown might be found for Murat one day, since he was a member of the Bonaparte family by marriage. Napoleon dismissed thoughts of his brother-in-law and continued.

'There is no question of Murat's being King of Spain. It is my judgement that you are the best man for the job. I am depending on you, Joseph. I need you to do this for me. I need a strong, wise man to take charge of France's southern flank. Who else can I trust? You have always looked out for me, for as long as I can remember. I have always depended on you. Will you fail me now?'

Joseph picked up a small bread roll and bit a corner off it as he stared out across the flat ground. He was silent for a moment and Napoleon tried not to appear anxious as he waited for his brother to speak. At length Joseph nodded.

'Very well. I will do as you ask.'

'I thank you, brother. You will not find me ungrateful.'

'On one condition.'

'Which is?'

'That you will not summarily announce my accession to the throne. You will not impose me upon the Spanish. Rather, the junta in Madrid must offer the crown to me. Freely if possible. With the appearance of freedom if not.'

Napoleon considered this for a moment. He would rather the situation in Spain was resolved as speedily as possible, even if that meant openly choosing their new king for them. All the same, he could see the wisdom in Joseph's suggestion. If the call for him to become king came from the junta in Madrid it would make Joseph's candidacy more acceptable to the Spanish people, as well as to wider public opinion across the continent. Of course, it would take a little time to persuade the members of the junta that it was in their interest to make the offer. Murat would have to distribute the required bribes and threats to ensure their compliance. Now that would be a far better use of Murat's abilities, Napoleon noted to himself with a smile. Still, it was a delay all the same and one that he knew would tax his patience. But what could he do? He wanted Joseph to take on the duty and therefore he would have to bow to his brother's will.

He looked up and nodded. 'Very well then, I accept your condition. I will send orders to Murat to prepare the ground.' He cleared the last morsel of meat from his plate and set it down in the grass. 'Now let's begin the day's entertainment.'

Seeing the Emperor rise to his feet the rest of the hunting party hurriedly put aside what was left of their luncheon and followed suit. The guns were brought forward as the guests were led to their posts along the slope of the hillock, where patches of gorse obscured some of the shooting stands from each other. Napoleon saw that Masséna was to his right, perhaps twenty paces off. To his left was Berthier. Across the flat marsh the distant figures of the beaters were visible on the far side, and once the signal was given they began to move towards the hillock, thrashing at the ground before them and using wooden clackers to scare the birds into flight. In case the targets should be too few, or too evasive, Berthier had taken the precaution of ensuring that a plentiful supply of pheasant and duck was held ready in small cages spread out amid the long reeds and grassy hummocks ranged before the hunting party.

The beaters edged across the marsh, scaring up the game, and as soon as he judged that the birds had come within range Napoleon reached for his gun. One of the servants behind him pressed it into his hand and he drew it up and settled the stock into his shoulder. He took aim into the air above the beaters. Movement flickered to either side of his vision as ducks rose up from the marshes, quacking in panic. With a sharp thud from his right, Masséna took a bird on the wing and there was a little explosion of feathers in mid-air before the duck plummeted to earth.

'Hah!' Masséna called out as he handed his weapon to one of his bearers and took a loaded replacement. 'First strike to me!'

A moment later a bird erupted from the reeds directly ahead of Napoleon and flew straight into his line of sight. He tracked it for a second and then began to lead the target before he squeezed the trigger. Instantly a cloud of smoke obliterated his view and the butt kicked savagely into his shoulder. As the breeze swept the smoke away Napoleon saw that he had winged the duck and it flapped pathetically for a little distance, losing height before it dropped into the marsh.

'One!' he shouted to Masséna, and reached for another gun.

As the day wore on more and more birds were frightened into the sky and were shot down by the imperial hunting party. When the beaters had exhausted the supply of birds in the marsh, they began to release those in the cages. Napoleon had become locked into a fierce competition with Masséna as each strove to score the most kills, and late in the afternoon Masséna was two birds ahead. Napoleon's arms were beginning to ache from holding his weapon as an uncaged pheasant flapped into the air slightly to his right, warbling in panic. Knowing that Masséna would be bound to claim the bird unless he shot first, Napoleon raised his gun and tracked the bird to his right. It flew low and fast and before he realised it Napoleon had turned almost ninety degrees to the side.

'Careful, sire!' one of the bearers cried out in alarm.

Napoleon snatched at the trigger and the weapon went off with a loud report. Almost at once there was a cry of pain and rage and when the smoke cleared Napoleon saw that Masséna was staggering back, hands clasped to his face as blood dripped through his fingers. After an instant's hesitation Napoleon began to run across to him, and behind came Berthier, racing towards the sound of Masséna's shouting. When the Emperor reached Masséna the marshal was down on his knees, groaning, and his bearers were standing over him. Napoleon brushed them aside. 'Get some bandages and water!'

'Yes, sire.'

'And see if there is a physician in the party.'

The bearer nodded and ran back up the hill as the shooting continued on either side. Berthier came running up, panting.

'What happened?'

'An accident,' Napoleon muttered. He pulled a handkerchief from his pocket and began to wipe away the blood on Masséna's face.

'Careful, damn you!' Masséna growled. He pulled the cloth from the Emperor's hand and mopped at the blood streaming down the left side of his face. Napoleon could see the small puncture wounds where the shot had struck, and blood and fluid seeping from the marshal's left eye. He heard the sound of footsteps rustling through the grass as the bearer returned with an officer, Dr Larrey, who had served with Napoleon in Egypt and Syria.

Larrey bent over Masséna and examined the wounds. 'What happened?'

'What do you think?' Masséna growled through clenched teeth. 'Some careless bastard shot me in the face.'

Larrey glanced round at the Emperor.

Napoleon felt a surge of anger at the clear accusation. He turned on Berthier and glared. 'It was you.'

'Me? But sire . . .'

'It was you, Berthier. It must have been. You lost sense of where you were aiming. It was an accident.'

Berthier opened and closed his mouth in numbed surprise. He looked to Larrey, and then at Masséna, and shook his head. 'I didn't . . .'

'Don't deny it, Berthier.' Napoleon grasped his arm. 'As I said, it was an accident. Masséna is wounded, but he will recover. Isn't that right, doctor?'

Larrey was examining Masséna's face closely, and did not meet the Emperor's stare. 'Yes, the marshal will recover, but he may lose the sight in this eye. I'll do what I can to save the eye, of course. Can you stand, sir?'

'Yes,' Masséna hissed. 'I was shot in the face, not my fucking legs.'

He struggled to his feet and Larrey gestured up the slope. 'Follow me, sir. We'll take your carriage back to Bayonne. I have my kit there and I can treat you.'

'Let's go then,' said Masséna, and then paused to glare at Napoleon. 'With your permission, sire.'

'Yes, yes, of course. Go.'

With the doctor gently guiding Masséna by the arm, the two made their way towards the crest of the hillock. Berthier coughed. 'Sire?'

'Yes. What is it?'

'Should I call an end to the shooting party?'

Napoleon turned to his chief of staff with a frown. 'No. There's nothing anyone else can do for Masséna. Let the guests enjoy themselves. Except you, of course. You've done enough harm for one day. Return to the carriages and wait for the rest of us there.'

For a second it seemed as if Berthier would protest, but the warning glint in Napoleon's eye challenged the chief of staff to defy him. He drew a sharp breath, clamped his mouth shut and bowed his head before turning to stride away. Napoleon watched him for a moment, and then turned back towards his hide and called out for another gun.

A week later, towards the middle of May, as the imperial party was preparing to return to Paris, a despatch arrived from Murat. There had been riots in Madrid and a mob had killed over two hundred French soldiers. Murat had responded by declaring martial law and ordering his troops on to the streets. Over two thousand Spaniards had been killed before order was restored. Napoleon lowered the report and stared at the staff officer who had brought it from Madrid.

'Major Chabert, isn't it?'

'Yes, sire.'

'Were you in Madrid at the time of the uprising that Marshal Murat tells me of?'

'Yes, sire.'

'Well, then, explain the situation to me in your own words.'

Chabert swallowed nervously. 'As you command, sire. I think the trouble began with some of our men. You know what they are like, sire. They have a bit of a drink, and then begin to help themselves.'

'Which is why I insisted that strict discipline be maintained, and that our men be restricted to the suburbs of Madrid.'

A look of surprise flitted across Major Chabert's face and Napoleon sighed bitterly. 'I take it that Murat did *not* quarter his men in the suburbs.'

'Well, no, sire. Many were billeted in the centre of the city.'

Napoleon closed his eyes briefly and winced. Once again Murat had failed to obey the express orders of the Emperor, and thousands of Spaniards and some soldiers had died as a result. Worse still, there would be a simmering atmosphere of resentment that would make it all the harder to ensure that the junta would call for Joseph to be the new King. Napoleon's first instinct was to recall Murat, have him brought in front of his Emperor and berate him severely. But that would only undermine French authority in Spain even further; and besides, whatever his occasional faults, Murat was his brother-in-law and had served with him from the early days. Napoleon knew that he had no choice in the matter. Murat had set the course for relations between the French army and the Spanish people for the immediate future. Any sign of weakness now would endanger whatever influence France still had over its neighbour. With a sigh Napoleon opened his eyes again.

'You are to return to Murat and tell him that he is to stamp on the slightest sign of rebellion. We will not tolerate disorder. He is also to apply pressure on the junta and impress upon them the importance of offering the crown to Joseph Bonaparte at the earliest possible opportunity. Is that clear?'

'Yes, sire.'

'Very well. One last thing, Chabert. You are to tell Murat, from me, that in future I will expect him to carry out my orders to the letter and that if he fails me again I will replace him with someone more competent, which should not prove to be much of a challenge.'

Napoleon hoped that a show of ruthlessness now would intimidate the Spanish people enough to prevent any further displays of resistance to the French forces stationed there. But in the days that followed news reached him of popular uprisings spreading across Spain. There were riots in Salamanca, Valladolid and Ciudad Rodrigo. The mayors of Cadiz, Cartagena and Badajoz, who had welcomed French intervention, were all set upon by mobs and butchered. The city of Seville had risen in open revolt against the French occupation and the revolutionary junta there had even had the temerity to ask the British governor of Gibraltar for arms and money to support their rebellion.

In Madrid at least, Murat retained control by judicious use of force. While he tamed the common people he worked on persuading the members of the ruling junta to strengthen their ties with France. Those members who proved to be intractable were offered bribes and threats until they came round, and early in April the junta issued a proclamation, in the presence of Murat and a company of grenadiers, to offer the throne of the kingdom of Spain to Joseph Bonaparte.

Napoleon felt a surge of relief as he read of the proclamation. He immediately sent for his brother, who had returned to Paris from Bayonne with the imperial party, and had not yet set out to return to his kingdom in southern Italy.

As Joseph sat in the Emperor's study in the Tuileries and read through the official invitation to ascend the Spanish throne, Napoleon paced up and down the length of the room. At length Joseph lowered the document.

'Well?' Napoleon crossed the study towards him and tapped the sheet of paper. 'You see, they want you.'

'In Madrid at least. I am not so sure that this sentiment is shared by the regional juntas.'

'Pah!' Napoleon waved his hand dismissively. 'Once they learn that the Madrid junta has made this offer, and that you have accepted it, they will quieten down and follow the lead from the capital.'

'I hope you are right,' Joseph responded doubtfully. 'I have heard that much of the country is in open rebellion.'

'Precisely because they lack a king,' Napoleon explained. 'Murat has handled his role with all the sensitivity of a common street butcher. Of course the people are resentful. They see only a French army of occupation and a French marshal acting as a dictator. But once they have a king, once civil government is restored and business can resume as before, they will settle down. Then you can offer them reforms to bring their backward institutions into the modern world. They will thank you for it, Joseph, and in a few years' time they will come to respect and love you. I am sure of it.'

Joseph nodded appreciatively. 'That would be something to be remembered for. Something I could be proud of, in the fullness of time.'

'Precisely.' Napoleon leaned towards him with an intense expression. 'Well, then. Your condition for accepting the crown has been met. Now you must keep your part of the bargain.'

'Yes.' Joseph nodded, then thought for a moment and looked directly at his brother. 'There is much to be done in Spain. May I count on your support? Your full support?'

'Of course, brother!' Napoleon smiled and patted him affectionately on the shoulder. 'No matter how long it takes, no matter how many men it takes, I swear that I will maintain you on the throne of Spain. I swear it.'

Chapter 42

Arthur

Dublin, April 1808

'Congratulations, my dear,' said Kitty as she leaned forward and kissed Arthur. 'It is no more than you deserve, and long overdue.'

He read through the letter from the War Office once more, just to make sure. The Secretary of State for War was pleased to inform Sir Arthur Wellesley that he was promoted to the rank of lieutenant-general in his majesty's forces with immediate effect. Furthermore, he was requested to attend a small investiture ceremony in London, and afterwards make himself available to the Foreign Secretary in order to offer his opinions with respect to the course of the war with France.

Arthur lowered the letter on to the table and shrugged. 'It is tempting to wonder if this might not have come a bit earlier had I not been held back by my service in India. Never mind. The promotion has come, and I am better able to serve my King and country as a result. That is the important thing.'

Kitty had returned to her seat and was fussing over the crib where their second child, Charles, was lying, tiny fists clenched as he waved them about furiously. The boy's birth had been one of Arthur's few consolations since his return from Denmark at the end of the previous year. Almost as soon as the convoy had put into port he had been summoned back to Dublin to resume his duties as Chief Secretary to the Duke of Richmond. He was back at his desk early in October, dealing with the same old problems that had beset Ireland for decades. The divisions between Catholics and Protestants were as pronounced as ever. There were more absentee landlords every year and the prospect of mass starvation due to the failure of the potato harvest constantly loomed.

Even as Arthur worked conscientiously to improve the lot of the Irish people, his mind was fixed on the political situation on the continent and his desire to serve his country in uniform again. Shortly after his return, news arrived of Bonaparte's attempt to seize control of the Portuguese navy and every man and woman in Britain had breathed a sigh of relief when they heard of the escape of the Portuguese royal family and their warships, two days before French troops occupied Lisbon.

Kitty cleared her throat and Arthur glanced across the table to see her watching him closely.

'What is it, my dear?'

'I was wondering how long you might be spending in London this time.'

'It is hard to say,' Arthur replied cautiously. He was conscious that Kitty had still not completely forgiven him for the cavalier way he had joined the expeditionary force setting sail for Denmark. He had given her no warning that he was involved with the planning and preparation for the campaign. 'But I promise that I shall write to you often and make every effort to return to Dublin as soon as I may.'

'As long as you promise that, I shall be content, Arthur.' She was quiet for a moment before she continued. 'You know that I miss you, and worry for your safety when you are not here.'

'I realise that, my dear,' Arthur replied patiently. 'But I am a soldier as well as a civilian official. As a husband and father, it is not always possible to balance the claims of all those duties, and those persons to whom I am obliged to give my attention.'

'I wish that you would give up soldiering,' Kitty responded with quiet intensity as she offered her little finger to Charles, who grasped it and squeezed for all he was worth, making his mother smile faintly. 'You have done enough active service for your country already. Surely it is the turn of someone else?'

'My dear, the long years of campaigning in India are precisely the reason why I am needed in uniform. I have valuable experience of leading men, and indeed entire armies, on campaign, and in battle. My country has profited from what I have learned. Would you deny Britain the benefit of that experience now, when we are almost within the grasp of the Corsican tyrant? Britain needs every soldier that can bear arms.' He smiled at her. 'If you must blame anyone for the demands made on me, then let it be Bonaparte.'

'Wretched man,' Kitty responded, with feeling. She was quiet a moment, thinking. 'What drives him to desire power without limit?'

It was an interesting question and Arthur gave it some thought before he attempted to reply. 'A difficult one to answer. There is a flaw

380

of character in some men, whereby they are never replete with the satisfaction that comes with serving one's country. Their sense of duty becomes corrupted by ambition to the extent that their only obligation is to themselves and hang the rest of it. I believe that Bonaparte is such a man. But he is also the child of a particular moment in history. Were it not for the revolution in France, I doubt that he would have attained any substantial rank in the French army.'

'Truly?' Kitty looked surprised. 'Surely the man has remarkable talents, otherwise he would never have risen to become Emperor.'

'Oh, he is remarkable enough,' Arthur conceded. 'But if there had been no revolution he would have faced the same restrictions on his advancement as I have in the British army. Indeed, given the obscurity of his social origins, I dare say he would never have been likely to rise above the rank of captain in the army that existed before the revolution. The revolution was the making of Bonaparte, just as it was of many of those who now hold powerful offices in France. It was the revolution that opened the doors of rapid promotion to so many men. It was the revolution that fashioned Bonaparte and fed him the opportunities for advancement that brought him to where he is today, and obliged the rest of us to fight him until the bitter end,' Arthur added with a mirthless smile. 'I wonder, if our positions had been reversed and I had been born in Corsica, how far I might have risen? Equally, if Bonaparte had been born here in Ireland, to my parents, he would have been fortunate to have attained the posts that I have and be sitting here talking to you, my dear.'

Kitty shuddered. 'The thought of being married to such a monster makes my blood run cold.'

'And so it should.' Arthur was silent a moment before he continued. 'Though I am not wholly certain whether he is what he is by defect of character, or by transformation afforded him by the revolution. I doubt we shall ever know. What a pity.'

'As long as he is brought low before too much longer, I don't care,' said Kitty. 'And as long as he is brought low without you or any of my brothers coming to harm I shall be happy. He is an evil man.'

'Evil?' Arthur considered the suggestion. 'I suppose he is . . . Yes, you are right. He is doing evil now. There is no question of it. He has changed the nature of war. There was a time when war had limited aims, when it was the last resort of kings and ministers when all else had failed. The army was the final servant of the nation. Now Bonaparte has made the Grand Army into the master of France and the country exists only to serve its soldiers, and their only purpose is to wage war. And war, to my mind, is the greatest of evils.' Arthur stared out of the window as images from the past burst, unwanted, into his mind. 'I have seen enough to know that. And to know the degree to which it corrupts the spirits of men.'

'Then why are you so keen to return to war?' asked Kitty plaintively.

'Keen? I am not keen in the slightest. I mean to do all I can to end this conflict, but there can be no end to it as long as Bonaparte rules France. Once he is defeated, then I can give up war once and for all.'

Kitty stared at him a moment. 'They are fine sentiments, Arthur, but there are times when I fear that you have become just as addicted to conflict as Bonaparte.'

Arthur pursed his lips briefly and nodded wearily. 'There are times when I fear that you may be right.'

London was buzzing with the news that the Spanish royal family had been ousted from the throne. It was clear to all that Bonaparte would replace them with a puppet ruler as soon as possible, and extend his grip on Europe from the Straits of Gibraltar to the Baltic Sea. Before his departure from Dublin Arthur had been sent some documents from the Foreign Office outlining possible campaigns that might be undertaken against Spain's possessions in the Americas. The schemes had all been hatched by a renegade, General Miranda, leader of the rebels in Venezuela who sought independence from Spain. During the journey to London Arthur had analysed the sketchy plans and could see that there was scope for some action in the Americas, but he was wary of backing wholesale revolution throughout the Spanish empire. Revolutions were tricky beasts whose nature and direction could never be anticipated.

As soon as he reached the house in Harley Street Arthur sent a message to George Canning announcing his arrival and preparedness to meet at the first opportunity. So it was that first thing the following day Arthur presented himself at the office of the Foreign Secretary. Canning was a slight man with brilliant eyes and a ready smile.

'Ah, Wellesley! Come in and sit yourself down.' Canning beamed from behind his desk. Arthur did as he was bid and settled comfortably into a soft leather chair opposite his host.

Canning leaned forward, hands folded together. 'First chance I have had to add my congratulations on your performance in Denmark. First of all, a vote of thanks from Parliament for your – what was the phrase? Ah, yes! Your "genius and valour". And then a formal note from the Danes expressing their gratitude for the honourable manner in which you negotiated their surrender of Copenhagen. Truly you are the coming man.'

'I thank you.' Arthur bowed his head modestly. 'I did no more than my duty.'

'Of course, of course,' Canning replied with a quick nod. 'Just as any officer would do.'

'Yes. That is what I would hope.'

Canning smiled and eased himself back in his chair. 'I have been authorised by the Cabinet to offer you a new command. An army is to be sent to liberate Portugal, and it was felt that you would be the most suitable officer to take charge of the campaign. Do you accept?'

'Indeed, sir.' Arthur's eyebrows arched in surprise at the suddenness of the offer. He felt elated, and did his best to hide it. 'Do you intend to extend the operation beyond the frontiers of Portugal?'

'The government considers that it would be most prudent to begin with Portugal. It is more easily supplied and defended, and should provide an admirable base for wider operations when the time is ripe. Only then you might consider Spain.'

Arthur's heart quickened at the prospect. This was the war he had dreamed of. The chance to tackle French troops directly on terrain favourable to the British. With the Spanish nation rising up against the French occupiers Bonaparte faced waging a war in the most difficult of conditions. His men, accustomed to feeding off the land, would be the targets of armed bands of peasants. The climate was hot too and Arthur well knew the particular strains of campaigning under the merciless glare of the sun. Nor would it be a theatre of war that the French Emperor could ignore. Having made his brother King, Bonaparte would be compelled to divert endless resources to Spain to support Joseph and prevent the humiliating spectacle of a member of his family being ousted from the throne that the Emperor had placed him upon. The situation was ripe with advantages for Britain and her new Spanish and Portuguese allies.

Arthur glanced at Canning. 'When do you want me to sail for Portugal?'

'The sooner the better. Best strike while the iron is hot, eh? I would like your force to land before the end of July.'

Arthur raised his eyebrows. 'That does not give me much time to prepare.'

'Really?' Canning frowned. 'How much time do you need? Our opportunity lies before us now, Wellesley. It may slip from our grasp unless you act quickly.' Canning paused. 'Of course, there are plenty of other general officers who might be able to act with greater alacrity.'

'I will be ready on time,' Arthur replied firmly.

'Good. Then your first task will be to defeat General Junot and drive him from Lisbon and out of the country.'

'Do we have any estimate of Junot's strength?'

Canning nodded. 'Our Portuguese spies tell us that he has no more than ten thousand men. Your command can handle that.'

'Yes. As long as the reports of your spies are accurate.'

'They are. Our agents in Lisbon had proved to be very reliable to date. You should have nothing to worry about. Now I suggest you set about making your preparations to leave as swiftly as possible.'

On returning to Harley Street Arthur immediately wrote a letter to Kitty to inform her of his new command. This time there was little likelihood of his returning to his duties in Dublin for a long time indeed. In which case, Kitty should move to London as soon as possible. He told her that this was the opportunity to serve his country that he had been waiting for for so many years, and that Kitty should be proud of him. Once she came to London, he continued, he would be content in the knowledge that his brothers would ensure that she was looked after, and help her run the family's affairs until he returned.

Having folded, sealed and addressed the letter to Kitty, Arthur next wrote to the Duke of Richmond to inform him of the coming campaign. He offered his profound gratitude to the Duke for the confidence he had shown in Arthur by appointing him to the post of Chief Secretary. However, his primary duty lay in serving his country on the battlefield, until peace was won. After Bonaparte was defeated Arthur pledged to return to his post in Dublin as swiftly as possible.

Once the letters had been written Arthur turned his attention to making a list of the preparations necessary for the coming campaign. There were staff officers to appoint, books to purchase. He must also arrange to meet a deputation from Spain, and representatives of the Portuguese government in exile. As the day wore on and dusk settled over London Arthur added further pages of notes to the growing pile, until at length, as a footman lighted a lantern to illuminate his study, Arthur sat back in his chair with a smile.

At last he could prove his worth to the world. With ten thousand men he would clear the French out of Portugal, and once that had been achieved the government must surely see that with adequate reinforcements there was ample opportunity of bleeding Bonaparte's army dry in the hostile plains and mountains of Spain.

The following weeks passed in a welter of details and meetings until early July, when all was ready. Kitty and the two infants had joined Arthur in London and on the eve of his departure he held a final private dinner for his brothers Richard, William and Henry. It was the first time for a number of years that they had gathered together, and as they chattered light-heartedly over the meal, catching up on each other's news, Arthur could not help thinking back to the days of their childhood when they had played in the gardens of Dangan Castle in Ireland. It seemed an idyllic interlude now. Carefree games on the lawn while faint notes of violin music issued from their father's recital room. Their mother would sit and sew in the shade of an oak tree and the outside world promised so much. Then came the French revolution and the war, and looking round the table Arthur was proud to note that each of them had risen to the challenge and served their country with distinction. At that moment he felt a surge of affection for his brothers and, slightly the worse for wear, leaned forward and picked up his glass.

'A toast, my brothers!'

Henry looked at him with an amused smile. 'A toast? Have you not yet drunk enough, Arthur?'

'A toast,' Arthur insisted. 'I give you family, honour and duty. Long may we hold true to those values.'

Richard nodded. 'Family, honour and duty.'

The others joined in as they all raised their glasses and then drained every drop.

Shortly afterwards William made his apologies and rose to leave, bracing himself against the table as the room spun round.

'Oh dear,' he muttered. 'I don't think I am very well.'

'Come, William!' Henry laughed as he stood up and moved round the table to support his older brother. 'Let me take you home. I must bid the rest of you farewell. Thank you for a fine meal, Kitty. God speed and good luck to you, Arthur. Teach those damned Frenchies a lesson!'

'I will,' Arthur replied. 'I promise. God save you, Henry, and you, William.'

When they had left Arthur turned to Kitty, who had been quiet all night. 'Are you all right, my dear?'

'I am fine. Quite fine,' she replied.

'Really?' Arthur looked at her closely. 'You are not sickening for anything?'

'No. I said I am fine, thank you.'

'Then why the long face?'

She looked up at him and now he could see the tears gleaming in the corners of her eyes. Her lips were trembling when she spoke. 'You are going off to war again. I don't know when you may return, if you return. So far fortune has spared you and sent you home to me in one piece. But can that last, Arthur? One day, a French bullet will find your heart, or a sickness will strike you down. Then I will be left a widow and your children will grow up hardly having known a father. And you ask how I feel?'

Before Arthur could summon a reply she had risen and hurried from the room, leaving her husband and brother-in-law staring after her in surprise.

'Bless my soul,' Richard muttered.

'I'll speak to her later. Put her mind at rest.' Arthur poured himself another glass of wine and stared into its red depths. The room was silent for a while before Richard spoke again.

'Your mood has changed. What are you thinking?'

'Hm?' Arthur stirred and looked at his brother. 'Oh, it just struck me that I have not faced the French since I was in Flanders, fifteen years ago. They were good then, and I dare say that with all the experience Bonaparte has given them they will be even more formidable. They have humbled every army in Europe, except our own. In addition, they outnumber our men overwhelmingly. It is quite a daunting prospect.'

Richard looked at his brother searchingly. 'Do you think you can beat them?'

'I think so. They have faced armies who were already unnerved by the prospect of fighting French soldiers. It is my belief that our men are made of tougher stuff. They are better trained, better led in most respects, and, above all, they have self-confidence. If the French manoeuvre against us in columns, as I have heard they always do, then I believe that our men, in line, will be steady enough to carry the day.' Arthur took a sip from his glass. 'If I am wrong then they will bury my cold body in some ditch in Portugal, and you will soon be learning the Marseillaise.'

Chapter 43

Mondego Bay, Portugal, 30 July 1808

The British fleet lay heaved to off the coast. In addition to the transports there was a squadron of warships assigned to protect Arthur's force. His strength had been increased by a further five thousand men under the command of Major-General Sir Brent Spencer, following further intelligence that Junot had up to twenty thousand men in his army. In the days before the transports had arrived off the coast of Portugal Arthur had been cruising along the coast looking for a place to land his soldiers so that they could march on Lisbon. A landing at the Portuguese capital itself was out of the question. The mouth of the Tagus was covered by a number of strong forts which commanded the approaches to the harbour. In addition, the British had discovered a squadron of eight Russian warships at anchor off Lisbon. With the treaty between France and Russia still in effect the Russian squadron presented a possible danger and was best avoided, Arthur decided. Sailing north along the coast from Lisbon it soon became clear that there were very few places suitable for landing his army.

Mondego Bay itself was covered by a centuries-old fort constructed from a pale yellow stone, and the British fleet was about to move on when a small boat put out from the shore and made directly for the British warships. On board was the excited representative of a group of students from Coimbra University. In broken English he explained that they had seized the fort from the small French garrison that had been posted there by General Junot.

'How long ago?'

'Two days.' The student grinned. 'Two days before, we kick them out.'

'Kicked them out? You let them go?'

'Yes!' The student nodded. 'They run like dogs with tails between legs.'

'Then they will have had time to report the loss of the fort,' Arthur mused. He turned to Admiral Cotton, the commander of the naval squadron. Cotton was a senior officer of long experience who approached his duty with caution. 'We have to ensure that the army is ashore before the French can retake the fort.'

Cotton looked surprised and gestured towards the shore, where a wide expanse of rough-looking surf pounded the sand. 'It is not a good place to land your army, Sir Arthur. The conditions are too difficult, too dangerous.'

'We'll land here,' Arthur replied firmly. 'We have already sailed a hundred miles up the coast from Lisbon searching for a suitable place. We cannot afford to keep looking or we will put too great a distance between us and our goal. We land here. Now, I would be grateful if you would send ashore a hundred of your marines to reinforce our gallant student allies.' Arthur patted the Portuguese youth on the shoulder and the latter beamed with pride as he puffed out his chest.

Admiral Cotton looked wearily at the student and shrugged his shoulders. 'As you wish. I will have our marines ashore within the hour.'

'Thank you, Admiral. Let me know the moment we are in possession of the fort. Then we can begin disembarking our troops at once. In the meantime I propose to entertain our young guest in the wardroom, if you don't mind?'

'Not at all,' Cotton grumbled. 'Be my guest.'

Arthur led the student down the gangway and automatically ducked as they went below deck. There was a bump and a groan behind him as the student learned the first lesson of naval architecture.

'Mind your head,' Arthur muttered unhelpfully.

As the student drank eagerly from the decanter placed before him, Arthur questioned him about life under the French. The student's cheerfulness faded as he told of the arrogance and cruelty of Bonaparte's soldiers. They stripped the land of food and valuables as they passed and punished any attempt at resistance by the Portuguese people with wanton severity. Five days earlier, so the student said, a French patrol had been set upon by the townspeople of Évora when the French had attempted to take gold and silver plate from the local church. In return, the commander of the nearest French division, General Loison, had marched a column to Évora and killed every man, woman and child in the town. There was nothing left there but bodies and ghosts, the student said with scarcely suppressed rage.

As Arthur listened to him, and shared his anger at the horrors of war, he could not help feeling a measure of satisfaction that the French had, as ever, managed to turn the local population against them. Now Arthur could be sure that the Portuguese would welcome the British soldiers about to descend on their land. Of course, it was essential that every man in the army knew how vital it was to behave in a way that would retain the support and loyalty of the locals. He decided that it was time to issue his first General Order, so that the troops would understand that Portugal was a friendly country and no liberties were to be taken with the property or persons of the Portuguese.

As the student came to the end of his account, there was a knock and a marine entered the wardroom and saluted.

'General, there's a brig joining the fleet. They've signalled that they have an urgent despatch on board for you.'

'Thank you.' Arthur turned back to the student and poured them both a glass before proposing a toast.

'To Portugal and Britain! Allies and sworn enemies of the Corsican tyrant.'

'Yes.' The student nodded. 'Death to the French!'

'Yes,' Arthur agreed. 'Even that. Death to the French.'

Once he had escorted the student back on deck and seen to it that the youth made it safely back aboard his boat, Arthur turned and looked for the brig. The small ship had hove to astern of the admiral's flagship and a small cutter was being lowered into the water. Four sailors took the oars and a midshipman climbed into the stern clutching a bag of despatches and letters. The small craft bobbed across the waves as the sailors rowed lustily, and a short time later the midshipman was standing on the broad deck of the flagship offering a sealed document to Arthur.

'From London, sir, War Office.'

Arthur returned the salute and took the despatch below to the wardroom, where he closed the door and broke the seal on the stitched canvas covering. Like most orders that were carried at sea, they had been covered with waterproofed canvas and contained an iron weight to send the message to the bottom of the sea if the vessel carrying them was intercepted. Placing the iron bar to one side, Arthur took out the envelope addressed to him and flipped it over to see that it had been sent directly from the office of Viscount Castlereagh, the Secretary of State for War. Arthur opened the envelope, unfolded the letter and began to read the contents swiftly.

Castlereagh reported that the latest intelligence received from British spies in Portugal was that General Junot's army might contain over forty thousand men. Accordingly, the War Office had decided to send a further fifteen thousand men to join Arthur's force in Portugal, and Castlereagh regretted to inform Sir Arthur that the combined force would be of such a size that a more senior officer would be required to command it.

Arthur felt the dead weight of disappointment settle on his soul. Once again fate seemed to have conspired against him. At the very moment when he was on the verge of commencing his first independent command in the European theatre of war, he was about to be trumped by a senior officer.

He read on. The combined force was to be placed under the command of Sir Hew Dalrymple. Arthur tried to recall what he knew of the man. Sir Hew must be nearly twenty years older than Arthur. He had seen very little active service, and even that was over ten years ago. Sir Hew was to be accompanied by Sir Harry Burrard and four other officers who would be above Arthur in the new chain of command. He clenched his fist and took a deep breath to calm his temper and ease the frustration that burned away inside. At length he read the final paragraph. He frowned, and read it again, slowly and deliberately, and then lowered the letter with a faint smile. The Secretary for War had concluded by ordering Arthur not to wait for his superiors to catch up but to continue his operation to seize Lisbon as speedily as possible.

'God bless you, Castlereagh,' Arthur muttered. There was a chance for him yet, provided he did not waste a moment. Folding the letter, he stood up swiftly and promptly whacked his head on the low ceiling. He emerged on deck, rubbing his crown, then jammed his hat on his head and strode across to join Admiral Cotton.

'I have just received orders from London.'

'So?'

'We are to land the army immediately.'

'Immediately? Why, half the day is gone already, Sir Arthur. My marines have only just taken charge of the fort. It would be best to wait until the morrow.'

Arthur shook his head. 'There is no time to waste. The army must be landed at once.'

All afternoon, and well into dusk, the boats ferried soldiers and supplies ashore. The surf was even more wild than it appeared from the ships, and some of the lighter boats were tumbled over as they attempted to approach the shore, casting the sailors and soldiers into the foaming spray where several were drowned. But, by nightfall, the first wave of Arthur's army was ashore and had moved beyond the red rocks lining the shore to make camp. Pickets were posted further inland. Arthur would have liked to send cavalry patrols out to locate the nearest enemy troops, but only a handful of horses had sailed with the expedition and they were still aboard the convoys, awaiting calmer conditions to be brought ashore.

A small tent had been erected for the commanding officer and by the light of a single lantern Arthur conferred with his new aide-de-camp, a young man recommended to him by the Duke of Richmond.

'So then, Somerset, how long will it take to complete the unloading?'

Lord Fitzroy Somerset consulted his notes in a calm, unhurried manner. 'We have three thousand men ashore. There're another twelve and a half to come all told. Food supplies and ammunition will come first, in case we encounter any of the enemy. Then the artillery and engineers. Given the available boats, and time taken to make a round trip, I have calculated that the landing will be completed in six days' time, sir.'

'I see.' Arthur nodded. It was not good news. General Junot was bound to learn of the landing before the following day was out and would instantly begin to concentrate his forces in an attempt to repel the British invasion. The army had to be ready to move before then. The main difficulty was that neither the artillery nor the cavalry had sufficient horses to march on the enemy. The War Office had anticipated that a ready supply of horses could be found in Portugal. However, as Arthur had quickly discovered, the small country was poor and good horses were scarce. Even mules were in short supply and as things stood the infantry would be required to haul some of the supply wagons by hand. Arthur glanced up at Somerset. 'Any word from our Portuguese friend yet?'

General Freire had been charged by his government in exile to co-operate with the British as fully as possible and had promised to join Arthur with food, horses and another six thousand Portuguese soldiers the moment the redcoats landed. Arthur had met Freire at Oporto when the flagship had stopped there on the way to Lisbon. Freire, like so many local officials, had offered an effusive welcome to Arthur and his staff officers, and had made wild boasts about crushing the French forces on Portuguese soil before joining with his British brothers and liberating Spain. Arthur had thanked him politely and persuaded Freire to meet him on the Lisbon road, at Leiria, and march on the Portuguese capital together.

Somerset shook his head. 'Nothing as yet, sir. Freire might have been delayed. Or he might not have sent out any messengers to advise us of his approach.'

'Tell me, Somerset, what did you make of Freire?'

Arthur watched his aide closely as Somerset quickly formed his judgement and made his reply. 'I was impressed by his sense of patriotism, sir. There is no doubting his desire to rid Portugal of the French. However, he did not seem to have any ready answers to your queries about where the supplies and the horses would come from. If I may be honest, sir?'

'Speak freely, Somerset. I will not have an aide humour me. I must be able to trust you implicitly.'

'Very well, sir,' the officer responded in a relieved tone. 'I fear that we may see very little of what he promised us when we reach Leiria. Naturally, I may be wrong.'

'I hope you are. If we cannot rely on our allies this army is going to be largely dependent on lines of communication that stretch from the shores of Britain to the coast of Portugal. Not a happy prospect, and when winter comes we can look forward to severe disruption of our supplies.'

'Yes, sir.'

Arthur looked at the map of Portugal that lay across his campaign desk. It was sparsely detailed and was all he had been able to obtain from the War Office before they set off. 'We will keep close to the coast as we advance on Lisbon. That way we can be resupplied by sea and can be evacuated if we suffer any serious reverse.'

Somerset glanced at the map. 'Yes, sir. That makes sense.'

'Thank you, young man. I know that.'

Somerset stiffened. 'Sorry, sir. Is that all?'

'Yes. You'd better go and get some sleep. You'll need all your strength for the coming campaign.'

'Yes, sir. Good night, sir.'

Once his aide had left him, Arthur concentrated his attention on the map again. Lisbon was over a hundred miles away. Perhaps seven days' march. There was every chance that Dalrymple would arrive and take command of the army long before Arthur had had a chance to prove himself. Be that as it may, he would still do everything in his power to prepare the men to march on Lisbon, even if another officer would take the credit for any success they might achieve. Arthur stood up, stretched his shoulders, left the stifling tent and emerged into the sweltering heat of a summer evening. The air had not yet cooled and was heavy with unfamiliar scents. Around the tent the shrill chorus of cicadas rose in intensity and then stopped dead, before beginning again and gradually building up once more. Arthur smiled to himself. He enjoyed this sense of strangeness, of getting away from the landscapes he took for granted in Ireland and England. He had few illusions about the discomforts of the coming campaign, but there was an undeniable sense of liberation in being so far from home, with all its petty and pedantic social demands, not to mention the endlessly shifting currents of the political scene. Arthur felt at home in the field. The goals were clear enough, the stakes were high, and if he and his men did their duty, then they would contribute to the salvation of their country. What greater satisfaction was there than that, Arthur reflected contentedly.

By the time the first week in August came to an end the army was ready to march. On the tenth, Arthur gave the order to break camp and the column set off for Leiria, some twelve miles away. General Freire had already sent word that he and his force had reached the town, but there was no mention of the promised horses and supplies, as Somerset had rightly suspected. As a precaution Arthur had used some of the gold that had accompanied the army to purchase enough horses and mules from the local people to ensure that the army could advance from its beachhead without having to rely on manpower to shift the guns and wagons.

The redcoats were not used to the midsummer heat of Iberia, and had had little chance to exercise in the close confines of the troopships, with the result that they suffered dreadfully on the first day's march. The rough cart track that passed for a road was baked solid and the dust and sand that had gathered on either side was quickly kicked up into a choking cloud that irritated eyes and caught in throats and added still further to the torments of thirst the men endured as they tramped along. Very soon, even the most spirited of them had fallen silent and the soft scrape and thud of boots was accompanied only by the shrill, grating protests from the axles of the wagons and carts carrying the supplies.

Late in the afternoon Arthur rode ahead with Somerset and a local man Arthur had hired to act as guide and translator. General Freire was waiting for them at Leiria, and had commandeered a fine house on the edge of the town and received his guests in a small courtyard where a fountain splashed invitingly in a tiled pond. As many of his men as possible had been quartered in the town, and sat silently in the shade as the British officers rode by, making no attempt to stand and salute.

'I apologise for the delay,' Arthur explained to Freire, pausing as his words were translated. 'But my army is far from its home, and I needed to ensure that everything my men required was ready before we marched.'

Freire nodded as he listened. He was a short, wiry man with a neatly clipped beard and moustache. His hair was grey and grizzled and cropped close to the skull. His eyes were deep set and dark and seemed to stare accusingly. As the translator finished he shot back a swift series of comments directed at Arthur.

'The general asks if all British armies are so slow, or is it that their generals are so cautious?'

Arthur drew a sharp breath before replying. 'Tell the general that my army would have advanced more swiftly if we had received the horses and mules he promised me when we met in Oporto.'

Freire shrugged nonchalantly when the comment was relayed to him.

'The general says that it was not possible to find any draught animals for you. He says the French had taken them all, and the few that remained were needed by his men.'

'And what of the supplies that he promised?' Arthur asked. 'Where are they?'

'The general says that without mules and horses he could not transport supplies. In any case, there were few supplies to bring after the French had passed like locusts across the land. What supplies he did find are needed by his men.'

'I see,' Arthur muttered, keeping his irritation under control. 'Please tell the general that we can manage without the things he had promised us for the moment. Now we need to discuss how we might best combine our forces to crush the French invaders.'

Freire raised a hand to stop Arthur and spoke again.

'The general says that his men are short of food and powder, and that you should supply them with both.'

'Now, just a minute—' Somerset started.

Arthur shot a look at his aide. 'Silence, if you please. Let me deal with this.' He turned back to Freire. 'Tell the general that I cannot supply his forces in addition to my own. I am not authorised to do it, and in any case we need all that we can carry as it is.'

'The general says that without supplies he cannot advance any further towards Lisbon.'

'Damn it, I will not be blackmailed,' Arthur said bitterly. 'Tell him that his government has instructed him to co-operate with me.'

Freire laughed.

'He says that the government's word means little to him. He says that his first duty is to his men. He will only co-operate with the British if they supply him with what he needs.'

Arthur clenched his jaws tightly together to avoid giving vent to his growing anger. He turned to Somerset. 'Can we supply his men?'

'To a degree, sir. But not for long. There might be a way round this impasse, sir.'

'Then speak plainly, man!' Arthur snapped.

'Yes, sir. Since we lack cavalry we are having to make do with light infantry for some of our scouting.'

'Yes. So?'

'Why don't we offer to feed and supply the general's light troops, in exchange for having them seconded to our army?'

Arthur considered the idea for a moment and then nodded to the guide to translate. Freire was quiet for a moment as he stroked his beard. Then he nodded and made his reply.

'He agrees, as long as you provide his men with full rations, and they still remain under his command at all times.'

'No,' Arthur replied at once. 'As long as I'm feeding 'em, they're mine to command.'

Freire made a great show of reluctance before finally conceding. Then Arthur moved on to address the matter of the advance on Lisbon. Somerset produced Arthur's map of the region and spread it out across the cool tiles in the shaded courtyard. Arthur indicated the coastal route leading from Leiria to the capital.

'This is the route I intend to follow. It is open country and the enemy might well take advantage of the fact to use his cavalry to harass my advance, but until the army is reinforced I must remain in contact with the British fleet following us along the coast. If we combine our forces, we should be able to cope with anything the French can put into the field against us between here and Lisbon.'

The Portuguese general looked at the map and tapped another route, further inland.

'He says that this is the best route. There are hills here that will conceal the advance. It is safer. He insists we should take this road,' the guide translated.

'Out of the question,' Arthur replied at once. 'It's too far from the coast. If it's mountainous it will only slow down my wagons and artillery. I am taking the coastal road. Tell him.'

Freire was adamant that he would march through the hills and re-join the British outside Lisbon to take part in the liberation of the capital. Then, rising to his feet, Freire announced that he was fatigued and the interview was over. He would give orders for his light infantry to join the British column. With a curt bow, he turned and disappeared inside the house.

Arthur stared after him for a moment. 'Charming fellow.'

'Quite,' Somerset said softly. 'I just hope this is not typical of the co-operation we can expect from our new allies, sir.'

'So do I.' Arthur took a deep breath and smiled. 'Well, at least we have some extra men to strengthen our army. Pass the word to Colonel Trant. I believe he has some mastery of the local tongue. He can command the Portuguese contingent. Now roll up the map and let us go and hunt the French. Even if our allies prove difficult I am sure we may at least rely on the enemy to be obligingly consistent.'

The British army continued marching south under the blazing sun. To their left, across a small plain, lay the hills where General Freire's column was supposed to be marching parallel to them, but there was never any sign of Portuguese patrols and Freire might as well be on the moon, Arthur reflected bitterly. To the right lay the sea, and some miles out the British fleet, under reduced sail, kept pace with the army. The sea was calm and sparkled seductively in the sunlight, so that the soldiers were constantly tormented by the prospect of a refreshing swim in the sea, and muttered sourly about the easy life of a sailor.

Towards the end of the fourth day, as they approached the village of Obidos, the faint crackle of musketry came from the direction of a windmill a few miles ahead of the main column. Arthur and Somerset rode ahead to investigate and discovered that a company of the 95th Rifles had driven off some French skirmishers and chased them a short distance before coming in sight of the main body of a sizeable French force.

Arthur felt his pulse quicken as he turned to Somerset with an eager glint in his eye. 'So it begins. With a bit of luck tomorrow will see the first battle of our campaign in the Peninsula. Now we'll see how well the French stand up against our boys.'

Chapter 44

The church tower of Obidos provided fine views towards the south, and through his telescope Arthur examined the small French army formed up in front of another village, Roliça, some eight miles away. One of the enemy skirmishers captured the previous day had revealed that the French were led by General Delaborde, a tough, experienced veteran. Even though the French were outnumbered nearly four to one, their commander had chosen a good defensive position. Roliça lay in a flat-bottomed valley surrounded by a horseshoe of steep hills that protected the enemy's flanks. The sun had risen an hour earlier and the slanting light bathed the landscape in vivid colours. Three columns of British soldiers were already setting off towards Roliça, and the dense ranks of red jackets gleamed brilliantly, like threads of blood flowing across the dusty landscape.

During the night a peasant had arrived from a village in the hills to the east. He reported that another French column, of perhaps five thousand men, was marching to join the force at Roliça. That news had determined Arthur to strike as soon as possible, and destroy General Delaborde and his men before they could be reinforced. His plan was simple enough. Two smaller columns of British troops had set off before dawn, marching swiftly towards the left and right of the hill. With luck Delaborde's attention would be drawn to the three main columns, allowing the others to scale the hills and fall on the flanks of the French force.

Satisfied that things were proceeding according to his intentions, Arthur snapped his telescope shut and turned to Somerset, who had just joined the small group of staff officers observing the deployment of the British army. 'Time to join the fray, I think.'

'Yes, sir.'

'Still no word from Freire, I assume?'

'No, sir. None of our mounted patrols could locate him.'

'Well then, he will just have to miss the battle. Too bad.'

Arthur called on his officers to follow him and descended from the church tower. They mounted the horses waiting in the street and rode off to join their commands. When Arthur reached the small rise behind the centre column that he had chosen as his command post he halted and watched as the three British columns formed into lines. The bands of each brigade began to play lustily to add to the spectacle that Arthur hoped would preoccupy the enemy's attention while the trap was closed. For nearly an hour the two armies faced each other, just beyond cannon range, while Arthur and Somerset watched for signs of movement along the crests of the hills that overlooked General Delaborde's flanks.

At length, Somerset thrust his arm out. 'There, sir!'

Arthur followed the direction indicated and saw the head of a column appearing over the crest of the right-hand hill. No more than a minute later the troops of the leftmost column came into view.

'Time to begin the attack.' Arthur nodded, then turned his attention towards the French. 'No, wait.'

'Sir?'

'Delaborde's seen the danger. Look.'

Already the single battery of French guns was being limbered up and then, together with the main body of French infantry, they began to retire. Delaborde's cavalry and skirmishers waited a moment to cover the retreat and then followed the rest of the small army as it marched past Roliça and made for the higher ground behind the village. By the time the flanking columns had descended from the slopes the last of the French had retreated out of danger.

'Damn,' Arthur muttered. 'Somerset, pass the word. The army is to advance to that village and halt. We'll have to make another attempt to bring Delaborde to bay.'

'Yes, sir.'

Once more the British army advanced, this time in line, and the formations rippled slowly across the dry stubbly grass as they entered the valley and moved towards the new French position. As they approached Roliça Arthur could see that it would be a hard fight. Delaborde's force was now arranged along the crest of a low hill with very steep sides facing the British. Here and there the slope was broken by a gully that led sharply up towards the crest. Arthur halted the army and sent fresh orders to the flanking columns to make another attempt to scale the hills on each side of the enemy. Now that the sun had reached its zenith the heat in the valley was stifling and a heat haze shimmered close to the ground. Thirsty and sweating, the two columns set off again, up towards the ridge. This time there would be no chance of surprising Delaborde. The French general could choose to retreat towards Lisbon through the narrow pass behind him, or stand his ground and fight, hoping that he might yet be rescued by the other French column somewhere to the east.

'Hello, what's Lake up to?' Somerset mused, and Arthur turned and saw that one of his regiments, the Twenty-Ninth Foot, was still advancing towards the French. 'Why hasn't he halted?'

Arthur watched in silence as the Twenty-Ninth continued towards a gully in the slope in front of them. A sick feeling welled up in his stomach and he gritted his teeth angrily. 'That damned fool, Lake. I fear he intends to scale that gully and break into their position.'

'He can't be serious, sir. Not without support.'

'You know Lake, bull-headed and keen to make a name for himself.'

'Yes, sir. As long as he doesn't seek to do it posthumously.'

'Get over there, and put a stop to that nonsense.'

'Yes, sir.' Somerset saluted and spurred his horse into a gallop towards the left of the line where the Twenty-Ninth should have halted. But, even as Arthur watched, Lake's men marched into the gully and began to clamber over the steep ground towards the French. Somerset was never going to reach them in time to prevent the coming tragedy. Arthur opened his telescope and began to follow the action as the first men from Lake's battalion emerged from the gully into the French line. At once the enemy turned to deal with the new danger, pouring volley after volley into the disordered ranks of the Twenty-Ninth as they clambered out of the gully. Soon the ground around the battalion's colours was littered with redcoats and the survivors were desperately returning fire at will. Then the steadily thickening gunpowder smoke obscured the view and Arthur lowered his telescope. He glanced to each side of the valley and saw that neither of the flanking columns would be in place to make an attack for at least another half-hour. Unless something was done immediately, the Twenty-Ninth would be wiped out.

He turned to the nearest of his staff officers. 'Simpson! Ride forward and pass the order for a general advance.'

'Yes, sir!'

Arthur took one last look at the unequal fight engulfing the Twenty-Ninth and then urged his mount forward, riding to join the rest of the army as it began to advance towards the waiting Frenchmen. With the skirmishers of the Rifles and the Light Companies of the other battalions leading the way, the British troops began to move up over the boulder-strewn slopes and gullies. As the skirmishers from both sides met there was a steady crackle of musket fire and shouted orders, and cries of pain and the wild exchange of insults and battle cries that echoed off the sides of the valley. Arthur joined the men of the central column as they struggled to advance with dressed ranks. The slopes were too uneven to permit the neat formations that the men had practised on drill grounds back in Britain. Slowly – too slowly, to Arthur's mind – they made their way up to the crest, while all the time the sound of firing from the direction of the Twenty-Ninth steadily diminished. Ahead of the British line the skirmishers continued to fight it out, but as the first ranks of the leading battalions emerged on to the crest the guns of Delaborde's single battery opened fire. Cones of lead balls tore through the ranks, opening gaps that were quickly closed by fresh men as the redcoats advanced on the main French position.

Now they were picking their way over the bodies of dead and wounded, British and French alike. A short distance ahead the British skirmishers had halted and gone to ground as they came up against the main French line. The British battalions halted to load their weapons and then continued forward until they were within effective musket range of the enemy, no more than fifty paces away. Then, as the French loosed their first volley and dozens of redcoats went down, the rest calmly halted, raised their muskets, thumbed back the firing hammers and waited for the order.

'Fire!'

Hundreds of muskets spat flame and smoke in a thunderous roar and then the sergeants bellowed the order to reload. The French fired again and Arthur heard balls zip through the air close by as he strained to gauge the progress of the fight through the eddying smoke. With a pounding of hooves Somerset came riding up, and reined his horse in sharply.

'How go things with the Twenty-Ninth?' asked Arthur.

'They've had it, sir. I wasn't in time to save them.'

'Had it? What, all of them?'

'Lake's dead. So are over two hundred and fifty of his men. The rest are wounded or routed.'

Arthur stared at his aide and muttered, 'Good God.'

One officer's vain moment of madness had cost the army half a battalion. Arthur was stunned. Then a fresh volley burst out from the British line and he collected his thoughts and stared towards the French positions. The enemy fire was already slackening, and as a breath of wind wafted down the valley the smoke cleared enough for Arthur to see that Delaborde's men were falling back again, making for the pass behind them. Now that the main battle line of the British army had reached the crest there was no choice for Delaborde but retreat to try to save as much of his force as possible.

'Keep the advance going!' Arthur called out to each side. 'Pass the word! Advance!'

All along the hill the line of redcoats pressed forward, straight into the volleys of French musket fire and the blasts from their six cannon. As Arthur followed the battle he saw that the French officers were handling their men well. The enemy companies kept their cohesion as they fired, fell back, and fired again, steadily giving ground as they came up on their own guns. Then the French gunners were ordered to withdraw, and started to limber their guns.

Arthur saw the chance at once. Now that the demoralising influence of French grapeshot was removed, it was time for the British infantry to use their bayonets.

'One last volley!' he called out. 'Then charge home, boys!'

The order was communicated to left and right, and after the last British musket had emptied its lead shot at the enemy the sergeants bellowed the order.

'Fix . . . bayonets!'

There was a distinct rattle along the line as the spiked bayonets were slotted over the muzzles and twisted into the locked position.

'Advance muskets!'

The front rank lowered their weapons and the triangular steel blades with their sharp points angled towards the French.

'Advance!'

In a staggered motion the entire line lurched forward, bearing down on the French, still hurriedly reloading their muskets a short distance away. Already a handful of the enemy were falling out of line, backing away from the approaching danger. More joined them as the others fired their last shots at the British.

'Charge!'

A deep ragged roar sounded from thousands of thirsty throats as the British surged forward. The effect of the bayonet charge was as Arthur had hoped and the French line broke. The enemy turned and ran for their lives, many throwing aside their weapons as they raced towards the mouth of the pass at the rear of their position. The French artillery crews had not completed limbering their guns as their comrades fled, and after a brief glance towards the wild faces of the British charging towards them they abandoned their cannon and followed the others. Only the cavalry, a regiment of dragoons, still remained formed up to one side of the track, and they now drew their carbines and formed a line across the pass to protect the last of the mob surging past them. They fired from the saddle, and though many shots went wide enough struck home to cause the British infantry to draw up. As soon as their weapons had been discharged the dragoons holstered them and unsheathed their swords.

'Prepare to receive cavalry!' The order passed along the British lines and the men instantly moved to rejoin their formations and close ranks, well aware of the dangers of being caught out in the open by enemy cavalry. Once the British battalions stood ready, in lines three deep, a stillness settled over the battlefield. Two hundred yards away, the dragoons stood equally still, glinting swords resting against their shoulders.

'Why don't they charge?' asked a staff officer close by Arthur.

'Because they don't have to,' Somerset explained nonchalantly. 'They know we won't risk charging again and breaking ranks. Not in the face of their cavalry. Equally, they won't risk attacking formed infantry. So we have something of an impasse. While the rest of their army escapes.'

'Impasse be damned,' Arthur growled. 'Order the line to advance! Close formation . . .'

Once again the redcoats stepped forward, at a measured pace so that the dragoons continued to face an unbroken line of bayonets. As the redcoats closed to within a hundred paces of the enemy a bugle call pierced the hot air, blasting out a series of notes, repeated three times, and then the dragoons sheathed their blades, wheeled round and began to trot away towards the track leading up to the mountain pass through which the rest of the army had escaped.

Arthur gave the order to halt and watched the retreating dragoons in frustration. The enemy had been broken, and had Arthur had a single cavalry brigade to unleash they could have been utterly destroyed in the ensuing pursuit. As it was, Delaborde would soon rally his men and they would be ready to fight the British again in a matter of days.

'A terrible waste,' Arthur muttered as he surveyed the thick carpet of bodies surrounding the mouth of the gully. Dusk was gathering over the battlefield and a working party from the Rifles was gathering up the bodies of Lake's battalion and carrying them to a mass grave that had been dug a short distance away.

'Indeed, sir.' Somerset sighed. 'And to such little effect.'

'Have they found Lake?'

'Yes, sir. He was near the bottom of the pile. Must have been killed almost as soon as he emerged from the gully.'

'Where is he?'

'I've had the body taken to Roliça for burial in a private grave, sir.'

'Very well.' Arthur nodded and then asked the question he had been avoiding. 'And the final butcher's bill?'

'Four hundred and fifty confirmed dead so far. Mostly from the Twenty-Ninth. Over seven hundred French accounted for, sir.'

'Not quite a pyrrhic victory then,' Arthur mused and then smiled bitterly. 'Here we are, somewhat less than fifteen thousand of us in Iberia against over a hundred thousand Frenchmen. Unless our soldiers can account for theirs at a ratio of one for ten, we have scant prospect of victory as things stand.'

Somerset shrugged. 'Then it is up to our generals to improve the odds, sir.'

Arthur looked at him and smiled. 'You are right. I will do my best.'

'I would expect nothing less, sir.'

Arthur awoke with a start as someone shook his shoulder. A figure with a lantern was standing over his camp bed. Arthur blinked and then squinted past the flare of light to see Somerset in a loose shirt and breeches.

'What time is it?' Arthur mumbled.

'Just past three in the morning, sir.'

'What's happened?' Arthur sat up and swung his legs over the side of the bed.

'Just had word from the fleet, sir. Reinforcements have arrived. Four thousand men. They will begin landing the day after tomorrow.'

'Where?'

'At the mouth of the Maceira river. Near the village of Vimeiro, sir. A day's march from here.'

Arthur smiled. Somerset must have been roused only shortly before he had come to wake his commander and had already marshalled the important details.

'Very well. We will move the army towards Vimeiro at first light to cover the landing.'

'Yes, sir.'

There was something in Somerset's tone that made Arthur realise there was more news, something altogether less agreeable. He looked up at his aide. 'Well?'

'There's a sloop following a day behind the reinforcements. Sir Harry Burrard is aboard.'

Arthur nodded wearily. So that was it then. It seemed his short tenure of command was about to come to an end. He sighed.

'Have my steward prepare my best uniform. I will need to report to Sir Harry the moment his ship arrives.'

Chapter 45

The sun was low in the sky and streamed straight into Arthur's face as he sat in the stern of the small launch. The last of the reinforcements had been landed hours earlier and was marching up to join the rest of the army encamped about Vimeiro. Anchored amidst the transports was the sloop *Brazen*, carrying Lieutenant-General Sir Harry Burrard. As soon as the sloop had arrived Arthur had ridden down to the shore and ordered the crew of the nearest launch to take him out to the *Brazen*. With weary obedience the sailors helped him aboard and then heaved the launch back into the surf, battling to get it some distance before clambering over the sides, unshipping the oars and rowing hard to propel the boat clear of the pounding surf and out to sea. The spray had drenched Arthur's uniform, but he made the best of a bad job by brushing off any sand and shingle that remained on his boots and the salt that had dried on the gold lace and black facings of his jacket.

As the launch approached the side of the sloop a naval lieutenant cupped a hand to his mouth and asked if she was bound for the *Brazen*.

'Aye, sir!' the coxswain called out. 'General Sir Arthur Wellesley comin' aboard!'

The launch pulled in towards the side of the sloop and the sailors shipped oars as a man in the bows caught the chains with the boathook. Arthur rose from his bench and worked his way awkwardly forward until he reached the boarding ladder. Two sailors stood by ready to help him up, but Arthur judged his moment and stepped on to the ladder as the launch rose on top of a small wave. He was greeted on deck by the lieutenant.

'The name's Swinton, sir. Welcome aboard the *Brazen*.'

'Good evening to you, Swinton. Would you be kind enough to take me to General Burrard?'

'Indeed, if you'd follow me, sir. The general has been given my cabin.'

Swinton led him down a narrow gangway and knocked at the small door at the end.

'Come!'

Opening the door, the lieutenant ducked inside and briefly announced

Arthur before he stepped aside. Arthur ducked through the door frame and stood with his neck bent forward under the low deck overhead. The cabin stretched the full width of the sloop, and was perhaps ten foot in depth, barely enough to accommodate the desk and chairs that seemed to take up most of the available space. The stern windows were hooked open to admit a cooling breeze that stirred the grey locks of the officer seated behind the desk. Sir Harry Burrard had taken part in the Danish expedition and smiled a greeting at Arthur as he dismissed the lieutenant with a curt wave of the hand.

'Wellesley! Good to see you again! Sit you down.'

Arthur did so, relieved to be able to straighten his neck. 'It is a pleasure to serve with you again, sir.'

Sir Harry shot him a knowing glance. 'Though not such a pleasure to be superseded by a superior officer, eh?'

Arthur did not reply and Sir Harry continued in an apologetic tone, 'That's the nature of the service, I'm afraid, Wellesley. Still, live long enough and you'll rise to the top of the pile in good time.'

'Yes, sir. Are you to take command of the army at once?'

'No need. Sir Hew is due any day. I shall remain aboard tonight and will probably come ashore tomorrow evening and take command then. Is that satisfactory?'

'Yes, sir. I will make the necessary arrangements at headquarters.'

'Thank you.' Sir Harry nodded, and then took a deep breath. 'So then, how are things progressing?'

Arthur had brought a report with him and now he placed it on the desk. Sir Harry glanced at it casually.

'I'll read that later. Now, if you don't mind, I'll hear it directly from you.'

Arthur detailed the events since the army had landed, then stopped and drew out a cloth from his pocket to dab at the sweat pricking out on his forehead.

'Sounds like you gave Frenchy a good thrashing.'

'Delaborde was outnumbered, sir.'

'But he had the advantage of holding the high ground,' Sir Harry countered. 'Don't be too modest, Wellesley. It is a positive handicap for a man of ability, and only a saving grace if a man is a complete fool.'

'I suppose so, sir. In any case, yes, General Delaborde was driven off.'

'And do you have any idea of the enemy's intentions?'

'I have heard reports that General Junot has gathered an army and is marching towards us from the south. As far as I can glean from our Portuguese spies, his strength is similar to our own. I have given orders for the army to be positioned along the ridge behind Vimeiro to meet any threat from that direction.'

'Excellent. It seems that everything is in hand, then.'

'I imagine that you will wish to continue the advance on Lisbon as swiftly as possible, sir. I understand that Junot is at Torres Vedras. If we marched to Mafra tomorrow, we could turn east and take Junot in the rear.'

Burrard paused a moment before shaking his head. 'No. I think we have chanced our arm enough for the present. It is my belief that you may have underestimated Junot's strength. The reports I read in London stated that he had over forty thousand men in Portugal.'

'I don't believe it is quite as high as that, sir. Besides, his forces are dispersed and many are tied down in garrisons. His field army cannot be much bigger than our own.'

Sir Harry shrugged. 'I think you put too much faith in our Portuguese allies' assessment of the enemy's strength.'

'I have learned to be circumspect in considering the information offered to me by the local people, sir. Even allowing for that, I believe my judgement of the strategic situation is sound. We have a good chance of defeating Junot and taking Lisbon in a matter of days, if we act quickly.'

'Perhaps. But even if you are right, what harm is there in delaying any advance until Sir John Moore arrives with his men? Then we shall outnumber the French beyond any question and should be able to guarantee a crushing victory.'

'Sir John may not arrive for some days, possibly weeks. That is more than enough time for Junot to receive overwhelming reinforcements from the French army in Spain. It would be far better to defeat the enemy now than to wait and risk a battle against far greater odds.'

Sir Harry clasped his hands together and leaned back in his chair with a weary sigh. 'I will not make any decisions before I have a full grasp of the facts. I will read your report in the morning and we will discuss the matter further when I take command of the army tomorrow evening. I thank you for taking the trouble to come to see me, and I suggest that you return to shore while there is still light. I bid you a good night, Wellesley.'

Arthur stared at the older man for a moment. Inside he was seething at the waste of the opportunity that Sir Harry was squandering through his caution. But there was no point in trying to persuade him to take action tonight. Best to let him read the report and then make another attempt to cajole him into action when he assumed command tomorrow. Besides, Arthur realised as he stared at the failing light outside the stern windows, Sir Harry had a point — it was getting dark and he did not wish to risk being rowed through the surf in pitch darkness. He stood carefully and bowed his head. 'Until tomorrow then, sir.'

For the second night running Arthur was roused from his sleep in the early hours by his aide-de-camp. He had established his headquarters in an inn on the edge of Vimeiro and had been looking forward to sleeping in a proper bed. However, the unsatisfactory interview he had endured with Sir Harry preyed on his mind and he had not fallen asleep until close to midnight. Now he glanced at his watch and saw that it was barely an hour into the new day.

'What now, Somerset?'

'Sir, I've had reports from our scouts in the direction of Torres Vedras. They say that Junot's army broke camp just after nightfall and started marching on Vimeiro.'

Arthur was out of bed in an instant, and hurrying to the large crudely constructed table he was using as a desk. 'Bring your lantern over here and show me.'

Somerset leaned over the map and pointed to the town of Torres Vedras. 'The scouts reported that the enemy were marching up to the right of the road to Vimeiro, sir.'

'To the right of the road?' Arthur frowned. 'Why not on it?'

'Perhaps they wish to avoid our patrols, sir.'

'Hm.'

'In any case, it appears that General Junot means to surprise us at first light.'

'Yes.' Arthur nearly laughed at the irony of the situation. Earlier he had been fretting about Sir Harry's not taking the fight to the French, and here was Junot saving him the trouble. Better still, he would reach the British lines and make his attack several hours before Sir Harry arrived to take command of the army. It seemed that fate had decided to give Arthur a chance to take on General Junot after all. He leaned forward and examined the map closely for a moment before tracing his finger along the line of a ridge that ran west to east behind the village.

'Here. This is where we will form our battle line. Send word to every commanding officer. They are to rouse their men and prepare for battle.'

The scent of myrtle filled the air as Arthur stood on the top of the ridge and waited for there to be enough light to show him the terrain to the south. The air was cool and refreshing and he allowed himself a moment to indulge the sensation. When morning came the heat would soon become oppressive but for now he relished the chill. Behind him, and spread out on either side, stood the eight brigades of his army. His army. He smiled at the phrase. They were his only until Sir Harry took command, but Arthur dismissed the thought. He would deal with that later. He must concentrate on the coming battle. His line extended to the right as far as the coast, to cover the shore where further reinforcements were due to land. The left flank rested on Vimeiro Hill, rising up just to the south of the village. It was a good position, strong enough for the British to repel any direct assaults up the slopes.

To the east the mountainous horizon was rimmed with a faint glow that slowly spread north and south and gained in strength at its centre until, with a sudden spark and distant flare of light, the sun began to rise. Very quickly the dark mantle that covered the landscape began to dissipate, shadow by shadow. Arthur raised his telescope and began to carefully scan the approaches to the ridge. Stunted growths of unused land were interspersed with occasional olive groves and vineyards and their quiet buildings, whose occupants were only just stirring, oblivious of the presence of the two armies preparing to clash over this panorama of tranquillity.

'I can't see any sign of movement,' Arthur said quietly. 'What about you, Somerset? Your eyes are younger than mine.'

There was a short pause, then: 'Nothing, sir. Do you suppose the scouts could have been mistaken?'

'Hardly,' Arthur replied with a wry smile. 'Either you see an army on the march or you don't. There's very little middle ground.'

'Well, what if they were mistaken about the direction that Junot was taking? Or what if Junot changed direction during the night?'

'It is possible,' Arthur conceded. 'We shall discover the truth soon enough.'

But as the sun climbed into the sky and burned off any lingering mist that hung in pockets of the ground there was still no sign of the French army approaching from the south, and the peasants who lived in the houses dotted across the landscape began to emerge and tend their crops and animals without any sign of alarm.

At length Arthur checked his fob watch. Just after nine o'clock. He turned to Somerset. 'In all the excitement I seem to have forgotten to inform Sir Harry of the night's events. Would you be so good as to send a runner to the beachhead to pass the details on?'

'A runner, sir? Wouldn't a rider be quicker?'

'It would, but we are short enough of mounted men as it is. No, I think a runner is all that can be spared at present. Now, don't delay, Somerset. Mustn't keep Sir Harry waiting.'

'Of course not, sir,' Somerset replied with a knowing expression. 'I'll see to it.'

Arthur nodded and returned to his examination of the surrounding landscape for a few more minutes. He was about to lower his telescope when he caught a glimpse of a flash, away to the east, amongst some trees on a ridge running past the British line. Arthur held his breath and steadied his telescope as best he could. There was another glint of reflected sunlight, and a faint tawny haze hanging in the air. Arthur scrutinised the ridge a moment longer before snapping his telescope shut and turning to his staff officers, a nervous flutter in his stomach.

'Junot has caught me napping, by God! He means to outflank us over there.' Arthur indicated the tree-covered ridge. 'He has already stolen a few hours' march on us so we must move swiftly, gentlemen.' He turned and indicated the ridge that ran at an angle from the village towards the east. 'That is our new battle line. Vimeiro Hill will now form our right flank and Acland, Bowes, Fergusson, Nightingall and Trant's Portuguese are to march on to the east ridge as quickly as possible, in the same order that they were positioned on the west ridge. Is that clear? Then move swiftly, gentlemen. The race is on.'

As soon as they had received their new orders, the five brigades hurriedly descended from the west ridge, marched past the village of Vimeiro and began to climb the slopes to their new positions. After a last careful examination of the enemy's dust cloud Arthur calculated that the French would not reach the redeployed redcoats until the latter were in position. Calling for Somerset, he spurred his horse into a trot and rode across to the east ridge. General Acland's brigade was the first in new line and Arthur touched the brim of his hat as he reined in.

'Well done, Acland. Your men have made good time.'

Acland was a dour, thin man, somewhat older than his commander, but he was gratified by the comment and smiled.

'Yes, sir. The lads are keen to have a go at the French.'

'And I am sure their keenness will be amply rewarded.' They shared a short laugh before Arthur raised his riding crop and pointed down the slope. 'Now then, I would like your Light Companies at the bottom of the ridge. The rest of your men are to stay up here and lie down.'

'Lie down?' Acland frowned. 'But the day's barely started, sir.'

'Easy, Acland. I am not indulging their indolence, merely trying to make them less of a ready target for enemy bullets.'

Acland was from the old school and he shook his head doubtfully.

'I'm not sure about that, sir. It's best to make 'em stand up to enemy fire. Last thing we want is to encourage any sense of self-preservation in the beggars.'

'While I agree with you, it is a fact that soldiers are less easy for his majesty to come by than they are for the Emperor. So let us preserve them as we may. Now, when those fellows of Junot's advance on the ridge, you must bide your time and wait for them to come well within range. Then have your men rise up and shoot them down. Then, in with the bayonet, when you judge the moment is ripe.'

'Aye.' Acland nodded. 'That'll please my boys well enough!'

'Then a good day to you!' Arthur spurred his horse and galloped on for a final inspection of his other brigades before returning to his command post. By the time he returned to the crest of the small hill south of Vimeiro, the enemy had swung round to the west and was forming columns in readiness to launch their assault. Arthur glanced north and was satisfied that the army was ready to repel any attacks they might face. The two brigades on the right flank were concealed behind the crest of Vimeiro Hill, on which twelve cannon had been positioned to cover the slopes. Down below, in the cover of boulders and folds in the ground, crouched the light infantry and two companies of rifles. Arthur nodded to himself with satisfaction. Now he would put his ideas to the test and see just how formidable the French assault columns really were.

A dull boom echoed up the slope and he saw a puff of smoke some half a mile from the foot of the ridge. Abruptly several more guns opened fire and kicked up small explosions of dirt, rock and small branches as the grapeshot tore up the ground along his skirmish line. After a few more rounds the French guns fell silent and a moment later the enemy skirmishers advanced to duel with their British counterparts. A steady crackle of musket and rifle fire drifted up the slope as the skirmishers of both sides contested the foot of the hill. Then, as weight of numbers began to tell, the British fell back, scurrying from cover to cover as they fired on their pursuers. A deep drum roll and tinny blare of trumpets carried across from the French lines as the assault columns edged forward and began to tramp up the slope behind their skirmishers.

'And here they come,' Somerset muttered casually.

There was a low fold in the ground just in front of the British cannon and the riflemen took shelter there as the other skirmishers ran back to their battalions and joined the main battle line. Then, as the first of the French skirmishers came into plain view, closely followed by the heads of the assault columns, the British guns opened fire. Arthur watched with keen interest the effects of the three howitzers he had deployed alongside the other guns. They were firing the newly developed shells designed by an artillery officer named Shrapnel, which were fused to burst over the heads of the enemy, spraying out scores of small iron shards. As Arthur watched, the first of the shells burst in a white puff over the leading ranks of the nearest column and at once a score of men went down.

'Not bad,' he mused, impressed by the effect. He could imagine the moral effect of being struck down from above as well as from the front, and made a mental note to fully endorse Shrapnel's innovation when he had the opportunity. Meanwhile the columns tramped forward remorselessly, straight into the withering hail of the case shot blasting out from the British guns. As each cone of shot struck home it was as if a giant fist punched into the French columns, knocking men down like skittles. Despite the terrible carnage Arthur could not help admiring the élan of the enemy as the gaps were swiftly filled with fresh men and the columns continued up the slope, urged on by the relentless beating of drums and shouts of encouragement from officers and sergeants.

As the front rank of the enemy came within musket range, the British gun crews fired one last shot and then fell back, running for the cover of the hill crest. At once the French began to jeer and shout their contempt and their pace increased now that they no longer had to fear being cut down by case shot. Ahead of them lay the abandoned guns and a short distance beyond them a small group of British officers on horseback.

Arthur raised his arm, glancing left and right to make sure that he had the attention of the two brigades either side of him, and then swept his arm forward. Orders were bellowed out and the men of the two brigades rose up from the ground, dressed their ranks and then advanced over the crest. To the French it looked as if they had risen up from the earth, and the assault column's pace faltered even as the slope began to level out beneath the leading ranks.

The British officers barked out the command, 'Halt! . . . Make ready to fire!'

The long thin line, two men deep, stopped dead, and then over two thousand muskets were lowered so that their muzzles pointed down the slope at the French, no more than fifty paces away.

'Cock your weapons!'

A ragged clicking rippled along the line, and then there was a pause, and a stillness that reminded Arthur of the tense anticipation between the flash of lightning and the crash of thunder.

'Fire!'

The roar was like a multitude of hammers striking a sheet of steel, and flame and smoke burst out along the British line. From his position slightly above and behind his men Arthur saw the terrible impact of the first volley as the heads of the French columns collapsed, leaving a crumpled line of blue-coated bodies across the bloodstained ground.

'Fire by companies!'

The flanks of the British brigades advanced round the heads of the French columns and then a rolling series of volleys crashed out as one company after another fired into the enemy. The French struggled to deploy from column into line amid the chaos of tumbling bodies and the whirr of lead passing through the air all around them. There was only the briefest of delays between the volleys, and the near continuous destruction being wrought on the French ranks shattered their cohesion and broke their spirit. Inevitably, they began to give way. Succeeding companies refused to advance into the place of their fallen comrades, and even began to edge back, down the slope.

As the commanders of the British battalions became aware that the enemy was recoiling, they gave the order to cease fire and fix bayonets. With a rattle and clatter the bayonets were fastened on to the ends of the muskets and then the red lines began to advance again. Arthur was struck by the difference between the two armies. The French, loud, brash and vociferous as they advanced, each man cheering, or singing along to the Marseillaise or another of their patriotic tunes. Facing them, the British soldiers were calm, ordered and quite silent, functioning like an implacable machine, so that when the final order to charge echoed along the crest of the hill, their sudden roar was quite terrifying and Arthur felt the hairs on the back of his neck rise in icy response.

The redcoats burst into a run, rushing down on their enemy, mouths wide open as they bellowed their meaningless roars of aggression. The more fearless of the Frenchmen stood their ground, bayonets lowered and boots braced, while others just froze in terror. Many more fell back then turned and ran as the British infantry burst upon them, stabbing with their bayonets and smashing the butts of their muskets into the heads and bodies of the enemy. It was a sharp, savage fight as Arthur looked on. The French were knocked down and impaled without mercy, adding still more corpses to those strewn along the hillside.

In less than a minute, it was over. The French soldiers were streaming down the hill and the British were left masters of the slope. Now it was their turn to shout their contempt for the enemy, and they bellowed insults and whistled mockingly before the sergeants called them to order and re-formed each company before marching it back over the crest of the hill. Meanwhile the artillery crews ran forward to their guns and recommenced firing after the fleeing mob of French soldiers until they reached the foot of the hill and scattered across the open ground beyond. The guns fell silent and Arthur surveyed the slope in front of his position. The attack had cost Junot as many as five hundred men, he estimated. In amongst the heaps of bodies lay an occasional redcoat, but the British losses had been slight indeed.

Even so, the French recovered quickly, and already a fresh column, preceded by the usual screen of skirmishers, was advancing up through the stunted trees that dotted the approaches to the hill. This time, though, Arthur could see that they were accompanied by light artillery pieces to provide close support for the attacking column. Clearly Junot had learned to respect his enemy.

The second attack suffered the same fate as the first, and most of the French guns were knocked out long before they could be deployed on the slopes. Once more the French battalions were badly cut up by British artillery before being stopped dead by a continuous fusillade of musket fire and then breaking as a wave of bayonets swept down the slope towards them, though this time they had exchanged a series of volleys with the redcoats and caused over a hundred casualties amongst Arthur's two brigades. Satisfied that there was no immediate threat to his position, Arthur trained his telescope on the east ridge and was pleased to observe that the French were being repelled there as well. So far, the British infantry had held their nerve and fought the enemy in fine style, as Arthur had always been confident they would. He lowered his telescope with a satisfied nod and returned his attention to the fight on Vimeiro Hill.

The British soldiers were returning to their protected position on the reverse slope of the hill when Arthur spied a party of horsemen riding up the hill from the west. As they drew closer he made out the gold braid and sash of a senior officer amongst them and realised, with a sinking feeling, that Sir Harry Burrard must have landed before the runner had reached the coast. Wheeling his horse about, Arthur turned towards Sir Harry and waited.

'Good morning to you, Wellesley!' Sir Harry called out as he rode up. 'It seems you have your battle after all.'

'Yes, sir.'

'So how is it proceeding?' Sir Harry surveyed the bodies littering the slope and the French below, massing for yet another attack, this time to the north of the hill, in the direction of the village of Vimeiro. Arthur quickly made his report and then hesitated before asking the obvious question.

'Do you intend to assume command here, sir?'

Sir Harry shook his head. 'I see no need. You have the situation in hand, Wellesley. Please continue your domination of the enemy.'

Arthur could not help smiling. 'Thank you, sir.'

Even though he could not but be conscious of his superior's silent attention, Arthur did his best to ignore Sir Harry as he watched for developments amid the scattered trees that covered the approaches to the ridge. He did not have to wait long. Once again, a thin screen of skirmishers emerged and warily began to make their way up the slope, to be met by the waiting light infantry and men of the Rifles. But this was no more than a feint. As soon as the musket fire had intensified on Vimeiro Hill a fresh column of French infantry suddenly marched into view, making straight for the village of Vimeiro, at the centre of the British line.

'Damn Junot,' Arthur muttered to himself. 'He means to cut my army in two.'

If the French general succeeded, then he would threaten to destroy each wing of the British army in turn. With a quick glance to the east to reassure himself that there was no sign of any further attempt to be made on the hill, Arthur called to Somerset and set off for Vimeiro at a gallop. The sturdy houses on the edge of the village had been occupied by light infantry and two companies of grenadiers. Behind it stood the survivors of the Twenty-Ninth Foot and the two hundred and fifty men of the Light Dragoons, the only cavalry available to Arthur since he had landed in Portugal. The two officers galloped into the main street of Vimeiro and the pounding of their mounts' hooves echoed off the whitewashed walls on either side of the empty street. The village's inhabitants had barricaded themselves in and were praying for a swift end to the battle.

When Arthur and Somerset reached the far side, they drew up behind a shoulder-high wall lined with British skirmishers who were already firing on the head of the French column. Rising in his stirrups Arthur squinted through the rolling haze of gunpowder smoke and saw that the leading enemy troops were no more than a hundred paces away. The crackle of muskets was underscored by the deep rhythmic rumble and rattle of drums. A handful of the enemy had been struck down, and as Arthur watched there was a white puff in the air above the column as one of the British howitzers on the hill found the range. Despite the losses the column came on at a quick step, and within a minute they had halted not more than thirty paces from the village to deliver one volley before charging.

Arthur felt a chill of terror as the enemy muskets foreshortened. The possibility that he could be shot at any moment filled him with a perverse excitement. Only good fortune could save him now, but if he lived he would have the satisfaction of having stood up to the enemy's fire. The French fired and the air was filled with the clatter of musket balls striking the walls. When the moment had passed Arthur looked round and was relieved to see that the only damage done was that one of his men's shakos had been shot off its owner's head. The soldier was now swearing bloody revenge at the French as he reloaded his musket, fired, and swiftly prepared the next round.

With a roar the French rushed forward.

'Sir,' Somerset called out. 'I think we should withdraw to somewhere less dangerous.'

He was right, Arthur knew. Commanding generals had no right to put themselves at risk when their men needed them. Yet this situation was different. If anything happened to Arthur, Sir Harry could take over the moment he heard the news.

'Just a moment,' he said.

The French had reached the wall and were locked in a desperate bayonet fight with the British soldiers defending the village. Badly outnumbered as they were, Arthur's men would have to give way eventually, he realised, and with a quick gesture to Somerset to follow him he wheeled his horse round and rode back through the village to where the Twenty-Ninth and the Light Dragoons were waiting. Arthur rode up to the colonel commanding the dragoons.

'Taylor, I aim to break the French attack once their formation is held up by the village. The moment I give the order I want you to charge them. Go in hard and fast and make as much of a show of it as you can.'

'Yes, sir!' Colonel Taylor's eyes glinted with excitement at the prospect. 'My boys will carve them up nicely.'

'No doubt. But listen here, Taylor, we have too few mounted men to waste. Don't let your men pursue the enemy too far. Rein 'em in once the enemy are making a run for it. Understand?'

'Yes, sir. You can rely on me.'

'Very well then.'

Arthur left the dragoons and trotted forward to the men of the

416

Twenty-Ninth. There were barely more than a hundred and fifty survivors formed up in front of the colours, yet the battalion must suffer still more grievously if the centre of the British line was to hold. Clearing his throat, Arthur addressed them.

'Men, I know you have tasted rather more of battle than you might like, but there is one last duty I would ask of you.' He paused and glanced along the lines of sombre faces. 'The French desire possession of Vimeiro. I will not have it, I tell you. So then, Twenty-Ninth, it is up to you to clear those rascals away!'

Someone in the rear rank laughed and piped up, 'We'll do it for you, Nosey!'

Arthur glared in the direction of the shout and feigned umbrage as he walked his horse to one side.

'By God, they lack manners,' he muttered to Somerset, and the latter smiled.

'That is so, sir. But I think they do not lack a degree of affection for you.'

'Indeed?' Arthur raised his eyebrows. 'Even as I send some of them to their deaths? A peculiar thing, is it not?'

The acting commander of the battalion, a captain, drew a breath and swept his sword out of its scabbard with a flourish. 'The Twenty-Ninth will advance! At the double!'

The small band of men surged forward, boots pounding along the dry lane that led into the village, towards the sound of firing. Some more of the howitzers had added their fire and the clear sky beyond Vimeiro was punctuated by the deadly puffs as the shells burst over the heads of the oncoming French, scything men down. Arthur turned his mount to one side and trotted up to the top of a nearby knoll, with a solitary tree upon its crest. From there he could see that the head of the French column had penetrated the village. The enemy had already suffered grievously and the ground in front of Vimeiro was dotted with bodies. A moment later there was a roar as the Twenty-Ninth charged into the fray. The musket fire intensified briefly and then the French began to fall back from the village. The men behind them stalled and the column ground to a halt in confusion as the men fleeing from the village ran into their comrades.

Arthur turned towards the dragoons and waved his hand to attract Taylor's attention. 'Now's your time, Taylor!' he yelled. 'Charge 'em!'

The bugler sounded the advance and the horsemen surged forward, riding round the flank of the village in squadron lines. As the smoke-shrouded French column came into view the bugle's strident notes sounded the charge and the dragoons spurred on, swords raised and flashing in the morning sun as they thundered over the dry ground towards the enemy. Only a few shots were fired as they charged home, and Arthur saw one of his men topple from his saddle and disappear into the swirling dust. Then the dragoons were in amongst the enemy, hacking to left and right. Within moments the column had ceased to exist as a formation and the French had turned and were fleeing across the open ground.

Arthur watched without expression. The effect of the dragoons' sudden appearance was all he had hoped. Taylor's men had smashed the column. Arthur trusted the man had sufficient presence of mind not to get carried away by the charge, and to call his men back in good time. But the bugler kept sounding the charge and the notes became more and more distant as the cavalry fanned out across the plain, running down isolated victims and avoiding those pockets of Frenchmen who had held together and were now retreating in good order.

'Damn the man,' Arthur growled. 'He should call his men back now, before it is too late.'

'I fear that it is already too late,' said Somerset, as he watched one of the clusters of infantry fire a ragged volley that carried three of the dragoons off their saddles.

Taylor's men were so scattered by that time that the French were turning on them, and now the disparity in numbers began to tell. At last, the bugler sounded the recall and the troopers broke off their pursuit and trotted back towards Vimeiro, singly and in small groups. The French continued to fire on them, causing more casualties, until they were out of range.

Arthur sighed. 'It seems we have a deal of work to do in disciplining our cavalry.'

'Yes, sir.'

'I don't know what it is about cavalry, that makes them stuff their heads with straw.'

Somerset smiled. 'You know how it is, sir. The brightest fellows join the engineers, and, failing that, the infantry. As for the rest . . .' He gestured towards the dragoons who had returned to Vimeiro and were slowly re-forming their companies.

'Quite.' Arthur nodded. 'At least they have repulsed the enemy. The field is ours. All that remains is to pursue Junot to his destruction.' Arthur paused and glanced up the hill. 'But that is an order for Sir Harry to give. Come on!'

He spurred his horse and galloped back up the slope to the crest of the hill. Sir Harry Burrard was where Arthur had left him. He smiled broadly as Arthur came pounding towards him.

'Damned fine work, Wellesley! The frogs are on the run.'

'Yes, sir!' Arthur panted. 'Now we must seize the fruits of victory, sir. Give the order to advance and Junot is finished. Lisbon will be in our hands within three days.'

Sir Harry smiled again, and shook his head. 'Fortune has smiled on us today, Sir Arthur. It would be rash to tempt providence. Let us wait until General Moore arrives with his men. Then we shall dominate the enemy.'

Arthur thrust his arm out towards the retreating French soldiers. 'But, sir, we already dominate them. You have but to give the word and we can run them to ground and compel Junot to surrender.' He paused as he swiftly considered the best way to change Sir Harry's mind. 'Think of the glory, sir. The man who forces Junot to surrender will be the hero of the hour.'

'And the man who throws caution to the wind and leads the army to disaster will be the villain in perpetuity, Wellesley. I will not be that man. Besides, we should wait and see what Sir Hew Dalrymple decides.'

'With respect, sir, Sir Hew is not here. If he was, then I am sure he would seize such a fine opportunity to destroy the enemy.'

'Enough, Wellesley,' Sir Harry said curtly. 'I have made my decision. There will be no pursuit. We will wait for General Dalrymple and the rest of the reinforcements.'

Arthur stared at his superior for a moment. His heart was crying out with frustration and despair, but there was nothing he could do. Sir Harry was the ranking officer, and his word was final. Trying hard to hide his feelings, Arthur turned away and gazed towards the escaping French. All around him he heard the cheers of his men, but there was no joy in his heart.

Chapter 46

The following afternoon Arthur visited the wounded in the makeshift hospital in Vimeiro. Even though the hard-pressed medical orderlies were doing their best to treat the men's wounds and find them shelter from the sun's searing heat, the cries and groans of the soldiers were pitiful and there were constant demands for water. All the while more casualties were being brought in from the battlefield, men who had been lying in the sun the previous day, left through the night and into the following morning. Many were suffering from sunstroke and were delirious, their cracked lips trembling as they babbled incoherently. As he moved from one room to the next in the small monastery Arthur was assailed by evidence of the true horrors of war. And it was not just the sight of the shattered limbs and bloodied dressings that caused him distress, it was the stench of urine, faeces, vomit and corrupted wounds that assaulted him.

As he emerged into the courtyard of the monastery Arthur breathed deeply to expel the foul vapours that had filled his lungs. He turned to Somerset. 'See to it that those men are fed and watered properly. They are to be made as comfortable as possible while they recover.' He paused. 'If they don't recover, at least they shall be comforted as far as possible in the time left to them.'

'Yes, sir,' Somerset replied.

Arthur noted the tremor in his young aide's voice and turned to look at him directly. 'The face of battle is grimmer than you had ever imagined, eh?'

'Yes, sir.' Somerset nodded, and Arthur saw that his face was quite drained of colour. 'It is my first real battle,' Somerset admitted. I had thought that the fight at Roliça was bad enough. But this . . .' He gestured towards the rooms lining the courtyard.

'This is the reality of war,' said Arthur. 'You had best grow used to it. Or try to.'

Somerset regarded his commander closely. 'Have you grown used to it, sir?'

For a moment Arthur was tempted to lie to make it easier for his subordinate, but then decided there was no point in hiding the truth. If

Somerset lived long enough he was certain to see far worse than the battlefield at Vimeiro. He shook his head. 'I have never lost a battle, Somerset, yet every victory has left a sour taste in my mouth when I contemplate the price that has been paid. Perhaps it is a good thing that war is so terrible. It would be dangerous if men got used to it.' He reflected for an instant before continuing. 'That is the real evil we are fighting. It is not France, nor the soldiers that are sent against us. It is the taste for war that Bonaparte and his followers have acquired. That is what we must defeat.'

'Yes, sir.'

'See to these men as best you can. I must report to Burrard.'

They exchanged a salute and Somerset strode off to find the officers of the supply commissariat and ensure they provided adequate food and water for the injured. Arthur waited a moment, drinking in the sweet smell of the herbs that grew in the flower beds running along the walls of the monastery. Then he sighed and made his way outside to where his mount was tethered. Unhitching the reins and climbing into the saddle, he turned the horse towards the cluster of tents on the crest of the hill and dug his spurs in.

As he dismounted and handed the reins to an orderly, Arthur heard a burst of laughter from inside the army commander's tent. The sentries on either side of the open flaps presented arms as Arthur passed through. The shade inside was welcome, as was the faint breeze that entered through the panels that had been removed on two sides. A group of officers stood about the large campaign table that dominated the centre of the tent.

'Ah, Wellesley!' A voice boomed from behind the table and Arthur saw that Sir Hew Dalrymple had arrived to take command. The third commander in less than a day, Arthur reflected wryly. Like Burrard, Dalrymple was a man with meagre experience of campaigning. Arthur saluted as he strode up to the table and then leaned across to shake his superior's hand.

Dalrymple pretended to look offended as he continued, 'It seems that you have done my job for me. Couldn't wait, eh?'

'I was attacked by Junot, sir. I did not seek to pre-empt your involvement.'

'Tsh! Don't be touchy, Wellesley. I am jesting. In truth you have won a fine victory and I shall be sure to give you full credit for it in my report to London.'

Arthur was momentarily tempted to mention that it might have been a far more complete victory had the army pursued Junot to destruction once the battle was won. But with Burrard standing at Dalrymple's shoulder and the evident bonhomie that filled the tent, now was not the time, Arthur told himself. Instead he nodded.

'That is most kind of you, sir.'

Dalrymple bowed his head graciously and then cleared his throat. 'Gentlemen, the task that faces us now is to complete the good work that General Wellesley has begun. Though we have bested Junot and sent him running off towards Torres Vedras, he still has more men under arms in Portugal than I have, at least until General Moore arrives. Therefore, having consulted with Sir Harry, I am of a mind to wait here and gather our strength before we continue the advance towards Lisbon.'

Arthur let out a faint groan before he could stop himself. At once, Dalrymple's eyes fixed on him.

'Do you wish to comment, General Wellesley?'

'Sir, I think we should push forward before Junot recovers from yesterday's defeat. We outnumber him at present, and he cannot concentrate his other forces quickly enough to save himself. If you pursue him, sir, I am sure that you can force him to surrender without conditions. If we delay then we simply hand the initiative to the enemy. And what if Junot is sent reinforcements from Spain? The enemy's strength in the Peninsula is such that they will always outnumber us. Our best chance is to defeat the French piecemeal. Sir, if you would end this campaign swiftly, then I urge you to move against Junot immediately.'

Dalrymple's expression hardened. 'I thank you for the lecture, Wellesley, but I think you misjudge our enemy. Junot's attack yesterday was clumsy and ill-considered. He underestimated the British army and paid the price. I will not repay him in kind. Who is to say that he is not preparing a trap for us even now? He has been in Portugal long enough to learn the lie of the land. We have been here a matter of days and I say it would be rash to throw caution to the wind and rush after the enemy. So we will wait until Moore arrives, and then consider the situation. That is my decision, gentlemen. If that is quite all right with you, Wellesley?'

Arthur felt anger pierce his heart. Dalrymple was evidently the kind of commander who was inclined to jump at the least shadow. He was wrong to sit here at Vimeiro and wait for more men, Arthur was certain of it. Even though the chance to crush Junot utterly had been lost the day before, the advantage still lay with the British, if they acted now. But

Dalrymple was his superior and he had made his decision. The matter was settled, whatever Arthur may think. So he kept his mouth shut and nodded.

'Good!' Dalrymple smiled and clapped his hands together. 'Now then, gentlemen, I suggest we repair to lunch. My staff have prepared a modest feast down on the shore, by way of a celebration of yesterday's battle.' He turned to Arthur. 'Now that at least will be to your taste, eh?' Then he laughed at his unintended pun, and Arthur forced himself to smile as the other officers joined in.

Before he could respond there was a sudden pounding of hooves outside the tent. A moment later a young infantry captain entered the tent and snapped to attention in front of Arthur, his chest heaving from his wild ride.

'Sir, beg to report that—'

Arthur raised his hand. 'I am no longer the commander of the army. You should address yourself to General Dalrymple.'

The captain glanced towards Dalrympe uncertainly and the latter frowned. 'What is it?'

'Sir, beg to report that the enemy has sent an officer to our lines with a flag of truce. He says that General Junot wishes to discuss an armistice.'

'An armistice?' Dalrymple looked surprised for an instant before a smile spread across his countenance. 'Already? By God, the campaign is as good as over. Have this French officer brought here at once.'

'Yes, sir.' The captain saluted and turned smartly on his heel to leave the tent. Once he had gone Dalrymple looked round at his senior officers. 'An armistice, then. It would seem that Junot is a beaten man after all. One battle and the enemy is humbled.'

That was stretching the truth a bit far, Arthur reflected. Junot had been given a reprieve, and would naturally seek to turn any truce to his advantage. Even though he had lost on the field of battle, he might yet secure a victory of sorts over the negotiating table.

Dalrymple dismissed all his officers save Arthur and Burrard, and passed the word for an honour guard to be assembled outside the tent. Shortly afterwards came the sound of horses approaching, and the British commander led the way outside to greet the French officer formally as he dismounted.

At a sharp word of command the company of grenadiers lining the approach to the tent snapped to attention and presented arms. The French officer pulled his sleeves down and straightened his jacket before striding towards Dalrymple. As he approached Arthur saw that the man was about the same age as himself and, judging from the proliferation of gold braid on his blue uniform coat, a general officer. His hair, streaked with grey, was tied back in a short tail, and though his features were heavy there was an intelligent spark in his eyes. He smiled slightly as he stopped in front of Sir Hew and bowed.

'General Kellermann at your service, sir.'

His English was good, Arthur noted, though there was a faint accent to it that he could not immediately place.

'Sir Hew Dalrymple at yours.' The British commander returned the bow with a nod and gestured to the two men at his side. 'May I present Sir Harry Burrard, my second in command, and Sir Arthur Wellesley.'

Kellermann's eyes fixed on Arthur for a moment before he turned his gaze back to Dalrymple. 'May I offer my congratulations on your fine victory yesterday, sir? I have never seen such magnificent troops as yours in battle. Steady as a rock and yet handled with a lightness of touch that does full credit to you, sir. I only wish our men had been equal to the occasion.'

'Ah, yes . . .' Dalrymple replied awkwardly. 'The truth is that I have only just arrived, General. You were defeated by General Wellesley.'

Kellermann glanced at Arthur with an appearance of surprise. 'I am confused. Surely in your absence General Burrard would have been the ranking officer.'

'General Burrard did not reach the field until after the battle was as good as won,' Dalrymple explained.

'Ah, I see.' Kellermann nodded, then turned very deliberately to Arthur and bowed. 'Then it is to you that I offer my congratulations.'

Arthur bowed in return, sensing the irritation of both his superiors.

Dalrymple cleared his throat. 'Yes, well, you'd better come inside the tent, General Kellermann.'

He led the way inside and the three British officers took their seats behind the table while Kellermann settled opposite them.

'Now then,' Dalrymple began, 'you wish to discuss terms for an armistice.'

'Yes, sir. My superior, General Junot, has authorised me to negotiate for the complete withdrawal of French forces from Portugal.'

Dalrymple's eyebrows rose. 'The surrender of Portugal?'

'In effect, sir, yes.' Kellermann nodded, then drew a folded sheet of paper from his pocket. 'The detailed terms are set out here. I have taken the liberty of translating them into English.'

'Your command of our tongue is commendable,' said Arthur. 'But I cannot quite place the accent.'

Kellermann smiled. 'I had the honour of representing my country at our embassy to your former colonies in America.'

'Ah!' Burrard nodded. 'That explains the coarseness of the accent.'

'For which I apologise.' Kellermann smiled again as he passed the sheet of paper across the table. 'Now, if you wish to consider the terms proposed by General Junot.'

Dalrymple looked at the document before passing it on to Burrard, and then Arthur read through it. Junot proposed to surrender every fortress and town in Portugal and evacuate the country. In return he asked that his gallant and generous British opponents should permit the repatriation of his army to France, together with all its equipment and property. When he had finished Arthur lowered the document and looked up at Kellermann with a feeling of concern. If Dalrymple accepted the offer, then the French army would be spared to fight another day. To be sure, lives would be spared, but the opportunity to truly humiliate the French would be lost. Junot had shrewdly calculated that he could at least save his army if he offered to quit Portugal without a fight.

Dalrymple slid the document back in front of him. 'This would appear to be a reasonable basis on which to proceed. Of course the precise details would need to be discussed.'

'Indeed,' Arthur added, fixing his gaze on Kellermann. 'To begin with, precisely how do you propose to repatriate your forces?'

'Alas, since the French fleet was defeated by your Lord Nelson our navy has not been equal to the tasks requested of it. So it would seem most reasonable to ask that the army is conveyed to a home port by British ships.'

'British ships?' Arthur was astonished. 'In British ships? Out of the question.'

'Restrain yourself, please, Wellesley,' Dalrymple said firmly, and spoke to Kellermann again. 'And why should we agree to such a suggestion?'

The Frenchman shrugged. 'It is the quickest way to remove our soldiers from Portugal. Of course, if you would be prepared to wait until a sufficient force of French warships was ready to carry them away . . .'

That would delay the surrender of Portugal for at least a month, Arthur realised. Plenty of time for fresh French columns to arrive from Spain and continue the struggle. The point was clear to all, and Dalrymple nodded.

'Agreed. There is a convoy of merchant ships, as well as Admiral Cotton's squadron, lying at anchor. They should suffice for the task.'

'That is good.' The Frenchman smiled. 'I am sure your navy will carry out the task with their customary efficiency.'

'You can count on it.'

'Now, is there anything else you wish to query, sir?' Kellermann continued. 'If not, then perhaps you and I might draft the armistice now.'

'Now?' Dalrymple was taken aback by the sudden challenge.

'I see no reason why not, sir. There is no need to delay the completion of your conquest of Portugal.'

'Liberation,' Arthur interrupted. 'We are here to liberate Portugal, not conquer it. We are not Frenchmen.'

'Tsk, Wellesley,' Dalrymple muttered. 'There's no call for that.'

'I disagree, sir. There is a world of difference between liberation and conquest. Or at least there should be.'

'Liberation then,' Kellermann conceded and turned his attention back to the British commander. 'May we commence with drafting the agreement?'

'Yes. Yes, I suppose so. You may leave, Burrard, and you too, Wellesley. Wait for us outside.'

'Perhaps it would be better for us to remain here, sir,' Arthur suggested. 'In case any of the finer points require further discussion.'

'I am quite capable of making my own decisions, thank you,' Dalrymple said coldly. 'Now be so good as to leave General Kellermann and myself to draft the document.'

Arthur stared back at him for a moment and then nodded slowly. 'Yes, sir.'

For the next hour Arthur sat in the shade of an awning a short distance from the tent. From there he had a good view over the slope that had been so hotly contested the day before. Today all was quiet, but the traces of the battle were plain to see: gouges in the earth and rock where cannonballs had thudded home, and the bodies of hundreds of men strewn across the stubble and clumps of gorse and myrtle. Most were French, and only a handful of British corpses had not yet been removed by burial parties. The French dead would have to wait until the last of the redcoats were interred. Some of the bodies were naked, their clothes and other belongings taken in the night by camp followers and the local peasants. A faint breeze stirred and carried the sickening stench of decay up to Arthur and he felt his stomach clench in revulsion.

It was not just the thought of the dead that occupied his mind. He was worried about the terms of the armistice. Although it would mean that the Portuguese campaign was over for the present, with no further loss of life, the prospect of allowing Junot's army to escape galled him. Worse still, he could imagine how people back in London might react to the news that a French army had been carried home in the holds of British warships. That was the kind of detail the newspapers and public opinion were bound to focus on, rather than the fact that the expeditionary force had achieved what it had set out to do, and expelled French forces from Portugal.

'Sir!'

He turned and saw a staff officer beckoning to him. 'Sir, the general wishes you to attend him.'

With a sigh Arthur rose to his feet and strode back across the top of the hill to General Dalrymple's tent. Inside he saw that his superior and Kellermann were sitting side by side on the far end of the table. Dalrymple indicated the seat nearest Arthur.

'Sit down, Wellesley. We have a draft for the armistice. Since you had the honour of winning the battle that led to this happy opportunity I feel it only fair that you should witness the fruits of your victory. So I will read the terms through to you and then you may comment on them, if you wish.'

'Thank you, sir.'

Dalrymple proceeded in a dry monotone and when he had finished he laid down the draft. 'Well?'

There was little deviation from the details they had discussed earlier, but there was one matter Arthur wanted clarification of. 'I do have a question for General Kellermann, sir. What exactly constitutes the "property" the French wish to take home with them?'

Kellermann stirred uneasily. 'Just a question of personal effects. The clause mostly concerns our officers, as you might imagine.'

'And what is the precise nature of this property?'

'It is hard for me to say.' Kellermann shrugged. 'I should imagine it comprises silverware, wardrobes, the odd painting or piece of statuary. Perhaps a carriage or two.'

'I see.' Arthur's eyes narrowed. 'Can I take it that none of these items were acquired during the course of the French army's campaign in Portugal?'

Kellermann stiffened. 'Are you accusing me, or my brother officers, of carrying off spoils of war?'

'Not if you can give me your word that your *property* is not loot.'

'Enough, Wellesley!' Dalrymple slapped his hand on the table. 'I will not have you undermine the armistice by making such accusations.

427

Now then, those are the terms. General Kellermann, will you do me the honour of signing first?'

'I would be pleased to, sir.'

Kellermann reached for a pen, flipped open the inkwell, dipped the nib and signed both drafts with a flourish. He was about to hand the pen to Dalrymple when he paused, and for an instant Arthur saw a crafty expression flash across the French officer's features before he composed his face into a respectful smile.

'General, I think that it would be appropriate for an officer of equal rank to sign on behalf of the British.'

'Really? Why is that?'

'Out of respect for your rank, sir. It would not be seemly for your name to appear on equal terms with my own.'

'Oh, I see. No, of course not.'

'In that case, sir, may I ask General Wellesley if he would do me the honour?'

Dalrymple looked up at Arthur. 'Well, what d'you say?'

Arthur was sorely tempted to refuse. He had had no hand in drafting the terms of the armistice, and some of the clauses were far too generous to the enemy. But if he refused it would only cause further ill will between him and his superior. He nodded, and took the pen offered to him by General Kellermann. Then the French officer slid the documents across the table and indicated the space beneath his own signature. Arthur dipped the nib in the ink, composed his hand and signed his name with neat, deliberate strokes. When he had finished he laid the pen down and sat back as the documents were whisked away. Kellermann handed one to Dalrymple and folded the other to tuck inside his coat as he stood up.

'I must return to General Junot and tell him the good news.'

Dalrymple and Arthur rose to their feet and exchanged handshakes with the French officer before Kellermann strode out of the tent, mounted his horse, and galloped away. As Arthur watched him go, he could not help doubting the wisdom of what his commander had agreed to. But at least the French would quit Portugal. Once Portugal was established as a base of operations the British army could turn its attention to Spain, and the next, far more ambitious, phase in the campaign to eject the French from the Peninsula.

A week later General Junot surrendered the Portuguese capital to the British. Dalrymple, reinforced by Sir John Moore and another fifteen thousand troops, moved south to occupy the city. There was a brief celebration in the streets as the inhabitants cheered the departure of the French garrison, but joy soon turned to disbelief and anger when it became apparent that the 'property' that the enemy were taking with them, with British consent, included gold and silver plate from Lisbon's churches and other loot taken from the royal palaces and homes of the wealthy. It was a bad business, and Arthur, who had signed the armistice, began to dread the manner in which it would be received in London. Worse still was the mood in the army. The plodding nature of Dalrymple, and the common knowledge that he had permitted the French to get the better of him, soured the mood of officers and common soldiers alike. The fact that they continued to report to Arthur in the first instance caused understandable resentment in his superiors. Arthur felt himself to be in a peculiar bind. On the one hand he had proved himself to be a fine commander who had the respect and affection of his men, which meant that it was impossible for him to serve with the army in a subordinate role. On the other, he did not wish to quit in case senior officers complained that he was unwilling to serve where he did not command.

The difficult situation was resolved for him late one afternoon in the middle of September when a message arrived from London. Somerset brought the despatch to Arthur's office in the Lisbon house he was renting, where he had been reading through the latest correspondence from home. His brother William was full of news of the public outcry over the armistice, and his letter included a newspaper clipping that referred to Dalrymple, Burrard and Arthur himself as cowardly curs. William urged his brother to seek leave and return to London to clear his name.

Arthur looked up as Somerset rapped loudly on the door frame.

'Come in!'

Somerset crossed the room, emerged on to the balcony and held out a sealed letter. 'From Castlereagh, sir.'

'Ah.' Arthur felt his heart sink a little, already guessing at the contents of the letter. He hesitated a moment before taking it from his aide and breaking open the seal. Unfolding the sheets of paper he read through them quickly and then looked out over Lisbon, glowing in the light of the late afternoon sun.

'Well, Somerset, it seems that my campaigning days may well be over.'

'Over?' Somerset frowned. 'Why, sir? What's happened?'

'I have been summoned home immediately, to face a military inquiry. Generals Dalrymple and Burrard are to follow. General Sir

John Moore is to assume command of the army. That's something, at least. Moore is a fine officer, and he'll keep his blade in the Frenchman's back.'

'I suppose so, sir.' Somerset frowned. 'But it isn't fair, sir. You are not at fault. The whole army knows it.'

Arthur raised a hand to quiet his subordinate. 'I must defend my part in the treaty. You have to hand it to that fellow Kellermann. He outfoxed us.' Arthur smiled bitterly as he recalled the manner in which he had been coerced into signing the armistice. 'Me most of all.'

Chapter 47

Napoleon

Vitoria, November 1808

The journey across the Pyrenees had been chilly and wet, and even though he had spent most of the day huddled beneath heavy fur robes Napoleon felt as if the cold had penetrated through to every bone in his body. His sour mood was not helped by the many hours he had spent reflecting on developments across the empire. Junot had failed him in Portugal, and now a British army had a foothold in the Peninsula. The bitter anger he had felt at the news had slightly abated at the gratifying storm of outrage the terms of Junot's treaty had caused in Britain. Napoleon could well imagine how it must have stuck in the throat of the British to have Junot's army given free passage back to a French port aboard the vessels of the Royal Navy. The memory passed and his mood became sullen again. He had met the Tsar at Erfurt in October and it had soon become clear that the cordial warmth which had existed between the two rulers following the meeting at Tilsit little over a year earlier was waning.

Napoleon had made lavish arrangements for the meeting, filling Erfurt with the very best entertainers to be had across Europe. But behind the glittering ceremonies, the fine theatrical performances and the spectacular concerts, the hard business of striking deals had not gone the Emperor's way. The Tsar was well aware of the difficulties Napoleon was facing in Spain. News of the loss of Portugal to the British and the defeat and surrender of General Dupont and his entire army to the Spanish at Bailén had echoed round Europe and given fresh hope to all who opposed France and her Emperor.

Accordingly, the Tsar had claimed that the Continental System was harming Russian commerce, and he argued that some concessions to trade with Britain had to be made. He had also demanded that Napoleon reduce the Prussian reparations by twenty million francs, and that Russian annexation of Finnish lands, as well as Moldavia and Wallachia, was recognised by France. Finally, the Tsar had made no secret of his designs to seize Constantinople and gain access to the Mediterranean from the Black Sea. In return for so many concessions by Napoleon, the Tsar had agreed to support Napoleon in the event of another war between Austria and France.

The reports from French spies in Austria were alarming. Every month more and more men were being recruited into the army. Hundreds of new artillery pieces were being cast and horse-buyers were travelling across Europe to secure the best mounts for the Austrians' growing number of cavalry regiments. It was clear to Napoleon that these were preparations for war, and if Russia could be induced to declare her support for France in such a conflict then it was possible that the Austrians might be discouraged from taking the final step. But Alexander's guarantees to France were unconvincing and Napoleon had little faith in his ally. The only good to come out of Erfurt was the appearance that the two rulers were still allies.

With his affairs in eastern Europe settled, for the moment at least, Napoleon concentrated his attention on Spain. Three of his finest marshals, Ney, Mortier and Victor, together with their veteran corps had been transferred from Germany to the Peninsula and it was these troops who formed the new Army of Spain. With such fine men at his back Napoleon was confident that it would require only a brief campaign to crush Spanish resistance and bring the entire Peninsula under French rule, in the person of King Joseph. Thought of his brother caused Napoleon to frown. Joseph had barely been in Madrid long enough to be crowned before he had abandoned his new capital and retreated. Clearly he lacked the ruthless streak that was necessary to cow the rebellious Spaniards. Yet Napoleon had set him on the Spanish throne and there was no question of replacing him, or letting him be driven out. Napoleon's prestige was at stake and he was firmly resolved to teach Spain that her people could not be permitted to defy the will of the Emperor.

It was dark when the imperial convoy at last entered the gates of Vitoria and made its way through the streets to the citadel that served as the army's headquarters. The four squadrons of lancers that had accompanied the Emperor's carriage across the mountains clopped straight to the stables, where the frozen riders dismounted and rubbed their stiff backsides and tenderly stretched their legs.

Napoleon's carriage lurched to a halt in front of a narrow flight of steps leading up into the central keep of the citadel. The steps were lined

432

with soldiers in greatcoats carrying torches in place of their muskets. The steam from their breath puffed out in little clouds as the Emperor climbed stiffly from the carriage and made his way up the steps to the entrance of the keep. A small group of officers, led by Berthier, waited to greet him formally.

'Sire, it is good to see you.' Berthier bowed his head. 'The army is keen to teach the Spanish a lesson.'

'Good,' Napoleon muttered. 'That's the spirit. Is everything prepared?'

'Yes, sire. There's food and wine in the hall and your quarters are ready to receive you . . .'

'Be quiet,' Napoleon said irritably. 'I meant is everything in readiness for the campaign?'

'Apologies, sire. I will brief you after you have eaten and rested, if you wish.'

Napoleon shook his head. 'You can do it as I eat. Show me the way.'

Berthier led him inside the keep and Napoleon relished the warmth as they entered the great hall, where a large fire was blazing in the hearth, casting a warm glow over the chamber and its furniture. A large framed map hung on one wall and was illuminated by a lantern hanging from a stand. Taking off his cloak and handing it to a footman Napoleon approached the fire and held out his hands, smiling as the blaze began to warm him through. At length he turned away and made his way to the table where there were several platters of cold meats, cheese and bread. A bowl of soup steamed at one end. Napoleon summoned a footman and pointed out his requirements.

'I'll have the chicken, this cheese and a bowl of soup. Over there, that seat to the left of the fire.'

'Yes, sire.' The footman bowed and started to gather the food on a plate bearing his master's crest. Meanwhile, Napoleon crossed over to a couch by the fire and gestured to Berthier as he eased himself down. 'Proceed.'

'Yes, sire.' Berthier stood in front of him, notebook in hand in case he needed to consult it, and cleared his throat. 'From the latest reports from our spies in Madrid it appears that the junta there is trying to take control of Spanish resistance to our forces. It's proving to be a challenge for them, sire, since other juntas and the leaders in the regions are not keen to subordinate themselves.'

Napoleon smiled. 'Already they are divided. They do our work for us, Berthier. Very well, if they choose to fight us separately then we shall destroy them one after the other. Good. Continue.'

The footman approached with a small table in one hand and a tray bearing the food in the other. He quietly set the table down and laid out the plate and cutlery as Berthier spoke.

'Based on the reports of our agents I estimate that the Spanish can field as many as one hundred and thirty thousand regular soldiers, with perhaps another seventy thousand militia. In addition, we face the British army in Portugal, under General Moore. He is thought to command more than twenty thousand men.'

Napoleon nodded as he tore some flesh off a chicken leg and chewed. 'It is well for us that the British government does not choose to reinforce Moore. Junot has told me how good their men are.' He shrugged. 'Maybe they are good. Or maybe Junot was never quite the general I had hoped he would be. No matter. We have two hundred thousand of our best men here in Spain. More than enough to deal with those who choose to deny the authority of my brother. Once they are swept aside there will be peace in Spain. And I need peace here,' Napoleon added wearily. 'The men need to return to Germany, and discourage any desire on the part of our Austrian friends to make war on us.'

Berthier raised his eyebrows and cocked his head to one side.

'You have something to say?' Napoleon asked. 'Speak freely.'

'Yes, sire.' Berthier chewed his lip for a moment before he continued. 'I fear this war in Spain will be different from those we have fought before.'

'Different?' Napoleon had finished his chicken leg and now turned his attention to a slice of cheese and a hunk of bread.

'Yes, sire. We are not just waging a war against regular troops. The people of Spain are against us too. Our soldiers dare not forage in small numbers. We have lost many men to groups of villagers, or those rebels who have formed bands and taken to the hills. Scores of our couriers have simply disappeared on the roads. Some bodies have been found, mutilated. As things stand, our commanders are obliged to send two or three squadrons of cavalry to protect their messengers.'

Napoleon swallowed quickly and lowered his. 'Then we must respond with the utmost severity. I want every act of rebellion met with reprisals. For every French soldier killed, the nearest village will be burned and ten of its inhabitants put to death. Send that instruction out to every one of our columns at once.'

'Yes, sire,' Berthier replied quietly.

'You disagree with my suggestion?'

'Of course not, sire. It's just that I do not see how it might help us to win the people round to supporting King Joseph.'

Napoleon stared at his chief of staff. 'Believe me, if we could win over their hearts then I would spare no effort to do so. But we do not have the time for that. I must have order in Spain as soon as possible. The only way to achieve that is by exercising ruthlessness. Spain must be whipped into submission, like a dog. Once these people accept our rule, then we can exercise a degree of leniency. But first we must break their will to resist.'

Berthier did not look convinced, but he responded, 'As you order, sire.'

Napoleon nodded sourly, and bit off another chunk of bread. 'Yes, as I order. Now then, what of these Spanish soldiers? Do we know how their forces are disposed? Are they still as they were when you reported to me last week?'

'Yes, sire.' Berthier approached the map and indicated the salient features as he spoke. 'The enemy appears to be trying to encircle our forces, from the west of the River Ebro, and here to the east at Tarazona. There is a third army to the south of the Ebro, blocking the route to Burgos.'

Napoleon wiped his hands on the napkin that had accompanied the plate, then joined Berthier in front of the map and examined it closely for a moment before he spoke. 'Since our enemies are insistent on dividing their forces and adding to their blunder by advancing to meet us, we shall make the most of their mistake.' He studied the map and then pointed at the Ebro, where it cut across the north of Spain, above Burgos. 'The army will cross here, and then Lefebvre and Victor will wheel to the right to cut behind the western thrust of the enemy. Once we are certain we have them trapped then Ney and Lannes can turn to the east and destroy the enemy's right flank. The rest of the army, under Marshal Bessières, will make for Burgos. As soon as our flanks are secured I will march on Madrid.'

'Yes, sire.' Berthier nodded, noting the Emperor's directions.

Napoleon's gaze switched towards the lands of Portugal and he tapped his fingers lightly on his lips as he thought. 'There is one thing that still concerns me.'

'Sire?'

'The British. If General Moore crosses the border into Spain he may cause us some difficulty if he can isolate any of our corps. Notify all our columns. I want any news of the British army's movements sent directly to me.'

'Yes, sire.'

'Very well then,' Napoleon concluded. 'If all goes well, the army will take Madrid before the year is out and Joseph will have his throne once and for all.'

The Army of Spain crossed the Ebro, but despite the simplicity of the Emperor's plan for the campaign, it was soon beset by problems. Bessières led his army forward at a snail's pace and Napoleon was forced to replace him with Soult before the vanguard was even in sight of Burgos. The Spanish garrison of the city, some ten thousand proud but foolish men, sallied out of the city to face the French host on a low ridge a short distance from the gates. There they put up a brief fight before being routed and cut to pieces. The following day Napoleon established his headquarters in Burgos and his troops set about sacking the town. Their Emperor hurriedly issued a general order forbidding pillaging and threatening summary justice for any men who defied the order.

As soon as Burgos was secured, the French columns moved west and east to clear the flanks of the Army of Spain. Then news of a battle fought at Tudela reached headquarters. Marshal Lannes had broken a Spanish army, though much of the enemy force escaped intact due to Ney's failure to cut off their retreat.

Napoleon was furious, and immediately sent an order for Ney to report to him at headquarters. Two days later Ney arrived, soaked through, spattered with mud and exhausted after a hard ride from Tudela. He was ushered into the imperial presence immediately and stood to attention under the glowering eyes of the Emperor as rain beat against the windows of the office.

'You have let me down, Ney,' Napoleon began. 'What is wrong with my commanders that they should fail me so? First Victor underestimates his enemy and leaves his corps strung out and vulnerable to counter-attack. I ask you, how could a man of his experience underestimate the worst army in Europe? Then Lefebvre sends his men in piecemeal attacks against entrenched troops. And now you do not arrive in time at Tudela and the enemy escapes. Tell me, Ney, what is your excuse this time?'

'This time?' Ney replied with evident ill-temper. 'And when have I let your majesty down in the past?'

'The past does not matter.' Napoleon dismissed the comment with a curt wave. 'You failed to move your army quickly enough. Because of you most of the enemy escaped.'

'Sire, you asked the impossible. When your orders reached me I was required to lead my corps one hundred and twenty miles in three days. Over mountains. It was impossible. No soldiers in the entire army could have done that.'

'It might have been possible had you not rested your men for two days at Soria.'

'It was barely a day, sire. Half the men were straggling. I had to let them catch up or I would not have reached Lannes with enough men to serve any purpose.'

'Rubbish! Davout managed an equally hard march before the Battle of Rivoli.'

'Sire, that was half the distance, over better roads,' Ney protested.

'You dissemble, Marshal Ney, and you know it.' Napoleon thrust a finger at him. 'Admit it, you failed to do your duty.'

'No, sire. I did my duty.' Ney's expression hardened. 'What I failed to do was the impossible. If you had considered the matter more closely before you sent me my orders you would surely have seen that.'

Napoleon breathed in sharply. 'How dare you speak to me in such a manner!'

But Ney was not cowed and nodded towards the wall. 'Look at the map if you don't believe me. Measure out the distance with those dividers you are so fond of. Then you'll see I speak the truth.' Ney paused a moment to control his rising temper. 'Sire, I serve you loyally. I am a soldier and I obey orders to the utmost of my ability. But if the orders are at fault then I will not take the blame for the consequences. Now, if you feel I have betrayed your confidence, or, indeed, you feel no confidence in my abilities, then dismiss me. I will not be held to account for the failings of another.' Ney stiffened to attention. 'Sire.'

There was silence as the two men glared at each other. The only noise was the rain at the window and occasional dull whirr as a gust of wind swept round the building. Napoleon gritted his teeth. He was enraged by Ney's defiance and for a while he was almost consumed by the desire to dismiss the marshal on the spot and send him back to France in disgrace. But he was forced to admit that Ney was a fine leader, and a capable subordinate. He had served his country bravely and loyally and been promoted to his present rank by Napoleon himself. Ney was a popular man, both within the army and with the French public. If Napoleon dismissed him now, his own judgement might well be called into question. That would not do. The latest reports from Fouché indicated that the people were becoming increasingly disillusioned with the almost perpetual state of war. Open dissent between the Emperor and his marshals would only increase unrest.

Napoleon relaxed his jaw. 'Very well then, Marshal Ney. I accept your explanation. This time. But do not fail me again.'

'I did not fail you this time, sire,' Ney replied gruffly.

Napoleon lowered his hands below the desk, out of sight, as he clenched them so tightly that every drop of blood drained from his knuckles. 'You were not where I wanted you to be, and the enemy escaped. However, on reflection, I will not hold you wholly responsible for that. You are dismissed. Return to your corps at once.'

'At once?' Ney glanced wearily towards the rain-streaked window and sighed. Then he bowed stiffly to the Emperor and turned to march out of the room, closing the door forcefully behind him.

Napoleon stared at the door for a moment. Then he picked up his dividers and walked across to the map. He adjusted the instrument to fit the scale and measured off the distance that Ney's corps had been ordered to march. The dividers passed over territory marked as mountainous and broken by many streams and tributaries. For long stretches there were no roads marked on the map. It was, as Ney had said, roughly a hundred and twenty miles. A fresh division of infantry might have encompassed it, Napoleon told himself, but a whole army corps, burdened by its wagons and artillery, could never hope to march such a distance in three days.

Why had he not seen this? It was a lapse of judgement. He would not have made such an error ten years ago, or even five. Was age making his mind less acute? He dismissed the thought. He was not yet forty, surely not old enough for that. But what if his judgement was at fault? What if the organisational brilliance that had made him the master of Europe had become corrupted by his success? It would not be the first time that a great man had fallen prey to the temptation to view every decision he made as infallible. The prospect appalled him. For a moment Napoleon was furious with himself for not making the correct allowances for Ney's movement. Then he forced the very idea of it from his mind. It could not be his fault.

In fact, he recalled that he had given the order without consulting the map. It had been a hectic night when he had dictated his plans to Berthier. Why had Berthier not mentioned the difficulties that Ney would face in keeping to the allotted time for his advance? It was Berthier who had failed him, not Ney. He decided that he must pay closer attention to Berthier from now on. Perhaps the man was growing too old, too weary, to carry the burden of being the Emperor's chief of staff. Berthier would have to be watched to ensure that he did not make any more such mistakes, Napoleon told himself sadly. Berthier was a good man, but he had let his Emperor down and caused him to blame wrongly a fine officer like Ney. Well, Napoleon comforted himself, his subordinates were only human. Once the campaign was over he would have a word with Berthier and suggest that the chief of staff apologise to Ney for making him the target of Napoleon's anger.

There was a knock at the door, and Berthier entered. Napoleon stared at him for a moment, uncertain whether to be angry with the man for causing the earlier scene, or to feel pity for Berthier's mortal failings. In the end he opted for the latter, and smiled condescendingly.

'What is it?'

'A report from one of our light cavalry regiments, sire. They have been scouting along the River Duero and have discovered that the British are on the march.' Berthier crossed to the map and tapped it. 'They are heading in the direction of Salamanca.'

'Salamanca?' Napoleon considered the map briefly. General Moore's army was thought to amount to little more than twenty thousand men. Hardly a critical threat to the Army of Spain. Yet one that could not be ignored. 'We could march towards Salamanca and defeat the British,' he mused. 'But it would mean leaving the conquest of Madrid until later.'

Berthier was emboldened by his master's thoughtful tone. 'That is true, sire, but I must admit the prospect of dealing a humiliating blow to the long-time enemy of France is alluring. It would be a fine thing to offer up a victory over Britain to the rest of Europe.'

'Yes, it would.' Napoleon scrutinised the map again and made his decision. Nevertheless, we can leave Moore until later. First we must crush these Spanish rebels and place my brother on his throne. So, then, we march on Madrid.'

Chapter 48

Before the Army of Spain lay the forbidding mass of the Guadarramas, a long barrier of hills protecting the northern approaches to Madrid. The weather had turned cold but the soldiers had been spared rain as they prepared to assault the Spanish forces defending the Somosierra pass. The night before, the enemy garrison in the village of Sepúlveda had abandoned the position and fled west, rather than face the mass of the French army drawn up before them. As dawn broke, skirmishers advanced through fog to capture the village, and soon afterwards the Emperor and his staff rode forward to climb the church tower, which rose above the fog, and inspect the defences of the main enemy force blocking the pass.

Through his telescope Napoleon followed the narrow road that wound up the side of the hill to the head of the pass. There he could make out the lines of Spanish troops waiting for the French. No more than ten thousand men, Napoleon calculated, in addition to twenty guns mounted in some hastily erected redoubts on either flank which covered the road from Sepúlveda. There did not seem to be any attempt to defend the slopes on either side of the pass and Napoleon briefly considered sending men into the hills to work round the enemy position. But that would cause delay, and he was determined to capture Madrid and settle matters in Spain as swiftly as possible. Besides, Spanish troops were no match for his veterans and would be brushed aside easily enough.

Snapping his telescope shut Napoleon curtly gave an order to Berthier. 'We'll use General Ruffin's division to clear the pass. They can advance up the road and deploy in line the moment they come within range of the enemy's artillery.'

'Yes, sire. How many guns shall we send forward to support them?'

'Guns?' Napoleon pursed his lips for an instant and then shook his head. 'It will be a quick affair, Berthier. Ruffin's men will not need artillery support.'

Berthier looked surprised, and seemed to be about to query the instruction, but nodded instead. 'As you wish, sire.'

Napoleon's head ached terribly this morning, something he put down to a lack of sleep since the advance from Burgos three days before. 'Give the orders, Berthier. I'm going forward with Ruffin as far as that hillock beside the road there, to view the attack.'

'Yes, sire.'

'Carry on,' Napoleon dismissed him, and thrust the telescope into the long pocket of his coat before descending from the tower. As he left the small church he was aware of some shouting a short way down the street and saw two soldiers approaching, with a third man held firmly between them. Behind them marched a young infantry officer.

'Let go of me!' the man shouted. 'Let me go, you fuckers!'

One of the men holding him suddenly lashed out and smashed a fist into the soldier's jaw. 'Shut your mouth!'

Napoleon paused in the street as the little party drew close to the church. As soon as they recognised him the soldiers halted and stared at him awkwardly.

'Well?' Napoleon glared at them. 'Don't you salute your emperor?'

The officer recovered first. 'Attention!'

The three men ahead of him snapped their arms to their sides and stood straight-backed, chins up. The man in the middle stood still as the blood oozed from his cut lip and dripped on to his white cross-straps. Napoleon strode up to them.

'What is the meaning of this? Lieutenant, what has this man done?'

'We caught him looting a shrine on the edge of the village, sir.'

'Looting, eh?' Napoleon turned to the middle man. 'What is your name?'

'Geunet, sire.' The man's gaze did not flicker as he continued to stare straight ahead. 'Jean Geunet, private, third company, first battalion, forty-second regiment of the line, sire.'

'One of General Ruffin's regiments then.' Napoleon nodded. 'And what did you manage to loot from the shrine, Geunet?'

'Sire, it was only an offering of food. Half a loaf of bread and a joint of lamb.'

'I see. And you are of course aware of my orders concerning pillaging?'

'Yes, sire.' The man straightened up. 'But it was not pillaging. I did not steal it from anyone.'

'But you did steal it from the shrine, did you not?'

The soldier nodded. 'I was hungry, sir. All the lads are. Almost starving.'

'But these men with you have not stolen anything, have they?'

The soldier's eyes met those of his Emperor. 'I don't know. Why don't you ask them, sire?'

'Because you were caught and they weren't. That's why, you impudent dog.' Napoleon turned to the lieutenant again. 'Is this man in your unit?'

'Yes, sire.'

'And where are you taking Private Geunet?'

'To battalion headquarters, sire.' The lieutenant held up a haversack. 'The bread and meat are in here, sire, and these two men witnessed the theft. The private's case will be heard by the colonel, and then he will be sentenced, according to your general order, sire.'

Napoleon frowned. 'Your colonel is about to be a very busy man. He has no time to deal with this matter.' Geunet puffed his cheeks out in relief and looked towards the Emperor with a grateful expression. In other circumstances Napoleon might have pardoned the man, but that morning, in the chill of the fog, with the ache in his head and several restless nights behind him, the Emperor's mood was surly and cold to the point of cruelty. He turned round and beckoned to one of the orderlies who accompanied him along with his personal escort of Polish light cavalry.

'Give me some paper and a pencil.'

'Yes, sire.' The orderly delved into his despatch bag and handed the requested materials to his Emperor with a bow.

'Turn round,' Napoleon ordered. 'Keep your back still.'

As the orderly did as he was ordered Napoleon held the paper to his back and began to write. *By the authority of his imperial majesty, the Emperor Napoleon, Private Jean Geunet has been found guilty of pillaging. In accordance with standing orders he is sentenced to summary execution. By order of Napoleon.*

He signed his name and handed the document to the lieutenant. 'There. Have it entered into regimental records. Now take Private Geunet back to the shrine and shoot him.'

'Sire?' The lieutenant stared back.

'Did you not hear my order?'

'Well, yes, sire.'

'Then carry it out immediately or I will have you charged with insubordination.'

'Yes, sire!' The lieutenant saluted and turned at once to his men. 'Take hold of him!'

Geunet's expression was one of pure horror. A moment earlier he had been convinced that the Emperor had been about to pardon him, or at least order a lenient punishment. Now he collapsed to his knees and clasped the hem of Napoleon's greatcoat.

'Sire! I beg you. Show me mercy. I have a family, in Toulon. A wife, two children.'

Napoleon looked down at him coldly. 'Get your hands off me.'

'Sire.' Geunet's eyes widened. 'Don't have me shot. Put me in the front rank. At least give me a chance to die with a musket in my hand. For my country. For you, sire.'

Napoleon ignored him. 'Take this man away, and carry out the sentence.'

Geunet's two companions grabbed his elbows and hauled him roughly to his feet before pinning his arms behind his back and thrusting him away from the Emperor, back down the street in the direction they had come from. Geunet struggled to twist his head round and called out, 'Sire! Don't let them shoot me. Please, sire!'

Napoleon ignored his calls and walked to the horse being held by a groom. Once in the saddle he spurred the animal forward and rode down the street that led towards the pass. The escort followed him in a rumbling cascade of hooves, and as the party left Sepúlveda behind them the sound of two musket shots rang out.

A short distance from the village the gradient of the road began to increase noticeably and within minutes they had emerged from the dawn fog and could clearly see the way ahead of them. Already some of Ruffin's skirmishers were advancing up the hill, on either side of the road, warily watching for any signs of their opposite numbers. But there was no movement below the summit and Napoleon was sure that the enemy had positioned all available men in the pass itself. He went forward with his escort along the narrow cart track that began to zigzag up the slope. When they neared the small hillock he had spotted from the church, he led them off the track and towards the crest. As Napoleon had hoped, the slightly elevated position gave a good view of the Spanish defences less than a mile ahead.

The Polish captain commanding the escort edged his mount closer to the Emperor and coughed. 'Excuse me, sire. But aren't we in range of the nearest battery?'

Napoleon glanced at the earthworks opposite and slightly higher than the hillock. 'It would be extreme range. I doubt they will waste the ammunition.'

'Even so, I would rather you did not take the risk, sire.'

Napoleon turned towards him and glared. 'We are safe here, Captain.

Besides, there is no other position from which to observe the fight. Now still your tongue.'

The captain opened his mouth, then nodded and saluted before walking his horse away to a respectful distance behind the Emperor.

Napoleon watched as Ruffin's division marched out of the fog and began to climb the road up to the pass. As the men passed the Emperor's position they cheered and Napoleon made himself raise his hat in acknowledgement, provoking fresh cheers from soldiers delighted by the simple gesture. As they neared the pass, the division halted and began to deploy in line. Ahead of them the skirmishers fired the first shots of the day at the enemy's light infantry, who were sheltering behind rocks and folds in the ground just ahead of their main position. Soon tiny puffs of smoke were blossoming across the slope. Napoleon watched the deployment with a growing sense of impatience, tapping the top of his boot with his riding crop. At length the drums rolled and the division edged forward. As soon as they came in sight of the Spanish guns the latter opened fire and the first balls tore through the French ranks, scattering bodies in all directions. Ruffin's men continued on towards the line of enemy infantry, the units on each flank taking the heaviest casualties as they approached the Spanish batteries. Inevitably, the line began to bow as the men being pounded by artillery slowed down, and finally stopped a short distance in front of the battery opposite Napoleon.

'Don't just stand there,' Napoleon muttered irritably. 'Get moving . . .'

The flanking battalion had suffered too many casualties and the men refused to advance any further. As the officers and sergeants tried to urge them on, the soldiers loosed off their muskets at the Spanish guns, which were shielded by their earthworks. It was a futile gesture that did not ease the storm of shot tearing the battalion to pieces. Then the first of the men fell back, away from the guns. More followed, and then the entire battalion was retiring, some of the men running, not stopping until the guns were out of sight. A lone officer remained on the bloodied ground, surrounded by bodies. He raised his sword and shouted, trying to shame his men into re-joining the attack. Then, as Napoleon watched, a round shot cut him in half. His legs stood still for an instant, before buckling and collapsing amid the carnage.

'Shit.' Napoleon clenched his fists as he glared at the scattered men of the battalion, then at the Spanish battery. Some of the gun crews had climbed on top of the earthworks and were jeering at the Frenchmen.

'Damn them!' Napoleon growled. He turned angrily in his saddle and pointed at the captain of his escort. 'Take that battery for me! At the gallop! Now.'

The captain looked up the narrow track to the pass, where it crossed the open ground in front of the enemy line.

'What are you waiting for?' Napoleon snapped.

The captain saluted and turned to shout orders to his squadron. The eighty men of his command formed up in column, four abreast. Drawing his sabre, the captain spurred his horse forward and galloped up the track. With cries to urge their mounts on and the jingling of bits the rest of the men pounded after him. Napoleon watched as the squadron charged up the road, past the men of the battalion that had broken earlier. As they reached the pass and came within range of the nearest Spanish infantry the enemy loosed off a volley, knocking several men from their horses. The horsemen slowed, veered away towards the shelter of a small outcrop of rocks and reined in. Napoleon rose up in his stirrups.

'What the devil? What are those cowards doing? Attack, you fools! Attack! How dare you cower in front of that gang of Spanish peasants?' He turned to one of his orderlies. 'You! Ride up there and tell them to continue the charge. Tell them that they shame themselves and they shame their Emperor. Go!'

The orderly saluted and spurred his horse forward. Bending low over the animal's neck he raced across the ground in front of the Spanish infantry and reined in with the surviving men of the escort, who were busy forming up in the shelter of the rocks. Napoleon saw the orderly gesturing back towards the hillock as he passed on the order. The captain of the escort seemed to argue for a moment and then turned away, making for the head of his small band of comrades. His sabre flashed as he raised it up, held it there for a moment and then swept it towards the nearest Spanish battery. The squadron burst out of the cover of the rocks and charged towards the enemy guns. As soon as they emerged, the Spanish artillery opened up, firing case shot into the charging Poles. The blasts tore men and horses apart, and ripped up the ground around them. The distance to the guns was no more than a quarter of a mile, and every shot struck down two or three men at a time as they charged towards their objective. The men's instinct for self-preservation caused their ranks to spread out so they presented a more open target as they galloped on, swords flashing, desperately shouting their war cries. It was all over in less than a minute. The last man reached the earthworks, spurred his horse up above the gunners, and was instantly shot from his saddle. The rest of his comrades, and their mounts, lay strewn across the ground in front of the battery.

Napoleon swallowed at the pitiful sight. They had died at his order. His temper had snapped and their lives had been thrown away. His headache was worse than ever and he reached up and rubbed his brow. Then he gestured to one of his remaining orderlies. 'Ride back to headquarters. I want a regiment of Guard cavalry brought forward. They are to wait below the pass until they are ordered to charge.'

As he waited for reinforcements Napoleon watched as Ruffin's men steadily fought their way forward again and began to take on the Spanish infantry in an unequal musket duel. Better training and discipline on the part of the French meant that enemy soldiers soon melted away. A dense column of chasseurs pounded up the road past Napoleon's hillock, formed into lines just below the crest and stood waiting with drawn sabres. Up ahead the smoke from the musket duel wreathed the pass, swirling away here and there as the wind carried it off. Through such a gap Napoleon saw that the Spanish line was wavering and immediately sent forward the order to charge.

The strident notes of cavalry trumpets echoed down the slope and then the horsemen swept forward in a rumbling wave, sweeping round the end of Ruffin's infantry and rolling up the enemy line before splitting in two and charging each of the enemy batteries. It was a brave sight. Too brave for the defenders, who threw down their weapons and their equipment and ran for their lives. Napoleon watched for a while longer until he could be sure that the pass was in French hands. Then, wincing at the pounding agony in his head, he turned his horse away from the battle and rode back down to the village of Sepúlveda. Berthier sent for his camp bed from the army wagon train and had it set up in a small cell built on one side of the church for the local priest. Napoleon gratefully collapsed on to his bed, fully dressed, and fell into a deep sleep.

Chapter 49

As soon as the last of the enemy was cleared from the pass the army advanced over the Guadarrama range and on to the plain beyond. The first French cavalry patrols rode warily into the suburbs of the Spanish capital the day after the Battle of Somosierra. They reported back to imperial headquarters that the Madrid junta had ordered the arming of thousands of the common people, and the construction of makeshift defences and artillery positions to cover the approaches to the capital's gates. In the first days of December the French army made camp outside the city and constructed their own batteries of siege guns ready to pound the hastily erected defences surrounding the entrance to Madrid.

While preparations for the assault were made Napoleon sent an envoy forward to demand the surrender of the capital. On the first day the envoy was rudely rebuffed, but on the second, the junta requested the opportunity to discuss terms. Accordingly, as evening fell over the plain and the soldiers began to light their fires, a small party of representatives rode out from Madrid and were shown to the gated estate that had been chosen for the imperial headquarters. Napoleon waited for them with his brother Joseph, and Berthier was with them to take notes, as ever. Once the representatives had been searched they were escorted into the Emperor's presence by a section of guardsmen, who remained in attendance, watchful for any sign of treachery from the Spaniards. Napoleon had decided to keep the encounter as brief and formal as possible and there were no chairs in the room. The fire had not been lit, but the room was brightly illuminated by scores of candles burning in the heavy iron holders suspended from the ceiling. The leader of the Spaniards, a tall, graceful man of advanced years, stepped forward to speak for the junta.

'I am Don Francisco Pedrosa of Castille, grandee of Spain and member of the Madrid junta, your imperial majesty.' He concluded with an elaborate bow. Don Francisco had studiously avoided looking at Joseph, as if he was not even in the room, and Napoleon felt his anger rise at this deliberate slight to his brother.

'Are you authorised to accept terms, or merely to discuss them?' he asked tersely.

'I speak and act for the junta,' Don Francisco answered. 'If we make an agreement here, tonight, it will be binding.'

'And these other men with you. Who are they?'

'Members of the junta and representatives of the Madrid councils.'

'Do they speak French?'

'They do. The junta insisted that negotiations be held in front of witnesses.'

'Really? But your witnesses are hardly impartial, Don Francisco.'

'Any more than yours are, sire.' The Spaniard smiled wearily. 'I doubt there is an impartial man left in Europe these days.'

Napoleon returned the smile. 'We live in difficult times, señor. Though that does not need to be the case. France and Spain are allies.'

'Allies? I think not, sire. You come here as invaders.'

'No. We come here to restore the rightful King of Spain to his throne and end the civil strife that is tearing his kingdom apart.' Napoleon placed his hand on Joseph's shoulder. 'You have but to acknowledge his legitimacy and set down your arms and I swear to you that my soldiers will leave Spanish soil.'

'All of them?' asked Don Francisco. 'And can you guarantee that they will not return?'

'They will not return of my volition. I have no desire to enter the territory of an ally, without that ally's express permission.'

'I see.' Don Francisco nodded. 'You will forgive me for asking, sire, but from whom would such permission be sought?'

'Why, your King, naturally.'

'Ah, there we have something of an impasse between us, since neither the Madrid junta, nor indeed any junta in Spain, recognises the authority of your brother.'

'Nevertheless, Joseph is your legitimate King.' Napoleon nudged his brother. 'Is that not so?'

'Yes.' Joseph swallowed nervously. 'That is so. After all, Don Francisco, the Madrid junta freely offered me the crown.'

'I beg to differ with your description of events, *monsieur*.' Don Francisco spoke the last word with heavy emphasis. 'The offer was only made after your Marshal Murat threatened the former members of the junta with prison if they did not offer you the crown.'

'That is also a matter of opinion,' Joseph countered. 'I rather suspect that they have since been coerced into making such a claim by you and the other rebels.'

Don Francisco drew a deep breath before he continued. 'We could argue the point for as long as you like, but the present reality is that you are not the King of Spain. You are a usurper. Your writ runs no further than the screen of French soldiers you surround yourself with. The rest of Spain will never accept you as their King.'

'They will!' Napoleon intervened. 'The moment we have eradicated the nests of rebels that challenge the authority of King Joseph. Those who take British gold to stir up unrest and provoke challenges to the rule of the rightful King.'

'Then I fear that you may well have to eradicate almost every man, woman and child in Spain, sire,' Don Francisco replied. 'For they are all against the imposition of a man who appears to be little more than the puppet of his brother.'

Napoleon felt the blood drain from his face. 'How dare you?'

'I am only telling you the truth, sire. Your brother can never be king here.'

'He is the King. You will honour him as such, or you will be considered rebels and traitors and treated accordingly.'

Joseph glanced at his brother in alarm and then spoke again. 'My dear Don Francisco, there is no need for such resentment. I swear to you now, as I swore on the first day of my reign, that I will be a just and fair ruler of Spain. There will be no reprisals against those who are currently in revolt against me. I have no desire to sow further seeds of disharmony. I truly wish to do no more than serve my people and see that they are offered the same opportunities for peace and enrichment as the rest of Europe.'

'That is all very laudable. But it is too late for you now. If you are imposed on Spain by force, then you can only hope to rule by force. The people simply will not accept you as King.'

'And whom would they choose?' asked Napoleon. 'Some fat Bourbon imbecile?'

Don Francisco shrugged. 'That is not for me to say, sire. But if that was their choice I would feel duty bound to honour it.'

Napoleon stared at him, and then laughed coldly. 'Then you are truly a self-deluded fool.'

'That is not helpful, brother,' Joseph protested.

'Be quiet!'

Don Francisco looked at them with raised brow and a faint mocking smile. 'Clearly I would be a fool if I imagined that Joseph would be anything more than your mouthpiece, sire. The moment he attempted to be his own man, you would call him to heel.'

Napoleon shook his head. 'I have had enough of this! Further discussion is pointless. Go back to the junta and tell them to surrender.

If they don't, I will start bombarding the city's defences at dawn tomorrow. Once they are breached I will let my soldiers sack the city.'

Joseph turned to him with a horrified expression. 'No, brother. You cannot threaten that.'

'It is my will,' Napoleon said firmly, his steely gaze fixed on Don Francisco. 'Now go back to your junta and tell them what I have said. If I do not have your surrender by first light, I will order my guns to open fire.'

Don Francisco returned the Emperor's gaze unflinchingly. 'I will tell them exactly what you have said, sire.'

He bowed, and the other representatives followed suit before they were escorted from the room by the grenadiers. Once the door was closed Joseph turned towards his brother.

'They will not surrender.'

'I know.'

Joseph was silent for a moment before he spoke again. 'And I will not be King.'

'Yes, you will,' Napoleon replied flatly. 'I made you King of Spain, and only I can choose to remove you from the throne, should I wish it. Not some antiquated committee of inbred aristocrats.'

Joseph cleared his throat. 'And what if I choose not to be King?'

Napoleon stared at his brother with a surprised expression, and then laughed. 'Why would a man not want to become a king?'

Joseph clasped his hands behind his back as he composed his thoughts. 'You misled me about conditions here in Spain. The people are not like those of other nations. They are profoundly inward-looking. They are suspicious enough of the people in the next village, let alone any foreigner imposed upon them as a king. I tell you what they are like, brother. They are like Corsicans.'

'Then you are surely the man to be their King!' Napoleon grinned, but Joseph's expression remained quite serious.

'No, brother. They will never be ruled by someone they have not freely chosen. You have made a grievous error in forcing me upon them. They will resist me until I am dead.'

'Let them try. I will not let you come to any harm, and I will not let them oust you.'

'But, Napoleon, can you not see that you have made a mistake? If you persist in this it may well be the greatest mistake of your life.'

'Mistake? Me?' Napoleon was hurt. His brother had never questioned his judgement so openly, or so honestly, before. 'I have thought this through. There is no mistake. Trust me. It is merely a question of the correct application of force for the appropriate length of time. Once the Spanish see that they cannot oust you, nor defeat French soldiers, they will see that it is pointless to continue the struggle.'

'You make it sound so simple.' Joseph turned away from his brother and wearily strolled across to the windows. He looked out over the surrounding landscape, which was dotted with the flames of Napoleon's army. 'How many men can you spare to keep Spain subdued?'

'Enough. You have my word on it.'

'Think on it. There will need to be strong garrisons the length and breadth of Spain. Every road used by our men will need to be protected. Every despatch exchanged between France and Spain will have to be escorted. None of our men will be able to forage alone, or even in small parties. And they will be attacked from behind every rock. That is even without considering any intervention by a British army. For that we will need a strong field army, over and above the men required for other duties.' Joseph turned back to face his brother. 'Your army will die the death of a thousand cuts here in Spain. And for what?'

'For you to be King.'

'Only until the day that the people finally triumph.'

'That will never happen. Brigands and outlaws can never overcome a modern army,' Napoleon asserted confidently. 'Trust me, brother. I know what I am talking about. I am a soldier to the core.'

'Perhaps that is the problem. You cannot conceive of the implications for an army forced to face the wrath of an entire people. Our men will not be fighting *a* war here. They will be fighting an infinite number of little wars. Against every man who can hold a weapon, every woman who can poison a well, every child who misdirects them or leads them into ambushes. In the end it will break their will, I am sure of it.'

Napoleon shook his head. 'You look too deeply into the hearts of men, Joseph. You always have. We will win here. You will be King and there will be peace.'

'Because you say so.'

'Yes, because I say so.'

'But I don't want to be King. I don't want to be the cause of the endless suffering of the people of Spain. I don't want to be responsible for the deaths of tens of thousands of those fine soldiers who now sit by their campfires. I don't want any of it.'

'It is too late for that, brother.' Napoleon moderated his tone as he continued. 'I made you King. I cannot afford to be seen to have made a mistake. Even if you are right in your fears for the future, I cannot be seen to be less than invincible. The other nations of Europe are like a pack of jackals circling France. The moment they scent weakness they will pounce. If that happens, it will not just be you that falls, it will be all of us, every member of our family, every friend and worthy comrade whom we have rewarded with promotions and titles. France will be returned to the Bourbons and the world will be the exclusive province of aristocrats again. Is that what you would wish for?'

'No. Of course not.'

'Then surely you must see why you have to be King here? If you give way, it will be as the first brick in a dam.' Napoleon's eyes glittered as he seized on the metaphor. 'That is what we are, brother. Bricks in a dam, shielding our people from the dark waters of reactionaries and religious fanatics. It is our duty not to give way. I know you are a good man. I know that you are an idealist, as I am. You will understand the role you must play here in good time. Your people will need you when the rebellion is crushed. You must lead Spain into the modern world. That is a task no Bourbon could undertake.' Napoleon smiled and clasped his brother's shoulder. 'It is a fit task for a Bonaparte, is it not?'

Joseph stared at him for a while in silence and then his shoulders slumped wearily and he nodded.

'Good! Then it is settled. Come, let us go and eat.' Napoleon ushered his brother out of the room, and because he went ahead Joseph did not see the look of contempt that hardened the Emperor's face.

On the fourth day of December the French guns opened fire. A barrage of heavy iron tore holes in the enemy's flimsy barricades, smashing those sheltering behind. One by one the guns in the batteries covering the capital's gateways were silenced as they were struck and dismounted in an explosion of splinters and slivers of iron that sliced through the gun crews. Once Madrid's outer defences had been pulverised, a column of French troops forced their way on to the Heights of Retiro that dominated the city. Several batteries of guns were moved up to the Heights and trained on the heart of Madrid. But there was no need to open fire. Before sufficient ammunition had been brought forward to begin the bombardment, a deputation of Madrid's councillors approached the French lines under a flag of truce to surrender. The junta had already fled, the moment they had seen the French guns being wheeled into position.

At noon, the first columns of French infantry entered the capital, the skirmishers warily picking their way along the main avenues and thoroughfares, searching the openings of each narrow lane for sudden ambushes. Behind them tramped the columns of line infantry, under their tricolour banners surmounted with the gleaming golden eagles of the empire. Once the route to the royal palace was secured, Napoleon entered the city on horseback, surrounded by a screen of escorts. He was struck by the silence and stillness that pervaded the capital, as if every living being had retreated within their houses, refusing to face up to the French presence on their streets. Napoleon stared about him in bitter resentment. The fools had been liberated from the dead hand of Bourbon rule. He had offered them his brother, as liberal and enlightened a ruler as any kingdom could wish for. Yet they resented their liberation and even now harboured a deep spirit of resistance to the new order.

Well, let them sulk, he reflected coldly. They would learn soon enough. The only real choice facing them now was acquiescence or death.

Chapter 50

Arthur

London, December 1808

'It was a mistake to ever send an army into Spain,' William grumbled as he poured himself another glass of madeira and settled back into his chair in the front parlour of Arthur's Harley Street home. 'Nothing good will come of it. How can General Moore hope to take on Napoleon's Grand Army with his puny force?'

'Oh, I don't know,' Arthur replied calmly. 'Moore is a fine officer. He might yet upset the plans of the Corsican tyrant. You'll see.'

William took a sip and looked across at his younger brother. 'If there was any justice, or common sense, in this world it would be you in command of that army.'

Arthur smiled slightly. 'Well, I don't know about the rest of the world, but there is precious little justice or common sense here in London at present.'

William nodded with feeling.

From the moment Arthur had stepped ashore following his return from Portugal he had been under attack from all those who opposed the treaty that had been signed at Cintra, allowing General Junot and his army to evade surrender. The image of the Royal Navy being used as a passenger service for the French army had humiliated the nation. The London newspapers had accused Arthur, Dalrymple and Burrard of everything from incompetence to cowardice. It had upset Kitty dreadfully and for the present she kept to the house rather than brave the hostile looks of Arthur's enemies, and the embarrassment of his friends.

Some politicians in Parliament, scenting the opportunity to settle old scores, had immediately seized the chance to extend the attack to the rest of the family. Richard was still denied government office and had fallen back into a mire of self-pity and whoring. To make matters worse he had approached the King to request that Arthur be ennobled as a reward for his victory at Vimeiro. Lesser generals had won smaller engagements and received far greater honours, yet the timing of Richard's approach was hardly ideal. With public opinion set against the generals held responsible for the Cintra treaty, now was not the time for the King to reward Arthur, and as things stood he doubted he would ever become Viscount Vimeiro.

Worse still, the enemies of the Wellesley family had finally convinced the government to set up a military inquiry into the events leading up to the Cintra treaty and it had been taking evidence for the last two weeks of November. Both Dalrymple and Burrard and their supporters had been busy laying the blame at each other's door, when they were not directing it at Arthur. For his part he had kept silent, reserving any comment for the moment when he would make his case in front of the panel of senior officers in the Great Hall of Chelsea College. The day appointed for him to give his evidence and face cross-examination was two days hence. Before that Arthur had been invited to a royal levee: an early morning reception by the King himself.

'Are you certain about tomorrow?' William suddenly asked, as if he had been reading Arthur's thoughts. 'It might be wise to stay out of public view, at least until the inquiry is complete.'

'I will go,' Arthur replied firmly. 'Neither the newspapers, nor the politicians, nor the London mob will have the satisfaction of having dissuaded me from showing my face in public.'

'I suppose that is a good thing,' William said doubtfully. 'In any case, I shall be coming with you. They might as well have two targets for their anger as one.'

Arthur laughed. 'Spoken like a true soldier!'

'God forbid.'

Several soldiers stood guard at the palace gates and a sergeant inspected invitations as each carriage rumbled to a halt. A small crowd of Londoners had braved the chilly morning air to gather round the gates to watch the great and the good arrive at the palace. As the sergeant read off the names on the invitations they raised a cheer for popular public figures, showed blank indifference to those without a reputation and booed and whistled at a handful of those who had incurred public displeasure for whatever reason.

'I don't like the look of that mob,' William muttered as he ducked back into the carriage.

'Ignore them,' Arthur replied calmly. 'They are as fickle as the wind.

Today I am dangled in front of them as a villain. In a year's time, who knows? I may be the darling of the mob.'

'Small comfort,' William muttered. 'It's today I am worried about.'

The carriage slowed to a halt at the gates and the driver handed over the invitation to the sergeant. The latter filled his lungs and bellowed out, 'Admit the honourable William Wellesley, member of Parliament, and Lieutenant-General Sir Arthur Wellesley!'

At once there was a chorus of boos from the mob and as the carriage rattled forward some muddy slime struck the carriage window. Arthur raised an eyebrow. 'Charming.'

They entered the inner courtyard of the palace and descended from the carriage to join the other guests climbing the steps into the reception hall. A number of footmen lined the route to the chamber hosting the levee. William nudged Arthur.

'Do you see that tall fellow ahead of us? The one with the fair hair?'

Arthur craned his neck and saw the man indicated. 'Yes. What of him?'

'That is Charles Franks, a parliamentary Whig. Those others he's talking to are some of his followers in the House.'

'Ah, yes,' said Arthur. 'I recall the name now. Recently elected, wasn't he?'

'Yes, and keen to make a name for himself.' William lowered his voice and leaned closer to his brother. 'Franks and those others have drafted a certain document. I gather that they intend to petition the King to have you tried for treason.'

'Good God, treason? The dogs. They'll never make that stick.'

'I hope not, Arthur. But in the present climate, who knows?'

The line of guests edged forward into the chamber and took up their places on either side of a broad red carpet leading up to a dais where an ornate chair awaited the King. When all were present, the royal chamberlain entered and rapped his staff loudly on the tiled floor to one side of the carpet.

'My lords and gentlemen, pray silence for his majesty the King and his highness, Prince George!'

The chamberlain stepped gracefully to one side and bowed deeply as the King entered the chamber in a dark blue frock coat, laced with gold. He wore several jewelled stars on his breast. Behind him came the Prince, also in blue, but with less decoration. They walked serenely down the length of the carpet, stopping here and there to exchange a brief word with friends and familiars. As they came abreast of Arthur the King suddenly stopped and turned to him.

'General Wellesley, is it not?'

'Yes, sire.' Arthur bowed.

'We are pleased that you have attended the levee, Sir Arthur. We are even more pleased that you have proved to the world that the armies of France are not invincible. Your country is grateful to you.' The King paused and smiled. 'At least, your country should be grateful, and they will be in due course, I have no doubt.'

'I thank your majesty.'

The King moved on. When he was out of earshot, Arthur muttered to his brother, 'It seems that at least one person approves of my actions.'

On the dais, the King coughed to clear his throat and addressed the chamber. 'Before the morning's entertainment begins I would like to take the chance to offer my profound thanks to the officers of the Navy and the army who are present here tonight. Our nation stands in an hour of great peril, and sometimes our people forget to show due deference and respect to those who risk their lives for their King and country. To which end I trust that those of us who are not in the services will join me in applauding our brave soldiers and sailors.'

He gently clapped his hands together and instantly the chamber was filled with the sound of applause. Arthur nodded his thanks to those on either side of him, as did the other guests who were in the services.

As the King folded his hands his guests quickly ceased their applause and the royal chamberlain nodded a signal to the small orchestra in the gallery. At once they struck up with a light piece of music and the guests slowly began to mill together, talking in an animated hubbub, as those who were to be presented to the King formed a loose queue to one side of the dais.

Arthur and William began to work their way through the guests, greeting old friends and acquaintances. Arthur was saddened by the coolness they met from many of those he had once counted as friends and political allies.

'What did you expect?' asked William. 'Richard is still waiting to be cleared of the accusations made against him from his time in India. You are about to go before a court of inquiry whose report may damn your political and military careers for ever. Who would want to be associated with a family like that? Failure and shame are contagious.'

'Sir Arthur! My dear fellow!'

The brothers looked round to see Castlereagh striding through the crowds towards them with a broad smile on his face. Arthur turned to William and cocked an eyebrow. It seems that we are not completely abandoned.'

'Not yet,' William muttered sourly.

Castlereagh took their hands in turn and pumped them vigorously. 'A bad business, this hue and cry over the Cintra treaty. But I am sure it will die away once the inquiry makes its report.'

'I hope so,' Arthur responded evenly.

'Speaking of which,' Castlereagh looked at Arthur with a mischievous twinkle in his eye, 'there is someone I think I should introduce you to. Do come with me.'

He took Arthur's arm and guided him through the crowd towards Charles Franks and his small entourage, who watched their approach with dismay.

Castlereagh waved his hand. 'Charles! Good to see you here. There's someone I would like you to meet.' Arthur's gaze met that of Charles Franks, and the men stared at each other frostily until Castlereagh continued in an ebullient tone, 'I don't think you have ever formally been introduced to Sir Arthur Wellesley, have you?'

'No, I have not . . .' Franks attempted to smile politely, but the tension between the dictates of good manners and the knowledge that he was hoping to petition the King to destroy Arthur tied the politician's tongue.

'Not what?' Castlereagh prompted. 'Not had the pleasure?'

'Yes. That's what I meant.' Charles Franks smiled weakly.

'Of course that's what you meant. Now then, it is my pleasure to introduce you to Lieutenant-General Sir Arthur Wellesley, the hero of Vimeiro.' He paused and repeated the words with heavy emphasis. 'The hero of Vimeiro. Has a nice ring to it, wouldn't you say?'

'I suppose so,' Franks replied uncomfortably, his eyes flickering towards Arthur. 'I congratulate you on your victory, Sir Arthur. However, it is a shame that so signal an achievement should be followed by so shameful a sequel.'

'That is a matter of opinion,' Arthur replied flatly.

'Yes. But I imagine you are just as keen to cast the blame on to Dalrymple and Burrard as they are to cast it on you.'

Arthur shook his head. 'I keep my opinions to myself. On matters relating to events that took place in Portugal, I reserve my words for the inquiry, which is the proper arena for such comments, as I am sure you would agree?'

'I suppose so, yes.'

Castlereagh clapped both men on the shoulder. 'Good! That's how these things should be done, eh?'

Charles Franks smiled weakly at the Foreign Secretary and then bowed his head. 'It has been a pleasure to meet you, Sir Arthur, but my friends and I must leave early. We have another engagement, so I bid you good day.'

His friends looked at each other in surprise before they echoed their farewells and the little band made its way through the crowd towards the entrance to the audience chamber. As he watched them depart, Castlereagh muttered, 'So much for their petition. I don't think it would have had much chance of support in Parliament. Still less now it is seen that his majesty evidently favours you.'

'Quite.' Arthur nodded, then turned to the minister. 'However, I still have to go before the inquiry.'

'Of course. But I am sure the panel will be persuaded that you cannot be held responsible for the Cintra treaty. Solely responsible, that is. Either all three generals will be condemned or none will.' Castlereagh shook his hand again. 'Good luck, Sir Arthur. And goodbye to you, William.' He turned and strode away to work another section of the crowd.

'Either all three condemned, or none,' William echoed. 'Was that supposed to be a few words of encouragement, do you think?'

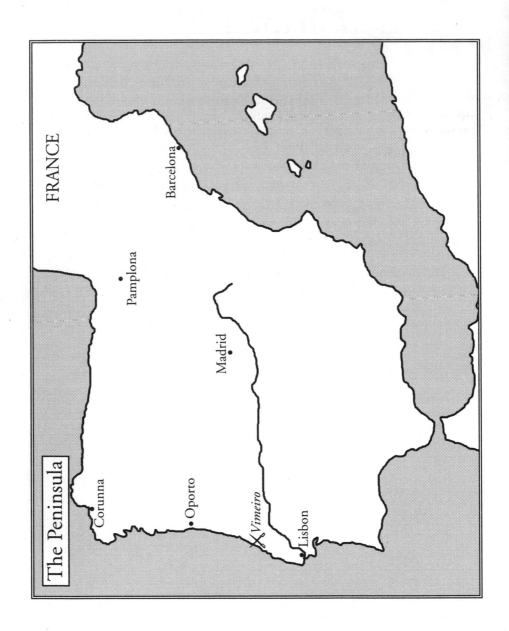

The Peninsula

FRANCE

Barcelona

Pamplona

Madrid

Corunna

Oporto

Vimeiro

Lisbon

Chapter 51

Arthur was wearing his best uniform when he presented himself before the members of the panel. Sir David Dundas had been appointed president of the inquiry and was assisted by six other generals, all of whom were now seated behind a long table at the end of the Great Hall. Several clerks and secretaries sat at small tables in the wings, organising documents and taking down details of what was said to provide an accurate record of the event. Arthur was shown into the hall and escorted to the single chair set before the inquiry panel. He bowed to each of the members and then took his seat. Dundas was an elderly general and one of the most senior in the army. His gaunt figure topped by a thin face, a long nose and white hair. Dundas had a reputation for being a strict disciplinarian and a stickler for rules and regulations.

'Sir Arthur,' he began formally, 'you have been called here to account for your actions in relation to the treaty signed at Cintra. Generals Dalrymple and Burrard have already given their evidence. You will answer all questions truthfully and to the best of your knowledge. Do you understand?'

'Yes, sir.'

'Very well then. It is the understanding of this inquiry that you were in command of the army for the duration of the engagement at Vimeiro. Is that so?'

'Yes, sir.'

'And yet General Burrard had reached the vicinity of the army the day before.'

'Yes, sir.'

'So, in your view, it would have been possible for Burrard to have assumed command of the army in time to fight the subsequent battle.'

'It was certainly possible, sir, but not necessary. The army had already won an engagement at Roliça, and it seemed that the enemy was retreating towards Lisbon. Sir Harry arrived in the afternoon and made the decision not to assume command until the next day. There was no expectation of a battle, and had the French not tried to surprise us, Sir Harry would have assumed command of the army in good time.'

'That may be so, General Wellesley, but let me ask you this. If you had been in Burrard's place would you have delayed taking command of the army as the senior officer present?'

Arthur paused. There was no way to answer this truthfully that did not undermine Burrard's position. He drew a sharp breath. 'No sir, I would not have delayed taking command.'

'And why is that?'

'It is my conviction that the initiative should be seized in all things, sir. If not, then you make a gift of it to the enemy, as we discovered.'

'Just so.' Dundas nodded, and then looked down at his notes for a moment. 'So, then, the French attempted to outflank your position. You changed your front to foil them, threw back their attacks and routed their assault columns.'

'Yes, sir.'

'Did you give the order to pursue the enemy?'

'There was little opportunity to do that, sir. What few cavalrymen we had were unequal to the task.'

One of the other members of the panel, a stout officer with florid cheeks, leaned forward and addressed Arthur. 'But surely you could have ordered your infantry to make a pursuit, and denied the enemy any chance at rallying his formations?'

'The order could have been given, sir. But it was not.'

'Why not?'

'General Burrard had reached the field in the course of the battle and was generous enough to permit me to retain command until the battle was over. Once the French had broken, I returned to my command position on the understanding that that was the point at which my authority was superseded.'

'I see.' Dundas nodded again. 'Did you suggest to Burrard that he should attempt a pursuit?'

'Yes, sir, I did.'

'As we know, there was no such attempt. Did Burrard offer you any explanation as to why he did not order a pursuit?'

'Yes, sir.'

There was a short pause before Dundas sighed. 'Would you be kind enough to explain his reasoning to the inquiry?'

'Sir Harry was of the opinion that we had insufficient intelligence about the enemy's strength and his dispositions. Therefore it would be prudent to await the arrival of General Moore and his men in order to ensure that we had the advantage in numbers before continuing our advance.'

'Did you agree with his opinion?'

'No, sir, I did not.'

'Why?'

'We had beaten General Junot. The information I had from my Portuguese allies was that Junot's army was the only enemy army between Vimeiro and Lisbon. Therefore it was my belief that we could have pursued him to destruction, before turning to liberate Lisbon.'

'As it was, the enemy was allowed to escape.'

Arthur hesitated a moment. 'Yes, sir.'

'Do you feel you were responsible for their escape?' Dundas asked in a very deliberate tone.

'No, sir. I urged Sir Harry Burrard, and Sir Hew Dalrymple when he arrived to take command, to march at once against General Junot. If they had, the French would have been defeated, and there would have been no armistice, and no treaty of Cintra.'

'And no inquiry,' Dundas added with a faint smile. 'Let us turn our attention to the armistice. You signed it.'

'Yes, sir.'

'Did you draft the agreement?'

'No, sir. It was drafted by Sir Hew and the French representative, General Kellermann.'

'So why did you put your name to it?'

'I was ordered to, sir. By General Dalrymple. My signature is a mere form.'

'I see. And did you agree with the terms of the armistice, as ratified at Cintra?'

Arthur swallowed nervously, but strained to keep his face calm, and his voice unflustered. 'There is no simple answer, sir. The object of the campaign was to capture Lisbon and eject French forces from Portugal. The treaty achieved that with no loss of life. To that extent I approved of the treaty.'

'However?' Dundas prompted.

'However, I contend that we should have accepted a few more casualties and pursued and destroyed Junot's army, and thereby damaged wider French morale and inspired our allies. In addition, I think the terms agreed were over-generous to our enemy and have damaged the reputation of Britain. Having defeated Junot, it was absurd to permit his army to be returned to France, rather than be taken into captivity.'

Dundas narrowed his eyes. 'You are a master of understatement, General Wellesley. However, I feel it only fair to inform you that Sir Hew Dalrymple is unequivocal in ascribing the blame for the treaty to you.'

Arthur felt a cold chill of anger grip his heart. 'I fail to see how I can be held to account for the treaty. If General Dalrymple refused to heed any of my advice in the conduct of the campaign, I am certainly not answerable for the consequences.'

Dundas looked away and conferred quietly with the other panel members, making a few more notes on the papers before him. At length he turned back to Arthur and continued questioning him on more precise details for the next hour, after which Arthur was permitted to leave.

For the next week other officers were called before the inquiry, and then the panel retired to consider the evidence and write their report. As Arthur waited, he made preparations to return to Dublin with Kitty and the children to resume his civilian duties at the castle, but he could not help considering his prospects. At best, he would be cleared of any blame, but he knew that the stigma of the Cintra treaty might stick to his name for many years to come, unless he had the chance to fight again and win a victory that would expunge his part in the armistice. At worst, he faced public censure and would be stripped of his post of Chief Secretary, with no hope of achieving high office at any future date.

Kitty and the boys went back to Dublin, but Arthur lingered in London, feeling he was in a peculiar state of limbo. His friends and acquaintances remained slightly at a distance, as if he had some kind of illness, and yet inside he felt certain that he would not be censured by Sir David Dundas and his colleagues. The fact that it had been a military inquiry, rather than a parliamentary one, was a considerable source of comfort in such politically partisan times.

The wait dragged by, and Arthur's spirits settled lower and lower, until three days before Christmas. He was taking breakfast, alone, when he heard a loud knock at the front door. A moment later a footman opened the door. There was a short, muffled exchange, then footsteps pounded down the hall and the door to the dining room burst open. William stood on the threshold, breathing hard, eyes wide with excitement.

'Good God,' Arthur exclaimed. 'What on earth is the matter with you?'

'Just . . . come . . . from my club.' William struggled to catch his breath, and swallowed before continuing. 'One of the others . . . brought news of the inquiry. They've just published.'

Arthur froze, knife and fork poised over his lamb chops. 'Well?'

'They've approved the treaty . . . six votes to one. There'll be no action taken against you or the others.'

Arthur nodded slowly. Inside he felt no joy or sense of vindication, only a sudden heavy weariness. It was over, then. Dundas and the others had decided to close ranks and protect their fellow generals, and the radical press and politicians would howl with protest that they had been denied their prey.

'You're in the clear,' William continued. 'You must show your face around London, and in Parliament. There's a reputation to rebuild. So what do you intend to do?'

'Do?' Arthur replied calmly. 'I intend to finish my breakfast. Then I shall complete my arrangements to re-join my wife and children in Dublin.'

Chapter 52

Napoleon

Madrid, December 1808

'And there's another message from his majesty the King of Spain and the Indies,' said Berthier, holding out a brief note towards the Emperor. Napoleon glanced sharply at his chief of staff, to discern whether Berthier was being ironic. It was out of character for Berthier, but Napoleon wondered if there was a feeling of disrespect for Joseph within the army. Certainly his brother had never shown any desire, or ability, for military affairs. It was possible that as far as the army was concerned the feeling was mutual. That pricked Napoleon's sense of loyalty to his older brother and he stared suspiciously at Berthier, who was still holding the message out towards him. Napoleon did not reach for it.

'What does my brother have to say?'

'His majesty asks to be informed when he might avail himself of the opportunity to enter his capital.'

Napoleon smiled to himself. That sounded precisely like the kind of message Joseph would send. He had trained as a lawyer in his youth and it seemed that the cumbersome turn of phrase of the legal trade had left its mark on him for ever.

Berthier cleared his throat. 'Do you wish to reply to his majesty, sire?'

'Yes. Tell him that I am still dealing with the arrangements for his reception here.' Napoleon paused an instant before continuing. 'Inform his majesty that I am in the process of reforming the institutions of his kingdom. Once said reforms are operative he may resume his occupation of the throne. Or something like that.' Napoleon smiled. 'That should keep him happy for now.'

'Yes, sire.' Berthier nodded. 'But I assume that his majesty's impatience to enter the capital cannot be assuaged for much longer.'

Napoleon's expression hardened. 'My brother will wait until I decide that conditions here are appropriate for his return. Before then the government must be reformed, the remaining rebels crushed, and the British chased back into the Atlantic. Now, if that is the last of the morning despatches, I have other matters to attend to.'

'Yes, sire.' Berthier bowed his head and backed away two steps before turning and leaving the Emperor's office. Once the door had closed Napoleon lowered his gaze to the notes on his desk. They concerned the tax system of Spain and had been compiled for him by one of the officials at the treasury. The arrangements were hopelessly complicated and inefficient and it was a wonder that any revenue was ever collected. Napoleon had been making his own notes alongside the official's to begin with but it was clear that the system was beyond redemption.

Accordingly, he had begun to draft his own system and would have it ready for implementation before Joseph took control of the country again. It was not that his brother lacked the wit to make such necessary reforms, Napoleon reflected, it was just that he lacked the iron will necessary to force such measures through. Given the present intransigence of the people it would be folly to attempt to negotiate the changes. Better to present them as a fait accompli and implement them by force if required. Particularly in view of the other reforms that Napoleon had planned.

The Inquisition was to be abolished, and the number of religious orders reduced, thereby cutting down the financial burden of the Church on the Spanish people. When Napoleon had announced his plans to Joseph's ministers they had reacted with horror, warning him that the people would not tolerate such changes, even though the reforms would undoubtedly improve the governance of Spain. Napoleon had addressed them firmly. The reforms would be made, and implemented fully. He had spoken.

It had been nearly two weeks since Madrid had fallen and Napoleon had spent most of the time devoting his energies to drafting his plans for Spain. Some eighty thousand men were camping in an arc round the south and east of the capital and another forty thousand were billeted in Madrid itself. Soon General Junot would be joining them, having marched directly from France the moment his troops had been repatriated by the British navy. Once he had attended to the political situation Napoleon would lead his armies in the next, and final, stage of his conquest of Spain and Portugal. There were only two enemy forces to deal with. A Spanish army concentrated around Seville, and the

British army of General Moore, which had emerged from its lair in Portugal to interfere with events in Spain.

As December wore on, the temperature steadily dropped and the nights were cold. The troops camped outside the capital had soon recovered from their march to Madrid and now that they were fed and rested they were keen to complete the campaign and return to France. The inhospitality of the climate, the hostility of the people and the scarcity of food to forage and property to loot had combined to undermine the morale of the French soldiers. They had complained to their officers, who had complained to their commanders, who had reported the mood of their men to imperial headquarters. The Emperor had long since discovered the best medicine for such disgruntlement and immediately gave orders for the army to hold a review in the centre of Madrid. That would serve the double purpose of raising the morale of his army as well as impressing upon the Spanish the might of the army they had dared to oppose.

The review was scheduled for the nineteenth of December and the day was overcast and chilly as the first division marched through the streets of Madrid towards the royal palace, where the Emperor and his staff stood watching on a balcony. With regimental colours raised high and buttons and boots polished to a high gleam, the men let out a lusty cheer that echoed back off the palace walls as they passed the Emperor and snapped their eyes to the right. Napoleon raised his hat to acknowledge them, with a smile. Once the entire division was formed up, he descended from the balcony and began a close inspection of his soldiers, stopping regularly to question individuals, and to award medals and other rewards to those who had been singled out for their courage by their superiors.

It was as he was handing a sword to the captain of the first company to enter Madrid that a staff officer came running up to Berthier and muttered something to him in a low voice. Napoleon was aware of the interruption but continued his congratulations to the captain before he passed on, with a brief gesture to Berthier to accompany him.

'What is the news?'

'A message from General Dumas, sire. He reports that his scouts have observed elements of the British army advancing towards Marshal Soult.'

'Soult?' Napoleon drew up and closed his eyes, visualising the disposition of his forces across Spain. Of all the major formations in his army, Soult's was one of the weakest, comprising twelve thousand infantry and two thousand cavalry. It was tasked with policing the regions of Castille and León. In a moment Napoleon grasped the danger to which he had exposed Soult. His eyes flicked open and he turned to Berthier. 'What else did General Dumas have to say?'

Berthier looked uneasy as he replied, 'Dumas has taken it upon himself to divert forces to support Soult. I have told his staff officer to ride back and order Dumas to halt his movements pending approval from imperial headquarters. He is also to send patrols out to find the British army and confirm their position.'

Napoleon considered Berthier's decisions for a moment and then shook his head. 'No. Cancel your orders. Dumas did the right thing. The British are more daring than I had thought. General Moore seeks to isolate and destroy Soult . . . Well then, we shall turn the tables on Moore. If we can move swiftly enough we can trap the British between Soult and the forces that are camped around Madrid.' Napoleon smiled. 'Imagine it, Berthier. The annihilation of Britain's only field army. Their government would not survive such a catastrophe. This could be the very chance I have always sought to bring this war to an end!'

He clasped his hands together and nodded towards the division standing silently behind the two officers. 'Cancel the review. Send word to all divisional commanders to have their men ready to march at once. And have all my senior officers summoned to the palace. The fates are with us, Berthier. Within a month we will have caught and crushed the British army.'

Orders for the redirection of the campaign flowed out of imperial headquarters over the following two days. The day after the news of the British move had arrived, Marshal Ney's corps was already on the march, climbing over the pass through the Guadarrama mountains to Villacastin. Napoleon remained in Madrid long enough to see his brother installed in the royal palace, protected by thirty-five thousand men under the command of Marshal Lefebvre. Joseph was left with strict instructions to ensure that the Madrid newspapers reported that the British army was trapped and would be crushed within weeks. Satisfied that he had set in motion a host of men to catch and trap the British, Napoleon set off from Madrid a day later.

Winter had set in with a vengeance as they approached the mountains, which were shrouded in a thick layer of snow. A biting cold wind was blasting down from the north and made the going tough even before the column reached the bottom of the route leading up into the pass. There they camped for the night, taking advantage of any shelter from the wind that they could find in peasant hovels and behind low walls and rocky outcrops. The men huddled round fires that flared and roared as they were discovered by stray blasts of the wind. It was almost impossible to sleep in the icy cold of the night, and before dawn thick flakes were borne down on the howling wind to swirl around the shivering men and horses of the French army.

As dawn broke faintly across the bleak landscape the men shook themselves free of the snow and prepared to climb up the slope to the pass. Napoleon watched as the infantry formed up in long shivering columns and the artillery train harnessed their horses to the limbers and caissons. The men were silent and any attempt at levity in the ranks died away almost as soon as it began. The dragoons of the Imperial Guard were the first to advance up the slope. Both men and mounts lowered their heads into the wind that howled down from the pass as they trudged forward. Napoleon had ridden a little way ahead and watched as the dragoons passed by with hardly a sound. The thick snow had deadened the sound of their progress and fresh flurries added to the drifts that had formed across the narrow winding track. They advanced slowly, and eventually the tail of the column disappeared into the snowstorm, as the first of the infantry battalions made ready to follow.

In less than an hour a messenger arrived from the commander of the dragoons. His breath burst from his lips in ragged puffs that were instantly ripped away by the wind as he reported to the Emperor.

'Sire, the colonel begs to inform you that his men can go no further. The colonel has halted to await orders.'

'Await orders? The colonel has his orders! Tell him to keep moving. I will not have my army held up because the colonel can't bear a little cold.'

The messenger bowed his head, and then looked up nervously. 'I beg your pardon, sire, but my colonel is right. It is not possible to advance any further.'

'And why not?' Napoleon asked tersely. 'Explain.'

'Sire, the conditions up there are far worse than they are here. The wind is so strong that our horses can barely stay on their legs, while the riders are nearly being swept from their saddles when the gusts strike. Then there's the ground, sire. There's ice under the snow, and now the first squadron's hooves have cleared the snow away the rest of the regiment are struggling to keep their footing.'

'Excuses!' Napoleon snapped. 'You ride back and tell the colonel to keep advancing. I don't care how strong the wind is, and I don't care about the ice. You tell him I don't care if he has to make his way across the pass on his belly, pulling his horse behind him. I don't care what he says. It is possible. It will be done. You tell him.'

The messenger looked as if he was about to make a further protest, but there had been a dangerous tone in Napoleon's voice, and he saluted instead. 'Yes, sire.'

Once the dragoon had turned his horse back to the slope and was trotting it carefully through the thicker snow along the side of the track Napoleon nudged his spurs in and walked his own mount on to the slope. Followed by his escort he began the ascent. The horses and men who had already passed that way had packed the snow down, and stretches of the track were already compacted into sheets of ice that gleamed like marble. The iron-shod boots of the infantry had some purchase on the ground, but the horses began to slither dangerously as Napoleon and his party pressed on.

'Clear the way there!' a sergeant called out as he saw the imperial party struggle to pass by. The infantry moved stiffly to the sides of the track. Napoleon noticed that there were none of the usual cries of 'Long live the Emperor!' as he rode through them. Instead, the men glared sullenly at him.

'Someone shoot the devil!' a voice called out when Napoleon had ridden by. He checked the impulse to turn round, and stared fixedly ahead. It would not do to try to find the man and punish him. It would only depress morale still further, and cause the advance to be delayed. Not one of the officers or sergeants amongst the infantry stirred at the man's cry. The Emperor bit back on his anger and pretended not to have heard as he continued up the slope.

'Will no one shoot him and put an end to this misery?' the voice called out again. 'You cowards!'

The track began to twist as the gradient of the slope increased, and Napoleon and his party came up with the battery of horse guns from the regiment of dragoons. They were stationary on the track, wheels wedged with rocks as the crews stood by and stamped their feet, hugging their arms about their chests, heads hunched down inside their greatcoats. At the head of the battery a team of horses was scrabbling for purchase on the icy surface, while men strained at the spokes of the wheels of a gun and limber. As Napoleon watched, they edged forward a few paces before one of the horses slipped and went down, dragging another with it. The limber and gun began to slither back down the track before a pair of sharp-witted gunners managed to slip some rocks behind the wheels and bring the transport to a sudden halt.

Napoleon reined in and called the commander of the battery over. He had to cup his hand to his mouth to make sure that his words were understood above the wind. 'Captain, double your horse teams up. Take the first three guns to the top of the pass and then come back for the rest.'

'Yes, sire.' The captain saluted and turned away to carry out his orders.

Whilst the men of the battery began to harness additional horses to the first three guns, Napoleon realised that the rest of the wheeled vehicles travelling with the army would have to adopt the same procedure. Some of the heavier guns would even need three teams of horses to negotiate the track. With a sinking heart he realised that it would be impossible to clear the pass before sunset. He steered his horse round the men struggling with the leading gun and continued up the track, soon coming up with the rear of the column of dragoons. Now the wind was violently blasting down the hill. The riders had dismounted and were bent almost double as they drew their mounts on. As the imperial party reached the dragoons a sudden flurry of snow struck Napoleon a stinging blow in the face. The blizzard roared around him and he felt the horse buffeted back a pace by the force of the wind. Then it lost its footing and staggered to one side, scrabbling for purchase on the icy ground. As it began to pitch over Napoleon released the reins, kicked his feet free of the stirrups and hurled himself to the side. He plunged into a drift in front of a large boulder and fetched up hard against the rocky surface, driving the air from his lungs.

'Sire!' the commander of the escort called out in alarm, dropping from his saddle and running through the snow towards him. Napoleon was gasping for breath and could not reply immediately as the officer leaned over him with a concerned expression. 'Sire, are you injured? Do you need the surgeon?'

Napoleon shook his head and struggled out of the snowdrift, his grey coat caked in snow. His hat, which he had jammed on to his head earlier, was still there, and as he swept the snow from his coat his breath gradually returned to him. 'I'm all right. But we'll have to continue on foot from here.'

One of the escort took the reins of Napoleon's horse and they trudged on, up the slope, passing stragglers from the dragoons. One man stood over his mount, which he had shot after it fell and broke a leg, busy stripping the horse of the saddlebags and anything else that could be carried away, and he did not look up the Emperor passed by, a few paces away.

Napoleon did not reach the pass until after midday, hours later than he had intended. Conditions there were as bad as they could be. The wind was now so strong that men were having to link arms to stay on their feet. Thick snow blanketed the ground and the combination of the altitude and the icy blizzard had driven the temperature down to well below freezing. The men's exhaled breath froze into tiny crystals on the front of the mufflers they had pulled up to protect their faces. The colonel of the dragoons was waiting there to urge his men on. He saluted as Napoleon shuffled through the snow towards him.

'Sire.'

Napoleon nodded a greeting and grasped the man's shoulder as he cupped his other hand to his mouth. 'Tough work, Colonel! How are your men faring?'

'Most have gone through the pass, sire. I'm just waiting here to send the last of them on their way. I've ordered the regiment to form up at the bottom of the slope.'

'Good. You'd better join them.'

'Yes, sire.' The colonel nodded and Napoleon released his grip.

The pass was a dreadful place under such conditions, and despite his layers of clothing and thick gloves Napoleon could feel his hands and feet beginning to grow numb. Leaving orders for some of his escort to stay behind and urge the rest of the army through the pass, Napoleon carried on, picking his way carefully down the far slope. He passed several more dead horses, and one dragoon who had been crushed when his horse had fallen on him. Already the snow had heaped up around the bodies and they would soon disappear beneath the mantle of white, there to remain until the spring thaw revealed their pitiful remains.

It took the rest of the day and through the night for the army to negotiate the pass and stumble into the town of Villacastin on the far side of the Guadarrama range. But there was little chance to rest the exhausted soldiers. Reports reached Napoleon that General Moore had begun to retreat to the north. A deadly race was on. The British seemed to be making for the port of Corunna where, no doubt, their navy would be waiting to evacuate them. But if Soult was still in a position to block their retreat then General Moore and his men were trapped and would be crushed. Napoleon took warm satisfaction from this chance to humiliate his oldest enemy. Such a catastrophe would rock Britain to its foundations and they would never dare to attempt another campaign in Europe on such a scale again.

So the Emperor drove his men on, often leading the pursuit at the head of a squadron of Guard cavalry as the army sped north. They began to pass the bodies of the first of the enemy's stragglers, cut down by the pursuing French cavalry. Then came the wagons, lying abandoned at the side of the road. Napoleon rode through towns and villages which had been looted by the British as their discipline began to fail. Some of the redcoats had been so drunk or exhausted that they could not continue and simply sat in the streets waiting to be taken prisoner. But the British were not the only enemies facing the French.

On the morning that Napoleon reached the town of Valderas, a mere two hours after the British rearguard had retreated from the town, they came across a small farm beside the road a short distance away. The farm was deserted, save for the bodies in front of the barn. Two French hussars had been staked, spreadeagled, on the ground. Their eyes had been gouged out and they had been mutilated and disembowelled. But they were the lucky ones, Napoleon reflected. Their officer, a lieutenant, had been nailed, upside down, to the door of the barn. Below him lay the smouldering remains of a small fire. His head and shoulders were burned black as pitch.

'Bastards,' someone muttered behind Napoleon.

The captain of the squadron edged his mount forward and cleared his throat. 'First six men, fall out and bury those bodies.'

'No!' Napoleon intervened. 'Leave them.'

'Sire?' The captain turned to him with a surprised look. 'Surely we can't leave them there, for all our men to see?'

'That's precisely why we are leaving them there. Let everyone in the army know what awaits them if they stray from their comrades to loot, or straggle.'

The captain thought about protesting, but then swallowed and nodded. 'Yes, sire.'

'Now let's go.' Napoleon spurred his horse on and the small column rode away, leaving the three bodies behind to serve as an example to the men who followed.

That night, as Napoleon ate his supper at a small inn just outside Valderas, Berthier came and sat opposite him with the evening despatches.

'I'm eating,' Napoleon mumbled as he chewed on a hunk of bread and then dipped some more into the remains of the stew in front of him. 'You read. Just the important items. Precis the rest.'

'Yes, sire.' Berthier had skim-read the messages and ordered them accordingly. He coughed and began. 'From Soult. He reports that he has skirmished with Moore's cavalry, and managed to evade the main force by a march to the east.'

'Evade?' Napoleon lowered the piece of bread and swallowed as quickly as he could. 'Evade? What the hell is Soult doing? I ordered him to hold his position, unless he had to manoeuvre in order to cut off the British line of retreat. If he goes east, Moore will escape. Why has he moved?'

Berthier scanned the message and replied, 'It seems that Soult is concerned that the survivors from La Romana's Spanish army is closing on him from the north-east. He did not want to get caught in a trap himself.'

'Pah! La Romana's army is little more than a band of brigands. Soult has nothing to fear from them.' Napoleon paused and projected a map of the area in his mind, together with the forces he had set in motion against the British. With Soult to the east the chance to trap Moore was gone. All that was left was the hope of overhauling the British army and forcing it to turn and fight. Napoleon ground his teeth in frustration at his subordinate's action and roughly pushed away the nearly empty bowl of stew. 'Have orders sent to every division. Tell them that the Emperor demands one last effort of them. They have but to catch General Moore and they will have brought Britain to her knees.'

'Yes, sire.'

'Now that Moore has escaped our trap we no longer need so many troops to continue the pursuit. Soult can deal with it. Reinforce him with Junot's men and the rest can return to Madrid. I'll follow Soult with the Imperial Guard as a reserve for the present.'

Berthier nodded.

'Next message.'

Berthier pulled out the next sheet. 'From your brother Lucien, sire.'

'Read it.'

' "Your imperial majesty, I write to you briefly to apprise you of certain unexpected developments in Paris which may well be innocent expression of the idiosyncracies of the characters in question, or a symptom of something more sinister. You well know the antipathy that has existed between Fouché and Talleyrand for many years . . ." '

Napoleon could not help smiling. It was an antipathy he had done much to cultivate in order to ensure that these two key ministers were kept divided.

' ". . . I write to tell you that I encountered the pair recently at the salon of the Hotel Monaco, arm in arm and talking in a most animated and friendly manner. Startling though such a sight was to me, I did not think anything sinister of it until Talleyrand began to be far more vocal about his opposition to his majesty's policies in Spain. Out of concern for the safety of your affairs in Paris I have taken the liberty of having my agents follow Fouché and Talleyrand and compile reports on whom they meet. I will report to you in more detail as soon as the picture is clearer. Your brother, Lucien." '

As Berthier lowered the letter Napoleon's mind was rapidly considering the significance of what he had heard. Fouché and Talleyrand arm in arm? Unthinkable. Barely a few months ago they would only have been prepared to walk so close to each other if their hands were round the other man's throat. This rapprochement was indeed unexpected, and suspicious. Napoleon did not like it at all. He chewed his lip for a moment before his gaze turned towards Berthier. 'I will ride to Valladolid. If Moore manages to break away from Soult then have the Imperial Guard march and join me.'

'Yes, sire.' Berthier made some notes and then looked at his master anxiously. 'Do you believe that Fouché and Talleyrand can be plotting against you, sire?'

'Plotting against me? Of course. I expect that. Plotting *together* against me is an altogether different issue. I don't like it.'

The next morning Napoleon, escorted by a complete regiment of hussars, the very least complement that could guarantee his safety, set off for Valladolid. On arriving in the city Napoleon sent word to Lucien that he would be returning to Paris as soon as possible. A second letter was sent to Josephine, relating to her the pursuit of the British, his certainty that they would be caught and defeated, and his desire to be back in her arms again. Despite the cooling of his passion some months earlier, Napoleon still had considerable affection for his wife. Enough to fire his desire to make love to her again. Once the letters were sent, Napoleon and Berthier settled to several days of planning for the continuation of the campaign in the Peninsula.

A week after he reached Valladolid the Emperor received a message from the Director General of the Post in Paris. A letter from Fouché and Talleyrand to Prince Murat had been intercepted. In it the ministers spoke of the widespread desire for peace that had taken hold of France, and wondered, if Napoleon perished in Spain, whether Murat would consider ascending the imperial throne.

When Napoleon read the message he knew at once that he must return to Paris immediately. There was no question of it now. A conspiracy was hatching, at the very time when Austria was building her army in preparation for war.

Chapter 53

Arthur

Dublin, January 1809

Even when the news reached Ireland that the senior officer of the British army, the Duke of York, had signed the report on the Cintra treaty, Arthur did not feel remotely like celebrating. He had come out of the affair somewhat better than either Burrard or Dalrymple. Those senior officers in the know at Horse Guards would ensure that the two generals were steered away from further field commands. Arthur had proved his ability to command at Vimeiro, and his services would be required again one day. He just hoped that the day would not be too long in coming. However high his stock with senior officers, he knew that his chief difficulty was that politicians have enduring memories, and it was likely that his enemies would protest if he was given a new command too soon.

Such a delay was a depressing prospect. Partly because he felt the injured pride of the wrongly accused, but mostly because he was honest enough to admit to himself that he was one of the most capable generals in the army. By rights his talents should be utilised in frustrating the enemy. Instead, it was he who was frustrated, and he regarded those who controlled Britain's political affairs with steadily growing cynicism.

Kitty and the two boys bore the brunt of his ill humour, which tended to manifest itself in a brooding silence and coldness to those closest to him. At first Kitty tried treating him with a forced cheerfulness and insistence on the most trivial of conversations in the hope that it might lift his spirits. But the harder she tried the more terse he seemed to become, and in the end she fell to matching his silences with her own. The long winter evenings of the first months of the year crept by under a cloud of mutual frustration and neglect.

Arthur's mood was not helped by the steady flow of bad news from London. The evacuation of the British army from Corunna and the death of General Moore had struck at the very core of the nation's morale. Then came word of a scandal involving the Duke of York. A former mistress of the Duke, Mary Anne Clarke, had revealed that she had been trading her sexual favours for army commissions and promotions, which she had sold on at a tidy profit.

'Rubbish!' Arthur growled as he tossed the newspaper down on the dining table. Night had fallen and he had been reading about the scandal after the dessert had been cleared away.

Kitty looked up from her coffee, licked her lips and asked, 'What is rubbish, my dear?'

'The allegations made by the Clarke woman, of course. Damn lies, all of it!'

Kitty had read the newspaper before Arthur had returned from his office at the castle. She took another sip of coffee before responding in a measured tone, 'It seems to me that her claims have some truth to them, and others corroborate what she says.'

Arthur frowned. 'I accept that she was selling offices on, but I cannot believe that the Duke of York can have been aware of it.'

'Why not?'

'Why not?' Arthur asked in an astonished tone. 'He is the highest-ranking army officer in the country. A royal. Why would he take the risk of exposing himself to such a scandal? It makes no sense.'

Kitty shrugged. 'He would not be the first man in high office to fall from grace because of a woman. The Duke should have known better.'

'But that is my point. She must have been selling the offices behind his back. Otherwise he would have known about it and dropped her at once.'

'Yes, that would make sense.'

'He is an honourable man,' Arthur insisted. 'I cannot believe he would be involved in such corruption.'

'Yet you accept that the Clarke woman was his mistress.' Kitty looked down into her coffee. 'It seems to me that if the Duke is capable of taking a mistress, who is to say that his immorality does not extend further?'

'Taking a mistress is one thing, Kitty. Taking liberties with one's office is quite another.'

'Both are immoral,' she replied. 'It is not what good people do.'

Arthur shook his head. 'Half the men in Parliament have mistresses. It is hardly uncommon. Yet they balance their physical needs with integrity in public office.'

'Really? And what about you, Arthur?'

He glared at her, lips pressed tightly together. In the bleak months since his return from Portugal he had visited a discreet club called the Game of Hearts on several occasions, and been entertained by Harriette Wilson. She had been good in bed, but he rather feared that his would be another name she bandied about in due course. He hoped that Kitty would not find out, and be hurt, yet at the same time he could not help wanting something more diverting than the stilted sex available at home. He was silent for a moment, and then said, 'My conscience is clear, and I'll thank you not to ask me that again.'

Kitty set her cup down with a sharp rap and folded her hands together. 'I ask it because of the way you are presently treating me, Arthur. I am your wife, yet you hardly ever speak to me. Never take any interest in me or my opinions. Lately, you have barely even acknowledged your children. Under such circumstances can you wonder if I should fear that you are seeking affection elsewhere?'

He pushed back his chair and rose to his feet. 'I will not discuss such accusations, Kitty, do you hear? And you are quite wrong about the Duke of York, as you shall see.'

Without another look at her, he left the room and retired to his private study. Pouring himself a large glass of port, he dropped into his chair and stared at the small pile of official papers and letters he had brought home with him from the castle. Almost all the latter were fresh requests for patronage, some specifically requesting positions that entailed few actual duties so that the incumbent could be assured of an income without the inconvenience of having to work for it. Arthur scowled at the papers for a moment and then took a hefty swig. The country was at war, and while every resource should be dedicated to providing the means to secure victory over France it seemed that many of his countrymen still placed selfishness above service to the nation. The situation was even worse in Parliament, where political factions spent their energies scoring points over each other, regardless of the wider peril that threatened to engulf Britain.

And now this business with the Duke of York. Arthur shook his head. Whatever the Duke might have done, he had a first rate talent for administration and making sure that his country fielded the best trained and equipped army in Europe. If the scandal that embroiled him was not quashed, Britain might very well end up deprived of his services. Simply because Mary Anne Clarke had decided to take her revenge on him for ending their affair. No doubt she was also being rewarded for her accusations by some Whig politician. At present the Whigs were spoiling for peace with France. Peace at almost any price.

It was madness, Arthur reflected. Bonaparte did not strike him as the kind of man who placed a premium on peace. The French Emperor was a soldier through and through and the conquest of nations and the subjugation of people had become his obsession. But then, Arthur wondered, did he himself not share something of that taste for war? He never felt so complete as when he commanded men on campaign. Gone were the duplicities of politics, the pretensions of London society and the endless ennui of domestic compromises that had come to define his life with Kitty.

As soon as the last thought entered his head the bitter taste of shame and betrayal soured his soul and he despised himself. He finished his port and set the glass down sharply on the table. His country needed him in the war against Bonaparte. He must embrace his true calling and return to the army. The longer he stayed in his present post, and partook of the slow poison of politics, the less chance he would have of serving his country in uniform. Now that the Cintra inquiry had cleared him, he must seek a new appointment in the army as swiftly as possible.

The next morning, Arthur strode purposefully to his office. Cancelling his morning appointments, he settled down in front of a sheet of paper and began to draft a letter to Castlereagh.

My lord, it appears to me that the war with France is swiftly approaching the point where the term crisis might be employed. The present scandal afflicting his grace, the Duke of York, and the recent ejection of our army from Spain, have caused public support for the continuation of the conflict to wither. Unless his majesty's government is resolved to continue direct confrontation of enemy land forces we cannot expect the nation to endure a state of war for much longer. Therefore, we must take it upon ourselves to overcome the French army in the field and prove, again and again, that the French can be beaten. Every victory we gain will sound through the rest of Europe like a rallying cry.

The French are intent on completing their conquest of the Peninsula by subduing Portugal, so that is where we may fight them. I have always been of the opinion that Portugal could be defended whatever might be the result of the contest in Spain. Once we have beaten off the French attacks we could then go on the offensive and drive them completely out of Portugal. At that point it may even be possible to extend the campaign into Spain.

Arthur paused, and thought over the requirements of his plan. If he suggested too few men, Castlereagh might deem the whole enterprise to be doomed from the start. If he requested too many Castlereagh would have a hard time convincing the rest of the Cabinet to undertake such a campaign when resources were already stretched. Arthur dipped his pen in the inkwell and continued.

In order for this project to succeed, the British army in Portugal must number at least twenty thousand, with four thousand of those being cavalry. The Portuguese army will also need to be equipped and trained from the British purse. Furthermore, we will depend upon the continued resistance of the Spanish in order to deny the French the chance to concentrate their forces against us.

Lowering his pen, Arthur read over his words and then puffed out a sigh. The next section was going to be the most challenging item for Castlereagh to accept, but there was no avoiding the recommendation. Arthur again set his pen to the paper.

Concerning the question of who should be placed in command of such an expedition, I shall make no resort to false modesty. It is my unshakable conviction that I have both the ambition and the necessary ability to best ensure our success in Portugal. I have already demonstrated the superiority of our men over the enemy at Roliça and Vimeiro. I have the confidence of our men and had garnered enough experience of campaigning in inhospitable terrain to give our forces the best chance of victory.

It was a bold claim, boldly expressed, but Arthur did not think that a word of it was unjustified. Besides, when he considered the other possible candidates for such a command, none matched his achievements. Of those who might have rivalled him for the command, Moore was dead and Baird had been severely wounded at Corunna.

Satisfied that Castlereagh knew him well enough to know that in such matters he would give honest recommendations, Arthur set his introductory note to one side and began working on a far more detailed memorandum concerning every aspect of the suggested campaign. He worked on through the day, and then, as dusk settled across Dublin, he called for a secretary and instructed him to write up the entire document in a fair hand, ready for despatch to London aboard the first available mail vessel.

While he waited for a response from the War Secretary, Arthur sadly continued to follow the news of the growing scandal that was engulfing the Duke of York. As more details dripped out it became clear that the

Duke had been aware of the improprieties of his lover. Even Arthur had to admit that there must be a minimum standard of morality observed by those who claimed high public office. In the end, the Duke felt forced to resign, and was replaced by Sir David Dundas as commander-in-chief of the army. Even before that had occurred, a fresh scandal, much closer to Arthur, had gripped the attention of London society.

Lady Charlotte Wellesley, the wife of Arthur's younger brother Henry, had eloped. She had left her husband for her lover, Henry Paget. As soon as he heard the news, Arthur travelled to London. Naturally he wanted to support his brother, but that was not the only thing on his mind as he arrived in the capital.

'You make a very persuasive case.' Castlereagh nodded towards Arthur's lengthy letter, lying on his desk. 'Frankly it is exactly the kind of far-sighted strategic vision that the Cabinet needed to consider.'

'You shared it with the Cabinet?' Arthur responded anxiously. Even though the Tories were in power there were still enough enemies of the Wellesleys within the Cabinet to undermine his suggestions and ensure that they were not given a wider circulation. 'Was that wise, if you don't mind my asking?'

Castlereagh smiled at him. 'You don't imagine I occupy this office by virtue of my naivety, do you? I withheld your name, as well as your claim to the job, until after the memorandum had been discussed. I passed it off as the work of a subordinate connected with my office. It took a while before I managed to convince them of the sagacity of your proposals, which was not easy, I can assure you. There are still some ministers who are wedded to the notion of only intervening in far-flung colonies, picking off French territories one at a time. I told them that if we pursued such a strategy it would be years, decades even, before it began to harm France.'

'Quite right.' Arthur nodded. 'We must pursue a more direct, more visible, line of attack on the enemy.'

'They accepted that argument, finally. So, once the plan for Portugal was approved, it only remained to appoint a commander for the army.' Castlereagh paused and flashed a mischievous smile at Arthur. 'That was when I mentioned who the author of the memorandum really was. Well, having approved the plan they could hardly not approve your being given the chance to implement it. Besides, I took the precaution of inviting Dundas to the meeting and he was happy to support my recommendation that you be offered the command. Faced with that, there was little scope for protest. And so there we are.'

Arthur stared at the Secretary for War, not quite believing his ears. 'I am to command the army?'

'Strictly speaking, I can't yet. The letter of appointment has yet to be written and sent to you, and then I must await your considered response to the offer. Only then will I be in a position to announce that you will command the army.' Castlereagh sat back in his chair and opened his hands. 'Of course, you could save me the trouble of waiting and let me know your answer here and now. Sir Arthur, will you accept the command of the Army of Portugal?'

Arthur grinned. 'Yes, sir. It would be an honour.'

'Alas, it is an honour that must be kept secret for the present. You may go about making the necessary preparations, of course. Recruit your aides, settle your affairs in Ireland and so on, but do not breathe a word of your destination. With luck we can have your army ready to march from Lisbon before the French are even aware of the danger.'

'I understand, sir.'

'Good.' Castlereagh's expression suddenly became deadly serious. 'Understand this too, Sir Arthur. You will be in command of our country's sole field army. You must ensure that it does not meet with disaster. After the fate that befell poor John Moore, our countrymen live in dread of another such defeat. You will take no unnecessary risks, and you will confine yourself to the limits of Portuguese territory. On no account are you to cross into Spain without the express permission of his majesty's government. Is that clear?'

Arthur nodded. 'Quite clear, sir.'

Castlereagh stood up and held out his hand. 'Then may I be the first to offer my congratulations, General Wellesley. I trust you will cause the enemy as much distress as possible.'

'You can count on it, sir.'

Even as he left the Horse Guards and marched across the parade ground, his mind was racing with the possibilities of his new command. He had told Castlereagh that Portugal could be defended. He had no doubt of that. But that was just the start. Once Portugal was safe, then the obvious progression would be no less than the liberation of Spain, in the course of which the cream of the French army would endure the same humiliation as had been visited on General Junot at Vimeiro.

Arthur smiled at the thought. Within months, the shadow of Cintra would be lifted and he would finally have enough men, and enough authority, to take the war to the French on his terms.

Chapter 54

Napoleon

Paris, 23 January 1809

The imperial carriage entered the city late in the morning, having been on the road for several days with only the briefest of stops to change the horses and drivers. Napoleon had taken advantage of such moments to step down from the carriage and stretch his limbs. As he walked up and down beside the coach he thought over the reports he had received on the journey from Valladolid. Soult had chased the British all the way to Corunna after an epic pursuit through the harsh terrain of the Cantabrian mountains. The British rearguard had fought like lions, contesting every step of the way along the ragged mountain tracks, and across wild rivers swollen by winter rain. At the end the British had abandoned almost all their wagons and many of their guns, and only just over half their original force was evacuated from Corunna. The news cheered Napoleon greatly. Such a repulse would strike a blow at Britain's desire to continue the war. It would have been even better if the entire army had been caught and crushed, Napoleon mused, but it was a French victory all the same, sweetened by the death of General Moore, struck by a cannonball on almost the last day of the evacuation.

There had also been further confirmation of the conspiracy of Talleyrand and Fouché. Prince Eugène, the Emperor's stepson, who was acting as his viceroy in Italy, had intercepted another letter to Prince Murat. The imperial crown was offered to Murat in far more explicit terms, together with an assurance that the people of France would be sure to back Murat's claim, *even if* Napoleon was not killed in Spain. Napoleon had felt the rage rising in him like a fire as he read Eugène's message. It was not that he felt surprised by their treachery. It was more to do with their ingratitude. Fouché and Talleyrand owed their high office, their titles and their wealth to Napoleon. It was he who had recognised their talents and raised them up to their current stations. Now they repaid him with treachery.

Looking out of his carriage window Napoleon studied the faces of the people he passed in the street. Most had stopped to watch the small procession of gaudily uniformed escorts and the gilded carriage pass by, and some had cheered when they saw the imperial crest on the door. But most had remained silent, their faces expressionless as they stared at their Emperor. It was a cold morning but even allowing for that Napoleon felt an icy tingle trace its way down his spine as he contemplated the mood of his people.

Once he reached the Tuileries he summoned his brother Lucien and strode anxiously up and down the length of his office until he arrived.

'Your majesty.' Lucien bowed his head. 'It is good to see you again.'

'The door is closed,' said Napoleon. 'You can dispense with the formalities, brother.'

Lucien cocked an eyebrow. 'Well, that is an interesting development. You must be more concerned about the situation than I thought.'

'How concerned should I be?'

'There is no immediate threat of open revolt. To be sure, Talleyrand carries the support of much of the nation. The people want peace, Napoleon, and we still don't have it. Can you wonder that they might want a change? Particularly in view of events in Spain.'

'The conquest of Spain is all but complete,' Napoleon replied irritably. 'We have beaten their armies. We have driven the British from the Peninsula. All that remains is for Joseph to mop up a handful of rebels in Seville and all is done.'

Lucien nodded faintly. 'So you say. However, there are reports reaching Paris that the common people of Spain are anything but conquered. They harry our men from every point of concealment and the writ of the new King carries no further than the nearest French garrison.'

'Those who say such things are liars. Worse than liars, traitors.'

'If that's the case, then perhaps there are rather more traitors in France than you might like.' Lucien smiled slightly. 'Sorry, Napoleon, but you have to know these things.'

'Yes,' Napoleon conceded and made a thin smile of contrition. 'Yes, I do. Apologies, brother. Please continue.'

'Very well. As I said, there is a strong voice for peace in France. Talleyrand is playing on that for all he is worth. But he knows that the army is behind you. While you have the loyalty of your soldiers there is nothing he can do. However, with the growing threat of war with

Austria, people are beginning to wonder what will happen to them if France is defeated. You will surely be removed from the throne, and those like Talleyrand and Fouché who have much to lose if the Bourbons return are fearful of losing their titles and their riches. So it seems to me that they are calculating that if they can find a leader who poses less of a threat to the rest of Europe, then France will be permitted to enjoy the fruits of peace.'

'And they think that Murat would make a good Emperor?' Napoleon asked incredulously.

'Not necessarily, but I am sure Talleyrand is convinced that Murat will be his puppet, and he would be a popular choice with the army. If Murat can be persuaded to make the concessions necessary for France to be at peace with Europe, Talleyrand and Fouché and their friends will continue to live very comfortably.'

'What if the other European powers will not make peace with Murat?'

'Then Talleyrand will align himself with the Bourbons and hope to be rewarded when Murat is defeated.'

'What makes you so sure our enemies can beat Murat?'

Lucien shrugged. 'Murat is a fine leader, but he is not you, Napoleon. There is only one man in France who can wield her armies with the genius that has defeated all our enemies these past years.'

Napoleon narrowed his eyes and stared at his brother, searching for signs of flattery, but Lucien seemed sincere enough.

'The current danger,' Lucien continued, 'lies in the confluence of Talleyrand and Fouché. They parade their unity before the public, almost as if they are inviting others to do the same. Talleyrand has found himself a powerful ally in Fouché. Fouché's agents are everywhere, and Paris is filled with his police. If called on, they might possibly overwhelm the soldiers you have presently guarding the Tuileries. I'd advise you to increase the size of your bodyguard at once. And make sure that those admitted to your presence are searched for weapons.'

'Assassination?' Napoleon shook his head. 'It is not Talleyrand's style.'

'I agree, Talleyrand would not dirty his hands with such business. But Fouché might.'

Napoleon considered this for a moment, and nodded. 'He's certainly ruthless enough. Very well, I will take the necessary precautions. Meanwhile, I need to move quickly to ensure that Talleyrand and Fouché are put in their places. It will probably be best to concentrate my wrath on Talleyrand. Fouché lacks his charm and could not proceed far on his own. Yes, it has to be Talleyrand.'

'When will you do it?'

'As soon as possible,' Napoleon decided. 'I want you to arrange a meeting of my senior ministers here at the Tuileries this coming Sunday. Then we shall prick the bubble of this conspiracy.'

'That is good,' Lucien agreed. 'Meanwhile, promise me that you will take due care for your safety.'

'Of course.' Napoleon flashed a smile at his younger brother and clapped him on the shoulder. 'I promise I will stay out of danger. After all, I must see my wife. So I shall go to Fontainebleau. That will keep me away from Fouché's police. I shall be safe enough there.' Napoleon paused for a moment. 'But I may as well be cautious. I will have a battalion of the Old Guard sent to protect me.'

'Thank you,' Lucien said quietly. 'I know you believe you are a child of destiny, but even destiny blinks from time to time.'

Napoleon laughed. 'I have survived shot and shell all these years, Lucien. I think I can survive the petty conspiracies of such men as Fouché and that milksop Talleyrand.'

'I hope so, brother. But don't ever underestimate the dangers of politics. It is as deadly as the battlefield, where at least you can see your enemies. Take care. I shall see you on Sunday, then.'

Napoleon clasped Lucien's hands and kissed his brother on both cheeks. 'Until Sunday.'

Josephine was entertaining her friends when Napoleon and his escort arrived at their château at Fontainebleau. She heard the commotion outside as the carriage and scores of horses crunched up the gravel drive and went to see who had arrived. Her eyes lit up as she saw Napoleon alight from the carriage and she hurried down the steps to embrace him. Napoleon closed his eyes and breathed in her scent, feeling the familiar increase in the beating of his heart as he held her close. They stood like that for a moment before she drew back and looked at him.

'So few letters from Spain, and so brief.'

'Believe me, my love, there was barely a chance to stop and even consider writing to you.'

There was a pained look in her eyes. 'I thought of you every day, many times. Praying that you were safe and would come back to me soon.'

'And here I am.' Napoleon forced a smile. 'Now let us go inside.'

'I have guests. A small gathering of friends.'

'Guests?' Napoleon stared past her at the entrance to the house for a moment, mindful of his brother's warning about his safety. 'Then send them away. I am tired.'

'I can't send them away just like that,' Josephine protested. 'It would be extremely ill-mannered. What kind of host would I be if I treated my guests so?'

'Nevertheless, send them away,' Napoleon replied firmly; then, as he saw her hurt expression, he softened his voice. 'My love, I have not seen you for some months. I would like to be alone with you this first night of my return, at least.' He pulled her close to him and kissed her on the lips, letting his arm slide down the back of her dress to the curve of her buttocks as he did so. For a moment Josephine was unresponsive, then she pressed her mouth against his and Napoleon felt the flicker of her tongue. At length she drew back and stared intensely into his eyes. 'I will send them away.'

Later, when it was pitch black outside, they lay in each other's arms in front of the fireplace in Napoleon's study. The flames had shrunk to a warm wavering glow and cast a dull orange light around the room. Josephine lay against a couch, her legs flat on the thick carpet. Napoleon lay beside her, head resting on her breast as the fingers of one hand idly stroked through her pubic hair. It surprised him that even now, after so many years of marriage, and so many other lovers on both sides, their lovemaking had been as passionate and pleasurable as it had ever been. Yet it wounded him that there was still no issue from their intercourse. There was no shred of doubt now that Josephine would never provide him with an heir.

'Tell me about Spain,' she said softly as she stroked his dark hair, noticing that it had started to thin around the temples.

'A hard country,' Napoleon replied. 'The people are poor and superstitious. You would find it hard to believe that a country on the very borders of France could be so mired in the past. I have done my best to set them on course towards a more enlightened future, but I fear it will take some time before they accept the benefits I hold out to them.'

'But they will in the end, I trust.'

'They will. As long as Joseph and my generals stand firm.'

'Good. Then there is no need for you to return there, is there?'

Napoleon turned to smile at her. 'Not for the present, at least.' Then his head rolled back on to the smooth flesh of her breast and he nuzzled her nipple as he gazed into the flames. 'Besides, I am needed here. It seems that the Austrian Emperor has taken advantage of my absence to push his forces right up to the borders of our territories on the Danube. He must be persuaded to draw back, before he provokes a war.'

'More war?' Josephine stopped stroking his hair. 'Are we never to see an end to war, my love, so that we can grow old together?'

Napoleon took her hand and gently kissed the palm. 'There will be peace.'

'I hope so. With all my heart. As do so many others. I do not know how a nation can endure war as long as France has. There must be an end to it soon.'

Napoleon was silent for a moment. At length, in a gentle tone, he said, 'Now that sounds like Talleyrand speaking.'

'I suppose it does.' Josephine smiled. 'Well, he has certainly been making no secret of his desire for peace recently. You know, for one of your most respected advisers, he certainly seems to share very few of your views. I don't know how you can tolerate it.'

'No. I sometimes wonder why I do,' Napoleon mused. 'Perhaps when he resigned as foreign minister I should have stripped him of all his offices. I doubt it will surprise you to hear that Talleyrand has been plotting to overthrow me. Plotting with Fouché and Murat.'

He sensed her stiffen, and quickly eased himself up and turned so that he was facing her. Josephine's eyes met his for a moment and then wavered before fixing on the flames over his shoulder. 'I had no idea it was as serious as that,' she said.

'But you had some idea of what he was plotting?'

'No. Not really. He talks a lot, but that's just the way it is. You never know how much to take seriously with Talleyrand. But plotting to overthrow you? Are you certain?'

'I have enough evidence to send him to the guillotine.'

Josephine was silent for a moment before she spoke again. 'And will you?'

'I don't know. He may yet be of some use to me, and I doubt the royal courts of Europe would thank me for extinguishing one of their brightest lights. But that is no reason to spare him, especially if there is any more to his treachery than I have already discovered. The difficulty is that Talleyrand and Fouché are my creatures. I raised them up. If I tear them down, that is to publicly admit that my initial judgement of their loyalty was flawed. That would be embarrassing. I will have to think about the matter before I decide their fate.'

The meeting of the Emperor's council of advisers took place, as scheduled, on the following Sunday in the Tuileries. Napoleon had ordered Talleyrand to give up the office of Grand Chamberlain two days earlier, and the ministers who gathered in the Emperor's private audience chamber sensed that there was something in the wind. Napoleon stood at the window with his back to the room, hands clasped behind him. For a minute or so there was complete silence and stillness as the ministers and advisers glanced warily at each other. Only Talleyrand seemed imperturbable, sitting close to the fireplace and gazing serenely into the hearth.

It was gloomy outside and Napoleon had a clear view of his guests reflected in the window. He had prepared for this meeting, to ensure that it had the appropriate impact on his subordinates. Taking a deep breath and clearing his throat, he turned round and strode back across the chamber to address them.

'Gentlemen, I had summoned you to discuss the growing threat from Austria, but first there is another matter that needs to be settled. A grave matter concerning the loyalty of two of my most important ministers.' He paused, deliberately avoiding the eyes of Fouché and Talleyrand. 'Two men who owe everything to me yet now seem determined to stir up public opinion against their Emperor. Well, they should be careful before they play with the sentiments of the people. Those who dabble in revolution are holding a wolf by the ears, and they are fools if they think that they would not be swept away in the first days of any popular uprising.'

Lucien rose to his feet, on cue. 'Sire, who are these traitors?'

'My chief of police, Fouché, and the former Grand Chamberlain, Talleyrand.'

There was an excited murmur amongst those assembled, while Fouché squirmed in his seat and glanced round desperately to gauge the balance of sympathy amongst the other ministers. Talleyrand simply stirred in his chair and turned to face Napoleon directly, his features devoid of surprise, fear or indeed any emotion.

Napoleon raised a hand to command silence from the council. When their tongues had stilled he continued, 'I have been handed clear evidence of their plot against me. Reports of their movements, whom they have met, letters they have exchanged with other plotters, most notably Marshal Murat, whom they have invited to take my throne once I have been removed.'

Napoleon at last turned to Talleyrand, his face twisting slightly into a cold sneer of contempt. His finger stabbed out as he raised his voice. 'You, Talleyrand, are a traitor and a coward. You believe in nothing but yourself. For that you have deceived us all and betrayed your country.

You have taken the coin of our enemies and sold your soul to them. Is there nothing you would not sell for your own personal gain? You have failed me, failed your people and failed yourself. You are contemptible. Even as you have enjoyed all the honours I have lavished on you, you have been attacking my achievements in Spain, lying to the people of Paris about what has been happening there.' He glared at Talleyrand. 'Well? What have you to say for yourself, you miserable cur?'

Talleyrand returned his gaze steadily and did not utter a word. Napoleon felt a genuine rage well up inside him at the man's insouciance. 'You heinous little cripple! You faithless husband! For all your pretensions you are nothing more than a pile of shit in silk stockings! You hear me? You turd! I ought to have you shot like that scum the Duke of Enghien. Shot, or hanged, or guillotined, and then have your body thrown to the crows. That is the least punishment you deserve. You and any other man who commits treason against his Emperor.'

As Napoleon shouted at his former foreign minister, the other members of the council were cringing in their seats, none more so than Fouché, who had slumped down and swallowed nervously throughout the tirade. Napoleon drew some comfort from that. As he had hoped, by turning the main weight of his rage against Talleyrand he had scared the others, and left Fouché in no doubt over the fate that might await him if he was ever again suspected of plotting against his Emperor.

With a last glare of contempt at Talleyrand, Napoleon abruptly turned and marched out of the audience chamber, slamming the door behind him so that the jarring crash made his advisers jump in their chairs.

'Do you think it has worked?' Napoleon asked Lucien two weeks later as they sat in the same room, on either side of the fire. Outside, rain lashed down on Paris so that the tiled roofs gleamed like fish scales.

'As well as it could,' Lucien conceded. 'Talleyrand has not made any more comments about your policy in Spain, or any form of criticism. The same goes for Fouché, who has even refused to be seen in the same room as Talleyrand for fear of being associated with him. People are being very careful about what they say in public at the moment. I think you can rest easy.'

'Good.'

'The thing is, I still don't see why you don't at least have them quietly sent into exile. They are dangerous men and should not go unpunished.'

Napoleon pressed his lips together briefly. 'It is enough for them to know that I am aware of their treachery, and that I can have them shot or thrown in prison at the click of my fingers. Besides, they serve as an example to the wider public that nothing escapes the Emperor's eye.'

Lucien was quiet for a moment before he spoke again. 'I still think you should have disposed of them. In time they are sure to be amongst your bitterest enemies.'

'Perhaps. In time. When that happens I will deal with it. At present I cannot bring myself to destroy them.' Napoleon looked up at his brother with a wistful smile. 'Call it a sentimental streak, but Talleyrand, Fouché and I have shared much over the years. Our fates are bound together, for better or worse.'

'Forgive me, brother, but that is madness. You cannot afford to indulge yourself in such obligations. You are the Emperor of France. If you fall then France will be crushed by her enemies. You are not free to place some misguided sense of mercy above the nation's interests.'

'Nevertheless, I will,' Napoleon replied firmly, and then frowned. 'No more of this, Lucien. There are other matters to attend to. Far more important matters. There is no longer any doubt that Austria means to make war against us. Our ambassador reports that the court of Emperor Francis is openly hostile. Our agents suggest that the Austrian army numbers well over three hundred thousand men. It seems that they have not forgotten, or forgiven, the shame they incurred at Austerlitz. They mean to have their revenge and crush me utterly.' He shook his head sadly. 'The thing is, they have never been in a better position to do it. I have one hundred and twenty thousand men on the Rhine. If we scour the garrisons in the German states and in France we might raise another eighty thousand. We are also short of officers, although we might make the numbers up by recalling those who have retired, or promoting sergeants.' He sighed wearily. 'The truth is that time is against us.'

'Time is always against us,' said Lucien. 'All that a man can do is acquit himself as well as he may, and not waste the smallest span of his life bemoaning the fact.'

'You are right, of course. If Austria wants war, then she shall have it.' Napoleon closed his eyes and after a moment he continued quietly, 'The greatest challenge I will ever face lies before me, Lucien. I had hoped that we might have subdued Europe by now, but that is not the case. The Tsar is building his strength, and each report from Moscow reveals that he is slipping further away from me. I have little doubt that Russia will seek again to humble us before too long. If there is a war with Austria we can be sure that Russia will join with our enemy.' Napoleon paused to contemplate the prospect. 'That will be war on a new scale. War such as no man has ever seen. And when it comes, I will lead the Grand Army to Moscow itself, if I have to, and burn the city to the ground.'

He turned to Lucien and smiled. 'The best is yet to come, my brother. The battle of the hosts, from which France will emerge triumphant, and the name Napoleon will be carved into the very bedrock of history.'

Chapter 55

Arthur

Lisbon, April 1809

'It appears that all of Lisbon has turned out to greet you, sir.' The captain of the frigate grinned as he gestured towards the crowd crammed along the quay. The waiting Portuguese were waving brightly coloured streamers and the national flag and their cheers carried clearly across the waters of the river Tagus.

'So it seems.' Arthur could not help smiling. Evidently the Portuguese had put the bitter experience of the Cintra armistice behind them. That was good. He had feared wasting valuable time rebuilding trust between Britain and her ally, but if this greeting was representative of the people's allegiance then Arthur would be able to put his plans into effect as swiftly as possible. Throughout the short voyage from Southampton he had been busy in the stern cabin the frigate's captain had let him use. It had been a hurried departure from Britain. His staff officers had been carefully selected; the latest books on conditions in the Peninsula had been purchased. His private stores for the campaign had been ordered and packed in trunks and sent down to the embarkation port. Then there had been a final round of social visits to make, as well as settling his family and political affairs.

Arthur had resigned as Chief Secretary of Ireland with some small measure of regret over unfulfilled ambitions to improve the lot of the common people. He had also given up his seat in Parliament. Henceforth, he would dedicate himself to his duties as a soldier, with a private resolve not to quit his new command until the French generals and marshals in the Peninsula had been humbled, or he himself had been killed in the process. He did not speak of this resolve to Kitty when he had informed her that he was off to war again.

Their parting had been emotional. This time it was likely that Arthur's duties would keep him away from home for years rather than months. Kitty had not been able to hold back her tears at the prospect and clung to him on the morning of his departure from their home in Phoenix Park. Once Kitty had overseen the packing of their possessions she would move to the house in London to await his return.

As he gazed at the sprawling tiled roofs of the Portuguese capital Arthur could not help wondering at the scale of the task he had set himself. If all went well, it would be a long time before there could be any prospect of returning to Kitty and he felt pricked by guilt at the satisfaction the reflection afforded. But he brushed the thought aside as the frigate dropped anchor and the crew lowered the launch over the side to convey the new commander of the British army ashore.

Escorted by a company of men from one of the regiments that had newly arrived from Britain, Arthur made his way through the crowd towards the reception committee of local dignitaries waiting on a small stage in a large public square decorated with ribbons and flags. He was relieved to see Major-General Beresford amongst them. Beresford had served under him at Vimeiro, and had, thanks to his command of Portuguese, remained in Portugal to train soldiers recruited from the local populace. The two officers exchanged a salute before Arthur grasped the other man's hand.

'Good to see you again, Beresford.'

'And you, sir.'

'I understand that you have been promoted in my absence. A marshal of Portugal, no less.'

'The rank serves its purpose,' Beresford replied self-consciously. 'At least the locals respect it. Makes my job of training them that much easier. Besides, I shan't be the only Englishman with such a fine rank bestowed on him.' Beresford turned to the local dignitaries and exchanged a few brief words with a small dapper man in a fine dress coat with a bright red sash across his shoulder.

'This is the High Chamberlain of the Royal Court, sir. The senior official left behind after the government fled to Brazil.'

Arthur bowed to the chamberlain and at once the man burst into speech, talking so rapidly that Beresford could not keep up and struggled to follow the man's address. At the end the chamberlain turned and clicked his fingers at one of his officials and the man stepped forward with an ornate case. The chamberlain took the case and opened it carefully to reveal a jewelled star on a purple ribbon, together with a gilded baton. He offered the case to Arthur with a deep bow.

'What's this?' Arthur asked Beresford.

'The acting head of the Portuguese government confers upon you the rank of marshal-general of the allied forces in Portugal.'

'And the rest of the speech?'

'Usual flummery, sir. And a nice bit about how you are going to crush the French armies in Portugal and Spain before you finally defeat the French Emperor himself.'

'Ah, well, yes,' Arthur responded awkwardly. 'Please convey my humble appreciation for the honour the chamberlain does me. Tell him that I give my word that the French aggressors will rue the day that they ever dared to wage war on the people of Portugal.'

Beresford translated, speaking loud enough for his words to be clearly audible to the element of the crowd closest to the stage. As he finished the crowd erupted in a great cheer and Arthur turned towards them and raised his hat to acknowledge their acclaim. When he had finished, he crammed his bicorn back on his head, this time front to back to indicate that he was on active service. He turned to Beresford.

'Better cut this as short as we can. There are matters to discuss, not to mention the usual formalities.' Before Arthur could assume command of the army he would have to present his authorisation to the current commander, General Cradock. It would be an altogether more formal affair than the occasion when Burrard had superseded Arthur on the battlefield of Vimeiro. It suddenly struck him that the worm had finally turned. This was the first time he had enjoyed the fruits of seniority.

'Yes, of course.' Beresford nodded. 'I will take you to the army's headquarters at once, sir.'

Arthur expressed his thanks, waved and bowed his head to the crowd once more, and then left the stage. With his escort in attendance, he followed Beresford through the crowd out of the square and along a street into the heart of Lisbon. As they walked, Arthur recalled his first impressions of the city from the previous year. He was surprised again by the squalor of many of its thoroughfares, where human urine and ordure mixed with that of dogs and other animals, since the inhabitants still slung the contents of their slop buckets into the streets from overlooking windows. As they progressed Arthur could not resist glancing up warily from time to time.

General Cradock's headquarters were situated in a large mansion overlooking the harbour. The position was elevated enough to ensure that a cooling breeze flowed through the house most of the year, and even though it was still only April the breeze was welcome, especially as it helped to dissipate the less pleasant odours of the city.

General Cradock and his staff were waiting in a large reception room overlooking the garden courtyard. After a formal announcement in front of these witnesses, Cradock surrendered his command. As soon as the brief ceremony was over Cradock relaxed and led Arthur down to the garden, where a small banquet had been prepared for the gathering of officers. As the others ate amid a hubbub of conversation, Arthur led Cradock to one side so that they might talk in confidence.

'What is the latest intelligence on the enemy?'

Cradock raised his eyebrows briefly as he composed his response. 'You have picked a hard time to take charge, Wellesley. Marshal Victor is at Mérida, not far from the Portuguese border. He defeated a Spanish army in March so we can't expect much help on that front for a while. Meanwhile, Marshal Soult still occupies Oporto and is awaiting reinforcements before renewing his attempt to conquer the rest of Portugal. It is most likely that Ney will march to join him the moment the rebels in Galicia have been subdued.'

'That may take rather longer than Ney might think,' Arthur responded thoughtfully, recalling the latest intelligence he had read on board the frigate. 'It seems that the Spanish who have banded together to fight the French are proliferating right across the country. Which makes my task easier. The more enemy troops they can tie down, the better our chances of picking off the French armies one at a time.'

Cradock looked surprised. 'Good God, you can't be serious. They outnumber you at least ten to one.'

Arthur smiled. 'Which is precisely why I must face them one at a time. Our soldiers are more than a match for the enemy. I proved that at Vimeiro. We can, and will, prevail.'

'I hope so,' Cradock said wearily. 'This war has gone on long enough. Perhaps it is time to tackle the bull by the horns.' He scrutinised Arthur for a moment and then added, 'And perhaps it is time for a new kind of general. I wish you good fortune, sir.'

Having despatched a small column to watch for any advance by Marshal Victor, Arthur left ten thousand men to defend Lisbon and set off to join the main body of his army. At the start of May he reached his forces camped in and around the town of Coimbra, five days' march from Oporto. A guard of honour greeted the new commander and his staff when they arrived, and after a brief inspection of the well-turned-out troops Arthur summoned all the senior officers to the army headquarters, a religious school on the outskirts of the town. The surrounding hills were covered in the greens of spring, and dotted with bright flowers and blossom on the trees. Despite a cooling breeze the air was hot, and inside the school's lecture theatre the British and Portuguese officers sat in sweltering temperatures, talking quietly as they waited for their new commander to arrive.

Outside the hall, Arthur paused to compose himself. The formalities of assuming command were now over. In a moment he would be addressing his officers and informing them of his plans for the immediate future. More immediate than many of them suspected, Arthur mused with a faint smile. It was vital that he struck the right note with his subordinates. After the fiasco at Cintra and the stalemate between the allied and French armies that had dragged on over the intervening months, he needed to inspire them with a new sense of purpose. All his plans for the future depended upon a high state of morale, an effective organisation of the army and confident leadership. He drew a deep breath, and entered the lecture theatre.

At once the officers quickly rose to their feet and stood stiffly to attention as Arthur crossed the stage and moved behind the lectern. He drew a small slip of paper from his jacket and set it down in front of him.

He looked up and round the theatre at the faces of senior officers: generals and colonels, mostly in red tunics, with a handful of blue-coated artillery men and engineers, and a few brown Portuguese uniforms, clustered about Beresford who would translate for his subordinates. There were many familiar faces here, men he had served alongside during his previous ill-fated campaign in the Peninsula. Men who had respected him and shared his frustration at the failure to capitalise on the success of Vimeiro.

'Be seated, gentlemen.' Arthur waited until they were settled and there was silence. 'The time has come to take the war to the enemy. For too long the French army has enjoyed a reputation for invincibility. The nations of Europe have come to believe in this, to the detriment of their ambition to frustrate Bonaparte. It is time for us to explode the myth of French superiority at arms. Therefore, it is my intention to have our army ready to attack Oporto in no more than ten days' time.'

The audience stirred and there was some excited muttering which Arthur indulged for a moment before continuing.

'From intelligence provided by a French deserter, I understand that Marshal Soult's army matches our own in size, almost man for man. It is my firm conviction that the coming battle will prove to everyone's satisfaction that we have the better men. Everyone's satisfaction save Bonaparte's, of course.'

The officers chuckled politely, yet their eyes glinted with eager anticipation, Arthur noted.

'Before we advance to meet the enemy, there is much to be done. Ammunition and equipment to be issued, artillery and supply trains to be assembled and loaded and final letters sent home. But there is more. From the moment I was appointed to this command I have been considering ways to improve the effectiveness of the army, and there are to be significant changes in the way we operate, gentlemen. One thing I have learned from the French is that there are advantages to operating in bigger formations than a brigade. Therefore, I am reorganising our brigades into autonomous divisions, each of which will contain five brigades. And, in order to distribute the best qualities across each division, a battalion of our Portuguese allies will be allocated to every British brigade. There will be no stronger or weaker elements in our battle line, gentlemen. Furthermore, having witnessed the effectiveness of riflemen at Vimeiro, I have decided that each brigade will have its own company of riflemen to stiffen the skirmish line.'

He paused to let his audience grasp the import of what he had said. It was a radical innovation and he knew that some of the older officers would be resistant to such changes, and some would even consider it unpatriotic to learn lessons from the enemy, no matter how valuable. Be that as it may, Arthur was convinced of the value of his decisions. When the allied army went up against the French in future, the fire of the skirmish line would be even more deadly, and there would be no doubts about the performance of each of the new divisions as the Portuguese battalions would be steadied by the example of the redcoats on either side of them.

'You will have your orders concerning this reorganisation before the end of the day. I have already chosen the commanders for the new divisions and they will be informed after this meeting. Gentlemen, by the time we face Marshal Soult, I want this army to operate as if we had always marched and fought in divisions. Now then, time is short. I will not waste it on florid appeals to patriotism and duty. We are here to beat the French and that is an end to it. Any questions?'

There was a pause before one of the cavalry officers rose to his feet. 'Yes?'

'What are your intentions should we beat Soult at Oporto? Where will the army march then?'

'After we have Portugal, it is my intention to seek permission to enter Spain.' Arthur paused. 'But, gentlemen, beyond Spain there is no mystery surrounding our final destination, though we may not attain it for many years. That destination I can reveal willingly enough.'

He paused and glanced round at the sea of expectant faces before he smiled. 'Paris.'

Five days after Arthur had arrived in Coimbra the allied army began its march north towards Oporto. The soldiers stepped out cheerfully, despite the hard going along dusty tracks beneath a hot sun. Many of them had been at Vimeiro and had told the rest that they had nothing to worry about with 'Old Nosey' in command. Arthur was pleased with their mood and keen to get them into contact with the enemy whilst it lasted. An army may march on its stomach, he reflected, but it fed on victory just as surely. The allied army descended from the hills of Coimbra and crossed the rolling country towards the coast where Oporto lay two miles from the Atlantic Ocean, on the bank of the river Douro.

On the eleventh, the vanguard of the army clashed with the first French outposts, and after a day of skirmishing the enemy were forced to abandon the south bank of the river and retreat into Oporto. It was evening before Arthur and his staff arrived in the sprawl of buildings that formed the small township of Vila Nova on the south bank. As light troops and riflemen pressed through the winding streets towards the ancient bridge that crossed the river, Arthur made his way to a convent that overlooked the city on the far bank. Emerging on to the terrace of the convent, the British officers had a fine view across the Douro.

To the left, a quarter of a mile upstream, a pontoon bridge constructed by the French engineers stretched across the river. The enemy still held a strongly fortified position around the end of the bridge on the south bank. Puffs of musket smoke pricked out along the palisade and from loopholes in the nearest buildings as the French rearguard and the British skirmishers fought it out. On the other side of the bridge the city of Oporto rose up from the banks of the river. To the left of the bridge the bank was lower, but to the right the bank gave way to rocky cliffs that tumbled down towards the water. The French had taken the precaution of moving every boat that could be found on to the northern bank and placing them under guard.

It was clear to Arthur that the bridge had to be taken if he was to get his army across the Douro and liberate the city. It would be a bloody business, as the enemy was bound to cover the crossing with every cannon that could be spared. He had little doubt that the crossing could be forced, but at what cost?

Turning to survey the southern bank he saw that the hills behind the convent were high enough to overlook Oporto. Arthur summoned one of his staff officers.

'Somerset, pass the word to the artillery train. I want three batteries of six-pounders placed up there. They can provide counter battery fire when we attempt to force the bridge tomorrow.'

'Yes, sir.'

'And have some of the howitzers brought forward as well, in case we have to deal with any enemy formations out in the open.'

Somerset saluted and ran off to do his general's bidding. Arthur turned to inspect the enemy's positions again as dusk began to settle over the land. As the light faded his eyes briefly passed over a large structure close to the river at the foot of the towering cliffs opposite. Some kind of convent or seminary, he guessed. There was no sign of life within, as if the building had been abandoned. Arthur's keen eyes searched the south bank as far up and downriver as he could, but there was no sign of a single boat on his side of the Douro.

As night fell, the struggle around the French bridgehead on the south bank died away until there was peace and quiet from that sector, broken occasionally when the men on either side called out to each other, offering items in trade, or simply ribald insults. Arthur had taken over the Serra convent to act as his field headquarters and had a desk set up on the terrace where he snatched a quick supper before settling down to read the evening reports, and then, shortly after midnight, draft his plans for the assault on the pontoon bridge. He had finished his notes and was in the act of handing them over to Somerset to have them copied up in a neat hand when there was a sudden brilliant flash from the direction of the river, then another, and at once a concussive blast that shook the terrace to its foundations.

'What the hell?' Somerset hurried across to the edge of the terrace, and Arthur rose to follow him. Small fires and flames flickered from the remains of the bridge and were gradually snuffed out as the pontoons sank into the current. By the light of the stars and a dim crescent moon Arthur could see enough to know that the bridge had been utterly destroyed. Only fragments remained, attached to each bank. The rest had been blown to pieces, or was already drifting away down the river towards the ocean.

Arthur stared at the scene a moment longer before he returned to his desk and picked up the plans he had made for the taking of the bridge. He held the sheaf of paper and slowly ripped it in half. Somerset joined him.

'What now, sir?'

'What now?' Arthur shook his head. 'Unless we find another way to cross the river, our campaign will have been frustrated almost as soon as it has begun.'

Chapter 56

As dawn broke across the river the full extent of the damage done by the French engineers was clear for all to see. Only the odd pile that had been driven into the river bed still protruded from the glassy surface of the Douro. Downriver the banks on both sides were littered with scorched and shattered lengths of timber and here and there a beached pontoon. Arthur regarded the scene stoically. The bridge had gone, and now his army would either have to march upstream to find a crossing place, or wait until the Royal Navy could be summoned to transport them across the mouth of the river. That possibility held its own risk as Soult would hotly contest any such landing.

On the far bank a party of French soldiers had climbed down to the water and stripped off their uniforms for a morning swim. Their excited cries could just be heard as they splashed each other in full view of the redcoats stuck on the other side of the river. Above the bank the tiled roofs of the city rose up the slope, crowding the narrow winding streets. Most of the buildings facing the river had been occupied by French soldiers, some of whom could be seen leaning on window sills, contemplating the opposite bank as they puffed on their pipes.

Arthur frowned. It was exceedingly frustrating. There was no prospect of a direct assault across the river without enduring heavy losses. But by the time they crossed upstream, Soult could have slipped away towards Galicia; or, worse still, he might steal a day's march on Arthur and head south towards Lisbon or Badajoz to link up with Marshal Victor. In either case, the tables would have been turned on the British.

As he stared across the river an officer came trotting across the terrace towards him and drew up breathless to stand stiffly to attention. Arthur recognised him as one of the Portuguese-speaking officers serving under Beresford.

'Colonel Waters, isn't it?'

'Yes, sir.'

The man's face was flushed with the effort of clambering up the hill to the convent, and his expression was animated as he drew sharp breaths to enable him to speak clearly.

'Beg to report, sir . . . I think I have found a way . . . to get across the Douro.'

'What's that? How?'

Waters turned and pointed upriver, to where the Douro curved round the steep cliffs opposite, just beyond the building Arthur had briefly observed the evening before.

'Just there, sir. I was down there this morning, scouting along the river bank looking for any boats the enemy might have missed. That's when I encountered a barber.'

'Barber? What nonsense is this?'

'The barber came from Oporto, sir. He crossed the river in a small rowing boat. He was quite excited and claimed to have discovered some unguarded wine barges on the far bank. There was a local priest and a handful of labourers nearby and I persuaded them to cross the river and help retrieve the barges.' Waters paused as he noticed the impatient expression on his superior's face. 'Long and short of it is that we now have four wine barges hidden in the reeds on our side of the Douro, opposite that convent there. I searched that too, sir. It seems to have been abandoned.'

Arthur raised his telescope and examined the section of river Waters had indicated. It was perhaps as much as four hundred yards wide, and any attempt to cross it in full view of the French would have been suicidal. However, that part of the river was not in full view of the enemy, Arthur realised. It was very likely that it was obscured by the tall cliffs on the far side. As he scanned the bank by the empty convent, he did not see any sign of French soldiers.

Snapping the telescope shut Arthur turned to Waters with a faint smile. 'Fine work. Well then, let the men cross.'

He turned to call Somerset to him and quickly explained the situation. 'Get the third regiment of foot down there as quickly as you can, but find a route where they won't be spotted by the French. They are to use the barges to cross and occupy that convent. As soon as that is done, we'll start feeding more troops across. With luck we'll be there in strength before Soult is aware of it.'

'Yes, sir.' Somerset hurried off.

Arthur turned back to Waters. 'I should imagine you will want to be involved in this?'

'Indeed, sir. Yes.'

'Very well, you may join the assault party. Good luck to you.'

Once Waters had made off Arthur turned to examine the far bank again through his telescope. There was still no sign of any life near the convent. None at all. It was something of a surprise that Soult had neglected to guard this stretch of river. But then perhaps Soult was the kind of officer who neglected to do a full reconnaissance of his position. Or perhaps he was so imbued with the contempt with which French commanders seemed to view their enemies that he was blind to the danger. Arthur smiled. If that was the case then Marshal Soult was about to receive a very rude shock indeed.

The wine barges could each hold up to thirty men, and as soon as they had crept down into the reeds on the near bank of the Douro the first company of redcoats clambered aboard. There were over six hundred men in the battalion, and the men of the following companies crouched low in the reeds to wait their turn to cross. The barges were propelled by two sweeps, long oars manned by two men, on each side, and once the barges had been punted free of the reeds and out into the river the men began to pull on the oars. Since they were soldiers and not sailors, the progress was slow and graceless, but within a quarter of an hour the first barge had grounded on the far bank. There was still no sign of the enemy as the soldiers of the Third Foot splashed into the shallows and surged ashore. Colonel Waters thrust his arm out towards the silent convent as the other barges grounded.

'Follow me, boys!'

He ran across the stony ground, which was broken by spiky clumps of aloe, and burst through the gates into the courtyard that surrounded the convent. The walls were solid masonry, covered in plaster, and stood eight feet high. To one side of the courtyard stood piles of timber and other building materials and Waters guessed that the structure must be undergoing some kind of renovation work.

'We need firing steps,' Waters decided, and turned to the nearest officer, a burly lieutenant. 'Get your men to work. I want firing steps around the perimeter wall. Fast as you can.'

Leaving the soldiers to set to work, Waters climbed the convent's bell tower and noted with satisfaction that the men who had been left to work the barges were already rowing back to the far bank to fetch the next company. It was going to be slow work, he realised. If the French spotted the danger and reacted quickly enough they could still hold the north bank, provided they could capture the convent that covered the landing point. He turned and looked down into the courtyard. The first company across looked like a pitifully small number to do the job. If only there was time to land an entire battalion before the French realised what was happening, they could hold the convent long enough to cover the landing of a force strong enough to assault the main French army in Oporto.

As the morning dragged on, the barges rowed steadily to and fro, bringing in more and more troops until over five hundred men were lining the walls of the convent, warily watching for the first sign of a French attack.

On the far bank Arthur watched their progress in a state of tense excitement. Incredibly, the crossing had not yet been detected, but even as he watched a sudden movement on the cliffs opposite drew his attention. Tiny figures in blue coats were picking their way along the rocks at the top. Sunlight glittered off gold braid, and raising his telescope Arthur saw that it was a party of officers. If they continued any further they must surely see the barges crossing the river away to their left. For a few more minutes he observed the French officers, until he saw one of them halt, stare for a moment and then thrust his arm down towards the river. The other officers hurried over, and their leader, whose uniform was gaudy with gold lace, gesticulated towards the convent. A moment later the party began to retrace its steps, leaving two of their number on watch.

Arthur snapped his telescope shut and swiftly gave orders for one of his orderlies to get down to the river and warn Colonel Waters that the enemy was now wise to the crossing. Then, quitting the terrace, Arthur hurried through the convent and mounted the horse waiting outside. He spurred it up the track leading to the heights on which he had positioned his heaviest guns the day before. The batteries were commanded by Major Harris, a thin officer in his forties, and he rose from the shade of an olive grove as his general came galloping up.

'Harris, do you see that track there?' Arthur pointed across the river. 'Leading down from the cliff to the convent. 'See it?'

Harris squinted a moment before he made out the route indicated. 'I see it, sir.'

'Good. Those men in the convent are ours. I expect the enemy to make an attempt to drive them out at any moment. But they will have to descend the cliff in order to reach the convent. Can your guns use case shot effectively at that range?'

Harris pursed his lips and squinted a moment before he nodded. 'The range is long, but it's possible, sir.'

'Good. You might want to try your howitzers on the enemy at the same time.'

'Yes, sir.' Harris rubbed his hands together. 'Scared them out of their wits at Vimeiro. Should do the same again here, sir.'

'That's what I'm counting on.'

Arthur remained with the artillery as Harris ordered his crews to train their weapons on the track leading down the cliff from Oporto. Harris went from gun to gun to ensure that they were well laid, and then the crews carefully loaded the first round and waited.

The French did not keep them long. Shortly after eleven thirty, by Arthur's watch, a dense column of infantry began to issue forth from one of the city's gateways and quick-march to the head of the track leading down the cliff. Arthur turned to Harris.

'In your own time, Harris. Make every shot tell.'

'Yes, sir.' Harris saluted and strode across to his guns. He stood behind the first six-pounder and squinted down the crude sights towards the head of the column. He stepped away from the gun. 'Open fire.'

The sergeant carrying the linstock lowered the glowing fuse to the small charge in the paper cone that poked up from the barrel. The gun bellowed as a jet of fire and smoke ripped into the morning air. There was a steady breeze blowing in from the ocean and the dense cloud of powder smoke swiftly dispersed. From his vantage point on the back of his horse Arthur was the first to gauge the effect of the cannon. Most of the cone of lead shot had smashed into the rocks above the track, dislodging stones and shredding the stunted plants that clung to the slope. Little puffs of dust marked the point of impact. One Frenchman was down, slumped over a boulder beside the track, and another was writhing on the ground as his companions marched on. Arthur could make out the white spots of their faces as they glanced nervously towards the guns on the far bank. As well they might, Arthur thought grimly as the other guns boomed out, raking the enemy column with their deadly scatter of small lead shot. Entire files of the leading French battalion were swept away and the track was soon littered with blue-coated bodies. But still they hurried on, down the track towards the convent, where the leading troops fanned out into a skirmishing line and began firing on the defenders lining the walls.

The wine barges were still ferrying troops across the river and these fed into the convent through a small side gate, out of sight of the enemy skirmishers. While it was an infantry only engagement Arthur was satisfied that Colonel Waters and his men would hold their position. The French commander must had reached the same conclusion because, as Arthur watched, a battery of horse guns emerged from Oporto and began to canter down the track.

'Harris!' Arthur called out, drawing the artillery officer's attention to the enemy battery. 'Stop those fellows before they can do any damage to the convent, or the barges.'

'Yes, sir!' Harris trotted over to his howitzers and gave orders to prepare to fire. The squat barrels were charged and the fuses cut to the appropriate length. Meanwhile the French battery had halted on a patch of level ground, protected from the British six-pounders by some large boulders beside the track, and was hurriedly unlimbering. Within moments they had begun to fire on the convent to support the troops now swarming about the courtyard walls.

Colonel Waters could not help flinching as the first of the enemy's cannonballs struck the bell tower, causing a shower of masonry and dust to cascade down into the courtyard. Looking up the track, beyond over a thousand Frenchmen who were gathering to attack the convent, he could clearly make out the battery of light guns that had begun to fire on his position. Bright flashes and puffs of smoke followed by sharp cracks announced the arrival of more shot, and Waters saw a section of the convent's wall explode into fragments, cutting down one of the redcoats sheltering behind it. The wall had been designed to keep prying eyes out, not to withstand the damage that could be inflicted by modern artillery. Unless something was done, the French guns would soon batter the walls down enough to provide a breach through which the waiting infantry could assault the convent. As Waters stared up at the French battery, he could see that they were sheltered from the British guns across the river by a rocky outcrop. It seemed that the French gunners would be able to continue their bombardment in safety.

With a sick feeling of inevitability in his stomach he climbed down from the tower and hurried across the courtyard to join the men defending the wall.

'Keep your heads down, lads, or the frogs will blow them off!'

Some of the men chuckled nervously. Others, who had never faced enemy fire before, hunched down with terrified expressions and waited for the end.

There was a jarring crash close by and another section of the wall collapsed in a cloud of dust. Mercifully, none of the defenders were injured, but as the dust settled it revealed a large gap just three feet from the ground. The rubble either side of the wall provided an easy ramp up into the breach. With a sudden deep roll of drums and a rising cheer that echoed back from the towering cliffs, the French surged towards the wall.

'Here they come, boys!' Waters yelled. 'Don't let them get inside or we're done for! Fire at will!'

Flame darted from the muzzles of the muskets along the wall, sending Frenchmen sprawling on to the stony ground, but the charge came on in a wave of blue uniforms and glinting bayonets. Waters jumped back into the courtyard as he saw a fresh wave of British troops enter the side gate.

'Over here, lads!' he called to them, waving desperately towards the breach. 'At the double, damn you!'

The men came running. Outside, the Frenchmen rushed on, boots scrabbling over the ruined masonry as they surged into the breach. Waters wrenched his sword out and turned to meet them, as the first of the new arrivals reached his side. Along the wall, the other men were firing and loading their muskets as fast as possible as they cut down the attackers. The enemy fire was just as deadly and all around men were dropping back from the wall, dead and wounded.

With a ragged cheer the first of the Frenchmen charged through the breach, straight on to the bayonets of the waiting redcoats. The man next to Waters gritted his teeth as he thrust his bayonet into the stomach of the leading Frenchman, the impact bending him double. Waters scrambled up the rubble and hacked at the face of another man, his savage blow only just blocked in time as the desperate enemy threw his musket up, taking Waters's blade on the stock, which splintered with a loud crack. Cursing, the Frenchman kicked Waters in the chest, sending him reeling back. Then, grasping the barrel of the musket like a short spear, the Frenchman tried to stab him. A musket crashed out close beside the British officer and his attacker spun round and fell on to the rubble. Waters did not have time to even nod his thanks as he rushed forward again to join the red-coated bodies struggling to hold the breach. On either side musket fire rippled up and down the convent walls. Then a voice cried out, 'They're running for it!'

Someone cheered and the cry was taken up.

The fight in the breach lasted a moment longer, and then the last of the Frenchmen turned and backed off a few paces behind his bloodied bayonet. Then he too turned and fled, joining the bluecoats as they retreated to cover. Waters joined in the cheers of the other men, until he recalled the enemy guns. Glancing up towards them, he saw that they were making ready to fire again, the moment their fleeing comrades had cleared the line of fire.

★

'How much longer is this going to take, Harris?' Arthur struggled to keep his voice calm. The first few rounds had either fallen short or gone too far and struck the cliff beyond the enemy battery before exploding.

The artillery major had just finished his latest adjustment to the howitzer's trajectory angle and nodded to the loader standing by with the next shell. As it was heaved into the stubby barrel, Harris turned towards his general.

'I think we have the range now, sir. It is usual to have to fire bracketing shots first in order to determine the range,' he explained patiently. 'But now we have the right charge, and the right angle, and the fuse length is good.'

'Kindly spare me the lecture.'

'Sorry, sir.' Harris turned back to the howitzer and ordered the crew to open fire.

With a deep thumping explosion the howitzer launched its shell. The muzzle velocity of the weapon was lower than that of a standard artillery piece and Arthur could see the faint dark smudge that marked the passage of the shell as it arced across the river towards the enemy battery sheltering behind the rocks. There was a sudden puff of smoke in the air just above the enemy guns and Arthur saw an entire gun crew topple to the ground, directly beneath the point where the shell had burst and scattered its lethal fragments of iron.

'Right on target!' Harris cried out. 'Range is good. Fire at will.'

Two of the next four rounds killed more of the men working the French guns, and then, as Arthur watched, their officer began to shout and gesticulate and the survivors hurriedly began to limber their guns and withdraw back up the track, though not before one shell struck down two horses in their traces, causing the whole team to veer sharply to one side so that horses, riders, limber and gun toppled over the edge of the track and tumbled down the slope in a shower of small rocks and dust before splashing into the river.

Arthur saw that the men in the convent were now out of danger, and the barges were safely and steadily feeding fresh troops into the fight. By contrast the French battalions joining the melee at the foot of the cliff were forced to undergo a steady hail of grapeshot fired at them from across the river before they even faced the muskets of the men of the Third Foot. It was no wonder that their attacks on the convent were half-hearted, Arthur reflected.

A fresh column of French troops had left the city and were making for the track to reinforce the assault on the convent. Three battalions of them, Arthur calculated. He turned to take a quick glance at the rest of Oporto and noticed that a small crowd of people had emerged on to the quays to the left of the remains of the demolished bridge. He examined them through his telescope and saw that they were civilians. More and more of them appeared, rushing out from side streets and racing towards the boats that Soult had ordered to be moved to the north bank. There was no sign of any French soldiers along the quay and Arthur guessed at once that Soult had been forced to strip men from that part of the city to send them against Waters and the men in the convent. The Portuguese swarmed aboard the boats and the first of them began to row across towards the south bank.

'Poor devils,' Harris muttered as he stood beside Arthur. 'Taking their chance to escape from the French, I imagine.'

'Escape be damned,' Arthur replied. 'They're coming to help us get across.'

He was back in his saddle in an instant and spurring his horse back to headquarters. As soon as he arrived he had orders sent to the nearest units to get down to the river as swiftly as possible and use the flotilla of small craft to get across to the far bank. When the orders were given Arthur rode down to the shore and watched in delight as the Portuguese hauled the waiting redcoats into their boats and desperately rowed them across to the north bank before returning for the next load. Soon the broad expanse of the Douro was dotted with craft of all sizes criss-crossing its glassy surface. A handful of French guns downriver of the city fired at long range, sending up spouts of water, but none of their shots struck home, and only one overloaded craft foundered as it was swamped by a wave from a near miss. Those on board panicked and the craft capsized, spilling them into the river. There were several soldiers on board, and only two of them managed to cling on to the upturned hulk with the Portuguese who had been at the oars. The others, weighed down by their kit, sank without trace.

Once the first two battalions had crossed the river and had begun to climb the streets leading from the quay into the heart of the city, Arthur handed his horse over to a soldier. Beckoning to Somerset, he climbed into a small launch and gestured towards the north bank. There were two civilians at the oars, and they nodded eagerly, bending at once to their work and stroking across the Douro as swiftly as they could. Somerset ducked as a round shot whirred close by and slapped into the water fifty feet upriver.

'Close,' he muttered.

Arthur's heart was pounding in his chest but he forced himself to keep his expression calm as he arched an eyebrow. 'But not too close, eh?'

Somerset stared at his general a moment before glancing away and shaking his head.

As soon as the boat thumped up against the base of the quay, Arthur stepped out on to the stone steps and ran to the top. On either side, redcoats were forming up in companies and being led up the streets into Oporto. Arthur and Somerset joined a company of men from the Twenty-Ninth Foot and the small force marched up a wide street, fronted by the counters of fish merchants and chandlers. The windows of the buildings on either side of the street were filled with women fluttering their handkerchiefs and crying out in shrill delight as they caught sight of their liberators.

'*Viva Ingleses! . . . Viva Ingleses!*'

Somerset waved back with a broad smile, but Arthur kept his gaze fixed ahead, watching for the first sign of the enemy. But they only encountered more and more of the excited inhabitants as they penetrated further into the city. When they reached the great plaza in front of the cathedral Arthur encountered a colonel of one of the first battalions to cross the river with the Portuguese. His men had occupied the square and were guarding the streets that led into it. In the centre, around a fountain, sat several hundred French prisoners.

'Hughes! Your report, if you please.'

'Yes, sir. I've got patrols searching the streets, but most of the frogs have gone. They've left their sick and injured behind, as well as wagons and supplies. Any Frenchmen we've encountered have just fired a shot and fled, or laid down their muskets and surrendered.'

'Very well.' Arthur nodded happily. 'Then I want you to take four of your companies to the east of the city. There's a track leading down to a convent held by our men. It's under attack by a French column. Have your men block the track and call on the French to surrender.'

'Yes, sir.'

'One last thing. Have you found Soult's headquarters yet?'

'Yes, sir, over there.' Hughes turned and pointed to a large building with an ornate facade that stood on one side of the square. 'Seems to be the seat of the local government.'

'Thank you.' Arthur and Somerset made towards it, accompanied by the men who had escorted them up from the quay. They entered the building cautiously, but there was every sign that it had been abandoned in a hurry. Bundles of bedding lay strewn across the entrance hall. Paintings that had been stripped from the walls were propped in the corner, Soult's staff presumably not having time to load them into wagons before leaving. From a balcony on the second floor Arthur had a clear view over the roofs of the city towards the north and east. Beyond the walls he could see the dense column of Soult's retreating column beneath a pall of dust. There was little sign of an organised rearguard, just a long tail of stragglers and overloaded wagons. For the moment the French were safe. There was no chance of mounting a pursuit until the next day, when the rest of the allied army would have crossed the river. Unlike Vimeiro, there would be no letting the enemy escape, Arthur resolved. This time he would harry the French all the way to the frontier with Spain.

Chapter 57

Throughout the night the people of Oporto celebrated their liberation and pressed food and drink on any redcoats they encountered in the streets. Arthur had paused only long enough to enjoy the meal that was still set for Marshal Soult on the table at the headquarters he had abandoned. Then he had returned to the quay to supervise the crossing of the rest of his army. All through the night, boats continued to ferry the rest of the infantry, the artillery and supplies over to the north bank. The cavalry had been sent upriver to find a crossing and do what they could to harry the enemy before rejoining the main body of the army in the morning.

Late in the night Somerset presented Arthur with the official casualty list.

'Twenty-three killed, ninety wounded and ten missing at present, sir,' Somerset read from his notes.

'Good!' Arthur responded with relief. Given the risks that had been taken, the cost had been light. Caught by the surprise crossing to the convent, Soult had panicked and abandoned the city, and much besides. So much for the myth of French invincibility, Arthur mused contentedly. 'What of French losses?'

'So far, four hundred dead and eighteen hundred prisoners, including the wounded they abandoned in the churches of the city. We've also taken twelve guns, two hundred wagons and a store of powder and artillery supplies.'

'Quite a haul,' said Arthur. 'Something for our people to celebrate back home.'

'Yes, sir.' Somerset nodded his head towards the centre of the city. 'And the locals seem rather pleased.'

'Good. Now we must prepare for the final stage of Soult's defeat. Send word to every battalion commander. I want their men ready to march at first light. There will be no drinking tonight. No one is excused duties, nor may they leave their formations.'

'The men won't like that much, sir. They'll feel they've earned the right to indulge themselves.'

'Then it is just as well that they don't have rights,' Arthur responded tersely. 'This is an army, not a democracy, Somerset. They will do as I damn well order.'

'Yes, sir. Sorry, sir.'

'Never mind. Just see to it that the order is given. We cannot afford any delay in our pursuit if we are to make the most of what we have won here today. Do you understand?'

'Yes, sir.'

'Then make sure that every man gets the message.'

The next morning dawned grey and overcast and the first drops of rain began to fall as the British and Portuguese troops tramped out along the road to the east, following the trail of Soult's corps. Almost from the outset there was clear evidence of the desperate state of the enemy. The British encountered abandoned equipment, scattered along the side of the road. Backpacks, broken muskets, and then the less valuable spoils that had been carried away from Oporto, and the heavier items. In amongst the detritus lay the wounded who had been left behind. At first Arthur gave orders for the enemy injured to be carried back to the city for care alongside his own casualties, but soon there were too many of them to tend to and he cancelled his order with a heavy heart, knowing their likely fate if they fell into the hands of the local peasantry.

The Portuguese people had already suffered much under French occupation and now their torments increased as Soult's retreating column pressed through their villages. The French soldiers were hungry and made free use of torture on any peasants they suspected of hiding food and drink. As Arthur's soldiers marched along in the wake of the enemy column, squelching through the mud as they hunched down under the steady downpour, they came across frequent examples of the enemy's cruelty. Bodies hung from trees. Mothers and infants had been bayoneted or shot in their hovels and young girls raped and left for dead. Villages had been burned so that faint columns of smoke and smouldering remains clearly marked the passage of Soult and his men. As he bore witness to these atrocities Arthur felt his heart grow heavy with a cold rage at the carnage endured by civilian bystanders of the war, and he vowed to do whatever he could to ensure that his own men did not follow the enemy's example.

Occasionally the British came across the bodies of French stragglers upon whom the Portuguese had wreaked their revenge. The luckiest had been killed out of hand, but others had been gutted, or partially flayed, and one officer's body had been discovered sawn in half, beside the bloodied blade of a tree-felling saw. In one village, during a brief lull in the rain, they came across a group of villagers standing round a circle of burning straw. In the middle a wounded Frenchman was screaming. Every time he tried to crawl out, the peasants drove him back inside the flames with their pitchforks, and threw more straw on to the fire. Before Oporto the British troops might have intervened to save the Frenchman, but they had seen enough of his comrades' handiwork to spare him little more than a cold-hearted sideways glance as they marched by.

Each night the sodden redcoats found what shelter they could and lit fires to warm their cold bodies and attempt to dry their clothes. Meanwhile Arthur read the reports of his scouts with a mixture of frustration and grudging satisfaction. Soult was marching at a faster pace than his own men could manage, but only at the price of steadily abandoning his guns and wagons. Soon all he would be left with would be his footsore infantry and the starving, lame mounts of his cavalry.

In an effort to prevent Soult's escape Arthur despatched a Portuguese column to try to march round the enemy's flank and block their passage across the hills into Spain. Another column, led by Beresford, blocked any escape to Vigo in the north where Soult might join forces with Ney. At last, the desperate French commander abandoned the roads and led his forces over the mountains of Santa Catalina. As soon as he heard the news Arthur realised the chase was up. It was five days since they had set out from Oporto, and without abandoning his own guns and supply train he could no longer pursue Soult with the main body of his army. Riding on with his cavalry, he followed Soult's tracks across the mountains and on the seventh day of the pursuit, as the cavalry descended towards the broken country of Galicia, Arthur halted his column.

No more than five miles ahead he could see the remnants of Soult's corps, moving like a band of beggars across the landscape. There was little sense of order in the straggling mass of humanity and only a handful of cavalry formations retained enough discipline to form a rearguard.

'We have them, sir!' Somerset said eagerly. 'We have but to charge and they will scatter to the winds.'

Arthur stared after his enemy for a moment and then shook his head.

'Sir?'

'Do you not know where we stand, Somerset?' Arthur gestured to the ground before them. 'That is Spain. I am forbidden from entering without the express permission of the Secretary for War.'

'But sir,' Somerset protested, pointing at Soult's ragged column. 'One charge and they will break.'

'Perhaps,' Arthur mused. He had seen enough of the British cavalry in action to know how hot-headed they were. Far in advance of the rest of the army it would be rash indeed to permit them to mount any wild charge against the enemy. Besides, Soult's men were hardened veterans of the Grand Army. Even now they would still form square and repulse any attempt by the British cavalry to break their ranks. He stiffened his posture in the saddle and continued to address his aide. 'There is much to be risked in an unsupported attack, and little to gain. Soult's men are beaten; he has abandoned every one of his guns. It will be quite some time before those men of his are ready to fight again. We have done our work, Somerset. Now it is time to retire. Time to turn and deal with Marshal Victor should he attempt to advance across the frontier.'

Somerset's expression was bitter and crestfallen as he stared longingly at the retreating enemy column. Then he composed himself and nodded. 'Yes, sir.'

'Then give the order for the cavalry to turn back.'

'Yes, sir.' Somerset wheeled his mount round to ride over to the colonel of the nearest regiment of dragoons. Arthur remained alone for a moment, staring out across the Galician countryside. For a moment his heart was heavy with the thought of giving up the pursuit. But for his orders he might have contemplated charging Soult's exhausted soldiers. He could imagine the excitement of the charge, the mad thrill of pounding across the open ground towards the enemy. Yes, it would have been exhilarating, he thought. But he was a general now and his army needed him. There was no one better able to defeat the French in the Peninsula. He had added to his reputation with victories at Vimeiro and Oporto, and had humbled two of Bonaparte's most valued commanders.

A fine start, he told himself. Yet there was more to do, much more, before Portugal and Spain were finally set free from their French oppressors. Arthur took one more look at the land of Spain and resolved in his heart that soon, very soon, he would lead his army into the heart of the Peninsula and succeed where General Moore had failed. He had no doubts about the magnitude of the task that lay ahead of him. Bonaparte had poured some quarter of a million of his men into Spain. But even though the British were outnumbered they had proved that they were the masters of Europe's battlefields. They had shown the whole of Europe that the blue-coated legions that marched under Bonaparte's eagles could be beaten time and again.

Arthur smiled with satisfaction. It could be done, as he had told Pitt, Castlereagh and the others. Soon, the French Emperor, safe in his palace

517

in Paris, would be casting his gaze towards Spain with a heavy heart and knowing the first stab of fear that his empire was starting to unravel. As he considered the future Arthur felt the unshakable conviction that his finest hour was yet to come. He allowed himself a moment of pride, in himself and his men, and then smiled self-consciously for a moment.

Then, with a click of his tongue, Arthur eased his horse round and galloped back to re-join his army.

Author's Note

Some historians consider the coronation of Napoleon, and his crushing victory at Austerlitz, as the high points of his astonishing career. Barely ten years earlier he had been a relatively unregarded artillery officer. At the time he became Emperor he was the master of Europe and commander of a formidable war machine. What is more, Napoleon had risen to the new throne on a combination of raw talent and plenty of luck. It is also important to remember that there was overwhelming popular support for Napoleon's elevation from First Consul to Emperor. Armed with such a mandate Napoleon reformed the admin-istration of France (and incidentally much of Europe) root and branch. Little escaped the attention of the workaholic Emperor who mastered a range of briefs to such an extent that he frequently surprised his min-isters and experts with the depth of his knowledge of *their* specialities. There is no question that many of the changes that Napoleon made to the governance of France were effective and necessary. Along the way he ensured that meritocracy was given as much opportunity to flourish in civil society as in the military. I wish there had been space in this book to cover some of these changes in more detail but, as ever, there were decisions to be made about how much to include and in any case much of the positive legacy of Napoleon's efforts only came to be fully appreciated in the years after his fall and are therefore outside the scope of this work.

Of course, there was an ulterior motive for much of his work. Napoleon's lust for glory meant that he needed an efficient and well-motivated society to support the French war machine. In pursuit of this aim Napoleon was not prepared to brook any opposition and there were severe sanctions for those that corrupted the system, or refused to play their part. There is also little doubt that the power vested in the new imperial throne exacerbated a deep-seated megalomania – a characteristic that Talleyrand correctly saw as the gravest danger posed to France. Napoleon had always considered himself to be singled out by fate for greatness. As a consequence he often had little regard for others, and the hardships he subjected them to. Such people were there to serve *his* interests. This included not only his wife, but also his brothers and sisters, who were the tools Napoleon used to extend his dynasty across Europe.

Being destiny's child had some unfortunate consequences for Napoleon. Firstly, it was increasingly difficult for him to accept that he could make a mistake. Accordingly, blame for his errors was lavished on his subordinates, instanced by the blaming of Berthier for the shooting accident with Masséna. Secondly, Napoleon believed so completely in his genius that he could not delegate easily, and frequently had to race from one crisis to the next in order to hold his empire together. The consequences of these flaws were soon to be exposed to all in the Russian campaign of 1812.

Unlike his rival, Arthur seemed to be as abandoned by destiny almost as often as he was favoured by it. After a gloriously successful series of campaigns that should have made a reputation that outshone that of Clive of India, Arthur returned from the subcontinent under something of a cloud, thanks to the political enemies of his older brother, Richard. That, coupled with the army's rigid system of seniority, worked to deny Arthur the chance to demonstrate his brilliance in command. Those who knew Arthur were in no doubt about his talent, but there were few opportunities to put it to the test in the field against the armies of France. Until the decision was made to intervene in Portugal and Spain, that is.

While many other British generals were overcautious, Arthur realised the need to take the fight to the enemy. This eagerness was tempered by the knowledge that Britain could not afford the same level of casualties that France could accept. The battle at Vimeiro was a foretaste of the tactics that would win Arthur the unmerited reputation for being a defensive commander. He had limited resources, and needed to husband them carefully. Yet, as the brilliant success at Oporto clearly demonstrates, Arthur was quick to seize any advantage and then exploit it to the full. The capture of Oporto fully justified Arthur's appointment to the command of the British forces in the Peninsula, and in the years to come he would prove time and again that the British soldier, well led, was more than a match for the men of the French Emperor.

As in *Young Bloods* and *The Generals*, I hope that I have presented this epic period of history as accurately as possible. In order to make the story flow freely I have been obliged to change some details, for which I apologise to those who are well read in this period. For example, I have described France's enduring enemy as 'Britain', yet the French habitually referred to the people and armed forces of the British Isles as the 'English'. It seemed sensible to simplify things by just referring to

Britain and the British, though even in modern times there is still a tendency in France to use the label 'English' for all those who live on the other side of the Channel.

Although this is a work of fiction, it is astonishing how often my research confronted me with instances where the reality was simply far more strange than anything I could have invented. So, dear reader, before you begin to have any doubts, let me just reassure you about one thing; on a sunny day in France, a small army of rabbits did indeed rout one of the world's greatest generals!

Simon Scarrow
November 2008